PROFESSOR MOLLY'S BIG BOOK OF MURDER

PART TWO

THE PROFESSOR MOLLY MYSTERIES

FRANKIE BOW

CONTENTS

PROFESSOR MOLLY'S BIG BOOK OF MURDER PART TWO

First edition. May 26, 2023.

Written by Frankie Bow.

FOREWORD

Dear Readers,

I am delighted to present Professor Molly's Big Book of Murder Part 2, featuring the second six Professor Molly mysteries and an exclusive bonus short story featuring Pat Flanagan and Harriet Holmes!

The Blessed Event: "Davison Gonsalves was a nightmare student—an obnoxious, entitled, cheating suckup. In a twist of fate that might seem hilarious if it happened to someone else, he was now my stepson." Professor Molly Barda is looking forward to a quiet summer in Mahina, Hawaii working on her research and trying to start a family with her new husband. But when a murder happens close to home, Molly wonders what she's married into—and realizes she might have a killer under her roof. If you're in the mood for a murder in Hawaii, you'll enjoy this tale of passion, paternity, and pawn shops in the middle of the Pacific.

Mother's Day: Mahina State University's powerful fundraising office tasks Professor Molly with a special assignment: To serve as the personal tutierge (that's tutor-concierge) to Jeremy Brigham, whose mother happens to be fabulously wealthy and gravely ill. Molly is not thrilled at having to babysit a spoiled rich kid. Especially not while she's battling morning sickness, a meddling mom, and (as always) the Student Retention Office. But once inside the historic Brigham House, Molly realizes something is very wrong. And she has to decide whether to mind her own business and keep her job, or risk everything to prevent a murder.

The Nakamura Letters: Professor Emma Nakamura doesn't believe in ghosts. So it doesn't bother her (much) when she learns of a long-ago suicide in her remote upcountry rental house. She's sure there's a logical explanation for the disappearing items and the strange sounds in the night. Fortunately (?), Emma's best friend Molly has news shocking enough to take Emma's mind off the hauntings. Now Emma and Molly have to rely on their strong reasoning skills and a weak internet connection to figure out how a body ended up in Molly's backyard. The Nakamura Letters is an island-style take on the Golden Age mysteries of Mary Roberts Rinehart and Agatha Christie.

The Perfect Body: When Professor Molly attends Mahina State University's exclusive donor dinner, she doesn't expect to share a table with the insufferable Stephen Park. Turns out it's one thing to invite your toxic ex-boyfriend to drop dead...it's quite another when he takes you up on it.

The Fever Cabinet: Through no fault of her own, Professor Molly just got promoted to department chair at Mahina State University ("Where Your Future Begins Tomorrow") in Mahina, Hawai`i. The Student Retention Office has her buried in paperwork. The college has just relocated to a former asylum, which is undergoing noisy renovations. Molly's dean has directed her to mentor the department's new star, the prickly Fiona Spencer, and to do whatever it takes to keep Fiona happy. At least nothing else can go wrong. And then Fiona finds a body in her office.

The Influencer: **There's no such thing as bad publicity. Until it happens to you.** Professor Molly's new renter is a social media star seeking privacy in remote Mahina, Hawaii. The arrangement seems to be working out—until the celebrity influencer vanishes. Molly and her best friend Emma Nakamura call in the Mahina PD and try to stay out of the way. But the unthinkable happens—the saturnine Detective Medeiros actually asks for Molly and Emma's help. As they confront nosy neighbors, fanatical followers, and the missing woman's has-been husband, Molly and Emma find themselves at the center of the story. And when fame creates its own reality, that's a dangerous place to be.

BONUS CONTENT: Death at the Effigy

It's 1984. Young Pat Flanagan gets his first reporting job at San Diego's second-coolest 'zine, *Voltaire's Quill*. But when Pat covers the opening night of a trendy new club, he witnesses a freak "accident" and has to choose: keep his eccentric editor Harriet and her advertisers happy, or find out the truth?

THE BLESSED EVENT

THE BLESSED EVENT

FOR EVERYONE MAKING an effort to be nicer than they really are

CHAPTER ONE

TODAY WAS GOING TO be a productive day. At least, that was my plan.

The living room curtains were shut, letting the hazy morning sun filter in, but blocking my view of the quaint pre-WWII bungalows and neat lawns on Uakoko Street. Not that my quiet neighborhood in downtown Mahina was exactly teeming with distractions.

I sat at my workstation in the corner of the living room, fresh cup of coffee in hand. The word processor and stats package lay open side-by-side on my computer monitor. My coauthor had just sent me the cleaned-up data file. Submitting the completed book chapter by the end of July would be a piece of cake.

Just as I congratulated myself on my anticipated productivity, a shadow fell across my keyboard.

"Eh, Molly, you busy?"

I pointedly kept my eyes on the computer monitor and my hands on the keyboard.

"Good morning, Davison. Yes, I am busy, actually. Did you need something?"

My name is Molly Barda. I teach in the College of Commerce at Hawai`i's Mahina State University, where, according to our radio spots, "Your Future Begins Tomorrow."

I've had many wonderful students during my time there. Then there was Davison Gonsalves.

In the first week of my Intro to Business Management course, Davison copied a classmate's paper word-for-word and turned it in as his own. My "student-centered" dean had blocked my report to the Office of Student Conduct and had forced me to give Davison a free do-over instead. For the rest of the semester, Davison came in late, missed deadlines, skipped class, and worse.

You may wonder what my least-favorite student was doing in my living room. In a twist of fate that might seem hilarious if it happened to someone else, Davison was now my stepson.

"You know where the coffee machine is. And we have Spam in the pantry, rice in the rice cooker, and eggs in the fridge if you want to cook some for yourself. Oh, and the paper bag on the counter is full of papayas if you want something sweet."

Davison was old enough to buy beer. He could certainly fix his own breakfast.

"No more, the eggs."

"The eggs are gone? I just bought a whole—okay, I'll pick some up at the store after I get some work done here. For now, you can fry some Spam, and there's rice."

"Rice is gone, too."

I worked for a while, ignoring my stepson, who continued to hover behind me. Finally, I swiveled my chair around and looked up to face him.

Davison was tall, like his father. He had Donnie's thick black hair and strong features. Thankfully, their personalities were nothing alike.

"I'm not hungry anyway," he said. "I wanna ask you something."

"Yes?"

"Where'd Dad get your ring?"

I glanced at the platinum band on my left hand.

"We bought our rings at Fujioka's Music and Party Supply."

"How come it's so plain? Didn't you want one all covered with diamonds an' li' dat?"

"No. This is the style I prefer. Why do you ask?"

"Could you drive me there, Molly?"

"You want to go to Fujioka's?"

"Yeah."

"What, right now? You're not even dressed."

Davison wore cutoff sweatpants and a tank top, whose purpose seemed to be to show off his muscles rather than to cover anything. The brown skin on his arms and the sides of his neck was blotched with pink where his father had made him get his tattoos lasered off, right before he had packed Davison off to military academy.

"I don't got a car, that's why. And Dad's not gonna be back from work till late."

"Davison, I'm at work, too. I just happen to work at home."

"You get summer vacation, but."

"No. Vacation is when you get paid and you don't work. I get summer unpaid, and I'm still working. It's the exact opposite of vacation. I still have to produce research, which I don't have enough time to do during the school year. Look, just hang on and let me finish this one thing."

I pulled down the "analysis" menu. I could sense Davison still lurking behind me.

"Davison, why don't you fix yourself a cup of coffee?"

"Nah. I'll wait."

I tried to ignore him for a few more minutes, and then gave up. I sighed, saved my work, and shut down the program.

"I still have to upload final grades before six. Don't let me forget. You're really ready to go? Right this minute?"

"Yeah, I'm ready." He lifted his elbow and sniffed his wiry black armpit hair. Evidently, the result was satisfactory.

I stood up and retrieved my purse from the hook by the front door.

"Okay. Let's get this done."

"I like drive the Thunderbird."

"Sorry. According to the Hawai`i State Motor Vehicle Code, you need a special license to drive any car built before 1960."

"Not."

"Do you want a ride or don't you?"

CHAPTER TWO

I DROVE THROUGH DOWNTOWN Mahina and then turned up a narrow street into an older neighborhood. The jungle had grown so lush, the tin-roofed bungalows were hidden from the road. Davison rolled down the window and propped his elbow on the doorframe.

"Let's put the top down."

"No. It's about to rain."

"Aw, Molly, you never put the top down. How come you went buy a convertible if you never put the top down?"

"Because when I bought this car on the mainland, I didn't anticipate moving to a town with four times the annual rainfall of Seattle."

I didn't care for Davison's calling me by my first name, but I couldn't think of a better alternative. He wasn't my student anymore, so I couldn't insist on the delightfully impersonal "Professor Barda." I wasn't about to let him call me "Mommy," something he occasionally suggested just to annoy me.

I took a deep breath and tried to feel less cranky. Life was going well. I could afford to be gracious to my irritating stepson. I'd just been awarded tenure, which was a huge relief. Contrary to popular belief, tenure didn't guarantee a job for life, but it meant the administration couldn't fire me without making up a good reason first. I wasn't stuck on any year-round committees, so I had the whole summer free to work on my research. And today was a beautiful, overcast day, the strong Hawaiian sun diffused through a layer of mist. Traffic was light. Just one dark blue pickup truck behind me, and no one ahead.

"Davison, buying a ring usually means something serious. Are congratulations in order?"

"I don't wanna say yet. It's gonna be a surprise."

"A surprise? So you're not going to tell me who the lucky lady is?"

"Nuh-uh. Not yet. Soon, but."

I felt a pang of foreboding. Not Sherry Di Napoli. Surely, Davison wasn't back together with Sherry.

"Okay. Here we are." I pulled into Fujioka's narrow parking lot alongside the compact cinderblock building. The exterior had recently been repainted white; red script lettering adorned the road-facing wall. Fujioka's Music & Party Supply since 1949. The abandoned lot behind Fujioka's was overgrown with skeletal Albizia trees and dense strawberry guava. Odorous maile pilau twined through the ramshackle chain link fence.

I checked my reflection in the rear-view mirror. A coil of hair had sprung free from my pony-tail. I undid the hair tie, pulled a brush out of my glove compartment, and fastened my hair back into place. Out of the corner of my eye, I saw the dark blue pickup truck enter the lot and pull into a parking spot near the door. Davison, demonstrating his usual gracious manners, hopped out of the passenger seat and went inside, leaving me alone in the car.

I locked up and followed Davison. The heavy glass door set off a doorbell tone from the back of the shop when I pushed it open. Davison was already at the far end of the store, examining the fine jewelry case under the watchful eye of a uniformed guard. I lingered by the door and watched the blue truck through the glass. No one got out. It seemed odd, the truck just idling there, waiting, but I shrugged it off. Maybe the driver was simply waiting to give someone a ride. As long as I was on a break from work, I might as well enjoy myself and have a look around.

While Davison perused the jewelry case, I examined the guitars and ukuleles displayed on the walls. The last time I'd really played guitar was in grad school. This summer might be a good opportunity to take it up again.

A small instrument caught my eye. At first, I thought it was an ukulele, but closer examination revealed six strings, not four. It was a scaled-down guitar. The body and headstock were black, and the neck was rosewood. The price seemed surprisingly reasonable. I took it down from the display and strummed a D-major. It wouldn't win any awards, but then neither would my playing. It sounded like a real guitar. And it was adorable.

Davison materialized at my elbow.

"Did you find anything you liked?" I asked.

"Nah. Everything they got here is too plain."

I looked down at my simple platinum band, identical in design to Donnie's. I liked it. It had been an easy choice to make, as no other wedding set in Fujioka's inventory was even remotely to my taste.

"Too plain? If you don't like plain, what about the gold nugget horseshoe ring?"

"Nah. That's a man's ring. I wanna get her something classy an' girly kine. Like all different color diamonds and li' dat."

"Well, I'm sorry you didn't find anything up to your exacting standards. Fortunately, this wasn't a wasted trip. I think I'm going to get this guitar,"

"That little thing? Looks like a ukulele. What about a real guitar? Like the one up there? Wit' the flames on it?"

"An electric guitar?"

"You could crank it, Molly."

"I don't need to crank anything. I'd prefer an instrument not dependent on electricity, so when the Zombie Apocalypse takes out our power grid, I can still play."

"You gonna try start up your grad school band again?" Davison grinned. "Whaddaya think Dad would say about it?"

"I'm not planning to start another band, but I'm sure your father would be fine with it if I did."

While Donnie and I were still dating, Davison found out about my grad school band. This was thanks to some sneaky internet sleuthing and the assistance of a much-smarter girlfriend—Sherry, in fact. He had gleefully ratted me out to Donnie, probably hoping to embarrass me and shock his conservative father.

To my amazement, Donnie hadn't seemed bothered at all. He actually thought my short-lived musical career was "cute." (And for the record, it wasn't my idea to call ourselves Phallus in Wonderland. The name was Melanie Polewski's idea. Ever since she'd discovered Lacan in our Psychoanalysis and Literature class, you couldn't shut her up about The Phallus.)

"Are you sure you didn't find anything you liked?" We stood at the counter. "Maybe you should go have another look. This is really the only place you'll find a proper ring."

A silver bell sat on the counter, a hand-lettered sign taped down next to it. Please ring for assistance. I hoped I wouldn't have to, but I didn't see any store personnel anywhere. I reluctantly tapped the button, sending a halfhearted ding reverberating through the store.

"Taking too long, these guys." Davison pounded the bell four times in a row. Wendell, the manager, emerged from the back room, glaring at me. He rang up my purchase without a word.

The blue truck still sat in the parking lot when we exited the building. I tried to get a glimpse of the driver out of the corner of my eye as we walked out to my Thunderbird. The truck's windows were too darkly tinted for me to see anything inside.

"So Molly, we going down to Modern Jewelers now?"

"Modern Jewelers closed when the Shigeokas retired, remember? Maybe you were away at school then. Fujioka's is the only jewelry store left in Mahina. It's why your father and I bought our rings here. Maybe you don't want to buy her a ring just yet. What about a nice pair of earrings or something?"

Davison grumbled, but he didn't argue. I was right. Fujioka's was the only game in town, unless he wanted to start visiting pawnshops. We climbed into my car, and I nosed out to the road, paused, and signaled left. I could see the blue truck in my rear-view mirror, still parked. The driver's side door cracked open.

"What are you doing?" Davison asked.

"Just waiting to make a left turn onto the road." If I told Davison about the suspicious truck, he'd probably turn around and stare. Or worse, hop out of the car and get into some chest-thumping dominance display with the driver.

"There's no cars, Molly. What are you waiting for?"

In the rear-view mirror, I watched a man jump down from the driver's side of the truck, and stand next to it, hand on the door, scowling at the back of my car. He looked to be in his forties, his solid prison-yard physique straining the seams of a green football jersey. Clipped black hair, broad nose, defined cheekbones and a strong chin. He might have been handsome if he didn't look so mean. I could practically feel his gaze burning through his black sunglasses.

Davison finally caught on, and as I had feared, cranked his head around to stare at the man. My car did not have tinted windows. I floored the accelerator and squealed out onto the road, almost cutting off a minivan.

CHAPTER THREE

"DO YOU KNOW THAT GUY, Davison?"

Davison took a moment to catch his breath. "Nah. I don't know him. Thought maybe it was one of your old boyfriends or li' dat."

"Very amusing. He was probably just interested in the car."

People often stared at my car. It was the only 1959 Thunderbird on the island, and the turquoise-and-white paint job made it especially eye-catching. Earl Miyashiro, my mechanic, kept nagging me to trade in my beloved Squarebird for something more practical. Earl was a decent mechanic, but entirely lacking in imagination. Also, considering how much I'd spent at Miyashiro Motors over the years, you'd think he'd make an effort to be a little less judgmental.

"Listen, as long as we're already out, I'm going to stop by the grocery store. I have to pick up some more eggs, apparently. Anything else we need?"

"You need more milk too," Davison said. "You ran out already. An' the rice, ah?"

I made a careful left turn onto the Bayfront Road. The sherbet pastels of the Old West style storefronts glowed under the gray sky. From a distance, in a moving car, Mahina's Bayfront looked cheery and vibrant and not at all shabby or termite-eaten. I pulled into a spot in front of the blacklight Bob Marley posters lining the windows of Sacred Herb.

We walked the few doors down to Natural High Organic Foods and stepped into the ginseng-and-five-spice scented interior. I grabbed a hand basket and headed toward the dairy refrigerator in the back.

"This place get beer?" Davison was close behind me. "If no, we gotta stop at Hagiwara's."

"I don't want to stop anywhere else. I want to go home and get some work done on my book chapter."

"Oh yeah, you gotta get more Spam, too. You're almost out."

I opened the glass door to the dairy case and savored the chilled air.

"So, you do eat Spam. I take it you're not doing your back-to-nature diet anymore then?"

"Nah. Too humbug."

During his previous visit, Davison had observed a strict dietary regime. It allowed organ meats and leafy greens but banned grains and dairy. Naturally, Donnie had catered to his son, cooking every meal to his new guidelines. It was a dark era of gizzard stews and salads bristling with husks and stems.

"Don't get the small milk, ah Molly. Gets used up too fast, that's why."

I sighed, put back the quart container, and pulled out a half gallon instead.

"Eh, what would you and Dad say if I didn't go back to school in the fall?"

I almost dropped the milk on the floor.

"Not back to school? What do you mean?"

"What if I took a break?"

"What? No. Why would you want to take a break? Do you not have enough money? We can lend you money. How much do you need?"

"Just like for a year." Davison followed me to the produce section.

"A year? Away from college? Where would you live for a whole year?"

I didn't like to be inhospitable, but Davison had been back for only two days, and I'd already had enough. He left wadded up shirts and dirty dishes everywhere. He ate like an army of locusts coming off spring training. Worst of all, he was just there all the time. Trying to enjoy alone time with my husband was pretty much out of the question with his obnoxious son thumping around in the next room.

"I thought you liked it at the academy." I tried to disguise the desperation in my voice. "And you get all four seasons back east. People love seasons. And if you drop out it'll be hard to get back in. Your father and I don't want you to lose your momentum."

"I could always come back to Mahina State."

The military academy was Davison's third try at college. He'd left Mahina State for a fancy liberal arts college in Southern California, where he'd goofed off, lost his athletic scholarship, and eventually gotten kicked out for cheating. Donnie and I had hoped the structured environment of his current institution would keep him on track.

"You don't want to come back to Mahina State. You should try to stick it out where you are."

I bustled around the store, trying to pick out snacks that were edible, but not so tasty they'd disappear right away. Plain yogurt. Frozen broccoli. Raw almonds, instead of roasted.

"You know lots of famous guys, they never finished college at all," Davison said.

"Now you're talking about not finishing at all? I thought you said you just wanted to take a break."

I checked out, and we exited to the sidewalk. Davison didn't offer to carry the bag, which was just as well. He'd probably stick his face into it and start eating the groceries.

"Dad never went to college," Davison persisted.

"Davison, you don't want to drop out and move back here. Look at everything you've already—"

"Look out," he shouted, but it was too late. I'd been focused on arguing with Davison, not watching where I was going, and I'd collided with a broad chest in a green football jersey. I looked up. No sunglasses this time. The man's eyes were flat, black irises revealing nothing.

He placed a heavy hand on my shoulder.

"Excuse me, ma'am." His voice was deep, with a local inflection. He kept the hand on my shoulder and turned to stare at Davison.

Davison glowered back. This went on for the longest two seconds I have ever experienced.

"I'm terribly sorry." I finally ducked out of the man's grip. I nudged Davison ahead of me with the bag of groceries. I could feel the stranger's opaque black eyes watching us as we hurried down the sidewalk.

Once we were safely inside the car, Davison decided to be brave. He unbuckled his seatbelt and grabbed the door handle.

"You wait here, Molly. I'm gonna go back there and kick his—"

"It's fine, Davison. No harm done. He didn't even break the eggs. And I was the one who bumped into him. Please buckle in so I don't get a ticket."

I twisted the key in the ignition a few times and pumped the gas pedal until the engine turned over.

I backed out of the parking space and drove the way we had come, watching the sidewalk, but I didn't see the man in the green football jersey.

"Eh, Molly, stop."

"No. I'm not stopping. The least I can do is not get you into a brawl with some stranger the minute we leave the house."

"It's Uncle Brian."

"Who?"

"Uncle Brian. What I just said."

Davison pointed to a dapper old gentleman strolling down the sidewalk. The man wore wide-leg trousers, a tan windbreaker, and a porkpie hat. His ensemble would have fetched top dollar at the trendy vintage place I used to shop at, the one just off La Brea.

"Who is Uncle Brian?" I pulled over and parked again.

Davison jumped out of the car and charged over to the man. I winced as my hulking stepson caught the frail senior citizen in a bear hug. Uncle Brian appeared unharmed, though.

By the time I joined them, they were chatting.

Davison switched from Pidgin to Standard American English as I approached. "Uncle, this is Dad's new wife. Molly, this is Uncle Brian."

Uncle Brian grinned, flashing a mouthful of perfect white teeth, and pulled me in for a hug. He smelled like wintergreen and hair oil.

"Looks just like Sherry, this one." Uncle Brian released me. "He like the Italian wahine, ah, your fadda?"

"She's not Italian, Uncle." Davison was clearly proud of his insider knowledge. "She's Armenian."

"Albanian. Very nice to meet you. How do you and Davison know each other?"

"Your husband, Donnie, was my brother's boy."

So "Uncle" wasn't simply an honorific in this case. Uncle Brian was Donnie's literal uncle. I absorbed this revelation as Davison and Uncle Brian resumed chatting, quickly lapsing back into Pidgin. I could follow the conversation but didn't have much to contribute. They speculated about mutual acquaintances, said some things to each other about sports, and discussed getting together now that Davison was back in town.

"He seems nice," I said evenly as we drove uphill from the ocean toward the house. "I didn't know your father had an uncle. Or any living relatives at all, besides his sister."

"Yeah, Uncle Brian's cool."

Donnie rarely talked about his family. I knew he had a sister, Gloria, who lived in the San Francisco Bay Area. Gloria was Davison's biological mother, but Donnie had adopted and raised Davison as his own. Why Davison's mother had given him up, and who Davison's biological father was, I had no idea. The most interesting (by which I mean sordid) part of the family saga had to do with Donnie's first wife, Sherry Di Napoli.

Sherry ran off when Davison was eight years old. Years later, Sherry and Davison reconnected, but neither one realized they had once been a family. Davison and Sherry were both reasonably attractive, and neither of them was ever going to end up in the Impulse Control Hall of Fame, so you can imagine how that went. By the time the truth was out, it was too late for either of them to be too bothered about it. As Sherry memorably said of her former stepson, "He's not a light bulb. I can't un-screw him."

Sherry had been in and out of Davison's life ever since.

I knew Sherry, and I got along with her, but I wouldn't trust her as far as I could throw my Thunderbird. Donnie acknowledged an "unhealthy attachment" between Sherry and Davison but preferred to remain in denial about the particulars.

I couldn't really blame Donnie for not wanting to acknowledge the Sherry and Davison situation. And perhaps Donnie's sister wanted to keep the circumstances of Davison's adoption private, which would explain Donnie's reticence on the topic. But it was curious, I reflected, that Donnie had never once mentioned his Uncle Brian.

CHAPTER FOUR

THE FIRST THING I DID was clear a place in the closet for my new instrument. According to the Fujioka's receipt, it was a "Guitalele," a term I had no intention of using. After I'd put away my guitar, I came back out to the kitchen. My unhelpful stepson had opened the milk, left the carton out on the counter, and disappeared into his room. I put away the groceries by myself.

Maybe I hadn't been as productive as I'd planned, and I'd let Davison take up way too much of my day, but I had a rare treat planned for the evening. Donnie and I had a dinner date at the Maritime Club, Mahina's oldest private club and possibly the last place on earth with Baked Alaska on the menu. My entrepreneurial husband (I've never cared for the term "workaholic," as there's no such substance as "workohol") had taken the evening off and scheduled one of his capable managers to cover the dinner shift at Donnie's Drive-Inn.

I planned to make sure to tell Donnie I'd taken Davison shopping. Donnie sincerely believed if I spent time getting to know Davison, I would learn to love my new stepson as much as he did. I didn't share Donnie's optimism, but I wanted to let him know I was trying. Naturally, I'd have to curate the day's events a little. I wouldn't mention the scary man in the green football jersey. We would probably never see him again anyway, and telling Donnie would only make him worry.

I went back to the bedroom to choose something to wear and glanced at the clock on the dresser. The deadline to upload final grades for spring semester was six p.m. I'd wait until a quarter till. I'd found if I released grades early, students would see it as an opportunity to open negotiations.

Niccolo Machiavelli advised that severities should be dealt out all at once, so that their suddenness may give less offense. Machiavelli's counsel more or less guided my grade-posting policy.

I pulled out three outfits from the closet and laid them out on the bed. My Lilli Ann cocktail dress required a corset underneath, which would interfere with my enjoyment of dinner. Also, this choice might require some stealth, as Donnie didn't know I even owned a corset, and I didn't feel like explaining it to him. My vintage fitted cheongsam in magenta silk looked stunning when I was standing up, but I wasn't sure I could sit down in it.

I decided to go with silver silk trousers and an ivory blouse. I was just hanging up the cheongsam when I heard Donnie's car in the carport, and then his keys in the door. I hurried out to meet him.

My husband was remarkably easy on the eyes. Even at the end of the workday, when he would walk into the house wearing his perfectly pressed red Donnie's Drive-Inn polo shirt, the armbands straining over his biceps, and he flashed me that gorgeous smile—sorry, where was I?

Right. Getting dressed for dinner. I intercepted Donnie at the door with a big hug. He looked around a little self-consciously, and then grinned and hugged me back.

"What'd I do to deserve this?"

"I'm just happy to see you. The semester's over. Grading is done. I'm not interim department chair anymore, and I'm looking forward to a nice dinner out."

"It's just the Chamber of Commerce awards banquet. Not exactly the most romantic surroundings."

"It's okay. I'm planning to enjoy it anyway."

"Did Davison behave himself today?"

"Yes. In fact, I took him shopping."

Donnie pulled back and beamed at me.

"Shopping? Where'd you go?"

"Oh, just Natural High for some groceries. And Fujioka's."

"The music store? What were you doing there?"

"I bought a guitar. Don't worry," I added quickly. "It was inexpensive."

Donnie had been worried about cash flow recently. Something about daily receipts at the Drive-Inn. When I asked him about it, all he would tell me was that it was just temporary, and nothing to be troubled about.

"Molly, I'm not concerned about the money. So are you going to start playing again?"

"I want to. Donnie, you have to see it. It looks like an ukulele, but it's actually a proper six-string guitar. It's adorable."

"A guitar that looks like an ukulele? Is there a name for it?"

"No, it's just a guitar. Okay, I know we have to go soon. Let me get the grades uploaded before we leave."

I sat down at my workstation and opened the Mahina State University Learning Management System.

"You're a little underdressed for dinner, Molly. Where's Davison?"

I realized I was sitting in the living room in my bathrobe. I'd have to get used to not having the house to myself.

"He's back in the guest room, I think. Oh, Donnie, speaking of Davison. Has he said anything to you about being in a serious relationship? Like buying an engagement ring serious?"

"No, he hasn't mentioned anything to me. Why? Is there someone you'd like to introduce him to?"

"No. I was just wondering if you knew why he might be ring shopping. He hinted there was someone special, but he wasn't specific. "

"I think Davison's a long way from being ready to settle down. He has to finish college first."

"I agree." I pressed the "upload" button to enter the final grades and stood up. "I have my outfit laid out already, so I'm just going to log off and—"

A "boop" sounded from my computer.

"It sounds like you have a new message," Donnie said. "Do you want to check it before we go?"

"It can wait. We should get going—"

"Boop," went my computer. "Boop."

"You're right. I probably should check my mail before we go. That way I won't be worrying about it over dinner."

CHAPTER FIVE

I SAT DOWN AT THE COMPUTER again.

"This is impossible. I just uploaded the grades. How did she get back to me so quickly? What, was she sitting by her computer refreshing the display every five seconds?"

"All capital letters?" Donnie peered over my shoulder. "This must be really important."

I HAVE 57% ON THE WRITTEN ASSIGNMENTS, 58% ON THE QUIZZES, 58% ON THE FINAL, 98% ATTENDANCE, AND 77% ON THE MIDTERM, SO MY TOTAL GRADE IS 347%. THAT IS A PASSING GRADE PLEASE FIX THIS ASAP.

I stood up. "I'm not dealing with this right now."

"I'm going to take a quick shower," Donnie said. "Do you think you can be ready in about twenty minutes?"

"Oh, sure, I—"

"Boop. Boop," went my computer as new messages popped up at the top of my inbox.

"What's going on?" Donnie frowned at my computer.

I sat down again. "Grade-grubbing season has begun. You think this is bad, you should see what Emma gets. She teaches introductory biology, so every semester she crushes the dreams of dozens of future doctors. It's so bad she's started carrying around a little pen recorder for when students claim she promised them extra credit or whatever."

"You're not going to try to answer all of these right now, are you?" Donnie glanced at his watch. "Can't you leave some of these for later?"

"I will. Oh, wait. Here's one from the marketing office. Do I want to continue being listed on the speakers' roster? Sure, why not. Yes, I'd be delighted, press reply, and sent. Okay. Done. Oh no, something else from the Student Retention Office about our new Humor Initiative."

"Can you ignore it for now?"

"Better than that. I'm deleting it."

I powered off my computer and followed Donnie into the bedroom.

"Your dirty Drive-Inn shirts are on the dresser," I said. "Did you want me to put them by the front door? When is the pickup again?"

"I'll take care of the shirts. Thanks for offering. I want to add this one, too."

Donnie pulled off the shirt he was wearing, rendering me momentarily speechless.

"You should put a vacation responder on your email." He folded his shirt neatly and added it to the stack on the dresser.

"How do you know about vacation responders, Donnie? I've never known you to go on vacation."

"I get them from other people sometimes. The person is out of the office until a certain date. If your matter is urgent, please contact the main desk at this number."

"You know what? That's a good idea. I know the Student Retention Office won't like it, because they think we should be at their beck and call twenty-four-seven, but I'm not getting paid over the summer, and they are. Donnie, do you mind if I just get these shirts out of the way?"

I retrieved the cleaner's bag from the closet, swept the stack of used shirts into it, and handed it to Donnie.

"Oh. Sorry. I'll bring this out to the car when we go. Hey, you don't have to let the Student Retention Office push you around anymore. You have tenure now." He disappeared into the bathroom.

"That's right," I called after him. "I do have tenure now. No more unpaid summer work. No more giving do-overs to plagiarists and cheaters."

I remembered who was occupying the guest room next door, and quickly changed the subject.

"I'm not going to think about work right now. I'm going to get dressed up and enjoy a lovely dinner."

I stood in front of the mirrored closet door and examined my face. My makeup was mostly intact, so I didn't have to wash it off and start over. I dabbed away under-eye mascara flakes with a Q-tip and blotted the shine from my skin. Good enough. I hung up my bathrobe, dumped baby powder into my armpits, swung my arms back and forth to disperse the powder, and pulled on the trousers and blouse. Then I rubbed a greasy dab of VO5 between my palms and pulled it through my hair a few times to define the curl.

"Oh, and Donnie," I called into the bathroom. "I'm going to wear those beautiful platinum earrings and necklace you gave me. Can I come in and get them?"

The shower was already running, and he couldn't hear me. I went into the steamy bathroom and checked the vanity counter for my necklace and earrings. They weren't there.

I went back out to the bedroom, knelt down, and peered along the floor. The hard maple was smooth and flat. Even a piece of lint would be easy to see, let alone a glittering earring. I stood up, brushed off my knees, checked behind the dresser, and then pulled the comforter off the bed and shook it, listening for a reassuring clatter.

Nothing.

I checked the top drawer of the dresser to make sure I hadn't put the jewelry away. I hadn't. The velvet boxes were empty.

I had a clear mental image of the two earrings with the pear-shaped diamonds, and the necklace, a delicate Edwardian confection of slender ribbons set with sparkling gems. I'd taken them out this morning and polished them with baking soda until they sparkled. And then set them down...where?

My jewelry had been here this morning. Now it was gone.

And the only people in the house were Donnie, Davison and me.

Davison, I recalled, was in the market for baubles.

It wouldn't be any use to accuse anyone of theft. Even if I was sure who the guilty party was (and I was sure, make no mistake), I had to play dumb and pretend I had no idea what had happened to my jewelry. According to Donnie, his wonderful son was incapable of wrongdoing.

The bathroom door opened, and Donnie emerged, a towel wrapped around his waist, a fragrant cloud of shower steam billowing out behind him.

"You look great," he said. "I'll be ready to go in five minutes."

"My jewelry's disappeared. We need to call the police."

CHAPTER SIX

WHILE WE WERE WAITING for the police to show up, Donnie searched the rest of the house with me. We went over the living-dining-kitchen area, the spare room next to the guest room, and the master bath. We even took the flashlight outside and examined every square inch of the lanai. The only place we didn't look was Davison's room.

By the time we heard the knock on the door, we'd been over the house twice. Donnie answered it. Davison hadn't come out of his room. He was either oblivious to the whole thing or, more likely, hiding out and hoping no one suspected him of nicking my jewelry.

The uniformed police officer came in and introduced himself as Andy De Silva. He already seemed to know Donnie. Of course just about everyone in Mahina knew the owner and founder of Donnie's Drive-Inn. Officer De Silva would have been difficult to describe to a police sketch artist. Mid-thirties to early forties, I guessed. Brown hair, beaky features, weak chin, generally unmemorable. He'd make a terrific spy. He could walk right by you, and you'd forget him immediately.

The three of us sat down on the couch, and Officer De Silva pulled out a tiny notebook. I was surprised he didn't have something digital.

"Shouldn't Davison be here?" I asked.

"Davison?" Donnie frowned. "He doesn't know anything about this."

"Donnie, I think Officer De Silva wanted to talk with everyone in the house."

"Davison's here?" De Silva said. "He might have seen something. You never know. I'll ask him if he knows anything about it."

Donnie went to get Davison from his room. When Davison emerged, he still wore the same outfit he'd had on earlier: cutoff sweats and a tank top. One side of his face was creased from where he'd been sleeping on it. No slumber-robbing pangs of conscience for him. As soon as he spotted the uniformed officer, he stood up straight and switched into suckup mode.

"Good evening, Officer De Silva. How may I help you?"

"Some jewelry is missing from your parents' bedroom. Did you see or notice anything unusual?"

"What? Molly, your jewelry is missing?"

"Yes, Davison. My platinum earrings and necklace. The set your father gave me. Have you seen them, by any chance?"

"No, I didn't see anything. My apologies, Officer. I wish I could be more helpful."

Officer De Silva nodded. "Okay. Thanks for your help."

Davison turned around and sauntered back to his room.

"Aren't you going to ask him anything else?" I entreated De Silva. "How did he know it was my jewelry that was missing?"

"Molly," Donnie said. "You're the only one in this house who wears jewelry."

It was true. Davison had gone through a pirate earring phase, and then an ear gauge phase, but since he'd been attending the military academy, he'd been letting the holes close up.

"Officer De Silva, maybe you should search his room." I avoided making eye contact with Donnie, who was trying to give me a look. "I'm suggesting looking in Davison's room because it's the only place we haven't tried yet."

De Silva made a note.

"Do you have any kind of housekeeping or cleaning service? Or anyone else who has a key to your house?"

"We do," Donnie said. "It's the same service I've used for the last fifteen years. I've never had any problem with them."

"And just to clarify, sorry to interrupt, Donnie, the cleaners weren't here today. I remember polishing the necklace and earrings just this morning."

"Do you have a house alarm?" Officer De Silva asked. I exchanged a glance with Donnie.

"No," I said. "We've talked about it, but what we've heard from other people about the number of false alarms, we didn't think it was worth the trouble."

"Usually in cases like this, it's rare to recover the items." De Silva stood up.

"Is there anything we can do?" I asked. Besides rifling through my stepson's belongings the minute he's out of the house, of course.

"Not really. Wait a week and see if it turns up. If not, report it to your insurance company. Maybe you could check the local pawnshops, but you probably won't have much luck. Someone steals something, they're not gonna try sell it in the same neighborhood where someone could recognize it. These people who come through and buy gold. It's where the stuff usually ends up."

"The ones with the big ads in the newspaper?" I asked.

"Those are the ones. The stolen goods usually end up off island pretty quick. So, how's Gloria doing? You hear from her lately?"

We were done with trying to solve a theft, apparently, and had moved on to small talk.

"She's fine. Her business is doing well."

"That's good." Andy De Silva seemed like he didn't want to leave yet. "She ever come back to Mahina?"

"I don't think she has any travel plans in the near future."

"Oh. Okay. Well, next time you talk to her, give her my love."

"Will do."

Donnie stood up. Not wanting to be the only one left sitting, I followed suit.

"Take care of yourself."

"Thank you, Officer," I added as De Silva clomped down the wooden steps of our front lanai.

"Oh, Mrs. Gonsalves," Andy called back as he opened the driver's side door of his police cruiser. "See you Monday, ah?"

It took me a few seconds to register that "Mrs. Gonsalves" meant me.

"I'm sorry. What's Monday?"

But he was already driving away.

CHAPTER SEVEN

"SEE ME MONDAY?" I ASKED Donnie. "What was that about?"

Donnie shrugged and closed the door.

"I feel like I'm the only person in Mahina who's never met your sister."

"She doesn't get back to Hawai`i very often. She and her husband are running their own business on the mainland. It's hard for them to get away."

"Well, I hope I get a chance to meet her someday. Oof, what an adventure. Officer De Silva seems nice, anyway."

"He's personable."

"Donnie, you know what sounds good right now? A nice glass of wine."

He nodded, went to the kitchen, and took down two wine glasses from the cupboard. Donnie's stemware collection was a far cry from the repurposed furikake cups I'd used during my single days.

"Sangiovese?" He pulled a bottle from the mini-cellar, a knee-high wine storage and cooling gizmo, which looked like a dorm fridge. Before Donnie had moved in with me, my preferred wine storage method had been to stack the boxes in the pantry.

"Sangiovese sounds delightful, thanks."

I sank onto the couch, the reasonably priced black leather one I'd bought at Balusteros World of Furniture when I first moved to Mahina. One of these days we'd get something nicer, but the couch had held up pretty well, and it was easy to clean. Even red-wine spills wiped off without leaving a trace.

"What kind of business does your sister have?" I took the glass from Donnie as he sat down next to me.

"It's a health spa."

"And she's in Palo Alto, isn't she?"

"Los Gatos."

"I wish I knew more about your family. I've barely even talked to your sister on the phone."

"You'll meet her one day, I'm sure."

"That'd be nice." I pulled a coaster off the stack and set down my empty wine glass. "Should we still go to the dinner? Or is it too late now?"

"I think we've already missed dinner. By the time we get down there, they'll be wrapping it up."

"Well, at least you got to see me all dressed up." I smoothed my silver silk palazzo pants and straightened my collar. "Even if I didn't have my beautiful platinum parure to set it off."

"You look beautiful." Donnie stroked my hair. "I can still take you to out dinner if you want."

"It's nice of you to offer, but it's late now. Everything's closed. Even the Drive-Inn is closed by now, isn't it?"

"I think Chang's Pizza Pagoda is still open." Donnie was volunteering to line the pockets of one of his main competitors, just so I wouldn't be disappointed.

"No, it's okay. What if someone sees us out when we were supposed to be at the Chamber of Commerce thing? It wouldn't look right."

"Good point. I'll throw something together for us. How about pasta?"

"Sounds great. Are you sure?" I was so hungry even the Maritime Club's iceberg lettuce and bleu cheese dinner salad seemed tantalizing.

"Very sure." Donnie gave me a quick kiss on the forehead and went into the kitchen.

"Davison," he called in the direction of the guest room. "You want something to eat?"

Davison emerged, wearing long pants and a dark blue hoodie. "Nah. I'm gonna go out."

"You need to borrow the car?" Donnie asked.

"You're going out now?" I said. "Where's there to go in Mahina? Everything's closed."

"No need. I got a friend coming by."

Off to fence my stolen jewelry, no doubt. There was nothing I could do about it, unless I wanted to tackle Davison on his way out and try patting him down.

"Why don't you stay and have a bite before you go?" I asked sweetly.

"Nah. You guys'll have plenty more chances to feed me. No worries."

Davison strolled out the front door and disappeared into the dark.

"Aren't you worried about him?" I asked Donnie. "Going out in the middle of the night by himself?"

"Molly, it's nice of you to want to mother him, but he is a grown man."

Donnie disappeared into the pantry and emerged with some dried pasta and an armful of jars. Garlic and fresh tomatoes materialized, and within minutes, the kitchen smelled better than any restaurant in Mahina. I carried our wineglasses to the counter and hitched myself up onto a barstool to watch Donnie work his culinary magic.

"Don't worry about the jewelry." Donnie pulled down various pots, pans and bowls and assembled them around the stove. "If it doesn't turn up, I'll find you a replacement."

"But you said it was irreplaceable."

"Unique, not irreplaceable. Only people are irreplaceable." He filled a pot with water and set it on the stove. Then he got out a cutting board and started whacking cloves of garlic with a broad knife blade to pop off the skins.

"Do you really think my jewelry's going to 'turn up'? You don't think someone took it, then?"

"You have been known to misplace things." Donnie lit the gas stove with a "whoomp." I was still getting used to having an open flame inside the house. Donnie had installed a propane stove to replace my electric range, not something one undertook lightly. The island was made of cooled lava, which was hard to dig through. Active volcanoes kept the ground in constant motion. The underground gas lines so common on the mainland would be impractical and dangerous in Hawai`i. For Donnie, cooking over a flame instead of an electric coil was worth the trouble of installing a propane stove and getting the tanks refilled.

"I looked all over the bedroom, Donnie. I know my earrings and necklace didn't fall behind the dresser or onto the floor. I would've seen them. And why do you say I misplace things?"

"Don't you remember the time I found your shoe boxes in your oven? I still can't figure out how those got in there. You must've been pretty distracted that day."

"Good point."

Before Donnie and I were married, I used my oven for overflow shoe storage. I'd never told him. It would have made me seem frivolous.

"Well, here we are." Donnie turned around and grinned. "It wasn't exactly the evening we expected, but we might as well make the most of it."

"The most of it? Sure." I wondered whether Davison was planning to sell my jewelry outright or drop it in the mail to Sherry. Unless Sherry was on the island, and he was meeting her now...

"...so why not celebrate?" Donnie continued.

"Celebrate?"

"Life is good. I have a beautiful wife. You have the summer off, and we have our son visiting. It's nice to have the whole family together, isn't it?"

I resisted the urge to make the obvious "two out of three" comment. "I'll take the compliment. But I don't exactly have the summer off. I have to turn a data file and a two-sentence abstract into a full-blown book chapter."

"Do you have to? You're not getting paid for the summer." Donnie brought the bottle of Sangiovese over to the counter, sat down next to me, and refilled our glasses.

"True, I'm not getting paid for the summer. But with my teaching load, summer is the only time to get my research done. So basically, I have twelve months' worth of work do to, but I only get paid for nine. I'm not complaining. It's still a good job. And I'm grateful I have tenure. Which, by the way, is not a guaranteed job for life."

Donnie set down his glass.

"I know. It just means they can't fire you without making up a reason first. So have you thought any more about our, you know, discussion?"

"Discussion? Oh. The baby discussion."

"How do you feel about it?" Donnie asked.

"You know, I never used to understand why people wanted children. Even my parents. They went way out of their way to adopt me. I'm glad they did, of course, but I never saw myself doing the same thing. All of the research indicates people are objectively happier without children."

"So what are you saying?" Donnie looked worried.

"Sorry. My mother always tells me I ramble. No, you know what? I do understand it now. Wanting a baby."

"Really?" Donnie took my hand and squeezed it gently.

In that moment, he wasn't the confident entrepreneur I knew. He was a supplicant, approaching me as if I were some sacred, forbidden temple. And bloody well right, too, as I was going to be the one doing all of the heavy lifting in this enterprise.

"Yes. I know it sounds kind of corny, but it's like you and I have all of this love for each other, and there's so much of it we almost need another little person here to help soak it all up. Kind of like when you have sauce left on your plate and you need more bread. Sorry, that's not a very good analogy. I must be really hungry."

"Sauce!" Donnie jumped up and ran to the stove, where the pot was starting to boil over.

CHAPTER EIGHT

DONNIE HAD LEFT FOR work by the time I woke up. A rectangle of hot sunshine lay across the white bedding. Despite a lingering headache and the memory of my missing jewelry, I felt pretty good. Donnie and I had enjoyed a nice dinner a deux the night before, and now I had the whole day in front of me. I planned to be productive enough to make up for yesterday.

I started by rearranging my workspace. I tried out various layouts of mouse pad, keyboard, and pencil cup. When I had attained a satisfactory configuration, I started up the computer. The library login was slow, so I went to the kitchen for a coffee refill. I finished logging in, finished my coffee, went to the bathroom, got a third cup of coffee, and checked my email. I was about to get to work on the book chapter when I heard a vehicle outside the house.

I pulled the curtain aside in time to see the mail truck pulling away. I knew I should close the curtain and get back to work. Time management experts advise ignoring both physical mail and email until after lunchtime. The problem was I didn't want to wait.

Working at home sounds like heaven to people who have never done it. Imagine rolling into the "office" in your pajamas, your only commute the distance from the coffee machine to the computer. Unfortunately, it gets lonely and boring pretty fast. I remember reading a study of "virtual" employees where one at-home worker reported the highlight of his day was when the mail came. Only a few days into my self-directed summer, I understood exactly what he meant.

Today's mail contained little to get excited about: a water bill, a flyer from Chang's Pizza Pagoda, and a thin white envelope from the Mahina Police Department. The latter was doubtless a copy of the police report. Had there been any good news about my stolen jewelry, they'd have called. I stuck the envelope from Mahina PD in the bill box. I'd send it along to our insurance company later. The Chang's Pizza Pagoda flyer went into the trash.

I knew I should get to work on my book chapter, but as long as I was thinking of it, maybe I'd have another look around for my missing jewelry. I had daylight and might see something I'd overlooked the night before. I took a small flashlight from the kitchen utility drawer, went back into the bedroom, and raked the light over the floor.

There was scarcely a dust mote in evidence, let alone a glittering pair of pear-shaped diamonds or a gem-encrusted necklace. I shone the light behind the dresser, illuminating a light coating of dust on the wall. Alas, no jewelry. I shone the light around the floor again, with the same result.

I hadn't heard Davison come in. He must have stayed out all night. This was my chance. If I found my jewelry in his room, I could just steal it back. What could he say about it? Donnie certainly wouldn't approve of my snooping, so I'd have to do it when they were both out of the house. This was my chance.

The guest room door was ajar. I knocked gently. When there was no answer, I knocked harder, and then pushed the door open.

I stood, listening for Davison clumping up the front steps. Or Donnie turning his key in the door. What if one of them walked in on me? I would simply say I was tidying up or looking for a spare fire extinguisher or something.

I tiptoed into the room.

The air was heavy with cloying cologne and a ripe, meaty aroma. Someone would have to launder the pile of bedding. That someone would probably end up being me. Davison's backpack lay in the middle of the floor, exactly where someone would be most likely to trip on it.

I picked up the backpack and shook it. It was disappointingly light. Inside I found a pen, a yellowed receipt, and a single sock, but no jewelry. I turned it upside-down, shook it again, and then searched for hidden pockets. Nothing.

Then I tried the chest of drawers. I rooted through the anarchy of socks and boxer briefs in the top drawer. Where better to hide something valuable? But I found nothing.

The next drawer down had a few rolled-up tank tops and a couple of pairs of shorts. The shorts pockets contained some loose change, lint, and a few crumbs of what looked like oregano. The next two drawers were empty. The closet was bare except for a few forlorn hangers.

There was one more obvious place to look. If Davison hadn't already fenced my jewelry, it might be hidden under the mattress. I paused and listened but didn't hear anything out of the ordinary. A car drove by; a lawnmower hummed in the distance.

I grabbed an armload of blankets and lifted them off the mattress.

I did not expect to see Davison lying on the bed in his boxer shorts.

I yelped and dropped the blankets back down on top of him. He pushed them out of the way and sat up, grinning.

"Eh, just let me brush my teeth first."

"What are you doing here? I thought you were out."

"What are you doing here, Molly?"

"I was looking for something."

He held his arms out, displaying his hairless, laser-blotched chest and his bristling armpits. A baby beer belly pooched out over the top of his boxer shorts.

"You find what you're looking for?"

"Stop it. Davison, why didn't you say anything when I knocked?"

"How come you're in my room?"

"I'm looking for a fire extinguisher. I don't have to explain myself."

I hurried out, slamming the door behind me.

CHAPTER NINE

A MUFFLED RING SOUNDED from the living room. I dashed over to my workstation and retrieved my phone. The Caller ID flashed Patrick Flanagan. Pat used to be a crime reporter at The County Courier. Now he taught introductory composition part time at Mahina State University, which was how I knew him. He also ran Island Confidential, Mahina's newsblog.

"Pat. What a nice surprise."

"Surprise? I hope not."

"What?"

"Aren't you dropping me off at the airport?"

"Yes, but that's not till the fourteenth, right?"

"Molly, today's the fourteenth. Are you okay? You sound out of breath."

I peered at the calendar in the corner of my computer screen. To my surprise, Pat was right. Today was May fourteenth.

"I'm fine. I thought today was going to be a lot more productive than it's been so far. I wasted a lot of time looking for some missing jewelry. Am I picking you up at your place?"

I hoped Pat would say no. He lived forty minutes up the mountain, at the end of a long dirt driveway, which during the rainy season turned into a rock-and-mud obstacle course. And on this side of the island, the rainy season was about fifty weeks long.

"I don't want to make you drive all the way up the mountain to get me."

"Oh, that's okay. I don't mind."

"No, I'll park down at the university. I know they don't have the manpower to monitor the parking lots over the summer, so I won't be towed. Just meet me there."

"Well, if you're sure. I'll meet you there in a few minutes."

I pulled into the parking lot by the dilapidated portables that used to house our music department. I inched along the buckled asphalt to avoid scraping the underside of my car, not relishing the thought of having to hunt down another replacement muffler. The worst part would be the inevitable lecture from Earl Miyashiro of Miyashiro Motors.

All this decay did have an upside. The beat-up portables and cracked, weed-infested parking lot now attracted a particular type of photographer, the kind that worked exclusively in black and white and specialized in images of decay. Now and then, I saw an image on social media with a title like "Desolation" or "Despair," with Mahina State University's Parking Lot B clearly recognizable in the background.

I hadn't been parked long before Pat showed up. I smelled Pat's car before I saw it. Pat drove a diesel Mercedes, which had been converted to burn cooking oil. Everywhere Pat went, he wafted the fragrance of fried potatoes behind him.

Pat stepped out of his car and unfolded himself to his full six-foot-plus height. He was not an approachable-looking man. Tall and gaunt, with his hair cropped to stubble length, he wore a tattered flannel shirt, ratty jeans, and black work boots. His luggage consisted of an over-stuffed, dirty green backpack.

He climbed into my front seat and placed the backpack between his feet. His filthy shoes were leaving dirt smudges on my floorboard carpet, but by the time I noticed, the damage was done. I'd have to clean it up later.

"So, what was stressing you out this morning?" Pat buckled in as I backed out of the parking spot and steered carefully to the exit. I told Pat about my missing jewelry and my unsuccessful search of Davison's room.

"I don't understand you, Molly. Why didn't you just tell Davison you were looking for your jewelry?"

"Because Davison would complain to Donnie. And then Donnie would get all upset at me for accusing poor innocent Davison of theft."

"Well, you snuck into his room and snatched off his blanket. What do you think he's is going to tell Donnie now?"

"I don't know. I told him I was looking for a fire extinguisher."

Pat chuckled.

"Wow, you two have some serious sibling rivalry going on there."

"What are you talking about? Who two?"

"You and Davison. You're worried about him telling on you. Like two kids fighting in the back seat. It's like you and him are in this ongoing competition for Donnie's approval."

"That's ridiculous."

We were at the main road now, left-turn signal ticking, waiting for an opening in the traffic.

"You know the thing you need to remember about your missing jewelry. When stuff like this happens, it's never who you think it is."

"Who else could have taken it? No one else was in the house. Unless it was the weird guy who was following me."

"A weird guy was following you?"

"Not really. Well, maybe."

I pulled out of the parking lot onto the road. "I was pulling out of Fujioka's and this guy was standing in the parking lot, just staring at us."

"Lots of people stare at this car."

"And then we bumped into him downtown. Same guy."

"This is Mahina. You always bump into the same people. Any idea who he was?"

"He did look kind of familiar."

"He did? So you've seen him before?"

"No. Maybe. I'm not sure now. He didn't look unfamiliar."

"Just promise me you won't get into any trouble while I'm gone. I hate missing all the fun."

"You won't miss anything. It's going to be a perfectly boring summer. And the fact that you're going out of town will make it even more boring."

"You're a respectable married woman now. You're supposed to have a boring life. Anyway, are you sure there isn't anything exciting going on around your home and hearth?"

I didn't want to tell Pat that Donnie and I had been talking about starting a family. Pat wouldn't be sympathetic. Pat was a lapsed Catholic and a devout misanthrope. As far as he was concerned, the sooner the human race died off, the better.

"Not really. I thought I'd like working at home, but I'm already getting cabin fever."

"Cabin fever? You're not enjoying your fabulous new remodel?"

"You mean Donnie's fabulous new remodel of my house."

"Ooh, territorial."

"It's true." I gunned the accelerator to make it through the yellow light, then slammed the brake when it turned red. "I won't deny it. I never realized how territorial I was until I got married. It's really my issue, not Donnie's. I have nothing to complain about. Donnie's a perfect roommate."

"A roommate who comes in and changes around your entire living space."

"We had to remodel. We couldn't live with just one bathroom. Maybe I shouldn't be trying to get all my work done at home—"

"Molly, don't do it."

"Do what?"

"No matter how bored you get, do not go into your office during the summer. Trust me on this."

I passed the Aloha gas station, a sign that we were nearly at the Mahina airport.

"No, I know. The minute you show your face, they rope you into doing unpaid administrative work."

"Exactly."

"Well, at least I'm not interim department chair anymore. Rodge Cowper gets to deal with it now. All the grade challenges and faculty grievances and paperwork for the Student Retention Office."

"They put Rodge Cowper in charge?" Pat turned to stare at me. "How can you sound so happy? The guy's completely useless."

Roger Cowper, "Dr. Rodge" to his students, taught only one course: Human Potential. HP was a wildly popular and utterly undemanding class Rodge designed himself. He gave no midterms or finals, and assigned no homework. Most of the class time was taken up with entertaining videos. To my knowledge, Rodge had never given a grade lower than an A-minus. Every year, the Student Retention Office nominated Dr. Rodge for the campuswide teaching award.

"Oh, I have no faith in Rodge's leadership abilities. But our department has so few resources and so little clout, he can't do much damage. And honestly, the less free time Rodge has on his hands, the better."

"Isn't he the reason you all have to keep your doors open when you have a student in your office?"

"Yes. The Rodge Cowper Rule. And enforcing it is no longer my problem. So exactly where are you going on this trip?"

"I'm renting a car at the airport and spending a few days in the City."

"Which city? San Francisco?"

"That's what I said. The City. Then I'm driving up through Oregon and Washington."

"Doing what?" I asked.

"Investigative reporting."

"Let me guess. Oh, I know. Northern California. Summer. You're doing an expose on the Bohemian Grove."

"The Bohemian Grove? No way. I don't want my headless torso to turn up in some motel bathtub."

"What then?"

"I'm doing a piece on Hawai`i expats on the West Coast. People who had to move away to get jobs. It's an important piece of the complicated story of Hawai`i's immigration and emigration patterns."

"Ah. In other words, you're visiting old friends in San Francisco and Portland. And you've figured out a way to make it tax deductible."

"Hawai`i's brain drain is a good story," Pat insisted. "The kind of thing that brings a lot of traffic to my site."

"You should look up Emma's brother, Jonah, while you're there. He's living in the Pacific Northwest now."

"Bellingham, Washington. He's on my list."

I pulled into the roundabout drive that serviced Mahina airport's single terminal and slowed when I saw the security line.

"Stay safe," I said to Pat as he climbed out of the car.

"I should say the same thing to you. Later, girlfriend."

I watched him amble over to the security line before I drove away.

CHAPTER TEN

DONNIE HAD OFFERED to take the morning off to accompany me to my appointment, but I'd assured him it wasn't necessary. I didn't know exactly what was going to happen, but I suspected it might not show me to my best advantage. I wanted to hang on to my aura of Feminine Mystery for just a little while longer.

The first thing on the agenda was a quick and painless pregnancy test. Then came the expected probing and prodding. Finally, I was allowed to change out of the paper gown and back into my clothes for a sit-down chat with the doctor. I would have preferred a female OB-GYN, but Mahina didn't have one. My HMO had assigned me the youthful and chipper Lane Ishimaru.

"You shouldn't be disappointed because you haven't conceived yet." Doctor Ishimaru patted my hand. "You know there are only a couple of days a month when you're fertile. And if even if conception is successful, it doesn't mean we can relax. You would be what we call elderly primigravida. That means—"

"Did you say elderly?"

"Oh." He laughed. "It's not what it sounds like. It's just a medical term for a woman who becomes pregnant for the first time after age thirty-four. This shows fertility by age."

He pulled out a laminated chart. It looked like a graph of AIG's stock price during the 2008 financial crisis.

"You should expect for it to take a while for you and your husband to conceive." He held up the chart so I could see the plunging line more clearly.

"Okay, I get the idea—"

"You can see here that at age twenty-two, you have a twenty-five percent chance of conceiving in a given month. By age thirty-two it's dropped below twenty percent, and by your age, it's barely—"

"Yes, I see. So what are our next steps? Just keep on, um, doing what we're doing?"

"Well I just said it might take a while, but we don't know when lightning will strike. I'd like you to set up regular appointments with my office. Best to be prepared. My nurse can schedule the times for you. And I want you to buy some prenatal multivitamins at the pharmacy on the way out."

As soon as I walked out to the clinic waiting room, a familiar voice hailed me from the pharmacy window.

"Hey, Professor. Howzit?"

The friendly pharmacist waving at me from behind the glass was a former student. Peter was one of our success stories. After graduating from the College of Commerce, he had gone on to earn his Pharm. D. His continued employment must have been due to his pleasant personality. It certainly wasn't his steadfast adherence to patient privacy laws.

"How'd the acyclovir work out?" he called across the waiting room.

A white-bearded man sitting in the waiting area lifted his head from the newspaper he was reading and looked me up and down. I hurried over to the window.

"Hi, Peter. It worked beautifully. Thanks for asking. The shingles disappeared in two days."

"Awesome. Yeah, I heard shingles can be a bummer. No fun getting older, ah? You know Mildred Shigeoka had probably the worst case I ever seen. All over the trunk. Both sides." He rubbed his hands up and down the sides of his white coat by way of illustration. "Remember the Shigeokas? They used to own Modern Jewelry. I think it's how come they retired in the end, too much stress. So what can I do for you today?"

"Oh, I was supposed to pick up some vitamin—actually, I don't need anything today. I just came over to say hello. Nice to see you again, Peter."

When I was in graduate school, back on the mainland, I could walk around town secure I would never encounter my students. The undergraduates traveled in their own circles. Those generally revolved around frat parties, football games, and a local sports bar with a famously laissez-faire attitude about checking IDs. My fellow grad students and I frequented indie bookstores and dive bars well away from campus, in places like Silverlake and Highland Park. (If that sounds pretentious to you, well, it was.) We never ran into professors or administrators. They, in our imagination at least, were busy dining at five-star restaurants and entertaining dignitaries during those brief interludes between international conferences when they were actually in town.

Of course, an important ingredient in maintaining our social segregation was our "town" was a megalopolis with ten times the population of the entire state of Hawai`i.

It was a different story in Mahina. I could scarcely leave my house without running into a current or former student. There was the cheerful and chatty young man who signed up for every one of my classes and always sat in the front row. He also worked as a cashier at Galimba's Bargain Boyz, a discovery I made one day only after I'd pulled up to the cash register with a cart full of bras and booze.

There was the quiet international student who couldn't find work in her home country. She returned to Mahina and found a job as a receptionist in my therapist's office.

A few of my accounting majors ended up working at my bank, so they all knew exactly how much money I had.

And of course, there was Peter. As my student, he would cheerfully derail class discussions with rambling digressions about the personal lives of his friends and relatives. Now he had access to everyone's medical records.

I'd heard that one shouldn't make a pregnancy public until the third month or so. I wondered whether such discretion were possible in Mahina.

On the way back into the house, I stopped to check the mailbox. My parcel from Honolulu must have been delivered right after I'd left for my appointment with Doctor Ishimaru. The brown paper was warm to the touch, as if the package had been baking in the metal box all morning. My lipstick was certainly melted by now. I brought the mail inside and put the unopened package in the refrigerator. When it re-solidified, I could still use it with a lip brush. I didn't want to go through the hassle of sending it back, and I wasn't about to throw away a forty-dollar tube of Russian Red.

In addition to the ill-fated lipstick, the mail contained a bill from the electric company and another flyer from Chang's Pizza Pagoda, advertising their new Kung Pao Pizza Rolls. I threw away the flyer and dropped the electric bill into the bill box, a repurposed lauhala tray that had once contained a gift basket of cookies and coffee.

I had never heard of a bill box until I met Donnie. My approach had been to tuck bills away in a drawer or someplace where they wouldn't clutter up the house, forget where I'd put them, and then swing into action when red envelopes started showing up in my mailbox. I had to admit, Donnie's approach was better.

I noticed the envelope from Mahina PD lying there unopened. As long as I was paying the electric bill, I might as well send in our insurance claim. Then the bill box and my mind would be clear. I could spend the afternoon working on my book chapter. I was about to pick up the envelope when my phone rang.

"Hello," said a woman's voice. "Who's this?"

"Who is this?" I knew better than to give out my personal information to some random caller I didn't know. She sounded faintly local, but the phone's caller ID showed a Bay Area prefix.

"This is Gloria," the voice said.

"I'm afraid you have a wrong number."

"Is Donnie there?"

"Donnie? How do you—Oh, Gloria. You're Donnie's sister."

"Yeah."

"This is Molly. Molly Barda. Donnie's wife. How are you?"

"Oh yeah, Molly. I'm doing great, thanks. Is Donnie there? Can I talk to him?"

"No, he's at work. Can I take a message and have him get back to you?"

"No need. He wasn't answering his phone. I'll keep trying."

"Good luck getting in touch with him. The Drive-Inn's probably busy right now. Gloria, I do hope we have a chance to meet in person at some point. You know you're always welcome to visit here."

Donnie and I hadn't really worked out a formal houseguest policy. In fact, this exact issue had come up recently because he seemed to think it was okay to invite Davison to stay with us without consulting me first. Davison, Donnie had explained after the fact, was "family." Well, Gloria was just as much "family" as Davison, and if Donnie could invite family to stay, so could I.

"In fact," I added, "Davison is staying here right now."

For a moment, I thought the line had gone dead.

"Davison is there?" I thought I heard Gloria's voice falter. "In Mahina?"

"As we speak. I guess he decided not to take the internship in Maine. I know. I was surprised, too."

"Molly, you mean it? I can come visit?"

"Of course. I'd be—we'd be delighted."

"Maybe I will, then."

"Well, great. Davison's staying in our guest room right now, but we have another spare room. Really, any time you want to come."

I normally wouldn't have welcomed the idea of my little house filling up with guests, but I wanted to meet Gloria. I was tired of Donnie being so secretive about his family. I know he hadn't had an ideal upbringing, and he probably wasn't keen to relive it. But here I was married to him, and he hadn't yet introduced me to a single one of his relatives. It was only by chance that I had met his uncle Brian.

"Are you sure it would be okay with Donnie?" Gloria asked.

"You're family. Of course it's okay."

I hung up the phone, immediately beset with second thoughts. Maybe there was a reason Donnie had been keeping his sister at arm's length. Should I congratulate myself for my generosity in extending our hospitality to Gloria? Or had I just committed an act of deliberate mischief, to get back at Donnie for springing Davison's visit on me?

I decided not to worry about it. You can tie yourself up in knots agonizing over stuff like this.

I dialed Pat Flanagan's mobile number. The phone rang a few times and then went to voice mail. He might be hiking in the Santa Cruz Mountains by now, or driving through the Caldecott tunnel.

"Pat, it's me. Molly. Hope you're safe and having fun. So, I just invited Donnie's sister to come stay with us at our house, and it sounds like she might actually take me up on the invitation. I don't know anything about her. Could you put on your news reporter hat for maybe an hour, check up on her, just to see if she's a nutcase, or what? Her name is Gloria..."

I realized I didn't know Gloria's last name.

"Her maiden name is Gonsalves, and she owns some kind of spa in Los Gatos. That's all I know. I don't mean to saddle you with extra work on your trip, but if you find out anything, please call me. Hope you're having a nice time."

I put the phone away and settled in to finish the bills. I paid the electric bill online, threw away the paper statement, and saved the envelope. Then I rummaged through the bottom drawer of the filing cabinet until I found our homeowner's insurance policy. I set it on the desk, and finally opened the envelope from Mahina PD.

It was not what I'd expected.

CHAPTER ELEVEN

I HEARD DONNIE PULL into the carport and was on my feet by the time he walked through the door.

"Thanks for picking up the mail," Donnie said. "Was there anything—well, hello to you, too."

I released Donnie from a tight hug. "I have great news."

His face lit up, and he hugged me back, gently, as if I were a raw egg.

"Oh, Molly, already? That's wonderful."

He kissed me on the mouth. Then he took my hand and guided me to the couch.

"How are you feeling? Are you all right? Can I get you something?"

"No, I'm okay." I sat down and waited for him to join me.

"Maybe you're hungry." He was still standing, hovering. "Are you craving anything? Are you thirsty?"

"Well, as long as you're offering, how about a glass of that Sangiovese?"

Donnie looked confused. "Wine? Are you sure it's okay? What did the doctor say?"

"The doctor? What does the doctor have to do with...oh. I see. Sorry, that wasn't my great news. I'm not pregnant."

"Oh. No, it's okay." Donnie's disappointment showed on his face.

I stood up and went into the kitchen. "I'll get the wine. So I had my first appointment with Dr. Ishimaru today."

"I've heard he's good."

"I hope so. He's the only OB-GYN on our plan."

"So how did it go? No, the glasses for red wine are to the right. They're the taller ones, with the round bowls."

"This isn't a red wine glass?"

"No, that's a chardonnay glass. Here, I'll do it. You sit down and rest."

I put my hands up in a gesture of "it's all yours" and sat back down on the couch.

"The office visit was okay, I guess. Ishimaru acted like trying to have a baby at my—under my circumstances was a big deal. It was as if I'd strolled into his office and announced I was planning to climb into a barrel and throw myself over Niagara Falls."

Donnie brought the two (proper) glasses of wine back and sat next to me on the couch. I pulled two coasters from the stack on the coffee table and set down my glass on one of them.

"So what was your big news, then?" Donnie asked.

I took a sip. "This is good. Must be because it's in the correct glass. No, really, thank you for the wine. My news is that Mahina PD wants to hire me."

Donnie slid a protective arm across the back of the couch. "What do you mean, hire you? Don't you want to stay at Mahina State? You just got tenure."

"Donnie, stop looking so concerned. No, I'm not giving up my job at the university. They're hiring me as a consultant."

"The police department?"

"It's not that strange. I already have a relationship with them, kind of."

"What relationship is that?"

"What do you mean, what relationship is that? As you know, there have been occasions where I've helped the police resolve an otherwise intractable crime. I mean, of course I wouldn't take all the credit, but no one can deny I've been helpful. And now, finally, they're taking steps to acknowledge it."

Donnie sighed. "Molly, they had to mount the biggest rescue operation in the county's history, just to pull you out of—"

"It could've happened to anyone. And I can't believe it was the biggest rescue operation. What about all of those tourists who fall into the lava every year?"

"I thought I'd lost you. I almost did lose you. Please don't do anything dangerous."

"It's not dangerous at all. Here, I'll read you the letter."

I retrieved it from the desk and returned to the couch.

"Dear Professor Barda," I read, "Thank you again for offering your consulting services to Mahina PD."

"When did you offer Mahina PD your consulting services?" Donnie asked.

"I don't remember, exactly. Maybe I mentioned it to Detective Medeiros at some point."

"Sorry for interrupting. Go ahead. What else does it say?"

"The purpose of this letter is to notify you of our new meeting time. We will meet Monday, May 18 at ten a.m. The location has not changed. New meeting time? That's weird. This is the first I've heard from them. I guess bureaucracies move in mysterious ways."

"What do they want you to do for them?"

"I assume I'll analyze evidence and statements," I said. "It'll probably be qualitative research. Like I did for my dissertation. Well, I think it's great news anyway. You don't seem particularly thrilled for me."

"Molly, if you're happy, I'm happy. I just want you to be safe."

"Thank you." I lifted my wine glass and touched it to his.

"Are you sure it's okay for you to drink that wine? While we're, um, trying?"

I set my glass down on the coaster. "Yes. I'm sure."

"Okay, as long as you—"

"A review of forty-six peer reviewed papers found consuming up to ten-point-four units of alcohol per week, while pregnant, was associated with no increased risk of miscarriage, stillbirth, premature birth, or birth defects. That's about ten small glasses of wine. I can print out the paper if you want to read it. "

"Okay, I was just—"

"Emma's the one who found the paper for me. Emma Nakamura is a biologist. She knows this stuff. Oh, Donnie, I almost forgot. Did your sister ever get in touch with you?"

"Gloria? No. Why? Is there a problem?"

"Not that I know of. She called and asked for you. It sounded like it was important."

"Hm. I suppose if it's so important, she'll try again." Then Donnie smiled. "I have some good news too."

"Wonderful. I love good news. What is it?"

"Davison is going to extend his stay."

"What? I thought he was just here for a couple of days. When did he tell you that?"

"This morning, right before I left for work. You were still asleep."

"This certainly is a surprise. Did he find a summer job in Mahina?"

"Not yet. But since he's here, I can get him started at the Drive-Inn. He needs to learn the ropes sooner or later."

"So, you assume Davison will take over the Drive-Inn?"

"Who else? If anything happens to me, I don't think you're going to want to run it. Davison is our only...oh. I see what you're saying. The baby."

"Well, there's no baby yet. I guess we can cross that bridge when we come to it."

CHAPTER TWELVE

I SAT IN MY CAR IN the parking lot of St. Damien's with the windows rolled down, watching the sanctuary through the open doors. The parishioners were just starting to retake their seats when my phone started to ring. Pat Flanagan was calling me back, finally.

"Do I have the time right?" Pat asked. "If my calculations are correct, you're down at church already, but you haven't gone in yet because you're waiting for the Passing of the Peace to be over."

"They're just finishing up. I didn't realize you knew my schedule so well."

"If you hate interacting with your fellow faithful so much, you should just do what I do. Never go to Mass."

"I'm not going to stop going to Mass. Just the Passing of the Peace stresses me out. Wandering around the sanctuary, beaming at people, trying to make eye contact, calculating whether you can get away with a handshake or you're going to get caught in a hug. You know how I feel about hugging strangers."

"Oh, honey, I hear you."

"And why do we have to walk around randomly? At least they could make an orderly line or something, like they do with Communion. So were you able to find out anything about Donnie's sister?"

"Yeah, that's why I'm calling. I'm in Los Gatos right now."

"Oh, great. Thank you, Pat. I knew I could count on you."

"It's not great. It's a yuppie hellscape of artisanal toy stores, overpriced coffee, and even more overpriced sandwich shops. I think I found Gloria's spa, though."

"Great detective work, Pat. What's it called?"

"It's called Gloria's Spa."

"Ah."

"Yeah, it looks like some New Age spa/lifestyle thing for hipster yoga moms."

"Dare I ask, did you venture in to this green-tea-scented oasis of serenity?" I envisioned Pat after a few days on the road, looking like a skinhead lumberjack who had been sleeping in his clothes.

"I did, and I asked for Gloria. She wasn't there. Her last name is Kealoha, by the way."

"Gloria Kealoha."

"Must be the same one, right?"

"I would imagine it's the right person. How many Hawaiian Glorias own spas in Los Gatos?"

"Entrepreneurial family you've married into."

"Yeah, somehow none of that drive and industriousness made it down to my stepson. Okay, I have to go into church now. Everyone's sitting down already. Thank you, Pat. Can I call you for updates?"

"You can try, but I'm going to be hiking in the Santa Cruz Mountains, and my cell coverage is going to be spotty. Molly, you should find another church if this Passing of the Peace thing stresses you out so much."

"No, I'm not going to. It's what the Protestants do. That's why there are a million Protestant denominations. Every time their church does something they don't like, they go off and start their own. I don't want to be a church-shopper."

"Imagine you, not wanting to go shopping."

"Not when it comes to this. To me, the Church is like, I don't know, a beloved elderly relative. Like, maybe he's a little out of touch, but he's your Uncle Konstandin, and you're going to invite him to Thanksgiving dinner again, even if your mother wants to lock him in the basement after the joke he told last year. That's just a metaphor, by the way."

"Hey, before I go, anything new in Mahina?"

"Yes there is and thank you for asking. The Mahina Police Department wants to hire me as a consultant."

"Molly, that's great. What are you going to be working on? I wonder if they're pulling one of their cold cases out of mothballs."

"I honestly don't know. I guess I'll find out more at the first meeting. Pretty exciting though."

"I know, keep me posted."

"Sure, as long as they don't make me sign a confidentiality agreement. Okay, I really have to go into Mass now. Pat, be safe, and don't worry. I'm sure nothing terribly interesting is going to happen before you get back."

I made it all the way through Mass without having to interact with strangers. I walked out in a good mood, looking forward to meeting Emma at the Pair-O-Dice.

"Mrs. Gonsalves?"

I paused at the edge of the parking lot and turned around.

The man looked familiar, but I couldn't place him. He wore church-appropriate attire, a red aloha shirt with a white pineapple print and khaki pants.

He held out his hand. "You don't remember me. Andy De Silva."

"Officer De Silva. I'm so sorry. I didn't recognize you out of uniform. I didn't know you attended St. Damien's. I haven't seen you here before."

"I'm here every week, as long as my schedule allows."

"Oh."

"You usually come in right after the Passing of the Peace, right?"

"Sometimes it's hard to get going on Sunday morning, but better late than never, right?"

"Do you prefer to be called Mrs. Gonsalves, or Professor Barda?"

"Professionally I go by Barda. You know, once you've started publishing under one name, it's not good to switch to another one. It can mess up your citation count. Actually, two-part last names like yours, De Silva, are tricky too. Sometimes they count the whole thing as one word, and sometimes just one or the other is listed as your surname, so it doesn't—sorry, that was probably more detail than you wanted. You can call me Molly. Or whatever."

"Maybe we'll stick with Professor Barda since you're working with us now."

"Oh, yes, I got the letter. I'm looking forward to it. So, will I be working on my own computer, or will you be providing the computing resources? I know there can be confidentiality issues as far as my doing the analyses at home."

"No need to talk shop at church. We'll have plenty of time tomorrow."

"Tomorrow?"

"The eighteenth. The letter had your starting date, yeah?"

Was tomorrow already the eighteenth? It was so easy to lose track during the summer.

"Yes, of course. So, where were we meeting again, exactly? At the police station?"

"No, we'll be next door. At the motor vehicle office, in their break room."

I wondered what kind of top-secret project would call for such cloak-and-dagger maneuvers. Maybe Pat was right about their revisiting a cold case. He had reported on the Karaoke Murders back when he was still a crime reporter at the County Courier, and to this day, they remained unsolved. Was I going to see the Karaoke Murder files?

This was getting exciting.

CHAPTER THIRTEEN

SUNDAY BRUNCH AT THE Pair-O-Dice Bar was a tradition for Emma and me. Pat normally joined us too, when he was in town, and not off hiking in the wilds of Northern California.

Donnie was not part of this happy ritual. Sundays were busy at the Drive-Inn. And Donnie wasn't fond of the Pair-O-Dice anyway.

Objectively, the Pair-O-Dice was a dump. Its one point of pride was its window-spanning neon sign. Swaying neon palm trees flanked the flourishing pink script spelling out "Pair-O-Dice." Underneath, animated neon dice tumbled from left to right.

Inside, the Pair-O-Dice was dark, and uncomfortably hot. The only climate control was a lone wobbly fan beating the humid air. The tables were rickety, the fries leathery, and the drinks watery. The bartender was probably the owner's son. He acted like he couldn't be fired, and he looked about seventeen years old.

On the plus side, the Pair-O-Dice attracted so little custom during the day it felt like our own private club. After the crush of Mass at St. Damien's, the quiet interior was balm to my jittery soul.

I pushed through the Pair-O-Dice's front door and waited for my eyes to adjust. Except for a furtive couple sharing one side of a booth at the far end of the bar, Emma was the only customer. It still took me a while to find her. Emma's black hair and black T-shirt faded into the dimly lit background, and she was so short her head was level with the back of her chair. By the time I joined her, she was halfway through a pitcher of Mehana Volcano Red Ale. A basket of fries and an extra glass sat on the table.

"Got a glass for you," she said as I sat down. "Want some fries?"

"I don't know." I poured myself a glass of beer. "I heard fries have a lot of carbs. I'm thinking I should cut back."

"How're things at home? You manage to go another day without murdering your stepson?"

"Barely. You know the platinum earrings and necklace Donnie gave me?"

"Yeah, those are nice. How come you didn't wear 'em to church today?"

"Because my beloved stepson stole them."

"Davison did? How come you think it was him?"

"I was polishing them Wednesday morning. By Wednesday evening, they'd disappeared. We called the police. Davison played dumb. And then late that night he went out to visit a friend. Or so he claimed."

"An' you think that's when he fenced your jewelry?"

"I can't think of another explanation. Who else would have taken my things? No one else had the opportunity."

"How come you never told me until today?"

"I guess I hoped the jewelry would turn up. Maybe Davison would hear Donnie and me talking about it, feel some remorse, and put the things back, or something. But no, my jewelry's still gone. Oh, and one more thing. Davison was looking to buy a ring."

"Davison was? You mean like an engagement ring?"

"Exactly. He pestered me into driving him up to Fujioka's that morning."

Emma set down her beer. "It's not Sherry, is it? I mean he wouldn't...would he?"

"Yes, I think he would. I think he is back with Sherry. And it sounds serious this time. Like I think he wants to marry her serious."

"Eh, not your problem." Emma emptied the pitcher into her glass. I looked around for the bartender, but he had abandoned his post. I probably could have walked up behind the bar and helped myself.

"It will be my problem. I'm going to be the one dealing with an extra-grumpy husband. Seriously, how do you think Donnie's going to react when he finds out his ex-wife and his son are going to get married? Think about it for a second."

"So Davison would be his own stepfather, yeah? That means he's gonna be your stepson and your brother-in-law at the same time."

"I can't even keep track. It's such a soap opera."

"Yeah, speaking of drama. You hapai yet? Hapai means pregnant by the way."

"I know what hapai means, thank you." I scooped the last few fries from the basket. They were chewy and lukewarm, but the fat and salt made them palatable. "And no. I'm not expecting. Not yet."

"Maybe it's time to start thinking about fertility treatments, Molly. You and Donnie are pretty old to be starting a family. I think you get at least one try covered by insurance."

"I don't know. I'm not sure how far I want to push the issue. I've seen couples get so obsessive about conceiving. Getting hormone shots, timing things down to the second, rushing home from work for...what sounds like the least romantic date ever. It seems like so much effort. I think we'd rather just take things day by day. If it happens, it happens. If not, it's not the end of the world."

"So what, you're doing the fatalistic Catholic thing now? You cannot just sit around and wait for things to happen."

"Oh, like Buddhists aren't fatalistic?"

"Only when it's something you can't do anything about. But this? You gotta get proactive. I'm telling you. Neither one of you's getting any younger."

I didn't bother to argue with her. Emma Nakamura was one of those driven people who went after things and got them. She always knew the direction her life would take. She grew up just outside of Mahina, moved to the mainland to earn her doctorate in biology, then beelined straight back to a tenure-track position at Mahina State with a new husband in tow. No postdoc purgatory for her. And despite Mahina State's heavy teaching load, Emma had been raking in grants and publishing like a fiend ever since.

"Who's your OB-GYN?" Emma demanded. "Is it Ishimaru? I heard he wasn't bad."

"It is Ishimaru. I guess he's okay. I don't know. He's young, but I still get this old school, Doctor Knows Best vibe from him. The office visit was like something out of the 1950s. It seemed like if I got too uppity or asked too many questions, they'd put me on tranquilizers. And if that didn't work, they'd schedule me for a lobotomy. I wish there were some other options."

"There's the LightSpirit Organic Farm and Natural Birthing Center, down in Kuewa."

"Really? It might be worth looking into."

"I don't think you'd like it, Molly. I was down there one time, to help them out with the rat lungworm disease problem they were having. The birthing center part is just someone's house with a redwood hot tub in the back. The water was all green, and there was a dead gecko floating in it."

"Oh well," I sighed. "I guess I'll take my chances with Doctor Headmirror."

"Hey, Molly, did you get something from the Student Retention Office about a humor initiative we're supposed to be starting in the fall?"

"I think so. I deleted the email."

"Know what we should do? We should get 'em to shut it down. When school starts again, I'll tell the refrigerator joke in class, and you can tell the canoe joke."

"Emma, why do you want to antagonize the Student Retention Office?"

"'Cause they're idiots."

"Yes, but thanks to their Foundation grant they're well-funded idiots, and you know what they'll do to anyone who gets in their way. Do you want to end up like the history department? Anyway, I can't tell the canoe joke. You tell the canoe joke."

"I don't like the canoe joke. I think it's gross."

"Get Pat to tell it, then. Hey, here's some interesting news I forgot to tell you. The police department is hiring me as a consultant."

"Our police department? Mahina PD?"

I nodded.

"Aw, that's great, Molly. How much they paying you?"

"I don't know yet. But after all of the times I've helped them out for nothing, it's kind of validating to have them acknowledge me."

"Good for you. Just don't let it distract you from your research. Hey, how's your book chapter going?"

"Not as well as I'd hoped. Working at home is kind of tough with Davison rattling around the house. You know, I don't have my own office at home, just a corner of the living room."

"Do not go onto campus during the summer, Molly."

"I'm not planning to go onto campus."

"I know you're tempted to go into your office. Don't do it."

"No, I know. Pat was telling me the same thing."

"Seriously. Anyone sees you there, you're gonna get roped into some time-suck admin work, and you're not gonna get any research done."

The couple in the far booth got up and exited toward the back. A glint of sunlight briefly illuminated the man's face. I realized I had just seen him at church. It was Andy De Silva.

I nudged Emma. "There's the police officer who took the report when my jewelry was stolen. And I was just talking to him at St. Damien's, right before I came here."

"How come you're whispering? Not like there's anyone around."

I looked around the Pair-O-Dice. Emma was right.

"Those two were up to something, though." Emma looked to where the couple had gone. "I bet at least one of 'em's married. You recognize the wahine?"

"No, I didn't see who the woman was. Well, what do you know? And right after Sunday Mass, too."

"Why, what day of the week are you Catholics supposed to schedule your fornication and adultery?"

"Where on earth is the bartender? Is there any ale left?"

"Too late." Emma turned the empty pitcher upside down to demonstrate.

CHAPTER FOURTEEN

MONDAY DAWNED RAINY and gray, but my mood was bright. Today was my first consulting appointment with the Mahina Police Department.

Donnie was already gone by the time I woke up. I showered and dressed, then slipped into the kitchen and quietly brewed and downed a cup of coffee. I tucked the letter from Mahina PD into my bag and slipped out the side door to the carport. It was a three-minute drive to the police station, and another ten minutes prowling for a parking stall big enough for my Thunderbird.

I entered the Motor Vehicle Department through the main entrance and picked the shortest line to wait in. When I reached the counter and told the woman why I was there, she was nice enough to close her window and help me. She led me through a door marked "Employees Only," and down a hallway to a bare-bones break room near the back of the building.

Sitting around a U-shaped walnut-grain table were half a dozen police officers in their late twenties or early thirties. They were heavy set, with close-clipped black hair, varying in height from five foot seven all the way up to five foot eight. The room itself was government-issue, with linoleum flooring and fluorescent lights. A single window, set high in the wall, revealed a patch of pearl-gray sky.

"Good morning." I smiled as I entered the room. The officers' expressions ranged from sullen to bored. I looked around for someone in charge, and at that moment, Andy De Silva burst in through the door. He was in uniform, and holding a clipboard.

"Doctor Barda. Good. You're here. Do you have slides? We have a projector." De Silva indicated an overhead projector sitting on the side table, its power cord coiled on the glass platen like a snake. It was designed to project transparent slides. I looked around, but De Silva was definitely talking to me. I did not have a presentation prepared, certainly not one compatible with their antique equipment.

I flashed what I hoped was a confident smile.

"I thought we could just talk today, and make introductions. This is my first time meeting with all of you, and I'd like to learn as much as I can."

"Good deal." De Silva grinned and nodded at me as if I had given the right answer. He took a seat in the remaining empty plastic chair. There I stood, with no chair, and seven of Mahina's Finest looking at me expectantly.

"So. Here we are. Thank you very much, everyone, for meeting with me this morning. I didn't realize we'd have so many people on the team. Officer De Silva, if you don't mind, I'd like to hear your take on this. What do you think are the salient facts?"

Andy De Silva flipped through the papers on his clipboard.

"This workshop is the centerpiece of the settlement in the case of Baker versus Mahina County PD."

I nodded knowingly, feeling utterly baffled. A settlement? Was this a cold case resurrected by a bereaved family member's lawsuit?

I turned to the officer next to De Silva, hoping for further explanation.

"Yeah, what he said." The officer jerked his head toward De Silva. "The settlement." The rest of them nodded in agreement.

"You said it was just gonna be introductions today," said another of the officers.

"Well, sure, that's what we're doing now. Just laying the groundwork." I hadn't even signed anything yet. I wondered how much I was going to get paid for this.

"How about you first, Professor?" The young policeman smirked and folded his arms. "Tell us what's your qualifications."

"Me?"

De Silva nodded at me.

"Right. Of course." I summarized my educational credentials, making sure to highlight my prestigious Ph.D. I spoke in broad terms about the qualitative methods that I'd used in my dissertation research, omitting the fact my degree was in literature and creative writing. Somehow, I sensed this wasn't a humanities-friendly crowd. Finally, I got to the important part: My Mahina connections.

"My husband, as you may know, is Donnie Gonsalves, of Donnie's Drive-Inn."

I could feel the tension in the room ease a little. Now they knew I wasn't just another earnest mainlander committing a drive-by let-me-tell-you-how-it's-done-back-home. Thanks to my relationship with Donnie, I was vetted.

Andy De Silva was the next to make introductions. He had grown up in Mahina. His father and uncles were police officers, and he had always known that he'd follow in their footsteps. The other six officers had also grown up with fathers, uncles, and grandfathers on the force. All of them had been born and raised in Mahina, except for one oddball whose family had moved from Maui when he was four years old.

When the session had finished, I knew everyone's biography, but I still had no idea what I was supposed to be doing for the Mahina Police Department.

Officer De Silva walked me out.

"You're gonna be starting the lectures tomorrow then, yeah?"

"The lectures? Listen, I'd like to make sure our expectations are aligned. I have my materials ready, of course, but I'd like to get a better idea of exactly what you envisioned." I hated myself for spouting corporate-speak at him, but I had no alternative. I had nothing prepared at all, and no idea what they wanted me to do. I'd assumed I'd be analyzing documents, not giving lectures.

"Alls you gotta do is what it says in the contract," De Silva said. "Simple."

"Officer De Silva, I never got a contract. Only a short letter. I think some of the important documents may not have reached me."

The look of panic on De Silva's face told me he had been the one responsible for sorting out the paperwork.

"No, no, it's fine," I assured him. "If we need to order another copy of the contract, we can do it. I trust you. I'll sign whatever I need to. In the meantime, maybe you can help me fill in some of the details. I haven't seen any written description of exactly what services I'm providing."

De Silva smiled, visibly relieved. "Oh, I got my copy right here. Here, Professor." He paged through his clipboard, unclipped a packet of papers, and handed it to me.

I read over it. Then I read over it again. And handed it back to him.

"Diversity training?"

"Yeah, cause that gender discrimination lawsuit. Works out good for us, too, 'cause we can get you for free."

"Did you say free?"

"Yeah, otherwise would cost us a couple thousand. When we was ordered to do this thing, boys was pretty unhappy about it, no lie. But our department admin called the university and found out there's this community speakers' bureau."

"The speakers' bureau. That's right. I volunteered for the speakers' bureau."

"Yeah, I dunno how come we gotta do this in the first place. I don't see what the problem is. You saw, it's all guys. How could we be discriminating if it's all guys?"

"Baffling," I agreed.

We walked through the low-ceilinged lobby of the Motor Vehicle department and out into the sunshine.

"So, Officer, will I be able to get a copy of the paperwork? Just for my records, to show my administration?"

"The info packet was sent on the twelfth," De Silva said. "That's how come I can't figure out how you never got it. We sent it to your office."

"It's on campus? Shoot. It's probably sitting in my mail cubby. You know, I'm flattered you picked me to teach your free seminar, but diversity training isn't my specialty at all. I teach IBM and BP."

"What's that?" De Silva asked.

"Intro to Business Management and Business Planning."

"Well we got all the speakers' bureau names an' took a vote. The boys picked you."

"Really?"

"Yeah, we gotta sit through this thing anyways. Rather look at a good looking wahine instead of some old guy with white hair."

"A gender discrimination lawsuit, you say?"

"I know, hard to believe, ah?"

"I'd better get home" I shaded my eyes against the sun. My turquoise and white Thunderbird gleamed in the parking lot. "I have some work to do before tomorrow."

CHAPTER FIFTEEN

I SPENT THE AFTERNOON trying to piece together the first day of my diversity workshop. None of the activities I found online sounded promising. The group itself wasn't at all demographically diverse, and they obviously knew one other pretty well already. So the get-to-know-you icebreaker exercises celebrating differences would probably fall flat.

Discussions of stereotyping would brush uncomfortably close to issues of profiling, and I didn't want to go there. Anything to do with gender would certainly put them on the defensive. Even the most introspective and thoughtful among us bristles a little when confronted with evidence of our biases. And I had no reason to believe these guys were exceptionally introspective or thoughtful.

I wondered whether I'd be able to provide an effective workshop at all. My husband was a local, which helped a little as far as gaining their trust, but I was clearly not one myself. There was still the danger I'd come off as the missionary, the educated white lady coming in to "civilize" them. As they say in politics, the optics were bad.

It was too late to back out now. I'd stupidly volunteered for the university speakers' bureau to show the administration I was a Team Player. I never dreamed I'd actually be called upon to do anything.

By mid-afternoon, I'd made exactly zero progress on tomorrow's diversity workshop and decided to take a break. I went back into the bedroom, pulled my new pint-sized guitar out of the closet, and tried playing some chords. My finger pads were sore within minutes. I'd have to build up the calluses on my fingertips again. And the guitar didn't sound great, although it was probably more my fault than the instrument's.

Maybe I could improvise. I'd just invite them all to talk about their feelings or something. If I did a horrible job, well, it would be embarrassing, and I wouldn't get asked back, but it wouldn't be the end of the world. After all, it wasn't like I was getting paid for it. I put my guitar away, returned to my computer, closed the library database, and pulled up the data file for my book chapter. At least I could make some progress there.

I stared at the screen. The chapter's main study had one glaring weakness: Our subjects were our own college students. This is more common than you might think. Two-thirds of American psychology studies are based on the responses of college students. The problem is the behavior of nineteen-year-old psych majors isn't universal. We had no way of knowing whether our results would apply to working adults.

That was it. I knew what I was going to do tomorrow.

When I had finished printing out everything I needed, I shut down my computer, and got up to start dinner. Donnie usually cooked, and he was much better at it than I. I liked to pitch in, though, so the burden wasn't always on him. I'd make Spam and rice tonight. It was simple and cheap. Davison could eat as much as he wanted without breaking the bank.

I cleaned out the pebbly old rice from the cooker and started a new batch. Then I sliced up two cans of Spam, one regular and one bacon flavored. I set two frying pans on the stove, poured out a little coconut oil into each one, and assembled the Spam slices. I set the Spam to cook on low heat and was in the middle of setting the table when I heard Donnie's key in the door.

I had forgotten how particular Donnie was about the table setting. Even after his thirteen-hour workday, he had the energy to rearrange the entire thing. He made sure to tell me, as he was clearing away the plates and moving the silverware around, how much he appreciated my having prepared dinner, so there was some consolation.

"You know, Donnie, this is the first time in my life I've been the Oscar. I've only ever been the Felix."

Donnie paused in mid-napkin arrangement. "What about an Oscar?"

"You know, Felix Unger and Oscar Madison? The Odd Couple?"

Donnie shook his head. "Doesn't ring a bell."

"Old TV show about two roommates. One's neat and fussy. The other one's a slob."

"Which one am I?"

"Are you kidding? You're Felix. The persnickety one."

"Persnickety? Me?"

"Little bit."

"Hm. I do have high standards." He grinned at me. "Obviously."

"Well, when you put it that way." I returned his smile, my momentary irritation forgotten.

Davison let himself in the front door as Donnie was setting out proper glasses for both water and wine. I moved the rice cooker to the table and set out the fried Spam slices on a platter. Donnie uncorked a cheap and cheerful red, and then Donnie, Davison, and I sat down to eat, just as a normal family might.

"How'd your meeting at the police department go today?" Donnie asked. "Are you allowed to talk about what you're working on?"

"You're working for the police?" Davison interrupted, in a tone one might use to ask whether an acquaintance has taken up murdering kittens.

"It's not anything to do directly with criminal investigation. It's more HR stuff. How do you guys like the bacon Spam? I think it's pretty good."

"I like the plain kind better," Davison said.

"So you're not working on anything dangerous." Donnie appeared to relax.

"Not at all."

"Sounds boring," Davison mumbled with his mouth full.

"Davison," Donnie turned to his son. "Did you get any interviews today?"

"I got stuff to keep me busy," Davison speared four more slices of Spam with his fork and transported them to his plate. He didn't look at Donnie.

"I want you to come into the Drive-Inn with me tomorrow. You didn't really answer me the last time I asked. What happened your last semester at school?"

"I got other things on my mind besides school, Dad."

Donnie and I exchanged a look. I was certain "other things" meant Sherry Di Napoli. I wasn't sure what Donnie was thinking, but I could tell he wasn't happy with Davison's deflection. I quickly changed the subject.

"Donnie, do you know what I forgot to tell you? I met your Uncle Brian. Davison introduced us. You never told me you had an uncle in town."

"Oh, yeah, that's right. Dad, he doesn't look too good. He got all skinny, and he's looking real old. Maybe we could—"

"We all get old," Donnie interrupted. "Molly, with all of the things you've been taking on this summer, have you had a chance to use your new guitar? I'd really like to hear you play one of these days."

Donnie didn't want to discuss Uncle Brian. I chatted about my sore finger pads and some of the challenging guitar pieces I was looking forward to learning. There was no point in pushing Donnie on the topic of his uncle. I'd have to wait until he was in a more talkative mood.

CHAPTER SIXTEEN

THE NEXT MORNING I awoke as Donnie was leaving for work.

"It's not even six." I squinted at the clock. "Donnie, you poor thing. You've been going in early and working such long days. No wonder you come home exhausted. Listen, I can put something in the slow cooker for dinner."

He popped his head back in the bedroom door.

"It's okay, Molly. I can make something. I don't mind cooking."

"You didn't like the Spam and rice?"

"No, no, the Spam and rice were terrific. Davison seemed to like it."

"Don't worry. I won't make anything too adventurous. I'll fix the tomato beef soup. You like the tomato beef soup, don't you?"

"I like cooking for you, Molly."

"And you're an amazing chef. I just feel like I should pitch in once in a while."

"Thank you Molly. Very thoughtful of you." He popped out again. Seconds later, I heard him descending the front steps.

Sometimes I suspected Donnie didn't like my cooking, although he seemed okay with the tomato beef. I got the recipe from Emma. She'd been trying out an amino-acid-optimizing regime. It was supposed to boost her paddling performance. She was never able to stick to the part of the diet where she was supposed to give up beer, though, so she eventually gave up.

I got dressed, went into the kitchen, and pulled out six big soup bones from the meat drawer in the fridge. I placed the meaty bones on the bottom of the slow cooker, dumped a jar of spicy arrabbiata sauce over them, and then added enough water to reach the top. I sprinkled in some garlic salt and turned on the heat. Easy.

The soup could simmer in the slow cooker for anywhere between twelve and twenty-four hours. Toward the end I'd throw in some vegetables or leftover meat, serve it over rice or noodles, whatever. It tasted good and it kept well. According to Emma, it was full of glycine and proline, which are supposed to keep you limber and springy. She had warned me to fish out any bone fragments before serving.

"You don't wanna get hit with some ungrateful guest's emergency dental bill," she'd explained.

Once the soup was on, I still had a couple of hours to kill. I started a load of laundry, balanced the checkbook, and mended the torn seam on a blouse. I checked over my handouts several times, then went back into the bedroom to practice my introductory remarks in the closet mirror.

I checked the soup again before I left and made the short drive to the Motor Vehicle Department. I got there early so I'd have time to settle in, but everyone was already in the break room by the time I arrived. I smiled at everyone. Only Andy De Silva smiled back, and then went back to doing paperwork. I stood and paged quietly through my handouts until it was time for the session to start.

"An important part of interacting with others," I began, "is understanding ourselves. First, if you don't mind, you're all going to sign a release form, indicating you consent to participate in these activities, and we'll fill out a couple of self-assessment instruments. After that, we're going to do a simulation. It's like a game."

The "game" was the behavioral experiment covered in my book chapter. In addition to the undergraduates already in our sample, I'd now be able to include results from working law enforcement officers.

"What are we signing here, Miss?" one of the young officers asked, as if I were his high-school teacher.

"An acknowledgement that the results of this exercise could be archived and might at some point be published. Without any identifying information, of course. These consent forms are a requirement of our Human Subjects board."

The young officer looked at Andy De Silva. Andy De Silva shrugged.

"What's the N-Scale?" someone else asked.

"I'll debrief you when everyone's done. Just answer the questions honestly and to the best of your knowledge."

If participants saw what the instrument measured beforehand—for example, if they knew the "N-scale" measured narcissism—I'd be unlikely to get honest answers.

After everyone had finished their self-assessments, I chose two of the officers at random as negotiating partners, and we ran the first "game." I was afraid they'd think it was a waste of time, but they seemed fine with it. They were probably relieved the session wasn't me lecturing the whole time.

When an hour had passed, I called for a break. This turned out to be the most popular deci-sion I'd made all morning. Andy De Silva sidled up to me.

"Interesting class, Professor. So when do find out how we did?"

I rested my fingers on the stack of filled-out forms on the conference table. "I'm going to score them tonight and bring back your results tomorrow."

"I just want you to know I see myself as part of the solution," De Silva said. "Not part of the problem. I'm an ally."

"An ally?"

"Yeah. I believe in gender. I think ladies should have rights and stuff."

"Well, I like having rights."

"I mean, people shouldn't get carried away with it or anything—"

"Eh, Sir," another officer interrupted him. "Something came up."

De Silva started to apologize to me.

"It's okay," I said. "Please. Go take care of it."

When we reconvened after the break, half of the small class was missing.

"They got called out," De Silva explained. "Cockfight."

"They needed to send three police officers to break up a cockfight?"

"There was about a hundred fifty guys. They counted twenty dead roosters so far. Confis-cated more than seven thousand in cash, too."

"Oh. How awful." I had envisioned three or four people standing around watching two roosters fight. "Can we continue the class without them? Or will they need to make it up?"

"We don't want 'em to miss out," De Silva said. "We got a lot done today anyway. I think everyone's kinda worn out."

The others nodded enthusiastic agreement.

"Oh. Okay. So, class dismissed, I guess?"

The remaining three officers disappeared so fast they practically left their Styrofoam coffee cups trembling in midair.

I came back to a quiet house, fixed myself a cup of coffee, and sat down to score the officers' self-assessments. I entered the results into the spreadsheet, then copied the individual scores into personalized feedback forms and sealed each one in an envelope. I'd hand back the envelopes first thing tomorrow, and we'd start the session with a discussion of what the results meant.

That was the first hour of class taken care of. What then? Maybe I could present my dissertation research. It was related to gender diversity, after all. Although my qualitative analysis of representations of masculinities in 'zines from the Orange County punk rock scene might be a little abstract for them. Maybe I could bring in the overview of employment discrimination laws I covered in Intro to Business Management. Something practical would be a better choice for this audience.

When I was finished preparing the next day's workshop, I fixed another cup of coffee and then sat down to go through my email. I had learned my lesson about rushing through my inbox. What had I been thinking, volunteering to be on a roster of volunteer speakers?

Dear Professor Barda, I just received my final grade...and I was just wondering if there is any way possible I could try to bring up my grade to pass the class.

I took a sip of coffee and clicked "delete."

"Oh sure," I said to the computer monitor. "I can think of no better use for my unpaid summer than to devote more time to your grade than you put in the entire semester. And let's not forget the inevitable complaints from all of your classmates the minute they heard you got a do-over. The decent, hardworking students who made the necessary effort to turn their work in on time. I'm sure they'd be thrilled to see you get special treatment."

The next email was from another dissatisfied customer.

Normally I would graciously accept my grade with the understanding that I did not put in as much effort as others, yet had I known the written assignments would have been counted as part of my grade, then perhaps my approach to your course would have been different.

Another one for the trash bin.

"Oh, do forgive me. How rash of me to assume students would know they were supposed to complete the writing assignments. When the only hints provided were that these assignments were, one, discussed at length and in detail in class, and two, posted on the course website with points and a grading rubric attached to them. Hey, and here's another hint. The class was designated writing intensive. They're called final grades, people, not opening bids."

I heard a lock turn in the door. Davison plodded into the living room, his backpack slung over one shoulder.

"Ho, Molly. You know the computer can't hear you yelling at it, ah?"

"No one is yelling." I scrolled down my emails, keeping my eyes on the monitor. "I don't know why anyone would think—are they freaking kidding me?"

The student who had contacted me earlier, claiming to have earned an overall score of 347% in my class, had filed a formal grade challenge with the Student Retention Office.

It would scarcely be edifying to reproduce my reaction verbatim. I fear I may have deployed some common (in all senses of the word) Anglo-Saxonisms as Davison disappeared into the guest room and quietly pulled the door shut.

According to the email from the Student Retention Office, the burden of proof was now on me. I had to demonstrate the complainant, an aspiring accounting major, really had earned the D I'd recorded as her final grade. I was going to have to go onto campus after all.

CHAPTER SEVENTEEN

I PULLED INTO THE LOWER campus lot and parked next to Pat's tan Mercedes. There was still no ticket on the windshield. With so few cars around, it probably wasn't worth it for security to monitor the lot over the summer. I sneaked up to my office, half-tempted to duck behind pillars and around corners as I went, like the Pink Panther.

Since I was on a nine-month contract, I would have been well within my rights to ignore my university email for the duration of my unpaid summer. I could be home now, working on my book chapter or taking a nap.

Had I chosen the course of inaction, however, Miss 347% would win her grade challenge by default. She would then be cleared to enroll in the next level of courses in the College of Commerce. I couldn't do that to my colleagues.

I darted into my office and pulled the door shut behind me, sealing in the still air. (The A/C was apparently on a nine-month contract, too.) I sat down on my yoga ball (it had been years since we'd had a budget for real office furniture) and bounced a bit to get settled. The ball felt a little flabby. I'd have to re-inflate it before the fall semester started. I switched on the computer and then jiggled the mouse impatiently as my operating system updated itself. Then the computer restarted, and I waited some more. Finally, I was able to log in.

I pulled up the Student Retention Office's online form and signed into the records portal, the one we could only access from campus. I filled in the SRO form, attached screenshots of the assignments in question, and submitted it.

There. Now all I had to do was dash back to my car without anyone seeing me. I hadn't noticed anyone around when I came in, so I assumed the coast was clear.

Unfortunately, Rodge Cowper, the new interim department chair (it had also been years since we'd had the funds to hire a permanent department chair) was lying in wait outside my office door like a rumpled, alcoholic spider.

Rodge had "just a few" questions about how to do the course scheduling and wanted me to "help" him. By "help" him, of course, he meant he wanted me to do the whole thing for him. He trotted next to me as I strode to my car, pleading for "just a couple minutes" as I kept walking, first to my mail cubby in the main office, and then back out to the parking lot.

"I don't have any fancy scheduling system," I explained. "What I've been doing is I just go around and ask everyone for their time preferences. Then I look at what students have to take, and I try to make sure classes they might take at the same time aren't scheduled against each other. Then I make a preliminary schedule and check it with the faculty. I go through several iterations until I reach something that doesn't make too many people mad."

"But your system would take such a long time," Rodge objected.

"Yes, serving as interim department chair can be quite time consuming." I did not mention how much of my own administrative time Rodge himself had consumed over the past couple of years. Rodge liked to think of himself as a professor who "connected" with his students. Rodge's favorites (who tended to be female, Asian, and under the age of twenty) were not uniformly comfortable with so much "connection," and occasionally brought their concerns to the department chair. I would then have to call Rodge in for yet another meeting, where he would once again express shock at the way his blameless behavior had been so grievously misinterpreted.

"I can't use last fall's schedule." Rodge huffed as he struggled to keep up with me, pieces of his gray hair sticking to his florid forehead. "Harrison's on sabbatical. And before you tell me I can just hire a lecturer to replace him, I can't. 'Cause when Harrison's gone, Schneider has some deal where he gets first dibs on Harrison's GM elective. But I don't know if Schneider wants GM in the fall 'cause he's not answering his email. If Schneider decides he wants GM, then I have to fill in whatever Schneider's not teaching."

"Oh right, the coveted Gender and Management elective. Do you know when I was first hired here, Harrison was afraid I was going to take the GM class away from him? Because, as you know, I was the first Person of Gender in the management department. Maybe I should put in to teach it one of these days. Just to shake things up."

"Molly." Rodge puffed. "Maybe you could just—"

"Well, I sure wish I could stay and guide you through the whole course scheduling process." I unlocked the car, swung the heavy door open, and slid into the bucket seat. "Unfortunately, I have to be at an important meeting across town."

I pulled the door shut, forcing Rodge to snatch his hand out of the way.

My cell phone rang as I drove out of the parking lot. I pulled into an empty space and dug my phone out of my purse. The caller ID showed Davison Gonsalves. Davison didn't generally call me just to chat.

"Davison? What's going on? Is everything okay? Did something happen to the house?"

"Eh, no worries. How come you gotta sound so stressed out all the time?"

"No one's stressed out. What is it?"

"Could you buy some vegetarian food while you're out?"

"Vegetarian food? Why? Did you convert to vegetarianism since this morning?"

"Nah. Uncle Skye's here."

"Who is Uncle Skye?"

"Aunty Gloria's husband."

"Aunty Gloria? Your dad's sister?"

"Uh-huh."

"And does your father know his sister's husband is visiting us?"

"I dunno. Dad's at work. That's how come I called you."

"Davison, listen. Is this person holding you hostage and forcing you to try to sound normal? Should I call the police?"

"Nah. We're cool. Oh, I hadda throw away the soup."

"My tomato beef soup?"

"Yeah, Uncle Skye said the meat smell was making him sick."

"Davison, you threw away my soup?"

"Eh, did what could, ah? It was making him all upset."

I rested my forehead on the cool Bakelite steering wheel.

"Okay. I'll be home soon."

I drove up to Donnie's Drive-Inn, and circled the block twice before I found a parking spot to accommodate the Thunderbird. It was the height of lunch hour in downtown Mahina. The red picnic tables were full, and behind the windows, I saw the workers racing to and fro.

I waited in line at the ordering counter. When my turn came, I didn't have to ask for my husband. The young woman in the red polo shirt knew who I was. She disappeared, and a moment later, Donnie emerged from around the back of the building, wiping his hands on a white dishtowel.

"Sorry to bother you when it's so busy, Donnie."

"No worries. This is a nice surprise. What's the occasion?"

"Davison just called me from the house. Someone named Skye has turned up on our doorstep, and he apparently made Davison throw away my tomato-beef soup."

"Skye Chaney?"

"I didn't get a last name. Do you know a Skye Chaney?"

"He's Gloria's husband."

"That's what Davison said."

"Is Gloria there too, or just Skye?"

"I don't know. Davison didn't say anything about Gloria. Oh, but Donnie? You know when she called a few days ago? I might have said something about how she was welcome to visit."

Donnie looked distracted. "Okay. Listen, I need to get back."

"So should I go pick up some kale and soy dogs, or what?"

"No need. I'll bring home a vegetable chow mein tray. Nice of you to offer." Donnie kissed me absently on the forehead and was gone.

CHAPTER EIGHTEEN

I CAME HOME TO FIND Davison sitting at the kitchen counter with a stranger. The man had pleasant, boyish features, chunky black glasses, and short, sandy hair. As soon as I was through the front door, the stranger set his beer on the counter, jumped down from the barstool, and approached me with his hand extended. With his madras shirt and his stylish stubble, he wouldn't have looked out of place in a nautically-themed fashion spread.

"Hey, you must be Molly. I'm Skye, Gloria's husband. Sorry to just pop in on you like this."

"Not a problem." I clasped Skye's outstretched hand. Definitely from the mainland. No one who grew up in Hawai`i would greet a family member with a mere handshake. At the very least, there would be a hug, and probably a big wet kiss, too. "Do you have a suitcase or...?"

"I put 'em in the other guest room," Davison interrupted. "Next door to mines."

"How very helpful, Davison. Thank you. Skye, can I get you something to drink—oh, right, you're all set."

"I got us beers," Davison said. "Uncle, come sit."

Not to be outdone in the hospitality department, I emptied some raw almonds into a bowl, which I set out on the kitchen counter. Then I got myself a glass of water from the tap and seated myself in the empty barstool between the two men.

"So what brings you to Mahina?" I asked.

Skye paused.

"Gloria's missing,"

"Missing?" I exclaimed.

"Huh?" Davison echoed. "Uncle, what?"

"Does she have a phone?" I asked. "Have you tried calling?"

"Oh, no, we don't carry cell phones. The electromagnetic radiation. You might as well put a microwave next to your head."

"But you think she's in Mahina?" I asked.

Skye closed his eyes and breathed deeply. "I don't know."

"Does Donnie know?"

Skye shook his head.

"I didn't call Donnie. I didn't want to worry him. I thought I was going to find her here. With you."

"How long has she been missing?" I asked.

"Two days. Since Sunday."

"Why didn't you call us right away?"

"We argued."

My sympathy for Skye shifted to suspicion. Maybe Gloria was running from her husband, and she wanted to disappear. Thanks a lot for welcoming this guy into my house, Davison.

"Arguing about what?" I asked.

Skye looked pained. "Iulani Malufau is out."

"Malufau." Davison stood up, looking like bad weather. Without another word, he marched back toward the guest rooms. We heard him slam the door.

I got up, dumped my water into the sink, and refilled my glass with wine. Then I sat back down at the kitchen counter.

"If I might ask the obvious question, who or what is Malufau? What are we talking about?"

"Iulani Malufau is Davison's biological father," Skye said.

"Ah. I did not know."

I had known Davison was Gloria's son, but Donnie had always been evasive on the subject of Davison's paternity. In the absence of concrete information, I'm afraid I'd entertained some lurid theories. It was a relief to find out the father was just some guy I'd never heard of before.

"He's out? Like he came out of the closet?"

"He escaped from prison," Skye said.

"Prison?"

Skye nodded.

"And he was in prison for...?"

"He was serving time for the robberies, I think. They couldn't make the murder charges stick."

"Murder charges? So where was he, the big facility on Oahu? What is it called?"

"You're thinking of Halawa. Actually, he was sent to the mainland. You know Hawai`i ships its prisoners out of state."

"So, he's escaped. And now Gloria is missing. I can see why you're worried."

"Malufau was bad news. Terrible temper. Gloria told me she once saw him run a guy over. Backed up his truck and ran over him again. She watched it happen. Couldn't do anything to stop it."

"Wow. And Gloria's afraid he's going to come after her now?"

"No." Skye rested his forehead in his hands. "No. She should be afraid. That's what we were arguing about. Gloria's fearless, and I love her for it, but sometimes..." He trailed off.

"Skye, I hope you don't mind my asking, but did Gloria give Davison up for adoption to get him away from this guy?"

"She didn't give him up. She hanai'd him. You know the Hawaiian practice of hanai is much more open than our Western system of adoption. And Donnie was her closest living relative irregardless. She didn't have many options when Malufau was convicted."

I refrained from correcting Skye on his use of the non-word "irregardless." You'd think people would appreciate getting helpful guidance about word usage from someone with a Ph.D. from one of the top ten literature and creative writing programs in the country, but I haven't found that to be the case.

"I know it would have been hard for Gloria as a single mom, but didn't she just put Donnie in the position of being a single dad? I don't understand how it was fair for Donnie to get responsibility for Davison."

"She didn't have much of a choice. Gloria was in a really bad place."

"Well. Lucky Donnie was there for them." I felt annoyed at Gloria. Thanks to her, I was now imagining Davison as an innocent toddler, and feeling sorry for him. "Skye, do you know this Malufau person? Would you recognize him if you saw him?"

Skye shook his head.

"I believe it's best to leave the past in the past. When you hold a grudge against someone, you're letting them live in your head rent-free."

I realized why the man in the green football jersey had looked familiar, even though I had never met him before. Not feature for feature. But something about his chest-out, chin-up, punch-first-and-ask-questions-later posture.

The man in the green football jersey was an older version of Davison.

"Molly, are you all right?"

I looked down to see shards of my wine glass sparkling on the floor, in a pool of dark red cabernet.

CHAPTER NINETEEN

AS I SCRUBBED WINE from the light wood floor (Why couldn't I be fonder of Chardonnay or some other colorless, non-staining beverage?), Skye told me more about his wife's disappearance. Gloria had heard the news of Malufau's escape, and had given Skye a story about having to visit relatives in Honolulu. Next thing he knew, she had packed her bags and disappeared. I kept thinking about the man in the green shirt, and especially about his hand on my shoulder— uncomfortably close to my neck.

"So Donnie and Gloria have relatives in Honolulu?"

"No. It looks like Gloria invented the Honolulu relatives for my benefit. The only family of Gloria's I know of is here in Mahina. It's why I came."

I wiped the glass fragments into a paper bag and dumped the wine-stained paper towels in after them. Then I rolled up the bag and dropped the whole thing into the kitchen trashcan.

"I think he's here, Skye. Gloria's ex. I think he's in Mahina."

"He's here? Why do you think he's here?"

I told Skye of the two encounters with the man I thought might be Gloria's fugitive ex.

"Skye, how does a guy who just escaped from prison manage to get on a flight to Hawai`i? Every time I fly, they ask for seventeen pieces of ID and a note from my mother."

"Those guys can get documents forged."

"An escaped prisoner with forged ID. Wow. And here I was hoping he was just interested in my car."

Skye got up and went to the fridge for another beer.

"If you ask me, I think he wanted to see Davison. He thinks he still has a right to his son."

"So what do you think he's planning to do now?"

"Planning to do?" Skye pressed the chilled beer bottle to his forehead. "What if he's already done it? What if he followed Gloria here, to Mahina? What if he—I don't even want to think about it."

"Okay, first of all, he might not be the man I saw." Although I was certain he was. "But if this guy really was this Malufau person, he was already here in Mahina last week. Gloria called our house after Davison and I saw him. So he couldn't have followed her here. He was here before she arrived—if she came here at all."

Or maybe she had followed him to Mahina. Looking for closure, or something else?

"Gloria called here?" Skye removed his hands from his face. "When? What did she say?"

"She wanted to talk to Donnie. We didn't really chat."

"Why did she want to talk to Donnie? What was it about?"

"I don't know. I'm sorry, Skye. I don't have a terrific memory. I can't even remember which day we—wait a second."

I retrieved my purse, pulled out my wallet, and leafed through my receipts until I found the one from Fujioka's Music and Party Supply.

"It was the thirteenth. Davison and I saw Gloria's ex, assuming this man was Gloria's ex, on the thirteenth of May. Have you contacted the Mahina police?"

"No." Skye took a gloomy swig from his beer. "Just Los Gatos PD."

I went to my workstation and found the envelope from the Mahina Police Department, the one I'd picked up from my office. A phone number for Officer Andrew De Silva was on it. I dialed it, and a woman answered. I gave her a brief summary of what Skye had told me about Gloria's disappearance.

"Is the husband there with you?" The woman asked.

"Yes. And another thing you should know is—"

"Just a minute. Is this person familiar to you? Are you sure this man is who he says he is?"

I glanced at Skye, who was distractedly eating almonds.

"Excuse me," I said to Skye. I took my phone out onto the lanai, closing the door gently behind me. After what Skye had just told me about avoiding cell phones, I imagined electromagnetic waves cooking my brain as I spoke.

"My stepson seems to know this man," I said, once I was safely outside. I related the conversation about Gloria's ex escaping from prison, and her bogus story about visiting relatives in Honolulu.

"Do you have any corroboration of this man's story? About the prison escape?"

"Well no, but—"

"What is the name of the missing person?"

"I don't know my sister-in-law's married name. Her maiden name would have been Gonsalves. Gloria Gonsalves. Wait a minute. It's Kealoha. She goes by Gloria Kealoha. It must be a business alias. Her husband's name is Skye Cheney."

"Alls you know is Gloria's husband is pursuing her. You don't know anything else about him."

"Well, what should I do? Do you think Gloria's in danger?"

"Of course, the decision is yours. But in general, we recommend not getting involved in a domestic dispute. In most cases of missing adults, the person has disappeared of her own volition. In all probability, she'll turn up, and she'll be fine."

Sure, just like my necklace and earrings. Thanks a lot, Officer Helpful.

"So you don't think it's worth having the police keep an eye out for her or something? Whatever you do in a missing person case?"

"Who was the other party? The one you think might have harmed her?"

"Oh, what was it again?"

I opened the front door and poked my head in. "Skye, what's the name of Gloria's ex again?"

"Iulani Malufau," Skye called back from the kitchen.

"Did he say Malufau?" The woman's voice softened. "You shoulda said so."

"Well I—"

"We already got an alert out for him. I'll pass this along, but. Good luck with your sister-in-law, ah? Hope she's okay."

CHAPTER TWENTY

I DISCONNECTED THE call and went back inside. Davison had come out of his room and was back at the kitchen counter with Skye. Both men put down their beers and turned to me expectantly.

"Well, I just talked to someone at Mahina PD. They told me there's already an alert out for Iulani Malufau."

"Do you have a headset, Molly?" Skye looked concerned. "You shouldn't hold the phone next to your head for extended periods of time."

"I do, somewhere, but I don't know where it went. Anyway, Mahina PD is doing what they can, it sounds like. They have an alert out for the ex."

Skye nodded.

Davison scowled at his beer.

"By the way, Skye? I didn't see the prison escape on the news. Was it reported anywhere?"

"Oh, you won't hear about it in the news. It's a private prison. Chronically understaffed. They're more concerned about profit than security. These breaches happen all the time, but it's not in their interest to publicize it, so they keep it quiet."

"How did Gloria hear about the escape?"

"I'm not sure. Someone called her, I think."

"Skye says you think it was him," Davison said.

"Sorry, what was that, Davison?"

"Ugly looking faka, wit' the blue truck. You think it was him?"

I considered asking Davison to watch his language, but I wasn't sure whether he'd uttered a bona fide swear word.

"I did tell Skye I thought it might be the same person. Davison, you didn't recognize him?"

"Nah. I dunno what he looks like. Aunty Gloria never like talk about 'em. I never even knew his last name till Uncle just said it today."

"Well, we've notified Mahina PD, and Donnie will be home in a few hours. I really need to get back to work. Skye, Davison, you'll be okay?"

Davison got up and retrieved two more green beer bottles from the fridge.

"Yeah, no worries. We'll be right here." Davison popped the top from one of the bottles and handed it to his uncle.

Skye chugged it gratefully.

I wasn't going to get any work done at home with Skye and Davison there. I grabbed my umbrella from the hook by the front door and made the short walk to the public library.

A couple of hours later, I came back to an empty living room. I poured some wine into a furikake cup, found the mystery novel I'd been reading, and got comfortable on the couch.

"Did someone come in?" Skye emerged from the guest room, wiping the sleep from his eyes.

"Just me." I set down my book and wine glass and sat up. "I still haven't heard anything new about Gloria. No one's called."

"Oh. I'm all disoriented. Guess I fell asleep. My internal clock is all messed up from the travel. You know, it's not good to cross time zones too fast. We're not built for it."

"Well, you're awake now." I stood up. "Want to help me set the table for dinner?"

When I'm a guest, I always appreciate being asked to help. Nothing's worse than sitting there, beaming uselessly at your hostess while she tells you to stay put and "relax."

"I wonder what Donnie's going to say when he finds out Gloria's gone." Skye folded the paper napkins in half diagonally, smoothing each one down so the apex pointed left. "I know they're really close."

"Close? Donnie and Gloria?"

That hadn't been my impression. If Donnie was in regular contact with his sister, it was news to me.

"You didn't tell him already, did you, Molly?"

"No. I haven't talked to Donnie since I saw you last. He's going to be home soon, though. We probably shouldn't hit him with the bad news about Gloria right away. Maybe when the conversation rolls around to the part where he asks you, 'So Skye, what brings you to Mahina?' You can tell him then."

Skye patted a napkin into place and looked up at me.

"Molly, since you mentioned it. What brought you to Mahina?"

"It's that obvious I'm not from Hawai`i?"

"Yup. Sorry, I didn't mean it to be insulting. Nothing wrong with being a mainlander. I'm one too, you know."

"No, it's okay. No offense taken. You're right, I didn't grow up here. I moved here to take a job at Mahina State...I guess it's been about eight years now."

"Do you speak Pidgin?"

"What, me? No. Never. Why would I do such a thing?"

"Shouldn't you try to learn the language of a place when you move there?" Skye said. "Hawaiian Pidgin is a language."

I handed him a stack of four dinner plates.

"I see what you're saying, but it's not like trying to learn French before you go to Paris or something. If you're not from here, and you try to speak it, it comes off sounding like you're either trying too hard, or you're mocking people, or something. You know, Donnie doesn't even speak Pidgin."

"Donnie doesn't?"

"At least I've never heard him. Then again, there's my friend Emma who teaches in the biology department. She speaks Pidgin. Although she kind of slips in and out of it, and she throws in some Yiddish too, now and then. In fact, I've noticed when Emma and Donnie are talking to each other, Emma dials up the Pidgin, and Donnie won't speak it at all. They both grew up here and they're both Hawaiian. Go figure."

Skye set out the last of the plates. "I asked Gloria if she would teach me. She laughed at me."

"I think Donnie would laugh at me, too if I—oh, hey, here he is now. Let's see. Donnie, what would you do if I asked you to teach me to speak Pidgin?"

Donnie paused in the front doorway, balancing a stack of three foil trays in one hand. "What?"

"Should I learn to speak Pidgin?"

Donnie laughed and shook his head. "These are still hot. I'm going to take a quick shower, and I'll be right back out. Hello, Skye."

Donnie set the trays down in the kitchen and disappeared into the bedroom to shower away the day's sweat and frying oil.

"Told you." I smiled at Skye.

Donnie, Skye, Davison, and I sat down to a dinner of vegetarian chow mein from Donnie's Drive-Inn. I did not care for the Drive-Inn's interpretation of chow mein. It contained crunchy carrot slices, stringy celery chunks, and bitter bamboo shoots, all coated in a salty white goo. Of course it was thoughtful of Donnie to bring home a vegetarian dinner, so no one else had to go to the trouble of cooking. I certainly wasn't going to complain.

Donnie was an amazing chef, at least when he cooked for us at home. But the people who frequented Donnie's Drive Inn weren't looking for culinary genius. They wanted gigantic portions of fried, sweet, and greasy, with big scoops of rice and macaroni salad on the side.

Skye had a shaker of powdered seaweed next to his plate, which he sprinkled all over his food. I wondered if it made the bland chow mein taste better or worse.

"So, Skye," Donnie said, "what brings you to Mahina?"

Skye and I looked at each other. This was our cue to give Donnie the bad news about his sister. Just as I opened my mouth to speak, we heard a knock on the door.

Donnie excused himself and went to answer it. I heard friendly conversational noises between Donnie and an unidentified woman. Then Donnie stepped back and let her in.

She was short and comfortably built, with straight, shoulder-length black hair and a round, impish face. She wore a white peasant blouse, snug jeans, and steep platform mules that made her tiny feet look like hooves.

"Hel-lo everyone," she sang out. Donnie walked in behind her, carrying a hard-sided animal-print suitcase.

Skye pushed his chair back and jumped to his feet. "Gloria."

"Oh, hey, Aunty. Howzit?" Davison didn't bother to get up. He'd been frantic with worry, but now that Gloria was safe, Davison was too cool to let on.

I stood up, too, and approached her.

"I'm Molly." I took Gloria's hand and then submitted to the inevitable hug. "I am so glad to meet you."

CHAPTER TWENTY-ONE

I WATCHED DONNIE ROLL Gloria's suitcase back to the guest room.

"Would you like something to drink?" I asked her.

"Just water, thanks, Molly. What's for dinner?"

"It's from the restaurant," Skye said. "But there's no meat in it, at least."

"Oh. Vegetarian. Great."

I ran her a glass of water from the tap. "We're having vegetarian chow mein. From Donnie's Drive-Inn."

I brought her the water, a plate, and a pair of chopsticks. Skye picked up her glass, sniffed it, and took a tiny sip.

"Is it filtered?" he asked. I thought I saw Gloria roll her eyes a little, but it might have been my imagination.

"No." I sat back down at the table. "But our county water is clean. I actually sent it in for testing, and it's quite safe. I think it tastes pretty good, too. Sorry, we don't have any bottled water."

"Oh, no. We would never drink bottled water. It's such a waste. All of the petroleum used in manufacturing the plastic bottles isn't healthy, not to mention your water is sitting in the plastic for weeks, with all of the poison leaching into it."

"You know what?" Gloria snatched her water glass back from Skye and set it down firmly. "I'd like some wine. Whatever everyone else is drinking."

Donnie emerged from the guest room.

"Excellent choice." He went to the kitchen and returned with a red-wine glass.

Before Donnie had moved in with me, I'd been perfectly happy to drink my wine from a repurposed furikake jar or even a coffee mug. Donnie didn't share my broad-minded approach to stemware. He had proper drinking vessels for every conceivable occasion. In addition to red-wine goblets, we had white-wine, dessert-wine, and chardonnay glasses, along with a set of what I assumed were either aperitif glasses or eyewash cups.

Now that we were all safely eating dinner, no one seemed inclined to bring up our earlier concerns about Gloria's safety. Donnie had no idea she had been missing at all, so obviously he wasn't bothered.

It seemed odd to me that Gloria had flown to Mahina without telling her husband. But who was I to question how other people conducted their relationships? There were things about me Donnie would probably never know. And Donnie didn't tell me everything, that was for darn sure.

"Skye, baby." Gloria reached over and patted Skye's hand. "Who you got watching the shop now?"

"Matthew and Alyssa can cover all the shifts for this week. But we should try to get back as soon as we can."

"Nah, nah, nah, they'll be fine. They know what to do. Long as I'm here, I like stay a while. See my brother, spend some time with baby boy." She reached over and squeezed Davison's stubbly cheek, which he seemed to take in stride. "And this is the first time I ever met my sister-in-law. Molly, it's the weirdest thing, you know who you remind me of—"

"Gloria," Donnie interrupted. "Do you have everything you need to stay the night?"

"We can make a run to the store if you like," I said.

"You don't have to drive us around," Skye said. "I rented a car. I was lucky. I got their last hybrid. Hey, it's great of you guys to let us stay here. I'd love to stay up and 'talk story' with everyone, but it's close to midnight my time. I think I might turn in. Gloria, what do you think?"

"You go ahead, baby. I'll be there soon."

"The bathroom's there, between the two bedrooms." Donnie pointed to the doorway leading to the guest rooms.

"I'll show you where the towels are." I led Skye to the guest bathroom and opened the floor-to-ceiling storage closet. "Right here. Towels, extra toilet paper, wrapped toothbrushes, little toothpastes, tiny floss. Every time we go to the dentist we get a bag of goodies, so we store them in here for guests."

"Thanks, Molly. I brought my own toothpaste. You probably want to think about investing in fluoride-free. You should look up the effects of fluoride."

"Good thing Gloria showed up when she did. What a relief."

"Yeah." His voice was devoid of enthusiasm. He should have been ecstatic about his missing wife showing up safe and unharmed. Maybe he was just tired.

"Do you think her ex might try to follow her here?"

"I don't know."

If I had been in Skye's place, I'd have been dying to know where Gloria had been. But Gloria was still chatting away happily at the dining table. It was almost as if she were trying to avoid having a one-on-one conversation with her husband.

"Are you going to be okay?"

"Sure." Skye nodded glumly. "Thanks."

When I returned to the dining room table, the conversation had turned to cars.

"I think you should save up for your own car this time," Donnie was telling Davison. I silently cheered. Donnie had paid for Davison's truck, but when his son moved to the mainland, Donnie let him pocket the proceeds from the truck's sale. I was happy to see Donnie trying to encourage some financial self-sufficiency in his spoiled kid. Better late than never.

"Do you really need a car here, baby?" Gloria squeezed Davison's hand. "This place is so close to everything. You can walk right down to the Bayfront in ten, fifteen minutes. You get a car, you gotta make car payments, pay the insurance, get your safety checks, so humbug. And as Skye would make sure to remind us, the less fossil fuel you burn, the better for the health of our planet." Gloria took a big swig of her wine.

"Ho, Aunty, you should tell Molly."

"What did I do?" I took my seat and reached over to the wine bottle. It was empty.

"I'll get another one." Donnie went to the kitchen and retrieved another bottle of Vino Nobile.

"Molly got a fifty-nine Thunderbird, Aunty." Davison lifted his bushy eyebrows for emphasis. "Three hundred horsepower. Eleven miles to the gallon. An' Aunty, guess what? She never let me drive it."

Gloria clucked and shook her head good-naturedly.

"If you need a ride somewhere important, like to a job interview, I'll be happy to drive you," Donnie said. "And I think Molly would be, too."

"To a job interview? Of course. I'd be delighted. Just let me know."

CHAPTER TWENTY-TWO

ANDY DE SILVA WAS LATE to my Diversity Seminar the next morning, so I didn't have a chance to talk to him until the break. I approached him as he poured himself a cup of coffee from the glass carafe on the side table.

He pulled a Styrofoam cup from the top of the stack and offered it to me.

"Thank you." I hadn't planned to drink the Motor Vehicle break room coffee, but I couldn't turn it down without seeming rude. "We had a little missing-persons drama at our house last night."

"Oh yeah?" De Silva tore open a packet of powdered creamer and shook it into his coffee. I related the events of the previous day, starting with Skye's arrival.

"And guess who showed up at our door, safe and sound, just when we were sitting down to dinner?" I concluded with a dramatic flourish. "Gloria."

"Hm."

"You don't sound very surprised."

After seeing Andy De Silva pestering Donnie for information about Gloria, I had expected him to show a little more enthusiasm.

"Most of the time, the missing person turns up safe."

"I understand you're on the lookout for her ex. He escaped from prison on the mainland, right?"

De Silva nodded.

"Any progress on finding him?"

"Not yet."

So, Gloria was safe for now, but her ex was still out there somewhere.

"I wouldn't recognize him if he came to our house looking for Gloria. Do you have his picture?"

In fact, I was pretty sure I knew what Gloria's ex looked like. I just wanted confirmation.

"Not on me. But yeah, we been running 'em on TV." De Silva took his coffee back to his seat. I followed him.

"You have?"

"They been showing it on the news."

I took the empty seat next to De Silva.

"I stopped following the news when school let out. It's always so distressing, and I can't do anything about any of it. I thought I might be more productive during the summer if I kept my mind clear."

"Well, we been putting out alerts." De Silva took out his phone and checked his messages, which seemed rude.

"Gloria and her husband are staying with us now. I don't know how long they'll be in town, but if you want to stop by and say hello, please come by any time."

De Silva nodded.

The break was drawing to a close, and my not-so-eager pupils started to take their seats around the U-shaped conference table.

"You know, Officer De Silva, I think I might have seen him. Malufau. Gloria's ex."

De Silva looked at me as if I'd finally said something worth his attention.

"You did? When?"

"May thirteenth. I remember the date because it was on my receipt from Fujioka's Music and Party Supply. He was in the parking lot of Fujioka's. He watched my stepson and me drive away. And later we saw him down on the Bayfront Road. I'd definitely recognize him if I saw him again."

"One week ago." De Silva looked listless again. "He could be anywhere by now."

"Sorry if that wasn't helpful. Anyway, if you have time, why don't you stop by for dinner? You and Gloria can catch up. I mean, we already have five at the dinner table. May as well make it an even six."

"Thanks anyway," De Silva glanced up at the wall clock. The break was over. "I think everyone's ready to get started, Professor."

CHAPTER TWENTY-THREE

DINNER WAS JUST THE four grown-ups. Davison had skipped out to spend the evening with friends. I felt a little indignant on behalf of Skye and Gloria. Not only were they our guests, but you'd think Davison would want to spend some time with his biological mother.

On the bright side, the meal was much more pleasant without Davison there. My stepson had horrible table manners. He would reach across me for the shoyu bottle instead of asking me to pass it, he would lick his fingers as he ate, and he was constantly overstepping the limits of appropriate mealtime conversation.

The first night back at our house, he'd treated Donnie and me to a vivid account of how he'd lost a toenail after dropping a weight on his foot. At one point, he'd grasped his ankle and lifted his bare foot, giving us an eyeful of his blackened toe. It had put me right off my gorgonzola gnocchi.

We dined on soggy tempura vegetables and pebbly fried rice, washed down with Donnie's excellent wine, and discussed the merits of local attractions like the Saturday Farmer's Market and the Mahina Public Library. Donnie, trying to be helpful, told Skye about all the soy-based meat substitutes available at Natural High Organic Foods. Skye responded with a lecture on the evils of dietary soy.

According to Skye, soy may have been considered healthful once upon a time, but those days were long gone. Modern soy was ubiquitous and genetically modified. Avoiding it was both urgent and practically impossible. Soy lurked in chocolate, cereals, Mexican food, Asian food, vitamins, sauces, chewing gum, cosmetics, and candles.

Soy's one benign form, Skye explained, was natto, soybeans fermented with a virtuous bacillus. I'd seen natto, but I never dared try it. To me, it looked like someone took a plate of beans and blew their nose into it.

Gloria interrupted Skye's informative monologue to complain that the tempura was chewy. Donnie tried to explain that at the Drive-Inn, it had to be fried in batches and stored under heat lamps.

"You shouldn't make tempura then." Gloria sniffed. "If you can't do it right."

"The sweet potato is nice," I interjected. Poor Donnie. I felt like I had to say something nice about the food, and my statement happened to be true. The purple Okinawan sweet potato was firmer than its orange counterpart and held up well to deep-frying. The flesh remained dense and sweet; it was nearly impossible to ruin.

"The eggplant's undercooked, too." Gloria made a face.

She was right about the eggplant. It squeaked like Styrofoam when I bit into it.

"Oh. There's okra in here." I set the other half of the fried okra pod back down on my plate. "Okra isn't my favorite." My words came out a little slurred thanks to the wad of fried okra stuffed into my cheek.

Gloria shrugged. "I like it okay."

"I didn't get any okra in mine," Skye said, not making any effort to remedy the deficiency.

"Excuse me." I stood up and hurried to the bathroom to spit out the offending vegetable (assuming a furry pod oozing with slime can properly be called a vegetable).

As soon as I was back at the table, I heard footsteps clomping up the front stairs. The front door rattled, and Davison let himself in.

"Everyone still eating? Good. I brought dessert." Davison held up a mason jar full of what looked like water. "Okolehao."

"Ho, where you get that, baby?" Gloria exclaimed.

"What is it?" Skye asked.

"It's the good stuff is what. Little after-dinner drink."

Davison dropped his backpack next to the door, sat down with us, and poured out a little of the clear liquid into each of our wine glasses.

"Okolehao is Hawaiian moonshine," Gloria explained to Skye. "You gonna like it."

"Where is this from?" Donnie asked. "Uncle Brian's bathtub?"

"You don't gotta be all sarcastic, Dad. You starting to sound like your wife already."

"I'm right here, Davison."

"Show some respect, Davison." Donnie scowled at him. "I don't like your tone."

"When did you see Uncle Brian?" I asked.

"Just now. He lives downtown, ah? Short walk from here."

"Good thing you weren't driving. Well, let's give this a try." Donnie raised his glass. "Saluti."

I took a sip. It tasted like bananas and gasoline. I set the glass down quickly, my eyes bulging.

"This is interesting. I don't think I've ever had anything like it."

"I've never met your Uncle Brian," Skye said to Gloria.

"I just met him for the first time a few days ago," I said. "Davison and I happened to run into him downtown. Donnie, have you talked to him lately?"

"I've been busy. The Drive-Inn takes up most of my time."

Donnie wasn't too busy for Chamber of Commerce events and Rotary meetings and Business Boosters lunches. Poor old Uncle Brian must not have been important to Donnie's business, so Donnie didn't think it was worth spending time with him.

This was an unpleasant side to Donnie I hadn't noticed before. And here I'd tried so hard to make him feel better about his tempura.

CHAPTER TWENTY-FOUR

FRIDAY WAS THE FINAL day of my Mahina Police Department Diversity Seminar. I stopped off at Mizuno Mart on the way over to pick up some treats. At first, the plan was to get donuts, but I decided actual donuts would be too on-the-nose for a group of police officers. Instead, I bought a warm bag of fresh malasadas from a van on the side of the road. Malasadas are pretty much donuts, except they don't have holes and they're called "malasadas."

The final class session was dedicated to debriefing. Each participant had the opportunity to share what he had learned in the seminar.

We were finished in well under an hour.

And so ended my brief consulting career with the Mahina Police Department.

It hadn't been a total loss. The malasadas were a hit. More importantly, I had collected some nice experimental data on how working adults responded to selfish behavior: much the same way college students did, it turns out. People will punish perceived injustice, even at some cost to themselves.

As I drove past the public library, I spotted a familiar figure sauntering up the street. He wore wide-legged trousers, a tan windbreaker, and a straw Panama hat with a black band.

I pulled into the parking lot of the public library, locked up my car, and grabbed my umbrella from under the seat. The rain had let up for the time being, but it would be back. The asphalt was wet, and the trees lining the street glowed green against a sky the color of steel.

"Mister Gonsalves." I hurried up the sidewalk. He turned around and touched the brim of his hat when he saw me.

"Oh, Sherry. Always a pleasure. You can call me Uncle. No need call me Mister."

"Okay. And you can call me Molly. I'm Molly."

I suppose I should've been pleased when people slipped up and called me by the name of Donnie's thin and pretty ex-wife. I wasn't, though.

"So, Uncle, what a coincidence, running into you like this."

We stood on the sidewalk and beamed at each other while I scrambled to think of something else to say. Finally, I hit on, "Um, listen, Uncle, are you busy right now? Do you have time for a cup of coffee?"

Inviting a near stranger for coffee was far out of my comfort zone. But Donnie's indifference toward Uncle Brian had bothered me. Maybe Donnie had his reasons for acting distant, but he hadn't told me what they were. If I wanted to find out anything about Donnie's family, I'd have to do the detective work myself.

"Aw, too late in the day for me to drink coffee. I like to have my coffee early in the morning. I meet the ladies down at the McDonald's. We get the senior special. Nice, the senior special."

"Well, it's lunchtime now. If you haven't eaten yet, how about we go across to Donnie's Drive-Inn, sit in the shade a bit? It's right there. And, you know, we could say hi to Donnie. Your nephew."

"I got a better idea. You know the Pair-O-Dice?"

It was a few minutes' walk from the library to the Pair-O-Dice Bar and Grill. We placed our order and sat at a wobbly table near the window.

"I wanted to say thank you for sending along the Okolehao. Davison brought us some last night, after dinner. Did you really brew it yourself?"

"Ah, you drank it, Missus? Not for beginners, that stuff."

"No, indeed. I've heard of it, but this was my first real-life encounter."

"Yeah, my own special recipe. What you think?"

"I think it might be an acquired taste. But I appreciated the chance to try it."

The bartender came over with our order. A double vodka for Uncle Brian, a house red for me, and a basket of fries to share.

I watched him dig into the fries before I spoke again. "You mentioned Donnie was your brother's son. You know, I don't know anything about Donnie's father. Not even his name."

"My big brother's name was Guy. Good man. Tried his best, you know."

"Where are Donnie's parents now? Are you still in touch?"

Uncle Brian stared at the ice glistening in his empty glass.

"Gone."

"I'm so sorry. I—oh, are you finished already?"

I signaled to the bartender, who acknowledged me with a sullen chin-jut.

"I miss him every day, you know."

"I understand."

I didn't understand, not really. I was an only child, and my parents were still very much alive. I'd never lost someone close to me.

"If I could ask...when did he pass away?"

"When Donnie and little Glory was kids."

The young bartender came over with the vodka bottle and refilled Uncle Brian's glass. He picked it up and took a gulp before going on with his story. "One night, they was all in the car, going around one of the horseshoe turns, up on the coast, you know? Must not've watched where he was going. No streetlights out that way, you know. Car went down a hundred feet. Little Glory was hurt pretty bad. Donnie was small kine buss up, but nothing broken. The parents, though."

"Did they..."

Uncle Brian nodded.

"Yeah. Glory was at the hospital a few weeks. Donnie was already working at da kine, Merrie Musubis, so he could help with the bills. They lived with me."

"Donnie was already in high school then?"

"Yeah. He wanted to go college, but with this thing, no can, ah?"

"That was a nice thing you did, to take them in."

"Hard, but. Never was married or had keiki of my own, now all at once I get two."

"I can imagine. So, do you still keep in touch with Donnie and Gloria then?"

Uncle Brian finished his second glass of vodka and gloomily signaled for a third. "Nah. But you gotta understand. I remind 'em of a hard time in their life, 'as why. Now they're grown up, they'd rather forget."

"But if it weren't for you—"

"Yeah, but you know how it is. Eh, did what could, ah? The boy keeps in touch, Davison. Good boy, him. That's how come I like help 'im out when I can."

My phone pinged. I reached into my bag and checked it. The reminder message on the screen read, "Rec letter for admin."

"Oh no. I completely forgot. I'm so sorry, I have to go."

"It's okay, Sherry. You go, get on with your day. I stay here and enjoy the ambiance."

"Uncle Brian, you can call me Molly."

"Molly? Doesn't sound right. You sure?"

"Yes."

"I'll be good here. Go, go."

I left two twenties on the bar and rushed out.

CHAPTER TWENTY-FIVE

I RACED OUT OF THE Pair-O-Dice, frantically scrolling through my recent calls in search of Andy De Silva's phone number. I paused outside the bar, in front of the window with the unlit neon sign. What did people do before online calendars were invented? I suppose they missed meetings, forgot birthdays, and got fired a lot.

I found De Silva's number and pressed the call icon.

Without the electronic reminder I'd set for myself, I would have completely forgotten to ask Andy De Silva to send a thank-you letter to my administration. The whole point of signing up for the university speakers' bureau had been to make a good impression on the higher-ups at my university. De Silva had agreed in principle to write me a letter of thanks, but in the rush to wrap things up, I'd completely forgotten about it. By this time, everyone would be gone from the Motor Vehicle Department break room.

I felt a raindrop on my cheek and retreated under the overhang, hoping De Silva would pick up. To my great relief, he did.

"I'm sorry to bother you, officer. I just wanted to remind you about writing the letter. And thank you again, by the way."

"The what?"

He had already forgotten.

"You were going to write a letter to my administration. To thank them for the free seminar?"

"Oh, yeah, yeah, I forgot. Happy to do it. You gotta get me the name and address, but."

"Of course. Should I give you the information now?"

"Nah, you can drop it off with—hold on, sorry, I gotta—what? Uh-huh. Yeah, it's her. What? f'real? Oh. Eh, Professor, the boys wanna know if you wanna go on a ride-along."

"A ride-along?"

I heard laughter in the background. It sounded like "the guys" thought it would be funny to bring me along on a real call and watch me faint or something. As if I were some fragile hothouse flower.

"I'd love to come along," I declared. "I'm just a few minutes from the station."

"Okay. Wait. Nah, you better meet us there."

De Silva gave me a downtown address and rang off. It seemed having to transport myself to the scene rather violated both the letter and spirit of a "ride-along," but I was curious. Also, I wanted to make a good impression on De Silva so he would write me a strong letter.

The address was only a block and a half from the Pair-O-Dice. My car was still parked way up by the public library. I ducked into the drizzle and walked over to the site. Two patrol cars were parked on the curb in front of one of downtown's Old-West-style buildings. The first floor housed a hair salon. Its windows were filled with faded, bluish posters of sullen models sporting geometric haircuts—probably cutting-edge style in the 1970s. Next to the hair salon was the empty storefront where Etsuko's Fashion Frocks used to be. A transient hotel occupied the second floor. The building had been an upscale hotel about a hundred years ago, but the current owner couldn't be bothered to keep it painted and termite-free.

De Silva stood next to his police cruiser, talking on his radio. He acknowledged me with a nod as I approached. He recited some numbers, whose significance I didn't understand. I did comprehend some of the other things he said. Like "unresponsive." And "unattended death."

He clicked off and tucked the radio back into his belt.

"In the empty lot." He jerked his head to the side. "Around the back."

I followed him through a narrow alley to the chained-off lot behind the building. The overgrown lot was enclosed by the unbeautiful backsides of downtown Mahina's more downmarket edifices. Two black dumpsters huddled next to the transient hotel. Beside the dumpsters, two young police officers stood talking, pointing up to an open second-story window. I recognized the men from my class.

"Techs are gonna be on their way soon," De Silva called out. I stepped carefully behind him, through the knee-deep weeds. As we got closer to the two officers, I noticed a dirty bundle lying along the bottom of one of the dumpsters.

One of the two nudged the bundle with the tip of his polished shoe and said something I couldn't hear. Both men laughed.

But it wasn't a bundle. As I got closer, I realized I was looking at the body of a man. The jeans and green football jersey were soaked from the rain. His head rested at an impossible angle.

I yelped and jumped back.

"'Samatter, Professor?" One of the young knuckleheads laughed. "You never seen a dead body before?"

I certainly had seen a dead body or two in my time. But unlike these two, I wasn't entirely devoid of empathy.

I glanced up at the open window above the dumpsters, and back down at the lifeless man. The window didn't look too high up, but maybe he'd hit a metal edge of the dumpster on his way down.

I forced myself to look directly at his face. It had been some days since the man's body and soul had parted ways, but I recognized him.

I motioned De Silva over. I wanted nothing to do with those other two. They had been the worst part of my week with Mahina PD, a pair of obnoxious jerks who wouldn't stop checking their phones and whispering to each other and generally acting like they had better things to do. It didn't help their attitude when they got back the results of their personality profiles, particularly their scores on authoritarianism (high), narcissism (very high), and hostile sexism (off the charts).

"You okay, Professor? You don't look too good."

"I think I know who this is, officer. It's Gloria's ex. The one who escaped from prison."

De Silva cast a skeptical look at the body.

"Iulani Malufau? You sure? He's been out in the rain a while, you know. After a few days—"

"I know. He's wearing the same clothes I saw him in earlier."

"Eh," De Silva called to the other two officers. "Professor just ID'd our John Doe. She says it's Malufau."

"Not what his ID says." One of the cops waved something at us. A dirty nylon wallet. "Driver's license says his name is Eric Northman."

"Could be fake," De Silva said to me.

"Could be," I agreed.

De Silva's radio crackled. He picked it up and had a terse conversation with a crackly voice on the other end. Then he put the radio back into its holder.

"Techs on their way now."

"I'd better get going." I started to pick my way through the weedy lot, going back the way I'd come in. De Silva hurried after me.

"Eh, thanks for coming, ah? Sorry you hadda see da kine."

"No, thank you for letting me share this unique experience." I wanted to remove myself from this unique experience as quickly as possible.

"Professor, you cannot tell anyone what you saw today. I mean, about the identity of the victim. Not till after we confirm, and then notify next of kin."

"Of course."

"Really. Not even your husband."

"I understand." I tried not to sound as disappointed as I felt. I hadn't planned to tell Donnie what I'd seen, but I did want to mention it to Skye. At least he could stop worrying about his wife's safety.

"Glad you understand. 'Cause it's not just to spare the family's feelings, you know Professor. If this is not Gloria's ex, then she might still be in danger."

"Oh. Good point."

"And we don't know if this was an accidental death or homicide. If it's homicide, it means someone out there killed him, yeah? And when you got a murderer at large, it's usually safer to stay quiet, know what I mean?"

CHAPTER TWENTY-SIX

I TRUDGED BACK UP THE street to the library parking lot. I didn't want to go back to the house, where I might have to make conversation with my houseguests. Or worse, sit alone with my thoughts.

I drove across town in the direction of the university, my eyes blurring. Malufau was a bad guy, I reminded myself, and the world was safer without him. It wasn't merely his death that bothered me. It was the thought of his remains lying in the rain, decomposing alone and unmourned.

I drove past the university. Soon I was all the way on the far side of town. And now, finally, I was hungry. Probably something about my adrenaline subsiding. I pulled into the Pōmaika'i Arcade, the little shopping center on the edge of Mahina. If I drove any further, I wouldn't see any more grocery stores or gas stations. Just dense jungle smothering tin-roofed houses, and the occasional hand-painted sign advertising homemade pasteles or fresh-caught ahi.

Donnie and I didn't have any rule against eating at restaurants other than Donnie's Drive-Inn. In fact, I thought it might be helpful for me to try one of his competitors. Conduct some culinary reconnaissance. Chang's Pizza Pagoda was in a bad location, tucked away behind the beauty supply store and hidden from the main parking lot. It wasn't much to look at either, just a few fake woodgrain tables on a tile floor, and glaring fluorescent strip lights overhead. The menu was on an illuminated board behind the counter with movable letters (mostly black, a few blue or red) stuck into the grooves.

Despite the charmless atmosphere, Chang's was packed. After waiting in a long but fast-moving line, I ordered the chow fun focaccia. It was one of the featured items from their new, expanded menu. The server plopped four generous bread squares into a Styrofoam clamshell container and handed it to me. I paid and waited for a seat to open up. Finally, a man in shorts and a baseball cap stood up from the counter against the wall, and I zoomed over to claim the space. I popped open the clamshell and took a deep breath. I got scents of garlic and frying oil mingled with faint acrylic nail fumes drifting in from the beauty shop next door.

From the first bite of spongy focaccia square, I felt rejuvenated. Maybe I'd just needed something on my stomach and a place to rest. I ate happily until a wadded-up napkin appeared on my lap. I turned to see a grinning, flailing toddler being restrained by a mortified young couple. I clicked my Styrofoam container closed and assured the apologetic parents I was about to leave anyway. As an aspiring parent myself, I was sympathetic.

The minute I vacated the seat, someone who had been hovering behind me slid into the chair.

On the way out, I almost collided with Mrs. Andrade from church. She and her husband ran The Snack Shack, a tiny beachfront hut popular with surfers and canoe paddlers.

"Oh, Mrs. Donnie." She examined my Styrofoam clamshell as if concentrating hard enough would give her x-ray vision. "What are you doing here?"

"I was just checking out the competition."

"Oh yeah. Me, too." She balanced a stack of Styrofoam containers, braced with her chin.

"How are things at the Snack Shack?"

"Little bit slow. You try the Kung Pao Pizza Rolls?"

"Not this time. Chow fun focaccia."

"Oh, I heard it's good, but I cannot. Noodles on top of bread, ah? Would send my blood sugar through the roof."

On the way back out to the parking lot, I stopped in at the beauty supply store. I didn't need anything from there, but it was air-conditioned, and the detour allowed me to put off going home for just a few minutes more. I wandered up and down the narrow aisles still holding my lunch leftovers. Judging from the display of curling irons and hair straighteners, hair-flattening technology hadn't progressed much since I'd moved to Mahina. In the tropical humidity of the island's windward side, ironing my hair straight was a Sisyphean endeavor. My curls would spring back within seconds. Worse, the heat damage would raise a nimbus of damaged strands that framed my head like an aura. I moved from the implements to the hair dye, perusing the swatches on display and wondering how I'd look as a platinum blonde. With my hair texture, probably like a sheep.

I perused the floor-to-ceiling nail polish display. From deep forest green to pale leaf, from black violet to lavender, every nail color one could possibly want was arranged in an orderly grid. After I'd spent a good half hour hanging around and soaking up the air conditioning, I knew I should buy something. It was only good manners. I settled on a bottle of nail lacquer in a shade of true red, reminiscent of Golden Age Hollywood.

On the way back home, I drove past Donnie's Drive-Inn. Most of the red picnic tables were empty. I considered stopping in to say hi, but the contrast between crowded Chang's and the deserted Drive-Inn was too uncomfortable to deal with at the moment. I kept driving, all the way back to the house.

I pulled into the carport and shifted into neutral. A sudden roar of rain on the carport's tin roof drowned out the Thunderbird's 300 horsepower engine. I rolled down the window, switched off the ignition, and sat. I hadn't wanted to stop at the Drive-Inn, but neither did I feel ready to go back into the house.

Andy De Silva had told me not to tell anyone what I'd seen. We weren't even sure the victim was Iulani Malufau. Of course, I would do as he said. Even if I had correctly identified the dead man, it wasn't my place to break the news. I certainly wouldn't say anything to Donnie, Gloria, Skye, or Davison.

Emma Nakamura, though, would be a perfect confidante.

CHAPTER TWENTY-SEVEN

I PULLED OUT MY PHONE and waited for the rain on the metal roof of the carport to ease up. As soon as it did, I dialed Emma's number.

She listened to my whole story, expressing surprise, disgust, or delight as appropriate.

"Sounds like things took care of themselves then," she said when I had finished. "Scary, but, the guy following you."

"I'm not sure things took care of themselves, exactly, Emma. Look. Gloria's ex escapes from prison. Then Gloria mysteriously disappears. Somehow, during her unexplained absence, the ex who has been such a blight on her life, and who now might be a threat to Davison, accidentally suffers a fatal fall."

"She real big, this Gloria?"

"No. She's almost as short as you, Emma. What I mean to say is she's petite."

"Oh, so what're you thinking now is Donnie's sister, this 'petite' wahine, tracks down her hard case ex who just escaped from prison. And then this lady, who from what you're saying keeps herself in fighting condition by giving aromatherapy pedicures to Silicon Valley yoga moms, throws the guy off a balcony."

"There was no balcony. It was a window looking out onto an abandoned lot."

"Okay, throws the guy out the window then. Is that what you're thinking, Molly?"

"Well yes, but you're making it sound ridiculous."

"It is ridiculous."

"And I don't think there's any such thing as an aromatherapy pedicure."

"Molly, you should just stay out of it and be glad nothing bad happened to you. Anyway, aren't you supposed to be working on your book chapter?"

"I am. I'm just trying to get my head clear." I switched off the ignition, let myself out of the car, and took the steps up onto my shady lanai. Instead of going into the house, I took the phone around to the back.

From the back lanai, I had a clear view of the graveyard. It was pretty, as graveyards go, a well-watered lawn studded with stone markers.

"Emma, do you think it's bad luck to live next to a graveyard?"

"Kinda late to worry about it now, Molly. How come you're asking?"

"The landscapers just cut the trees back. I can see it clearly from the back lanai. I wasn't ever able to see it before."

"So what, you superstitious now?"

"No. Of course not."

"Quit thinking up new things to worry about. Remember you're supposed to stay calm and serene so you can get your 'elderly' eggs fertilized."

"Thanks for the tactful reminder. I wasn't supposed to say anything about the murder to anyone, by the way. So don't tell anyone."

"I'm not gonna say nothing. Anyway, what's to tell? And you don't know for sure if it was murder."

"Speaking of murder. Emma, I really am not enjoying having houseguests. Ever since Gloria's husband got here, we've been eating nothing but—"

"Ho, calm down, Molly. This is in-laws you're talking about. You always gotta suck up to the in-laws."

"I know. And they're nice enough people, but—"

"Nah, nah, no 'but.' Anyways, aren't you the one who invited the sister?"

"Maybe."

"Well, it's not forever. You just gotta suffer through it. Same thing I gotta do when Yoshi's parents come visit. Oh, an' seriously, Molly. De Silva's right. Don't say nothing about the dead guy. He might not be Gloria's ex, an' you don't wanna get anyone's hopes up."

I was a model of discretion at dinner. I said nothing about my ride-along adventure and little about anything else. Skye held forth on the topic of food additives for a good long time. Then Davison managed to steer the conversation around to pig hunting. Gloria reminisced about when she used to eat bacon. Skye seemed not to hear her. He lectured Davison on the topic of animals and their feelings, pointing out pigs don't like to get shot with arrows any more than people do. Donnie tried to change the subject back to food additives. I ate quietly, glancing now and then at Gloria's biceps and trying to estimate her upper-body strength.

After dinner, I spent some time working on my book chapter, trying to make up for the hours I'd missed during the day. By the time I showered and made it to bed, Donnie had fallen asleep. He had left the light on with a recent economics bestseller open on his night table.

Donnie was always looking for ways to become better informed. He'd tried taking night classes, but they didn't fit his schedule, so instead he would check out edifying books from the library. My night table had books on it too, but mine were mostly lightweight murder mysteries.

I switched off the light and tried to slip into bed quietly. Donnie stirred and dropped his arm over me.

"You okay?" he murmured.

"Sure."

He propped his head on his hand, fully awake now. "You seemed quiet at dinner."

"There was plenty of conversation. I didn't have much to add."

"You just felt like not saying anything tonight?"

"The conversation seemed to be humming along perfectly well without me."

"Anything happen today?"

I momentarily forgot about my chance encounter with Uncle Brian; I had a much more interesting news item to share. And really, was it reasonable to expect me to conceal what I'd seen from my own husband? I decided it was not.

"I went out on a ride-along with Andy De Silva."

"A ride-along?" Donnie turned his head toward me. I couldn't see his expression in the dark. "I thought you were just doing diversity training for them. How did it turn into you going on a ride-along?"

"Donnie, have you ever seen a dead body?"

"Why, what happened today?"

"You know the guy that I thought was following me?"

Donnie sat up. "Someone was following you?"

"Maybe I forgot to mention it. Well anyway, you don't have to worry about it because I saw the guy today. No, it's okay, because he's dead. It was the same guy. Don't tell anyone, though, because Officer De Silva said I wasn't supposed to say anything. They have to notify next of kin first."

Donnie pulled me into a tight hug. "Molly, please, please keep yourself safe. Please. You have a family now."

"I am safe," I murmured into his chest. "Really, Donnie. You don't have to worry about me."

He sighed. "I hope you're right."

CHAPTER TWENTY-EIGHT

THE NEXT MORNING, I got up early, fixed myself a cup of coffee, and started working on my book chapter. Today was going to be productive. I wasn't going to let anything stop me. I would make up for all the time I'd lost the day before plying Uncle Brian with double vodkas and looking at dead bodies and driving across town to eat at Chang's Pizza Pagoda.

"Molly, you got a internet connection we can use?" Gloria was at my elbow, hands on her hips. "Me and Skye gotta book our return tickets."

"This computer is the only one..." I started, but then I remembered my conversation with Emma. She was right. I was the hostess, and it was my job to be patient and gracious with my in-laws. Besides, I had invited Gloria here in the first place, so I had only myself to blame. "How disappointing your visit is ending so soon. Of course you can use my computer. It'll just take me a minute to finish this one thing, and then it's all yours."

"Okay. You finish up." Gloria walked to the kitchen. "Donnie said you guys got some bacon."

I was looking over the email from Andy De Silva, a draft of his letter of thanks to my administration.

"In the pantry. You can have whatever you like. Help yourself. Wait. Aren't you guys vegetarians?"

Gloria muttered something I couldn't quite hear.

To whom it may concern,

Began Andy De Silva's letter to my administration.

Thank you for sending Professor Barda to conduct the Diversity Seminar. She was very friendly and nice and not like a real Professor. We would use her again if we have to.

With Warmest Regards,

Andrew De Silva, Mahina Police Department

This was not at all what I'd hoped for. I sent De Silva a reply.

Dear Officer De Silva,

Thank you so much for your kind letter, and for allowing me the opportunity to comment. If I might make a few suggestions:

I rewrote the letter from top to bottom and sent it back to him. Then I logged out of my email account.

"Gloria?" I stood up. "Here you go. The computer's all yours. Gosh, I hope you and Skye don't have to leave right away."

"Not right away." She came over and plopped down in my chair. "Sometime in the next few days, though. We gotta time it for whenever we can get a good price on the airfare."

I left her to tap away at my workstation. I went back into my bedroom, pulled a book from the stack on my night table, and went back to the living room to read on the couch.

"Skye, baby," Gloria called out. "My credit card's maxed. Can you come here and finish this up?"

Skye emerged from the guest room and took Gloria's place at my workstation. Gloria stood and disappeared back into the guest room.

Skye addressed me over his shoulder as he typed. "Should I shut it down when I'm done?"

"No, leave it on," I said. "I'm going to use it when you guys are done."

"That's not bacon I smell, is it?" Skye asked me.

"We got the Wednesday flights, yeah?" Gloria came back into the living room.

"You're leaving Wednesday?" I exclaimed. "So soon."

I hoped I sounded suitably disappointed. In fact, I was eagerly anticipating getting my living space back and being able to eat what I wanted.

Gloria and Skye decided to make the most of their remaining time. They rousted Davison from his room, and the three of them went out to the Saturday Farmer's Market. As soon as they were gone, I retrieved the leftover chow fun focaccia from its hiding place in the vegetable drawer. I heated it in the microwave and sat down at the kitchen counter to enjoy a solitary breakfast and think over recent events.

I was certain the dead man was Iulani Malufau, Gloria's ex and Davison's biological father. But what if he wasn't? Suppose the corpse in the vacant lot was a random individual. Who coincidentally bore a physical resemblance to Davison. And had been following him.

Sure, that was likely.

So then what if the dead man was Davison's biological father? He escaped from prison, evaded capture, and made it back to Mahina—where he accidentally toppled out of a second-story window.

I supposed an accidental death was possible. More likely than little Gloria overpowering him and shoving him out of the window, anyway.

Why was I worried about this? No one else was, as far as I could tell. Skye and Gloria seemed to be on good terms now. Who knew what story Gloria had come up with to explain her temporary disappearance, but whatever it was, it seemed to be good enough for her husband.

I wondered if I should have a look inside the second guest room, where Skye and Gloria were staying. I immediately pushed the temptation away. Snooping hadn't worked out too well for me the last time I'd tried it in Davison's room. Leave it alone. They'll be leaving soon, then everything will be back to normal, and none of this is your problem anyway.

In the meantime, the visit had had its good points. I'd learned a little more about Donnie's family. I'd met Donnie's sister and her husband in person, and I now knew the story behind Davison's adoption. Gloria had been young and in a bad situation, and Donnie had stepped in. Donnie had his faults, but piecing together this story reminded me of what I loved about him. Sure, he could be a little bit inflexible at times, but when it came down to it, he was a decent, unselfish human being. He had uncomplainingly taken in a toddler when he was struggling to build his new business.

I really couldn't figure out how someone capable of so much compassion could be so cold to his Uncle Brian.

I stuffed the Styrofoam clamshell from Chang's into the trash, refilled my coffee mug, and went back to my workstation. I now had additional data from my sample of working law enforcement officers. The sample size was small, of course, but I could spin it as a pilot study and mention it in the Directions for Future Research section. If I buckled down, I could get all the information from the paper forms entered into my spreadsheet before everyone came back from the Farmer's Market.

Skye had left the browser open on my computer. I was about to close it, but my bad angel had other ideas.

CHAPTER TWENTY-NINE

I MAXIMIZED THE BROWSER window and saw two tabs open. Skye and Gloria had traveled to Mahina under different reservations. I clicked over to Gloria's confirmation number and then to her full itinerary. Hey, I was just sitting at my own computer. It wasn't like I was sneaking into someone's room and rummaging through their sock drawer.

According to her itinerary, Gloria had taken a redeye from San Jose to Honolulu and then to Mahina, arriving on the morning of the seventeenth. Sunday. I remembered the date because Monday the eighteenth was when I had started my diversity seminar for Mahina PD.

And Gloria didn't show up at our house until after Skye arrived. When was that? It was the day we had to cancel the second half of the session because half the class was called out to break up a cockfight. Tuesday. Gloria had arrived in Mahina two days before she showed up at our front door.

I closed the browser window and got to work. I was entering data for about an hour before my right eye began to throb. Outside it looked cool and overcast. I slipped my umbrella into my bag and started on the ten-minute walk to Donnie's Drive-Inn. I'd get an early lunch there to make up for the previous day's gastronomic disloyalty at Chang's. I walked out to the main road, turned right at Laukapu High School, and started downhill. When I reached the Drive-Inn, it wasn't even eleven o'clock yet, and hardly anyone was there. Lunch could wait. I went a block and a half farther down the road toward the ocean. Then I turned into the narrow alley and went into the vacant lot, retracing the previous day's steps.

The lot was empty. There was no indication a man had lost his life here unless you counted a few patches of trampled weeds. The second-story window was shut. The dumpsters were empty, their lids propped open. I stood there and looked around the soggy lot for a few moments. Then I turned around and walked back out through the alley.

I found Donnie at the Drive-Inn, wiping down the shiny red picnic tables.

"Hey." He grinned at me. "The family was here for breakfast. I missed you."

"I was working on my book chapter all morning. I didn't know they were coming here, or I would've tagged along. I thought they were just going down to the Farmer's Market."

"Not a lot of customers right now." Donnie looked around. "I can take five minutes."

I sat down at the picnic table. Donnie disappeared and then returned with two Styrofoam cups and a plate of hard chicken katsu strips.

"So everyone else went out to have fun, and you stayed home?" He set the food down and slid onto the bench. "You're a hard worker, Molly."

"I've got nothing on you. Besides, I have to keep publishing. Publish or perish, you know."

"What about the guy you work with, Rodge Cowper?" Donnie dipped a katsu plank into the plastic tub of brown sauce. "From what you and Emma say, he doesn't seem to have much on his plate."

I took a piece of katsu and decided to forego the ketchup-and-Worcestershire dipping sauce. I liked the crispy crust, and thought the sauce just made it soggy.

"I don't want to be like Rodge Cowper, Donnie. Rodge is a master of strategic incompetence. No one will even put him on committees anymore because he'll just tell one of his jokes. And then he gets pulled off whatever committee he was on and sent to sensitivity training."

"So, what is this research that's taking all your time? Can you explain it to a non-expert like me?"

"You want to know what I'm working on? Really?"

"Yes, I do." Donnie rested his handsome chin on his hand.

"Well. All right. If you insist. Have you heard of the ultimatum game?"

"No."

"It's basically a demonstration of how pride and spite override self-interest. There are two players. Say you and I are playing. I get a hundred dollars, and then I have to split the money between the two of us. So I could split it fifty-fifty, or I could keep ninety-nine dollars and give you one. Then you could choose to accept the deal or reject it. If you reject it, though, neither of us gets anything."

"I think you'd split it fifty-fifty."

"Donnie, how do you know?"

"Because I know you."

"Pretend we don't know each other. I'm just some random selfish jerk who wants to keep most of the money. But remember: If I propose a split and you reject it, then neither of us gets anything."

"So you have to propose something fair," Donnie said. "Otherwise, we both lose out."

"Aha. But why? Econ 101 would say as a rational being, you would accept an unfair split because you would still get something, which is more than nothing. But let me ask you. Would you accept an unfair payout? Would you take one dollar if the other person gets ninety-nine dollars? Or would you turn it down, and get nothing?"

"What would I do? I think...hmm. I think I'd reject the deal if I thought it was unfair."

"Exactly. You just described what happens in real life, as it turns out. People will reject an unfair settlement, even if it costs them a little money to do so, because it's more important to punish their greedy partner."

"No, I didn't say I wanted to punish anyone. I just wouldn't take an unfair split."

"Anyway, that's what Betty and I are working on. We're trying to describe the phenomenon a little better. We're looking at how personality affects the way people play the game. And beyond that, we're going to look at whether we can tweak some of the conditions to affect peoples' responses. Maybe we can make certain aspects of their identity salient, or even threaten their self-concept in specific ways."

"So what does this game have to do with management?"

"Oh, that's easy. Classic example. An employee thinks they're being treated unfairly. So they walk out, leave their employer hanging, even if they don't have another job to go to. On the face of it, it's irrational, right? But people do it."

Donnie nodded.

"It's called cutting off your nose to spite your face."

"You're right. I guess you could say that."

"I'd like to think my employees don't feel that way."

"I'm sure they don't. I'll bet you're a great boss."

"I try." He smiled.

"You know Skye and Gloria bought their return tickets this morning."

"They told me."

"Well, I'm glad I finally got to meet your sister. And her husband. Did you ever find out what the story was with her going missing?"

"I think it was just some miscommunication between the two of them about their travel plans. At least they got it straightened out."

He looked around and seemed to be doing a head count of the few customers sitting around the picnic tables.

"Everything okay?" I asked.

He nodded absently.

"Yeah. Fine."

CHAPTER THIRTY

THAT NIGHT AT DINNER, we discussed how Gloria and Skye might best spend their remaining three days in Mahina. Skye wanted to make the drive down to unincorporated Kuewa to tour the LightSpirit Organic Farm and Natural Birthing Center, the one with the algae-coated birthing pool. Gloria hoped to find some locally-made soaps she could sell at Gloria's Spa. Donnie suggested a walking tour of downtown Mahina's historic buildings, which I thought was a sound idea.

At first glance, downtown might not seem like much of a beauty spot. But Mahina's century-old buildings still had a certain faded glamor. Downtown also boasted a number of grassy parks, which used to be neighborhoods until successive tsunamis had washed the buildings away.

Gloria liked the idea of a downtown stroll and began to reminisce about some of her favorite Mahina haunts. Donnie then had the sad duty of reminding her that many of the old businesses she might remember were now defunct. Places like Tatsuya's Moderne Beauty, Etsuko's Fashion Frocks, and Modern Jewelers were gone, the storefronts either vacant or occupied by social-service agencies.

Skye tried to move the conversation into a debate about mixed-use development and high-density urban housing, but he didn't have much success. Davison, who could usually be counted on to contribute his opinions (however uninformed) to any discussion, seemed preoccupied and uncharacteristically quiet.

"Something on your mind?" Donnie asked Davison.

"Huh? Oh yeah." Davison came back from wherever he was daydreaming. He pushed his chair back and stood up.

"Everybody, I got a big announcement." He lifted his glass and looked around the table.

We all lifted our glasses in response, ready to join him in a toast. Maybe he'd found a summer job—I could get on board with celebrating Davison's gainful employment. He could save up for a housing deposit, and then move out and get his own place. Donnie and I would finally have our house back. Maybe this summer wasn't going to be so bad after all.

"I'm a father," Davison declared.

I set my glass down quickly to avoid dropping it.

Gloria broke the stunned silence.

"Baby, that's wonderful. Aw, congratulations."

She stood up and squeezed Davison in a hug, pinning his arms to his sides as if he himself were a giant infant. He reddened a little but looked more pleased than embarrassed.

"Congratulations." Skye offered his hand. Davison fist-bumped him.

Davison and Sherry had a baby now? Of course, they were both adults, and if Davison wanted to be his own half-brother or whatever, it was their business.

Unfortunately, Donnie wouldn't see it that way. When Donnie found out the whole story about his ex-wife and his son—well, Donnie couldn't find out, that was all there was to it.

"Where is she?" I asked Davison. "The mother? Shouldn't you be with her?"

"What did you just say?" Donnie was staring at Davison and looking pithed.

"Her and the baby's staying with her family now. She'll be here soon, but."

"She's coming here?" I exclaimed.

"Boy or girl?" Gloria asked.

"Do you have a name yet?" This was Skye.

"It's a boy. His name is Davison Hiapo Keali`i Junior. That's just the first part. We didn't pick out the rest yet."

"Great news, son." Donnie choked on the words. He obviously didn't approve, but neither did he want to spoil his son's proud moment.

"Bet you wasn't expecting that, ah Dad? Beat you to it." Davison sat down, beaming.

I realized I was the only one at the table who hadn't made congratulatory noises yet.

"Well, I'm speechless. Congratulations to you and the mother. Donnie, are you okay?"

"Just swallowed something the wrong way. Excuse me." Donnie jumped up and rushed over to the kitchen sink to refill his water glass.

Now what? I imagined Sherry showing up at our front door, diaper bag slung over one shoulder, baby over the other, cigarette in her mouth. I grabbed the wine bottle from the middle of the table and filled my glass to the top.

"Eh, Molly," Davison said. "You gotta cut back your drinking if you gonna try come hapai too."

"You and my brother trying for a baby, Molly?" Gloria smiled encouragingly (and, in my opinion, a little condescendingly). "Aw, good for you."

"If we'd known, we would have brought some of our Fertili-Tea blend. I'll send you some when we get back."

"Aw no, she's not gonna like the Fertili-Tea, Skye. It's the one was making the ladies all gassy."

I looked helplessly in the direction of the kitchen sink, but Donnie couldn't hear the conversation over the running water.

"She should try the Super Cleanse capsules at least," Skye said. "I brought a box with me. Molly, let me get you a sample. You'll like it. Very energizing."

"Thanks Skye, you don't have to get it right now. Maybe after dinner—"

"No problem. Before I forget."

Gloria watched her husband disappear into the guest room.

"I already put everything away. He's never gonna find it." She stood and followed him out, leaving me alone at the table with Davison.

"So, how's the baby doing?" I asked, to make conversation.

"He's doing real good. Was born premature, you know. Less than six months along."

"Oh, Davison, I'm so sorry." I set down my wine. "And they sent him home already? Is he going to be okay?"

"No worries, Molly. It's all good. 'Cause the mother took care of herself, that's why. Cut down on her smoking an' everything. Baby boy weighed more than eight pounds when he was born."

"Your son was born three months early, and he weighed eight pounds?"

"Yeah. Her and me hooked up Christmas Eve, that's how come I know the date."

"I see."

"What are we talking about?" Donnie asked as he sat back down. "And where'd Gloria and Skye go?"

"We were discussing the importance of good prenatal care," I said. "Speaking of which, here are Skye and Gloria with my Super Cleanse pills."

Skye handed a small glassine bag to Gloria, who handed it to me. It contained four gelatin capsules filled with a sinister-looking dark green powder. I thanked them both and slid the bag under my plate.

"So Davison." Donnie had composed himself now. "Who is the young lady?"

"You're gonna meet her soon." He grinned. "Molly, you know her."

Donnie shot me a questioning look. I shrugged. I was not going to get in the middle of this.

"Mom and baby can come stay with us, Davison. Whenever you're ready. We have plenty of room."

"But Donnie," I faltered, "where would they stay? Do you think all three of them want to be crammed into the one little guest room?"

"The guest room is perfect for them, Molly. There's already a queen-sized bed, and room for a crib." He smiled indulgently. "We don't want to keep a young mother out in the cold."

"Mahina's not cold," I reminded him.

"Young mother" was similarly off the mark. Sherry and I were born in the same year.

We were still absorbing Davison's announcement when we heard a knock at the front door. Donnie answered.

"Davison," Donnie called back to the dining table. "Someone wants to talk to you."

"Who is it?" Davison didn't get up.

"Police."

"What? I didn't do nothing," Davison grumbled, but he stood up and went outside.

Donnie closed the door gently behind Davison and came back to join us. We sat and watched the door.

"What do you think all this is about?" Gloria asked.

I shrugged as if I had no idea, but in fact, I had a few. This visit could be about my missing jewelry. Or it might concern some other infraction Davison had committed. Or a third possibility: it could be about Davison's biological father turning up dead in a vacant lot.

After a few minutes, Davison came back in, looking dazed.

"Everything okay?" Donnie asked.

"Aunty Gloria." He came back to the table and sank into his chair.

"What is it, baby?"

"He's dead, Aunty. Iulani is dead."

So it was Door Number Three.

Gloria lifted her chin as if to say something noble and consoling.

"I hope he's burning in hell," she announced cheerfully. "Donnie, go open up another bottle of wine."

CHAPTER THIRTY-ONE

ANDY DE SILVA INTERCEPTED me on the way out of Mass the next morning and motioned me over to a quiet spot next to the sanctuary door. I watched my fellow worshipers streaming out into the sunny parking lot, and hoped Officer De Silva wouldn't make me late for my brunch with Emma. Maybe he had a question about the thank-you letter he was supposed to be writing for me.

"You got the next of kin notification yesterday." It was a statement, not a question.

"You weren't there?" I asked.

He shook his head no.

"Someone from Mahina PD came by and talked to my stepson out on the front porch. Then he came back inside and told the rest of us. He seemed pretty shaken up, actually. So the, uh, the deceased really was Iulani Malufau."

De Silva nodded. "Those kinds of notifications are one of the hardest things we do. Was Gloria there?"

"She was." I wondered why De Silva hadn't been there, and whether he had wanted to be.

"How'd she take it? Finding out her ex died?"

"I think she was overwhelmed." Overjoyed was more like it, but I didn't think it would be appropriate to tell him all the details. "People all deal with grief in their own ways, don't they? Oh, by the way, I'm going to meet my friend Emma over at the Pair-O-Dice. You're welcome to join us if you like. Or not, if you're busy."

I wasn't just trying to be friendly, although De Silva seemed nice enough and I'm sure Emma wouldn't have minded a third at our table. I wanted to give him fair warning. If he was planning to spend another Sunday morning canoodling in a dark booth at the Pair-O-Dice with a mysterious female companion, Emma and I were going to be right there gawking at him.

"Thanks for the offer, Professor, but I'm working today. Maybe next time."

"Yes, definitely." I smiled at him and hurried off to my car. This wouldn't have been a good time to bring up the thank-you letter. There was plenty of time to straighten it out later.

Emma was waiting for me at the Pair-O-Dice. I told her about the events of the previous night, and of Gloria's glee at her ex's demise. Then there was Davison's blessed event and his secrecy about the mother's identity. Finally, I told Emma what I'd learned from Uncle Brian about the car crash that had killed Donnie's parents.

"I had been so eager to find out more about Donnie's family," I sighed. "And come to find out, it's just one tragedy after another. Donnie's sister has this rotten ex, who goes and dies. Then I find out Donnie and Gloria's parents died, poor old Uncle Brian took them in, and now they barely acknowledge the man."

"Know what, though, that's just how life is." Emma placed her bare elbows on the sticky table and leaned forward. "People suck. What did you think you were going to find out when you started poking around? You thought your husband was secretly descended from the Romanovs or something?"

"Hardly."

"Secretly descended from Kamehameha the Great, then. And Davison's Johnny Appleseed all of a sudden? Man, that came out of nowhere."

"I know. Here Donnie and I have been trying so hard to start a family, and meanwhile Davison has a healthy eight-pound infant just drop into his lap."

"So what, it's a contest?"

"No, Emma, it's not a contest, it just seems so unfair—"

"Aha. It is a contest. It's like total sibling rivalry between you two."

"No, it's not—"

"Yes, it is. You're all like, 'How come Davison got a baby? How come I can't have a baby? I never get anything, and he always gets whatever he wants.'"

"He does always get whatever he wants."

"So who's the mom? How come he won't tell...? Aw no, not Sherry, is it?"

"I think it is Sherry. Davison says his mystery woman is someone I know. Oh, and she smokes. And the baby isn't even Davison's. I mean, who else could it be?"

"It's not right." Emma shook her head. "The stepmother-stepson thing. Kinda unhealthy if you ask me."

"You think?"

"Does Donnie know about Davison and Sherry?"

"He knows they've reconnected. But he's in complete denial about it involving anything more than filial affection. I think he just doesn't want to believe it."

"So he's gonna be pretty upset when he finds out there's a baby involved."

"No kidding. Oh, Emma, did you order yet?"

"Nah. I just got here about a second before you did."

"Speaking of Donnie, how would you feel about going over to the Drive-Inn? We can walk up. Probably won't take five minutes."

"They serve booze there now?" Emma asked.

"At the Drive-Inn? No. But now we're talking about Donnie. I'd like us to support him. I think business at the Drive-Inn hasn't been great lately. Please don't say anything to him about it, though."

"Oh, 'cause Chang's Pizza Pagoda, that's why."

"Emma, what do you know about Chang's Pizza Pagoda?"

"They been advertising their new menu. They got two-for-one specials, and they're open later than anyone else."

"They have two-for-one specials?"

"Yeah. Big portions, too. I don't know how they're making any money. Okay, we can go to the Drive-Inn."

"You're fine with the Drive-Inn?"

"Yah, sure. Just a second."

Emma went up to the bar and returned with a covered twenty-ounce Styrofoam cup.

"They have coffee at the Drive-Inn, you know."

Emma gave me a look.

"Coffee?"

"Oh. Hey, Emma, can I have a sip?"

CHAPTER THIRTY-TWO

"MAN, MAHINA'S REALLY gone downhill." Emma rapped her knuckles on the glass of a blank window with a sun-faded For Lease sign propped in the corner. "Everything's so junk now."

"I think downtown looks cool."

"Yeah, you and Pat like it for some reason. I don't see it."

"It's because you grew up around here. You take it for granted. You don't find the picturesque decrepitude quite as enchanting as Pat and I do."

"I hadda watch it get all junk, that's why. Back when we still had the sugar plantations, Mahina was a real city. Everyone went to the Mahina College basketball games—"

"Mahina College?"

"Yeah, was Mahina College back then, before it became Mahina State University. We had roller derby, too, and stock car racing, and sumo. Mahina was the place to be, believe it or not. We even got big-name bands on tour stopping by."

"Really? Touring is expensive. How many people lived in Mahina back then?"

"Not much more than now. The bands were probably here for the high-quality pakalolo more than the ticket revenue, to be honest."

As we were about to turn onto the main road going uphill, I nudged Emma. "Here's where they found the body. Right behind this building."

"Aw, no." Emma stopped walking and took stock of the building. "When did this happen? Etsuko's Fashion Frocks went out of business? My mom used to take me there when I was a little girl."

"I can't imagine you wearing a fashion frock." I had rarely seen Emma in anything fancier than jeans and a free T-shirt she'd picked up from one of her conferences. Today she was wearing a green shirt advertising a brand of PCR primer, whatever that was.

"Yeah, well, I was like, eight years old." Emma and I turned up the busy main road. We passed the abandoned bank building and the downtown post office, and then the Drive-Inn was in our sights.

"Whoa." Emma laid a hand on my arm. "This is sad."

"I know."

Objectively, it didn't look like anything was wrong with Donnie's Drive-Inn. The bright noontime sun washed the building white, and the sky glowed blue above the white corrugated metal roof. The empty picnic tables gleamed in the cool shade, clean and inviting. The problem was, at this time of day there shouldn't have been any empty tables.

"Emma, don't say anything to Donnie about how deserted it looks. We should just pretend we don't notice anything's off."

Emma socked my arm. "Gimme some credit, ah? I do have some tact."

We placed our order at the window and took our food and drinks to one of the many available tables. We had just begun to dig in when Donnie joined us.

"Ho, bradda," Emma exclaimed. "Hardly anyone here. What happened? Chang's got all your customers?"

I rested my face in my hands.

"Business is down, a little." Donnie didn't sound particularly offended. I supposed he must be used to Emma by this point.

"So what're you doing to fight back then? You know Chang's Pizza Pagoda got a new menu, and some of the stuffs, not bad, ah? You were telling me, Molly, their chow fun focaccia—"

"I heard they had chow fun focaccia," I interrupted. "Bread with noodles on top. Doesn't it sound revolting?"

"I just started running an ad in The County Courier." Donnie pulled a folded piece of newsprint from his back pocket. "Either of you see today's paper?"

"We don't get The County Courier," Emma said.

"I brought in the paper this morning," I said, "but I haven't had a chance to read through it."

"This is the ad." He unfolded the paper and smoothed it out for us to see. The ad showed Donnie framed in the Drive-Inn's ordering window, smiling stiffly and holding out a tray of Spam musubis to the camera. The picture was underexposed and had been taken with a harsh flash, making him look dark and shiny.

"Whoa, is this you?" Emma exclaimed. I kicked her under the table.

"Who else would it be? It's a great ad, Donnie. It makes the Drive-Inn look really welcoming."

"Our establishment is centrally located near the Mahina Public Library, Laukapu High School, and the Downtown Farmer's Market," Emma read. "Enjoy our daily specials."

"Donnie, is the street address on here anywhere?"

"It's not there? Oh. I didn't notice. Well. Everyone knows where the Drive-Inn is."

"You know Chang's got those buy-one-get-one coupons in The Island Shopper." Emma obviously didn't know when to stop. "And they got a lotta ads on Island Confidential too. You got an ad in Island Confidential? Ow! Molly, what the—"

Island Confidential was Pat Flanagan's newsblog. Pat and I had already been friends by the time I met Donnie, and the two of them had never warmed to each other. When Donnie and I tied the knot, Pat gave me a copy of Charlotte Perkins Gilman's The Yellow Wallpaper as a wedding present.

"I think The County Courier was a great choice." I smiled at Donnie and then glared at Emma.

"Eh, bradda, you married to one business professor, remember? She can find out whatever you gotta know about marketing an' sales an' da kine. You gonna let her save your `okole or what?"

"I do have access to a lot of good information through our library, Donnie. We have industry reports, and marketing journals, all kinds of things. I'm happy to help you find whatever you think might be useful."

"I know you're always willing to help, Molly. Thank you. Oh, Emma, did Molly tell you the big news?"

Emma and I looked at each other. I had told her a lot of big news.

Donnie reached across the table and took my hand tenderly, a rare public show of affection.

"Molly and I have a grandson."

"We what?"

"Oh, yeah, Molly told me all about it. She couldn't stop talking about how happy she is for Davison. Right, Molly?"

"Sure," I stammered, stunned at my sudden promotion to grandma.

"And I appreciate you being so understanding about letting Davison's new family stay with us." Donnie beamed at me.

"Understanding? Yes. That's me. Very understanding."

"They're coming here to stay with you?" Emma made big eyes at me. "The mom, too?"

"Donnie insisted." I shrugged. "Hey, if it's what he wants, it's okay with me."

CHAPTER THIRTY-THREE

I PULLED INTO THE CARPORT, got out of my car, and paused. A repetitive squawk sounded from inside my house. It sounded like an insistent duck. I tiptoed up the steps, unlocked the door to the mudroom, and eased it open.

The sound got louder. It reminded me of squeaky bedsprings, an explanation as unlikely as it was distasteful. Our beds were all memory foam. Was it my computer? A propane tank? A nēnē goose? And how would an endangered bird have gotten trapped inside my house? I'd never actually heard a nēnē. For all I knew, they didn't even quack.

I poked my head out of the mudroom. The kitchen lay straight ahead with the living-dining area to my left. Everything looked as I'd left it that morning, except for one thing. Parked in the middle of the living room was a crib.

Inside the crib, bright-eyed and awake, lay a prosperous-looking baby. He had chubby pink cheeks and a big round head with tiny wisps of black hair. I assumed "he" was the correct pronoun. The baby wore a blue terrycloth onesie, and Mahina wasn't the kind of place where people encouraged their infants to upend gender norms.

The baby made little spastic motions with his tiny fists as he yelled. He wasn't crying, exactly. It was more like he wanted to practice making loud noises. When I approached the crib, he quieted down, looked me in the eye, and said, "Bah."

I looked around, wondering how an unattended baby had managed to move into my house. A gentle buzzing sound alerted me to Davison, asleep on the couch. I grabbed the arm of the couch and shook it.

"Davison. Davison."

He sat up slowly and wiped his hand across his eyes.

"Davison, there's a baby in our living room."

He turned and blinked. "Oh, Molly. That's Junior. Aw, how come you wen' woke him up?"

"He was awake when I came in. He was crying."

Davison lumbered over to the crib, picked up the baby, and plopped back down on the couch with Junior in his lap. He produced a bottle and popped it in the baby's mouth. Immediately the baby's eyes closed, and his cheeks started to pulsate. Chubby little fingers clasped the bottle.

"He is adorable. Poor little thing. Where's the mom?"

"Resting at home. She pumped a bunch a milk so I could bring Junior over to meet everyone. Eh, Junior, this your tutu Molly."

"Where are Gloria and Skye?"

"Went out to buy more diapers an' da kine."

"Does Donnie, does your father know the baby's here?"

"Nah. Didn't wanna bother him at work. He'll meet 'em when he gets home. It'll be a surprise."

"Well, there's nothing your father likes better than surprises."

I spent the rest of the afternoon at my computer, trying to work on my book chapter. Skye and Gloria returned, laden with baby supplies. I did my best to tune out the grownups bickering and the baby squawking and the pervasive odor of baby poop. When I'd taken yoga sessions down at Laughing Lotus, one of the instructors had scolded me for having "monkey mind." It was a fair description. I had been unable to stay focused on the lesson for more than a few minutes at a time. Today, my monkey mind kept leaping back to the scene of the dead man lying in the rain-soaked lot.

I could probably rule out Gloria as the murderer, and not just because she was bustling around and acting all grandmotherly now. Gloria was much too small to pitch the hulking Malufau out of a window. On the other hand, brawn wasn't everything. She might have rigged a trip wire, or something similarly clever. And there was the matter of her having gone missing for two days. Right around Malufau's time of death. On the third hand, if she was guilty, she'd have tried to feign grief at the news of Malufau's death, instead of celebrating.

Even if Gloria were in the clear, three other people in my house had a motive to get rid of Malufau: Gloria's husband, her biological son, and her brother. All of them would have wanted to protect her from Malufau. Any of them could have slipped away and made the short walk downtown to take care of things. The killer could have been back home—or in Donnie's case, back at the Drive-Inn—before anyone noticed he had gone.

Of course, if Malufau was as bad as everyone said, then his circle of enemies would certainly extend beyond my household. Maybe his past had caught up with him in a way that had nothing to do with anyone in my family. The officers who found him in the vacant lot sure didn't seem too torn up.

There was also the possibility Malufau's fall had been an accident, but I didn't believe that for a second.

When Donnie came home, it turned out I was the one who was in for a surprise. I watched him turn into a doting grandfather right before my unbelieving eyes. He insisted on holding Junior, who contentedly nestled into Donnie's arms and rested his fat cheeks on Donnie's shoulder. Donnie didn't even seem to mind when Junior spit a stream of curdled milk down the back of his red polo shirt. Donnie tenderly lifted the baby, dabbed the spit-up from his face with the front of his shirt, and kissed his chubby cheek.

Then he passed the baby to me. I looked around, panicked, but no one else stepped forward. Donnie, Gloria, Skye, and Davison just stood there beaming at me. I told myself to calm down. Humans had been doing this for millennia, and what kind of mother was I going to be if I was afraid to hold a baby? I had to get used to this sooner or later.

The second I took Junior in my arms, he stiffened and started to scream. Gloria quickly snatched him from me and calmed him down. I backed away and sank down onto the couch, temporarily deaf in one ear and feeling like a failure.

CHAPTER THIRTY-FOUR

THE FOLLOWING MORNING I didn't even try to get any work done at home. I walked down to the library, where I spent the rest of the morning at an ancient but serviceable terminal and made acceptable progress on my book chapter. At lunchtime, I packed up and crossed the street to Donnie's Drive-Inn. The air smelled of frying oil, plumeria blossoms, and rain.

A few customers were scattered around the Drive-Inn's gleaming red picnic tables. At this time of day, it should have been at capacity.

I seated myself at an empty table, and within a few minutes, Donnie appeared with a Drive-Inn Jumbo Meat Platter. I gratefully attacked it, starting with the Portuguese sausage.

"What did you think of Junior?" Donnie asked.

"He's the most productive worker I've ever seen." I took a bite of the spicy sausage slice. "Did you notice Gloria was changing his diaper like every twenty minutes? The principle of conservation of mass means nothing to the kid. And he is cute, I have to admit. Those chubby cheeks."

Donnie beamed. "Our grandson. Do you believe it?"

"No." I swallowed the sausage and stuffed a strip of fried chicken into my mouth.

"I hope Davison can bring him by again tonight. I'm really curious to meet the mother. Davison says you know her."

I shrugged. "I heard him say it, but I'm not exactly sure who he's talking about."

Two people at another table finished their lunch and walked away, leaving Donnie and me the only people sitting at the Drive-Inn's picnic tables.

"It doesn't seem like the ad in The County Courier worked very well." Donnie picked up a curly slice of teriyaki beef and examined it. "I don't know what's wrong. I'm not doing anything different."

"It might just be a matter of doing a little more marketing. Chang's Pizza Pagoda is being very aggressive. Lots of advertising, two-for-one specials. Maybe the Drive-Inn could try some of the same things."

"I don't know, Molly. I didn't even like doing The County Courier ad. I've always relied on word of mouth."

"Let me just look into it. I'll see what I can find, maybe put some ideas together, and if you don't like it, you don't have to use any of it."

"Sure." Donnie gave me a pained smile. "Thank you, Molly. Listen, I'd better get back. Did you want to take some food back to the house?"

"Am I allowed to take meat inside, with Skye there?"

"I'll find something vegetarian."

"It's okay," I said. "I checked the fridge before I left. We have plenty of leftovers."

I sensed something hovering behind me at the same time Donnie said, "Hey buddy."

I turned around. Davison stood there, holding the baby like a football in the crook of his arm.

"Thought I'd bring him down to say hi. Here, you can hold him, Dad."

Donnie took the baby and stood up. Immediately three red-shirted Drive-Inn employees, two girls and a boy, surrounded Donnie, cooing and prodding Junior. Fortunately, they didn't have much else to do.

Davison looked around with a puzzled expression.

"Ho Dad, business is junk, ah? Nobody here. Molly, that's how come you was looking up restaurant marketing an' da kine."

"How do you know I was looking up restaurant marketing?"

"You left the search up on your computer."

"I was looking at some marketing ideas for the Drive-Inn." I dropped my hands into my lap. "I'm thinking of outlining a very basic social media plan."

Davison plumped down next to me on the bench.

"'Cause Chang's Pizza Pagoda?"

I scooted away from him to reclaim my radius of personal space.

"Yes. I think Chang's is the main problem. They've expanded their menu, they're spending a ton on advertising, and they have these two-for-one coupons I think are loss leaders." I looked up at him. "They can't be making money. I think they're buying market share. It's going to be like what happened to Aloha Airlines. They're going to keep this up until one of their competitors goes under."

"You tried their new menu items?" Davison noticed a spot of baby droll on his forearm and wiped it off with the hem of his shirt.

"I tried their food one time, in fact. For research purposes."

"Dad doesn't wanna fight dirty." Davison glanced over at his father, who was expertly burping the baby over his shoulder.

"No one should fight dirty. Your father is right." The employees went back to their stations, and Donnie returned to the table.

"Donnie, it looks like Junior was a big hit with the staff."

"That's our boy. Listen, I should get back. Here you go, buddy."

Davison took Junior and hoisted him up so he faced backwards, his little frog legs making climbing motions on Davison's chest. When Donnie had disappeared into the cooking area, Davison said, "Molly, remember that case we did in your class?"

"Yes, Aloha Airlines. It's the one I was just talking about."

"Nah, not that one. The drug company. The pills got cyanide in 'em and some people died? They handled it good, but they hadda spend a bunch of money to send out replacement products an' li' dat."

"Yes," I said cautiously. "The Johnson and Johnson case. No one's putting cyanide in Chang's chow fun focaccia, Davison."

"Nah, nah. Alls I'm saying is, what if Chang's gets one big PR problem? Like, someone finds a big cock-a-roach in the food? And then the picture goes online, an' all their friends—"

"No. That's not how your father does business. It's not how we do business. And—"

A thunderous noise resounded from Junior's diaper. My eyes started to water.

"Oof. Time to change. Let's go, little guy. Your mama's gonna wonder where we been."

When Davison was gone, I sat at the picnic table and watched the few customers come and go. Most did takeout, some sat down to eat, and no one had to wait in line or share a table with strangers. At this rate, I doubted the food purchases were even covering the employees' salaries, let alone the rent, utilities, and the rest of it. And I knew Donnie paid himself last, after everything else was covered.

The trade winds had pushed the clouds inland, revealing a shiny blue sky. I walked back across the street to the library, signed out another computer terminal, and got to work. Donnie didn't want my help, and I couldn't force it on him. But he couldn't stop me from doing my own research.

CHAPTER THIRTY-FIVE

MY SEARCH FOR RESTAURANT marketing ideas turned up a lot of information. It was both enlightening and daunting.

When Donnie built Donnie's Drive-Inn, it had been enough to offer fast, friendly service, giant portions, and popular menu items.

But word-of-mouth, Donnie's marketing tactic of choice, was no longer sufficient. In these days of smartphones and short attention spans, a restaurant had to have an online presence. It had to build a "brand," a distinctive personality. A restaurant's online presence had to entertain and inform. Overt self-promotion turned customers off. Any "selling" was done by positive reviews on restaurant review sites.

I navigated to the top restaurant review site—I don't know why I'd never thought of doing this before—and pulled up Donnie's Drive-Inn. I saw two five-star reviews, and a single one-star review:

Just okay. If you want real plate lunch, try Chang's Pizza Pagoda.

I clicked over to Merrie Musubis next. It had two five-star reviews, one four-star review, and a one-star:

Use to be good. No more. Try Chang's Pizza Pagoda instead.

So Chang's Pizza Pagoda was doing more than just offering some two-for-one specials. Right after I'd scolded Davison for thinking about playing dirty, I found out Chang's was doing exactly that.

I would have liked to believe diners were too smart to be taken in by those obviously fake reviews, but unfortunately, I knew better.

A couple of years ago, our administration decided the results from a popular professor-rating website should be used in tenure and promotion decisions. Linda Wilson from the Student Retention Office had announced the new system to the faculty with great enthusiasm. She went on to explain this method drew on the wisdom of crowds, which she called "crowd-surfing."

Of course, the faculty objected. What about the negative (and poorly spelled) reviews, which predictably popped up whenever you busted a student for cheating? What about the fact that anyone, anywhere in the world, could leave reviews for professors they'd never met? But the administration had made up its mind, and the system went into effect immediately.

Pat Flanagan, Emma Nakamura, and I did the only sensible thing: We started posting positive reviews for one another. You might call it "gaming the system." We called it "self-defense."

I created an account on the restaurant review site and left an honest, positive review for Donnie's Drive Inn. I cited the Drive-Inn's massive portions and reassuring cleanliness. Then I navigated to where Chang's Pizza Pagoda was listed. I perused the dozen or so positive reviews (most of which were short variations on "try Chang's") but I didn't add one of my own. I was tempted, but as I had told Davison, "We don't do business like that."

I did an online search for a model social media marketing plan and found one that seemed doable. Just as I was mailing it to myself, I felt a tap on my shoulder. It was the librarian. She was one of those lucky people who can wear a cardigan when it's eighty-seven degrees and seventy percent humidity.

"We close at five," she said. "I hope you found what you needed."

"It was very informative." I stood and gathered my things. "Thank you."

Rather than heading straight home, I walked back across to Donnie's Drive-Inn. I'd get a soft drink, sit down, and enjoy the occasional puff of ocean breeze from the Bayfront. I might even have a chance to see Donnie again if he wasn't too busy. Which he probably wouldn't be.

"Good evening, Missus." The young woman in the red polo shirt smiled as she handed me my 32-ounce diet root beer. "He's out back."

I went around to find Donnie loading several large, covered foil trays into the back of his SUV.

"Are you leaving work already?" I asked.

"Yeah, it's been pretty slow today."

"I don't think we need that much food for dinner."

"It's left over anyway. We miscalculated and made too much. I don't want to trash it. The employees are taking home the meat dishes."

"We'll have a nice big dinner then." I smiled. "Can I help?"

"No, this is the last one." He slid in the tray and pulled down the hatch. "Did you walk down? Or do you have your car?"

"I walked."

Donnie opened the passenger door for me, and then climbed into the driver's seat.

"When do you think we'll meet the mother?" Donnie pulled out onto the main road.

"The baby's mother? Oh, we shouldn't rush them. She'll meet us when she's ready. We don't need to insert ourselves into Davison's private affairs."

"She must be really haole, the mother," Donnie said.

I'd always thought haole was a slur, but Emma told me haole just means a person of European extraction. Unless it's prefaced by an obscene gerund. Then it's an insult.

"Why do you think the mother is 'really haole'?" I asked.

"Junior's pretty fair-skinned. He didn't get that from Davison."

"Probably not. Oh, I ran across something interesting online today. It was about restaurant marketing and how online reviews and social media are so important nowadays. Have you checked the Drive-Inn's online reviews?"

"No. If you have a quality product, you shouldn't need all the hype."

"It might be something to try. I mean, it couldn't hurt. And I'd be happy to help. I know you're busy at the Drive-Inn, but I can set up a plan, get you a website, set up some social media accounts, maybe spend a little on advertising—"

"It's nice for you to want to help, Molly. But it's not necessary. And it sounds like it'll take a lot of time. Don't you need to work on your research?" Donnie pulled into the carport, next to my Thunderbird.

"I'll help you carry the trays in," I said. "Let me do that, at least."

CHAPTER THIRTY-SIX

DONNIE AND I CAME HOME to a haphazard dining table. Sloppily-folded paper towels served as napkins. The drinking vessels were a motley assortment. Forks had been placed to the right of the plates.

"Who set the table?" Donnie asked.

Davison emerged from the side hallway "I set the table, Dad. Looks good, yeah?"

"Thanks, Son. Nice job."

I stared at Donnie.

"Nice job, Donnie? Really?"

"What?"

"Davison, why are there six places? There are only five of us. Is the baby joining us for dinner?"

Davison held his finger up, as if to say, "Just a minute," and disappeared into the guest room.

"Donnie, whenever I set the table, all you say is, 'thank you for trying to help,' as you rearrange all my place settings. But this you call a 'nice job?'"

"I'm just doing what you told me, Molly. Remember? Positive reinforcement. Praise him when he helps out around the house."

Donnie placed the food trays on the kitchen counter. I'd probably eat a little bit of everything except for the mac salad. (The idea of macaroni salad and rice cohabiting on the same plate still struck me as contrary to the laws of nature.)

"Some positive reinforcement is helpful." I peeled the foil back from one of them. "But it seems unfair to give Davison a pass on the table-setting when I..."

The aroma of fried rice enveloped me. I had skipped lunch, but that wasn't the only reason it smelled so enticing.

"Donnie, are you sure this fried rice is vegetarian?"

"This should all be vegetarian."

"Well, I think there's char siu pork in this. Isn't that what those little red pieces are?"

Donnie came over to examine the fried rice and sighed.

"I picked up the wrong tray."

"Hey, I'll eat it."

"All right, we won't set it out tonight. I think we have enough for dinner without it."

"Let's cover it and hide it in the fridge. I'll have some for breakfast."

I re-sealed the foil around the fried rice tray and slid it into the bottom drawer of the refrigerator.

"Everyone ready to eat?" Donnie called out.

I got to work, ferrying plates from the kitchen to the dining table. Gloria came out from the guest room, with Skye right behind her.

"Where's Davison?" Gloria asked.

"He said he'd be right out," Donnie said. "Please. Everyone sit down."

As soon as we were all seated, we heard rustling and baby squawks coming from the hallway. Then Davison's voice: "Shh-shh. Okay, now."

Davison walked out, carrying a squirmy Junior.

"Okay babe," Davison announced as Junior tried to grab his nose. "Everybody, I want you to meet my fiancée."

I felt my appetite shut right off. This was going to be ugly. What had I been thinking, imagining I could keep the news about Davison and Sherry from Donnie? I should have told Donnie everything—all of my suspicions—as soon as I had the chance. Now Donnie was going to wonder what else I was keeping from him, and whether he could trust me at all.

I held my breath, wishing I could slide under the table.

And out she came.

She was shorter than I remembered her, and she looked tired without her makeup, but I recognized her right away.

"Tiffany." I leaped up so fast I almost knocked over my chair.

"Eh, where's your ring, Tiff?" Davison asked.

Davison was engaged to Tiffany Balusteros. Not Sherry Di Napoli. Cue the angel chorus.

"Fingers too fat right now." Tiffany held up a bare, slender hand. Gold charm-studded magenta fingernails glowed against her brown skin. "Can't get it on past my knuckle. Gotta pee out all the water weight first."

Tiffany had not been among my star students. She had been absent so often I'd barely managed to learn her name before the end of the semester. She had shown up for the exams (or at least someone who looked like Tiffany did) and in the end, had done well enough on those to squeak through Intro to Business Management with the lowest possible passing grade.

Recognition dawned on Tiffany's pretty face as she focused on me.

"Ho, I thought you was joking, baby. Barda's your stepmom f'real?"

"Congratulations, Tiffany." I beamed at her. "It's really nice to see you."

CHAPTER THIRTY-SEVEN

I WOKE UP EARLY THE next morning with my head pounding. I was never good at sleeping through noise, and we now had four adult houseguests and one outspoken baby staying with us.

I eased myself out of bed and went into the bathroom for some ibuprofen and a glass of water. The house was quiet now. I supposed everyone was resting up. It must have taken a lot of effort to stay up all night slamming doors, flushing the toilet every ten minutes, and knocking pot lids onto the kitchen floor.

I pulled on a pair of pajama pants and an old Alice Mongoose t-shirt, and shambled zombie-like into the kitchen. Donnie had left the coffee machine on for me. I found my favorite mug, a sixteen-ouncer with a wraparound illustration of Chicken Boy. I brewed a serving, futilely shush-ing the machine as it hummed. Then I eased the fridge open to get the cream and stirred cautiously to avoid clanking the spoon against the mug. I was trying not to wake anyone, which I thought was very considerate of me.

I padded over to my workstation, sat down, and jiggled the mouse to wake up my computer. Then I lifted the mug to my face, inhaled, and prepared to take a sip. My serene moment was shattered by what sounded like a herd of cattle clattering up the steps to the front door.

Bong! The doorbell sounded. I froze. Good. The doorbell didn't wake the baby. What did wake the baby was the raucous hammering on the door right afterward.

I hurried over to look through the peephole as Junior's wails filled the house. I saw Andy De Silva, in uniform, and Detective Ka`imi Medeiros, in plainclothes, which this morning was a bright turquoise floral aloha shirt in size 4XL. Medeiros's expression was a grim counterpoint to his festive attire.

I invited the two officers in. Detective Medeiros looked around to discern the source of the crying. De Silva sniffed the air and winced.

"We have a new baby. Not mine," I added quickly. "He belongs to my stepson, Davison, and Davison's fiancée, Tiffany Balusteros."

"Balusteros?" Medeiros asked. "The Balusteros World of Furniture family?"

"Yes. I believe so." As a student, Tiffany had displayed all of the initiative and drive one might expect from someone who already had a guaranteed job in the family business.

"Donnie's Drive-Inn and Balusteros World of Furniture?" De Silva grinned. "It's like on da kine, the show. Two powerful dynasties coming together."

"I never thought of it like that. Is there something I can help you with?"

"We'd like to talk to your sister-in-law," Medeiros said. "Gloria Kealoha. Is she here?"

I excused myself into the side hallway and tapped on the door of the second guest room.

There was no answer. I knocked again, and finally I heard Gloria's voice. "We're sleeping."

"Someone's here to see Gloria," I said.

"Okay, okay. Hold your horses." Skye mumbled something, and I heard Gloria say, "Nah, Baby, you stay here."

Medeiros and De Silva were standing in the living room exactly where I'd left them, when I came back.

"Gloria will be right out. Please have a seat." I indicated the couch, the only piece of furniture I was confident would accommodate Detective Medeiros safely. The men seated themselves, De Silva occupying one cushion, Medeiros taking up the other two.

The baby's crying finally petered out, and blessed quiet settled over the house.

"Please let me get you some coffee while you're waiting," I said.

De Silva looked at Medeiros as if for approval.

"Thanks, Professor," Medeiros said. "Black, please."

"I'll have the same," De Silva said.

As the three of us waited for Gloria, Junior started wailing again, and then settled down to satisfied glup-glup noises. A moment later, I heard Tiffany shriek. Then Davison mumbled something I couldn't hear.

"Little baga wen' bite my nipple off, is what." Tiffany's voice rang though the house.

I reflexively hugged myself and smiled weakly at the two officers. They were both examining their coffee cups with intense interest.

I made a mental note to ask Donnie about putting a soundproof door on the entrance to the hallway.

Gloria eventually appeared. Her face was freshly powdered, and her straight black hair was brushed to a high shine.

"Good morning, Officers." Her smile faltered briefly when she caught sight of Andy De Silva. Medeiros braced his beefy hands on his knees and rose to a standing position. De Silva stood up and looked at the floor, shifting from one foot to the other. From the way Andy De Silva had asked after Gloria, I'd assumed the two were good friends. But now he looked uncomfortable, and Gloria seemed to be ignoring him. I didn't want to stand and gawk, so I quietly retreated into the short hallway leading to the master bedroom.

"Ma'am, we just have a few questions for you," I heard Medeiros say before I closed the bedroom door behind me.

Now I was stuck in my bedroom without my computer. I pulled out my little guitar, sat on the edge of the bed, and tuned it. Then I tried playing "Judy Butler Did It," one of Phallus in Wonderland's original compositions. I had some trouble with the F chord, but then I've always had trouble with the stupid F chord. I switched to "Song of the Subaltern," which was much easier to play, as it only required the D-minor and A chords. When my finger pads had had enough, I put the guitar away and tried to take a nap. The house started shaking just as I was drifting off to sleep. Detective Medeiros and Officer De Silva were descending the front steps. Through the sliding glass door that faced the street, I watched the men climb into the police cruiser and drive away.

Gloria and Skye were sitting on the couch when I came back out. Skye was glowering; Gloria's features were tense.

"Everything okay?" I asked.

Skye opened his mouth to say something, when Davison popped out into the living room.

"Where you guys put the new diapers?"

"In the pantry." Gloria stood up. "I'll show you."

People were putting diapers in my pantry now?

"They told us we had to cancel our flight back home," Skye said to me.

"Are you going to do it?"

Gloria returned to join us. "No, we are not going to cancel anything. Skye, this is just harassment."

"What's harassment?" Davison called from inside the pantry.

"Nothing, baby." Gloria squeezed Skye's hand. "Don't you worry about it."

"Is there anything I can do to help?" I couldn't imagine how I could actually be of any use at the moment, but it seemed like the right thing to say.

CHAPTER THIRTY-EIGHT

WHILE EVERYONE ELSE was busy with Junior, I grabbed my bag and slipped out through the kitchen to the carport. It was sunny but not yet unbearably hot, the quiet street fragrant with mowed grass and gardenia blossoms.

The Drive-Inn was emptier than I'd ever seen it. Only one service window was open, doing double duty as both ordering and pickup. Donnie must have seen me approach. He came out from the back with two Styrofoam cups of coffee.

"Taking a break?" he asked.

"I missed you so much, I couldn't stay away. Do you have a few minutes to sit?"

Donnie smiled. "I guess it's hard to get your work done with so many people in the house."

"I'll tell you what really makes it hard to concentrate." I set my bag down on the nearest table and swung my leg over the bench. Donnie sat down opposite. "When the police stop by."

"The police?"

I told him about the morning's events.

"Why did they want to talk to Gloria?"

"I don't know. I didn't hang around and eavesdrop. But from what I heard, they told Gloria and Skye to cancel their flight and stick around for a while."

"After they went to all the trouble to arrange their flights back. It's unfortunate."

"Oh, don't worry. Gloria is not planning to comply."

Donnie sighed. "Gloria's a good kid. But she's so—stubborn. She gets it into her head she's right about something, and she just charges ahead. She doesn't compromise."

I nodded. "She's no pushover."

"She needs to learn to go with the flow a little more." Donnie placed his hand on mine. "Like you, Molly. I mean, you can be opinionated and stubborn too, just like Gloria, but when it comes to important things, like when you were negotiating for tenure, you're...how do I put it?

"Refreshingly unprincipled?" I suggested.

"You know what I mean. I know you've given the police a hard time, but you'd never do it just to prove a point. I'm worried Gloria might be making things harder for herself. It wouldn't be the first time. What did they want to talk to her about?"

"I don't know. I assume it was about her deceased ex. I kind of wish I'd eavesdropped now."

"I think you're right. When you go around announcing that you want to kill someone, and then he ends up dead, you have to expect the police are going to want to talk to you."

"Gloria said she wanted to kill Malufau?"

"Many times. Gloria doesn't exactly keep her opinions to herself."

He glanced around, checking to see if any customers required attention. None did.

"This has been a real learning experience for me, Donnie. Having your sister and her husband staying with us. I feel like I'm finding out a lot about your family."

Donnie squeezed my hand. "I didn't realize it was important to you. If you want to know something about me or my family, all you have to do is ask. Don't look like that, Molly. What have I ever kept from you?"

"What have you ever—Donnie, I didn't even know your middle name until we did our marriage license paperwork. And you still won't tell me what kind of name 'Muraco' is."

"Donnie Muraco was someone my father admired." Donnie took his hand back and ran it through his neat salt-and-pepper hair.

"Was this Donnie Muraco, what, a teacher?"

"No."

"A great-uncle or something?"

"He was a professional wrestler. My father didn't know him personally."

"Oh. Okay. Well there's nothing wrong with that."

Donnie laughed a little. "If you really thought there was nothing wrong with it, then you wouldn't have to say it."

"You know something, Donnie? I don't think I told you this. I saw him."

"Saw who?"

"I saw Malufau. When he was alive. He's the guy I told you about. Who I thought was following us."

"Are you telling me Iulani Malufau was following you? And you never thought to mention it? Molly, I can't believe you were just accusing me of being secretive. Why didn't you tell me any of this before?"

"I wasn't sure, and I didn't want you to worry unnecessarily. Anyway, in retrospect, he must have been following Davison, not me. I'm not defending him or anything, but think about it. If you were in his situation, what would you do? You get shipped off to prison, and the last time you've seen your son, I mean your biological son, is when he's a toddler. Obviously, Davison's your son, you're the one who raised him, but that wouldn't stop Malufau from wanting to see him."

"If I were Malufau?" Donnie looked thoughtful. "Maybe I'd want to get revenge on whoever I thought was responsible for putting me in prison."

"Oh. I guess that makes sense, too."

Donnie rested his forehead in his hands.

"I don't know what to think about all of this, Molly."

"Well, as long as I'm throwing all this stuff at you, let me give you one more thing to think about."

"What?"

"Gloria left her flight itinerary open on my computer. I saw it."

"And?"

"And you know how she showed up at our house last Tuesday? The nineteenth? Right after her husband came to us frantically looking for her? Well, according to her itinerary, she arrived in Mahina on the seventeenth. Two days earlier."

Donnie looked stricken. "Do the police know this?"

"I have no idea what the police know. I didn't say anything to them, and I don't know if they've already figured it out. Do you have any idea what Gloria was doing between the time she arrived in Mahina and the time she showed up at our door?"

"What are you saying, Molly? Do you think she flew into Mahina, killed her ex, and then showed up at our house like nothing happened?"

"No, that's not what I'm saying. I don't even see how it would be possible. I mean, Malufau, he was a big guy, and he looked really fit. I mean, not that I was checking out his physique or anything...let me start over. What I'm saying is Gloria couldn't have pushed a big guy like him out of a second-story window, at least not without some help. I don't know what's going on here. I just wanted to tell you what I know. Donnie, do you think Gloria killed Iulani Malufau?"

"What?"

"Do you think Gloria did it? Why else would the police have told her not to leave town?"

Donnie shook his head. "Molly, I don't know what you expect me to do about any of this."

"I don't expect you to do anything. I'm just—should I not have said anything?"

"No, of course not. It's not what I'm saying. It's just—Gloria's worked really hard to build a life for herself. She's had some setbacks. I don't want her to lose everything because of some bad choices she made when she was young."

"No, of course not."

"How did Malufau find Davison in the first place?" Donnie asked. "How could he know Davison would be back in Mahina, and not at his college?"

"Probably social media. You know how people post things like, 'Here's a picture of me about to eat my Donnie's Drive-Inn Sumo Saimin Bowl.' 'Here we are at Galimba's Bargain Boyz buying a trampoline.' People broadcast everything they do. There's no challenge to being a stalker anymore. Hey, speaking of which, did you take a look at the social media plan I sketched out for the Drive-Inn?"

"No." Donnie ran his fingers through his hair again. "Not yet. Sorry. I've been busy."

Busy was exactly what the Drive-Inn wasn't. But Donnie had his own way of doing things, and badgering him wasn't going to get me anywhere. His sister Gloria wasn't the only one who was stubborn.

CHAPTER THIRTY-NINE

DONNIE DIDN'T BRING home any big foil trays from the Drive-Inn that evening. Instead, to my delight, he stopped by Mizuno Mart and bought ingredients to make vegetarian pasta from scratch. As he worked his magic in the kitchen, I sat at my computer and sorted through my email.

Andy De Silva had sent back another iteration of his thank-you letter to my administration. Rather than simply sign his name to my template, De Silva had crafted an entire second draft in his own voice.

"Why does De Silva think it's a good idea to tell my administration I'm not like a 'real' professor? It's exactly what I'm constantly fighting against. Even my students think a 'real' professor means you have to be an old silverback like Hanson Harrison. This is not helping."

"De Silva probably meant it as a compliment," Donnie called out over the sizzle of garlic in olive oil. "He's saying you're down to earth and approachable."

"It would've been a lot more helpful if he'd said I was competent and effective. At least he took out the part about me being 'cute.'"

"Does it matter? You have tenure now. Who do you need to impress?"

I stood up and went to the kitchen counter.

"Yes, I am a tenured associate professor now. But I have one more promotion to go. If I can keep my students happy and get some good pubs other people cite, I might get promoted to a full professorship."

"Do you have to get promoted again? What about—"

"Please don't say Rodge Cowper. Rodge is, in Emma's words, a complete waste of carbon. I do not want to be like Rodge Cowper. Also, I'll get a raise when I'm promoted to full."

"How much of a raise?"

"I think it's six percent."

"Just a minute." He turned the pan down to simmer, disappeared into the bedroom and returned with his calculator.

"How many summers until your next promotion?"

"Between five and seven. Donnie, what are you doing?"

Donnie pulled out the bar stool next to mine and sat down.

"Let's say six summers, and then if you get your promotion, how many years until retirement?"

"Donnie, what is your point?"

"Let's say twenty-five. Assume your promotion to full professor gets you an extra six percent for each of the twenty-five years until you retire. Present value...assume inflation...have you worked this out already?"

"Worked what out? What are you doing?"

He pushed some buttons and raised his eyebrows at the result.

"If you're working full time over your unpaid summers hoping for a six percent pay bump six years from now, your hourly salary works out to a little less than what I pay my lowest-paid employee. If you get the promotion. If you put all this work in and don't get the promotion, then of course, your summer pay is zero."

"It can't be. Are you saying I could work every summer as a fry cook and end up with as much money in the end as if I get the raise and promotion six years from now?"

"Not every summer. Just the next six summers, and then you're done. Actually as a fry cook, you'd make more. At least at the Drive-Inn."

"Are you sure?"

Donnie handed the calculator to me. I waved him off.

"Okay. I believe you. If I were the kind of person who sat down and figured out these cost-benefit things in advance, I probably wouldn't have gotten myself a Ph.D. in literature and creative writing in the first place."

Donnie poised his fingers over the keys.

"And no, please don't calculate what that cost me."

That evening we dined on penne with roasted mushrooms, zucchini, and eggplant. I was thrilled to be eating Donnie's cooking again instead of Drive-Inn food. In fact, everyone seemed to be in a decent mood. Skye and Gloria were much less grumpy than they'd been right after the police left. Davison and Tiffany didn't seem to realize anything out of the ordinary had happened at all.

"This has been an amazing trip." Skye speared a chewy forkful of pasta. "I almost wish we didn't have to go back so soon. Mahina is such a beautiful, special place."

Go back so soon? So Skye and Gloria were sticking with their original travel plans. Maybe they'd worked out something with the police, and everything was going to be fine. I did so want to believe it.

"Well it was nice to have both of you to visit." I beamed at my houseguests. "And Donnie, this pasta is amazingly good." It was. The vegetables were tender, the marinara sauce piquant.

"Glad it's acceptable." He gave me a little smile.

"Aw, I'm gonna miss Junior," Gloria said. "Tiffany, what's with your shirt?"

Tiffany wore an oversized black t-shirt with a green marijuana leaf printed on the front. Junior's chubby legs stuck out from under the shirt, kicking with delight.

"Not mines. It's Davison's. I hadda find something big to cover the baby when he ate."

I remembered seeing the shirt in Davison's drawer when I'd searched his room for my missing necklace and earrings.

"Eh, no big deal, Aunty." Davison's mouth was full of pasta. "Gonna be totally legal here soon, guarantee."

"I think you're right, Davison," Skye said. "And Hawai'i has a great reputation for high quality product. If your tourism people are smart, they'll jump on it."

A knock on the front door made us all turn and look. Donnie got up to answer it, and Ka'imi Medeiros walked in without waiting for an invitation. Right behind Medeiros was a uniformed officer I didn't recognize.

We all laid our silverware down and stood up. All except Tiffany, who was feeding Junior. She glowered at the two officers.

"Gloria Kealoha," Medeiros said. "AKA Gloria Farrah Bysentenyl Gonsalves. You are under arrest for the murder of Iulani Malufau. You have the right—"

"I know my rights." Gloria stood up and pushed her chair back in rather harder than necessary. She strode out between the two policemen, radiating hostility. Skye and Donnie followed them. I ran to the front window and watched the police cruiser take off slowly down the street. Donnie's SUV pulled out and followed it.

Davison, Tiffany, and Junior disappeared into their room, leaving me to clear the dishes by myself.

I was asleep when Donnie returned from the police station. In the light slanting from the bathroom, I watched him peel off his Donnie's Drive Inn polo shirt and fold it.

"Donnie, what happened?"

"Molly. You're awake. Fortunately we made bail."

"Was it a lot? Did we pay for it?"

"Yes, it was a lot. No, we didn't pay it. Skye's parents did. They're getting an attorney for Gloria. Skye and Gloria had to cancel their flight out of Mahina, of course. They'll be staying here for a few more days."

He disappeared into the walk-in closet and switched on the light.

"So where is everyone? Did Gloria come back with you?"

"We all got back just now," Donnie said from inside the closet. "Sorry, I didn't mean to wake you."

"No, no, it's okay. I want to know what's happening. Donnie, wait, I don't understand. Medeiros said Gloria was under arrest for the murder of Iulani Malufau. How on earth do they think she did it?"

"Malufau's blood alcohol was high. I don't remember the exact number, but they said at that level you can barely walk. So it wouldn't take a lot of strength for someone to throw him off balance."

"They think Gloria got him drunk and pushed him out the window?"

"It seems to be their theory. More or less."

"Donnie, wait. They think she went to see this guy in his room, alone? I can't imagine going to confront someone like him by myself." Of course, Skye had said Gloria was fearless.

"There was something else too. The bottom of the window in Malufau's room was low, close to the floor. Even more evidence for their theory someone Gloria's size could have pushed him out."

"Donnie, do you think she did it?"

Donnie came to the closet door and stood silhouetted against the light. "Doesn't matter what I think."

"When did this all happen? Do they know?"

"They calculated the time of death as the morning of the nineteenth." Donnie came over and sat down on the bed. "Ka`imi says you're the one who first ID'd Malufau. How did you figure it out?"

"When Skye told me Malufau had escaped, I remembered the guy who was following us, and I put two and two together. It was a lucky guess. So where was Gloria before she showed up here at the house?"

"I don't know." Donnie shook his head. "It's something she'll have to discuss with her lawyer. She didn't tell me anything."

CHAPTER FORTY

THE NEXT MORNING FOUND me at my computer, revising the social-media marketing plan for Donnie's Drive-Inn.

My first draft had been too detailed. It probably looked like a daunting amount of work to my overworked husband. Maybe I could simplify it a little, spell out the details of the campaign week by week, so that Donnie could follow it with little effort.

A small part of my brain, the sensible part, told me I was wasting my time. Donnie didn't want me to rescue him. Still, I felt like I had to do something, and as Emma had pointed out, what was the point of his being married to a business professor if he wasn't going to take advantage of my expertise?

"Molly?"

There were no other chairs around my workstation, so Skye perched in a rather familiar fashion on the edge of my desk.

"Oh, Skye. Good morning. Donnie told me everyone got back safe and sound last night. How are you holding up?"

"We had the dubious pleasure of experiencing the coercive power of the state apparatus. At least we managed to find a good lawyer."

"Good. About the lawyer, I mean. Who is it?"

Skye frowned, trying to remember. "Some guy named Feinman. Have you heard of him?"

"Alika Feinman?"

"That sounds right."

"Sure. He's a local celebrity. My friend Emma Nakamura in the biology department says when she finally snaps and strangles her incompetent dean, Feinman is going to be the first person she—uh, it sounds like you've made a great choice."

"Well, we have one little problem. Feinman's in Costa Rica right now. Is it okay if he calls Gloria here?"

"We don't have a land line. We just use our cell phones in the house."

"I know. Gloria gave him your number. He's going to call in about five minutes. Okay?"

"Alika Feinman is calling here?" I got up and retrieved my phone from my purse which hung by the door.

"Sorry, Molly. Things have been so crazy. Thanks. We appreciate it."

"No, no, I'm happy to help. Of course I am. You should know that the reception's not great in this neighborhood. You might need to go outside if you want privacy. The reception in the room you're in is almost nonexistent."

I unlocked my phone and handed it to Skye. He took it back into the guest room, apparently not believing what I'd told him about the reception in that part of the house. Within a minute, Gloria was back out in the living room.

I tried to work on the Drive-Inn's social media plan, while behind me, Gloria conducted a stage-whispered conversation I could hear perfectly well.

"We are cooperating," she hissed. "We already postponed our flight, didn't we? How come they're so sure it wasn't an accident anyway? Oh yeah? Who was the little snitch who told 'em I said that? What? Well they're all lying, is all I know. No I did not. Yeah, and it's none of their business."

Gloria's side of the conversation went on in the same vein for a good half hour. Had I been the one racking up Alika Feinman's fees, I'd have done a lot more listening than talking.

"Molly. Here's your phone."

Gloria dropped it on my desk and walked away. A thank you might have been nice.

While I just didn't think it was fair for her to take it out on me, I could understand her being upset. The police could have written off Iulani Malufau's death off as an accident. Why had they settled on Gloria as the murderer—just because someone overheard her making ill-considered comments about her ex? Who hasn't done that? And you'd think having a friend like Andy De Silva in the department would have helped her.

I should get Pat Flanagan's take on this. Pat was always interested in a good news story, although he probably couldn't publish this one in Island Confidential. I picked up my phone and went out onto the front lanai. Pat's number went straight to voicemail.

I stepped into the middle of the road, where the reception was strongest. I dialed again and got transferred to voicemail again. I decided to leave a message.

"Pat, listen carefully, because I'm going to drop some bombshells on your voicemail right now."

I checked up and down the quiet street for cars. There were none.

"Okay, here we go. A man named Iulani Malufau escaped from prison, turned up in Mahina, fell out of a window, and died. Who is he and why do you care? He's Donnie's sister's ex, and he's also Davison's biological father. Now Donnie's sister Gloria has been arrested for Malufau's murder. Gloria's husband is Skye Chaney, family is loaded, so they posted bail and hired Alika Feinman to defend her. Yes, the Alika Feinman. Now here's the thing. They think Malufau died Tuesday, May nineteenth. Gloria appears to have arrived in Mahina on the seventeenth, but she didn't show up at our house until the evening of the nineteenth, which is the same day Malufau died. It doesn't look good for Gloria. Could you poke around and see what you can find out? Maybe the date on her itinerary is wrong, or somehow she has an alibi for the nineteenth, or something. Anything you can find out. Just in case."

I heard a click, and then a woman's mechanical voice. "The message length has been exceeded."

A golf cart puttered up the road, and I stepped out of the way. The three teenage boys inside the cart waved as they went past. They were taking their skateboards to the cul-de-sac at the top of the tree-shaded street.

This would be a nice neighborhood to grow up in.

I put my phone away, smiled, waved back at the boys, and went into the house.

CHAPTER FORTY-ONE

DINNER WAS TENSE. JUNIOR fussed incessantly as his relatives passed him around the table, trying to find the magic key to appeasing him. He didn't calm down until Donnie took him. He kissed the baby's fluffy round head and then held him, stroking his back. Junior dozed off immediately and spent the rest of dinner drooling contentedly on Donnie's shoulder.

Through all this, Gloria made sure to appear very put-upon. Every so often, she would contribute a deep, heartfelt sigh or a despairing shake of the head to the conversation.

Skye enabled her, acting grave and solicitous.

I had to remind myself I wasn't the one on the hook for murder. Had I been in Gloria's place, I'd have been cranky too. I reminded myself of Emma's advice: You always gotta suck up to the in-laws.

I hoped Pat could use his reporter skills to find something out about Gloria's situation, preferably something exculpatory. Then Gloria and Skye could go home, and everyone could get on with their lives. Any such information would have to be handled with care, though. Gloria seemed like the type to resent people intervening on her behalf.

After dinner, Davison and Tiffany took Junior back from Donnie. Gloria went to lie down on her fainting couch while Skye fanned her with a palm frond and fed her peeled grapes. (Actually, I only saw them disappear into their room; I'm assuming the rest.)

Donnie and I cleaned up the kitchen and went to bed.

By the time I got out of the shower, Donnie was dead asleep. It was a warm night, so I turned the ceiling fan to the highest setting and pushed the comforter down to the bottom of the bed. I glanced over at Donnie to see if my jostling had accidentally woken him up, but no, it had not. I pulled the sheet over me and watched the ceiling fan spin in the dark. Donnie snored serenely beside me, and Junior's wails reverberated throughout the house. At one point, someone stomped out into the kitchen to rummage noisily in the refrigerator. I heard something clatter onto the kitchen floor.

Apparently, the best way to prevent the arrival of a new baby was to have another baby already in your house. It must be some kind of Darwinian adaptation, like the way baby sand tiger sharks gobble up their siblings while still in the womb.

The next morning, Donnie drove us to Mahina Hospital. Doctor Ishimaru had called to tell me he'd signed us up for birthing classes, just in case our plans came to fruition sooner than expected.

"You'd normally wait till you're pregnant," he'd explained, "but at your age, you never know what's going to happen. And there's an open spot in the class. Might as well get the lay of the land now."

We weren't even out of the car, and I already felt like an impostor. To make things worse, Donnie was missing work for this.

"Are you feeling okay?" Donnie glanced at me and then turned his attention back to the road.

It was right after the morning rush, so traffic was pleasantly sparse. I'd been surprised at first to find that Mahina had a rush hour. Or a rush half-hour to be precise—short, nasty and brutish. It was usually over by eight-fifteen.

"Sure." I sighed. "I guess Doctor Headmirror's program is better than the hot tub with the dead gecko floating in it."

"What?"

"Oh. Emma told me about this birthing place she knew about down in Kuewa. The same place your sister's husband wanted to tour. Sky Light or something?"

"Are you thinking of LightSpirit? There's a LightSpirit Organic Farm and Natural Birthing Center."

"Right. That's the one."

We took the elevator to the third floor as we'd been instructed and stepped out into an abandoned-looking hallway. The air conditioning was on overdrive. It was freezing.

"Are we in the right place?" Donnie asked. Why was he asking me? Was I suddenly the expert?

"I don't know. I see an open door down there. Let's check it out."

I walked into a conference room with about a dozen metal folding chairs lined up on one wall. A few teenagers hung around, including some young and very pregnant girls. A counseling class for troubled adolescents, I assumed. I went up to a woman who looked like she was in charge, a sun-weathered blonde in a floppy orange-and-yellow rayon batik dress. She was fiddling with a boom box, trying different kinds of serene mood music.

"Excuse me. I'm sorry to bother you, but we're here for the birthing class. Can you tell me where it is?"

"The birthing class? Are you here with your daughter?"

"My daughter? I don't have a daughter. I'm here with my husband."

"Oh. Well, welcome. We'll get started in just a minute. I'm your instructor."

I walked out to the hallway, where Donnie was waiting.

"We're in the right place. If there's an after party, I guess we'll be buying the booze."

Donnie followed me into the room, looking grim.

"Donnie it was supposed to be a joke."

"That lady looks about our age." Donnie indicated the one woman in the room, other than the instructor, who looked old enough to buy alcohol without getting carded.

Donnie and I sat down on two of the metal folding chairs against the wall, but our instructor was having none of that. She urged us to join our limber young classmates on the floor.

I was flexible enough to sit on the mat, thanks to my recent yoga lessons. Donnie, who was dressed for work, looked less comfortable.

Kara introduced herself to the class and launched into a speech about the weighty responsibility of bringing a new life into the world. She warned us against a number of pastimes I wouldn't have dreamed of pursuing, pregnant or not. After the fire-and-brimstone intro, we went into some breathing exercises, which were supposed to calm us. These went on for what seemed like hours.

The instructor finally called for a break, and the round-bellied girls all leaped to their feet and stampeded out. It took Donnie and me a little longer to get up, but we managed. The "older" woman came over to us and struck up a conversation. She, as it turned out, was not expecting. She was there to give moral support to her pregnant fifteen-year-old daughter, who was out in the hallway with the rest of the mothers-to-be, in line for the ladies' room.

"I had her when I was sixteen." The woman shrugged. "I told her it was hard having a kid when you're still in school, and she should wait. But here we are. Eh, you da kine, ah? Donnie from Donnie's Drive-Inn."

"That's right." Donnie flashed his charming smile. "Home of the Lolo Lunch Plate and the Sumo Saimin Bowl."

"Yeah, baby girl and me used to go there all the time. Lately we been going Chang's Pizza Pagoda though. You seen their two-for-one specials?"

"Yes." Donnie's smile faded. "I have."

The second half of the class was devoted to diet and lifestyle. We were warned against eating junk food, forgetting to take our vitamins, petting cats, taking acne medicine, drinking lukewarm tea, or touching hair-loss pills. But it was the injunction against new tattoos and piercings that set off groans of disappointment throughout the room.

When the instructor had listed all of the ways we could accidentally cause lasting and irreparable harm to our unborn babies, she went on to explain how important it was to keep our stress levels low.

"Some of you are the kind of women who always have to be achieving something." She looked directly at me as she said this. "And that's great when it comes to your schoolwork or your career. But now is not the time to be a martyr. Now is the time to surround yourself with calm and serenity, and to remove yourself from anything that causes you stress. You have to be a little bit selfish. Starting right now."

I raised my hand.

"How does one manage that, practically? For example, my husband and I have a house full of guests. I can't exactly pack a bag and check into a hotel."

I felt Donnie giving me a look. I ignored him.

"Can't you?" She smiled at me. "What's stopping you?"

Everyone in the class was staring at me now.

"Costs money, that's why," someone else said, and the spotlight was off me.

CHAPTER FORTY-TWO

"DID YOU THINK THE SESSION was useful?" Donnie asked as we were driving home.

"I don't know. You don't need to go anymore if you don't want to."

"Do you really want to leave our house and check into a hotel?"

Packing a bag and retreating to a private hotel room sounded delightful. Not only would I not have to scurry around picking up after my houseguests, someone would clean up after me.

"No, of course not, Donnie. I only asked her the question to show how unrealistic it is to try to create a perfectly serene environment. She should have given us concrete ideas we could actually use. Like how to get a good night's sleep. I haven't slept through the night since your sister—well, for a while now."

"I didn't know you were having trouble sleeping. Do you think you should see a doctor about it?"

"Donnie, we have four adult houseguests, a crying baby, and thin walls. It's not a medical mystery. You seem to be able to sleep through all of it. But I sure can't."

"Maybe we can stop at Long's and get you some over-the-counter sleeping pills."

"Don't you remember when she was talking about what you can and can't take? She said there aren't any sleep aids considered completely safe for pregnancy."

"But you're not pregnant yet. Are you?"

"No. You're right. I'm not. Oh, Donnie, I almost forgot to tell you. Seeing the library reminded me. I ran into your Uncle Brian."

Donnie glanced at me and then turned his attention back to the road.

"You told me. When you were downtown with Davison."

"No, I saw him again. Later."

"Hm."

"I guess I don't understand how your father's brother can be right here on the island, and you don't even want to talk to him."

No answer.

"He told me what happened to your parents."

Donnie didn't seem any more eager to talk about Uncle Brian than the last time I'd brought him up, but I plowed ahead anyway.

"Didn't you and Gloria live with him for a while?"

"Yes."

"Davison seems to get along with him. I don't understand why you and Gloria are both so distant. Didn't he take you and your sister in after your parents passed away?"

"Is that what he told you?" Donnie's voice was level, but he was gripping the steering wheel hard.

"Is it not true?" I asked.

"No. It's true. He took us in. He treated us well. He was generous."

"So what, then?"

Donnie shook his head.

"Come on, Donnie. You know all about my family. You've met my parents. Why are you being so secretive?"

Donnie blew out a breath.

"My father had a drinking problem. He was trying to find his way back. Make things right. He enrolled in a program. They didn't call it rehab back then. They called it 'drying out.' He talked our mother into taking him back."

I nodded, which was pointless. Donnie was watching the road.

"When he came back, it was supposed to be a new start for all of us. We were going to be a normal, happy family. And we were, for two days. Then on Saturday, Uncle Brian had us over. All four of us, a few of Uncle's friends. Gloria and me, we ate and watched TV. When it was time to go, Dad was drunk. He wanted to drive. He insisted on driving, and he was mean when he didn't get his way. No one could argue with him. I couldn't do anything. I didn't have my license yet. Next thing I remember was waking up in the hospital."

"Mahina hospital? Where we just were?"

"M-hm. And I found out my mother and my father...my little sister's in intensive care, and my parents are gone."

"Oh Donnie, I'm so sorry."

"Did you know that when you detox, your tolerance goes down?"

"I have heard, yes."

"Well, Uncle Brian didn't know. Neither did my father, it seems. They thought you could pick up where you left off. You can't."

Donnie and I came home to find Tiffany at the dining room table, doing something on her phone while she nursed the baby. An empty glass sat on the table in front of her.

"Let me fill this up for you," I took the glass to the sink.

"Eh, thanks, ah?" She glanced up from her phone. "Makes me so thirsty, this thing. Like one termite, him, always hungry."

"Where's Davison?" Donnie asked.

"He's in the room."

"Okay, I have to go back to work." Donnie gave me a quick kiss and left.

"I see you're wearing your ring," I said to Tiffany. "It's nice. That's quite a diamond."

"Oh, yeah, my hands not so fat anymore. I could wear it finally." She held out her hand, and I leaned in to admire the ring.

"Davison got it for you?" The band was rose gold, supporting what looked like a round three-carat diamond.

"Yeah, it's so big. I hope I don't lose any more weight, otherwise the thing's gonna get too loose and fall off."

Junior began to make cranky noises, jerking his head back and forth.

"Ow, ow, greedy baga." Tiffany pulled her hand back and switched Junior to the other side. He settled in and resumed gulping.

"Eh, Professor, one a my friends says they saw you at the birthing class."

Apparently, the news had managed to reach her faster than Donnie and I could drive the mile and a half back down the hill.

"Yes, we were there." I set the full water glass in front of her. "And you might as well call me Molly. Davison already does."

I heard Skye's voice from the guest room:

"Someone saw you there."

Gloria shouted something, but the only words I could make out were,

"...think he is."

I pretended I hadn't heard.

"Where did Davison find the ring? I didn't see anything like it at Fujioka's Music and Party Supply."

Tiffany glanced down at her left hand, which now supported Junior's round head.

"I dunno. I wasn't with him when he got it."

At least he'd fenced my jewelry for something of comparable value. The diamond looked huge on Tiffany's delicate hand.

"Something, something lawyer," Skye shouted.

A door banged open, and Gloria stormed into the living room.

"Well you weren't doing nothing about it, were you? And that stupid lawyer doesn't know when to shut up an' mind his own business." She glared at us.

"I'm going out," she announced, to no one in particular, and shouted one more time back toward the guest room, "And nobody's perfect, you know. Nobody."

She stomped out and slammed the door behind her. Junior wrenched his head away from under Tiffany's shirt and started bawling. Tiffany yelled out a bad word and clapped her hand over her chest.

"I'll take him." I held my arms out. "Here."

Tiffany hurried off to clean up her injury. I held Junior and walked around the living room. He was inconsolable. He wailed furiously as I tried walking, rocking, sitting, and standing. Finally, I hit on something that worked: deep knee bends. Junior relaxed, cooed, and spit up on my shoulder as I pliéd frantically.

Tiffany eventually returned from the bathroom, relieved me of Junior, and repositioned the baby under her shirt. I sank down onto a chair, my quadriceps trembling.

My good angel reminded me Gloria had been through quite a lot lately and could hardly be expected to be on her best behavior, what with the violent ex and the murder charges and all. My bad angel disagreed, pointing out that Gloria was an entitled pill who probably deserved to rot in prison. I thought my bad angel had a point. Everyone was trying to help Gloria. Her husband's family was shelling out a fortune for the best lawyer around. What was she doing? Pouting and slamming doors.

Davison came shambling out of the back room.

"What happened?" He rubbed his face and looked around warily. "Sounded like a bomb went off."

"Your Aunty Gloria. She wen' left an' slammed the door."

"I'll get the rice started." I stood up and busied myself in the kitchen. Davison sat down next to Tiffany.

"Get me more water, baby," Tiffany said, and Davison did.

Skye came out of the back bedroom.

"Everything okay?" I asked him.

"No. No. Everything is not okay. We have to step up the fight. There's a terrible injustice happening."

"Did Gloria say where she was going?"

"She just went out to get centered." Skye went over and stood behind Tiffany and Davison.

"I'm not going back to California until Gloria is a free woman," He put one hand on Davison's shoulder, and the other hand on Tiffany's. "I'm staying in Mahina for as long as it takes. And I know Davison and Tiffany are with me on this. Right?"

"Yeah, sure." Davison sounded like he was still half-asleep.

"Whatever," Tiffany agreed.

"Okay. I'm going to check on Gloria." Skye went out the front door.

"You two have lunch yet?" I asked.

Tiffany and Davison shook their heads.

"Rice'll be ready in about half an hour. I'll heat up some leftovers. Davison, could you please refill Tiffany's water glass?"

"I just did."

"Eh, you wanna do this?" Tiffany pointed at her chest with her free hand. Davison got up and took her empty glass to the sink.

I wondered whether Pat would be able to find anything useful about Gloria's whereabouts during the time of the murder. I hoped so. Otherwise, my houseguests were never going to leave.

CHAPTER FORTY-THREE

I'D MANAGED TO GET a few hours of sleep the previous night, so I woke up the next morning feeling optimistic.

Gazing out across the lanai onto the quiet street, I realized I had a lot to be grateful for. I lived in one of the most beautiful places on earth. I had a loving husband, good health, and tenure. This situation with Gloria would be straightened out eventually, and things would go back to normal. Skye and Gloria would return home. Tiffany and Davison and little Junior would find a place of their own. My earlier impulse, to move out and stay at a hotel, now seemed like a petty overreaction.

I padded out to the kitchen, humming to myself and not watching my step. Halfway to the coffee machine, I tripped over a noisy baby toy, setting it a-jingle. Startled, I stumbled sideways, planting my foot firmly on a squishy used diaper and squirting the contents in all directions.

I cleaned up the diaper mess and washed my hands with soap and water, running the water until it was as close to boiling as I could stand. Baby poop aroma tickled the roof of my mouth. I realized the smell came from the kitchen rubbish can, so I took out the garbage and put in a new liner. Then I washed my hands again, scalding myself with the now-heated water.

By the time I made it to the coffee machine, my good mood was gone.

As I sat down to start work on my book chapter, I heard a key turn in the lock. Gloria and Skye came in through the front door.

"Good morning. Did you go out for breakfast?"

"We had to find a pay phone to call Feinman," Skye said. "I didn't want Gloria using the cell phone again."

Gloria ignored Skye and me and stomped back toward the guest room.

"That was an early call."

"I know." Skye went into the kitchen. "Feinman's still in Costa Rica. It's four hours later there."

Junior was up now. I could hear his babbling coming from Davison and Tiffany's room. The adorable baby sounds set me on edge. I knew they could escalate without warning to eardrum-shredding shrieks.

I stood up from my workstation.

"Skye, I'm going to the store. Do you want anything?"

"I'll come with you," he said quickly.

"You want to come shopping with me?"

"If you don't mind, yes. Can I bring my coffee?"

"I'll wait while you finish it. I don't have cup holders in my car."

Skye didn't say anything when we pulled into the parking lot of Galimba's Bargain Boyz. I hoped he wasn't disappointed. The building's corrugated siding was touched with rust, and the "temporary" Galimba's banner had hung over the entrance for the last decade. None of this had dissuaded Mahina's thrifty shoppers. The parking lot was packed.

"Molly, this is great."

"It is?"

"It's the real Hawai`i. The one the tourists never get to see. I wish I'd brought my camera."

We got out of the car and followed the crowd to the entrance. I yanked a gigantic shopping cart free and wheeled it to Galimba's audio section as Skye followed. I picked out a pair of noise-cancelling headphones. They cost more than I had planned to spend, but if they worked, they would be worth it.

"So, any other insights from Feinman?" I asked Skye. "What's the latest?"

"It's not going great. Feinman was trying to tell Gloria that she's automatically going to be a suspect, because of her history with the deceased. They always look at the ex first. That's what he said."

"I've heard the same thing."

"Well, Gloria didn't like it when he told her she had to come up with an alibi. And then Feinman said it was her own fault she was in trouble to begin with, and she should never have given false information to the police."

"She gave false information to the police?"

Skye shrugged. "I don't know what he was talking about. Anyway, she told him to mind his own business and do his job."

"I don't understand why she needs an alibi." I eased the cart back from the headphone display and headed down the aisle. "Even if she was right there when he fell out of the window, she could easily say it was self-defense."

"She says she wasn't there at all. She claims she never even saw him. I believe her. This whole thing is so frustrating."

"I get it. Do you need anything while we're here?"

Skye bought a cheap pair of rubber slippers (he called them flip-flops), a box of loose green tea, and a twelve pack of Mehana Mauna Kea Pale Ale.

As we stood in line with our giant shopping cart, I heard, "Oh, I thought it was you."

I turned around to see the woman from our childbirth class. I had forgotten her name, so I introduced myself and my brother-in-law, Skye.

"I'm Jennifer," the woman said. "This is my aunty. Sorry, I forgot your name. So much to think about, getting ready for baby girl's new baby."

Jennifer wielded a cart loaded with super-sized boxes of baby wipes, canned formula, and newborn diapers.

"Your daughter's due soon then?" I asked.

"Oh, any minute now. What about you, Molly? You barely even showing yet." Jennifer patted her own flat tummy.

Skye started moving the contents of our shopping cart to the counter, turning the UPC labels face-up to make the items easy to scan.

"What a beautiful necklace," Jennifer's aunty said to me.

I touched my throat to remind myself which necklace I was wearing. It was a costume piece made of base metal and glass bits colored dark gray to resemble marcasite. On especially muggy days, it left traces of green on my skin, but I liked the style.

"Is it an antique?" the older woman asked.

"It's vintage. I bought ages ago, at a little consignment store on La Brea."

"It reminds me of the things you could buy at the shop, before they closed." Jennifer's aunty wrinkled her forehead. "What was it called? They always had the nicest things, even though it was just a pawnshop. You remember the place, Jen? From when you were small?"

"You mean Modern Jewelers?" she asked.

"No, no, no, Modern was the Shigeokas' place. Royal Pawn. That's the one I'm thinking of.

The owner was Brian Carvalho. So charming, the man, and always dressed to the nines. Was it Carvalho?"

"I don't know what store you're thinking of, Aunty," Jen said.

"We're up." Skye bought his items, and then I paid for my headphones.

"It was nice to see you, Jennifer," I said. "Best of luck with everything if I don't see you in class."

"You too, ah?" She nosed her brimming cart forward.

"It was Gonsalves," Jen's aunty exclaimed.

"What?" I turned around, surprised to hear the familiar surname, although Gonsalves isn't exactly uncommon in Mahina.

"What I'm saying, Carvalho." The older woman frowned. "It was Brian Gonsalves, Royal Pawn. I can see the name written on the glass door. Remember, Jen?"

Jennifer was busy hauling items from the cart onto the counter for the cashier to scan. Diapers, six-packs of formula cans, and something called a noise machine, which seemed a little coals-to-Newcastle for a household with a new baby on the way.

"I don't remember, Aunty." She lifted a pillow-sized pack of gauze burp cloths out of the cart.

"Royal Pawn. I remember now. Too bad he went out of business. I found such pretty things there. Better than the other stores. Nicer even than Modern Jewelers."

"Brian Gonsalves is my husband's uncle," I said.

Jennifer moved the last item from her cart. It was a lavender magnum of baby wash, enough to shampoo a battalion of infants.

"Oh yeah, Aunty. Her husband is Donnie, from Donnie's Drive-Inn. Small world, ah?"

"Home of the Sumo Saimin Bowl and the Lolo Lunch Plate," I said.

Jennifer's aunty smiled apologetically.

"You know, we mostly go Chang's Pizza Pagoda now. Cannot beat the two-for-one specials."

CHAPTER FORTY-FOUR

MY PHONE STARTED TO ring as I was unlocking the Thunderbird.

"Hey, Pat." I slid into the driver's seat and reached way over to open the passenger door for Skye. "Everything okay? What's up?"

"I dug up some interesting information about your sister-in-law," Pat said.

I glanced over at Skye. He was busy with the seatbelt.

"Listen, Pat. Can I call you back? Maybe in about twenty minutes?"

"You can try. Why, is someone there?"

"Absolutely." I clicked the phone off and dropped it back into my bag.

"Are these the original seat belts?" Skye got the two sides lined up and clicked them shut.

"No, but they're the closest thing. The original seat belts were rotting. I had to mail order these from the ends of the earth, and then find someone to install them. It wasn't easy to find them in turquoise."

"They look like they belong in the car. Very authentic. Almost like airplane seatbelts."

"They're exact reproductions of the originals. And thank you for noticing. Hardly anyone appreciates this car as much as I do. Donnie keeps telling me I should get something newer and more reliable. And Earl Miyashiro, my mechanic? Don't get me started on him—"

My phone rang again. I dug into my bag to find it.

"Sorry, Skye, let me get this. It's Donnie. Uh-oh. He never calls when he's at work. Donnie, what's going on? Are you okay?"

"I'm fine. Where are you?"

"I'm in the parking lot of Galimba's Bargain Boyz. Skye is with me. What's up?"

"Can you come by the Drive-Inn?"

"Can we stop by the Drive-Inn?" I asked Skye. "Do you have to be anywhere?"

Skye shook his head.

"Okay. We're on our way."

I turned the key in the ignition and pumped the gas pedal twice, lightly. The Thunderbird's 352 cubic inch V-8 rumbled to life.

"Is there a gasoline smell?" Skye asked.

"Earl says it's an oil leak, which is impossible to fix completely because of the way some joint is configured or something. He says he can do a workaround, but I'd have to get a custom part made, and it would be really expensive. So I just top up the oil every week or two. I admit it might not be the best thing for the environment."

I pulled out of the parking lot and turned right toward downtown.

"What's going on at the Drive-Inn?" Skye asked.

"I don't know. I hope nothing bad has happened. You know, business at the Drive-Inn has been, well... Remember what the lady at the store, Jennifer's aunty, said? They've stopped going to the Drive-Inn, and are going to Chang's Pizza Pagoda instead. Unfortunately, it's not the first time I've heard the same thing."

"I can't believe she came right out and said it to you. Although, no offense to Donnie, people really shouldn't be eating that kind of food all the time. How's the other place getting your customers anyway?"

"Chang's has been marketing very aggressively. They send out flyers. They're on social media. They advertise two-for-one specials. You name it. I'm pretty sure they've been gaming the restaurant review sites, too. And the result is, you'll pardon the expression, they've been eating Donnie's lunch."

"We had a situation like that with the spa. A competitor moved in, started offering these spa packages at prices we couldn't match. We knew they were either taking a loss or breaking employment laws."

"So, what did you and Gloria do?"

"My parents kind of helped us out."

"How nice of them. What did they do?"

"Bought them out."

"Just bought the entire business?"

"M hm."

"And then did what?"

"I don't know. I think there's a Vietnamese restaurant in the space now."

"Well, that's one way to deal with the competition. And here we are."

I made a left, and then another quick left to park behind the Drive-Inn. We got the last spot in the parking lot.

The place was packed.

We found Donnie out front with two of his red-polo-shirted employees. They were clearing and wiping tables as customers finished and others crowded in to take their place. Donnie spotted us, peeled off his latex gloves, and dropped them into the red oil drum trashcan.

"Donnie, this is great. Look at all these people. Where did they come from?"

Every table was occupied, and people stood around waiting for empty seats to open up.

"Way to go, man." Skye fist-bumped him.

Donnie grinned.

"This is the busiest Friday we've had in three months."

"So, did you follow the marketing plan? You did the social media outreach and everything?"

"Oh. No. Sorry, Molly, I haven't really gotten around to reading your plan."

"Then what happened?"

He shrugged.

"I guess people just got tired of Chang's. The novelty wore off."

"Really? Just all of a sudden, people started coming here again? Do you think it was your ad in the newspaper?"

"Maybe. One of my workers told me that someone found a cockroach in one of Chang's Kung Pao Pizza Rolls, but that's kind of hard to believe."

"It's crazy the kind of rumors that can get started," Skye said. "Lucky it's your competitor and not you, though."

"Someone was eating at Chang's and just happened to find a cockroach in their pizza roll?" I exclaimed. "That is weird. I can barely believe it myself."

I drove Skye back up to the house, went into the bedroom, and pulled my little guitar out of the closet. I sat on the bed and tuned it as I tried to organize my thoughts. Davison had ignored my good advice and had gone ahead with his numbskull plan to sabotage Chang's Pizza Pagoda. It was a clumsy effort that would inevitably be traced back to him. Donnie's business, and his reputation, would be ruined.

I played half a song. When it got to the part with the F-chord, I gave up and put the guitar away. I went back to Davison and Tiffany's room, to find the door closed. I could hear Junior making baby noises, so I knew he wasn't asleep. I tapped lightly and then nudged the door open. Tiffany lay on the bed, on her back, her phone in one hand. Junior was on the bed beside her, tucked under her arm.

"What?" Tiffany kept her eyes on her phone.

"Where's Davison?" I whispered. Junior stirred a little, and then settled down.

"Probably at the gym. My cousins and him was gonna go work out today. Good thing, too. He's getting da kine, ah? Davison. Beer belly."

"Have you and Davison been to Chang's Pizza Pagoda?" I asked.

"Yeah."

"Did he ever take a picture of his food there and post it online?"

"I dunno."

Junior was making soft buzzing baby snores, his face buried in Tiffany's armpit. I wasn't going to get any details from her about this cockroach-in-the-pizza-roll situation. For that, I'd have to confront Davison directly. But maybe Tiffany could help me solve a different mystery.

"Tiffany, can I show you something?" I reached into my purse, pulled out my phone, and searched through the photos until I found the one I was looking for.

"Do you recognize these?" I turned my phone toward her.

She sighed and set her phone down. "That's you an' da kine."

"Yes, it's Donnie and me at dinner. Do you see the earrings I'm wearing in this picture? There's a necklace too, but you can't see it."

"Oh, yeah. I see 'em."

"Do you have a pair of earrings like this, by any chance?"

"Those?" Tiffany wrinkled her nose. "Nah, those are old lady earrings. I never wear ones like that."

"Have you ever seen earrings like these?"

"Yeah, you just showed 'em to me."

I sighed and dropped my phone back into my bag. I don't know what I'd expected. If Davison had fenced my jewelry to buy Tiffany's ring, she wouldn't necessarily know about it. And if memory served, retaining information wasn't exactly Tiffany's strong suit.

CHAPTER FORTY-FIVE

MY PHONE VIBRATED INSIDE my bag. I'd forgotten that I was supposed to call Pat back. I rushed out of the guest room before the sound woke the baby.

"Did you see this thing from the Student Retention Office?" Pat asked.

"The Student Retention Office? Did they track you down all the way over there in California?"

"No, I was just catching up on my email while I was waiting for you to call back. We're supposed to start telling jokes in class now?"

I slipped out the front door and pulled it shut behind me.

"Oh, that stupid Humor Initiative. Emma and I think you should tell the canoe joke in class. That'll put a stop to it."

"Yeah, and get me fired."

"So, find out anything about Gloria?"

"Yeah. Molly, your sister-in-law's a jailbird."

"You know, you could have told me to sit down first before you sprang something like that on me."

"Molly, maybe you want to sit down."

"I think I will."

The rattan chair creaked as I settled into it. The heat had subsided, mellowing to an evening sultriness. The sun hung low in the sky, poised to drop behind the mountains. This was the best time of day to relax on the lanai. The mosquitoes wouldn't be out for another hour.

"Okay, I'm nice and comfy now. What did she do? Donnie's sister has a bit of a temper, it turns out."

"She went to prison for robbery."

"Robbery?"

"You sound surprised."

"I am surprised. It seems out of character for her. I thought you were going to tell me she handbagged someone and got charged for assault."

"Technically she was sentenced for aiding and abetting. A jewelry case disappeared from a private plane on Maui, and somehow ended up in the trunk of her car. She claimed she didn't have anything to do with it. Her boyfriend must've put it there without her knowing."

"So how long was she in prison?" I asked.

"She got fifteen years."

"Fifteen years!"

"The boyfriend was sentenced too. And they had a son."

"Oh. Davison."

"Uh-huh. According to the records, the son was three years old when Gloria Gonsalves started serving her sentence."

I watched the golf cart putter up the street. The boys jostled each other happily, excited about one more skateboard ride down the hill before dinner.

"Molly, are you there?"

"I'm here. I was just thinking. When Skye said Gloria handed Davison over to Donnie because she was in a 'bad place,' he literally meant she was in a bad place."

"Yeah. She only served part of her sentence, though. A group of law students got interested in her case and managed to get her exonerated. It's how she met her husband, by the way. Skye Chaney was one of the law students. Hey Molly, I have to go. Listen, keep this information to yourself, okay?"

"Of course. Who am I going to tell? I'm sure Donnie knew about it anyway. I didn't know people still said 'jailbird.'"

I came back into the house to find Davison sitting at my workstation, arms folded, glowering at my computer monitor.

"Where did you come from? I was just looking for you."

"Bathroom."

"Oh. Glad I asked. What are you doing at my computer?"

"I gotta talk to you, Molly."

"What a coincidence. I need to talk to you, too." I plumped down on the couch.

Davison swiveled the chair around to face me. He seemed nervous, although I couldn't fathom why. "Tiffany said you came in our room just now."

"Yes, I did."

"And you was asking her all kinda questions."

"A few. Is there a problem?"

"You scared her, that's why."

"I scared Tiffany? I doubt it very much."

Davison ran his hands through his buzz-cut hair and folded his arms again. "You gotta problem, Molly, you can talk to me." He swallowed, setting his Adam's apple bobbing.

It took me a moment to realize what was going on. Davison was trying to step up. He was defending his delicate fiancée from his terrifying stepmother.

"Fine," I sighed. "You're the one I need to talk to anyway. I was just down at the Drive-Inn. It was packed."

Davison folded his arms tighter, as if he were trying to hug himself into invisibility.

"That's good news, ah, Molly? You should be happy the Drive-Inn's doing good."

"Yes, it would be good news if it had come about honestly."

"What? How come you're grilling me? What's your problem?"

"What is my problem? I'll tell you what my problem is. Did you learn nothing in my class?"

Davison's neck reddened beneath his tattoo scars.

"Eh, I posted that review long time ago. How'd you know it was me?"

"I—what? Never mind about that. I'm not talking about your online reviews. I'm talking about you planting nasty rumors online about Chang's Pizza Pagoda."

Davison's gaze shifted away. He couldn't look me in the eye.

"I knew it. Davison, what you did is not okay. Your father has been working to build this business his whole adult life. He's always run things ethically and honestly, and if this gets out, his reputation, everything he's worked for, is going to collapse. Did you think about that at all?"

Davison folded his hands in his lap and assumed an innocent expression. His bushy eyebrows tilted up in the middle. "I dunno what you're talking about."

I leaned forward, and he rolled the chair back until it bumped against the desk and wouldn't roll any more.

"What I'm talking about is you put a dead cockroach in one of Chang's Kung Pao Pizza Rolls, took a picture of it, and uploaded it to a review site. I know you just wanted to help your father, but Davison, how is it going to look when everything comes out? Because it will come out. What do you think your father's going to say?"

He shrugged and stood up from my chair.

"Too late. Cannot do nothing about it now. And you see the crowd down at the Drive-Inn today?"

CHAPTER FORTY-SIX

I MADE AN EFFORT TO smile through dinner. Donnie was in a good mood, and I didn't want to spoil things for him. Let him enjoy a few moments of success before everything came crashing down. Of course I wasn't annoyed at Donnie for ignoring the well-researched and completely ethical marketing plan I'd put together for him. He was a busy man, and it was hard for him to find the time. Although, if he had actually read and followed my plan, the Drive-Inn might have recovered sooner. And Davison wouldn't have felt the need to pull his stupid cockroach stunt in the first place.

At bedtime, I thought Donnie and I might spend some time making progress on our family plans. But Donnie pleaded fatigue (so many customers today) and asked for a rain check. He dropped right off to sleep, and within seconds was snoring peacefully.

I lay awake, listening to Junior's fussing and the rumble of arguments coming from the guest rooms. The guest toilet seemed to be flushing constantly, sending water coursing through the walls.

This was ridiculous. I was never going to be able to provide a growing baby with a calm and serene environment as long as we had all of these noisy houseguests. Okay, there wasn't a growing baby yet, but what about a calm and serene environment for me? I got out of bed, went into the walk-in closet, found my little overnight bag, and started to pack.

Perhaps I wasn't as quiet as I might have been. Donnie stirred.

"Molly? What are you doing?"

"I'm going to the Lehua Inn."

"You're what?" He sounded wide-awake now.

"I can't sleep here."

"You're leaving? Now? You can't go. It's too late."

I came out of the closet to face him. "I just need to sleep through the night. Just one night. Please, let me have this."

"Molly, what are people going to say when they wake up and you're not here?"

"What was that you said, Donnie? Did I hear you say, 'Please don't go, Molly. I'll miss you terribly'? Or maybe what you said was, 'Let's see what we can do to make sure you can sleep through the night at least once?' Wait, no, you didn't say either of those things. My mistake."

I stomped back into the closet and resumed packing, only faster and more angrily.

"Molly, why are you doing this?"

"I need a serene environment to ready my body for our growing baby," I called out to him. "This is not serene. I'm so sleep-deprived I'm afraid I'm going to lose it. And you know, I put this whole social media marketing plan together for you, and you ignored it, and that's why this cockroach thing happened."

"Molly, I looked at your plan, I promise I did, but there were a lot of things in there I didn't understand."

"Sure, marketing is hard work. It's a lot easier to let Davison sabotage Chang's with his faked-up cockroach photo."

"What are you talking about? What is it with you and Davison, anyway? What do you have against him? He doesn't have any problem with you."

"That's where you're wrong. Did you know he wrote an online review of my class, claiming he didn't learn anything? Although come to think of it, he's not wrong."

I stuffed one last bra into the overnight bag, zipped it shut, and stomped out of the closet.

"You're going out in your pajamas?" Donnie said.

"These are not pajamas, Donnie. I'm wearing sweatpants and a T-shirt, which is perfectly acceptable for casual wear. Don't you try to gaslight me. Oh, and I packed the rest of my jewelry too. So your poor, misunderstood son can't steal any more of it."

Donnie got up out of bed, looking magnificent in flimsy sleep pants and nothing else. I averted my eyes and willed myself to stay strong.

"That's a serious accusation, Molly."

"Yes, it is serious. And true."

"You can't just drive away in the middle of the night."

"I certainly can. Are you trying to tell me I may not leave? Are you trying to forbid me to leave?"

"Molly." Donnie's voice was warmer now, conciliatory. He stepped around the bed toward me. "I know it must be upsetting for you that you haven't been able to get pregnant, and Davison already has Junior. But it's not fair to take your frustration out on him."

Less than ten minutes later, I was pulling into the parking lot of the Lehua Inn. I parked my Thunderbird, locked up, and kept an uneasy eye on the Hanohano Hotel as I hurried into the Lehua's well-lit lobby.

The semi-abandoned Hanohano, standing right next to the Lehua Inn, looked especially creepy at night. Decaying scaffolding clung to the building like a disease. Skeletal fingers of rebar protruded skyward from the unfinished top floor. The Hanohano Hotel had once been a charming single-story plantation house. An overambitious local developer decided to bulldoze and "rebuild" it. The money ran out sooner than expected, leaving the hulking eyesore half-finished.

That stupid hotel is exactly like my life. I was doing just fine on my own, and then I had this big bright idea to go and get married, and change everything around, and now look at me. I'm fleeing my own house in the middle of the night. I never had to do this when I was single.

I had planned to check in to the Lehua under an assumed name, but the lady at the front counter greeted me as "Mrs. Gonsalves," so there went that idea. I let her take my credit card information and then went up to my second-story room. Before I did anything else, I wiped down the sink, phone, and doorknobs with rubbing alcohol. Not that the room didn't look clean, but I always do that when I check into a hotel. Then I pulled the bedspread off and piled it in a corner, checked under the mattress for bedbugs, and finally crawled into bed. I settled into the best sleep I'd had in weeks, lulled by the murmur of traffic on Hotel Drive.

CHAPTER FORTY-SEVEN

THE DIGITAL CLOCK ON the nightstand read 10:01. It took me a few moments to remember I was in a room at the Lehua Inn. I felt a pang of regret when I remembered the previous night's unpleasantness with Donnie, and it felt strange to wake up alone. But it was impossible to stay in a bad mood when I'd enjoyed such a refreshing sleep. I wasn't really that mad at Donnie. I had just been desperate to sleep through the night for once.

I swung my feet onto the floor, stood up, and pulled open the light-blocking curtains. I could hear the traffic from Hotel Drive below, but the road itself was hidden by the canopy of hundred-year-old banyan trees. The rolling greens of the golf course were bounded on the far side by a forty-foot hedge of ironwood trees. I had opted for an inland-facing room over the more expensive ocean-side accommodations. It had been a good choice. I still had a beautiful view.

The interior was equally delightful. A potted Phalaenopsis, or moth orchid, sat atop the dresser. The broad petals were yellow-green, veined and speckled with vibrant magenta. The walls, bedding, and drapes were bright white, suffusing the room with reflected sunlight. Donnie would like it here, I thought.

I didn't want to get dressed and go out. I wanted to nestle in the floral chintz armchair, reading mystery novels and ordering room service all day. Unfortunately, I still had to work on my book chapter, and I hadn't brought my computer.

The public library didn't have air conditioning, just louvered windows open to let the breeze through to the courtyard. It was too warm to buckle down and focus. Maybe all I needed was a short break.

I wandered into one of the side rooms, where I found a display of manga paperbacks, sorted by series. Some of the titles were in Japanese. Others contained English words but were equally incomprehensible. A shelf further back featured old videotapes few people had the equipment to play anymore. Next to that was a stack of free books, library holdings, which had rotted in the humid climate. One of them had an actual, honest-to-goodness bookworm tunneling through the pages. And then I saw the yearbooks along the back wall.

Why not? I wasn't getting any work done anyway, and now I was curious. I'd never seen pictures of Donnie other than as an adult. I knew Donnie's date of birth, and calculated which years he would have been in high school. Mahina had two cross-town rivals: Mahina High, directly across the street from Mahina State University, and the older Laukapu High. I pulled down both yearbooks for what would have been Donnie's freshman year. A quick search of the index showed Laukapu High as Donnie's alma mater. I took down the next three years of Laukapu High School yearbooks, wondering how a high school in rural Hawai`i had chosen Vikings, of all things, as their mascot.

Donnie's freshman portrait showed a skinny kid wearing a crewneck t-shirt and a serious expression. He hadn't yet grown into his ears, and was still a long way from handsome. Donnie's sophomore yearbook yielded a bonus. Donnie's younger sister, Gloria Farrah Bysentenyl Gonsalves, appeared in the freshman section. Her curly hair was pinned behind one ear with a red hibiscus.

By his junior year, Donnie had matured into looking more like his adult self. That issue of the Laukapu High yearbook also had a photo of Gloria at the junior prom with Andy De Silva.

Cute. The budding ex-con and the future cop. Young Andy gazed at Gloria adoringly, his gawky features aglow with delight. Gloria looked happy too, but in a way you might be happy if you were having a fun night out with a friend.

I briefly wondered whether it was Gloria I'd seen at the Pair-O-Dice with Andy De Silva. But that didn't jibe with De Silva's standoffish attitude toward Gloria when he'd been in the same room with her.

On the other hand, maybe De Silva's impersonal demeanor didn't mean anything, and was simply a necessity for someone who had to police the same community he grew up in. How awkward would it be to bust your math teacher for possession, or to be called out on a domestic involving your high school buddy? He probably ran into old acquaintances all the time in Mahina and acted detached as a matter of course.

The yearbook for the following year didn't have Donnie's photo with the rest of the senior class. He was still enrolled but hadn't made it in for picture day. Where his senior portrait should have been was a gray box, captioned with his name: Donald Muraco Gonsalves. There were no memorable quotations or favorite memories underneath where his photo would have gone.

Gloria's junior portrait was where it was supposed to be, but she had no more prom pictures. She had apparently lost interest in high school proms. Or in Andy De Silva.

I put the yearbooks back on the shelf. I knew patrons weren't supposed to re-shelve books, but I remembered where they went, and I didn't want to make extra work for the librarian. Looking over Donnie's old pictures made me realize I missed him, a little.

I glanced at the library's wall clock. I still had some time to decide whether to check out or stay another night.

I left the library and walked down toward the Drive-Inn, past the little stone house with the chiropractor's office, and then the tiny shopping center with the defunct toyshop. Of course, I wouldn't tell Donnie how much I enjoyed my stay at the Lehua Inn. I didn't want him to think I was glad to be away from him. But I would tell him about flowers in the room, the vintage koa furniture, and the calming view of the golf course. Once this murder charge was cleared up and all the houseguests were gone, Donnie and I might spend a weekend at the Lehua inn as a mini-vacation.

I was thinking about the yearbook pictures, which led to doing some quick arithmetic. Gloria had gone to prison when Davison was three years old. When Davison was three, Donnie was twenty. From the yearbook, I knew Gloria was one year behind him, so she was nineteen. She had been sixteen when Davison was born. Well, at least I'd figured out why she skipped her junior prom.

Poor Andy De Silva. He thought he had a shot, and next thing he knew, Gloria was off having babies with Iulani Malufau.

There it was. Why hadn't I seen it before?

I stopped, pulled out my phone, and called Emma. She wasn't picking up. I considered leaving her a text message, but I was almost at the Drive-Inn. I'd tell Donnie what I'd just figured out.

CHAPTER FORTY-EIGHT

EXHAUSTED FARMER'S Market shoppers filled the Drive-Inn's picnic tables and lined up at the order windows. I had to stand and wait for an empty seat, but I didn't mind. This crowd was good news, as long as it lasted.

Finally, a couple with a baby stood up from a table, and I hurried over to claim the space. I pulled out my phone and tried Emma's number again, but before it rang, I felt someone sit down across from me.

I looked up at Donnie. He didn't seem particularly glad to see me.

"Hi Donnie." I put my phone away. "Listen, thank you so much for letting me get an uninterrupted night's sleep. Just one night's sleep makes all the difference. I feel better than I have in ages. It's so important in my delicate condition. I mean, I'm not in a delicate condition yet, but we want me to be, right?"

"I suppose." Donnie was avoiding eye contact with me. I wanted to tell him I'd figured out who murdered Iulani Malufau, but I sensed I should probably deal with whatever was bothering him first.

"Donnie, are you mad at me?"

He sighed.

"Am I supposed to act like everything's fine? How would you feel if I walked out and spent the night who knows where?"

I thought about it.

"If you did it for no reason, then sure, I'd be upset. But since we're playing what-if, how would you feel if, I don't know, I got my old band together, and then let them practice in our living room all night? I think I'd understand if you needed to go somewhere else to get some sleep."

"It's not the same thing. I can't just tell my family to leave. Especially not now, with the trouble Gloria's having."

"I didn't ask you to tell your family to leave, because I know it would be impolite and you would never do it. So I found another solution. I got to sleep through the night, and you have a cheerful wife. I believe it's called a win-win."

Donnie shook his head and made a move to stand up.

"Donnie, wait. Don't go. I have to talk to you about something important."

He sat back down.

"You know what? Even when you're grumpy, you're still very handsome."

"Molly, this really isn't the time—"

"Sorry, that's not what I wanted to talk to you about. It's about Gloria. And the murder."

"I'm listening." He seemed to be half-listening, if that. He was making the whole table vibrate with his impatient leg bouncing.

"It was Andy De Silva, Donnie. De Silva is the murderer. He killed Iulani Malufau. I just figured it out when I was walking down from the library."

"Officer Andy De Silva? That's impossible."

"Andy and your sister were high school sweethearts, right?"

"I don't know if I'd say they were sweethearts. They knew each other. They might have gone out a few times."

"They went to prom together in Gloria's sophomore year."

Donnie shrugged. "Maybe? I don't remember. Why?"

"Their prom picture was in your high school yearbook. All the yearbooks are at the public library, which by the way is a valuable and underestimated community resource. Anyway, I think Andy De Silva was smitten with her."

"How do you know that? And even if he was, how does that make him the murderer?"

"Just listen, please. Okay, cut to junior year, and Gloria is not only with Iulani Malufau, she's having a baby with him. How do you suppose young Andy felt about that development?"

Donnie drummed his fingers on the table but didn't make a move to get up and leave. He knew what I was saying made sense, but he apparently didn't want to admit it.

"Donnie, listen." I leaned forward so I could speak quietly. "When Malufau escaped and came back to Mahina, Andy De Silva saw his opportunity. Part one, he kills Malufau. Part two, he lets Gloria take the blame. It's a perfect way to get revenge on both of them. And I do mean perfect, because even though I've figured it out, what can I do about it? Nothing. I can't call the police, right?"

Donnie looked like he was about to say something to contradict me, so I spoke quickly.

"You're going to ask what proof I have, right? Well, I don't. Sorry. But what about this? First, De Silva seems like he's senior in the department. In a case like this, with no witnesses and no evidence to speak of, De Silva could probably influence where suspicion fell. Oh, and he's the one who invited me on that ride-along, when we found Malufau's body. He knew very well who Malufau was, but he had me there so that I could ID the body. I said, 'I think that's Iulani Malufau,' and then De Silva announced I'd identified the John Doe. I bet it was part of the plan too, to have me there to ID the body, maybe to make it look like he hadn't been stalking Malufau and planning to kill him, even though, of course, it's exactly what he'd been doing."

"Was it De Silva who invited you? I thought you said it was those other guys who wanted you to come along."

"Well, I'm sure De Silva engineered it or encouraged it somehow."

"How did De Silva know you'd be able to ID Malufau? In fact, how were you able to identify him? I'm still not clear myself. You just guessed?"

"I told you already. Because he was the guy who followed Davison and me into Fujioka's parking lot. And then he happened to bump into us downtown later the same morning."

"But how did you connect the man with my sister's ex? What made you think it was the same person?"

THE BLESSED EVENT   121

I knew "the unmistakable family resemblance" wasn't the right answer. Oh, because Davison looks so much like his real father Felon McMurderpants.

"An educated guess. Putting two and two together. Induction."

"Don't you mean deduction?"

"No, I mean induction, Donnie. Stop trying to trip me up. Induction is where you ask, 'What are the circumstances that led to this situation?' As opposed to deduction, which is, given the present circumstances, what are the likely consequences?"

"I'm not trying to trip anyone up," Donnie said, "and since we're playing detective. Would Iulani Malufau let Andy De Silva, a cop, get near him? Let alone into his room, where De Silva could do anything, and it would be Andy's word against his?"

"De Silva could've gone to visit him pretending to be someone else. Or maybe he just followed Malufau home one night and cracked him over the head. The whole falling out of the window thing could have been staged."

"But why would Andy let Gloria take the blame?"

"Because she hurt him by choosing Iulani Malufau over him, and he's been stewing about it all these years. Now he's getting his perfect revenge. Why do you seem surprised?"

"Molly, who holds a grudge from high school?"

"Are you kidding? Everyone."

"You think Andy would want to hurt my sister? It doesn't make any sense."

"Wow, Donnie, you really do have a much more charitable view of human nature than I do. Anyway, you know Gloria's not helping her own case. I don't know why she doesn't just cooperate with Feinman. Here Skye's family just bought her the best lawyer in the state, and instead of working with him, she's giving him attitude."

At that, Donnie stood up. "You and I should stay out of this."

"What, and leave it to the police? Who might be trying to frame her?"

"Why don't we just let Gloria's attorney do his job? It's bad enough having Skye rattle on about how the police are spying on us. I don't need you hopping on the paranoid train, too."

"You want your sister to spend the rest of her life in prison? She's not a first-time offender, you know. This doesn't look good for her."

Donnie sat back down. "Molly. Please, let's stay out of this. Our getting involved is not going to help. It'll only make things worse."

CHAPTER FORTY-NINE

I WAS COMPLETELY OUT of options now. I couldn't call the police and tell them what I'd told Donnie. It would get right back to De Silva, and then all of us would be in danger. Had Donnie believed me, he could have tried to work his Mahina connections to fix the situation. Maybe get De Silva transferred or something. But he was being stubborn again, refusing to listen to reason. Just like when he'd ignored my marketing plan.

And if we did "stay out of this," best case? Gloria would sabotage her own defense and end up in prison. Skye's parents would finance endless appeals. Skye (and Davison and Tiffany and little Junior) would heroically rally to fight for her freedom. And in the meantime, of course, they'd all need someplace to stay. Donnie wouldn't dream of turning them away...

"Okay, I'm going back to the house." I stood up.

"Good. Thank you, Molly. I'm glad you're coming home. You're making the right decision."

"I'm just going to grab some fresh clothes. I might be at the Lehua Inn for a while."

The mail hadn't arrived yet, but there was a brown paper parcel from Donnie's laundry service on the front porch. I picked it up and let myself into the house. The rental car was gone, so Skye and Gloria were out somewhere. Strategizing with Alika Feinman, I hoped. Squawky noises and bilious aromas signaled Junior was home, with (presumably) at least one of his parents.

I set the parcel down on the kitchen counter, took out my phone, and dialed Emma's number. It clicked over to voicemail.

"Emma, it's me. Listen. I know who—"

Wait. Donnie had said, "Skye keeps rattling on about how the police are spying on us." Skye might be paranoid, but that didn't mean he was wrong. Someone could be listening in right now.

"Emma, I need to talk to you. It's about the, um, the set of slipcovers I was going to order? It's urgent. Please call me back now. I'm at the house, heading out to—uh, the hotel I like."

That was probably more secrecy than necessary. The Lehua Inn's desk clerk had recognized me right away. By this time, half of Mahina probably knew I was staying there.

I picked up the laundry parcel and took it back into the master bedroom. After the tense conversation Donnie and I had just had, I felt like doing something nice for him. I could put away his shirts, sparing him a minor inconvenience when he came home later.

I tore off the brown paper to find a dozen red Donnie's Drive-Inn polo shirts, Size Large. Each one had been cleaned and pressed, hung on a paper-wrapped wire hanger, and sheathed in clear plastic. The twelve wire hangers were fastened together with a rubber band, from which hung a white letter-sized envelope. Gonsalves was written across the envelope in black marker.

I hung up the shirts, and then pulled the envelope off. Hey, it just said Gonsalves on it, not Donnie Gonsalves. The flap was sealed shut. Inside was something substantial, bigger than just a stray button. The contents seemed heavy for their size, and slithered as I tipped the envelope back and forth. I tore open the flap and dumped the contents onto the bed.

My platinum necklace and earrings gleamed on the white duvet cover. The delicate ribbon of the necklace was bent in one spot. Otherwise, the jewelry looked unharmed. Not only that, it was sparkling clean from a trip through the laundry's industrial washing machines.

I stood, flummoxed, for a few moments. Then it came back to me. I'd put the jewelry on top of the dresser in anticipation of going out that evening. Donnie had folded his used shirts and stacked them on the same dresser. When I'd swept the shirts into the cleaner's bag, the necklace and earrings must have gone with them.

Had I accused Davison of this theft outright, I would owe him an apology. Of course I hadn't, so I didn't. I went to the closet and pulled out a few of my own shirts, an extra pair of trousers, and some underwear. I placed the necklace and earrings back in the envelope and rolled the envelope inside my bundle of clothes. Then I tucked the bundle under my arm, closed the front door quietly behind me, and hurried back down to the library to get my car.

I pulled into the lot of the Lehua Inn and jogged into the lobby. This hotel room was an investment in my mental health, and I was going to get my money's worth. Skeptical husbands, ungrateful sisters-in-law, and crooked cops could do their worst. I was going to enjoy a relaxing afternoon reading a mystery novel in my room. Afterward, room service and another heavenly night of uninterrupted sleep.

Housekeeping had already tidied my room and made the bed. Every surface sparkled. Even the potted orchid looked clean. I plugged in my phone to charge and hung up my fresh clothes in the closet. Then I pulled out the white envelope with my jewelry still in it. I opened the night table drawer and tucked it into the back, behind the Mahina phone book, the Protestant Gideon Bible, and The Teaching of Buddha.

I longed to crawl between the crisp sheets, but like Esther Greenwood in The Bell Jar, I couldn't bear to do it without getting cleaned up first. Walking from the library to Donnie's and then up to my house and back to the library had been sweaty work. I went into the bathroom and took a long, luxurious shower. I toweled off and slipped my clean body into clean sweats and a fresh t-shirt. It felt marvelous. I wrapped the towel around my hair turban-style to soak up the extra moisture and opened the bathroom door.

To see Andy De Silva standing there. Right in my room, with his fist raised, as if to knock on the bathroom door. Or strike me.

CHAPTER FIFTY

I SLAMMED THE BATHROOM door shut and locked it.

"Professor?" I heard De Silva say through the door.

How had he found out? Donnie must have called Gloria and told her about my suspicions. And Gloria, heedless of her safety or mine, must have called De Silva right away, telling him she was onto him and blabbing everything.

De Silva would have denied it, of course. But then he came right down here, looking for me. He was wearing an aloha shirt and trousers, not his uniform. This was a bad sign. It meant he wasn't on duty. He was here on his own time.

"Professor?" He knocked on the door. "It's me. Andy De Silva."

"How did you get in?" I yelled.

"Your room door was open."

He was lying. Or maybe he wasn't lying. I'd been having trouble pulling that heavy door shut. Had I made sure to close it all the way when I came in? I couldn't remember now.

He knocked again.

"Professor? You got a minute?"

I had stupidly assumed that I would be safe from the outside world here. And now look.

Instead of protecting me, the hotel staff had probably told him exactly which room I was staying in. If I lived through this, I'd never hear the end of it from Donnie.

"Professor, please. I gotta talk to you."

"How did you know I was staying here?" I shouted through the door.

"Went by the Drive-Inn, talked to your husband just now."

He certainly didn't seem too worried about covering his tracks. Maybe he was planning to go back and murder Donnie, too. Or perhaps he'd already murdered Donnie, once he had the information he needed.

I considered yelling for help, but it was no good. The Lehua Inn was sturdy. Even at close range, De Silva's voice was muffled by the solid door between us.

My phone. Where was my phone? Out in the room. On the night table. Charging.

I had to signal for help somehow. Maybe if I banged on the faucet, it would set the pipes ringing. I had to hit it with something hard. The most solid-looking object in the bathroom was the blow dryer. I picked it up and brought it down hard on the faucet.

The first two times I hit the faucet with the blow dryer, it made an unimpressive plinking noise. On the third hit, a big plastic piece broke off and skittered across the floor.

This obviously wasn't going to work.

"Professor?" De Silva called. "You okay?"

"I'm getting help. You'd better leave right now."

"What?"

I stopped the bathtub drain and opened the faucet to full volume. Then I plugged in the blow dryer and turned it on. The cord was long enough. Maybe I could get the attention of hotel security by plunging the Lehua Inn into darkness. When the tub had filled to a depth of about six inches, I switched on the blow dryer. Despite having a piece broken off, it was still working. I held the roaring blow dryer in both hands and tossed it into the tub, bracing for an explosion.

Instead, I heard a click as the dryer shut off. The safety mechanism was working flawlessly. Great.

I unplugged the dryer, fished it out of the bathtub, shook the water off, and placed it back on the counter.

The bathtub. I could flood the place. It would take a while, but when water started dripping into the room below, surely someone would come up to investigate. I would still have a chance to escape with my life, if not my dignity.

More knocking.

"Professor, you okay? Your husband was worried about you, you know."

Sure he was, you murdering liar.

I stuffed a washcloth into the tub's overflow hole, opened the faucet, and watched the water rush out and fill the tub. When it got to a depth of about six inches, it was no longer colorless. It was a luminous greenish blue, like my Thunderbird. That's why the color's called aqua, because it's the color of water. If I lived through this, I could share my mildly interesting observation with Emma.

The water in the tub brimmed and then sloshed over the side.

"I'm flooding the place," I called out.

De Silva didn't answer me. I pressed my ear to the door, hoping he wouldn't shoot through it. I heard voices, albeit faintly.

De Silva had brought an accomplice with him? This was even worse than I thought.

I sat on the closed toilet, cross legged, and watched the water gush over the side of the tub. It coursed across the floor in waves and disappeared under the door. Sorry, Lehua Inn management, you're going to have to replace the carpet. But it's better than having to mop up a murder scene, right?

De Silva was banging on the door again. I squeezed my eyes shut and hugged my knees tight. I'd wait him out. As long as he didn't start shooting, I'd be fine.

Then I heard someone else with him, and the pounding intensified. I thought the door was going to rattle off its hinges.

"Molly. You crazy or what?"

I stared at the door.

"Emma?"

CHAPTER FIFTY-ONE

I PULLED THE PLUG ON the bathtub to let it drain.

Andy De Silva, Emma, and I pulled all the fresh towels down from the rack and laid them on the floor to soak up the water.

"We should open the sliding door," Emma said. "Let the room dry out."

Andy hurried over to open the door to the balcony.

"Molly."

"What?"

"What were you doing in the bathroom?"

I glanced at De Silva, who was struggling with the lock on the sliding door.

"He showed up in my room. I was alone and trying to signal for help. What would you have done, Emma?"

De Silva yanked the door all the way open and came back to join us, trailing a warm breeze from outside.

"Aw, sorry, ah Professor? Didn't mean to scare you."

"I wasn't supposed to be scared by a man lurking outside my bathroom door? What was I supposed to think?"

"Sorry," he repeated.

"Officer De Silva called me, you know." Emma tapped her temple. "He thought you'd lost it."

"How did you know to call Emma?" I asked him.

"I redialed the last number on your phone. I got Professor Nakamura."

"Oh, now you're picking up the phone, Emma? Wait a minute. Officer, if you thought I'd 'lost it,' why didn't you call for backup or something? In fact, why aren't you in uniform? You're not on duty, are you?"

"Can we talk about this somewhere else?" De Silva looked uncomfortable. "It's all wet in here."

I didn't realize how hungry I was until we walked into the pancake-scented Lehua Inn Coffee Shop. Emma and I scooted into one side of the booth. Andy De Silva sat opposite, facing us. We all ordered coffee and pie.

"Eh, nice earrings," Emma said. "Those the ones you thought Davison took?"

"Yes, they're the same earrings. I didn't want to leave them in the room."

"Those the earrings you reported missing?" De Silva looked them over. "Lucky they turned up."

"Well?" Emma propped her elbows on the Formica tabletop. "Who's gonna tell me what's going on?"

"Sorry, Professor Barda. Didn't know you'd get so scared when I showed up. I just wanted to talk to you about Gloria. She's in big trouble, you know."

"Eh," Emma chimed in. "How come you're asking Molly about it? If anyone can help her, it's you, officer."

"I wanna help her. But cannot."

"How can that be?" I asked. "She has a friend on the force, the best lawyer money can buy, and the least sympathetic victim imaginable."

De Silva shook his head hopelessly.

"You really want to help Gloria?" I asked.

He nodded.

"Not watch her rot in prison?"

"Prison?" He looked stunned. "Why would I want that? I lo—I don't want her to go to prison."

"Officer De Silva. Why did you sneak into my room?"

"I didn't sneak. You didn't answer when I knocked, and the door was open, so I came in. I wanted to talk to you."

"Why me? I'm not a lawyer."

"Yeah," Emma echoed. "Why her?"

"Look. Remember when you told us in the class what to do when you got a difficult problem that needs a creative solution? You gotta get different people on it, with their diverse points of view and life experiences."

"I did say that." I nodded.

"So that's what I'm doing. Hoping you could help."

"You're asking for my help?"

"Exactly, yeah."

"Uh oh," Emma said.

"I have some information, officer. But I'm not sure it'll help Gloria. I saw her flight itinerary.

She came into Mahina a couple of days before she showed up at our house. And no one knows where she was when Iulani Malufau was killed. Not even her husband. Or her lawyer."

"Yeah, we know all about it."

"You do?"

"It's how come she's in trouble to begin with. She gave a false statement to the police as to her whereabouts. If it wasn't for that, they mighta wrote it off as an accident. But her giving the contradictory statement made everyone suspicious."

"Why'd she do something so dumb as lie to the police?" Emma demanded.

De Silva's voice was soft.

"She didn't have a choice, you know. When her ex escaped, Gloria was worried he might come after her brother."

"He was going to come after Donnie?" I said.

"And the boy, too. She thought Davison was safe at his college on the mainland. But when she called here to warn her brother, you answered the phone, Professor. Remember? You told her the boy was right here in Mahina. Staying at your house, even."

"She flew out here and killed da kine to protect Davison?" Emma said.

"Nah, nah, nah. She never killed him. She came to me for help."

"You killed 'em then," Emma said.

"No," De Silva objected. "I never."

"She was with you, wasn't she?" I said. "The days she was missing. She was the woman you were with at the Pair-O-Dice."

De Silva nodded and stared into his coffee.

"I'm Gloria's alibi. That's how come the missing day and a half. She wasn't killing Iulani Malufau. Neither was I. But we cannot tell anyone."

"How come you're telling Molly, then?" Emma demanded.

"He's telling you too, Emma," I pointed out.

"Maybe she can figure out how to stop all this without Gloria getting in trouble. Professor Barda's family. She sees Gloria every day. And I can trust her."

I was about to thank De Silva when he added, "The consulting contract has a confidentiality clause. I know Professor Barda's not gonna tell anyone about our conversation. She'd get sued, that's why."

CHAPTER FIFTY-TWO

EMMA TURNED TO GLOWER at me. "Molly, did you even read that thing before you signed it?"

"Emma, I always keep class discussion confidential. We all have to, because of FERPA. Why would I think this would be any different? Oh, and you can't say anything about this conversation either, because it might get traced back to me."

"Why'd you even sign up for that stupid community speaker da kine anyway?"

"Listen, I've learned my lesson."

"Never volunteer."

"Emma, I know."

"Professors," De Silva interrupted. "I'm not trying to make trouble. But you gotta help me."

"So let me get the timeline straight," I said. "Gloria called to warn Donnie that her ex had escaped—"

"She gotta do this every time," Emma stage-whispered to De Silva. "She got a real orderly mind, OCD kine."

"Emma, you're not helping. Anyway, when I told Gloria Davison was in Mahina, she decided to come here in person. Because she was afraid for Davison. But she didn't bother to tell Donnie. Even though it would've been the first time they'd seen each other in years."

De Silva nodded, encouraging me to go on.

"Why wouldn't she let Donnie know she was on her way? Why didn't she tell me, 'Thanks, I think I will take you up on your invitation to visit Mahina'?"

"'Cause your husband's such a boy scout, he'd never help her get rid of her ex like she wanted," Emma said. "He'd tell her, 'Leave it to the authorities. They'll take care of it. Don't get involved.'"

"Too true." I sighed. "So officer, when you found the body, did you know it was Malufau before I identified him?"

He shook his head. "I didn't even recognize 'em until you said it was him. He didn't look much like his picture by the time we found 'em."

"How did you know it was him?" Emma asked.

"I recognized his clothes first. I'd rather not think about it, if you don't mind."

"Fine. So officer, Gloria comes to you, says eh big boy, help me get rid of my pilau ex, and then?"

"I couldn't do anything for her. There already was an alert out for Malufau. Wasn't much more I could do than tell Gloria we were already looking for him."

"I can't imagine she was satisfied," I said. "So what happened?"

"I told her, 'Stay with me as long as you want.' Then right afterward, her husband Skye showed up in Mahina, and then you made the call reporting her missing. She knew she had to leave my place then, so she went over to your guys' house."

"You must have known her husband would notice that she was missing," I said. "Did you know she was married?"

"Did she?" Emma chimed in.

"Aw, come on. We knew it wasn't right. It was just—you know how it goes. She called me, said she was here, and could I get her at the airport. We started talking about old times, kinda reconnecting like, and then you know how it is, yeah?"

"No," Emma and I said in unison.

"So you're Gloria's sole alibi?" I asked.

"Right. I am her alibi. But I cannot say nothing. Unless I wanna ruin her life."

"You two should come clean," Emma said. "You know what'll ruin her life? Spending the rest of it in prison."

"You could say you were with her," I suggested. "That doesn't mean you were with her. People won't necessarily assume the worst."

De Silva looked hangdog.

"The husband doesn't trust me."

"Why not?" I asked.

De Silva's cheeks flushed pink.

Emma widened her eyes at him.

"Oh, you and Gloria hooked up before?"

De Silva tugged on his collar.

"Me and her go way back, you know. We got a connection, like. So, Professor, what can I do?"

"I really don't know what to tell you, officer. I'm stumped."

"You gotta think of something. Please." He glanced up at the coffee shop's wall clock. "I gotta go report for my shift. Sorry again for the misunderstanding, Professor Barda."

When De Silva left, Emma moved to the other side of the booth, facing me.

"Thanks for coming down to rescue me," I said.

"You didn't need to be rescued from De Silva. He called me when you tried to flood the hotel. If anything, I rescued you from your own lolo self."

"How was I supposed to know De Silva was harmless?"

"Yeah, fair enough. Sure, I'll take the credit for saving your life. Oh thanks, ah?"

Emma and I moved our cups out to the edge of the table so the waitress could refill them.

"I was sure De Silva was the murderer." I took a sip of the coffee. The mild Kona blend paired perfectly with the luscious apple pie. "And I really thought he was framing Gloria. I guess it was silly to think he'd been holding a grudge since high school."

"Nah, that's not silly. There's still people I hate from preschool."

"Well, his story fills in a lot of gaps. Gloria was with De Silva between the time she landed at Mahina Airport and the time she showed up at our house, so there's one mystery solved. And it explains why she won't tell anyone where she was. At least not while her husband is around."

"So speaking of husbands," Emma said. "You gonna stay here another night avoiding Donnie or what?"

"I should at least call him. Tell him Gloria has an alibi."

"You really wanna tell Donnie his sister's been cheating on her husband?"

"What, am I supposed to keep it to myself?"

"Yes, you're supposed to keep it to yourself. Cause look. Either Donnie already knows, or he doesn't." Emma counted off the possibilities on her stubby fingers. "If he already knows about it, he's just gonna be upset you found out about it, too. And if he doesn't, and you're the one to tell him, how do you think he's gonna take it? Ever heard of shooting the messenger?"

"Good point. And what can he do about it, anyway? Nothing. Maybe I should talk to Gloria directly."

"Nah, Molly, don't do it. She already knows she has an alibi. If she doesn't wanna use it, that's her business. I mean, if it was me, I'd come clean, and just take the consequences with my husband finding out."

"Wait a minute," I said. "Gloria can't come clean."

"Why not? Of course she can. She's just gonna have a lotta 'splaining to do."

"No, because Skye's parents are the ones who are paying for her fancy lawyer. If it comes out she was spending the night with her old boyfriend, I doubt the parents will keep footing the bill for Alika Feinman."

"Oh, the in-laws. Yeah, that's a whole 'nother kettle of worms."

"Fish," I said. "Kettle of fish. And 'nother isn't a word."

"Aw, come on Molly, that doesn't make any sense. What's bad about a kettle of fish? A kettle of worms, now that's gross. Geez, and here you are an English major and everything. Anyway, my point is, if Gloria admits she was with Andy De Silva, her rich in-laws are gonna stop paying for her fancy lawyer, and then she's sunk for sure."

"That wasn't your point, Emma. It was my point."

"So you gonna go home and tell Donnie about this or what?"

"No, you're right. Donnie doesn't want to hear it. And I don't want to go back home tonight."

"You at least gonna tell him you found the earrings and the necklace?"

"Eventually."

CHAPTER FIFTY-THREE

I MET EMMA AS USUAL after Mass the next day. I should have been in a buoyant mood, having enjoyed another night of uninterrupted sleep at the Lehua Inn, but I missed Donnie. Emma was the only customer in the Pair-O-Dice. She had a copy of the Sunday paper and a pitcher of beer in front of her.

"You read the paper today?" she asked as I sat down.

"No. I drove right over to Mass, and then came here. I didn't see De Silva at Mass, by the way."

"Probably too shame to show his face after yesterday. You hear from Donnie?"

"I saw he sent a text yesterday afternoon saying De Silva was looking for me and he hoped I was safe."

"You talk to him at all?"

"No. I was afraid if I called him, he'd take the opportunity to scold me for staying another night at the hotel."

Emma smoothed out the newspaper in front of her. "You know the picture of the cock-a-roach in the Kung Pao Pizza Roll? At Chang's Pizza Pagoda?"

"Oh. Don't remind me. Yes, the one that drove all the customers back to Donnie's Drive-Inn."

"It's on the front page." Emma pushed the Sunday paper over to my side of the wobbly little table. The below-the-fold headline read, Chang's Pizza Pagoda Victim of Corporate Sabotage.

"They did some CSI stuff on the photo and found out it's a fake."

"The County Courier did? I'm impressed. How?"

"It wasn't too hard, actually. The location was embedded in the photo. Chang's got some kind of experts to look at the post, and they found that it wasn't even sent from Chang's. The location information placed it at a 'major competitor.'"

"Oh, no. I knew this would happen."

"Well they didn't come right out and say who the 'major competitor' was."

"Emma, everyone's going to know who it is. The County Courier doesn't have to spell it out. Come on, this is Mahina. Donnie's rotten kid just destroyed the family business."

"Yeah, I know. Sorry, Molly. This is really gonna test your 'for better or for worse' clause, huh?"

"Yeah. It is. Maybe I should make an effort to be extra nice to Donnie right now."

After the Pair-O-Dice, I stopped by the Drive-Inn. It was still crowded, so the news of Davison's sabotage apparently hadn't become common knowledge just yet. I ordered a diet soda and stood next to the pickup window until a space opened at one of the picnic tables.

Donnie eventually came out to say hello, looking grumpier than ever.

"Business is still good," I said. "That's a relief."

"It doesn't matter. My wife isn't here to help me celebrate my success. What happened to for better or for worse?"

"Whoa, deja vu. Donnie, I'm not abandoning you. I just wanted to get some sleep. That's all. Although my stay at the Lehua Inn hasn't been quite as peaceful as I'd hoped."

"Molly, are you sure you really want a baby? If Junior makes you want to run away from home, maybe motherhood isn't for you."

"Junior's adorable," I said. "Really. But if I'm going to have my life expectancy shortened, and make no mistake, having kids is associated with a shortened lifespan, I'll do it for my own kid. You can't expect me to take years off of my life for someone else's."

"I was looking into the sleep thing," Donnie said. "There's something called a white noise machine. It puts out constant noise to drown out things like babies crying and toilets flushing. If you can sleep through the traffic on Hotel Drive, maybe it can help you."

"You were researching ways to help me sleep?"

"I was. Molly, of course I want you to be able to sleep through the night. And I want you back home with me. Yes, I miss you."

"Oh. Well, thank you for saying it. I miss you, too."

"Did Andy De Silva find you, by the way? He was looking for you. I had to tell him you were staying at a hotel."

"I'm sure he had more important things on his mind than passing judgment on our marriage. Yes, he found me."

"What did he want?"

"He wants to help your sister, Donnie. He was hoping I could think of something. That's all. By the way, did you see today's paper? About a competitor sabotaging Chang's with that cockroach photo?"

"M hm. I already knew about it."

"You did?"

"We've hardly talked about anything else at the MRA meetings."

"The what?"

"The Mahina Restaurant Association. Whoever uploaded the picture really messed up. They didn't realize the location information was embedded in the photo."

"Did you say 'whoever' uploaded the photo? They haven't traced it back to an individual yet?"

"No, but the location was Merrie Musubis."

"See, I knew this would…did you say Merrie Musubis?"

"Merrie's management says they had nothing to do with it, but they can't deny the evidence. They're going to have to pay a settlement to Chang's and publish a public apology. Molly, are you okay?"

"Wow. I guess he's smarter than I thought."

"What? Who are you talking about?"

"What? Oh, I was just thinking about what you said. About the, uh, the noise machine. The one to help me sleep. In fact, I'm going to stop by the store and get one right now. I'll bet Galimba's has them."

"Does this mean you're coming home?"

"Yes. Is it okay if I put the noise machine in our bedroom?"

"Of course it's okay."

I stood up, leaned over the table, and planted a kiss on Donnie's mouth. It seemed to catch him by surprise.

"I have to run, Donnie. Checkout time's at noon."

I dropped my suitcase in the bedroom and went out to the kitchen to get myself a glass of wine. Davison was at the sink, running hot water over a baby bottle to warm it.

"Did you see today's paper?" I asked him.

"Nuh uh. Too busy wit' Junior."

I uncorked a new bottle of Sangiovese. "It's on the front page. You posted the picture of the Chang's pizza roll from Merrie Musubi and left the geolocation on. You slandered Chang's, and implicated Merrie Musubis. You hurt your father's two major competitors in one go."

"Dunno what you're talking about, Molly. That's like evil genius three-dimensional chess kine stuff. You think it was me, did all that?"

"It was clever, I have to admit." I filled up my sixteen-ounce Chicken Boy mug about halfway.

"Eh, Molly, there's real wineglasses up there."

"This is my preferred stemware."

"You can call it stemware when it doesn't gotta stem?"

"I don't know. And stop trying to change the subject. Listen. You have to be a role model now. For Junior. It's not just about you anymore."

"Molly." Davison shook the contents of the bottle onto his wrist. Satisfied with the temperature, he shut off the water and turned to me. "It wasn't me. I'm serious. Guarantee."

It took me a minute to register what he meant.

"Wait a minute. You're not saying...Tiffany?"

He shrugged.

"Are you trying to tell me Tiffany Balusteros is the mastermind behind this?"

"How come you don't believe me?"

"Davison, Tiffany tried to tell me once that the sun isn't a star because stars have five points."

"Eh, maybe she's not some big-time astrologer, but she's real smart, that girl."

"Astronomer," I said, but Davison had already gone back into the guest room.

CHAPTER FIFTY-FOUR

IT WAS NICE TO BE BACK in my own bathroom, with all of my familiar unguents and supplies. I moved my head from side to side and watched the earrings sway and catch the light. They were a simple design. A round cut diamond at the earlobe with a long baguette suspended from it and a teardrop-sized diamond hanging from the bottom of the baguette. The necklace was a delicate platinum ribbon studded with tiny diamonds.

I had assumed Donnie had inherited the parure from his mother. But his parents had been taken suddenly. They hadn't made a will, and probably hadn't even thought about the disposition of family heirlooms.

It was much more likely, I realized, that the set came from Uncle Brian's Royal Pawn inventory.

"I found such pretty things there," Jennifer's auntie had said, in the Galimba's Bargain Boyz checkout line. "Better than the other stores. Nicer things even than Modern Jewelers sometimes."

I removed my earrings and unclasped the necklace. I held the jewelry in my hand, admiring how the diamonds sparkled under the bright pinpoint lights. I snapped open the velvet box and carefully replaced them. I hadn't given it a second thought at the time, but now I wondered: Why did Uncle Brian's pawnshop have a better selection than the other stores? Maybe it didn't. Maybe Jennifer's auntie had simply fancied Uncle Brian, and her assessment of the wares on offer at Royal Pawn was the result of some kind of halo effect.

Still, I thought it might be worth following up.

I dug out my phone and called Pat. This time he picked up. I caught him up on everything that had happened so far, shoving aside any concerns about any confidentiality contracts I may have signed.

"Did you try to search for information at all?" he asked.

"I've been staying at a hotel. I didn't have internet there."

"Why were you at a hotel? You and Donnie finally getting divorced?"

"No, we are not getting a divorce. I was dealing with chronic sleep deprivation, and I had to do something. It turns out, it's hard to get your beauty rest with a crying baby in the house, not to mention four self-centered adult houseguests. Actually, Skye's okay. I should say three self-centered houseguests and one bewildered brother-in-law who's probably wondering what kind of nightmare he married into."

"That's harsh," Pat snickered.

"Sorry. Anyway, don't you have special journalist access to some database of court cases?"

"My special journalist access is I pay the subscription fee. Do you know the district or circuit where the case was filed?"

"No idea. Whatever it would be for Mahina, I guess. Although maybe I shouldn't assume Malufau only operated in Mahina. In fact, the robberies must have taken place somewhere else. I'm sure he didn't want buyers in Mahina recognizing their stolen jewelry."

"Okay, I have his name. I can use the case locator to narrow it down."

I heard tapping noises in the background.

"Hey, Molly, speaking of stolen jewelry, you ever find yours?"

"Oh, the jewelry. In fact I did find it."

"Where was it?"

"It's a long story."

"Here he is," Pat said. "Bingo. Ooh, assault, terroristic threatening, abuse of a family or household member, extortion. Nice guy, your stepson's dad."

"So? Was he active outside of Mahina?"

"He had one case over in Honolulu District Court. And before that, one in Maui. And those are just the times he got caught. Yeah, just from what I can see here, it looks like Malufau was operating all over the state. Not just in Mahina."

As soon as Pat rang off, I called Mahina PD, and left a message for Officer Andrew De Silva. Then I called Emma.

CHAPTER FIFTY-FIVE

EMMA PARKED IN FRONT of my house, and together we made the short walk downtown to Brian Gonsalves' apartment building. It was a 1960s stucco box with lava rock siding, the walls surrounding a dim interior courtyard. In the alcove, an ancient black label with raised white letters indicated Uncle Brian's apartment number. A locked gate blocked our access to the stairs. Emma and I loitered innocently and then slipped in behind the next person that came in, a young man in a fast-food uniform.

Uncle Brian seemed pleased to see us, and not at all surprised.

"Nice to see you again, Sherry." He grinned, showing off his perfect dentures, and gestured us inside.

"Molly," I corrected him.

"I'm Brian." He clasped Emma's tiny hand in both of his. "Brian Gonsalves. Donnie's uncle. Although Donnie, don't see him much no more. His boy Davison, but. Good boy, him. Getting married, you know. Gotta keiki too, him."

"Nice to meet you Uncle. Emma Nakamura."

"Nakamura? Oh, you're Masuo's girl. You still working at the pakalolo clinic?"

"No, that's my brother Jonah. I teach at the university."

"Ah, right. You're the smart one."

"You going somewhere, Uncle?" Emma asked. She indicated the hard-sided red suitcase sitting by the front door.

"Yeah, I'm going Vegas. Taxi's gonna be here any minute. You girls like a quick drink?"

"Sure." Emma caught my look. "I mean, no. No, it's okay."

My genius plan now didn't seem so bright. Emma and I were standing in this man's apartment, unarmed, and where was Officer De Silva? I went ahead anyway.

"Your niece, Gloria's ex, Iulani Malufau, is dead," I said.

He shook his head and clucked disapprovingly.

"I tried to tell her the boy was no good, but she never listen. 'You're not my father,' that's what she said to me. 'You're not my father.' She shoulda stayed with the other boy, Andy. I liked Andy. Nice family. Father was a policeman, you know."

"They arrested Gloria for murder," Emma said.

This seemed to come as a surprise to Uncle Brian.

"Little Glory?" He stepped back from the door and sank down on the shabby tan couch that dominated the tiny living room. "They arrested Glory?"

"Uncle Brian, if there's anything you know to help her?"

He gestured at us impatiently. "Sit down, girls. Sit down."

Emma and I took our seats in two Danish Modern style chairs across the low coffee table from where Brian sat.

"Gloria didn't kill anyone. If Iulani fell out of a window, it was his own fault. I would consider the possibility the man must have had too much to drink."

Emma and I looked at each other.

"Uncle, how'd you know Iulani fell out a window?"

"You must've told me, 'as why."

"I'll be honest," Emma said. "Sounds like the world's a better place without Iulani Malufau in it."

"He was a nasty piece of work," I agreed.

"A what?" Brian Gonsalves said.

"Pilau," Emma explained.

"Exactly," I agreed. "He seems like the kind of guy who would break out of prison, track down his former business partner, and try to shake him down for money. No one would blame the former business partner for trying to defend himself. I believe it's called justifiable homicide."

"Young lady," Brian said mildly. "That is quite an accusation. Are you saying I killed the boy?"

"If you was over at his place, they can tell now, you know," Emma said. "All they need is to find one little hair or skin cell or something. If you was there, you cannot keep it secret."

That police-procedural level of scrutiny wasn't going to happen, of course. Malufau's death was just another run-of-the-mill domestic as far as the prosecutor's office was concerned. The room where Malufau had spent his last minutes on earth had already been rented to someone else. Uncle Brian didn't know that, though.

"Greedy baga," Brian Gonsalves sighed. "Mean, too. Never could hold his liquor, though."

A soft beep sounded from the street, and the old man rose to his feet.

"There's my taxi. California Hotel, here I come. Eh, you wish me good luck, ah?"

He shooed us out of the apartment in front of him and refused our offers to help with his luggage. We followed him down the stairs and watched him climb into the cab. It took the driver several tries to shut the taxi's trunk over Uncle Brian's massive suitcase.

"Looks like he packed for a long trip," Emma said. "You think he's still got some of the jewelry from back in the day? When he was running the pawn shop?"

"I'm sure he does. In fact, I'll bet Uncle Brian gave Davison the enormous engagement ring Tiffany's wearing. No way could Davison afford a huge diamond like that by himself."

"Yeah. Seems like he's pretty close to Davison."

"From what I can tell, Davison's the only family member who's still speaking to him. So De Silva never showed up." I glanced down the empty street.

"That's okay. You want that old geezer in prison? Anyways, with De Silva here, Uncle never woulda told us what he told us."

Emma and I stood on the sidewalk and watched the tiny white taxi drive off in the direction of Mahina Airport.

"I'm going to call the police department again." I fumbled in my bag for my phone. "I should've gotten De Silva's direct number."

"No need. Speak of the devil."

A police cruiser pulled up and parked next to us on a stripe of red curb in front of a fire hydrant. De Silva stepped out and joined us on the sidewalk.

"Got your message," he said to me. "What's going on?"

"You know Brian Gonsalves?" I said. "Gloria's uncle?"

"Uncle Brian? Yeah, sure. What about him?"

"Uncle was there when Malufau fell out the window an' wen' makē." Emma completely ruined the buildup I had planned. "He get all buss, that's why. Probably uncle's home brewed Okolehao."

"That Okolehao is amazing," I agreed. "You drink it, and you think you're fine, until you stand up and your knees start bending the wrong way."

De Silva pulled out a note pad, all business now. "You're saying Brian Gonsalves was present when Iulani Malufau died?"

"You got it," Emma said.

"We think Brian Gonsalves and Iulani Malufau were working together. Malufau stole jewelry from high-end resorts and private planes, and Uncle Brian sold the stolen merchandise in Royal Pawn. When Malufau went to prison, it broke Royal Pawn's supply chain, which is why he closed the store."

"Then Malufau escaped and came back to shake down Uncle Brian. Probably thought Uncle owed him. It was self-defense, though. You're not gonna put an old man in prison for defending himself, are you, officer?"

"Where's Brian Gonsalves now?" De Silva asked. "Is he here in the building?"

"You just missed him," Emma said. "He's going Vegas. Eh, if I had good luck like him, that's where I'd be headed too."

De Silva hurried back to the cruiser and leaned into the driver's side.

"They'll intercept him at the airport," De Silva said when he came back "But I don't know if they'll want to pursue this. The prosecutor thinks he has a good case against Gloria. If Brian Gonsalves won't corroborate your story... I guess we wait and see."

Emma reached into her back jeans pocket and pulled out a pen.

"Maybe this'll help."

"Is that your pen recorder?" I asked. "You had it on the whole time? Is that legal?"

"Yeah, in Hawai`i only one party has to agree to recording. I checked with the university lawyers before I started carrying this around to record my whining students. Here, officer. Play this for whoever needs to hear it. Just make sure you get it back to me."

Emma handed De Silva the pen recorder. He studied it for a couple of seconds and then slipped it into his shirt pocket.

CHAPTER FIFTY-SIX

THE CASE AGAINST GLORIA was dropped within the week. Emma's recording persuaded the prosecutor that Iulani Malufau's death was accidental, and that Gloria was not even present. Uncle Brian was able to relocate to Hawai`i's "ninth island" without incident. I understand he's now a resident of the California Hotel in downtown Las Vegas. It's not cheap to live in a hotel, but I suspect the contents of his red suitcase will sustain him for a while.

Happily, Uncle Brian doesn't have to live out his golden years far from family. Tiffany is managing the new Las Vegas location of Balusteros Baby World. Davison is taking evening electronics classes at a local community college and watching Junior during the day.

I got my book chapter submitted a full week before the final due date. That evening, Donnie fixed us a celebratory meal of green salad with vinaigrette and pasta puttanesca. Afterward, we relaxed on the couch, sampling a fancy single-malt whisky Donnie had received as a Christmas gift from one of his vendors.

"It feels strange to relax." I took a deep breath. "I feel like I should be working on something."

Donnie smiled and slung an arm across the back of the couch. "Spending quality time with your husband is important, too."

"You're right. And it's so nice to be here, just the two of us. I adore your family, of course, but it's such a relief to have the house to ourselves again."

"I'm really impressed with Alika Feinman. Things looked hopeless for Gloria, and then all of a sudden, all the charges were dropped. Molly, are you okay?"

I cleared my throat. "Sorry, this whiskey is really smoky. It tastes like burning tires to me. Sorry. I know it's really expensive. I guess I don't have very refined taste."

"Molly, what aren't you telling me?"

"Me?"

"You have a terrible poker face. This isn't about the whiskey. What do you know about Gloria?"

"Oh, Donnie, we don't have to talk about this now. I mean, everything worked out. Everyone's safe—"

"Molly, please. Don't keep things from me."

"Okay. Fine. You want to know? I'll tell you."

And I did. I told Donnie the whole story, including Gloria's shenanigans, Uncle Brian's confession, and my attempt to flood the Lehua Inn.

"So, you're telling me Gloria had an alibi the whole time? Why didn't she tell anyone?"

"Because if she told the truth, her in-laws would stop paying for her legal defense."

"And what made you think of Uncle Brian?"

"I figured it out after a woman we met at the birthing class, well, her aunty, told me Royal Pawn always had such nice things on offer, so much nicer than the other shops. I wondered why. Well, it turns out Uncle Brian had Malufau stealing jewelry from all over the state. From private planes, top resorts, people whose insurance would cover the theft. So, of course, no one in Mahina would ever recognize it as stolen merchandise."

"But how did you put it together? It's not obvious to me."

"Because of this." I touched the platinum necklace at my throat. "You got this jewelry from Uncle Brian, right?"

"No. I bought it from a respectable jeweler who specializes in estate pieces."

"Oh. Well, I guessed wrong about that part, then."

Donnie looked troubled. I should've kept my mouth shut. Whose bright idea was it anyway, couples telling each other everything?

"Donnie, look. Emma and I accomplished the impossible. We got your sister's murder charges dropped. Without revealing her bad behavior to her husband. We did what her lawyer couldn't. No one's in jail, and everyone can go on with their lives. Why are you acting grouchy about it?"

"Am I?" Donnie laughed. "I suppose I am. I'm sorry. I'm being, what's the word you like to use? Petty. I'm being petty."

"What do you mean?"

"Molly, I love Gloria. She's my baby sister, and I'd do anything for her. But one thing about her—maybe you didn't notice—she's a little bit spoiled. Entitled, I supposed is the word I'm looking for."

"You don't say."

"She does whatever she feels like doing at the moment, throws everyone else's life into chaos, and she gets away with it. Every time. This is just another example."

"Do you wish things had turned out differently?"

"No. Of course not. I feel a little sorry for Skye, though. You want me to get the Jameson?"

"I don't need any more whiskey. I'm fine."

"Here, let me get you a glass of wine."

"No, no, it's okay. I don't need wine."

"Did you just say you don't need wine? Molly, are you feeling all right?"

"Me? Mostly. I have been a little bit queasy. Especially in the mornings. Oh, Donnie, that reminds me. There is one more thing I need to tell you."

MOTHER'S DAY

MOTHER'S DAY

For my wonderful children, who would never dream of murdering me.

CHAPTER ONE

I WASN'T HAVING a great day. There was the usual beginning-of-semester chaos, of course. The last-minute scramble to hire adjunct instructors, the confused students caught between payment deadlines and late financial aid checks, and the ongoing struggle to interpret the administration's latest half-baked "student success" initiatives.

Now throw in an unexpected summons from administration, a case of round-the-clock "morning" sickness, and the coup de grâce: a call from my mother. Who thought I needed to be reminded (once again) how risky it was to have a child at my age.

"Although to be fair," she added, "they're finding out the father's age has something to do with it too. Donnie's no spring chicken either. That's why you have to be doubly careful. Molly, you sound like you're out of breath. Do you need to lie down and rest?"

"I'm fine," I panted. I didn't tell my mother I was marching in place, a tactic to disperse stress hormones. "And thank you for the helpful information, but I'm already pregnant. Listen, Mom, I'm kind of stressing out about this appointment with administration. I'm supposed to report to the Death Star in half an hour, so I—"

"Molly, I know it's tempting to poke fun at your administration, but please be wise. Things always get back to them. That's why I never say anything negative about our medical director, no matter how craven and incompetent he may be."

"Mom, I wasn't—"

"Really, dear, it's nice you have tenure, but those people know how to get around it. Mahina State's already the bottom of the barrel. Who's going to hire you if you lose your job there?"

Marching wasn't dissipating enough stress. I began doing high kicks, careful to avoid the living room furniture.

"Not that your father and I aren't immensely proud of you, dear, so please don't take it so negatively."

"We're real proud of you, sweet pea!" I heard my father shout in the background.

"And we think it's wonderful that your due date is Mother's Day. That way you won't forget the date again."

"Mom, it was that one time. I already said I was sorry."

"Of course, due dates are merely estimates, so don't be disappointed if Baby doesn't come exactly when you planned."

"I know that, Mom. Thanks."

"Well, the good news is that mixed-race children are healthier than average. They call it hybrid vigor. And the Polynesians are very strong people, so it seems you've made a good choice there."

"That's great, Mom."

"Also, they're finding the mother's education level tends to predict the children's life outcomes. So it's a good thing you have a Ph.D., even if it is only in English."

I switched from can-can kicks to deep-knee bends.

"Yes, it's actually good for something. Who would have guessed?"

"Let's hope it makes up for Donnie's being a dropout."

"He's not a dropout, he just never had time to go to college. Doesn't he get any points for, you know, building and running the most popular casual dining spot in Mahina?"

"I sent you a copy of *What to Expect When You're Expecting*. Did you get it?"

"Yes, I did, thank you. It's very thick."

"I tried to find a large print edition, but they don't make one. I imagine most new mothers aren't at the age yet where they need reading glasses. Do you want me to send you a pair of reading glasses?"

"I don't need you to send me reading glasses, but thank you for asking. Listen, Mom, I really have to go. The Death Star—I mean Victor Santiago's office does not tolerate tardiness."

I could never remember Victor Santiago's actual job title. As far as I could tell, his duties involved cozying up to potential donors and scolding faculty members whose unruly behavior threatened to tarnish our Institutional Image.

"Professor Barda." Victor half-rose as I entered his office and shook my hand, in precisely the way you'd greet someone you could barely stand. "Please. Have a seat."

I sat down as directed and stared at the plaque on Victor's desk, trying (once again) to memorize it:

Victor Santiago, (M.Ed., MBA) Vice-President for Student Outreach and Community Relations.

Alas, I'd forget it (again) as soon as I walked out the door.

"We're rolling out an exciting new program," Victor said, without any excitement whatsoever. Victor did not waste his charm on faculty members. "We call it the Young Leaders Program. It's a targeted, high-touch, boutique program for our valued student stakeholders."

"Sounds great."

"We're piloting the program this semester with a student named Jeremy Brigham. You're familiar with the Brigham family, I assume."

I shook my head.

"Jeremy's late father was Alexander Brigham, a direct descendant of Hiram Brigham."

"Hiram Brigham, of course." I vaguely recalled something about a planter son of a missionary who had married a Hawaiian princess. The confluence of money, land holdings, and political connections had catapulted the Brigham family into Hawaii's elite.

"Jeremy Brigham has had to withdraw from his classes due to illness."

"I'm sorry to hear it."

"Fortunately, under our new Young Leaders Program, Mr. Brigham will receive daily tutoring sessions to keep him on track for graduation."

"That sounds like a great idea," I said. "Very compassionate."

What does all this have to do with me? I wondered. If Jeremy Brigham were a management major, I'd know his name by now.

"Is Jeremy Brigham a management major?" I asked.

"No. Psychology. But they can't spare anyone, so we're inviting you to serve as Mr. Brigham's tutierge."

"Me? Excuse me, his what?"

"Tutierge. Tutor-Concierge."

"I see. Well, that's immensely flattering. But I'm the chair of the management department. Why would you choose me for such an important job?"

I wondered how Victor would manage to answer this question without saying anything positive about me. He did not disappoint.

"Your elective didn't fill. Your participation in our pilot of the Young Leaders Program gives you a way to discharge your teaching obligations. Without having to pay part of your salary back."

"Pay my...what? I thought I just had to do more research or something if my class didn't make. I have to pay my salary back if my class is canceled?"

"Your union agreed to the terms, Professor Barda. To those of us without tenure or summers off, it seems more than fair."

I didn't bother to reply that my summers were unpaid, which was very different from having summers off. Especially when I always got stuck doing work over the summer anyway. And tenure was great, but it didn't mean I couldn't get fired. It only meant the administration had to put in a little more paperwork to do it.

"No, that sounds great," I said. "I'd be thrilled. What am I teaching him?"

"Statistics."

"Stats? I've never even taken a stats class, let alone taught one."

"It won't be a problem for you. It's the intro class. I'll have my assistant send over your schedule and textbook. You and I will make the initial visit together. And remember, Professor Barda."

Victor fixed me with his unsmiling gaze.

"Your students don't care how much you know, until they know how much you care. We'll start on Monday. Meet me here at my office at seven-thirty."

"In the morning?"

"Yes. In the morning."

CHAPTER TWO

RUSSIAN ROAD WASN'T far from campus, and I would have been happy to meet Victor there. But he clearly didn't trust me to find my own way.

And he insisted on driving. I believe he would have preferred to commit seppuku rather than show up at a donor's house in my turquoise-and-white 1959 Thunderbird. I sat in the passenger seat of his Lexus and checked my email as he drove. Then I texted Donnie:

ME: With Victor from marketing. On my way to be a tutierge.

DONNIE: I know you'll do a great job. Darlene brought in a book for you.

ME: Who is Darlene?

DONNIE: the shift manager

ME: Is it what to expect etc.?

DONNIE: Yes how did you know?

ME: My mother sent me a copy already

DONNIE: I'll keep this one then. If your mother recommends it must be good. BTW she called me, would like you to call her back. Have to go. Love you.

Then I texted my friend Emma Nakamura. Between her paddling practice, her teaching schedule, and some book project she was working on, I hadn't seen much of her since the semester began.

ME: With Victor from marketing. On my way to be a tutierge.

EMMA: [emoji of a round yellow face, barfing].

As much as I loved my husband, sometimes Emma understood me better.

We turned onto Russian Road, the most beautiful neighborhood in Mahina (in my opinion, anyway). The mansions ranged from lacy white Victorians to earthy Craftsman bungalows with deep porches and tapered pillars. The vast, velvety lawns needed no sprinklers; Mahina had enough rainfall to keep the landscape green and vibrant. I cast a longing look at the old Brewster House as we drove by. At one time, I'd considered buying the Brewster House, and for a time, it seemed tantalizingly within reach. But alas, it was not to be. Pink Garisenda roses twined around the white pillars of the porte-cochere, and the mullioned French doors glittered in the morning sun. I reminded myself that my remodeled plantation house on Uakoko Street was perfectly nice, and tried my best not to boil with envy.

Victor drove in silence. Probably imagining all the ways I could screw up this deal, I thought.

"Are there any dos and don'ts for me to remember?" I asked. "I'm not really experienced with fundraising."

"We don't call it fundraising, Professor Barda. We call it friendraising."

I started to laugh, but a quick glance at Victor's stony profile made me choke it off immediately. He was not joking.

"Mrs. Brigham is a very distinguished member of our community and a great friend of the university. She's in poor health as well. I believe she's worse off than Jeremy, sadly. Ah. Here we are."

He pulled up in front of a vacant lot that was overgrown with sixty-foot-tall trees and garlanded with vines. We got out of the car, and I stared at the wall of jungle.

"Where's the house?" I asked.

"The Brigham House is right through there. There's a path to the front door."

Victor walked ahead of me and parted a curtain of vines.

"I don't see any ..."

"Follow me."

"Right. I'll follow you."

I could barely make out the black lava-rock stepping stones set into the ground, obscured as they were by moss and foliage. I watched my feet as I followed Victor down the overgrown path. Sure enough, there was a house there in the middle of the lot. It was neither Victorian nor Craftsman, but a simple design with a steep gabled roof, and walls of mortared black lava rock. It looked more like an old church than anything else.

Victor lifted the knocker, and then we waited.

The door was opened by a gray-haired man wearing a blue-and-gray aloha shirt and a stern expression.

"Please come with me." He led us a short way down a dark hallway and showed us into a cramped parlor.

Victor and I sat uncomfortably side by side on a koa bench that looked like a refurbished pew. Rather, I should say I was uncomfortable. Who knows what Victor was thinking?

"The man who let us in didn't introduce himself or ask us who we were," I said.

"They're expecting us," Victor replied, completely overlooking the fact that I might have liked to know who the man was.

I quickly traced the cloying odor that permeated the room to a dish of gardenias on the windowsill. I normally tolerated the scent of gardenias. But to my pregnancy-sensitized nose, it was the olfactory equivalent of getting handbagged with a giant bouquet. I wanted to take my phone out and check my e-mail to distract myself, but I didn't feel right doing that with Victor sitting right there.

I decided to amuse myself by trying to catalog the smells in the house. Aside from the gardenias, I picked up coffee, a trace of mildew, and a raw vegetal smell that reminded me of my grad-school roommate's green juice fasts.

The gray man materialized in the doorway.

"Bernardine is ready to meet you," he said.

Because Victor had warned me about Bernardine Brigham's failing health, I expected her to be bedridden. But she was in the kitchen, chopping vegetables.

I recognized her right away. Twenty years ago, Bernardine McCrae had modeled for a preppy label and cultivated a golden surfer-girl image. Now she had transformed her look to Bohemian Dowager. Her tan had faded, and she wore satin and crushed velvet in jewel tones. Her grey-streaked hair was piled atop her head in a way that invoked Klimt's Judith holding the Head of Holofernes. She had always been slim, of course, but now she was emaciated; her famous cheekbones looked like they could slice paper.

"Bernardine!" Victor beamed and held out his arms.

"Victor, darling!" She set down her chopping knife, embraced him, and offered her cheek. He kissed it.

"Please, sit down." She indicated the sturdy maple table that occupied the center of the kitchen.

"Bernardine, this is Professor Molly Barda," Victor said as we seated ourselves. "She's the chair of the management department, and one of our most popular teachers."

The last part was news to me. I assumed Victor was improvising.

Bernardine briefly acknowledged me and then turned her attention back to Victor, who had apparently flipped his personality switch to "on" the minute we entered the kitchen. He asked Bernardine about her herb garden (she was enjoying a bumper crop of sorrel), made delicate inquiries after her health (she had good days and bad days, she said) and finally brought the conversation around to the matter at hand: Jeremy, the one-man inaugural class of Mahina State University's Young Leaders Program.

"Jeremy's not feeling his best today," Bernardine apologized. "That's why he's not here to meet you. But he'll be ready for you tomorrow, Miss Barda. I'll make certain of it. Honestly, Victor, I don't think it's worth all this effort. Jeremy was never that interested in school. But Edward insisted, so here we are."

We didn't stay long after that. Victor and Bernardine exchanged gentle gossip about mutual acquaintances in town, then the older man (Edward, I assumed) returned and showed us out.

When we were back in the car, I asked,

"Were we supposed to meet Jeremy today?"

"He wasn't up to it, as you heard. You'll have the chance to meet him tomorrow. I won't be able to be there for every visit, so you'll have to do it on your own."

"I'll try to manage," I said, and then immediately regretted it. It came out sounding much more sarcastic than I'd intended.

"Is Edward the name of the gentleman who answered the door?" I asked.

"Yes."

We drove on in silence for a few minutes and then Victor asked,

"Are you in touch with Emma Nakamura?"

"Sort of?" The question surprised me. Emma and Victor weren't exactly buddies. Of course, Emma wasn't on particularly good terms with anyone in administration.

"What do you know about her book?" he asked.

"Not much. I know she was working on some kind of book project, but she hasn't told me much about it."

I wasn't being coy with Victor; Emma had been secretive about her book project, which was unusual for her.

"These are interesting times," Victor said, after a few moments. "There's a lot of focus on the university. For better or for worse. Now, of course academic freedom is a bedrock principle of Mahina State University. We would never tell Professor Nakamura—or anyone—what they could and could not publish."

"But?"

"Freedom comes with responsibility. Emma's published under her real name. Her university affiliation is public. Take a look at the book and see whether you might have a word with her."

And that was all Victor said for the rest of the uncomfortable drive back to campus.

CHAPTER THREE

I STARED OVER EMMA'S shoulder at the electronic image of her book cover.

"Emma, this is your book?" I leaned in to take a closer look. "Did you check this with anyone at Mahina State before you published it?

"Why would I do that?"

"Because they've spent the last few years sending us out to the high schools to tell the kids that college is for everyone. And your book is called *No, you can't be an astronaut: Why College Isn't for Everyone.*"

The cover illustration was a line drawing of an astronaut with a red circle and slash superimposed on top.

"Yeah, so? What's the big deal?"

"What's the big deal? How do you think your students would feel if they saw this? It sounds like you're saying some of them don't belong here. Emma, you published this under your real name!"

Emma shrugged. "Know what I say? Prove me wrong. Show me you can do the work. Hey, where's your coffee machine?"

"I put it into storage. I can't stand the smell of coffee these days."

"Aw man, coffee's the whole point of coming to your office."

"You can always go to the coffee machine in the English department. If you don't mind your coffee tasting like chicken soup and hot chocolate."

"When are you gonna be done with your morning sickness?"

"It usually doesn't last past the first trimester, thank you so much for your compassionate concern. Anyway, this book."

"So Santiago really had his goatee in a twist about it, ah?"

"He was concerned, yes. And I can see why. Why did you write a book like this anyway? This doesn't have anything to do with biology."

"It was gonna be a biology book at first. I had this whole section on genetics. I was trying to explain it to my editor how it worked, how you can't take a bunch of nineteen-year-old dimwits and turn 'em into Nobel laureates like the Student Retention Office keeps telling us we gotta do."

"Emma, I don't think the Student Retention Office would—"

"Or, say, turn you into an elite runner. Just not gonna happen. So anyway, she thought my ideas were 'provocative,' she took it back to the publisher, and they wanted me to expand on that. So I did."

"So what is this book about, exactly?"

"*No, You Can't Be an Astronaut* is a hilarious and heartbreaking account of a local girl from the islands who comes back home to teach college but gets a rude awakening when she encounters the Trophies for Everyone generation."

I peered at the screen.

"You memorized your book description."

"Look, I'm addressing a genuine societal crisis. We're pushing more and more college graduates out the door, and it's not like there's a bunch of great jobs out there waiting for them. How many times have you run into one of your former students waiting tables or working a cash register or whatever?"

"Sometimes people want to stay in town after they graduate."

"You think it was worth it for them to take years of their life and get into a bunch of debt just to keep working the same job they had since high school?"

"But maybe credential inflation's gotten so bad that if they didn't get the degree they'd get pushed out of their barista job by someone who did. Anyway, congratulations on getting published. I hope your book does well."

Emma drummed her fingers on my desk and bounced on the yoga ball that I used in lieu of a proper office chair (Mahina State no longer has a budget for faculty office furniture).

"I got a problem, though. My preorder numbers are junk. I'm selling maybe a copy a day, based off my Amazon ranking. Oh, excuse me, based *on*, not based *off*, geez, Molly, let it go, you're so fussy."

"Me? I didn't say anything."

"I could tell you wanted to."

"If you know 'based off' is wrong, then don't use it in the first place. Anyway, a copy a day sounds pretty good to me. My advisor told me half of published academic papers never get read by anyone other than the author and the reviewers. Plus unlike an academic paper, you're getting paid for what you wrote. How much are you getting paid, anyway?"

"Pfft. About a nickel a book. At this rate it's gonna take me about three hundred years to earn back my advance. I need some publicity. Molly. How do I become a best-seller?"

"Do you have three-quarters of a million dollars to spend?"

"Are you crazy?"

"If you do, there's a company that can get you on the New York Times bestseller list. But marketing's not really my area of expertise. Doesn't your publisher take care of advertising? What are they doing?"

"Bupkis. They're telling me I gotta do all my own publicity."

"I was hired to teach business communication, and even that's a stretch for me. I—"

"Yeah, yeah, you got your degree from one of the top ten literature and creative writing programs in the country. I know."

"I wasn't going to say that. Anyway, I'm not sure I want to associate myself with anything called *Why College Isn't for Everyone*. Especially now that Victor's got me giving special tutoring to this rich kid who would otherwise wash out. Sorry, I mean tutierging, not tutoring.

"The kid can't just take online classes?"

"Apparently that's not high-touch and boutique enough for a prominent family with a sick matriarch."

"A-ha. So we're trying to weasel our way into her will before she kicks the bucket, is that it?"

"Victor calls it friendraising, but yes, that's what we're doing."

"Who's this prominent family anyway?"

"Brigham. Do you know them?"

"Brigham? Whoa. What, do you not know them?"

"Victor told me the family was one of those planter-missionary-Alii families," I said.

"Yeah, there's a story there." Emma did not relinquish my yoga ball, so I went around to the other side of my desk and sat in the plastic visitor chair. "There were two sons, a little older than us. One of them married this haole girl from the mainland."

"Was her name Bernardine?" I asked.

"Yeah. Bernardine McCrae."

"I knew it! The model, right?"

"That's the one. So she married Alexander Brigham, but the word is she had a thing with the older brother Cyrus."

"Where are the brothers now?"

"Died in a car crash. And the older brother, Cyrus, you know, the one she wasn't married to? Come to find out he left everything to her. Her husband, Alexander, was the one who was driving. You gotta wonder if he knew what was going on and crashed 'em on purpose, ah? Eh, you got time to get lunch?"

"Thanks for asking, but I can't stand the cafeteria smell these days. I'm going to stay in my office and have pickles for lunch."

"So it's true you like to eat pickles when you come hapai? What about ice cream?"

"I don't think anyone likes pickles and ice cream together. But they're both good when your stomach's feeling touchy. Pickles have that refreshing vinegary crunch that distracts me from my queasy stomach. Ice cream is creamy and soothing.

"Whatever. I'm going to the cafeteria to get loco moco. Come on, doesn't that sound good? Brown gravy, nice meaty hamburger patty, egg yolk soaking into the rice—"

"Just go. Enjoy yourself. And please don't tell me about it."

CHAPTER FOUR

"WE DON'T NEED THE MONEY," Donnie said. "You should quit and take the penalty. I'm sure your classes will fill next time."

Donnie and I were having a nightcap in our living room. Wine for him, decaf green tea for me.

"I already agreed to do it. I can't go back on my word."

"You should try to minimize your stress right now. In What to Expect What You're Expecting, they say stress can make morning sickness worse."

"Oh, and if I gave pregnancy-related stress as a reason for backing out, I'd be ruining things for every woman of childbearing age for the next twenty years. Can't trust those ladies with anything important, they'll just get pregnant and quit. And I do want to help. I mean, we're getting budget cuts from the state every year, most of the faculty with big grants have left, we're not allowed to raise tuition and our students couldn't afford to pay more anyway. Fundraising —sorry, friendraising—is the only thing we have left to keep us afloat."

"So you do want to do it then."

"I feel like I should. But the kid, Jeremy? All these grownups are racing around accommodating him, and he didn't even come out to meet me."

"Didn't you say he was sick?"

"That's the pretext for our providing the individual tutoring, yes. Mind you, students who get sick and don't happen to have rich mothers with one foot in the grave don't get the VIP treatment. Do you know the Brigham family by any chance?"

"I know of them. They have the lava rock house on Russian Road, don't they?"

"Yeah, but their lot's so overgrown you can't even see it from the street. And when you go inside? There are all these weird smells. It's hard to spend a whole hour in there."

"Your sense of smell is heightened right now. It said in the book that that was normal."

"Or maybe their house is especially stinky."

"Molly, you could tell I was showering with scented Dial from across the house."

"Yeah, I was surprised how strong the smell was to me. Good thing they make unscented. They should call it the marriage-saver. Donnie, I know this is something universities do all the time, cozying up to wealthy families, but I have to admit, with Mrs. Brigham obviously in poor health, it feels ghoulish to me. Victor Santiago is obviously hoping she'll put Mahina State in her will."

"Do you get a commission if your university gets a donation?" Donnie asked.

"No. I get to keep my job. Boy, I'm not looking forward to spending the semester tutoring little prince Jeremy."

"You're being kind of hard on him, Molly. He's young. Remember, Davison took a while to find his stride."

Davison Gonsalves had been one of my worst students, an unrepentant cheater who thought he could talk his way out of anything. When I married Donnie, Davison became my stepson. Thankfully, Davison was married now, busy with a new baby and living thousands of miles away in Las Vegas.

"You're right," I said. "But everything worked out well in the end, didn't it? I mean, Davison settling down and having a family and everything."

"Everything did work out." Donnie grinned at me. "And you became a grandmother before you became a mother."

"Just as amusing now as it was the last few times you pointed it out. Hey, speaking of things that people probably shouldn't say out loud, did you know Emma wrote a book?"

"Did she? That's interesting."

"What do you mean, that's interesting?" I got up and dumped my tea into the sink (I thought it tasted slimy) and got myself a cup of lime seltzer water instead.

"Well, I don't usually eavesdrop on my customers, of course."

"Can't imagine why not, but okay. So what happened?"

I sat down on the couch again.

"It was a group of kids at one of the tables. They looked like college students, you know, about that age. I overheard someone say 'Emma Nakamura,' so of course I was interested. And then someone else said something about 'the action,' and something about how an anonymous donor was going to pay for a lawyer. Then I heard someone mention Honey Akiona."

Honey Akiona was my former student. She had gone on to law school, then had come back to Mahina where she'd established a successful criminal law practice. I myself had used her services when I'd ended up on the wrong end of a little misunderstanding.

"So someone needs a lawyer? What'd they do?"

"Nothing yet. Will it bother you if I get another glass of wine?"

"No, not even craving it. Help yourself. So they're planning to do something illegal and someone's hiring a lawyer in advance for them?"

Donnie came back and sat next to me.

"From what I could hear, they're going to protest Emma's book. She's giving a reading, right?"

"She is giving a reading. Donnie, I have to warn her."

As I stood up, Donnie said,

"Your mother called me again today. She says she can't get ahold of you and your phone is turned off."

"I'll get to it. But I have to call Emma first."

Instead of being worried, Emma was dismissive of my warning.

"My little book?" she said. "I should be so lucky."

"It sounds like they're planning to protest your Faculty Spotlight talk."

"Molly, have you ever seen more than ten people show up for one of those?"

"Well, then why are you doing this talk to begin with if you don't think anyone's going to show up?"

"Cause my agent said I should get some footage of me giving a talk, so I could post it on my website. She said it doesn't matter how many people show up, just edit it so it looks like it's well-attended. Oh, that reminds me. Are you gonna be able to go?"

"Sure, if I'm not getting clobbered by morning sickness."

"My talk's not gonna be in the morning."

"I know that. Morning sickness can last all day, it turns out. But yes, of course I'll go."

"Could you video it for me? I got a pretty good video camera."

"Not saying I'm not happy to help, but what about Yoshi?"

"He's on the mainland. Some graphic artist convention."

"When is it again?"

"Tomorrow night. In the Yamashiro auditorium. Hey, how's it going tutoring Richie Rich?"

"Not good. I'm supposed to be there every day, and I'm not looking forward to going back tomorrow."

"I thought you liked old houses."

"The house itself is great. It looks like an old church. The problem is it's filled with tension and sickness and bad smells."

"That's okay. You have my talk to look forward to afterward."

"Yes, something to live for."

CHAPTER FIVE

WHEN I DROVE MYSELF to the house on Russian Road the next day I saw an expensive electric car parked in front of the Brigham lot. I wondered whose it was; there weren't a lot of those kinds of cars in Mahina. I picked my way through to the front door, knocked, and was greeted once again by the elderly man who I was pretty sure was named Edward.

I smiled.

"Hello, I'm Molly Barda. I was here yesterday with Victor Santiago. I'm here to tutor Jeremy."

Edward assured me that he did indeed remember me, and once again, he led me to the side room to wait. Without Victor there to judge me, I felt free to take out my phone. I didn't usually open the Student Retention Office's emails, but I didn't have anything better to do. I clicked on,

Are you a dream-killer?

I already knew what this was about. Our recruiting office had been doing a great job going out to the local high schools convincing the kids that science and engineering were fun. As a result, we'd had an influx of enthusiastic freshmen who thought engineering meant building cool toys from kits and had no idea math was involved. The ones who stayed on and stuck it out in the engineering major burned a lot of their financial aid by repeatedly failing out of precalculus.

Apparently some unnamed "dream-killer" (most likely the precalc instructor) had suggested to a few of these students that they pursue a different course of study. It was clear from the e-mail that although Mahina State believed in Academic Freedom and faculty teaching their courses and discharging their advising duties as they thought best, no one ever should tell a student that they should not major in engineering. Not when our STEM Education grant was up for renewal next year. The situation had escalated to the point that the administration was now engaged in a shooting war with the math and engineering departments over the issue of course prerequisites.

As chair of the management department, I didn't need to get involved. All I had to do was wait for the aspiring engineers to run up against calculus, at which point many of them would come flocking to my department no matter what anyone told them. Ex-engineering majors were the main reason the College of Commerce never hurt for enrollment.

And speaking of dream-killers, the next announcement was about Emma. She would be giving a reading from her new book at our monthly Faculty Spotlight. Faculty Spotlight was an event meant to raise the profile of our university, build the town-gown relationship, and probably do some "friendraising." It was usually modestly-attended, a low-key and pleasant occasion for faculty to show off their latest research, and community members to enjoy free cookies and coffee. I put the date on my calendar and wondered whether the administration realized No You Can't be an Astronaut was an entire book in support of being a dream-killer. If so, they were more committed to Academic Freedom than I had given them credit for.

"Are you ready, Professor Barda?"

Edward was standing in the doorway. "You'll be in the sunroom today."

As we passed a closed door I heard voices. It sounded like two men and one woman talking, but we walked on too quickly for me to hear anything.

"Where is your restroom?" I asked the man quietly.

He gave me a complicated set of instructions involving going down a side hallway and up some stairs. I'd figure it out if I needed it later. I hoped I'd make it through the session.

I followed him to a room flooded with hot sunlight and thick with a cloying, fruity smell that made my stomach rise up in protest.

"Please, have a seat," he said. "Jeremy will be right out."

I sat down at the table and pulled out the textbook, some worksheets, sharpened pencils, and my notebook, and arranged them on the table. A few minutes later, Jeremy came shambling in, holding a tall glass of something that looked like green swamp sludge. He was slight and pale, with black hair and large black eyes.

"You're Barda," he observed.

"Yes. I'm Professor Barda. It's delightful to meet you. Victor Santiago told me they sent you some diagnostic worksheets for you. Should we go over those first?"

He slouched into the chair and plunked the glass directly on the koa table, ignoring the stack of coasters. It wasn't my house or my table, but I still flinched a little.

"I didn't do it. I got too tired."

"That's fine. We'll start at the beginning." I tugged at the collar of my blouse. The sunroom felt infernally hot, although Jeremy seemed comfortable in his sweatshirt. "Now, the first section goes into describing data. Before we analyze anything, we need to have a good handle on what we're looking at—"

"I heard no one likes teaching this class," he interrupted. "Is that true?"

"I'm sorry?"

"That's what I heard. They always get the young teachers to teach stats cause no one else wants to do it. You don't seem that young, though."

"This is no ordinary stats class," I shot back as I pulled out a worksheet. "This is the Young Leaders program."

"Young losers program, you mean. The only reason Mahina State cares so much is they're hoping Bernardine puts them in her will."

"You call your mother Bernardine?"

"That's her name."

He slurped his disgusting green smoothie, and I felt my mouth flood with salt water. I swallowed hard and stared at the table.

"She doesn't even care if I get my degree or not," he went on. "She just likes that guy that comes over and flirts with her. The one that looks like Tony Stark."

"Well, I'm sure she has a lot to deal with right now. Are you ready to get started?"

Jeremy opened his mouth and let out a smelly belch, which sent me dashing out in search of a bathroom.

I couldn't remember the old man's complicated directions to the servant's bathroom or wherever it was I was supposed to go, so I headed back down the hallway hoping to find something off the main hallway. I got there just in time. I rinsed my mouth and was heading back down the hallway when I again heard the rumble of voices from Mrs. Bingham's room. The phrase, "family trust" caught my ear. The fancy car out front must belong to a lawyer, I thought. Bernardine Bingham was putting her affairs in order.

"And Jeremy?" I heard a man ask.

I paused. His Majesty wouldn't be heartbroken if I was thirty seconds late. I told myself that I was keeping my eyes and ears open as part of my assignment, but the truth is I was madly curious myself.

Mrs. Bingham said something, but in a low tone, so I couldn't hear.

"Nothing at all?" The man exclaimed.

I held my breath.

"I don't wish to give the boy any further reason to look forward to my passing."

Her voice quavered. I couldn't tell if it was sadness, fear, or something else.

As I headed back to rejoin Jeremy, I patted my belly.

"Hey, Baby," I whispered. "When it's time for me to go, at least try to act sad about it, okay?"

CHAPTER SIX

I DROVE BACK TO CAMPUS, but as I neared the Yamashiro Auditorium I saw police cars, lights flashing, blocking off the entrance. I drove around to the lower end of campus and parked in the lot closest to my office and walked back up. But the crowd was so thick, I couldn't even get close to the building.

I moved onto the grass some distance from the noisy crowd and texted Emma.

ME: What's going on?

I scanned the crowd. Aside from the small knot of noisy protestors, about a hundred restless people were milling around.

The text alert on my phone beeped.

EMMA: Hardly anyone here. Where are you?

ME: Protestors blocking the entrance.

EMMA: They're setting up a live feed for me so you can watch from outside.

I caught sight of Victor in the crowd, then noticed Bernardine Brigham sitting on a bench beside him. Her head was pulled back in a way that made her look regal and vaguely like a swan, a pose I supposed they taught in modeling school. I wasn't sure whether I should go over and say hello, but Victor caught my eye and motioned me over.

I fought my way through the crowd, which reeked of body odor and carport-dried laundry (hardly anyone in Mahina owns a dryer).

I found Victor in full donor-charming mode.

"Professor Barda," he greeted me, with a rare smile. "Bernardine, you remember—"

"Of course I do, Victor," she simpered. "My memory's not gone yet."

She must not have been much older than me, but out here in the daylight, she looked shriveled and frail. A whiff of the overripe floral smell from her house reached my nose.

"Isn't this exciting," she went on. "I've attended the Faculty Spotlight talks since they began, but I've never seen anything like this. When someone wants to prevent me from hearing something, it just makes me all the more curious."

Victor's smile tensed a little. He probably wasn't thrilled at the idea of Mrs. Brigham hearing Emma explain why students like Jeremy Brigham didn't belong in college.

"And how is Jeremy's tutoring going?" Mrs. Brigham asked me.

"Very well, thank you. We had our first session today."

"Yes, you must excuse me for not greeting you. I was in a meeting."

I tried to look appropriately surprised.

"Your house is lovely. And I really enjoyed meeting your son..."

Bernardine Brigham's expression soured. Victor immediately bent down and whispered in her ear, pointing at the monitor mounted on the wall. It was the one usually used to post announcements, but it had been hooked up to project the inside of the auditorium. Emma was standing on the stage, wrestling with a stand mic to make it short enough for her to talk into. The sound wasn't on yet, but the image was clear. I hoped Mrs. Brigham was worse at lip-reading than I was.

"Excuse us for a moment, Mrs. Brigham." Victor motioned me to follow him a short distance away.

"What did I say?"

His oleaginous charm was gone. He shook his head curtly.

"We were afraid you might say something to disturb Mrs. Brigham if you had too much information about the family. But I see now we've given you too little information."

"I only said she had a lovely house and I enjoyed meeting her son. So yes, I would appreciate knowing what I said wrong."

"Let me give you some background," Victor said. We'll have to trust you to be discreet. The Brighams are a very distinguished family."

Of course they were. Victor wouldn't be friendraising them so hard if they weren't.

Victor told me more or less the same thing Emma had—that Mrs. Brigham's late husband Alexander and his brother Cyrus had died in the same car accident. Victor had more details: It had been raining, he told me, and no one else was in the car aside from the two brothers.

But the story ended the same way; Cyrus and Alexander Brigham died shortly after they reached the hospital.

"How sad," I said, wondering what this had to do with my mystery faux pas. I glanced over at Mrs. Brigham, still sitting on the bench, watching the monitor over the restless crowd. Vice President Marshall Dixon was speaking now, but the hubbub and chanting made it impossible to hear her.

"Certain facts emerged when the will was read," Victor continued. "Cyrus was not married, so most of Cyrus's estate—and it was significant—was left to his brother Alexander, Mrs. Brigham's husband. And there was a stipulation that in case his brother failed to survive him, the full legacy as bequeathed to Alexander should go to his widow and any of their children."

"And that was Jeremy?"

"Please let me finish. Alexander's death, as I have already stated, preceded his brother's by several minutes and consequently, Bernardine became the chief beneficiary. But when Alexander's will was read, it was discovered that he had fathered a child outside of the marriage."

"Oh. Mrs. Brigham must not have been happy about that."

"No. And they already had a son of their own. But she did the noble thing and took the boy in."

"Where is Jeremy's biological mother?"

"I don't know. But I do know Mrs. Brigham was now a widow with two sons to raise. When the boys were eleven years old, they went swimming in the Hanakoa River without her knowledge or permission. Her own son was swept away and drowned. Jeremy survived."

"Oh, how awful. So Jeremy is her stepson." And a daily reminder of her husband's infidelity.

"That's right."

I wondered whether Mrs. Brigham blamed Jeremy for her son's death. I also wondered whether an eleven-year-old could engineer his stepbrother's drowning.

"Can I ask, sorry, I know this is tactless, but what is Mrs. Brigham's illness?"

"It's not contagious if that's your concern." Victor had just told me to mind my own business *and* accused me of being a hypochondriac, in one short sentence.

He excused himself and went back to ooze around Mrs. Brigham. Emma was back on the monitor now, but I couldn't hear a thing she said. Her voice was drowned out by boos and chants and occasional shouts of "Let her speak!"

The protestors barricading the entrance wore tall paper dunce caps, presumably a reference to Emma's assertion that not everyone was college material. I observed the spectacle until I heard the smash of breaking glass, then decided it was time to leave.

CHAPTER SEVEN

WHEN I ARRIVED AT THE Brigham House the next morning, it was with the uneasy feeling that I knew far too much about the family. I almost wished Victor hadn't told me that Jeremy was Bernardine's unwanted stepson, or that Bernardine's son had drowned.

And Bernardine, too, was dying. Victor thought so, in any case.

When Edward answered the door, I asked how Mrs. Brigham was doing.

He shook his head.

"Too much excitement yesterday. She should be resting. But she's in the kitchen again."

My tutoring session went as expected. Jeremy's attention drifted, and it was impossible to keep him on task. It was only when I was packing up to leave that things took an interesting turn.

He fixed me with his dark eyes, and said,

"I'm not ready to go, Professor."

"Oh, you don't need to go anywhere. I'm going. I'll see you tomorrow, okay?"

"I mean I'm not ready to die."

I paused and sank back into the chair. I had been through suicide prevention training. I knew that I had to ask the question. Not the polite question, are you thinking of hurting yourself? People who want to commit suicide aren't thinking of it hurting. On the contrary, they are hoping to make the pain end. I had to ask the uncomfortable question, the one that was so hard to say out loud:

"Jeremy, are you thinking about killing yourself?" I scrambled to remember my suicide prevention training. I had memorized the number of the suicide hotline, and I wrote it down for him.

Jeremy rolled his eyes.

"I don't think I'm going to outlive her."

My mind flashed on a suicide-by-cop story I'd seen in the Honolulu paper.

"Jeremey?" I said, "I'm going to get in touch with someone on campus who can help you. Okay?"

"Whatever," he scoffed.

After the tutoring session, I went straight back to my office, pulled up the online Student of Concern form, and filled it out on Jeremy's behalf. When I had taught my classes and finished my last meeting, I went to Emma's office, only to find it closed. A paper sign on the door read:

Class and office hours canceled today

So I drove up to her house.

I expected to see Emma looking frazzled, but when she came to the door, she was in her sweatpants, looking relaxed and holding a coffee mug.

"Want some wine?" she asked.

"Not for me, thanks. Maybe just a glass of water if you don't mind."

"Oh yeah, I keep forgetting. You're not showing yet, that's why. Hey, you get to see my talk last night?"

"I was there, but I couldn't get in. There was a big demonstration outside, and some people in masks and dunce hats were blocking the door. Looks like you really stirred things up. When did you start drinking white wine?"

"When I was getting ready for my talk. Red stains your teeth. I wanted my smile to look good on camera."

"I saw you on the monitor, but I wasn't really paying attention to your teeth. What with the protestors and everything. Plus Victor Santiago was there with Bernardine Brigham."

"Oh man." Emma plopped down at the table. "I guess he's gonna give me a hard time now."

"I don't know. Mrs. Brigham seemed to be enjoying the spectacle. So what have you been doing today? I saw you canceled your classes."

"Yeah, security told me to. I've been watching my book rankings. They're going up, you know. I'm getting a bunch of reviews too."

"What are they saying?"

Emma shrugged.

"Depends on whether you're talking about the five-star ones or the one-star ones. My publisher says more reviews are better no matter what they say. Eh, speaking of the Brighams. How's your tutierging going?"

"Well, for one thing, I still don't know the difference between tutierging and just plain tutoring. But I'm a little worried about Jeremy. He seems...off."

"Anyone would be off, shut up in that weird house all day with their dying mother."

"Emma, I think I overheard Mrs. Brigham talking to her lawyers, or someone, about making sure Jeremy doesn't get anything when she dies. Now, what if Jeremy decided he's going to kill her before she can change her will?"

"Doesn't Victor want her to change her will to leave everything to Mahina State?"

"I don't think he expects her to leave everything, but I think he'd like something, yes. So it would be in Victor's interest for Bernardine to survive long enough to change her will. I can't imagine what he could do about it, though."

"So we're rooting for Victor now? That's funny."

"Why should it be funny?"

"Cause you don't trust him."

"I never said that."

"You don't. Otherwise you would've told him about all this already."

"I do trust Victor. I *trust* he'd find some way to make me feel like an idiot for bringing it up. Anyway, in this case, yes, I guess we are rooting for Victor."

"Cause we want the university to get the money?"

"Because we don't approve of people murdering their stepmothers, Emma."

"Stepmothers?"

"Jeremy is Mrs. Brigham's stepson, apparently, not her biological son."

"Oh, I did hear something about that. There was some scandal, yeah?"

"Emma, someone might be planning a murder. Don't you think we should do something?

"What do you mean we, white man?"

"Dang it. I knew you were going to say that."

"It's funny cause you're white."

"Yes, very amusing. So what do I do about Jeremy wanting to kill his stepmother before she can change her will?"

"Look, Molly, I know you love butting into other people's business, but I think you should let this one go. The Brighams are a big deal on this island. You don't wanna get on their bad side. If Little Lord Psychopath wants to slaughter his family, let him."

"Emma, do you think it's too dangerous? Should I quit?"

"What, and have to pay back a quarter of your salary? No way. Besides, you got a front-row seat to the best reality show around. I want you to keep your eyes open and tell me all about it. Just don't get yourself murdered."

CHAPTER EIGHT

THE NEXT TIME I WENT to the house on Russian Road, Edward was holding a tray with a single glass perched on it. The glass was filled with a frog-colored liquid that smelled like raw broccoli stems.

"Is that one of Mrs. Brigham's smoothies?" I asked, ferociously hoping it wasn't meant for me.

"Bernardine has always been interested in nutrition," he said as he led me down the hallway. "She was a model, you know, so she's always had to be careful about her figure. She's got all kinds of vegetables and herbs in here and I think she'll put in a whole apple now and then. She'd like me to drink them too, but I tell her, just take care of yourself, Bernardine. I don't know. I don't think she's going to pull out of this one."

"I'm so sorry to hear it."

Victor wouldn't be, though.

The man paused at the doorway to let me enter the room first, then followed me in and placed the tray on the table.

"Bernardine doesn't trust doctors," he said. "Not for herself, and not for Jeremy. Oh, here he is now. Jeremy, I have your drink."

"So how did that problem set go?" I asked Jeremy when he was seated.

"Didn't do it."

"At all?"

"Don't take it personally. You're not that bad of a teacher. I was too tired, that's all."

I put on a faint smile. Mahina State better get a giant payday out of this, I thought. I'm certainly not doing any good here otherwise. Although maybe encouraging Jeremy to take the long view would help to motivate him.

"So you're a psychology major," I said casually as I unpacked my books and papers. "What are you planning to do after you graduate?"

"I'm probably not going to finish."

I paused and looked up.

"Don't say that. We'll get you through your stats class."

"I dunno. I think fate has other plans for me."

I hope you're not counting on a big inheritance, I thought.

Jeremy produced a silver gadget and brought it to his mouth. Immediately he was enveloped by billows of white vapor. The artificial-cherry odor was overwhelming.

"May I ask you not smoke, please?"

He looked at me and slowly exhaled, and even more vapor poured out of his nose and mouth. He looked like a scrawny, insolent little dragon.

"I'm not smoking," he said when he'd emptied his lungs. "I'm vaping."

"And I'm pregnant," I shot back before I had time to think about it.

My voice reverberated in the sunny room. I had not intended to disclose my condition. Except for Emma, no one at work knew yet (and for some reason, Emma didn't quite believe it). I wasn't even planning to tell my regular classes. Sure, after a certain point they'd figure it out on their own, but explicitly announcing it seemed one step removed from strolling in and declaring I HAD SEX!!

Jeremy stared at me and slowly, resentfully, shut the device down and put it away.

Too bad. If he wanted to complain to Victor and get someone else to tutor him, he could be my guest. I didn't know what was in that vapor. And darned if I was going to avoid wine and undercooked eggs and restaurant tea and cats for nine months, only to have my unborn child done in by some vaping doofus.

Fortunately, we finished the lesson without further incident. After we had finished and Edward had shown me out, I sat in my car and called my obstetrician's office.

I didn't want to call from my office as our walls are thin enough to hear everything. I knew this because I used to hear every embarrassing word of Rodge Cowper's self-affirmation tapes as clear as day.

I noticed the expensive electric car was gone; the lawyers, or whoever they were, had left.

"I was around someone who was vaping," I said as soon as the nurse was on the line. "Should I worry?"

"Probably no harm from just once," she said. "Just make sure you don't ingest the liquid. It's got a high concentration of nicotine. If you drink it, it can kill you."

I WAS WATCHING EMMA'S talk online when Donnie came home. He crept up behind me and kissed me behind the ear, which made me yelp with surprise and yank off my headphones.

"Sorry to interrupt, but I thought you'd be hungry. I brought home some chicken katsu. I made sure to get an extra-crispy batch because I know that's how you like it."

He peeled the tinfoil back from the tray. The meaty odor made me want to clap my hands over my face and run out of the room. But I didn't want to hurt his feelings.

"That was so thoughtful," I squeaked, trying not to breathe, "But I don't think my stomach can handle meat right now."

"It's chicken, not meat." Donnie looked crestfallen. "And we brine it beforehand to pull all the blood out."

I jumped up and dashed to the bathroom, leaving him standing next to my toppled chair.

Later that evening, I was able to make a meal of a small bowl of cereal with plain yogurt instead of milk. Donnie had eaten already and packed up the rest of the chicken katsu in the freezer. Over dinner, I told him about my suspicions about the Brigham family.

"And I know you're just going to tell me not to get involved," I said. "But I think Jeremy Brigham's trying to kill Bernardine Brigham before she finalizes the will."

Donnie set down his wine glass.

"Okay, let's look at it this way. What if one of your students came to you with this story? What would you say?"

"Like if they were trying to weasel out of a deadline? I'd say, that's a new one, you already kill off all your grandparents?"

He laughed.

"You're starting to sound like Emma. No, what if you had a student come to you with exactly the story you're telling me? And they asked you, Professor Barda, what do you think I should do?"

"I guess I'd say, if you think someone's in danger, tell the police, and don't go back to that house."

"Hmm." Donnie took a sip of wine.

"Okay, maybe I'll talk to Victor about getting someone else to do the tutoring, and we can figure out another way for me to make up that class. I don't really have anything solid to take to the police, though. I know Bernardine Brigham's health is mysteriously declining, I know she wants to cut Jeremy out of her will, and if I were Jeremy I'd want her to die before that happened. And she's a perfect person to poison because she refuses to see a doctor."

"You're sure she's being poisoned? How do you know she isn't actually sick?"

"Well, no, that's the thing. I'm maybe sixty percent sure. Seventy-five percent. Maybe you can mention it to Detective Medeiros. You know, offhandedly. You still see him at the Drive-Inn, don't you?"

"He comes in for plate lunch. Molly, if you see evidence of a real crime, you should call the police yourself. If I tell Ka`imi what you just told me, all that is, is gossip. By the way, I saw you were watching a video of Emma. Was that her book talk?"

"Yeah. Boy, you weren't kidding about the protest. I tried to warn her, you know."

"I didn't realize how bad it was till I saw it on the news. I'm glad you didn't get hurt. Have you talked to Emma since then? Is she okay?"

"Is she okay? With all the controversy her books are selling like hot malasadas. Maybe I should write a book and instigate a protest against myself. Then I really could afford to quit this stupid tutoring job."

"Molly, I don't want to tell you what to do, but we're not hurting for money. You can quit this tutoring thing if you want."

"I am tempted. It's not like I don't have two other classes to keep me busy, not to mention the stuff I have to deal with as department chair. I had to get the Title Nine officer to come down and explain to Rodge Cowper that no matter what her initials are, it's not okay to address a full-figured young lady as 'Double-D' in front of her classmates."

"Maybe you can take the weekend to think about it. I just want you and our baby to be safe."

"Hear that, Baby?" I said to my stomach. "We're on your side. So please don't poison us when you grow up, okay?"

"That reminds me, your mother called me again. She asked me why you're not returning her calls. I told her I'd have you call her back."

"I will," I promised. "Eventually."

WHEN I SAW JEREMY BRIGHAM on Monday I could see right away that something was wrong. He was paler than ever, and seemed to be having trouble focusing his eyes.

"Did you have a nice weekend?" I asked as I flipped the pages of the textbook. A vile odor hit my nostrils. I looked up to see Jeremy unconscious on the table, his cheek pressed into a spreading pool of vomit.

"Help!" I yelled, but quickly realized there was no one in the house who could help. I'd have to risk the doctor-hating Bernardine's wrath by calling 9-1-1. Fortunately, the dispatcher knew where the Brigham house was. I waited next to Jeremy until I heard the whoop of the ambulance out on the road.

I followed the two blue-shirted paramedics as they wheeled a gurney down the dark hallway. From behind a closed door, I heard Mrs. Brigham call out, "Edward?"

"Keep going," I urged them. "Your patient's down there."

It was reassuring to see how quickly they swung into action. It seemed to take seconds for them to get Jeremy cleaned up, lying on the gurney, and fitted with an oxygen mask.

"Has he had thoughts of suicide or self-harm?" the woman asked me as the man fastened Jeremy down for transport.

"I don't know. He did say some strange things to me last week."

"Such as?"

"Pinpoint pupils," the man said. He was bending over Jeremy, shining a flashlight into his eye.

"He said he might not finish school because fate had other plans or something. I filed a student of concern report with the university. I should say I submitted one, but I just got a message back saying they couldn't take it because he's not officially enrolled this semester."

"Was he drinking this?" She indicated the half-finished green smoothie on the table, which looked exactly like the pool of green liquid that was now dripping onto the tile floor.

"I believe so, yes."

She nodded to the man, who took out a plastic bag, dropped the entire plastic tumbler into it, and sealed it up.

"And you're the mother, correct?" she asked as we started back down the hallway.

I opened my mouth to answer, then stopped myself. If I said no, I feared they wouldn't be able to take Jeremy to the hospital until they found an actual relative who would agree to it.

"Jeremy?" I heard Mrs. Brigham call from behind the same door as we went back down the hallway. "Edward, where is Jeremy?"

"I don't need to ride in the ambulance," I assured them as they wheeled Jeremy out the front door. "I'll drive down separately."

When Jeremy had been safely taken out on the gurney, I went back and knocked softly on the door of what I inferred was Mrs. Brigham's room.

Edward opened it.

"Bernardine's not well," he said quietly.

Over his shoulder, I saw Mrs. Brigham. She was in bed, lying back on her pillow and looking frail.

"Jeremy was sick," I whispered to the old man. "I called 9-1-1. Do you have a cleaning service?"

"What's going on?" Mrs. Brigham called from her bed. "Edward, tell me what's going on."

I went over and sat in the chair next to the bed. The room smelled of disinfectant and ripe human, but the French doors to an enclosed herb garden were open. Piney smells of rosemary wafted in on a warm breeze.

"Jeremy fainted, Mrs. Brigham. He's ill." I hoped I hadn't just saved the life of her would-be murderer. But I couldn't stand by and do nothing. I guess what I'm saying is if you want to send someone back in time to kill baby Hitler, don't pick me.

"How is Jeremy? Please tell him to come in and see me. Can you do that for me, Miss Barda?"

I looked to where Edward had been standing, but he was gone.

"He's not here, Mrs. Brigham. The paramedics took him to the hospital."

Her eyes widened with fear.

"I have to see him," she pleaded. "Please, go get Edward. Ah, there he is. Edward, help me get dressed. I'm going to see Jeremy."

"Bernardine, you can't go there. Your immune system's weak, and the hospital is full of sick people."

"I know what a hospital is, Edward," she snapped. "I'll wear my gloves and mask."

"Okay," I said awkwardly as I backed out the door. "I, uh, hope everyone feels better soon."

CHAPTER ELEVEN

I HAPPENED TO HAVE a prenatal appointment scheduled, so I drove up to the Mahina Medical Center and checked in early. Then I went down to the first floor where the phone reception was decent and called Victor Santiago to let him know what had happened to Jeremy. I could tell it was a struggle for him not to blame me.

"What other choice did I have?" I defended myself. "The paramedics thought he was bad enough to take him to the ER."

"No one's blaming you, Professor Barda," he said in a blaming tone. "It's simply unfortunate. I'll get in touch with Mrs. Brigham. Please wait to hear from me before you do anything else."

"Do you happen to know whether Mrs. Brigham has changed her will?" I asked.

"You know I can't discuss that with you, Professor Barda."

If Jeremy knew (or at least believed) he'd already been cut out of the will, maybe he wouldn't be in such a rush to have Bernardine Brigham kick the bucket. Maybe someone should tell him.

On a whim, I went over to the main information desk to ask after Jeremy Bingham.

Unlike the paramedic, the receptionist did not assume I was Jeremy's mother. She informed me that due to patient privacy laws, she couldn't tell me the condition of the patient, where he was, or even whether he was there at all.

I went back up to the second floor to wait for my prenatal appointment, took a seat in the little waiting room, and pulled a book out of my bag.

A flash of purple in my peripheral vision made me glance at the doorway. I stood up and stepped out into the hallway. Sure enough, there was Mrs. Brigham, dressed in flowing purple, slowly making her way down the hallway toward the Intensive Care Unit.

I followed her as quietly as I could as she tottered along, steadying herself on her cane. She was so focused that I didn't have to work very hard to be invisible to her. When she approached the nurses' station of the Intensive Care Unit, I walked in right after her and lurked behind her, shamelessly eavesdropping.

"Your son's in with the doctor right now," the receptionist told her. "It'll just be a moment. He's in room five."

There was no way for me to talk to Jeremy with Bernardine right there, so I went back to the prenatal unit to wait for my appointment.

As I walked out to my car afterward, I thought about Mrs. Brigham. Why wasn't she wearing a mask and gloves, as she'd told Edward she would? She really did look sick, and I couldn't imagine her immune system was in any shape to fend off the kinds of nasty bugs that lived in hospitals.

I knew I shouldn't stick my nose into these people's business any deeper than I already had. But Russian Road was just down the hill from the hospital. If Edward was still at home, he could bring Bernardine the mask and gloves that she'd forgotten.

When Edward opened the door I said,

"I just saw Mrs. Brigham up at the hospital."

He nodded sadly.

"I told her not to go, but she called a cab. Come in. Would you like a beer?"

"No thank you."

"Scotch?"

"That's very kind, but maybe just water."

The table and floor in the sunroom had been scrubbed down and smelled faintly of bleach.

"Mrs. Brigham forgot her mask and gloves," I said. "She's in the ICU now. I can drive them up for her if you like. She must really care for Jeremy to take that risk to see him."

"Please have a seat, Professor Barda. Bernardine took a taxicab up there. Against my advice."

Edward had gotten me a can of Coke. I took a sip and felt the sugar and caffeine perk me up immediately.

"I've always done my best to protect Bernardine," he said. "I still think of her as a baby. I was in college by the time she was born."

"Bernardine is your sister?"

"Yes. She's had some ups and downs. A very successful career, of course, and a wonderful marriage, for as long as it lasted. It was very hard on her when she lost her husband and then found out about Jeremy. Do you know the story?"

I shook my head.

"Jeremy is not Bernardine's son. Her husband was running around with a woman from a Honolulu hostess bar, and Jeremy was the result."

I nodded, trying to look mildly surprised.

"Bernardine was terribly distressed about it, of course. And what made it worse was she and Alexander had their own son. Alexander Jr. was born just a few months earlier than Jeremy."

"Oh, dear. How awful." I couldn't imagine Donnie running around on me while I was recovering from childbirth and nursing a sickly infant.

But if he did, I could easily imagine wanting to murder him.

"Bernardine didn't know about Jeremy until her husband passed away. The boy was mentioned in his will."

"What happened to his mother?"

"I don't know. I believe Alexander's parents either paid her off, got her deported, or both. So the boy had nowhere else to go. And then not long after that, a swimming accident claimed Alexander Junior. I was staying with them at the time. After the accident, I simply stayed on."

He blinked back tears, stood up, and left the room.

I wasn't sure what to do, so I stayed put. Edward returned with a highball glass filled to the top with amber liquid.

"I don't know how Bernardine could have known what was in Cyrus's will," he said, mystifyingly.

"Cyrus?"

"Her husband's older brother."

"Oh?"

"I was here when she got the call. Alexander and his brother were driving back from a day out fishing. They went over the side into a gulch. I was going to go with them, you know. But I had woken up that morning with a bit of a cold, and I told them to go ahead without me..."

Edward took a gulp of whatever was in his glass—whiskey, by the smell of it—and stared at a point in the distance.

"Even if they had been at the most advanced medical facility in the world, I don't believe there was anything that could have been done," he said, finally. "Bernardine asked whether we could spend some moments with them alone, and they obliged us. This was down at the Kuewa Clinic, now. Well, I went out on the lanai to give Bernardine some privacy, you understand. So she could say good-bye to her husband. I happened to turn around, and..."

Edward drained the glass.

"She had her hand on Alexander's face. At first I thought she was touching his cheek, or some such thing. But from where I stood, I could swear she held her hand over his nose and mouth."

I stared at him.

"You know when the person doesn't breathe for a while, the machine makes the high-pitched sound, and people come running in. Well, as soon as that happened, Bernardine pulled her hand away. What do you think, Professor Barda? Do you think my sister killed her husband?"

"I...why would she want to do that?"

"Well, now, I'm not a lawyer, but as I understand it, Alexander's passing first was very advantageous to Bernardine. Cyrus had stipulated that if Alexander predeceased him, Alexander's widow would inherit most of his estate, which included this house. The only surprise was when Alexander's will was read. That's when Bernardine found out about Jeremy."

"And she took him in."

"Yes."

"So why does your sister not want Jeremy to get anything when she dies?"

If he was surprised, he didn't show it. I suppose he had too much on his mind to worry about how I knew the terms of Bernardine's will.

"Jeremy's existence is a daily humiliation to my sister," he said slowly. "A reproach. And I believe...Jeremy was so unloved, he became unlovable."

"Is she afraid of him?" I asked.

"She wishes he were dead."

"What?"

Edward met my gaze.

"Bernardine is prepared to go. She's ready. But the one thing she can't bear is the possibility that he might outlive her. If he does, she wants to make sure his life is unbearable."

"Maybe we should call the ICU and alert them."

I called the Mahina Medical Center main number and was instantly put on hold by their automated phone service.

"It'll be faster if we drive." I stood up.

He shook his head slowly.

"I'm in no condition to get behind the wheel, Professor Barda."

"My car's right out front. I'll drive."

"I HAVE TO SEE JEREMY Brigham," I panted to the ICU receptionist. I wasn't that pregnant yet, but my weight had already redistributed to the point that running made me wobble like a raw egg.

"And you are?"

"His uncle," Edward said.

She looked at me.

"And aunt," I added, improvising.

She narrowed her eyes at me. What was the problem? The paramedic thought I was Jeremy's mother. That was unlikely to carry much weight with the ICU receptionist, unfortunately.

A man in turquoise scrubs came out of the double doors, and I took the opportunity to dash through before they closed behind him.

"Ma'am? Excuse me, ma'am?" I heard the woman calling after me.

I hurried to Room Five and peered through the rectangular window, but someone had pulled the privacy curtain across the bed. I shoved the door open and yanked the curtain aside.

Jeremy lay on his back. A tangle of wires and tubes tethered him to an IV bag and a beeping monitor. He had regained consciousness, but barely. He turned his head toward me and mumbled something I couldn't understand.

Bernardine Brigham was seated on the far side of the hospital bed, lips pursed, glaring at me. This, I assumed, was not a facial expression they taught in modeling school.

Thankfully, Uncle Edward caught up to me at that moment.

"Don't worry, Professor Barda," he said, "I told her you were with the family and convinced her not to call Security."

"Edward?" Bernardine exclaimed. "What on earth is going on?"

"I'm sorry, Bernardine. I was worried you'd come up without your mask and gloves."

"Well that's very thoughtful of you, but I'll be perfectly fine. And you didn't need to bring Jeremy's tutor. As you can see, he's not in any condition do his lessons."

"I offered to drive," I said, feeling sheepish. What an embarrassing mistake. Jeremy looked dazed and uncomfortable, and probably wanted nothing more than to rest.

Then Bernardine shifted in her seat, and I caught a glimpse of something white in her lap.

A pillow.

Jeremy's pillow. That's why he looked uncomfortable. He was lying flat on the bed because Bernardine had taken his pillow.

"Maybe I can drive everyone back," I said. "As long as I'm here. Mrs. Brigham, would you like to come back with us?"

"Forgive me if I don't get up." She gave us a tight smile. "I'm very tired. Edward, you go on back home. I'll take a taxi when I'm finished here."

I could see that Edward was about to do what she suggested. Leaving Bernardine to smother her stepson as soon as we were gone.

And maybe it was none of my business. After all, Jeremy might have been trying to kill Bernardine first. It would be self-defense.

But then I recalled what Edward had told me about Alexander Brigham's final moments.

I darted into the room, leaned over Jeremy's body (noticing briefly that my belly was in the way) and yanked all of the connectors out of the heart rate monitor as Bernardine screamed and clawed at my arms.

As the alarm shrieked, I took advantage of the confusion to slip out. I had a tense moment strolling casually past two hospital security guards who were running toward the direction I had just left.

On my way out of the building, I reached out to the dispenser for a puff of hand-sanitizing foam and smeared it on the scratches on my arms. Then I walked slowly to my car and drove directly home.

I didn't notice how much my arms stung until later, when I was on the phone with my mother.

Yes, I called her back. My mother wasn't really that bad, I realized. All things considered.

And no, I didn't tell her anything about what had happened on Russian Road. I'm not an idiot.

BERNARDINE BRIGHAM passed away at home two days after the hospital incident. The cause of death was given as pancreatic cancer. I knew the disease moved swiftly, but still; she'd been pretty strong when she'd torn my arm up in the ICU. Possibly with Jeremy under medical care, she realized things weren't going according to plan, and decided to hasten her exit.

She did leave a generous bequest to Mahina State University. So generous, in fact, that the psychology building was renamed Brigham Hall, and the next few times I saw Victor Santiago on campus he actually said hello to me.

Emma's book continued to sell briskly and ended up on the New York Times bestseller list. One day over lunch, she let it slip that she'd already made ten times over what the protester's legal fees had cost her.

"Did you say cost *you*?" I demanded. "You paid the protestors' legal costs? The anonymous donor was you!"

"I had to do something," she said with not a trace of remorse. "My publisher wasn't doing bupkis, and you wouldn't help me either."

"You obviously didn't need my help. No wonder you weren't stressed out about the protest. You orchestrated the whole thing."

"Did I mention my book's on the New York Times bestseller list?"

"Several times. Emma, you're the one who should be teaching in the College of Commerce, not me. You're like the Lee Atwater of book marketing."

Emma swallowed her bite of sandwich.

"I don't wanna teach in your college," she declared, with her usual grace and tact. "Your students are even dumber than mine."

Jeremy recovered quickly and was able to petition for late registration only three weeks into the semester. Our tutoring sessions were converted to a standard directed-reading course. This was a great relief to the registrar, who'd had no idea how to deal with Victor's "Young Leaders" program.

I nearly didn't recognize Jeremy when he came into my office. His face had filled out and gained some color, his black eyes were lively, and he moved with energy, not the slothful motions I'd seen earlier.

I told him how sorry I was about Bernardine's passing. I added that it was wonderful to see him up and about, and asked him how he was feeling.

Jeremy was eager to tell me everything. I'd like to think I had won his trust and confidence, but I suspect he simply wanted to run out the clock on his tutoring time. Family drama is far more interesting than T-tables and standard deviations.

He was building up his strength by taking walks in the morning. Soon, he told me, he'd be lifting weights again.

"You're staying in the house on Russian Road?" I asked, knowing Bernardine had left no part of her estate to Jeremy. And why should she, if she was planning for him to die before she did?

"It's Uncle Edward's now. He says I can stay as long as I want. He let me move into Bernardine's room, too. It's way bigger than my old one."

"That's a lovely room, with the herb garden outside."

"The garden's gone, you know."

"Gone?"

"Yeah, while I was at the hospital, Uncle Edward got a contractor to dig it up and pour concrete over it. It was kinda sad to come back and see it tiled over. But someone told him it was the green smoothie that was making me sick. So Uncle Edward decided to get rid of the whole garden, just to be on the safe side."

"Did they tell you which one of the herbs was making you ill?"

"Opioids."

"She was growing poppies?" I asked.

"No. Regular painkillers. They had to fully detox me. Man, I don't understand how people take those things for fun. I felt like crap all the time. And when they were tapering me off, I thought I was gonna die."

"How were you getting the opioids?"

"From the smoothies. Weird, huh? I guess Bernardine must've been mixing her painkillers into her own glass, and then I guess she mixed up the glasses a few times."

"I can imagine when you're that ill, you can get forgetful," I said.

"You know, Professor Barda, between you and me? The way Bernardine treated me sometimes, I thought she hated me. Especially after Junior died. I felt like she blamed me. But then at the end...even though she was so sick herself, she tried to take care of me. She made me those smoothies every day and made sure I drank them. I guess she did care after all."

"She certainly did," I agreed.

"I guess sometimes you don't even know it when people are looking out for you."

"No argument there." I rubbed the scratches on my forearm, which by now had faded to pink lines. "In fact, I care very much about your passing the stats exam. Did you remember to bring your worksheets this time?"

THE NAKAMURA LETTERS

THE NAKAMURA LETTERS

For the scientists, the discoverers, and the noodges.

ACKNOWLEDGEMENT

Thanks to the Hawai'i Department of Land and Natural Resources Division of State Parks, without whom the inspiration for this story would not exist.

ONE

EMMA KANO'OPOMAIKA'I Nakamura <emmakn@mahina.edu>
   to Molly
   Molly,
   So I just got here and haven't even unpacked yet, but I'm writing you first thing just like I promised.
   So here I am in my exotic sabbatical location a 2-hour drive from Mahina. We'll see how long it takes this email to get to you. I'm writing it at 2:54pm on Monday. The only internet access I have here is through my cell phone. The signal is junk, but least there's a landline. At least I think there is, I'll have to try the phone later to make sure it works.
   The fridge is old and has rust on it but the temp is fine and there's enough room for my samples.
   The water's catchment, they got one big old concrete tank out back. There's no UV filter, so I gotta boil all my water just to be safe.
   No idea why someone decided to build a house way up here a hundred years ago or whenever, or how the park ended up owning it, but it works out perfect for my research.

So you getting used to being a mom yet? Say howzit to Donnie for me. (Just kidding I can't imagine you saying howzit. Say Good Morrow, Dear Husband or whatever it is you call him.)

Hope you appreciate your fast internet and clean county water. And your warm temperatures too, did I mention I'm freezing my okole off up here? I'll call you tomorrow and you can try get my landline number from your caller ID. I can't find the phone number anywhere. If it was ever on the phone it wore off years ago. Did I mention this place is old?

PS did Kayla start yet? You'll like her, Molly. Once you get some regular help with the baby you'll start to feel human again.

Emma Nakamura, PhD
Professor of Biology
Mahina State University
mahina.edu
SOME OF THE MOST FUN people I know are scientists.
Mae C. Jemison (b. 1956)

TWO

EMMA KANO'OPOMAIKA'I Nakamura <emmakn@mahina.edu>
  to Molly
  Eh Molly,

No worries about being cranky. I guess I'd be cranky too if I had a bunch of guys revving up their chainsaws outside my window all day while I was "housebound, leaking from every orifice, hooked up to wheezing pumps like a dairy cow, and at the round-the-clock beck and call of an insatiable eight-pound nipple-crushing lamprey." I actually wrote down what you said for the next time Yoshi brings up having kids.

Good thing you guys are finally cutting back that hedge though. I can't believe how fast that thing grew, it was taller than your house last time I was over there. That's the thing about gardening in Hawaii though. You bring over some well-behaved plant from the mainland and it gets here and suddenly it's out of control and climbing all over everything. Kind of like our exchange students.

You'll be glad you got the hedge cut down though. It was making your house kind of dark, and plus there'll be less places for coqui frogs to hide.

That's one good thing about staying way up here, there's a lot less coquis. I heard one or two last night, but it wasn't even close to being as bad as it is down at sea level.

I don't think you need to worry about Kayla telling everyone on campus about your private life. First of all, your private life isn't that interesting. Especially not for the first six weeks, if you know what I mean. Second, Kayla's doing an official practicum through the school for her early childhood ed program, so if she does anything unprofessional like blab all your secrets (if you had any) she'd get kicked out. Third, and most importantly, you live in Mahina, Molly, what secrets do you think you have left?

I still don't understand how come you don't get some kind of leave or something for the baby. That's so messed up. At least they're letting you teach your classes online so no danger of you showing up to class and accidentally spraying the front row with breast milk.

There was a freak lightning storm today so I was stuck inside. It gave me a chance to look around the house some more. Molly, I don't think anyone's been here for like decades. I found some Yardley of London (?) lipstick in one of the bathrooms. It looked super retro and smelled like old crayons. This whole place is creepy. You'd love it.

I can't believe how long it took for my last email to get to you. I guess my emails cue up and don't get sent out till an angel flies overhead at just the right altitude or something. Well at least you're getting them.

How was Kayla's first day? She's good, yeah?

Emma Nakamura, PhD

Professor of Biology

Mahina State University

mahina.edu

SCIENCE IS THE GREAT antidote to the poison of enthusiasm and superstition.

Adam Smith (1723-90)

THREE

EMMA KANO'OPOMAIKA'I Nakamura <emmakn@mahina.edu>

to Molly

Honestly Molly I don't think you're doing this mother's helper thing right. If you feel like you have to stay and watch Kayla whenever she's watching the baby, why have her there at all? And no I don't believe she's after Donnie, that's your hormones talking. Come on Molly, she was one of my best students, I wouldn't have told you to hire some sleaze.

Seriously, leave the baby with her and Donnie for a couple days and come up to visit me here.

Oh and when you come up, bring pizza, cause no one delivers all the way up here. I already checked.

OK, guess you'll get this when it QUEUES up, not cues up, is that better? (I still think CUES up is right. Like, it's your turn, that's your cue. But yeah, I'll give you the less vs. fewer thing. Fewer coqui frogs, not less coqui frogs. Happy?)

Emma Nakamura, PhD

Professor of Biology

Mahina State University

mahina.edu

SCIENCE AND EVERYDAY life cannot and should not be separated.

Rosalind Franklin (1920-1958)

FOUR

EMMA KANO'OPOMAIKA'I Nakamura <emmakn@mahina.edu>

to Molly

So I forgot to tell you, Yoshi actually got that residential fellowship he was applying for. I know, I couldn't believe it either. He's gonna be on the mainland for three months, freezing his okole off in the woods working on his Vision or whatever. I told him he could come up here and stay with me if he wanted, it's plenty isolated, but then I found out they're paying him so I was like, bon voyage honey, see you when you get back.

It's weird, usually people bug me (not you so much, only sometimes) but it's so isolated up here, I feel like I'm about to go nuts. At least there's a park ranger. She came by today to say hi (probably check on me and make sure I'm legit). She seems okay. She told me her name, but I forgot it right away. For some reason she thought it was important to tell me that the owner killed themselves here in the house, before it became part of the national park. And then she goes, yeah, people are upset by that but why be upset at one suicide, what about all the other people who died in this house over the years, probably in the exact bed you're sleeping in.

Guess I'll sleep well tonight...

P.S. and yes, it is unreasonable and paranoid of you to forbid Kayla from wearing shorts at your house. It's freaking hot in Mahina, Molly.

Emma Nakamura, PhD

Professor of Biology

Mahina State University

mahina.edu

THERE IS NO ADEQUATE defense, except stupidity, against the impact of a new idea.

Percy Williams Bridgman (1882-1961)

FIVE

EMMA KANO'OPOMAIKA'I Nakamura <emmakn@mahina.edu>

to Molly

The weather cleared up today, so I was able to get some samples. I'm not going to go into a bunch of detail cause I know you wouldn't understand the technical details, but I'm feeling pretty good about it. Oh yeah, and there's a little church down the road, closer to the highway, although I don't know who goes there, there's no other houses or anything around here. Oh, and good thing I brought the generator cause the power went out practically as soon as I'd gotten everything in the freezer. I'm typing this in the total dark in the middle of the living room, with my ear plugs in cause the generator's so loud.

Oh yeah, remember I got that billion-lumen whatever flashlight to bring up? Good thing I did. It's my only light now, besides my phone, so I'm walking down the hall to the bathroom hoping not to get the attention of any ghosts like I'm in The Sixth Sense or something. By the way, not like you asked for my advice, but unless you're going for sainthood (that's a thing Catholics do, right?) I don't think you should have to keep teaching your classes while you're on maternity leave. If your department doesn't have the money to run the classes your students need, that's the administration's problem, not yours. If you keep doing unpaid work for them, they'll just keep expecting it.

Of course I'm one to talk, look where I am. For sure no one's paying me extra to spend my sabbatical up here on the set of Friday the 13th:The Wilderness Years.

I was wondering whether I should tell you this or not so here goes: Last night when it was raining I thought I heard someone crying outside.

I'm sure it was a feral cat or something, but it kind of freaked me out. Just goes to show how your mind can go all weird on you when you're isolated.

OK, time for me to go to bed in complete darkness and try not to think about all the people who died in this house. I'll write again as soon as I can cause I don't want you to go crazy bored at home and end up sticking your head in the oven. I don't need you haunting me on top of everything else I have to deal with.

Emma Nakamura, PhD

Professor of Biology

Mahina State University

mahina.edu

A SHIP IN PORT IS SAFE, but that's not what ships are built for.

Grace Hopper (1906-1992)

SIX

EMMA KANO'OPOMAIKA'I Nakamura <emmakn@mahina.edu>

to Molly

You'll never believe it, I had another visitor today. Wow, two whole people in the space of three days, it's practically Grand Central Station up here. So I was out all morning. I came back kind of tired but I put away my samples, fixed some lunch, cracked a beer, and I just settled in to relax and catch up on my reading, and next thing I know there's someone's knocking on the door. So I thought maybe it was that park ranger again (I still can't remember her name) reminding me to expect to see blood running out of my faucets or furniture flying around the room or whatever, but no, it was this little old haole lady in a big straw hat. At first I thought she was a tourist who got lost. But no, she came to this house on purpose. The Hodges House, she called it. I didn't know it actually had a name, but according to her it did. She was so excited I was staying here, she told me she was sure the house was lonely with no one staying there for such a long time. So that was creepy. (At least she didn't say the house was hungry, I guess that would have been worse. Cause by this point I could totally imagine this place chewing me up and spitting out my bones.)

So I invited her in and asked her how she happened to be in the neighborhood and she told me she'd been visiting the graveyard (??). I was all, graveyard, but I guess it's in back of that little church. I told you about that, right? Betty (that's her name) said her grandfather was a minister at that church so she has a bunch of family buried there.

Seriously, Molly, you should come up here and see this place. Bring Pat too, he'd love to do a story on it for Island Confidential I bet.

And bring pizza. And beer! I thought I packed plenty beer but I'm already running low.

Emma Nakamura, PhD

Professor of Biology

Mahina State University

mahina.edu

WE MUST HAVE PERSEVERANCE and above all confidence in ourselves. We must believe that we are gifted for something and that this thing must be attained.

Marie Curie (1867-1934)

SEVEN

EMMA KANO'OPOMAIKA'I Nakamura <emmakn@mahina.edu>

to Molly

Oh, you think Donnie would be "worried" about you and Pat making that long drive in your "delicate" condition, huh? Riiight. I gotta talk to that boy. He knows there's no chance of you and Pat running off together, doesn't he? Maybe he's still holding a grudge about Pat giving you that copy of The Yellow Wallpaper for your wedding gift. Donnie shouldn't take it personally though. Pat would've given you it no matter who you ended up marrying.

Hey, at least your husband likes having you around. Yoshi wasn't even considering coming up here with me cause he says he needs a reliable internet connection. I think the real reason is he doesn't like the idea of just him and me in the middle of nowhere with nothing to do but hang out with each other. Well, he's off in Indiana or someplace now, doing Art and getting a stipend and I guess atoning for his MBA years.

Tho to be fair to Yoshi (which I always am) he didn't want me to come up here either. He said he didn't think it was "wholesome" whatever that means. Probably he thought it was barbaric to stay somewhere with no cell phone service.

Wait a minute, did you actually ask Donnie if he minds if you come up for a visit? Or are you just assuming you know what he'd say? (You know what happens when you "assume," right?) Ask him, Molly! Bet he says yes.

By the way there is a cat that hangs around here. Brown with stripes, cause I guess a black cat would be too on-the-nose. Anyway that's probably what I heard that night that sounded like someone crying.

Emma Nakamura, PhD

Professor of Biology

Mahina State University

mahina.edu

ABOVE ALL, DON'T FEAR difficult moments. The best comes from them.

Rita Levi-Montalcini (1909-2012)

EIGHT

EMMA KANO'OPOMAIKA'I Nakamura <emmakn@mahina.edu>
   to Molly

Oh, Donnie said it was fine with him for you to come? Told you he'd be OK with it. Yeah, I get the whole thing about you having to pump milk, in case you forgot I am a BIOLOGY PROFESSOR.

So pack your dairy equipment and get up here with my pizza and beer. Tell Pat to get his skinny tochas up here too. I miss you guys. There, I said it.

   Emma Nakamura, PhD
   Professor of Biology
   Mahina State University
   mahina.edu
   LIFE NEED NOT BE EASY, provided only that it is not empty.
   Lise Meitner (1878-1968)

NINE

EMMA KANO'OPOMAIKA'I Nakamura <emmakn@mahina.edu>
   to Molly

Eh Molly, you better get up here quick before I totally lose it. Stupid landline rang last night. One ring, and then nothing. And the technology's so old I don't think I can put any kind of caller ID on it. Something else, I managed to lose my reading-glasses and they turned up later in the weird little bathroom I never use. Ever since then I've been imagining that things aren't exactly where I left them, although why would a burglar break in just to move my things and not steal anything?

At least Nettie seems happy with the service I'm providing. She left me a tip this morning. I tried attaching a picture but no can. Stupid data. So I'll just tell you, it's a dead rat.

(Nettie is the cat. If she was going to keep hanging around I thought I might as well call her something, so I decided to name her after Nettie Stevens.)

So yeah, after all this time I actually have a pet, kind of. I know, you're thinking where's Emma and what have you done with her, right? When the cat starts talking to me that's when you can call the guys with the butterfly nets.

And speaking of the guys with the butterfly nets, this might sound crazy, but with the phone calls and my stuff getting misplaced, I'm going to try an experiment: Sprinkle baby powder on the floor tonight and see if there are footprints tomorrow morning. I got the idea from Scooby-Doo.

   Emma Nakamura, PhD
   Professor of Biology

Mahina State University

mahina.edu

THERE ARE IN FACT TWO things, science and opinion; the former begets knowledge, the latter ignorance.

Hippocrates

TEN

EMMA KANO'OPOMAIKA'I Nakamura <emmakn@mahina.edu>

to Molly

so it's morning and the results of the baby powder are...drum roll please...FOOTPRINTS!
Whose footprints you ask?

Stop drum roll, start sad trombone: MY Footprints. That's right. I guess I went downstairs in the middle of the night to check on something and forgot about it.

Molly, get your milk-soaked carcass up here before I totally lose it.

P.S. HOW had you not heard of Nettie Stevens? The discoverer of sex chromosomes? What are they teaching English majors these days?

Emma Nakamura, PhD

Professor of Biology

Mahina State University

mahina.edu

MY MOTHER ALWAYS TAUGHT us that if people don't agree with you, the important thing is to listen to them. But if you've listened to them carefully and you still think that you're right, then you must have the courage of your convictions.

Jane Goodall (b. 1934)

ELEVEN

EMMA KANO'OPOMAIKA'I Nakamura <emmakn@mahina.edu>

to Molly

So my new friend Betty Brewster came by again today. Remember, the little old haole lady with the giant straw hat? She practically invited herself in and acted all buddy-buddy with Nettie, who she called Balthazar (!?) (like any self-respecting cat would put up with that!)

Anyway all I had to give her was protein bars and instant coffee (yes, instant coffee. I know you're on your fainting couch right now). I gotta tell you, the kitchen's nothing to write home about (except I just realized that's exactly what I'm doing right now: Irony!) a 1950s stove, old cabinets, and a wooden floor that gives you splinters when you walk barefoot.

Even boiling water is kind of a pain because it turns out one of the burners goes on maximum heat when you turn it on no matter where you set the dial, one of them doesn't heat up at all, and the other two kind of turn on and off randomly.

I'm getting pretty sick of this place already, to be honest, but I'm nowhere near collecting all the samples I need. I want to just get it over with and then walk away. I should probably do a shopping run pretty soon, but it's like a forty-minute drive down to the Hashizaki Store, and another 20 to the closest town. I feel like if I'm gonna drive two hours I should just drive back to Mahina.

Hey, you know what would be perfect? HALLOWEEN PARTY! This house is spooky enough for anyone. And you know there won't be any trick or treaters coming by so we can just hang out and drink all night, just as nature intended.

Update:

Right after I went to bed the phone rang. I ran downstairs answered it and I think I heard breathing, then it went dead. Say what you want about conserving energy, I'm sleeping with ALL the lights on tonight. WHEN ARE YOU COMING UP TO VISIT

Emma Nakamura, PhD

Professor of Biology

Mahina State University

mahina.edu

IF YOU KNOW YOU ARE on the right track, if you have this inner knowledge, then nobody can turn you off... no matter what they say.

Barbara McClintock (1902-1992)

TWELVE

EMMA KANO'OPOMAIKA'I Nakamura <emmakn@mahina.edu>

to Molly

Molly, you will not believe this. So you know I was complaining about the long drive I'd have to make to get more beer and food and stuff, but I figured I might as well just get it over with. So I drove down the access road toward the highway and right past the church there was a barricade with the guys in orange vests, the whole thing, and know why? Turns out there was an accident with a propane truck down on the highway RIGHT at the corner of the access road. MY access road.

You remember last time a propane tanker caught on fire here? In case you don't it burned for DAYS. Now I'm totally stuck. I can't get down, you can't come up. There's no other way out.

At least the power's on, and I have enough gas for the generator, for now.

Emma Nakamura, PhD

Professor of Biology

Mahina State University

mahina.edu

I HADN'T BEEN AWARE that there were doors closed to me until I started knocking on them.

Gertrude B. Elion (1918-1999)

THIRTEEN

EMMA KANO'OPOMAIKA'I Nakamura <emmakn@mahina.edu>
  to Molly
  Eh Molly,

So here I am stuck in this old haunted house, miles from civilization, and who should stop by but my old friend Betty Brewster! Like, I'm stranded here by a flaming propane truck and somehow Betty manages to find her way here, how does that happen? And yes, it's her in person and no I'm not hallucinating. So first thing I asked was, where'd you come from and how'd you get up here? Did they put the fire out already? The answer was no, because of course it wasn't, the fire's inside the tank and they have to let it burn itself out. So she knew what was going on. Then she said, get this, she was camping up here. Come on, she just HAPPENS to be camping close to the house? Call me paranoid, but I think she's keeping an eye on the house now that I'm here.

And now that I think of it, I even think she might be the one who's ringing my phone.

So anyway I asked her if there was anything she needed (I'm sure it wasn't my instant coffee that lured her back). She said, well, you know it's Sunday. I actually didn't know off hand (I lost track of the days honestly) but I just nodded like I was keeping up. She said because the church is on the access road and blocked off from the main highway, the pastor and the audience can't get up there so she wanted to go down there with her.

It didn't really make sense to me but it's not like my social calendar was exactly bursting with thrilling activities. I told her sure, I'll go down there with you. In fact I'm leaving in a few minutes. So if this is the last email you get from me, you know where to tell the authorities to look.

OK she's done freshening up talk 2U later if I'm not murdered.
Emma Nakamura, PhD
Professor of Biology
Mahina State University
mahina.edu
THERE IS NO LAW EXCEPT the law that there is no law.
John Archibald Wheeler (1911-2008)

FOURTEEN

EMMA KANO'OPOMAIKA'I Nakamura <emmakn@mahina.edu>
  to Molly
  OK first thing is you'll be glad to know I'm still alive.
  OR AM I...?
  I guess I probably wouldn't be able to type this if I was a ghost so yeah.

Second thing, how am I supposed to know it's called a "congregation" and not an "audience?" Plus I'm not sure you're right about that. What about when people have an audience with the Pope? I've seen it on TV. He stands out on the balcony and there's like an AUDIENCE of about a million people out there to see him.

But hey, I'm not the lifelong Catholic around here so sure, we'll call it a "congregation."

Now I know you're wondering, is Betty Brewster any relation to the Brewster House on Russian Road, the one you wanted to buy? Well I asked her and she said probably but they haven't been able to find the connection.

But that got her talking about her family. So I learned all about Miss Brewster's family history today, cause I can be a good listener when I have to. Anyway what else were we gonna talk about? It's not like I was gonna start lecturing her about my phylogenetic analysis.

So anyway I don't have all the names and dates, but here's the deal. They're all descended from one of the old missionary families, but not one of the famous ones you've heard of.

Betty had two cousins, a brother and sister. They're the ones that lived in the house where I'm staying now.

Their dad and his dad and probably his grandfather were all pastors at that little church. The brother was going to be next in line (no women pastors, it was one of those super old school New England kine churches where the guys wear buckle hats and burn witches). But I guess the brother was kind of a black sheep and it didn't work out. Of course I wanted to know more details about that, but she wouldn't tell me. Instead she goes:

Oh, my dear, Titus was bad enough in his ordinary way. But Priscilla...

Right, now I remember their names. Titus and Priscilla. So of course I ask, what about Priscilla, what did she do? (Remember the park ranger told me about a suicide in the house? I really wanted to ask Betty about it but if it was one of her cousins who killed themselves I'd really kick myself.)

Anyway, instead of dishing the dirt about Priscilla, Betty gets all evasive. She said, well, her life was hard, she buried her father and then her brother, and she sold the church to the Methodists.

Oh, and she told me this: Titus, the black-sheep brother, had a collection of "terrible" books that the father didn't know about, and would've have approved of. So like I said the father died, then Titus was lost at sea, and Priscilla boxes up the books in a big crate.

Then what do you think she does with them?

Sell them? Donate them?

Nope, she gets a couple guys from town to drive the box down to the coast and dump it into the ocean.

I told her I thought it was a waste, but then Betty says,

"When a man believes there is no afterlife, he can be as wicked as he likes. She had to rid the house of all that wickedness, you see."

I didn't argue with her but come on, really? I mean look at me, I'm agnostic so I guess you could say I'm not convinced there's an afterlife. And I don't even cheat on my husband even though no one who knew him would blame me.

On the other hand, maybe that is true for some people. Like you, Molly, no offense but if it wasn't for your Catholic guilt I know some people who'd turn up missing pretty quick.

Hey that reminds me, how's it going with Kayla?

Emma Nakamura, PhD

Professor of Biology

Mahina State University

mahina.edu

IT IS NOW QUITE LAWFUL for a Catholic woman to avoid pregnancy by a resort to mathematics, though she is still forbidden to resort to physics and chemistry.

H. L. Mencken (1880-1956)

FIFTEEN

EMMA KANO'OPOMAIKA'I Nakamura <emmakn@mahina.edu>

to Molly

No of course I didn't know, how would I? I was just joking, seriously. Was it an accident? How did it happen?

Emma Nakamura, PhD

Professor of Biology

Mahina State University

mahina.edu

WHAT WE KNOW IS REALLY very, very little compared to what we still have to know.

Fabiola Gianotti (b. 1960)

SIXTEEN

EMMA KANO'OPOMAIKA'I Nakamura <emmakn@mahina.edu>

to Molly

Of course I'd come down if I could but unless I can get a helicopter and a winch to lift me off the mountain, I'm stuck here for now.

Okay, obviously after what happened you can't go anywhere, especially now you don't have anyone to watch the baby.

I'll admit you were right about one thing. Looks like Kayla lied about being a nonsmoker. I thought the smoke smell was your imagination but I guess not. If Kayla was sneaking a smoke that explains what she was doing in your shed.

(Unless someone planted a cigarette on her? Why would they do that though.)

I can't believe Kayla's dead. Are you sure it was really her? Did you see the body?

The police don't seriously think you had anything to do with it, do they? Maybe you need to call in Honey Akiona again. Is she still practicing in Mahina?

OK, believe it or not, I have something that'll take your mind off your problems, no disrespect to poor Kayla.

Pay attention, I'm not making this up.

I was trying to figure out once the road opens back up if there's a way to add a phone extension without spending a fortune to get someone up here (it's a fortune, believe me. I already called.) I was poking around and in the drawer of the night table way in the back was this old piece of paper stuck to the underside of the table top, if that makes sense.

I don't have the bandwidth to send a picture but here's what it says:

To the one who finds this:

I have taken a woman's life.

Pray for me. I fear I am beyond salvation.

The signature looks like it could be Priscilla Hodges. The sister half of the brother-sister pair that lived in this house. (And maybe the same person that hanged herself in the living room? I still wish the friendly park ranger hadn't told me about that.)

Was she talking about her own planned suicide? She wouldn't have been talking about her brother, because she said I've taken a woman's life, and anyway the brother was lost at sea.

So assuming the signature really is Priscilla Hodges. Who did Priscilla murder?

(Whoa, hold up, I mean WHOM did Priscilla murder, not who, geez, Molly, what are you, like the human spell-checker? Don't you have more important things to worry about, like feeding your baby and staying out of prison?)

I don't think Mahina PD will be interested, but if you think it's worth passing along to them go ahead. Or maybe just keep this email in case I'm murdered by ghosts.

Now the note could be a prank or a fake, and I'm not saying I think it's necessarily real. But on the other hand, why would anyone write this note then stuff it into the back of a drawer? Get that big brain to work, Molly, and figure it out. Also this will keep your mind off the whole Kayla thing.

Poor Kayla. I still can't believe she's dead. So weird.

Emma Nakamura, PhD

Professor of Biology

Mahina State University

mahina.edu

THE IMAGINATIVE CHILD will become the imaginative man or woman most apt to create, to invent, and therefore to foster civilization.

L. Frank Baum (1856-1919)

SEVENTEEN

EMMA KANO'OPOMAIKA'I Nakamura <emmakn@mahina.edu>

to Molly

The park ranger came by to check on me. Her name's Ellie. I thought about showing her that letter but I decided not to. She said the truck's still burning, and they didn't think it was worth the risk to try move it. So no one's going anywhere anytime soon. I asked Ellie if she checked on Betty Brewster cause Betty had told me she was camping nearby, and she said yeah, Betty's fine. So she didn't think it was weird that a 90 year old lady was camping by herself in the middle of the forest. It sounded like she knew Betty though, so maybe it's actually normal for her.

I did ask Ellie if she knew anything about the brother and sister that used to live here, and if it was either one of them who killed themselves here, but she said she didn't know much, cause the house reverted to the park way before her time, and she thinks the suicide story's just a rumor anyway.

THANKS FOR TELLING ME THAT NOW, HELPFUL PARK RANGER, YOU OWE ME LIKE FIVE NIGHTS OF SLEEP.

And then she tells me she's glad someone's finally making use of the house because in all the years she's been working up here no one's stayed here until me. So once again, very reassuring.

Hey, I know you're busy fighting off murder charges and everything, but you get a good internet connection. Can you check a few years back for suicides and murders on the island? I kind of want to know if any of this is true, the suicide and the supposed murder in the note I found.

I sure hope you made the right decision talking to Detective Medeiros. You know on detective shows you're always supposed to lawyer up and then they can't do anything to you. Did you get any idea from them how Kayla died? I think you have every right to ask, the whole thing happened right in your backyard.

Emma Nakamura, PhD

Professor of Biology

Mahina State University

mahina.edu

DO NOT UNDERTAKE A scientific career in quest of fame or money. There are easier and better ways to reach them. Undertake it only if nothing else will satisfy you; for nothing else is probably what you will receive.

Cecilia Payne (1900-1979)

EIGHTEEN

EMMA KANO'OPOMAIKA'I Nakamura <emmakn@mahina.edu>

to Molly

Eh, thanks for the article on false confessions. I didn't even think of that angle. I guess it puts things in perspective. So maybe Priscilla Hodges, if that's who wrote it, had a guilty conscience about something. She might've even blamed herself for her brother's death or something.

I can't remember exactly what it said now. Did she literally write that she killed someone, or did she just say she was responsible for someone dying? I guess I should just haul my lazy carcass upstairs and find the note so I can check for myself.

...

Well now I can't find the stupid note. I thought I remembered putting it right on top of the nightstand but now it's not anywhere. Nettie comes into the house sometimes. Maybe she was doing that thing cats do where they go onto a shelf and bat everything onto the ground. Last time (and I do mean the last time cause I'm not going there again) I went to visit my college roommate, her cat got on the bathroom counter and swatted all my stuff off. I found my deodorant floating in the toilet.

Oh I know what though. I can drive down to the church and check the gravestones to see when the brother Titus Hodges died. Then if I ever find the stupid note I can compare the dates. Not sure what that'll tell us, but it's something to do anyway. Long as I'm stuck up here thanks to the stupid burning truck.

Now, let's go over what you told me:

So it's two in the afternoon, you hear banging on the back door, it's your gardener. He says he found Kayla in the shed unconscious with a burning cigarette on the ground next to her. (OK, you were right about that, she was sneaking out to smoke. Chalk one up for your suspicious mind.) Now, was she lying on the ground, sitting up, what? See if you can find out. I can't think of any biting insect here that could kill someone, but maybe that's something to look into.

Does the gardener have a motive? I mean probably not, but you can look into it.

Unfortunately your gardener messed up the crime scene when he moved her. Probably left his footprints all over the place.

What happened to the cigarette? Did the police take it? If I could get down there I could bring it into my lab and see if there's anything in there that shouldn't be. Did someone poison it?

DID YOU? JK I know you didn't. Probably.

Did you look inside the shed after they took the body away? Better yet let Donnie do it, just in case there's something toxic in there. He's not breastfeeding.

Anyway, I still haven't found the Confession Letter. But: I was looking in the storage closet in the back for a trowel, and there was an inside door that's locked. I brought my bolt cutters (the ones I told Yoshi the Women's Studies department was handing out, he still believes it LOL) and cut off the lock and guess what was inside: No not skeletons or anything like that but a big pile of old books. Holy anticlimax! They look pretty old, though so they're probably worth something.

Emma Nakamura, PhD
Professor of Biology
Mahina State University
mahina.edu

IN SCIENCE IT OFTEN happens that scientists say, 'You know that's a really good argument; my position is mistaken,' and then they would actually change their minds and you never hear that old view from them again. They really do it. It doesn't happen as often as it should, because scientists are human and change is sometimes painful. But it happens every day. I cannot recall the last time something like that happened in politics or religion.

Carl Sagan (1934-1996)

NINETEEN

EMMA KANO'OPOMAIKA'I Nakamura <emmakn@mahina.edu>

to Molly

Remember I told you I found a closet full of old books yesterday? I didn't like seeing them outside where they could get moldy so I brought them in. The books...are not what I'd expect at the home of a pastor, let's put it that way.

I actually went out to look for Betty's camp today. Is that weird? I wanted to ask her if she knew anything about the books. I mean, if those were the ones she didn't throw away, I sure would like to know how bad they'd have to be to get tossed over the cliff.

But before I could find Betty, the park ranger, Ellie, found me.

I still didn't want to tell her about the note, especially now that I don't have it anymore cause she'd think I was just making it up. So I cleverly told her I thought Betty had said something about a murder although I could've misheard, and I asked her had she heard anything about it. She said no, but also that this place was pretty isolated and lots of stuff could've happened without anyone noticing. Then she told me even now she's pretty much the closest thing to law enforcement we have up here, so that was really reassuring.

I was going to tell her about the books I found but I decided not to. Cause when you think about it, how is that even worth talking about? Oh, I was in a house and guess what I found BOOKS. And if I told her I cut off a padlock to get to them then that sounds like I'm confessing to B&E. So I just kept my mouth shut.

I also didn't tell her that someone has been calling me on the stupid landline EVERY SINGLE NIGHT (yes, it's true) and that I heard crying outside the house again and I'm pretty sure it wasn't the cat. Cause that would make me sound crazy.

I did ask her if she'd seen Betty and whether Betty was okay (between you and me I don't think she's okay at all; I think Betty's the one who's been calling me and hanging up, and I wouldn't be surprised if she'd let herself in and was poking around too. Who knows how long it's been since the keys were changed?) Anyway Ellie said she'd check on Betty later, and that was that.

So I didn't get to ask Betty about the books. I really want to talk to her now. This is what I'd ask her:

1. Who was the woman Priscilla (thinks she) killed?
2. Where is the body, if there is one?
3. What was the motive?
4. Did you take the note from my bedroom?
5. What's the deal with the books?

Emma Nakamura, PhD

Professor of Biology

Mahina State University

mahina.edu

THIS IS AN ERA OF SPECIALISTS, each of whom sees his own problem and is unaware of or intolerant of the larger frame into which it fits.
Rachel Carson (1907-1964)

TWENTY

EMMA KANO'OPOMAIKA'I Nakamura <emmakn@mahina.edu>
to Molly

I'm so sorry I had to miss Kayla's memorial service. I hope you told everyone I'm literally stuck behind a burning truck, otherwise I would've come down for sure.

So Donnie finally went to check out the shed? That's good, although he doesn't have your obsessive attention to detail. I'm not surprised he didn't find anything out of the ordinary.

But yeah, I get why you don't want to go in there. I mean, Kayla died in there and we still don't know what killed her.

So:

Gardening tools, an old bicycle, hedge clippings, pesticide, weed killer.

Seems like the only thing in there that might kill someone without leaving a mark would be the pesticides. Although you didn't see her close up, did you?

I'm sure it was some kind of accident or natural causes. Who would want to murder Kayla? But if getting a house alarm makes Donnie feel better you should probably let him do it.

Emma Nakamura, PhD
Professor of Biology
Mahina State University
mahina.edu
I HOPE WHEN I GET TO Heaven I shall not find the women playing second fiddle.
Mary Watson Whitney (1847-1921)

TWENTY-ONE

EMMA KANO'OPOMAIKA'I Nakamura <emmakn@mahina.edu>
to Molly

Did someone say house alarm? Turns out I'm the one that should have a house alarm, not that it would do any good way up here.

I had a break-in last night. I heard some noise last night and thought it was the cat, but someone got into the office. They pulled books off the bookshelf and messed up my desk (shut up I know when someone's moved my stuff). At least none of my things seemed to be missing when I checked.

So I called the police right away and told them what happened, and also that there's only two people who could've done it, Ellie the park ranger and Betty Brewster. I said it has to be one of them cause no one else can get up here cause of the road being blocked. So the lady I talked to said hold on let me check something, then she came back and said, they cleared the truck away early this morning.

So the bad news is the burglar could be anyone. Although somehow I don't think so. I know I didn't leave any doors unlocked. Whoever it was must've had a key.

The good news is the road's finally open again so I'm gonna make a trip to Mahina. I can bring my samples down to the lab, and let the house sit empty for a couple days. That way the burglars can come back and take whatever they want and leave me out of it.

Of course I'll come over to your place. Can you drink yet? Beer's supposed to be good for nursing mothers, right? I'll bring a couple six packs.

And before you ask, no I haven't told Yoshi about any of this. I'm gonna wait till he gets back from his retreat. That way we'll have something to talk about for a week or so at least.

Emma Nakamura, PhD
Professor of Biology
Mahina State University
mahina.edu

[THOSE] WHO HAVE AN excessive faith in their theories or in their ideas are not only poorly disposed to make discoveries, but they also make very poor observations.

Claude Bernard (1813-1878)

TWENTY-TWO

EMMA KANO'OPOMAIKA'I Nakamura <emmakn@mahina.edu>

to Molly

Well, that was a fun trip back down to civilization. I'm back up at the haunted house now. I can see why it would be hard to travel with the baby, wow, does she ever stop eating? When she gets older are you going to tell her that her nickname was "the termite?"

It's still kind of weird seeing you as a mom, but even weirder seeing Donnie as a doting dad, don't tell him I said that. And not that I wasn't happy to see him, but I couldn't exactly snoop around your shed looking for clues with him there, could I?

But the good thing is it sounds like Pat's on the case. (That's one super annoying thing about the bad connection here, I can't get Island Confidential. But I know he's snooping around!) It looks like Donnie's OK with Pat hanging around now. Progress, right?

So I had a visit from a nice police officer and I couldn't identify anything that was taken, except the letter. I showed him the picture I'd taken of it on my phone. But it wasn't my property to begin with, he was all like, whatever. He said I should change the locks, couldn't really help me with anything else. I guess I need to talk to Ellie the park ranger about that since the house is part of the park now. Oh and I asked him if he'd heard about your case and he said yeah but he can't tell me anything about it. He knows your friend Detective Medeiros though. He said everyone remembers that time when Medeiros got everyone on the island involved in rescuing some haole lady who'd gotten herself stuck down in a lava tube on an abandoned property. Have you ever heard of such a thing LOL

Emma Nakamura, PhD

Professor of Biology

Mahina State University

mahina.edu

I BELIEVE THERE IS no philosophical high-road in science, with epistemological signposts. No, we are in a jungle and find our way by trial and error, building our road behind us as we proceed.

Max Born (1882-1970)

TWENTY-THREE

EMMA KANO'OPOMAIKA'I Nakamura <emmakn@mahina.edu>

to Molly

I had Ellie the park ranger come over today. The phone reception's so bad up here I had to text her. I told her I wanted to put in a request to have the locks changed. The cop that came to talk to me confirmed there were no signs of forced entry. So someone has a key.

Of course if Ellie's the one who broke in then that was a stupid thing to ask.

But why would Ellie want to poke around the house now, when she could've done it before I moved in? And what happened to the confession letter, did the same person break in earlier and steal it?

Ellie told me Betty packed up camp and went back down to her house on the coast, wherever that is. She didn't know.

Emma Nakamura, PhD

Professor of Biology

Mahina State University

mahina.edu

MANY RECEIVE ADVICE, only the wise profit from it.

Harper Lee (1926-2016)

TWENTY-FOUR

EMMA KANO'OPOMAIKA'I Nakamura <emmakn@mahina.edu>

to Molly

I hope Donnie's feeling better now! Poor dude, I've never known him to get sick before.

I guess it was too much to try to clean out the shed on top of everything else. (What happened to the gardener anyway? Traumatized by finding a dead body? And what the heck was in that shed? You should ask him if he handled any pesticides. Some of those old-school ones are pretty scary.)

Things are getting back to normal here. As normal as things can be stuck in the mountains hours from civilization. The good news is, there's been no more break-ins, no more weird phone calls in the night, and no more spooky sobbing outside.

Funny how all that stuff stopped after Betty Brewster left. Hmm.

Of course it could have been Ellie doing that stuff and trying to pin it on Betty Brewster.

Or someone I haven't thought of.

Or, you know, ghosts.

Anyway, I'm taking advantage of the peace and quiet and getting a lot done.

Emma Nakamura, PhD

Professor of Biology

Mahina State University

mahina.edu

I DO NOT LIKE IT, AND I am sorry I ever had anything to do with it.

Erwin Schrödinger (1887-1961), speaking of quantum mechanics.

TWENTY-FIVE

EMMA KANO'OPOMAIKA'I Nakamura <emmakn@mahina.edu>

to Molly

Okay, Molly, normally I'd tell you stop being paranoid but that is weird that your gardener came down with the same symptoms Donnie did. How's everyone now? How are you feeling? What about the baby?

Are you sure Donnie didn't get splashed by any liquids while he was cleaning out the shed? Were there any leaky old buckets or containers?

What else is in your backyard? You know what, I bet there's someone up at the Ag College who can help. They have people they send out to help with contamination whenever someone wants to use an old sugarcane field. (You wouldn't believe some of the nasty stuff sugar cultivation left in the soil. Dioxin, arsenic, you name it. I'm not saying all that stuff's in your backyard, but then again, I'm not saying it isn't.)

Ellie told me Betty Brewster's in the hospital. It might be a huge mistake but I think I'm going to visit her.

Emma Nakamura, PhD

Professor of Biology

Mahina State University

mahina.edu

WHEN WE TRY TO PICK out anything by itself, we find it is tied to everything else in the universe.

John Muir (1838-1914)

TWENTY-SIX

EMMA KANO'OPOMAIKA'I Nakamura <emmakn@mahina.edu>

to Molly

Well I got some news. Want to hear it?

Yes, I know you do.

I visited Betty Brewster in the hospital up in Waimea.

(I didn't just barge in, I bought her some flowers from the gift shop. I'm not a monster, Molly.)

I was surprised to see how frail she looked all of a sudden. I mean sure she was old, but she was healthy enough to spend like a week camping in the forest. I know you wouldn't do that.

So I felt kind of bad taking advantage of her weakened state to grill her but I got over it. I figured I'd start by asking her about the letter. And just as I'm about to open my mouth to say something I see this folded piece of paper on the little table next to her hospital bed...IT WAS THE LETTER! She had it with her right there! The letter that was in the house next to MY bed! Well, not my bed but the bed I was using, you know what I mean.

So I sat down on the chair and I reminded her who I was and asked her how she was feeling. So she goes,

"I am not long for this world."

So I said,

"Sorry to hear it. Can I do anything for you?"

She didn't say anything, so then I go to pick up the letter, and I'm about to ask her where she got it, and she grabs my wrist—holy old lady strength Molly, I don't think I have a grip like that even in the middle of paddling season!

Then I said,

"Did your cousin Priscilla really kill someone? Like she claims in that letter?"

Betty just looked away and didn't answer me. So I figured I'd ask something simpler. So I asked,

"Did you break into the house?"

Still she doesn't answer. So then I say, look. I'm here, no judgement, I got nowhere to be and neither do you, why don't you tell me what's going on?

She kind of snorts and then she says,

"I cannot abide wickedness."

Well, Irony Alert ahead, Molly. Go pour yourself a glass of wine, fill up your water bottle, get Baby clamped on, and get ready.

Are you back? Okay.

So Titus, the black sheep brother with the naughty books (yes, those were his books I found, and by "naughty" I mean like Voltaire and Jefferson) was supposed to be next in line to be the pastor. You know, of the little church where their dad was pastor, and his dad before him, etcetera. But like I said, he was the black sheep, and not only was he rebellious and full of heretical ideas, turns out he got someone pregnant.

Well the dad set the girl up with the kid on another island and sent her checks to keep it all quiet. Now Priscilla's doing a slow burn this whole time. Why does she care? Cause first of all her brother and her used to be pretty close, and now they're not close anymore, cause he has this whole other family now. And it's not like she has anything going on. Second it's not like the family had a lot of money to begin with, and she sees the family fortune going to support her brother's little love nest.

Okay, so she spends years fuming about it, and then the final insult was that when the father died, he left Titus all the money and the church building and he left Priscilla the house and no cash. And all these years she'd been the one taking care of the father while Titus was out doing whatever, and I guess Priscilla decided she'd had enough. She made her brother a cup of laurel tea, which I guess is poisonous? You should look it up cause you have a good internet connection. I guess I could've stopped into a Starbucks and used their Wi-Fi but I didn't think of it until I got back home.

And he drinks the tea and dies! So he wasn't lost at sea like it says on his gravestone!

Although in a way he was...

Priscilla packs her brother's body in a crate and tells everyone he was lost at sea. Then she calls one of the parishioners who knows the family. She says Titus left behind all these awful books and she's already boxed them up and wants to get rid of them. So he helps her put the box in the truck and they drive down to the cliffs and dump the box into the ocean.

Meanwhile, this is back before the internet and cable news, so it takes the news a while to get to Titus's girlfriend. But eventually she does learn that Titus has died, and she comes to claim her part of the inheritance for her daughter. So she shows up at Priscilla's house.

Now, here she is, this woman who's stolen Priscilla's brother from her. So you guessed it, Priscilla invites her in for a cup of tea. This time she stages a suicide. She leaves a note saying she can't live without Titus.

So if you're keeping track: Father dies, leaves the house to Priscilla and everything else to Titus. Titus is "lost at sea" so Priscilla inherits his money. Baby mama and love child are out in the cold. Baby mama comes to ask for her share, Priscilla kills her and stages it as a suicide.

Now here's where it gets interesting: the mother of Titus's child was his first cousin. She and Priscilla looked enough alike that people thought the dead woman was Priscilla.

The cousin's name was Betty Brewster.

So I said, genius that I am, but you're Betty Brewster.

And she goes,

I'm Priscilla Hodges, you idiot. I thought you'd have figured it out by now.

So I asked, what about Betty Brewster's daughter?

She doesn't know any of it, Priscilla / Betty said. She was an innocent. I made certain she was raised by a respectable family. And she'll be well provided for when I'm gone.

Did you come into the house and take the letter? I asked. Did you move my glasses?

It was my house, she said. She sold it to the county, and somehow the national park ended up taking care of it, but she still thought of it as hers.

So it was her poking around in the house, which was the house she grew up in. She just felt entitled to it, I guess, and no one had ever changed the locks.

She died later that night. The name on her chart was Betty Brewster. I think I'm the only one who knew who she really was. It's too bad. I wish I could've gotten to know her better. I've never been friends with a real murderer before. That I know of, anyway.

Emma Nakamura, PhD

Professor of Biology

Mahina State University

mahina.edu

...THEY ARE ILL DISCOVERERS that think there is no land when they can see nothing but sea.

Francis Bacon (1561-1626)

TWENTY-SEVEN

EMMA KANO'OPOMAIKA'I Nakamura <emmakn@mahina.edu>

to Molly

Eh Molly,

I can't believe I been to your house all those times and never noticed your hedge. I mean I did, but I didn't really think about what kind of plant it was. So I'll take the credit for inspiring you to find the information, but I guess you really need to thank the late Betty Brewster aka Priscilla Hodges for bringing it up.

Yes, an enclosed space like your shed full of laurel cuttings would definitely release enough cyanide gas to kill someone, especially someone tiny like Kayla. And yes, you did the right thing telling Detective Medeiros. Don't worry, when he checks with his experts he'll realize you're right.

Good thing you found out now. You don't want a poisonous hedge with a baby in the house. A fence is probably going to be lower-maintenance anyway.

It's weird to be packing up now. I'm almost used to being here. Ellie the park ranger stopped by to make sure everything was okay before I checked out. She's the one who told me "Betty Brewster" passed away. And maybe you saw this coming, I didn't.

Ellie's a rich woman now. "Betty Brewster" left everything to her. Ellie thought "Betty" was just someone who loved the outdoors as much as she did. She doesn't know "Betty" was her aunt. Not to mention the person who murdered Ellie's biological parents.

So there you go.

I should be back in Mahina by tomorrow afternoon. How about I just come over and we can order in a pizza?

Emma Nakamura, PhD

Professor of Biology

Mahina State University

mahina.edu

HAPPY IS HE WHO GETS to know the reasons for things.

Virgil (70-19 BCE)

THE PERFECT BODY

THE PERFECT BODY

TO THE SLEEP-DEPRIVED new parents whose lives feel like a blur of diapers and poop.

CHAPTER ONE

"ARE YOU OKAY, MOLLY?"

Donnie squeezed my hand a little tighter as we made our way up the worn steps of the old Mahina Memorial Hospital. My normally-stoic husband seemed nervous about our first time leaving the baby alone with the sitter. But instead of coming out and saying so, he kept asking me how I was feeling.

"Donnie, it's fine. Remember I've known Margaret since she was a student. She's probably the most conscientious person I've ever met. And besides, she's already watched Francesca lots of times."

"During the day. With you there."

"That's how I know how good she is with the baby. She's probably reading to Francesca right now from her CPA study guide. Come on, this is our first dinner out together since the baby was born. Let's enjoy it. It's kind of exciting to be out at night, isn't it? Well it is when you've been stuck in the house for two months."

I don't normally look forward to work functions, but the Mahina State University Donor Dinner was different from the team-building retreats our administration regularly inflicted on us. The purpose of tonight's event was to woo and celebrate our donors. There would be no "inspiring" PowerPoint presentations about doing more with less, no mind-numbing exegeses about the distinction between Mission Statements and Vision Statements, no lectures from the Student Retention Office about crafting a "customer-friendly" classroom.

All I had to do tonight was dress up and enjoy a rare dinner out with my handsome husband.

We followed the crowd through the double doorway into the reception area of the old hospital. The building was in mid-remodel. Here and there you could see a patch of unfinished wood, or wires protruding from the wall where a light switch would be. The tang of fresh drywall cut through the food smells wafting from the dining room.

The old Mahina Memorial Hospital had stood empty for years, accumulating graffiti, termite damage, and ghost stories. Last year, the county had "generously" donated it to the university. It was our white elephant now. But as white elephants went, it was gorgeous.

Donnie and I followed the crowd under one of the two curving staircases that bookended the vast entryway.

"I've always wanted to see what was inside this building," I said. "Look at this. It's like something out of an old movie set."

"It doesn't look ADA-compliant," Donnie remarked. "How do people get upstairs? Is there an elevator?"

That's the kind of thing Donnie would notice. When I enter an old building like this I see glamor and history and long-forgotten craftsmanship. He sees code violations. I would never say it to Donnie, but I think being an entrepreneur eats away a little piece of your soul.

"There's a creaky old elevator somewhere," I said. "You know, the kind I wouldn't ride on a bet. That probably gets us a pass on ADA. Oh! Did you know, Dan, my dean told me he would try to get some space over here for our college? Wouldn't that be amazing?"

"Molly," Donnie said, *"you're* amazing."

He placed his arm around my shoulders as we took our place at the end of what I assumed was the check-in line. I couldn't see the reception table, but from the speed of the line, I assumed there was only one person staffing it.

"You don't like this place," I said.

"It's distinctive," he replied diplomatically. "No offense, but it reminds me a little bit of a horror movie."

"Oh yeah, I can see it. Out of the corner of their eye, someone notices the wallpaper moving. Did they really see a tormented soul screaming? No, it's just the wisteria print. *Or is it?*"

"I thought you didn't like scary movies," Donnie lifted his chin to get a better view of the dining room as we inched forward in line. "This is a distinguished crowd. I see our mayor, two state senators, and a football coach. And there's the prosecutor. Did you know the prosecutor's office used to be in this building?"

"That must have been before I moved to Mahina. This building has been abandoned as long as I can remember."

"You're right. I think the last time anyone was in here was right after I graduated high— graduated *from* high school."

Being much shorter than Donnie, I didn't have the same view he did. But I did get a glimpse of the vast dining room. White-shirted wait staff circulated from one table to the next, refilling water and wine glasses.

"Nice event," he said.

"Don't be too impressed. I wasn't the one who was invited, originally. It was supposed to be

Dan, my dean. But he's stuck at an accreditation conference, so he asked me if I wanted to come in his place. Ooh, look at that stamped tin ceiling. Do you think it's original?"

"I suppose so."

I noticed someone waving from a table inside the dining room. I waved back.

"That's Betty Jackson from the psychology department," I said. "She's the one who helped me with the Student Retention Office paperwork. She had a copy of the memo that said we only had to update the Teaching Philosophy Statements once a semester, not every week. It's only the Customer Interaction Reports that every faculty member has to generate each week—"

"Molly?" Donnie interrupted. "We're up. You need to sign in."

"Professor Barda?" I recognized the woman at the registration table as someone who worked in fundraising. Her name tag was hidden behind her hair. "You're at Table Four. Near the entrance, just like you requested. You'll be seated with Miss Dorothy Pfaff and her companion."

"Oh, that'll be nice," I said. "I've met Miss Pfaff. She's delightful."

I hoped it didn't sound like I was namedropping, but it didn't matter in any case. The woman had already turned her attention to Donnie. I was now invisible.

"Congratulations, ah? Donnie. The baby." Apparently, she thought Donnie had managed to produce a baby all by himself. "Aw, I bet she's beautiful. Get pictures?"

Two things about Donnie. One, he's extremely easy on the eyes. Two, he doesn't seem to realize when people are flirting with him.

I do, though.

"Let's not hold up the line." I slid my arm through Donnie's, smiled at the woman, and moved us toward the dining room.

CHAPTER TWO

TABLE FOUR WAS, AS promised, close to the entrance. In case of a baby emergency, we could make a quick getaway without disrupting the dinner.

When I saw who was already sitting at Table Four, I wanted to make that getaway immediately.

"Isn't that your old friend, the music teacher?" Donnie asked. "What's his name again? I don't remember."

"Stephen Park. He teaches theater, not music, and he is not my friend."

I wish *I* could forget Stephen Park's name. When I first moved to Mahina, Stephen and I were briefly an item. We broke up after he stood me up on my birthday. Infuriatingly, whenever I've run into him since then (impossible to avoid on our small campus), he's always acted like he's the wronged party.

"And that's Bee Corcoran sitting with him. She's the new kinesiology professor I was telling you about."

"The one who keeps telling you to work out more?"

"Yes. Nothing a new mom loves better than unsolicited life advice from someone who's never had kids."

"She doesn't look like a man."

"She's not a man. She identifies as a woman. She is a woman. You shouldn't treat her differently or anything. And I'm not sure she wants people to know, so don't tell anyone."

"Then why did you tell me?"

"You're my husband. We're one flesh, remember our wedding vows?"

"Is that the rule?"

"Yes. You tell me everything, right?"

"Sure."

"Come on. It'll be fine. When Dorothy Pfaff shows up she'll talk about her latest skydiving adventure or her affair with Ernest Hemingway or something and we won't have to say a word."

CHAPTER THREE

I DIDN'T DISLIKE BEE Corcoran, exactly. I just didn't want to sit with her. Bee seemed to think I wanted to hear her views on how much to exercise (excessively), what to eat (practically nothing), and how to sleep (for eight uninterrupted hours, "no excuses." Because a baby who wakes up hungry every hour is apparently an "excuse.") I'd never say it to Bee, of course, but I kind of resented getting fitness advice from someone who grew up without thigh fat.

"Molly!" Bee grinned, exposing blue-white teeth. When she reached across the table to grasp my hands, I saw her arm muscles slithering under her skin. She put me in mind of a toothy blonde shark sizing up a plump seal.

"Bee, this is my husband Donnie. Of Donnie's Drive-Inn. Donnie, this is Bee Corcoran, our new kinesiology professor."

"Donnie. Hel-*lo*." She turned her high-wattage smile on him and reached out to take his hand.

"Stephen Park, Donnie," I interrupted, "I believe you've met."

This forced the two men to acknowledge each other.

It was only after we were all seated that I noticed Stephen looked different. His black dress shirt was snug over his shoulders, and his neck was thicker (either that or he'd shortened his bolo tie). He looked like he'd been lifting weights, something I'd never known him to do before.

Aside from the new muscles, he was the same old Stephen Park. His jet-black hair was pulled back in a ponytail, as always. Defying the usual order of things, his hairline had advanced, rather than receded. Stephen's parents owned Park Beverly Hills Aesthetic Center. Each time he flew to Southern California to visit them, he came back looking a little younger.

But I noticed glints of silver at Stephen's roots. The eternally-youthful Stephen Park was finally going gray.

It had been a long time, I realized. Years. Maybe it was time to let old resentments go.

"We're very lucky tonight, Bee," Stephen started in as he reached for the bread basket. "We get to sit with the world's happiest couple. Isn't it marvelous?"

Apparently not everyone was letting things go.

Stephen liked to poke fun at my "bourgeois conformity." I had moved on and gotten married, he hadn't, and this was his way of getting back at me. Well, I wasn't going to take the bait. The only thing to do was to maintain a dignified silence.

"Wow, Stephen," I said, "it looks like you lost all of that weight you gained after rehab. Between that and the gray hair, I almost didn't recognize you."

"Oh, he's just eating clean and moving around a little more," Bee said, before Stephen could respond. "Getting in shape's not super hard. You just have to make it a priority. Now, Molly, how about you? Are you taking those walks with the baby?"

"Yes, I am. It's quite invigorating," I said, referring to the times I walked Francesca between the playpen in the living room and the changing table in the nursery. Moving around the house was still moving. "And Francesca loves being carried."

"Be careful about carrying her too much," Bee warned. "You don't want her to get lazy."

"She's two months old, Bee. She's not even going to start crawling for another—"

"Oh, I bet she's *adorable*."

"Well of course she's adorable." Stephen managed a thin smile. "Look at her parents. The ideal family. All they need is one-point-seven more kids and a white picket fence, and the dream is complete."

"The cliché is two point *five* kids, Stephen, not two point seven. So, Bee, how do you like the new building? This is the first time I've been inside. It's so beautiful. They don't build places like this anymore."

"Our Bee is fearless," Stephen proclaimed. "Aren't you, darling? The ghost stories don't rattle you at all, do they?"

"Hey, I'm just glad to get the lab space I need, finally," Bee said. "I didn't realize how hard it was going to be getting this place up to compliance. We're getting there, though."

"They say if you come here after dark, you can hear babies crying," Stephen said.

"Oh, Stephen, stop trying to scare me!" She dealt him a playful slap on the shoulder, which sounded hard enough to hurt. Stephen didn't seem to mind. "Let's talk about something happy. Do you two have any baby pictures?"

Donnie got there first. He pulled out his smartphone to show off a picture of Francesca in her pink, blue, and white striped knit hospital cap.

"This is Francesca the day she was born." He swiped to the next picture. "And here she is the day we brought her home."

"Oh, she's so cute!" Bee enthused. "Look at all the black hair! She got it from her dad, didn't she? Donnie, you're Hawaiian, aren't you?"

"Hawaiian, Portuguese, Chinese, Scottish, and German," Donnie said.

"I knew it. Lucky girl, there's so much college money out there for Native Hawaiians. You know some of the scholarships I see my Hawaiian students coming in with, wow. I mean I wish *I'd* had—"

"It's a little early to think about college," I said quickly. Donnie's own college plans had been scuttled in high school when his parents died. "We're just happy to have her. We think she's adorable."

"Yes, *adorable*," Stephen sneered. I wanted to kick him in the shins, but was distracted by a dangerous prickling in my chest. Seeing Francesca's face on Donnie's phone had triggered the letdown reflex. I grabbed my purse and stood up so fast I almost knocked my chair over.

"I have to call the babysitter," I announced, and hurried away, leaving poor Donnie to make conversation with my toxic ex-boyfriend and his tactless companion.

CHAPTER FOUR

I RACED INTO A BATHROOM stall, whipped off my blouse, and checked my pads. I was just in time. Another minute or two and they would have been soaked through. What reckless impulse had led me to wear a red silk blouse? I grabbed a wad of toilet paper and pressed as much moisture out of the pads as I could. In my rush to get out of the house and arrive at the dinner on time, I hadn't even thought about packing an extra pair of breast pads.

Emma Nakamura, my best friend at Mahina State, had advised me not to come to this dinner at all. As I repositioned my bra and bent over to shake everything back into place, I wondered whether she might have been right.

"It's summer," Emma had warned me. "Don't be a schnook and work for free when you should be catching up on your research. It sets a dangerous precedent." (Emma grew up in Hawaii but went to graduate school in New York. This, in her mind, entitles her to throw in a little Yiddish when she feels like it.)

The flaw in her logic was that doing research is work too. But Emma doesn't see it that way. She lives for her research, which has something to do with plant DNA.

Also, Emma and Yoshi don't have kids, so she has no idea how hard it is to get anything done with a baby in the house. Looking after a baby is like trench warfare—long stretches of boredom punctuated by moments of terror. And like trench warfare, it wears you down. A dinner out, even a work-related one, was a treat.

The donor dinner *should* be a treat, I reminded myself. And I wasn't going to let Stephen Park ruin it.

I tugged my blouse straight, checked the soles of my shoes for stray toilet paper, and headed back out, determined to enjoy my dinner.

CHAPTER FIVE

WHEN I GOT BACK TO the table, I saw we'd been joined by Geoffrey Gunderson, Mahina State's new Arts and Sciences dean. He was thin, balding, and sixtyish. Emma liked to complain about him, referring to him as "that dithering medievalist with his glasses on his forehead." As far as I could tell, he wore his glasses the usual way. I think Emma only said those things because she resented answering to someone from the humanities.

"Dr. Gunderson," I said.

"Please call me Geoffrey." He stood, beaming, and shook my hand vigorously. "Geoffrey, as in Geoffrey Chaucer, and spelled the same way. Well, of course *you* get the reference, Molly. Molly's secretly one of us, you know. One of these days we might talk her into coming back over from the dark side."

"The dark side?" Bee asked.

"The business school," I explained, as I took my seat. "My Ph.D. was actually in literature and creative writing."

"I bet there's an interesting story there," Bee exclaimed.

"No. Not really."

I had earned my doctorate from a top-ranked program, fully expecting to land a job at an exclusive campus in a trendy city. But the openings simply weren't there. My graduation was followed by a desperate year of gradually broadening my horizons (or "lowering my standards" if you prefer) until I finally landed a position teaching business communication at Mahina State University.

Upon which my dissertation advisor (who has tenure, a pension, and health insurance) wrote to tell me how disappointed he was in me.

"The thing about going over to the dark side," Stephen drawled, "is it pays so well. And who really needs a soul these days?"

"Well," Geoffrey Gunderson rubbed his hands and beamed at us. "What a marvelous concentration of talent we have at this table."

"Geoffrey was sharing some good news about your campus," Donnie said.

"I didn't even ask to be nominated for the system research award." Bee flashed her Sports Illustrated swimsuit smile at her dean. "I'm as surprised as anyone. Honestly."

Stephen reached over and rubbed Bee's back. But he wasn't looking at her. His eyes were on me.

"She's amazing, isn't she?" he said.

A real academic, he may as well have added. Not some phony who couldn't get a literature position and had to settle for teaching business majors how to pad their resumes.

I ignored him and turned to Donnie. But Donnie was glaring at Stephen. A little muscle in Donnie's jaw was twitching.

"Well, I didn't only stop by to crow about our accomplishments." Gunderson was rubbing his hands so vigorously now, I half-expected to hear cricket noises. "As impressive as those may be, it's my sad duty to inform you that Miss Dorothy Pfaff won't be joining us tonight after all."

"Oh, what a shame," I said, with genuine disappointment.

"Is Miss Pfaff not feeling well?" Donnie asked.

"No, no, nothing of the kind," Gunderson assured us. "Miss Pfaff is in fine fettle. She's on her way to Buenos Aires right now for a, I believe it's a tango competition of some sort. Her assistant got the dates mixed up. In any event, I wanted to let you know what was happening. But please, stay and enjoy your dinner."

He looked around and lowered his voice. "Please do stay. We need to keep empty seats to a minimum."

"Ah," Stephen said. "Like the Academy Awards."

"Precisely. Precisely," Gunderson said, and then scuttled away, no doubt relieved to escape our dysfunctional table. Donnie reached over and gave my hand a sympathetic squeeze. With Dorothy Pfaff on her way to Argentina, we were staring down the barrel of a long evening with Stephen and Bee.

For a moment I considered faking going into labor. But I'd just had a baby two months ago, so that particular ploy would probably fool very few people.

And then my phone rang.

CHAPTER SIX

"IT'S MARGARET," I SAID to Donnie.

"I can take it." Before I realized what was going on, Donnie plucked the phone from my hand and was gone.

I couldn't really blame him.

"That was the babysitter calling," I explained.

"Molly, you're so lucky," Bee said. "Donnie seems like such an involved father."

And I'm a very involved mother, although I don't suppose it would occur to anyone to praise me for it.

"He is," I said. "He's wonderful. You're right. I do feel very lucky."

"Indeed," Stephen put in. "I mean, look who you *could've* ended up with."

"I know, right? Bullet dodged." I took a sip of water and didn't look at either Bee or Stephen. What was taking Donnie so long?

Fortunately, a server rolled up to our table with a silver drink cart. She opened her mouth to say something, made brief eye contact with Stephen, and then looked away quickly.

She was tall, slim, and young, with bronze coloring and startling green eyes. Surprisingly, Stephen didn't try to flirt with her.

"Nothing for me," Stephen said flatly, his eyes fixed on the tablecloth in front of him.

Maybe he was afraid Bee would snap him in half if she caught him gawking.

"We'd like green tea," Bee instructed the server.

"Sure thing." The young woman set a box of tea bags on the table. She looked familiar, but I couldn't place her. She wasn't one of my former students. And was it my imagination, or was she looking everywhere except at Stephen?

"What kinds of wine do you have?" I asked.

"Chardonnay, Merlot, and Pinot Noir."

"I'll have Pinot Noir, please."

"They have tea, Molly," Bee said.

I pretended not to hear her.

"Wait," I called to the server as she turned to go. "*They'll* want some too."

"Pinot Noir for them as well?"

"Sure. Yes. Thank you."

I watched the server fill Donnie's glass, and then the glasses at the two empty place settings.

"Impressive, Molly," Stephen said, when the young woman had gone.

"I think the word you're looking for is *thoughtful*, Stephen." I picked up my glass and took a sip. "How would Donnie feel if he came back to an empty wine glass?"

"You know, Molly," Bee said, "if you're concerned about milk production, wine doesn't really help. The thing about wine and beer is a myth. All you need to do is drink plenty of water. The milk glands—"

Stephen pushed his chair back. "It's stuffy in here. I'm going out for a smoke."

"Stephen..." Bee began. But Stephen was already gone.

Now only Bee and I remained, staring at each other across the round table. This was not what I had in mind when I'd talked Donnie into attending the donor dinner with me.

"Love how Mr. Edgy Avant-Garde has to run for the smelling salts the minute someone brings up breastfeeding."

"What was that?" Bee asked.

"What? Oh, nothing, I was just thinking out loud. Apparently. Um, Bee, I notice Stephen's really gotten into shape. Have you been coaching him?"

"Not much. A few tips here and there. But he's very self-motivated. Oh, thank you."

The server had returned with a pot of hot water for the tea.

"One thing, though, he really has to stop smoking," she continued when the young woman had left. She opened the teapot, lowered in three teabags, and closed it again. "I know it's hard to quit, but smoking's about the worst thing you can do for your health. Besides being inactive."

"But they're not *real* cigarettes, Bee." I mimicked Stephen's why-is-everyone-so-stupid inflection. "They're *clove* cigarettes."

"Those are just as bad," Bee said earnestly.

"No, I know about clove cigarettes, I was just..."

Fortunately, Donnie reappeared.

"What did Margaret say?" I asked him. "Is everything okay?"

"Francesca is asleep, but there's only one bottle of breast milk left, and Margaret wanted to know, what if the baby wakes up and drinks the rest of it? I told her go ahead and use the formula. Didn't we go over all that with her before we left?"

"We did." I took back my phone. "But you know Margaret. She has to double-check everything. This is why she's going to be a great CPA."

"Good for you, Molly, sticking with the breastfeeding," Bee said. "You know, you're going to start losing weight eventually if you keep at it."

Once again, I felt an ominous prickling in my chest.

"I'm sorry." I stood up and pushed my chair back under the table. "Will you excuse me for a second?"

"Is it something I can take care of?" Donnie asked, a little too eagerly. I sympathized, but there was nothing to be done.

"No. It is not. I'll just be a second."

Talking about Francesca's feeding had re-activated the letdown reflex. I scurried away, holding my arms up in front of me praying mantis-style.

This time I was too late. As I burst into the ladies' room I saw my reflection. Two maroon splotches bloomed on my red silk blouse.

I cleaned up as well as I could and then poked my head out of the ladies' room to make sure the coast was clear. It was not. Geoffrey Gunderson stood in the entryway between the hallway and the dining room, chatting with someone I couldn't see.

I couldn't walk past Gunderson. Attempting to scrub the milk off my blouse had only made the stains bigger. And I'd had to throw away my soaking-wet breast pads. To replace them I'd used folded paper towels, which gave me a sort of Cubist silhouette.

Instead of turning left toward the dining room, I turned right to continue down the hallway toward the EXIT sign. The door opened directly to the moonless night outside.

Good. A walk around the building would give my blouse a chance to dry off.

I stepped out onto the rickety landing and let my eyes adjust. It was still warm outside, and a little drizzly. We had walked in on the ground floor, so I was surprised to see several flights of wooden stairs between me and the ground. The dining room was level with the front entrance, but because of the slope of the lot, I was twenty or thirty feet up.

I wasn't sure the stairs would hold my weight. And with no lights and no visible moon or stars, it was completely dark. Fine. I'd go back the way I came, praying-mantis arms and all, and hope no one noticed my stained blouse.

I pulled on the door handle to go back inside. But the door had locked behind me.

Okay, no problem. I'd stick with Plan A. Walk down and around the building and go back through the front entrance. I picked my way down the creaking steps and, happily, made it to the bottom without incident. I switched on my phone light and followed the dirt path, watching the ground for potholes and rocks. The last thing I needed was to trip in the dark and break something.

I caught a whiff of Indonesian clove smoke, and I looked up to see the glow of the end of a cigarette about twenty feet above me. It had to be Stephen up there on the terrace, smoking his stupid cigarettes. I kept my eyes on the ground and kept walking.

"Molly!" I heard Stephen call out above me. I sped up my pace.

"Oh, drop dead, Stephen," I muttered. Whatever he was going to say to me, I didn't want to hear it.

And then I heard something I'd remember for a long time.

Floomp. A heavy sack-hitting-the-pavement kind of sound.

I looked up at the balcony again and strained to see the glow of the cigarette. It wasn't there.

I turned around and shone the light behind me.

What I saw nearly made me drop my phone.

CHAPTER SEVEN

I KNOW I DIALED 9-1-1. But only because it's in my call history. I have no memory of making the call.

I remember sirens, and then pulsing blue and red lights in the darkness.

I remember Donnie (how did he get out here?) asking me over and over whether I was okay. I don't remember what I said to him.

I remember Bee Corcoran rushing over to the covered gurney as it was being loaded into the back of the ambulance, and Detective Ka'imi Medeiros stepping in front of her, coming between her and Stephen.

I remember thinking, no one is supposed to touch the body. Bee should know that.

At some point Donnie must have taken me home. Although I don't remember that either.

The next thing I recall was waking up in my own bed, to the sound of a ringing phone. I was wearing sweatpants and a worn-out T-shirt.

Donnie was standing in the bedroom doorway, the baby over one shoulder, holding the handset of our phone.

"You're looking for Molly?" Donnie announced loudly. "Just a second, Dan. Let me see if she's here."

I shook my head. No, I was not in any condition to talk to my dean.

"Sorry about that, Dan." Donnie came over to the bed and let me take the baby from him. "She's not available. Can I have her get back to you?"

"Your dad is awesome," I whispered to Francesca as Donnie went off in search of a scrap of paper and a pen.

CHAPTER EIGHT

THE BABY OPENED HER mouth wide, giving me a glimpse of the sharp tooth breaking through her lower gum. She waggled her head back and forth to find the optimal position and clamped on. Immediately her panic melted away, and her eyelids fluttered and drifted closed. She was motionless except for the plump cheeks, which pulsed gently as she applied an eye-popping level of suction.

I wasn't exactly comfortable, but the baby was happy, which was something.

"Look at you two," Donnie smiled as he came in. "You look so serene."

"I guess," I said. "If 'serene' is a synonym for the sensation of someone clamping a sawtooth binder clip on your nipple. She's having fun, anyway."

Francesca bit down harder and kicked her chubby legs with delight.

"A sawtooth binder clip? What's that?" Donnie sat on the chair next to the bed.

"I don't know. What did Dan want? Was it about what happened last night?"

"No, it was something about moving your office. I don't know if he knows about last night. He didn't say anything about you-know-what."

"It's fine," I said. "We can discuss it in front of the baby. She's not paying attention. She's busy doing her food-processor imitation."

Donnie stroked my hair. "How are you feeling? It must have been hard for you. Having to see what you saw."

"Uh, yeah."

Here is the horrible truth: I felt more relief than grief at Stephen's death. I was not about to tell Donnie, of course. He'd think I was a heartless monster.

But it was freeing to realize I could show up at the next department chairs' meeting without having to endure an hour of Stephen's passive-aggressive barbs.

"It's kind of jarring to have someone die right in front of you," I said.

Donnie leaned forward and laid his hand on mine.

"You saw it happen?"

"Well, okay. He didn't literally die in front of me. He died *behind* me if you want to be precise about it."

"Molly, what were you doing back there? I'm not saying it was your fault or anything, I'm just curious."

"You really want to know? Fine. I was trying to avoid running into Geoffrey Gunderson. He was standing right where the hallway opens into the dining room."

"So, you went out the back door instead?"

"Yes. And then the door closed behind me and I was locked out, so I couldn't go back inside."

"But why? I know you don't like talking to people, but you were doing fine. I thought you were very charming."

"The front of my blouse had two big milk stains on it. Plus I was covered with those little paper shreds you get when you try to dry your shirt with a paper towel. Donnie, would you mind...?"

"Sure."

Donnie got up and came back with a pillow and a tall glass of ice water. I positioned the pillow under the baby to ease the strain on my back and downed half the glass in one go.

"Thanks," I said. "Much better."

Donnie sat back down and looked at me with a concerned expression.

"Molly, I—"

"Donnie, you don't have to take the day off. Go take care of the Drive-Inn. Margaret will be here soon."

"That's not what I was going to say."

"You weren't offering to stay home with me?"

"I will if you want me to."

"No, it's fine. What were you going to say?"

"I just wanted to say I know you're naturally a curious, inquisitive person, and I love that about you."

"But?"

"When you set your mind on something, there's no stopping you. But now we have Francesca, it's not just the two of us. We have to think about—"

"Donnie, can you get to the point? Sorry, that sounded kind of snappish."

"Kind of," he agreed.

"Look, I have an angry little customer here chewing up my tender bits. *Ow*, baby, hang on. Next course is coming right up."

When I had switched Francesca to the other side, I turned my full attention to Donnie.

"Yes? What would you like to tell me?"

"I'm worried you're going to get curious about what happened to Stephen Park, and you're going to get mixed up in something dangerous," he said. "I'm asking you right now. Please don't."

"You're asking me not to look into Stephen's death?"

Donnie nodded.

"Okay."

"Really?"

"Yes, really. Please don't worry. I have no desire to get involved with this. Besides, I didn't even..."

I stopped myself before I could say, *I didn't even want to have anything to do with Stephen Park when he was alive.* It would have come off as callous, I think.

Donnie reached over and squeezed my hand.

"Thank you. Molly, I don't like coming off like I'm telling you what to do. But if it's a choice between that and some crazy murderer pushing you into a lava tube—"

"I guess I'm never living *that* down..." Francesca grunted and jerked her head back and forth. "*Ow*! Come on baby, let's latch you on properly. Geez, what kind of baby starts growing teeth at two months?"

I repositioned Francesca as Donnie averted his eyes.

"It's okay," I said, "You're allowed to look."

"I know. I just don't want to get shot in the eye again."

"Look. I didn't do it on purpose. I had no idea it could squirt so far. Nobody warns you about those things. Hey, do you want to hear a joke Emma told me? What's a pirate's favorite letter of the alphabet?"

"Molly, you're trying to change the subject—"

"You'd think it would be *Arrrr*, but they're really in love with the C."

"Molly? You mean it about not getting involved?"

"Oh yes. I mean it. And I really would rather not think about it anymore."

Stephen Park had already benefited from my uncompensated emotional labor while he was alive. He wasn't getting any more from me just because he was dead.

"I only want you to be safe. Both of you." Donnie stood up and went into the walk-in closet. "Are you sure you'll be okay with me going to work today?"

"Fine. Totally back to normal already. Accidents happen."

"You think it was an accident?" Donnie said from inside the closet.

"Probably. But what do I know? It's not my job to figure out what happened. Like I said, I don't want to think about it."

I flashed back to the sight of Stephen lying lifeless on the ground. I *hoped* it was an accident. If not, someone had just gotten away with murder.

CHAPTER NINE

MARGARET SHOWED UP at exactly two minutes to nine to take over baby duty. Francesca greeted her arrival with a well-timed (from my perspective) diaper explosion. Margaret took the baby from me and went to change her while I settled down at my computer.

One of the persistent myths about academia is that professors get summers "off." Our summers are unpaid, and technically the university can't require us to do anything they're not paying us for.

However. There are things that need to get done, whether it's summer or not. And many of these things fall to the department chair (me).

During the school year, faculty members are supposed to turn in regular reports to the Student Retention Office. These reports don't always get done, because there is no way to force faculty members to take attendance, record student engagement levels, or update their Teaching Philosophy Statements. When the faculty in my department take principled stands against administrative overreach by refusing to fill out the forms, I then have to spend my summer completing the forms myself. Because I had no information to work with, I found myself using the sophisticated data interpolation method known as "making stuff up."

For this course session, please list

a) The date, room assignment, and instructor of record,

b) The current enrollment expressed as a whole integer,

c) The average engagement level on an eleven-point scale, rounded to two decimal places.

d) The average student success level (letter grade on a four-point scale), rounded to two decimal places.

Fortunately for me, the management department was small—only four full-time faculty including me. But multiply that by three or four classes per faculty member times a sixteen-week semester, and it left me with a pile of reports to fill out before fall semester.

I was having some trouble focusing on my task, so when I heard Margaret clear her throat, I welcomed the interruption. I swiveled my chair around to face her.

"Sorry to bother you Professor, but I was wondering if I could ask you something?"

"Sure. Have a seat. Margaret, you can call me Molly. It's been how many years since you were my student?"

She perched on the arm of the couch with Francesca on her lap.

"Sorry, Professor, I guess I'm just used to it. I mean Molly, sorry. I heard about what happened last night. Poor Professor Park. It must have been awful for you."

"Yes. It was. Thank you, Margaret. You're very compassionate."

"You shouldn't feel bad about it, Professor. It's perfectly normal to throw up when you see a dead body. I'm sure everyone understands."

"Margaret, did you have something you wanted to ask me?"

Margaret hitched the baby up onto her shoulder.

"I hate to bother you, but Keola? You know, my boyfriend?"

"I've heard you mention him."

"His job ended, and he's looking for something else. He was working as a lab tech. He has a biology degree. If you know of any opportunities?"

"I can ask around. In fact, Emma Nakamura might know of something. I'll ask her when I see her."

"Thank you so much, Professor. That would be so nice of you!"

"Where was he working before? I know Emma will ask me. She'll want to talk to his previous supervisor."

"Oh, that's the thing." Margaret absently rubbed the baby's back. "He doesn't feel like he can ask Professor Corcoran for a recommendation."

"Professor Corcoran? Is this Bee Corcoran? In Kinesiology?"

Margaret nodded.

"I see. He doesn't want to bother her while she's grieving. Understandable."

"Grieving?"

"Because Bee and...never mind. Why can't he ask her for a recommendation?"

"She kind of fired him."

"Ah. Do you know why?"

"There was a disagreement about the lab animals. I told him, don't contradict your boss, but I guess he didn't listen."

"Was she mistreating the animals?" Bee could be tactless, but she didn't strike me as someone who tortured helpless creatures.

Margaret shook her head.

"No, it wasn't animal cruelty. You have to report animal cruelty. It was just that Professor Corcoran sometimes got the rats mixed up. Keola would find them in the wrong cages. She didn't want to listen to any of his suggestions for keeping records. I told him, Keola, bosses don't want to hear *your* ideas. They want you to take *their* ideas and make them successful."

"That sounds pretty cynical, Margaret. Where did you hear that?"

"Your Intro to Business Management class."

"Huh. Really?"

"Professor, Keola didn't do anything wrong. He was just trying to help. He loves animals."

"Okay, I'll talk to Emma about it."

"Oh, thank you so much Professor!"

She started to stand up.

"By the way, someone told me you don't get paid in the summer. Is it true?"

"It is true. I'm on a nine-month appointment."

"But you're still working?"

"Yep."

"What are you working on? Sorry, I'm not trying to be nosy. But Keola thinks he might want to be a college professor someday."

Margaret held the baby on her shoulder and swayed rhythmically.

"Sure, I don't mind telling you. Research, prep for fall classes, student petitions, search committees, course scheduling, and whatever's currently on fire in my in-box. Right now, it's paperwork for the Student Retention Office that the other faculty members didn't do during the school year. If I weren't department chair maybe I could take some time off. Travel, or just drop off the face of the earth. Like everyone else in my department seems to be doing."

"So why did you want to become department chair?" Margaret asked.

"I don't know that I *wanted* to. Harrison and Schneider refuse to do it. Every time the dean tries to make them, they threaten to retire. So that leaves Rodge Cowper and me, and I'd rather be department chair than have Rodge be in charge. Sorry, I've probably given you way more information than you wanted."

"No, it's good to know." Margaret stroked Francesca's head, which was resting heavily on her shoulder. "No offense, but honestly? I'm glad I'm going to be an accountant."

CHAPTER TEN

DONNIE STOPPED IN AT home after the lunch rush to check on the baby and me. We sat out on the front porch, enjoying the view of Uakoko Street. It had been raining all morning, so the air was pleasantly cool. Donnie fed Francesca from a bottle.

"Well, the news is out," I said. "Margaret already heard all about what happened last night."

"M-hm," Donnie said to Francesca. "Look at her. What a champ. She's not letting that bottle go until she's killed it."

"It's funny," I said. "Francesca's whole world is about consuming the bottle. She's being utterly selfish right now, and it's the most adorable thing imaginable. But imagine a grownup acting the same way. Not adorable at all."

"My customers are a little bit like our baby. They show up, they're hungry and cranky, we feed them, and then they're happy."

"So how are things at work, speaking of your customers? Has anyone asked you about last night?"

"Everyone," Donnie said. "They already knew I was going to the donor dinner because I left work early last night."

"Right. You don't usually take off work."

"People are letting their imaginations go wild."

"What do you mean?"

"Park was relatively young and in pretty good health. And you know, a place like the Old Mahina Memorial Hospital, with its history, people are going to, you know. Assume things."

"Do you mean people think it's haunted?" I asked.

"When you ask people straight out, they say *they* don't believe in ghosts or anything like that. But then they tell you everyone else does."

"Hey, I don't even believe in ghosts, and you wouldn't have a hard time convincing me the old hospital is haunted. Although it is gorgeous. Did you see the ceiling in the dining room?"

Donnie checked his watch and set the baby bottle down on the rattan table. Francesca had fallen asleep in his arms.

"Okay, I have to get back. You two going to be okay?"

I reached out to take Francesca. She woke up and fussed until I popped the bottle back into her mouth.

"We'll be fine," I said. *"Our* house isn't haunted. Also, Emma might stop by later."

"Good. I feel better knowing you have company."

Donnie gave me a quick kiss, and I went back inside. I got Francesca to sleep in her rocking bassinet and was able to answer a few emails before someone rapped on the front door.

"The baby's asleep," I whispered as I let Emma in.

"Nah, she's not," Emma contradicted me. "She's wide awake. Oh, hey little girl!"

"She's awake *now*," I said.

Emma knelt next to the bassinet. Francesca beamed at Emma.

"Aw, she's smiling at me. Look, she wants me to pick her up." Emma picked up the baby. "That okay with you?"

"Sure. Want coffee?"

"Yeah, thanks."

"Want a burp cloth?"

Emma had hoisted the baby onto her shoulder and was marching her around the living room. Francesca giggled and cooed.

"Nah," Emma said. "If she spits up on me I'll just throw my shirt in the wash. Like I did last time."

"Like last time? Oh, you mean you'll make *me* wash it and then you'll take one of my shirts. Oh, before I forget. Can you use a lab tech?"

I told Emma about Margaret's boyfriend.

"You're asking me do I want to hire some little boy who's gonna come in acting like he knows more about running my lab than I do? Yeah, I think I'll pass."

"Well, I told Margaret I'd ask you about it."

"You can tell her I said eff off with that."

"I'll paraphrase."

"Eh, how come she didn't just come ask me? She knows who I am."

"Why didn't the shy, high-strung accounting major approach you directly? I don't know, Emma. It's a mystery. Hey, so I never told you what happened last—"

"Oh yeah, last night! Big news, ah?" Emma was talking to the baby, not to me. "Isn't that *right*, Francesca? Oh, yes, it is."

"Okay, let me go get coffee. You okay watching the baby out here?"

"Auntie Emma wants to hear all about it," I heard Emma tell the baby. "Miss Constance gave mean old Stephen Park what was coming to him, didn't she?"

I brought our coffee back out to the living room.

"Sounds like you heard about Stephen already. What was that you were telling the baby? Emma, don't tell her Stephen Park got what was coming to him. That's not right."

Emma touched her nose to Francesca's.

"Oh, your mommy thinks Aunty Emma's being too mean, but she's wrong, because Stephen totally deserved it, didn't he? I think we need to remind your mommy about the time Stephen forgot all about her birthday because he was too busy—"

"Emma, Stephen might not have been my favorite person, but you can't say someone deserved to die."

"Oh yeah? What about Hitler?"

"Stephen Park was a self-important, faithless poseur, but he wasn't a genocidal dictator."

"As far as you know."

"No, I'm positive he wasn't. He didn't have the initiative."

Emma gave Francesca's chubby cheek a kiss and placed her back in the bassinet. Francesca dropped off to sleep immediately.

"That schmuck broke your heart, Molly. I'm talking about Stephen Park, not Hitler."

Emma examined her shoulder and rubbed the fabric.

"Oh look, baby left me a little blurp. So, tell me from the beginning what happened."

"First you tell me. Who's Miss Constance?"

I handed Emma a coffee mug. She took a sip.

"Mm, I like this one. Good choice, Molly."

"Emma?"

"Oh yeah, Miss Constance. People see her around the old hospital at night sometimes."

"Who is she?" I asked. "I mean, besides a ghost, I got that. But was she a patient? An employee?"

"She was a patient. I heard she was from a rich family and as soon as she got married her husband had her hospitalized for nerves or whatever. Then he went out and partied and spent all her money. You know back in those days that's how it was. Your husband could lock you up in the loony bin and take everything you have and there was nothing you could do about it."

"Yeah, the good old days. So, whatever happened to her?"

"She killed herself," Emma said.

"Oh, how awful."

"Yeah, but she got the last word. Her husband was riding the train—"

"Here? On this island?"

"Yeah, we used to have a train until a bunch of the tracks got washed away by a tsunami. Anyway, his car derailed and fell into the ocean. Him and a bunch of his party buddies were never seen again."

"Wow." I took a sip of my coffee. It had gotten cold. "And people think Constance did it?"

"Uh huh. And that wasn't enough for her. Cause they say she's still around, taking revenge on—"

"Men?" I asked.

"Nah, not all men. Just, you know..." Emma glanced at the sleeping baby.

"Eff-boys," she stage-whispered.

"What boys?"

"Useless idiot party boys," she explained. "You know, like your stepson."

"Ah. Your words, not mine."

"How come I never hear about Davison anymore by the way?" Emma asked.

"Ever since he moved to Vegas he's been too busy to call or visit. It's like he doesn't even exist. It's wonderful."

"Aw, who says there's no happily ever after in real life? Anyway Molly, you were there. Last night. What happened? Tell me everything."

"Okay but first let me put on some fresh coffee. I'll bring out the pot."

CHAPTER ELEVEN

"THEY HAD THE DINING room open to the terrace?" Emma exclaimed.

"You know the layout of the building?" I asked.

"Kinda. Me and my friends used to go exploring there. That terrace is where they say Miss Constance killed herself."

"Ooh. That just gave me a little shiver."

"And now you're telling me Stephen died in the exact same place? Yeah, chicken skin for real. What were they thinking, letting people go out there?"

"It's not like we were encouraged to," I said. "They didn't have any lights on. But they hadn't exactly closed it off, either."

"Why did they have a dinner in the old hospital at all? It's kind of morbid, ah? All those people suffering and dying and losing their minds in there—"

"Oh, but Emma, the building is beautiful."

"Seriously?"

"Inlaid marble floors, big sweeping staircases, there's nothing on the island remotely comparable. I can see why they wanted to have a donor event there, haunted or not."

"They should've at least had lights on." Emma tipped up her mug and then refilled her coffee.

"That reminds me," I said, "Wasn't there supposed to be some big project to catch up on our deferred maintenance and bring all our buildings up to code? Wasn't it part of the deal when the county gave us the building?"

"Old news, Molly. Don't you remember what happened the last legislative session? The ledge zeroed out all our maintenance funding."

"I thought they gave us some money in the end, though."

"We got three million dollars for football," Emma said. "Everything else got cut."

"Seriously?"

"Seriously."

"See, that's why I don't follow the news. Ugh."

"Molly, that's probably how come they had the donor dinner up there in the first place. So the high maka makas could see for themselves all the work that needs to be done and open up their checkbooks."

"If that was their plan, it backfired. No one was pulling out their checkbooks that night, believe me."

Emma and I drank our coffee in silence for a few moments.

"So, the old hospital building's been closed for decades," I said. "They open it up and the first event they have there, Stephen Park wanders out onto the terrace, the same place where Miss Constance supposedly killed herself, what, a hundred years ago. Next thing you know, he's dead."

"Yeah. Creepy, ah?"

"Ghost stories aside, though. It's not impossible that there was someone up there with Stephen."

"You see or hear anyone?" Emma set down her coffee cup. I lifted it and slid her coaster underneath.

"No. I was just remembering how dark it was out there. Yeah, it was probably an accident. Stephen called my name, and when I didn't answer he leaned too far over the railing and fell."

"Oh yeah, if you hadn't walked by, Stephen wouldn't've tried to get your attention, but you ignored him, so he leaned over to try again, and he fell down. You shouldn't blame yourself for Stephen dying, though."

"It hadn't occurred to me to blame myself, Emma, but thanks ever so much for bringing it up."

"You know, if there wasn't someone else up there with Stephen Park? You're the only one who saw what happened."

"But that's the problem. I didn't see anything. Stephen fell behind me, after I'd already walked past. I only saw him after I heard him fall and turned around."

"You remember anything that happened just before?"

Emma stood up and took our coffee cups into the kitchen.

"Emma, you know what? We should talk about something else. This isn't our problem to solve."

"Sure," Emma called from the kitchen. "As long as you can honestly say you're a hundred percent sure that whoever killed Stephen Park will never kill anyone else."

"Emma, no one killed Stephen Park. Ghost or human. It was an accident."

"Oh yeah? Would you bet your life on it?"

I placed my hands over my eyes, relaxed into the couch cushions, and let my mind float back to that evening. It was a practice I'd learned from Stephen, of all people. Memories want to be found, not forced, he'd said. This technique had never helped me remember my student's names, and it sure hadn't stopped Stephen from forgetting my birthday, but I didn't have any other tricks up my sleeve.

I recalled the glow of Stephen's cigarette and the scent of burning cloves. It was dark, and Stephen had been drinking. No, wait. I was the one who had been drinking. Stephen and Bee had green tea. So, what happened? Either Stephen really wanted to get my attention and lost his balance, or someone had been waiting up there to give him a little shove. Someone who had been pushed to his limit.

I moved my hands off my eyes and pressed my fingers into my temples.

"Got some fresh coffee..." I heard the clunk of cups on the bare wood of the coffee table, but I couldn't will myself to open my eyes, much less do anything about it.

The couch cushion jumped as Emma plunked down next to me.

"Ooh, Molly, you okay? Got one of those ice cream headaches?"

"Ice *pick* headaches," I groaned. "Ice cream. I should be so lucky. Okay. I think it's gone."

I slowly released the pressure on my temples, opened my eyes, and sat up.

"What aren't you telling me?" Emma demanded.

"What do you mean? I'm telling you everything." I avoided looking at her and concentrated on putting coasters under the coffee mugs.

"I know you, Molly. You only get those headaches when you get da kine. Too many ideas in your head fighting with each other."

"Cognitive dissonance." I picked up my cup and held it under my nose. The coffee aroma made me feel a little better. "Emma. Do you think Donnie is jealous?"

"Of what?"

"Not *of* something," I said. "I mean is he jealous in general. Like Othello."

"The 'who's on first' guy?"

"Donnie was not happy about having to sit with Stephen."

"Molly, what guy would want to have dinner with his wife's ex?"

"I know. Maybe I'm overthinking it. Is the baby still asleep?".

Emma leaned over the arm of the couch to check.

"Uh-huh. She's out."

"Good. Thanks. You know, I'll be honest. I wasn't thrilled about having to sit there either."

"Oh yeah, having to sit next to Bee the Body right after you had a baby? I don't blame you."

"Bee the Body? Who calls her Bee the Body?"

"Everyone," Emma replied. "You gotta admit, she's hot."

"I guess, if you buy into Eurocentric, ageist, thinness-privileging—"

"So in other words, you admit she's hot."

"It's not fair. That low level of body fat is completely unattainable for...most women."

"Oh, you thinking *Donnie* killed Stephen Park?" Emma said.

"No, I I'm not saying I think Donnie did it. It's just—"

"Then look me in the eye instead of talking to your coffee."

I set my mug down and angled myself to face Emma.

"Stephen was really getting under Donnie's skin that night. I could tell."

"Yeah, Stephen's annoying. No argument there. But Molly, Donnie is not a hothead. When has he ever made an impulsive decision? Besides marrying you."

"He made a point of asking me not to investigate Stephen's murder. I hadn't even mentioned investigating anything. Why would he do that?"

"Cause he knows you like to go poking your nose into things, and he doesn't want some crazy idiot shoving you into a lava tube and leaving him widowed with a baby to take care of."

"Why does everyone keep bringing up the stupid lava tube incident? I make one little mistake—"

"What about Stephen's ex-girlfriends?" Emma interrupted. "You know if anyone was stalking him?"

"I don't know about his ex-girlfriends. I don't get involved in Stephen's personal affairs."

"What? How about the girl he was cheating on you with? You broke 'em up, don't forget."

"I did nothing of the kind. All I did was let it slip that Stephen Park was not, in fact, part-Korean."

"And she dropped him like a maggot sandwich."

"Wow, what a disgusting expression."

"But accurate. Eh, sounds like Donnie's home."

"I don't think so. This is peak lunch hour at the Drive-Inn. Besides, it doesn't sound like Donnie's car."

CHAPTER TWELVE

DETECTIVE KA`IMI MEDEIROS strode into the living room, the floorboards straining under his weight. His demeanor alone would have been intimidating enough, even if he had been the size of an ordinary man, which he wasn't. His aloha shirt could have doubled as a slipcover for one of our armchairs.

Emma, the coward, quickly made her excuses and skedaddled, leaving the baby and me alone with the plainclothes Goliath.

I offered Medeiros a cup of coffee. He refused.

"Did you want to talk to Donnie? He should be down at the Drive-Inn." I took my seat on the end of the couch next to the baby's bassinet. Medeiros carefully lowered himself onto one of the aforementioned armchairs.

"Actually, I was hoping to ask you a few questions, Professor. About the events leading up to Stephen Park's death."

"Oh. Wonderful. Okay. You did get my statement that night. Was there more?"

Medeiros reached into his shirt pocket and took out a tiny notepad and pencil.

"Just following up on a few details. Can you describe the interaction between your husband and Stephen Park prior to your discovery of Park's body?"

Was this the part where I was supposed to clam up and demand a lawyer? No, that would have been silly. A lawyer for what? I wasn't in trouble.

"Civil, I suppose? I guess it's no secret Stephen Park and I used to date."

"No. It's pretty well-known."

"Oh, good."

"To your knowledge did your husband have any conflict with the deceased?"

"Donnie gets along with everyone," I said.

"It didn't bother him that you had been in a romantic relationship with Park?"

"It was over before I even met Donnie."

"But is it possible there was still some jealousy?"

Ouch. I had to hand it to Medeiros. Despite having been friends with Donnie since elementary school or whenever, he wasn't shying away from the hard questions.

"Detective, Donnie is a devoted husband and father, an honorable businessman, and an outstanding human being. Stephen Park was a narcissist, a predator, a fraud, and Donnie's inferior in every possible way. Donnie had absolutely no reason to be jealous of Stephen Park."

Medeiros wrote in his notebook for what seemed like a long time.

"How about you, Professor?" he said finally.

"Me?"

"How did you get along with Stephen Park?"

"Fine, I guess."

"Can you be more specific?"

"I mean, I didn't socialize with him. But I saw him now and then around campus. He was the theater department chair, and I'm the chair of the management department in the College of Commerce. Mostly I'd run into him at department chair meetings."

"You called him a predator," Medeiros said. "Why?"

"Oh, that. He dated students."

Whimpering sounds came from Francesca's bassinet.

"Would you excuse me, please?"

"Yes, of course," he said.

I picked up the baby and the nursing pillow and took a seat on the chair next to my computer. With my back to Medeiros, I got Francesca latched on. All the action was hidden under my baggy t-shirt, so there would be no possibility of indecent exposure.

"How did your relationship with Stephen Park end?" Medeiros asked as I swiveled to face him. His eyes flicked briefly to the baby legs sticking out from the bottom of my shirt, but his expression remained neutral.

"We went our separate ways," I said.

He held his pen above his notepad and waited.

"He stood me up on my birthday," I said, finally. "He claimed he'd lost track of time, and I found out later that he'd been with, yes, one of his students. But it was a long time ago, Detective. I've moved on. I mean, look at me. I'm married with a baby. The whole situation with Stephen Park, it's over. It's not something I dwell on."

He nodded and wrote on his tiny notepad.

"And the worst thing about it was," I continued, "Stephen wasn't even a little bit contrite. The fact that he left me waiting for him, on my birthday, was my fault somehow. Like *I* was being unreasonable for expecting him to keep his appointments or something. Because *his* time was valuable, and mine wasn't."

"How did your husband feel about the fact that you had contact with Stephen Park at your workplace?"

"I don't think it bothered him. I doubt he ever gave it a thought."

Underneath my shirt Francesca squirmed and tugged. I tried not to grimace.

"In your view, is it possible that your husband, if provoked, might have gotten into an altercation with the deceased?"

"Detective, you know how even-tempered Donnie is. He's the last person in the world who would get pulled into some chest-thumping nature-show display with his wife's ex. Now if you're looking for someone with a motive to kill Stephen Park—"

Just as I was hitting my stride, I heard the garage door open. Donnie was home. The lunch rush at Donnie's Drive-Inn must have ended early. The sound made Francesca fussy. I struggled to get her calmed down while she did her best to rip my nipple from its moorings. Medeiros kept his eyes on his notepad.

"Donnie, hi!" I said as he came into the living room. "Look who stopped by for a chat!"

Medeiros stood, and they greeted each other with a hand grip. Donnie was almost as tall as Ka`imi Medeiros, but Medeiros beat Donnie hands-down in the width department.

"Coffee," Donnie offered.

"Thanks, ah?"

Donnie went to the kitchen to make coffee and Medeiros sat back down. Why had Medeiros accepted coffee from Donnie, but not from me? The man had never trusted me, that I knew, but did he think I was going to poison him?

"Who do you think had a motive to kill Stephen Park?" Medeiros asked as I wrangled the squirmy baby.

"Well, let me say straight off that I don't want to speak ill of the dead." Like any good Catholic, I know you're supposed to make that disclaimer before you launch into speaking ill of the dead. "But as I mentioned, Stephen did have a habit of getting involved with his students. I'll bet there are a few angry parents out there that you might want to talk to."

Medeiros nodded.

"You already mentioned Stephen Park dating his students. Any particular individuals I should follow up with?"

This was where a better memory for names would have come in handy.

"There was an Alyson. No, Alicia?"

"Last name?"

"I'm sorry, I don't remember."

Donnie came in with two cups of coffee on a tray with a cream pitcher and a sugar bowl.

"I can go into the back room if you want to talk out here," I said. Donnie declined my offer, so I wouldn't have to pick up the baby and move. Instead, the men went out to the lanai. I stayed indoors, nursed the baby, and watched cat videos on my computer. Then I went to bed early.

CHAPTER THIRTEEN

I WAS ASLEEP BY THE time Donnie came to bed, and I didn't have much luck the next morning trying to find out what Medeiros had asked about. I followed him into the bathroom, hoping to get him to talk.

"So what did you two talk about last night?" I asked. "You were out there for a while."

"Nothing too interesting," Donnie said.

"Did Medeiros tell you how Stephen died?"

"You know Ka`imi. He doesn't tell you much."

"So, what did he ask you?"

"Just the normal things. Probably the same questions he asked you. Right, Francesca?"

I held Francesca so she could watch Donnie shave. She stared at him with big eyes as he leaned into the bathroom mirror and ran an electric razor over the lower half of his face. He stood up, tapped the razor against the sink, then rinsed it and wiped it down. All of this fascinated the baby.

Then he turned around, kissed the top of my head, bent down to kiss the baby's chubby cheek, told us he'd see us for lunch, and headed out to work.

I decided to use the time between Donnie's departure and Margaret's arrival to take a walk. It was still cool outside, so it would be pleasant for Francesca as well as good weight-bearing exercise for me.

I trudged uphill toward the dead end of the street and reviewed the events of the past two days. The fact that Medeiros was asking questions meant that Stephen's death wasn't considered an accident. And I didn't like what he was asking about Donnie and Stephen. It was one thing for me to wonder what Donnie might be capable of. But for Medeiros to suspect Donnie seemed paranoid and wrong of him.

A car went past, and I stepped off the road onto a neighbor's lawn. I liked my little street, but sometimes I missed the big-city amenities. Like sidewalks, streetlights, and roads wide enough to fit two cars at once. Fortunately, traffic was sparse, and my neighbors didn't seem to mind the occasional pedestrian on their lawn.

I stepped back onto the asphalt and resumed stewing about Detective Medeiros.

Maybe Medeiros didn't believe I'd tell the truth on my own and assumed he had to rattle me. To shake loose whatever I might have been keeping to myself. Medeiros has always mistrusted me, ever since the first time Emma and I found ourselves accidentally mixed up in a murder case. Neither of us had ever wanted to get involved. Every time it happened it was because of some weird chain of coincidences that no one could have predicted. But as any hard-boiled detective novel will tell you, men like Ka`imi Medeiros don't believe in coincidence.

Or maybe Medeiros's suspicions had nothing to do with me. Maybe someone put the idea in his head, about Donnie being jealous of Stephen. But who? There was Geoffrey "Chaucer" Gunderson, the arts and sciences dean. He sat with us long enough to have perceived the tension at our table. And the young woman who came by with the tea and wine, who wouldn't look Stephen in the eye (and vice versa). It didn't take much imagination to guess what was going on there. The poor girl must have been one of Stephen's discarded conquests. But what possible reason would either of them have to direct suspicion toward Donnie?

Then there was Bee Corcoran. Maybe she was so upset at losing Stephen that she was looking for someone to blame. Or maybe she had a more sinister motivation for misdirecting Detective Medeiros? No, I was letting my imagination get ahead of the evidence now. I stopped to readjust the baby carrier and work the kink out of my back. I had hoped to get in shape by carrying the baby around, but she was gaining weight much faster than I was gaining strength.

Stephen's death was an accident, I told myself. Medeiros would poke around and disrupt people's lives for a while until he figured it out, and then everything would go back to normal. It was highly unlikely that there was a murderer on the loose.

It occurred to me then that I should reach out to Bee Corcoran. Just to see how she was holding up in the aftermath of Stephen's death. Bee hadn't been at Mahina State that long, and as far as I could tell, Stephen was her only friend there. From what Stephen had told me, Bee was estranged from her family. A friendly call from a coworker wouldn't be amiss at a time like this. Of course, I wouldn't ask Bee any inappropriate questions, like what she remembered from the night of Stephen's death, or who might have wanted to kill him. That would be bad form. But if she wanted to talk things through with a sympathetic colleague, I'd be there to listen. She'd even given me her phone number and told me to call any time if I had questions about getting my pre-pregnancy body back. Why would she have given me her number if she didn't want me to call her?

I'd be doing Bee a kindness by calling. A mitzvah, as Emma would say.

I took out my phone and turned my back to the sun so I could see the screen. Francesca watched, fascinated, as I dialed Bee's number. While the phone rang I debated how I would start the conversation. Bee picked up the phone before I could decide.

"Hey Molly," she said.

"Oh. You knew it was me calling?"

"The Caller ID gave you away. How are you holding up? Are you taking care of yourself?"

*Darn it, she's got me off balance already. I was going to ask *her* how she was doing.*

"I'm fine," I said. "Taking a walk with the baby. How are you?"

"I can't pretend everything's okay, but this grant report is keeping me busy. Oh yeah, and I had to fire one of my student workers."

We spent a few minutes trading student worker horror stories. Then a pause in the conversation gave me the opportunity to introduce a new topic.

"Has Detective Medeiros talked to you?" I asked. "About what happened?"

"Medeiros?"

"He's a big, tall guy, maybe forties or early fifties, short black hair, he was wearing a red aloha shirt with a yellow taro leaf print?"

"Oh, yes, of course. I remember him. He was great. So friendly and comforting."

"What?"

"It was one of the worst nights of my life and he really put me at ease."

"Are we still talking about Detective Medeiros?"

"I can't believe it, Molly. Stephen's really gone."

"It is kind of surreal," I agreed.

Francesca and I had reached the top of the street. Although it was not yet nine o'clock, the sun was shining hot, and my belly was sweating where the baby carrier covered it. I adjusted the baby's hat to shade her face, turned toward the sun, and started back down to the house.

"Detective Medeiros doesn't think Stephen's death was an accident," I said.

"What do you mean?"

Medeiros hadn't sworn me to secrecy or anything. I couldn't think of any reason why I shouldn't tell Bee about my interview with him.

"He was asking me about Donnie's, my husband's, interaction with Stephen that night. You didn't see anything, did you? No raised voices or anything like that?"

"Well...I mean, it's totally understandable," Bee said.

"What's understandable?"

"Your husband not being crazy about Stephen. I mean, what guy wants to sit across the table from his wife's ex?"

Why did she assume it was Donnie who disliked Stephen? Donnie had been patient and gracious throughout the whole ordeal, while Stephen had pouted and snarked like a middle-schooler. But Bee apparently remembered things differently.

"I'm *Stephen's* ex," I pointed out. "And you don't seem to have any animosity toward me. What's so funny?"

"Stephen and I were friends," she said, suppressing her laughter. "But I would never...I mean, that was all. We weren't romantically involved. I can't even imagine...I'm sorry, I shouldn't laugh. It's not funny. I'm sorry. I don't mean to disrespect the dead."

"It's okay. You have a lovely laugh." It was true, she did. Just the right mixture of throaty and silvery. "Wait. You and Stephen weren't a thing?"

"No. You can have a male friend without it being a 'thing', can't you?"

"Well, sure. I mean, I'm friends with Pat Flanagan. You don't know him—"

"The news blogger? Island Confidential?"

"Yes. That's him. Okay, I guess you do know him."

"Just from reading the blog. His haunted Hawaii stories are great. I'd love to meet him sometime."

"Sure. So, really? You and Stephen weren't an item? He seemed to think pretty highly of you."

The few times I'd run into Stephen over the past semester, he'd unfailingly brought the conversation around to the topic of Dr. Bee Corcoran and her amazing awesomeness. Bee, according to Stephen, was a triathlete, a fitness model (which I gather is like a regular model but with even less bodyfat), and a research superstar. Stephen would never fail to mention how *brave* Bee was to claim the life she wanted for herself, and how despite "everything," she was the most *feminine* woman he'd ever met.

Why hadn't I noticed that Stephen had been getting more muscular? Because I had been trying my best to ignore him. It was only at the dinner that I'd been forced to look at him for any length of time.

"No. I told you, we were buds, that's all. Besides, it was pretty clear he still wasn't over you, Molly."

"He...what?"

"I mean, I guess I can understand why you dumped him for Donnie, but honestly? He had a hard time accepting it."

I sputtered for a moment and finally managed to form words.

"I dumped *him*...is *that* what he told you?"

"I guess it doesn't matter now, sad to say. Hey Molly, did you remember to drink your lemon water this morning?"

"Not yet." I was barely paying attention to what Bee was saying. I was furious at Stephen for selling Bee his preposterous story with himself as the wronged hero. And me as the heartless villain, or course. But if I tried to set the record straight now, I would just sound petty.

"Just one glass of lemon water in the morning," Bee said. "It'll keep you from overeating."

"Right. I remember."

"Don't worry, Molly, you'll lose that baby fat. Just keep at it."

"Thanks, Bee. So glad I called."

CHAPTER FOURTEEN

I HAD BEEN LOOKING forward to my usual late lunch with Donnie, but after Margaret left, he called home to cancel.

"We're slammed," he explained. "The lunch rush usually dies down by now. Not today."

"Oh. But that's good, right?"

"If people were only showing up to buy lunch, yes, it would be. But I think a lot of people are here because of the...incident. Word's getting out that I was at the dinner when Park died. And people are asking me about it. It's a little uncomfortable, to tell you the truth."

I'd become accustomed to the Mahina rumor mill, aka the Coconut Wireless. It used to bother me, but I've long since given up on any expectation of privacy.

"Rubberneckers?" I asked.

"You mean like people who slow down to stare at a car accident? Exactly. That's the feeling I'm getting from a lot of them."

"But are they buying food?"

"I suppose so."

"Doesn't seem like a problem to me then. Let me rephrase that. It seems like a silver lining to an otherwise tragic situation. Want me to write you some talking points?"

"No, it's fine. I'll be okay. I just wanted to let you know what was going on. You two stay safe, okay?"

"Listen, Donnie, I was talking to Bee Corcoran this morning—"

"Molly, I'm sorry, I have to get going. I'll see you tonight. Love you both."

I wanted to talk to someone besides the baby. I called Emma to see whether she could come over.

A few minutes after I hung up, Emma knocked on the door.

"I'm glad you called, Molly," Emma swept in and made a beeline for the refrigerator. "I gotta talk to someone who understands. In other words, not Yoshi. You know they say the only thing worse than being married to another academic is being married to a non-academic. You got any beer?"

"Just wine. Can you pour me one too? And a big glass of water while you're there?"

"Water? Oh yeah, the baby. Okay, sit down. I'll be right there."

Emma brought three big mugs out to the living room, set two of them down in front of me, then sat down and took a big gulp from hers.

"I'll go first," she said. "Friggin' Bee Corcoran."

"Bee Corcoran! That's funny, I just...what about Bee?"

"I think Gunderson's gonna nominate her research for the system life sciences award." Emma narrowed her eyes. "Which means I'm out."

"But Emma, your research...I mean, I'm not an expert, but what you're doing seems really important. To the environment and everything. Right?"

"That's what I thought." Emma lifted the mug to her mouth and kept tilting it back and drinking until it was upside-down.

"Is it just one nomination per campus?" I asked.

"Uh-huh."

"Ohhh. Hm. I saw Geoffrey Gunderson at the dinner. I think he did say he nominated Bee."

Silence fell over my living room.

"I need another glass," Emma said, finally. "You?"

"I'm fine."

I waited for her to come back from the kitchen.

"You've been spending years on it, haven't you?" I said. "Mapping the family trees of native plant species, right?"

Emma lifted her mug in a mock toast.

"Yeah, pretty much. Not bad for an English major, Molly."

"I'll take it. So, what's Bee doing that's more impressive than what you're doing?"

Emma set down her mug.

"You know about DNA, right?"

"Yes, I do, thank you for asking. That's what you study, yes?"

"Yeah. I study plant DNA. But us humans have DNA too."

"Emma, I'm not a complete moron. Plus, I've seen GATTACA. I know humans have DNA."

"Sorry about assuming you're a moron, Molly. I've been spending too much time talking to administrators, that's why. Like my dean."

"Come on, Emma, Geoffrey Gunderson seems perfectly nice."

"Have you ever tried to explain gene mapping to a medievalist?"

"I have not. Go ahead and tell me about DNA."

"Okay." Emma set down her wine mug. "You know how your eye color, earwax, stuff like that is determined by your DNA, right?"

"Earwax?"

"Yeah. You probably have wet earwax."

"How would you know that?"

"Don't get distracted when I'm trying to explain stuff. Look. Muscle, right?" Emma held her arm up and tapped her meaty bicep. "You know how you work out, you grow more muscle?"

"Theoretically, yes."

"So you have these processes in your body that work to build muscle, yeah? But how come your muscles don't just keep growing and growing forever?"

"Well, there must be some natural limit—"

"Ha! Exactly. So these other processes that keep the growth under control, so you don't grow too much muscle. That's what Bee's researching."

"Oh. So if you're a bodybuilder, you'd want to find out what's keeping your muscles from getting as big as possible, right?"

"Yes."

"And you'd want to slow down or stop that process."

Emma pointed at me.

"Exactly. And not just bodybuilders. If you can get a handle on the mechanism, you can treat people with muscle wasting conditions."

"She can't be the only one working on that," I said. "There must be a huge market for a treatment like what you're describing."

"That's the thing. People have been trying to crack this for years. But somehow, apparently, she's finally nailed it. Molly, how can I compete with that?"

Francesca had dozed off, so I set her down into the bassinet. She immediately woke up and started fussing. I slid the bassinet next to me and rocked it gently with my foot, which seemed to calm her down again.

"Has Bee actually published anything?" I asked. "About this research, I mean? Maybe it's just vaporware."

Emma pointed at me again.

"Exactly! It has not been peer-reviewed."

"Interesting."

"She presented it at a conference, and it got a bunch of publicity. I'm surprised you didn't hear about it, Molly."

I looked down at Francesca, who was starting to stir.

"I've been a little busy," I said. Then something struck me.

"Stephen!" I exclaimed.

"What about him?" Emma asked.

"When I saw him, he looked like he'd been working out."

Emma snorted.

"Stephen Park? Isn't he way too cool to go to the gym and sweat in front of everyone?"

"Exactly. But he was definitely more muscular than I'd ever seen him. He had the shoulders and everything. Do you think he was Bee's guinea pig?"

"What? Testing a treatment like that on human subjects? Aw, no way. She'd never get that approved. Our IRB doesn't let us do bupkis."

"What if it wasn't approved," I said, "but she did it anyway? Think about it. You know how Stephen is about his appearance. Was. He was so self-conscious when he gained weight after rehab."

"I guess," Emma said. "I don't think I would've noticed, except when he started wearing capes to cover it up."

"Maybe Stephen found out something about Bee's research," I said, "and was going to make it public. So she had to stop him."

"Ooh, are you saying she killed him?"

"No, Emma, I don't know. I'm just brainstorming."

"Nah, I like it. Go on."

"Okay. Maybe she was doing something unethical, or at least something the IRB didn't approve in advance. Maybe she was experimenting on Stephen, and he consented at first, but then he got some side effects and changed his mind. Oh, great, she's awake."

I picked up Francesca and popped her under my shirt. She latched on right away. I was getting good at this. I was also suddenly desperately thirsty.

"Emma, can you get me another glass of water?"

"What? Oh, sure."

Emma disappeared into the kitchen and returned with a big tumbler.

"Your idea's a little out there," Emma said as she handed me the glass. "But I can see it. If someone didn't kill him then the only other explanations are either he fell on accident or Miss Constance got him."

"It was so weird to see Stephen Park looking like he'd been lifting weights," I said. "I was like, when did you turn into such a basic bro?"

"Eh, there's nothing wrong with lifting weights." Emma plunked down on an armchair. "You should try it."

"Try it? Hey, I'm lifting weights all day, every day." I looked down at the baby latched to my chest. "Boy, I hope she doesn't grow up to be like Stephen. You know, Stephen's parents aren't bad people. And his sister's perfectly nice. But Stephen. How does someone grow up to be so entitled and arrogant?"

"Stephen was spoiled, that's why. He always got everything he wanted."

"Ah, that reminds me. Not everything. When I talked to Bee this morning—"

"You what?"

"Yeah, I called her. Anyway, she told me she and Stephen were just friends. No romance."

"What? Nah." Emma leaned forward, interested. "Maybe he was trying to get jacked to impress Bee then."

"Maybe? It seems unlike him to make that much of an effort."

"So, let's flesh out our theory." Emma leaned back into the chair and folded her hands behind her head. "Stephen is using Bee's treatment to get all jacked. He might be the first human subject to try it."

"He'd be all over that," I said. "He loves to think of himself as a risk-taker."

"Okay, but then he starts to get some bad side effects. He tells her to fix it. She says sorry, she can't. He gets upset and threatens to report her. She knows she can't let that happen. So she acts all nice to him, that way he won't get suspicious. But the whole time she's waiting for an opportunity, yeah? When he goes outside for a smoke, she sees her chance. She sneaks out after him and shoves him off the terrace. Then she comes back in and pretends to be surprised when she hears the news."

"Sounds plausible to me," I said.

"She could've sent 'im over with one push, too," Emma said. "You see her arms, yeah?"

"Oh yes. She was wearing a sleeveless top at the dinner. She looked like a golden statue of Athena come to life. It was appalling."

"So we solved it. Bee killed Stephen Park to keep her secret safe."

"If I didn't know better, I'd think you wanted Bee to be guilty of murder so she won't get the research award."

"It was your idea to begin with, Molly. Anyway, you don't know what it feels like to lose that research award."

"True, because I've never had a research award. They don't really expect us to bring in grant money in the College of Commerce."

"Man, why didn't I become a business professor?"

"Because it would be so contrary to your nature that your every waking minute would be a torment of self-loathing?"

"Yeah, something like that. Molly, I'm gonna get more wine. You want some?"

"Not right now, thanks," I said. "But could you refill my water?"

CHAPTER FIFTEEN

EMMA'S FEARS ABOUT the research award were confirmed a few days later. A university-wide email from the chancellor's office announced that the system life sciences award had been granted to Dr. Beatrice Corcoran of Mahina State University for her research on muscle metabolism.

I heard the news first from Emma. She called while Donnie was home for lunch. I invited her to come over. She accepted.

"Emma." Donnie half-stood to give Emma a careful hug without tipping the baby out of the sling. "Congratulations. I heard Mahina State won the system life sciences award. You beat out all the other campuses."

I was shaking my head at Donnie and mouthing the word "no" at him, but he didn't see me until it was too late.

Emma pushed him away and stormed into the kitchen.

"No congratulate me, bradda. Molly, you explain."

I was glad we didn't have a door between the dining room and the kitchen. Because if there had been a door, Emma would have slammed it.

"Emma thought she had a shot at that award," I said quietly."

Donnie's face fell.

"Sorry," he whispered.

"Eh, no need whisper, you two," Emma called from inside the kitchen. "I may be washed-up useless deadwood, but I'm not deaf."

"She shouldn't take it personally," Donnie whispered even more quietly.

"What was that?" Emma yelled. "No secrets, ah?"

"It's hard not to take it personally," I replied. "It was up to each dean to pick the nominee for their campus. So she can't even blame some faceless committee on Oahu. Emma's own dean backed Bee's research and not Emma's. And get this, Bee claims she didn't even apply. Gunderson thought Bee's research was so impressive he put in the application for her."

"That's right." Emma burst back into the room, holding my sixteen-ounce Chicken Boy coffee mug. She pulled out the chair next to Donnie and plunked down into it. "That's who chose the 'most promising or impactful life science research at the university.' A frickin' medieval studies professor with holes in his sweater and his glasses on his forehead who couldn't tell Gregor Mendel from Josef Mengele."

"Emma, Gunderson wears an aloha shirt like everyone else. Where does the sweater with the holes in it come from?"

Emma took a long drink instead of answering me.

"You're just throwing around random humanities professor stereotypes, aren't you?" I asked. "Is that wine?"

"It's water. Ha! Just kidding. It's gin."

"Straight gin?" Donnie asked.

"Nah. I put ice in it." Emma moved the mug back and forth, so we could hear the ice clink. "Come on. I'm not an animal."

"By the way, Emma, it wasn't Gunderson who didn't know the difference between Mendel and Mengele. It was Linda from the Student Retention Office. Don't you remember? You emailed the whole campus about it."

Donnie glanced at his watch.

"Do you have to get back?" I asked.

"Pretty soon. Francesca's sleeping so nicely. I don't want to disturb her."

"Not that I don't respect Bee," Emma said. "I mean, right now I hate her guts of course, but she's doing a heck of a job promoting herself and picking a sexy research topic. How can mapping plant genomes compete against inventing a magic muscle pill? Man. I guess I knew this was coming. But it still hurts."

Francesca whimpered in her sleep. Donnie stood up carefully.

"I'll change her and put her in her crib," he said.

"Thanks!" I called after him.

Emma took another swig from the mug.

"Just between you and me, Molly? I think it's shibai."

"What is?"

"This whole thing. Gunderson promoting her research. Her acting like it's a big surprise, like who, little old me? There's gotta be some kind of gaming the system going on."

"You really think so? Or are you just saying all this because you're mad and you hate Bee's guts?"

"Nah, Molly. I've been looking into the research and where it's at now. Number one, Bee's results are really preliminary. She doesn't even have any *in vivo* studies published yet. Number two, no one's been able to get close to where the press release says Bee is. What are the chances someone at Mahina State is suddenly gonna crack the code when researchers at the top universities and the big pharma companies haven't been able to?"

"To be fair, the big pharma companies can't develop every possible drug. The approval process takes so long that they need to bring out profitable drugs that people take for their entire lives. Like cholesterol drugs. If Bee's muscle treatment is just going to be used by hardcore bodybuilders and people with rare diseases, it won't bring in enough money to cover their initial investment."

"Oh, so now you're the big expert on the pharmaceutical industry?"

"I wouldn't say I'm an expert, but I do know something about—"

"I guess anyone can be an expert these days, ah?" Emma interrupted. "Like Geoffrey Gunderson, sitting in front of his fireplace, sucking on his pipe and deciding whose life science research is the most impactful."

"You gave him a fireplace and a pipe now?"

Emma rattled the ice in her mug, frowned at it, and took another gulp.

"Anyway," I said, "the pharma example is from one of the cases I use in my Intro to Business Management class."

"Fine, blah blah blah business reasons. Still doesn't explain how come someone at another university hasn't done it yet."

"Good point. So, you say you examined the research. Do you have any evidence that Bee faked her results?"

Donnie came back out, wiping his hands on a paper towel.

"Faked results? That escalated quickly." He came over and gave me a kiss. "Francesca's changed and asleep. I'm going back. See you tonight. Bye, Emma."

"Laters." Emma watched him leave and then turned to me. "Molly, the more I think about it, the more I'm sure I'm right. There's no way Bee's research is as far along as she says."

"Do you mean, the more you stew about it the more you want to do something to get back at Bee? Emma, if you want to blame someone, blame Gunderson. He put in the application for her, and then he picked her application to forward to the system."

Emma set her cup down harder than necessary and pointed at me.

"Exactly. Favoritism. Predetermined outcome. The whole thing stinks."

"But it worked, didn't it? Out of all the campuses in the system, we got the award. When was the last time Mahina got the system life sciences award?"

"Let's see. The last time we got it was...never."

"So, it sounds like Gunderson made a smart—"

"That's it," Emma declared. "I'm gonna blow the whistle."

I reached over and slid the mug away from Emma. Too late. It was almost empty.

"Emma. Blow the whistle on what, exactly?"

"Are you saying I should keep my mouth shut?" Emma challenged me.

"No, I'm saying don't go accusing people unless you have actual evidence. It's one thing to sit around and spin wild stories, but...look, what if you're wrong, and Bee's discovered something that works? It would alleviate suffering and might even bring the university some income. Imagine, we could travel to conferences. Get the air conditioning working. Finally fix that leaky toxic waste storage shed next to your building, or whatever that thing is. Emma, this could be good."

Emma grabbed back the Chicken Boy mug and glared at me.

"Molly, you are not being a good friend right now."

"What do you want me to say? If you have evidence of fraud you should report it. Otherwise, let Bee do her thing and bring our university money and glory."

Emma stared into her mug.

"It's not right, Molly. That's all I'm saying. It's not right."

CHAPTER SIXTEEN

A RINGING SOUND INTERRUPTED us. I looked at Emma, and she looked at me.

"That's not my ringtone," I said.

Emma shrugged. "Mine either. Don't you have a landline?"

"Oh, that's right. We do. No one ever calls it, though." I pushed the chair back and sprinted to the computer desk in the corner of the living room.

The handset Caller ID flashed a 310-prefix number that I didn't recognize at first.

"Probably a junk call. Hello?" I expected to hear a recorded voice imploring me to call for important information about my car's extended warranty. Like anyone would sell an extended warranty on a 1959 Thunderbird.

"Is this Molly?"

There was no mistaking the bracing Brooklyn accent.

"Tiffany! Ohhh, wow!" I tried to disguise the panic in my voice as enthusiasm. *Stephen's mother*, I mouthed to Emma. She grimaced. Not because she had anything against Stephen's mother, but because she knows how adept I am at negotiating delicate, emotionally-fraught situations.

"Tiffany, how are you? I'm sorry, I shouldn't ask how you're doing. Not good, of course, how could you be? What am I saying? Poor Stephen. I can't imagine..."

Emma shook her head and took the mug back into the kitchen.

"Oh Molly, it's awful," Stephen's mother said. "Just awful. *You* must be absolutely devastated!"

Stephen's parents had been convinced that Stephen and I were going to get married. Even after our breakup, which they seemed to believe was a temporary bump in the road.

"Och, Molly!" Stephen's father, Angus Park, was on the phone now. "How are ye holdin' up?"

Stephen's father sounded even more Scottish than the last time I'd talked to him. This despite his having lived in Los Angeles for decades.

"Angus, I am so sorry. I can't even imagine. Is there anything at all I can do?"

"Well we'd love to see you," Stephen's mother said.

"Yes, of course, me too. But I don't think I'll have the chance to travel to California anytime soon—"

"Oh, Molly, I'm not talking about coming out to California," Stephen's mother said. "We're here,"

"You're here? You mean you're here in Mahina?"

Emma was on her way back from the kitchen. She nearly dropped her drink but managed to set it on the table just in time.

"Aye," said Stephen's father. "An I don't mind telling ye, it's no what we expected."

"It's like the third world here, is what he means," Stephen's mother added. "I guess you're not supposed to say that now. I don't mean it in a bad way. It's just the kind of thing Stephen would have liked, isn't it, Angus? But the hotel is pretty primitive."

"Where are you staying?" I asked. "I can recommend a place if you like."

"It's called the Lehua Inn." Stephen's mother pronounced it "Le-hwa."

"Oh. Sorry, that's pretty much our nicest hotel."

"Can we come now? Give us your address and we'll punch it into the GPS. We'd invite you to meet us here, but they won't let us check in yet. You're not near the lava, are you?"

"No, we're nowhere near the lava flow. But really, you don't have to—"

"Oh, what am I thinking? I have your address right here."

"You do?"

"Stephen had you as his local emergency contact. Okay, we'll be over in a few minutes."

I replaced the phone and came back over to sit with Emma.

"Stephen's parents are coming here," I said.

"Yeah, I heard the whole thing."

"And he had me as his local emergency contact. Why me?"

She slid her mug over and I took a big gulp. Which I quickly regretted.

"Warm gin?" I sputtered.

"The ice was diluting it too much. Molly, Stephen's parents like you a lot, ah? It's weird. How come they like you so much?"

"My delightful personality and sterling moral character. What a ridiculous question."

"Nah, for real though."

"I think they liked the way I'd clean up Stephen's messes. And the fact that I'm the daughter of a prominent OB-GYN. Also, I'm not underage."

"Bee's not underage."

"Bee's not his girlfriend."

"When you put it that way, I guess you do look pretty good on paper. Do they know you're married and have a kid?"

"I don't know. I haven't been in touch with them. Who knows what Stephen told them?"

"I bet he let them believe what they wanted to believe. What if they think you're the bereaved fiancée? Someone should let them know, Molly."

"You're right. Someone should. I wish it didn't have to be me."

I heard Francesca fussing in the bedroom and went back to see what she wanted. I had just brought her back out and gotten her latched on when the phone rang again. Emma brought the handset over to me.

"Molly." It was Stephen's mother again. "We're trying to find your house, but the GPS has us next to a big graveyard."

"Yes, that's right." I harbored a wild hope that this would put them off. "I am right next to the cemetery. When the hedge is trimmed, you can see it from our back lanai. It's huge. Gravestones as far as the eye can—"

"Oh, never mind. Angus, this is it. Number twenty-five. We're here."

CHAPTER SEVENTEEN

A FEW SECONDS LATER came the knock on the door.

"I'll get it," Emma said. "Don't worry, I'll take care of everything."

"Thank you. Thank you so much. I owe you." I stood slowly, carefully keeping the baby in position. She clamped down so hard that I was convinced if I let go of her, she'd still be latched on like a circus acrobat.

"Please tell them I'll be right out," I said. "You're sure you can handle it?"

"You leave it to me, Molly."

I sank into the big glider chair in the master bedroom. It would be a while before the baby went to sleep. She was wide awake and hungry. Through the bedroom door I heard Emma let Stephen's parents in. I couldn't make out any words, just the rumble of conversation. Emma's tone and inflection seemed perfectly normal. You wouldn't know she'd been drinking straight gin for the last hour. I don't know how she does it. If it were me, I'd be dragging myself around on my elbows by now.

Finally, Francesca drifted off to sleep. I detached her, placed her in her crib, checked the mirror to make sure everything was dry and in its proper place, and went out to face the music. At least Emma would have filled them in by now. I wouldn't have to break the news about my getting married and having a baby.

Emma, Tiffany, and Angus were sitting around the coffee table in the living room. Emma had not only made coffee, she had placed all three mugs on coasters and set out a bowl of almonds.

"The university's poormouthing," Stephen's mother was telling Emma. "They're giving us this big story about how they get less money from the state every year and they're not allowed to raise their tuition. They're trying to make us think they don't have any money to pay...Molly!"

Stephen's parents looked younger than I remembered them. Angus's hair had thickened and blackened with time, and Tiffany had a lovely new nose, long and slender to fit her face. Her former nose had been a sweet-sixteen gift from her parents. It had had the sharp-tipped, ski-jump shape that now looked dated.

Stephen's parents stood to greet me. We took turns hugging Los Angeles-style, with air kisses instead of actual lip-to-cheek contact. Emma stayed seated and sipped her coffee.

"Tiffany," I said, "you look beautiful." I knew she'd be pleased that I'd noticed her remodeled nose. Stephen's parents were proud of the work their clinic did, and always eager to show it off.

"It's the new nose. I'm glad you like it, Molly. You have such good taste. Well of course you do, that's why you picked our Stephen, right Angus? You know, some people call this an aquiline nose, but that's wrong. I notice you didn't make that mistake."

"Aye," Angus agreed. "Aquiline means ye've a conk like an eagle, wi'a wee bend in it."

Angus's hair wasn't the only thing that had gotten thicker over the years. And why not? Americans adore a Scottish accent. The clients of Park Beverly Hills Cosmetic Center were surely no exception.

"There's no one shape that's right for everyone," Tiffany said.

"So true," I agreed.

I wasn't sure where to take the conversation from there, but a wail from the bedroom decided it for me.

"What on earth was *that*?" Tiffany exclaimed. "It sounds like a baby crying."

I widened my eyes at Emma. She grimaced and shrugged. With all of her chatting and coffee-pouring and almond-setting-out, my whole married-with-a-baby situation apparently hadn't come up.

"Emma," I said, "would you mind bringing everyone up to date? I'll be right back."

I turned and hurried down the hallway before Emma had a chance to wiggle out of it.

When I came back out to the living room, the mood had changed. Stephen's parents looked stricken. Emma had done her job and delivered the news. This was my problem now.

"Molly." Tiffany's voice was uncharacteristically quiet. "You're *married*?"

"I told the lad, didn't I, tae fish or cut bait," Angus said. "It's nae Molly's fault, Tiff."

I held the baby tight to me and shook my head. *No, it most certainly is not my fault.*

"At her age, she canna wait forever," Angus added.

"But Stephen wanted children," Tiffany objected.

"Yeah. He wanted to *date* them," Emma muttered.

I frowned and shook my head at Emma. Fortunately, Stephen's parents hadn't heard her.

Stephen's mother marched up to me, grasped my shoulders, and looked me and the baby up and down.

"No one told us you were a *mother*, Molly. Why didn't anyone tell us?"

Francesca cooed and batted her chubby arms at Stephen's mother. *Don't rub it in*, I wanted to tell the baby.

"I don't know. I guess Stephen...hm." I was going to say, *I guess Stephen didn't keep you up to date*. But that would sound like I was blaming their dead son.

I guess Stephen has been too busy to tell you about it? No, that would be worse. It would sound like I was still blaming Stephen for not telling them, only being sarcastic about it.

Maybe he did, and you just forgot.

Nope, that wouldn't work. I gave Stephen's mother a shrug and a weak smile.

Tiffany released me and sat back down.

"Angus and I have always appreciated what you did for Stephen," she said. "Nothing changes that."

"Aye," Stephen's father agreed.

"Thank you." I sank into the closest armchair.

Come to think of it, I *had* done a lot for Stephen. Organized his portfolio for him when he went up for promotion. Packed him off to rehab and arranged a cover story for him at work when his addiction got out of control. Refrained from murdering him when I found out why he'd stood me up on my birthday.

"Well," I said, "would anyone like more coffee?"

"Oh yeah," Emma took the cue. "Coffee? Or tea? Molly has tea somewhere, you have tea, right, Molly? Where do you keep your tea?"

Stephen's parents weren't so easily distracted.

"Look at you, Molly. *Married*. And a *baby*." Tiffany had taken on the hearty tone of the runner-up who is trying hard to be a good sport. "So. Are we going to meet the man who stole you away from our Stephen? He must really be something."

And right on cue, we heard the side door open. Donnie came in through the kitchen. He wore the same work uniform as his employees, a red polo shirt with the Drive-Inn logo. I don't want to be vulgar, so let's just say that Donnie is in excellent physical condition and his shirt was on the close-fitting side.

"Eh, Donnie!" Emma lifted her mug in a sort of greeting.

"Wow," Stephen's mother blurted out. "Is that him?"

"You're home early," I added, unnecessarily.

CHAPTER EIGHTEEN

I MADE QUICK INTRODUCTIONS as Donnie took the baby from me. Donnie expressed his condolences to Stephen's parents and dispensed handshakes and hugs as appropriate.

"Donnie, what a pleasant surprise," I said. "This is so nice that you could come by."

"It was a little slow at the Drive-Inn, so I thought I'd stop in and see how everyone was doing," he explained.

It was only later that he confessed to me he'd been concerned by how much Emma had been drinking. He'd come back to make sure the baby was safe, and no one was passed out on the floor.

"Will you be joining us for an early dinner, Donnie?" Stephen's mother asked hopefully. This was the first I'd heard of anyone going to dinner.

"Tiffany, I'm sure the man's busy," Angus said.

"I have to get back," Donnie said. "You go, have fun. I'll take Francesca."

Donnie hoisted the baby onto his shoulder, grabbed the diaper bag, and left. Emma made her excuses and followed him out. It was just as well, as it turns out.

The Parks' attorney was waiting for us at the Lehua Inn Coffee Shop. He was conspicuously drab among the colorful tourists, and probably the only person in the hotel who was wearing a suit.

I slid into the vinyl booth next to the man and introduced myself. He told me his name and handed me his card. *If I run into this guy in the street tomorrow*, I thought, *I probably won't recognize him.* His forgettable-ness was certainly deliberate; he probably had many clients like Stephen's parents, who would not tolerate being upstaged.

"Shall we get started?" he asked. He had a fresh yellow legal pad next to his plate, blank except for the date written at the top of the page. The handwriting was like the man himself, small and spidery.

"Let's get something to eat first," Stephen's mother said. "I'm starving."

I realized I was hungry too. The Lehua Inn's pancake and coffee aroma was tantalizing.

The Lehua Inn's coffee is mediocre and always smells better than it tastes. (Like sin, as the saying goes.) But their pancakes are divine. Give me a stack of golden, hubcap-sized pancakes topped with a foamy ball of butter, bring out a warm, sticky pitcher of maple-flavored syrup to glug over the whole mess, and I can endure anything.

Even a conversation with the parents of my dead ex about suing my employer.

The lawyer took down my name and contact information and asked me to tell him what I could recall.

"From the time you entered the old Mahina Memorial building," he said. "Please include anything you may have noticed about the condition of the building."

I told him what I could, uncomfortably aware of Stephen's parents sitting across from me. I was telling a story whose grim ending they already knew.

"Why did you exit the building after you visited the washroom?" the lawyer asked.

"I had tried to wash a stain off my blouse. I wanted to give it a chance to dry off a little before I went back to join the others."

No one at the table needed to know about my makeshift paper-towel breast pads. I'd sure learned my lesson that night, though. I now had four pairs of proper pads stuffed in my purse.

"Anyway, when I went outside the door locked behind me," I went on. "So, at that point I had to go around the building. I didn't have a choice. Oh, I did notice that the stairs felt pretty rickety. It might have been termite damage, or rot."

The attorney nodded and made a note.

"How was the lighting?" he asked. "Could you see where you were going?"

"There was no lighting. I don't remember whether the moon was out or anything. Whatever it was doing it was covered up with clouds. That's not unusual for Mahina, though. I had to use the light from my phone to find my way."

He kept writing as I spoke. Then he underlined something.

"And it seems you are...married?" He looked at Tiffany for confirmation. She pursed her lips and nodded.

"But you attended this dinner with Stephen Park."

I stared at him.

"No. I went with Donnie. My husband. We just all ended up at the same table. It was assigned seating. We didn't know in advance who else was going to be at our table."

"What is your husband's full name?"

"Donald Muraco Gonsalves."

"Unusual middle name," the lawyer said.

"It was the name of a famous local wrestler." I spelled the name for him. "His sister's middle name is Bysentenyl. Like two hundred years, except spelled in a unique way. Their parents apparently liked unusual...I guess it's not important. Sorry."

"So at dinner, it was just you and Stephen and your husband?"

"And Bee Corcoran. There were supposed to be two other people sitting with us, but there was a scheduling mix-up and they couldn't make it."

The waitress came by and doled out our giant plates of food. I said grace, crossed myself, and dug in. As soon as my mouth was full of pancake, the attorney cleared his throat.

"Now, I want to ask you about access to the terrace outside. How difficult would it have been, in your view, for someone to gain access to the outdoor terrace?"

He'd caught me off-guard with my cheeks full of pancake. I took a quick gulp of coffee. It didn't have much flavor, which was good, because the flavor it did have was kind of nasty.

"I don't know whether they wanted people going out there," I said. "But there wasn't anything stopping them. There were these tall French doors at the far end of the dining room. I don't remember seeing any velvet ropes or signs that said, 'stay off the terrace' or anything like that."

"Were the doors locked?"

"I don't think so. They must have been unlocked for Stephen to get out. So I guess my answer is that it was probably pretty easy to gain access to the terrace."

More writing. Lots of underlining.

"So, a reasonable person would have concluded that it was acceptable to exit the dining room and go out onto the terrace?"

"Probably. Sure."

I was doing exactly what Stephen's parents wanted: putting the university at fault. And the university was at fault. They owned the building, they had decided to open it for an event while they were still doing renovations, they had set up the dinner, and they had left the terrace accessible to guests.

I wasn't sure how to feel about it. On the one hand, I sympathized with Stephen's parents. I couldn't begin to imagine what they were going through. And the university should not have let people wander out onto an unlit terrace with a potentially fatal drop.

On the other hand, Stephen's parents had plenty of money. And the university, my employer, didn't. Except for that big student success grant. Which had so many restrictions on it that it was no help at all.

"When Stephen left your table to go outside, did he go alone?"

"Yes."

"Was there a particular reason he left?"

In fact, he'd turned green and bolted the minute the topic of breastfeeding came up. I decided it wasn't necessary to share that particular detail. It would have disappointed his parents, I think.

"He said he was going outside for a smoke."

"He told us he'd quit," Stephen's mother objected.

"Was anyone else out on the terrace?" the lawyer asked.

"No. At least, not that I saw."

"After Stephen left the table to go outside for a smoke, when did you see him next?"

Oof. Who thought it would be a good idea to discuss this over dinner?

"When I went outside I saw Stephen up on the terrace, smoking."

"You said it was dark outside," the lawyer said. "You're certain it was Stephen you saw?"

"I recognized the smell," I said. "He smokes those clove cigarettes. Then when I looked up, I saw the glow of the cigarette. Then I heard him calling my name. No, wait, first I heard him say, 'Molly' and that must have been why I looked up...I'm sorry. I'm getting mixed up about the exact order of things."

"You say he called you by name?"

"Yes."

"Did you recognize his voice at that time?"

"Yes."

"And when he called out to you, what did you do?"

I stared at my plate to avoid looking at Stephen's parents.

"Nothing. I kept walking."

"You heard Stephen call out to you, you looked up, and you kept walking?"

"Yes," I said to my pancakes.

"Did you say anything to him?"

I shook my head. Nothing he could have heard, anyway.

"Now, I'm sorry to have to ask this," the lawyer said to Stephen's parents. "Did you see him fall? Please think carefully."

"I didn't. I didn't see anything until I turned around. And then he...and then I called for help. And then things happened quickly. Police, and ambulances, and I guess someone must have told the people inside. Bee came running out, but it was too late. She wasn't allowed to touch his body—she wasn't allowed to go near him."

"Who is this Bee person?" Stephen's mother asked.

"Beatrice Corcoran," I said, glad to be the bearer of good news for once. "One of our rising stars. She just won a systemwide research award. She's very impressive." She had also told me that she had no romantic interest in Stephen, but his parents didn't need to know that.

"What does she do?" Tiffany asked.

"She's an assistant professor of kinesiology."

Stephen's mother turned to her husband.

"That's just great. Our son was dating a P.E. teacher."

Stephen's father decided this would be a good time to go pay the bill, and Stephen's mother went to freshen up. This left me sitting next to their attorney.

I cleared my throat. "May I ask you something?"

The attorney paused his writing and looked up, which I took as a "yes."

"What exactly killed him? Stephen?"

The lawyer looked at me like he wasn't sure he'd heard me right.

"He fell from a height of ten meters onto a hard surface," he said slowly.

"No, I know that. But I mean, if he hit his head first, it would've been over quickly. But if it was internal injuries...you know what I'm saying? Stephen didn't suffer, did he? I guess that's what I'm asking."

The furrows on the man's forehead cleared.

"Oh, I see. I don't have that information. We'll know more when the autopsy's done."

It hit me then that Stephen Park was really gone. It must have been the word "autopsy" that got me. I was suddenly desperate to escape the crowded coffee shop with its cloying pancake smell. Stephen's parents were making their way back to the table. As they approached I made a show of glancing at my wrist. Only to remember I wasn't wearing a watch.

"Thank you so much for dinner." I stood and sidled out of the booth. "It was wonderful to see both of you again, very nice to meet you Mister...well. I should be getting back."

"Are ye gonna walk?" Stephen's father asked, surprised. Right. Stephen's parents had driven me over to the hotel.

"I have a ride," I improvised, and before anyone could stop me, I rushed out to the lobby and called Emma.

CHAPTER NINETEEN

IT DIDN'T TAKE LONG for Emma's Prius to zoom up to the front of the Lehua Inn. She was of course dying to know everything that had happened at dinner.

"How about we get down to the Maritime Club before happy hour ends, and you can tell me everything." Emma screeched out of the parking lot and made a two-wheels-off-the-ground left turn onto Hotel Drive.

"Sounds fun, but Donnie has the baby with him at work," I said. "I should probably go pick her up."

"They'll be okay," Emma declared with the confidence of an expert. Which she most definitely is not when it comes to babies.

"I'd feel better going back and relieving Donnie," I said. "I'm not sure a fast-food restaurant is the best place for a baby, and he's not off work for a couple more hours at least. Besides, happy hour at the Maritime Club? What has your poor liver ever done to you?"

"I am very nice to my liver," Emma said.

"Didn't you just drink up all our gin?"

"It wore off already. So fine, no Maritime Club today. Tell me what happened at dinner."

I told Emma everything I could remember.

"I used to get so frustrated with how Stephen's parents would enable him," I said.

"They did enable him," Emma agreed. "Remember that thousand dollar a night rehab or whatever it was? You know it wasn't his theater professor salary paying for it."

"But now that I have Francesca, I understand why they did what they did. He was their child, and he—"

"Nah, you were right the first time," Emma said.

"Okay, maybe he was spoiled. But I didn't realize one of the things about having a baby is, it never stops. By the time your baby's approaching middle age and has tenure, Stephen's parents should've been able to stop worrying about him. But no, you never can stop worrying. Having a kid is a life sentence."

"You should stitch that onto a throw pillow," Emma said. "Having a kid is a life sentence. Anyway, you enabled him too, you know,"

"I know. Thanks for giving me something else to feel bad about."

"Don't feel bad Molly. Stephen's dead."

"How is that supposed to help?"

Emma pulled into the Drive-Inn's lot, and I hopped out to look for Donnie. I found him inside, among the sizzling griddles and bubbling pots that made me so nervous. Francesca wasn't there with him.

"Where's the baby?" Emma asked when I returned to the car empty-handed.

"At the house with Margaret." I pulled the door shut and buckled in. "He could've let me know before we came all the way here. I walked in and there he was, empty-handed, no baby. I practically had a heart attack."

"How was he supposed to let you know?" Emma pulled out and made a daring left turn into traffic in front of a truck lifted so high the driver probably didn't even see us.

"Emma?" I said. "We just missed getting run over by that truck."

"Nah. We woulda gone right under him. Anyway, don't blame Donnie. You know what it's like when the restaurant's busy. He was running around with his head cut off the whole time, it was probably hard enough for him to get ahold of Margaret."

"Emma, the expression is running around like a *chicken* with its head cut off."

"You know what I mean."

"But now I have the image in my mind of Donnie running around with his head cut off. It's very upsetting. And I've already had an excruciating day."

"See, Molly?"

"See what?"

"You shoulda drank some gin when you had the chance."

I came home to find Margaret at the dining room table. She was balancing Francesca on her lap and reading to her from her CPA review book. I came over to take the baby. Francesca lit up when she saw me. Then she smacked me in the face with her damp little fist and pawed at my blouse.

"I'll get you a glass of water." Margaret jumped up and headed to the kitchen as I got settled on the couch.

"Thank you, Margaret!" I called after her. "And thank you for being available on such short notice."

"I heard you had dinner with Professor Park's parents." She set a tall glass of ice water in front of me. I picked it up and drank most of it before I answered her.

"Well, that news traveled fast. Yes, I did."

"Do you mind if I fix myself a hot chocolate?"

"No, of course not. Help yourself."

Margaret was one of those thin women who always feels cold. I envied her that. I'd love to be able to wear a stylish sweater or jacket now and then without risking heatstroke.

Margaret returned with a mug of hot chocolate, and a second glass of ice water for me. She sat on the couch and hunched over, her slim hands clutching the mug for warmth.

"So..." she asked timidly. "How was it?"

"Seeing Stephen's parents? They're devastated, as you can imagine." I touched Francesca's pulsing cheek. She drew her eyebrows together and ramped up the suction. She apparently didn't appreciate being bothered while she was eating. Fair enough, neither did I.

"It's really nice that you still get along with them even though you aren't seeing Professor Park anymore."

"They're suing Mahina State."

I didn't see any reason to hide the news from Margaret. She was obviously connected to the coconut wireless. She'd heard about it before long anyway.

"Why are they suing the university? What did Mahina State do?"

"It's what we didn't do. We didn't block off the terrace, we didn't put up lighting, and the railing height wasn't up to modern code. Apparently, it was only twenty-four inches high. Oh, would you mind getting the tape measure from the drawer next to the fridge? I'm curious now."

Margaret disappeared and came back with the tape measure. She measured out twenty-four inches and touched the end of the tape measure to the floor.

"It's low," she said. "Just above my knees."

"Stephen's a little taller than you. And men are more top-heavy because they carry their weight in their shoulders, not their hips. I can see how he would have fallen over."

"So, it was an accident?" Margaret asked brightly.

"Of course it was," I assured her.

Margaret stared into her hot chocolate.

"Why?" I persisted.

"Professor Park was seeing a friend of mine before he started going out with Dr. Corcoran."

"Stephen was seeing a friend of yours?"

Margaret nodded.

"Your age?"

"Yes."

"Ah. Disappointed but not surprised. Have you talked to her since this happened?"

"No. We haven't been in touch." Margaret blew over the top of her mug.

"Why not reach out to her?"

"I don't think she really wants to hear from me. The thing is, I told her it was a bad idea to get involved with Professor Park. I mean, if I were about to make a big mistake, I'd want someone to try to stop me. That's the only reason I said anything. But I guess she didn't feel the same way."

"You didn't approve of her getting involved with Stephen?" I asked.

"It wasn't just getting involved with him. She turned down a full-ride scholarship to a graduate program in actuarial science. Just to stay in Mahina to be with him."

"She turned down a full ride?"

Margaret nodded vigorously. I could tell she was still upset about her friend's decision. I didn't blame her. I didn't even know this young woman, and now I felt the urge to go shake some sense into her.

"Professor, do you think I should tell Professor Park's parents?"

"That Stephen had been seeing your friend?"

She nodded.

"I don't know. What would it accomplish now? Would it make them feel any better?"

"They would know that somebody loved their son," she said "Sorry, I mean, you must have too, of course, but...I don't know."

"I'm not sure they're ready to deal with anything else at this point. If you don't mind my asking, who is this 'friend' you're referring to?"

I couldn't imagine that Margaret herself been one of Stephen's conquests. She seemed far too sensible to fall for him. But then again, so did I.

"Her name is Verna Jackson-Brown," Margaret said.

"Her last name is really Jackson Browne?" I asked.

"Yes. Why?" Margaret asked.

"Like the singer?"

Margaret shook her head.

"Who?" she asked, which made me feel very old.

"Wait a minute." I rested my hand on Francesca's fuzzy head. "Verna Jackson-Brown? Isn't Verna the name of Betty and Niall's daughter? Betty Jackson, in psychology. Is that your friend's mom?"

"Verna's mom is a psych professor," Margaret said brightly. "Yes, I think that's right."

"Stephen Park was dating Betty Jackson's *daughter?*"

Margaret shrugged. "I guess so?"

"Does Betty Jackson know?"

"No, I don't think so. She said they'd kick her out if they knew. Um, can I get more chocolate, Professor? It's really good."

"Of course. Help yourself. And please call me Molly. You're not my student anymore. Unless you're more comfortable calling me Professor...I don't know, do whatever you want. But if you're going into the kitchen, can you refill my water glass?"

"Were those really Professor Park's parents you had dinner with?" She called back from the kitchen.

"Yes, why?"

"My friend who works at the Lehua Inn told me they were both haole."

"They are."

"But Stephen is Korean. Is he adopted?"

She came back with two glasses of water for me. I picked up one and drank half of it in a single gulp.

"Thank you," I said, "That's perfect. I can't believe this is coming up again. Who told you Stephen Park was Korean?"

"Verna. She said she and Stephen had that in common, their mixed background."

I suppressed a snort.

"Park is a Korean name," Margaret added, a little defensively. "Isn't it?"

I touched Francesca's little nose. "Well Stephen Park is just a big poser, isn't he?" I cooed. "Park is a Scots name. Stephen let people assume he was half-Korean because in his mind it's cooler to be half-Korean than just a plain old white guy."

Margaret looked puzzled.

"So he's not hapa? I mean, he wasn't?"

"He was Scottish and Jewish, if you want to call that hapa, but he was not even remotely Korean. He just liked to let people think he was."

"What? I don't understand. Why?"

"I guess in his mind being Korean was trendy or something. I don't know."

"But didn't that hurt his parents' feelings?" Margaret asked.

"I don't think they knew. And I'm sure not going to be the one to tell them."

CHAPTER TWENTY

IT WASN'T UNTIL DONNIE came home that night that something clicked into place in my memory. I sat at the counter holding the baby, while he was busy trying to fit foil trays of leftovers into our refrigerator. Donnie lets the staff take home extra food at the end of the day, and whatever they leave, we get.

"Donnie, do you remember Betty Jackson, who I waved to last night?"

Donnie wrote *Chicken Chow Fun* on a length of blue masking tape and pressed it onto the end of the foil tray.

"Betty? Yes. Your friend, the psychology professor. Her husband's name is Niall Brown. And they have...four kids?"

"Wow, good memory! *Five* kids, though. The oldest is named Verna. I just found out she's already graduated from college. Donnie, I think she was the one who waited on us at the donor dinner."

"Who?" Donnie asked from inside the refrigerator.

"Betty Jackson's daughter. Verna Jackson-Brown. Remember, pretty girl, tall, green eyes? She poured the wine? Maybe you were away from the table. Donnie, what would you do if one of baby Francesca's professors tried to date her? When she's in college, I mean. She obviously doesn't have any professors now, because she's a baby."

Donnie stood up and looked at me over the refrigerator door.

"I'd kill him," he said evenly, and went back to fridge-arranging.

"Not literally, though," I said. "You mean you wouldn't be happy about it. You're exaggerating for effect, right?"

"Maybe," he replied.

"Yeah, I know what you mean." I watched the baby sleeping in my arms, her little chest rising and falling evenly. If someone ever tried to harm Francesca, or take advantage of her the way Stephen Park took advantage of his students, I would destroy him.

I wondered whether that might not be very Christian of me. I made a mental note to mention it the next time I happened to go to Confession.

Donnie finished fitting everything into the fridge, poured two glasses of Sangiovese, and came over to sit with Francesca and me.

"Why are you talking about Francesca's professors trying to date her?" Donnie reached over and gently stroked the baby's fuzzy black hair. "It would be terrible. I don't even want to think about it."

"Me neither. But Verna, Betty and Niall's daughter? The one who was serving us? Apparently, she was dating Stephen Park."

Donnie shook his head.

"Do the parents know?"

"I don't know."

Donnie raised his eyebrows.

"Were you thinking your friend Betty Jackson might have had something to do with Stephen Park's death?"

"What? I wasn't even thinking of that," I lied.

"When you asked me how I'd react, isn't that what you had in mind?"

"I don't know. I know I'm not a detective, it's not really any of my business who killed whom, but the thing is I know everyone involved in this, so it's kind of hard not to think about it. But Donnie, just follow me here. Betty Jackson is sitting at her table at the far end of the dining hall, right?"

"I remember she waved to you."

"Exactly. So she's over there, she sees Stephen is at a table across the dining room, her daughter Verna is working for the catering company waiting tables, Betty watches her daughter interacting with Stephen—"

"Interacting in what way?" Donnie asked.

"The daughter came around to refill drinks. I don't know, it seemed there was some kind of weird eye contact. Or non-contact, because they wouldn't look at each other. Anyway. Betty knows Stephen is there. She waits for him to go out for a smoke and follows him onto the terrace, and then...what? Waits until he's distracted by the sight of someone walking by underneath? And sneaks up, shoves him over the edge, and runs back inside?"

"That 'someone' walking by being you?" Donnie asked.

"Yes. It's been bothering me, to be honest. Donnie, if I hadn't been walking by at that exact moment—"

"Molly, it wasn't your fault."

"Thank you for saying that. I've been thinking about it a lot. If I hadn't walked by right then, Stephen might still be alive."

"Maybe not," Donnie said thoughtfully.

"If Betty Jackson were planning on killing someone," I said, "which seems highly unlikely, but let's just say she wanted to protect her daughter, which I can understand. Betty would have a much better plan than just running out and shoving Stephen over the railing. Think of how many ways it could've gone wrong. What if Stephen had called for help, or shouted, *Hey, Betty Jackson from the psychology department, why are you pushing me to my death?*"

"Are you sure it was Stephen's voice you heard calling you?" Donnie asked.

"I don't know. At the time I was sure it was Stephen. Who else could it have been?"

"Someone who killed Stephen Park and wanted you to think he was still alive?"

"Ew, that's grotesque. Someone imitates him and then drops his dead body onto the ground?"

"Sorry, I'm not as good as you and Emma at thinking about murders."

"No, you're quite good at it. Disturbingly good. Donnie, should I tell Betty? About her daughter and Stephen?"

Donnie glanced at the baby.

"I think a few months ago if you'd asked me, I would've said to stay out of it. But now, I'd want to know if it were Francesca."

CHAPTER TWENTY-ONE

THE IDEA OF HAPPY HOUR at the Maritime Club had been growing on me ever since Emma suggested it. We used to go all the time before the baby came. So the next afternoon I arranged to meet Emma there. It would be just like old times, I thought.

The Maritime Club was exactly as I remembered it. Weather-beaten clubhouse, an unparalleled view of the blue ocean, and waves crashing on the rocks so close that we got misted with salty seawater. Emma had bought a membership because she thought her husband Yoshi might like it. Yoshi had just moved to Mahina and made no secret of how unimpressed he was. He would say things like, "an Ivy League MBA doesn't belong in a place like this." Yoshi's mellowed a lot since then. He gave up on finding a "suitable" job, took up canoe paddling, and now spends most of his time at the bayfront. These days he thinks the Maritime Club is too pretentious.

The Maritime Club's menu probably hadn't changed since Hawaii became a state. Today's complimentary happy hour snack was rumaki and greasy egg rolls, served with a red-and-yellow yin-yang of ketchup and mustard. To avoid disturbing the other diners we sat outside on the lanai, where the sound of the waves crashing on the rocks would compete with any baby noise. Francesca kept trying to wiggle out of my arms and onto the floor (which was not going to happen). She fussed when I thwarted her, and she also needed a few diaper changes and feedings, but overall, she was an exemplary baby.

"Well, that was an experience," Emma said as she signed the check.

"It was nice to get out," I said. "We should do this again."

"Yeah. Maybe fifteen or twenty years from now."

"Don't you worry about Auntie Emma," I cooed as I wrestled Francesca's car seat into the base. The Thunderbird's soft top didn't leave me much room to maneuver, but I had to keep the top up if I didn't want the baby getting rained on. "It's been a long time since she was a baby. She doesn't remember what it was like. When you're being held, you want to go explore. When you're out exploring, you want someone to hold you. I understand."

"Beh," Francesca replied.

I had just gotten buckled in and was about to turn the key when a diaper blast shook the car. Then, like thunder follows lightning, came the smell. I unbuckled myself, unbuckled the baby, grabbed the diaper bag, and went back inside to change her in the bathroom. By the time we got on the road, I was feeling fairly frazzled.

When we arrived home I was surprised to see Donnie's car in the garage. I felt the hood. It was cool. He'd been here for a while. Very odd.

We came in to find Donnie on the living room couch, a glass of whiskey in his hand. The bottle was on the coffee table. He looked shell-shocked.

"Donnie?"

It seemed like he didn't even hear me. I put the sleeping baby in her crib, turned on the baby monitor, and came back out to the living room.

"Molly," he said, as if he had just noticed I was there.

I sat down next to him, gently took the whiskey glass from his hand, and sipped it.

"That's the one you don't like," he said as I started coughing.

"Donnie. You're home early, you look like someone pithed you, and you're drinking this stuff that tastes like a tire fire. What is going on?"

"It's peated."

"What?"

"They burn peat to dry the barley. That gives it the smoky flavor."

"Donnie."

He turned to look at me, finally.

"I was arrested," he said.

"What? Why? For what?"

Donnie took the tire-fire whiskey back and downed it in one gulp.

"For killing Stephen Park."

"They arrested you? They didn't drag you out of the restaurant, did they?"

Donnie shook his head.

"Medeiros called and told me to come down to the station."

"So he literally phoned it in."

"It was a courtesy."

"So did you go?"

Donnie nodded.

"But you're here. I guess they figure you're not a flight risk. They released you on your own recognizance?" I was proud of myself for remembering the correct legal term.

"It wasn't quite that easy. Bail was fifty thousand."

"Fifty thousand *dollars*? Donnie, where on earth—"

"The home equity line of credit."

"That we were going to use for Francesca's college? Oh, listen. She knows we're talking about her."

Francesca's gentle fussing crackled through the baby monitor. I went back to get her.

"Here. Say hi to your daughter. She missed you."

I plopped the baby into Donnie's arms and went to pour myself a glass of wine. Thus equipped, I returned to the living room and sat next to my husband and daughter.

"Do you think it's okay having all this alcohol around the baby?" I asked.

"She's not drinking it."

"Fair enough." I clicked my glass against his.

"Where did you go this afternoon?" Donnie asked. "I thought you'd be here."

"We went to the Maritime Club for happy hour."

"With the baby?"

"Yeah. Emma and I hadn't been in a while. It wasn't as relaxing as I remember it. Donnie, what is going on? Why, and how, were you supposed to have killed Stephen Park? I was there with you at the donor dinner. I can vouch for you."

"No, you can't, Molly." Donnie stroked the baby's head.

"Well, okay, maybe they won't take my word for it because I'm your wife. But Donnie, you were nowhere near Stephen when he fell. You only left the table the one time to take Margaret's phone call."

Donnie shook his head.

"Okay, maybe I left the table two times. But Bee Corcoran was there. She should be able to tell them where you were that night. Anyway, what's your motive supposed to be?"

Donnie frowned a little.

"You," he said.

"What?"

"That's their thinking."

"Me? You mean because I briefly dated Stephen, like a hundred years ago when I first came to Hawaii, before I even met you?"

Donnie nodded.

"Well, that's an idiotic theory, and it doesn't make any sense. Unless you believe that your wife is like a pair of shoes that you don't want anyone else trying on before you buy them. Even then, you don't go track down the person who tried on your shoes and kill them. You just disinfect your shoes...never mind. I'm not sure where I was going with that. Donnie, my point is that we'll just have to find one of the servers or someone at another table who can attest that you didn't go anywhere." I stood up. "Look, you've just been through a lot. Maybe you should get something on your stomach. Have you eaten? I'll go warm up some Korean chicken."

"Go ahead and get some for yourself. I'm not hungry. We'll be right here. The baby and me."

I sat back down.

"Donnie, is there something you're not telling me?"

CHAPTER TWENTY-TWO

I SAT IN THE DARK LIVING room, nursing the baby. Donnie had finally gone to bed, but I couldn't sleep. (This was fine with the baby, who was awake and hungry.)

I had assumed that Donnie had been nowhere near Stephen that night.

According to Donnie, I was wrong.

Donnie told me he had been bothered by Stephen's waspish comments, but felt he couldn't say anything because he didn't want to make a scene. When I left the table for the second time, only Donnie and Bee remained; Stephen had already gone out for a smoke. Then someone Bee knew came over to chat with her. No longer obliged to make conversation with Bee, Donnie had gone outside to confront Stephen.

"But as soon as I stepped out there I said to myself, this is crazy," Donnie told me. "I went back inside right away."

"Did you see Stephen out there?" I asked.

"I didn't see anything. It was dark."

I told myself I believed Donnie. I accepted his story the way I accept that radio waves can travel through empty space. Even though I can't get my mind around the idea that a wave motion can travel through a vacuum when there's nothing there to move.

But at the same time, I could understand why the police might not have been so credulous.

Stephen had been especially unpleasant that evening. There was his usual snide banter about my being a bourgeois business-school sellout, but that had been going on for years. It had started back when The County Courier was still doing actual reporting, and they'd published the salaries of Mahina State's employees. Stephen discovered I out-earned him, and never forgave me for it. Like it was my fault the business school paid better than the theater department.

Then there was the needling about my being complicit in The Patriarchy by getting married and having a baby. After Stephen ditched me for his teenage student I guess he expected me to sit around lighting candles in front of his picture or something. Instead I moved on and married Donnie. Which was also unforgiveable in his book.

But something had been different this time. Stephen hadn't blunted his poison barbs with his characteristic "just kidding" smirk. He scowled the whole time, as if it literally pained him to share a table with me. A few times he even rubbed the back of his neck (we get it, Stephen. Having to sit with us is a pain in the neck, so clever).

I didn't blame Donnie for wanting to have a word with Stephen. I could have pushed him over that railing myself. Not that I would share these thoughts with Detective Medeiros.

My phone jangled, startling the baby in the middle of her meal (ouch). I answered it as quickly as I could.

It was my mother. A woman with years of top-notch medical training and experience, who still didn't get the concept of time zones.

"Mom. Is everything okay? It's so early."

"It's seven-thirty, Molly. How late do you usually sleep?"

"It's four-thirty in Hawaii."

"AM or PM?"

"AM. If it were four-thirty in the afternoon, I wouldn't have said it was early."

"Well, you sound alert. It seems I didn't wake you up." This was as close to an apology as I would get.

"No, but the ringing phone scared the baby. Don't worry about me. Who needs two nipples?"

"Molly, that Stephen Park's parents called me. What on earth is going on over there?"

"Stephen's parents...right, well there has been some unfortunate news, but I didn't tell you because I didn't want to worry you—"

"They told me Stephen is dead. Is it true?"

"Yes. Sorry."

Why was I apologizing? I didn't kill him.

I tried to predict what I was going to get scolded about next. Either my mother was going to ask why she didn't hear it from me first and make me feel guilty about keeping her in the dark, or she'd take the opportunity to warn me about lurking dangers in my life that I couldn't be trusted to navigate and that were also somehow, vaguely, my fault.

"I must say the news rather caught me flat-footed. Stephen's parents seemed to assume that you had already told me, which of course you didn't."

"Well, this whole thing just happened, and things have been a little hectic—"

"It seems your university does a terrible job of maintaining their buildings. They're very unsafe. Are you sure your building is safe? Remember, you're a mother now, with a helpless little human depending on you. You can't just live for yourself anymore."

So one from column A, one from column B.

"Mom, I didn't tell you because I didn't want you and Dad to worry. Hi Dad."

"Hiya sweet pea. How'd you know I was here?"

"Lucky guess." Whenever my mom calls, my dad is lurking cheerfully in the background. Always.

"How's little Frankie?" he asked.

I looked down at Francesca, who had recovered from the interruption and was once again happily chowing down. Her eyes were closed, but her cheeks were pulsating furiously.

"That's not really her nickname, Dad. We just call her The Baby." I disliked the name Frankie, but I didn't want to hurt his feelings.

"She's right dear," My mother said. "It's not very feminine."

"The Baby just fits her better," I said. "Although I guess it'll only work until we have another one. If you have two babies you can't just call one The Baby."

"Molly, your optimism is wonderful, but let's stick to reality, shall we? You were just under the wire with this one. It would be madness to try again at your age."

"Thank you for the tactful reminder, Mom. But we could always adopt like you guys did."

"Oh, no, I would never recommend adoption," my mother said. "Not if you have other options. It's like buying a pig in a poke. You have no idea what you're going to get."

"Okay. Thanks, Mom."

"Just do your best for little Fanny. Oh, and send a card or something to Stephen's parents. I don't want them to think we've raised a boor."

"I'm sure that's their main concern right now. Don't worry, I won't forget. And her name isn't Fanny either."

It wasn't long before Donnie was up and getting ready to go to work. He fixed himself a coffee and sat down at the counter. I put the sleeping baby down in her crib and came back out to join him.

"How are you feeling this morning?" I asked.

He pulled me close and kissed my forehead.

"Better. I got in touch with Honey Akiona. I'm thinking of asking her to represent me. If it's okay with you."

"Yes, of course it's okay with me. Why wouldn't it be? You should have a great defense lawyer."

I had known Honey Akiona since before she went off to law school and returned to become one of Mahina's most prominent criminal defense attorneys. She had taken an introductory business class from me years ago. Even back then she had been smart, fearless, and not particularly concerned about coloring inside the lines.

"It's going to cost some money," Donnie said.

"Donnie, what is money for if not to influence the criminal justice system in one's own favor? Besides, you hired Honey to represent me that time I was in a wee spot of trouble. Don't you remember?"

Donnie smiled a little.

"How could I forget? But we weren't married yet. It was just my money then. Now it's our money. That's right, you *were* in pretty deep—"

"Yes, well, I didn't mean to rehash all that old news right now, but my point is, even though this is a silly misunderstanding, it's best to hire someone who can help us get through it as quickly and painlessly as possible."

"Okay." Donnie gulped the rest of his coffee and stood. "I need to get going. I'll see you two this afternoon. Hopefully there won't be any more surprises between now and then."

CHAPTER TWENTY-THREE

BY MIDMORNING THE HOUSEHOLD was back to its usual routine. Margaret was reading accounting rules to Francesca, and I was neck-deep in Student Retention Office paperwork, when the phone rang.

It was Betty Jackson calling.

I wondered whether she knew what Margaret had told me, about her daughter Verna being involved with Stephen Park. Should I tell Betty? I'd want to know if it were my daughter. On the other hand, I didn't want to be the one to deliver the news.

"Molly," Betty said, "I heard about Donnie's arrest. Are you okay?"

"Yes, just a minute."

I took the phone out onto the front porch, where the reception was better. I had long gotten over any worries about my neighbors seeing me in sweatpants and a ratty t-shirt. I felt too jumpy to sit, so I paced.

"Thank you for asking," I said. "I'm doing as well as can be expected when one's husband's been arrested for murdering one's ex-boyfriend."

"Sounds reasonable," she said. "Is this a good time to call? I didn't even ask."

"No, it's nice to be interrupted. I was just trying to figure out how to do a particular data query for one of my Student Retention Office reports."

"Do I want to know?" Betty asked.

"No, but I'll tell you anyway. I'm supposed to show that students have greater success in classes with 'engaged' professors. Regardless of class size, student preparation, or whether the professor is part-time or tenure-track."

"They tell you what conclusion they want, and you're supposed to find it? Oh lordy."

"They tell me what conclusion the *foundation* wants, and if we find it, we keep our grant funding for another year."

Betty Jackson is a psychometrician. She specializes in measuring things like student success and is a coauthor of one of the field's most popular textbooks. Her name was even on the original grant application that funded the Student Retention Office. I don't know the whole history, but I do know that nowadays the Student Retention Office won't even let her see their data.

"Just out of morbid curiosity," Betty said. "How are they measuring student success?"

"By the student's final grade in the class."

"And how do you know which professors are 'engaged'?"

"Easy. They're the ones who give out the highest grades."

"Uh huh. And they're going to use your results to...?"

"To show that handing out those tablets with the proprietary software increases faculty engagement and student success."

"I thought the Student Retention Office gave those tablets to everyone."

"They did."

"So there's no comparison group."

"Nope. Because if you had a comparison group, you might find out that your ground-breaking innovation doesn't make a difference. And that would be an unacceptable result."

"Oh, don't I know it. Look on the bright side, Molly. It's not every day you find such a perfect real-life example of 'begging the question.' You still like being department chair?"

"Hate it."

"Okay."

"But if I step down, Rodge Cowper becomes chair and that would be even worse. How did you hear about Donnie's arrest by the way? Was it in the paper already?"

"The online police blotter on *Island Confidential*. Didn't you see it?"

"I guess not."

"Molly, I thought you of all people would have kept up with *Island Confidential*. You and Pat haven't had a falling out, have you?"

"I guess when the baby came I got out of the habit of reading it. I wanted to avoid bad news. Wow, I haven't talked to Pat Flanagan in ages, come to think of it. Not since the baby was born."

"It happens when you have kids," Betty said. "It's easy to drift away from your friends."

From the back side of the house I heard the revving of a distant lawnmower. They were mowing the graveyard.

"I should call Pat," I said.

"You should, Molly. He's on good terms with Mahina PD and can give you the scoops, so to say, on Donnie's case. But I called for another reason. Do you remember my daughter Verna?"

What would I say when she asked me what I knew about her daughter and Stephen? I wasn't even certain it was true. I'd let Betty tell me, and then I'd try to act surprised.

"Uh, yes. She was one of the servers at the dinner, wasn't she?"

"Yes, she was. Verna is working part-time at a catering company. That quarter-million-dollar liberal-arts degree sure is paying off. Anyway. Since then, she did a dinner event at the Maritime Club. Dean Gunderson, have you met our new Arts & Sciences dean?"

"I talked to him at the dinner," I said. "He seems nice."

"Yes, doesn't he? Well. He happened to be sitting with Ray Pang."

"The prosecutor?"

"M-hm. I will repeat to you what Verna claims she overheard. I do not vouch for its authenticity or truthfulness, and I will deny having told you any of this."

"Disclaimer noted." I tried to sound calm, but I noticed my pacing had picked up speed.

"It seems that Gunderson was lobbying the prosecutor to put Stephen's death down to murder, rather than accident."

I peeked in the window to make sure Margaret wasn't listening in. She wasn't. She was sitting on the couch, reading to Francesca from her CPA exam flashcards.

"Why would they want to do that?" I asked.

"I have my own theory. But I'd like to hear what you think."

I considered it for a moment.

"They want Stephen's death to be a murder. Hmm. Because if they can pin Stephen's death on the jealous husband of his victim's ex, then they're not liable and they don't have to pay anything to the bereaved parents?"

"Bingo," Betty said. "Do you have another call coming in?"

I did.

"Dan Watanabe," I said. "I'll swipe it to voice mail."

"Your dean? You're not on duty over the summer, are you?"

"No. He's probably trying to get me to serve on some committee for free. I'm going to ignore him and let him call the next sucker. I'm already spending too much time on these stupid Student Retention Office reports."

"Good plan."

"Betty, thank you for telling me about this. What do you think I should do? Should I tell Stephen's parents?"

"Well, that's up to you," Betty said. "I'm just passing it along because I thought you'd want to know. I'm sure you'd do the same for me."

Dang it.

"Um, Betty? I was actually going to call you. To tell you something I'd heard. I have no idea whether it's true or not, but, you know, just like you told me, and I appreciated it..."

"Sure. What is it?"

"It's about Verna."

"Ah. Does it have to do with the late Stephen Park?"

"Kind of. Someone told me they were romantically involved."

"Yes. I knew about that."

"You did?"

"But thank you for telling me."

"Does your daughter know you know?"

"She's never said anything to me. But if I didn't know before, I'd have to ask myself why she was so interested in listening in on a conversation about Stephen Park."

"Well, he did die. I guess that makes it interesting."

"What I don't understand is, why arrest Donnie of all people?" Betty said. "Donnie is the most level-headed person I've ever met. Niall and I have as much of a motive as anyone, Stephen breaking our little girl's heart like he did. And I was there at the dinner. Why didn't anyone arrest me?"

"Donnie admits he followed Stephen out onto the terrace," I said.

"Oh my. That is unfortunate."

That evening, after dinner, I told Donnie what Betty had told me. His arrest was a deliberate act of misdirection, I said. The university just wanted to avoid paying for Stephen's death.

He sat and rocked the baby and nodded as if he were listening, but it seemed like he wasn't really processing it.

"Donnie," I persisted, "I know it's second- or third-hand information, but this is 'Pay-to-play Ray.' The prosecutor who made our chancellor's DUIs magically disappear. It's not like it's out of character for him to go along with something like this. Maybe you want to tell your lawyer about it? That the university is looking for a fall guy so they're not liable?"

Donnie shook his head.

"I can call her myself," I offered. "That might be even better. You might not remember all the details."

"Please, Molly, don't...let's just let her do her job. She's going to be getting in touch with you anyway to take your statement. I'm going to bed."

"Donnie, it's not even eight o'clock."

I took Francesca from him.

"Thanks," he said, without looking at me. He stood up and headed down the hallway to our bedroom.

CHAPTER TWENTY-FOUR

I DIDN'T TAKE ACTION until the next day. Donnie had left, and Margaret was supervising the baby's tummy time. Francesca was supposed to sleep face-up, but not spend all of her time that way lest she develop a weak back and a flat head. Francesca didn't particularly enjoy tummy time. She struggled to lift her head (which, admittedly, was massive compared to the rest of her). Francesca always seemed relieved when her exercise sessions were over. In this way she was truly her mother's daughter.

I set down my coffee cup and found my purse.

"Margaret?" I said.

"Francesca, look up here at Aunty Margaret. Good job, baby! Sorry, what?"

"I'm going out for a few minutes."

"Oh. Okay. Baby's doing a good job with tummy time, yes she is."

I went to the garage, started up the Thunderbird, and dug around until I found the business card I was looking for.

Ah, here it was. I pulled out the card and called Stephen's parents' attorney. I left a message detailing what Betty had told me: that Geoffrey Gunderson had conspired with the county prosecutor to pin Stephen's death on Donnie. Donnie had told me not to talk to *his* lawyer. He hadn't said don't tell *any* lawyer.

Then I called Emma and caught her up.

"Molly, forget about working this morning," Emma said excitedly. "We gotta brainstorm."

"Margaret's here at the house," I said.

"Can she hear you?"

"No. I'm calling from my car."

"Let's meet somewhere. Not here. Yoshi's got his t-shirt printing junk everywhere. How about the Pair-O-Dice?"

"The Pair-O-Dice? Is that place still around?" Every time I had gone there, the place had been practically empty. I had no idea how they stayed in business.

"Whaddaya mean is that place still around? Molly, the Pair-O-Dice is like four blocks from your house. How do you not know it's still there?"

"It's three quarters of a mile from my house. And I haven't had a lot of opportunities to go strolling around downtown Mahina lately."

"You're not gonna bring the baby, are you?" Emma asked warily.

"I told you, she's with Margaret."

"Until when?"

"Until this afternoon. Around two, whenever Donnie comes home for lunch. I can be down there in half an hour."

"Never takes half an hour to drive from your place."

"I'm going to walk. I don't want to deal with parallel-parking the Thunderbird downtown. Besides, it's not raining, and I can use the exercise."

I went inside and checked on Margaret and the baby one last time to make sure they were okay. Everything seemed fine. Margaret was sitting in one of our big armchairs, holding Francesca in her lap and reading to her from the CPA exam flashcards.

Donnie's Drive-Inn looked crowded when I passed. The lines at the order windows were three or four deep, and people were standing around waiting for one of the picnic tables to clear. Good. We were going to have to sell a lot of plate lunches to pay for Donnie's lawyer. I continued downhill, past the Victorian post office building. By the time I passed the park and reached the intersection. my surroundings had gone from quaint to charmingly sketchy. Rain-battered old-West style storefronts mingled with disused gas stations, ramshackle plantation houses, and makeshift hostels with hand painted signs.

By the time I reached the Pair-O-Dice Bar & Grille, I was out of "charmingly sketchy" territory and had entered plain old "sketchy." When the Pair-O-Dice's festive neon sign was turned on, the pink dice tumbled, and the green palm trees did a stop-motion sway. But now, in the drizzly midday, the sign was merely a scribble of dusty tubing in a black window. Sun-faded flyers taped behind the glass announced concerts and craft fairs that had taken place months ago.

Once my eyes adjusted to the Pair-O-Dice's dark interior, it took no time at all to locate Emma. She was the only living soul there. She was most of the way through a tall glass of beer.

"Emma, It's not even lunchtime." I took a seat at the wobbly table and popped the tab of the canned club soda Emma had procured for me. She knows I'll only order canned drinks here.

"Not that I'm judging," I added. "Thanks for this."

"The Pair-O-Dice has its own time zone." Emma pointed to the darkened window. "Once we're on this side of that neon sign, it's eternal happy hour. You're okay? Baby's squared away?"

"The baby's fine. When I left, Margaret was reading something to her about par versus book value. I'll have to borrow her note cards for when I have trouble sleeping. Emma, guess what I just found out. Apparently Verna, Betty Jackson's daughter, turned down a grad school scholarship in actuarial science to stay in Mahina with Stephen Park."

Emma tilted her head.

"What does Betty Jackson's daughter have to do with Stephen?"

"Oh, I guess I never got a chance to tell you. Betty's daughter and Stephen Park were a thing."

"Ew!" Emma set down her beer and shook her hands as if they were covered with bugs.

"Didn't I tell you?"

"No!" Emma cried. "I think I would've remembered. Poor Betty."

In any other establishment, Emma's outburst would have turned heads. But there were no heads to turn at the Pair-O-Dice. Even the bartender was mysteriously AWOL. At least as far as I could tell, although it was dark enough that someone might have been standing behind the bar without my realizing it.

"I didn't tell you? I guess I told Donnie about it," I said.

"Oh, and that's the same as telling me about it? Cause we all look alike to you?"

"Yes, you and Donnie look exactly alike to me. That's the explanation. Actually, I think it's because you're both in my 'close confidant' category."

"Well, tell me then. What's the deal with Park and Betty's daughter?"

I told Emma everything I could think of that she might have missed.

Emma shook her head.

"Man. I don't even have a kid, but I can tell you, if it was my daughter? I'd want to kill him. You sure Betty or Niall didn't shove him off that balcony?"

"No, I'm not sure. Nor would I blame them."

"But they think they can pin it on Donnie," Emma mused. "It's weird. With all the people around who had something against Park, how come they focus on Donnie? He can prove he was inside when Stephen fell."

"Actually, he can't."

"What?"

"He told me he went outside to talk to Stephen."

"He did what?" Emma slammed her beer down on the wooden table. I picked up a napkin and wiped beer foam from my eye.

"He didn't like the way Stephen was talking to me. But he didn't do anything to Stephen. He told me as soon as he was outside he realized he was making a mistake. He changed his mind and came back inside."

"Molly, how come you're keeping all the interesting stuff from me? I thought we were friends."

"And that's why we're here," I reassured her. "To get caught up. I've been replaying that night in my mind. So we were at Table 4—"

"Whoa, table four?"

"You don't have to be sarcastic, Emma."

"I'm not. Four is unlucky. It means death."

"What?"

"In Japanese, four is pronounced *shi*, which sounds like the word for death. That's how come you're not supposed to give gifts that are in sets of four."

"Oh good. Yet another opportunity for me to make a horrible social blunder without realizing—hang on."

I reached for the ringing phone in my bag. Dan Watanabe's office number flashed on my screen.

"Speaking of deans. *Dang* it. What does Dan want now?"

"Don't answer it," Emma urged me. "He's gonna try put you on a committee."

"He's tried calling already," I said. "Maybe it's important."

"And he can't get another sucker, so he's trying you again. Molly, don't. It's a trap."

But I had already pressed the answer button.

CHAPTER TWENTY-FIVE

DAN WASN'T TRYING TO press-gang me onto a summer committee. In fact, he had called to do me a favor. He had negotiated space in the new building for the College of Commerce, he said, and he was going to let me pick out my office.

"The other faculty members are bugging me about it," he said, "but I said I'd let the department chairs have first dibs, and I'm keeping my word."

"Thanks Dan," I said. "I appreciate it."

Across the table from me, Emma turned her head sideways like an owl.

"Well, I appreciate what you guys do too, Molly."

"You mean like work for free during our unpaid summers?"

"Yeah. Like that. Management department has the top floor, by the way," he added.

"The top floor, huh? Because we're the most important?"

Emma rolled her eyes and stood up for another trip to the bar.

"Because you're the smallest department, and there are only four usable offices up there. This way you're all together."

"Only four *usable* offices? What are the unusable offices, where they store their old straitjackets and lobotomy icepicks?"

"I couldn't say. They're not quite done fixing up the building."

"Yeah, that was pretty evident at the donor dinner." I didn't know whether Dan had heard about Stephen Park's death. Serena, his secretary, would tell him if she hadn't already. "Too bad you couldn't be there, by the way. I mean it."

"Yes, I heard what happened, Molly. I wasn't sure whether to tell you I'm sorry for your loss."

So he had heard.

"It's not my loss, particularly, but it's a shame."

"By the way, you mentioned the donor dinner? We're not in that building."

"We're not? We don't get the fabulous entryway with the curving staircases?"

"No, we have the building behind the main hospital."

"There's another building? Where? I didn't see it."

"Directly in back, a little further down the hill. It's kind of overgrown back there. You wouldn't notice it unless you were looking for it. It used to be the nurses' quarters or a leprosy ward or something."

"I wish you had just said nurses' quarters."

Emma came over and sat back down. She had a tall glass of beer in one hand and a miniature wine bottle in the other.

"Seems like you need this." She handed me the wine.

"Is that Emma Nakamura?" Dan asked. "Tell her hi for me. You guys keeping up your coffee breaks this summer?"

Dan knew Emma well. During the school year she made a habit of hanging around my office and mooching coffee from my espresso machine.

"Yes," I said as I unscrewed the top from the wine bottle. "Can't let that coffee break tradition go. So, when should I go pick out my office?"

"Sooner's better than later. I'd go today if I were you. If anything's locked, you can call security to let you in. Make sure you have your ID."

"See?" Emma said, as soon as I hung up. "Told you it was a good idea to answer the phone."

"Uh-huh. Hey, thanks for the wine."

"You're lucky," she said. "Your dean's a decent guy."

"I know."

Emma lifted her glass, clinked it against my little wine bottle, and drank.

"Want another one?" she asked.

"No thank you. I just started this one. Emma, we have some time. Margaret has the baby. Want to come help me pick out my new office?"

"Sure. Might be fun." Emma picked up her glass, realized she'd already emptied it, and set it back down again.

CHAPTER TWENTY-SIX

"SO I'VE BEEN THINKING," I said as I climbed into Emma's undersized front seat. "About our theory of Bee Corcoran being the one who killed Stephen."

"Yeah, I dunno about that," Emma said. "If there was any evidence against Bee that made her look guilty, wouldn't Gunderson be trying to get the prosecutor after her, instead of Donnie?"

"Unless Gunderson has his own reasons for keeping her out of trouble, like being complicit in her research fraud. Maybe he doesn't want her flipping on him."

"Ooh, Molly, I like it."

"I thought you might. Anyway, when someone's murdered, it's usually the spouse or significant other, isn't it? It wouldn't be the first time someone killed their cheating boyfriend."

"But he wasn't her boyfriend."

"So she says."

"Wait a minute, Stephen was cheating? With who?"

"I don't know. I can't think of everything. But Emma, it's Stephen we're talking about here. He was probably cheating with someone."

"Okay," Emma said. "Speaking of jealousy as a motive, how about Betty Jackson's daughter?"

"I like that idea a lot less," I said. "Verna is just a kid."

"Yeah, I agree. But Stephen dumped her and wrecked her life and now she's working this junk job and she has to see him sitting there with his new da kine."

"Exactly, Betty's daughter was working," I said. "She didn't have time to follow Stephen outside and push him over the railing. Besides, I don't want it to be Betty's daughter. I like Betty."

Emma started the car and shifted into reverse.

"I like Betty too, but everyone's got their limit, ah? In fact, I'd say it's more likely Betty killed him. Betty's daughter gave up her scholarship for Stephen Park, and then Stephen Park dumped Betty's daughter for Bee Corcoran. He broke the girl's heart and even worse, wrecked her career."

Emma peeled out into traffic inches ahead of a battered minivan.

"Eh, you think Betty Jackson is capable of murder?" Emma asked.

"No," I replied. "But neither is Donnie."

Emma swore and slammed on her brakes.

"I'll assume that wasn't directed at me," I said.

"Nah. Babooze in the minivan tailgating me. Yeah, I can't see either Betty or your husband going crazy an' killing someone. If I was making a movie called Attack of the Level-Headed Logic People, I think I'd cast Betty and Donnie in the leading roles."

"What about me? I'm a level-headed logic person."

Emma snorted.

"You? With your Italian temper?"

"Emma, you know very well I'm—"

"I know, I know, everyone thinks you're Italian but you're really Albanian."

"I'm *Albanian*, Emma...wait. That's what you just said."

Emma sped up at the yellow light and accelerated into a screeching left turn.

"Of course it is. How come you're surprised?"

"It's just that you usually get it wrong and say 'Armenian' or 'Angolan' or 'Azerbaijani' or something like that."

"Only cause it's hilarious how mad it makes you."

"I don't get mad. I just correct you. It's not the same thing. Oh, how about Niall? Betty's husband?"

"I thought he was out of town," Emma said.

"Betty *says* he's out of town. I don't want it to be him either, though. Hey, maybe Bee will be in her office,"

Emma shot me a look.

"Why do we care if Bee's in her office, Molly? We're not going around interviewing suspects, right?"

"No, of course not. But it would be short-sighted of us to close ourselves off to readily-available information, don't you think?"

"Whoa, Molly. I said yes to seeing your new office, but talk to Bee? About what? Tell her, ha-ha, here we are, unarmed and no one knows we're here, just wanted to let you know we think you're the murderer. Hope you don't kill us now."

"Aha, so you agree Bee could be the murderer."

"Nah, I just don't wanna make her mad. She could jack us up. You seen her arms?"

"Yes, we've already been over the topic of Bee's arms. Look, I'm not saying I'm going to throw her office door open and point at her and declare, *j'accuse*!"

"Oh good. That's a relief."

"And she probably won't even be there."

"Yeah. Let's hope not." Emma gripped the steering wheel and accelerated around a slow sedan.

"But what if I just stop by to say hello and share the sad news about my husband getting wrongfully arrested because the university's looking to blame someone for their negligence?"

Emma was already shaking her head, but I pressed on.

"And now we're spending Francesca's college fund to hire an expensive lawyer to defend him. She'll realize what she set in motion, and I think she'll consider changing her story."

"You're counting on someone you think is a murderer to have a sense of decency, Molly?"

"No, not at all. In fact—"

"Sounds like you are."

"No. Here's the thing, Emma. I tell Bee that we hired Honey Akiona to defend Donnie. Everyone knows Honey has the best investigators around. Her people are famous for finding out things the police missed. If Bee's guilty and she knows Honey Akiona is on the case, she might consider confessing before the truth comes out."

"So you're saying suppose Bee's guilty, knowing Donnie has a smart lawyer might make her think twice about trying to keep things covered up."

"Exactly."

"Yeah, I dunno. Bee had lots of opportunities to kill Park. Why would she wait to kill him at an event with so many people around?"

"To make people doubt that she did it, just like you're doubting. To make sure there are witnesses who saw the two of them getting along all lovey-dovey kissy-face in public. That's what I'd do if I wanted to kill someone."

"Good to know. Eh, you know who we should've invited today?"

"Pat!" we said in unison. Emma leaned forward and reached for her back pocket.

"You drive," I said quickly. "I'll call him. That's a great idea, Emma. He's always on the lookout for Haunted Hawaii stories for *Island Confidential*. Besides, I haven't seen him in ages."

The façade of the old Mahina Memorial Hospital was pure Victorian grimness. At the donor dinner, with the lights blazing and the conversation humming, the old edifice had felt festive. But in the gray afternoon, with black mold streaking the gray stucco, it was easy to believe the building was teeming with tormented souls.

"So, this is where Miss Constance is supposedly floating around?" I asked Emma. "Pushing people off balconies?"

"Sometimes she just scares 'em to death," Emma said. "Or makes 'em go crazy. Or derails their train. Eh Molly, where do I park?"

"College of Commerce isn't in the main building," I said. "Dan told me we're around the back."

Emma cut over from the main driveway to a narrow access path that snaked around the side of the old hospital building. We descended as we made our way around, so by the time we reached the back of the hospital we were a good two stories lower than the front. Emma stopped in front of what looked like an ancient loading dock. Wide bay doors were boarded up with plywood. The hospital had its best face to the street. Viewed from the back, it looked like a strong wind could blow it apart.

My glasses fogged up the minute I stepped out of the car, thanks to Mahina's humidity. Downhill to our left, half-embedded in the jungle that had overtaken the untended edges of the property, was a boxy building. It was a dirty white, and completely bereft of Victorian adornment.

"Darn it," I said. "We don't get a fabulous Victorian building. That thing looks like it could've been built in the thirties as part of the EUR."

"What's the EUR?" Emma asked. "Something bad, it sounds like."

"An un-fabulous suburb of Rome. Built by Benito Mussolini."

"I think you're approaching this with a very negative attitude, Molly. Eh, is that where it happened?" Emma pointed upward.

Around twenty or thirty feet above us a balcony jutted from the main hospital building, surrounded by a low railing. I quickly looked down at my feet to see what I was standing on. An old concrete pad, half-buried in charcoal-gray dirt and dried leaves.

"It looks higher up than I remember." I looked up at the balcony again, and down at the ground.

Floomp. I wished I could forget the sound. "Well, we don't have all day," I said brightly. "Let's go find my office."

"Eh, careful, ah, you two!"

Emma and I looked up to see a young woman peering over the railing.

"Honey?" I called up.

"Stay right there, I'm coming around."

"What do you think Honey Akiona is doing here?" I said to Emma. "It must have something to do with Donnie's case. I hope so, anyway."

"You tell her about what Betty's daughter said?" Emma asked. "About our dean talking with the prosecutor?"

"No. Donnie asked me not to get involved."

"What? And you listened to him?"

"Look, he specifically said to me, don't contact her, just let her do her job."

"Wouldn't she do her job better if she knew about the university wanting to frame him for Stephen Park's murder, so they can minimize their own liability?"

"If you ask me, yes. But Donnie thinks I'll go blundering in and mess everything up."

"Yeah I can see his point," Emma said as Honey Akiona came around the corner of the building. "Donnie's right. You shouldn't say anything to her."

"What?"

"But that doesn't mean I can't tell her."

"Ah. Well, tell her whatever you like. As long as it's clear you didn't hear it from me."

"You got it. Eh, Honey, howzit?"

Honey Akiona cut a striking figure. Her leather pumps boosted her to six feet tall, and a navy-blue pantsuit flattered her Junoesque contours. She had cut her dark hair to chin length, where it hung in a glossy bob. She embraced Emma first, planting Emma's face directly in her impressive bosom. I got a hug too, and then we got down to business.

"Professor, you get my messages?"

"Messages?" I pulled my phone out and saw the icon for un-played voice mail messages in the corner of my screen. "Ooh. Sorry about that. I've kind of been behind on my voice mail."

"I was trying to set up a meeting with you to go over your statement, see if you could remember anything else about that night. But now that you're here, you got some time to talk?"

"Sure," I said.

"I get something," Emma said eagerly.

"Professor Nakamura. Were you at the event?"

"Nah. Molly only went cause her dean couldn't make it. But you gotta hear this. My dean, Gunderson, and the prosecutor are framing Donnie so the university doesn't have to pay Stephen Park's parents."

As the three of us stood in the chilly shadow of the old hospital building, Emma told Honey Akiona about the overheard conversation between the arts and sciences dean and the county prosecutor. I was impressed by Emma's memory for detail. I couldn't think of a single thing to add to her account.

Honey listened with her arms folded, staring at the ground as Emma spoke. She seemed to find the news distasteful, but not surprising.

"I suspected something wasn't right," she said, when Emma had finished. "Pang won't touch a case unless it's an easy win, or there's something in it for him. Good thing I came out here when I did."

"Honey, what are you doing out here?" I asked.

"Taking measurements and pictures. That way if the university tries to fix that railing after the fact, I have visual proof of the way it was before they changed it."

"Wouldn't the police have pictures of the scene?" Emma asked.

"I've found it's better not to rely on someone else." Honey was looking at a spot on the ground about ten feet away from where we were standing. The leaves and dirt had been washed away and one patch was lighter than the surrounding concrete, as if it had been bleached. It was a little disorienting to see it in the daylight, but I still had a pretty good idea of what we were looking at.

"Is that where it happened?" I asked quietly.

Honey nodded.

"Oh, by the way—"

"You remembered something else?" Honey asked.

"Well, not exactly. But Emma and I were talking, and we have a theory."

"Oh." Honey's enthusiasm had vanished.

"Molly," Emma said, "maybe now's not the time—"

"We think you should look into Bee Corcoran," I persisted.

"No, not we," Emma interjected.

"She has two possible motives," I went on. "One, she was committing research fraud and Stephen found out. Two, he was cheating on her."

"I agree something was weird about Bee's research results," Emma said. "But the other stuff, we were just kicking some ideas around."

"Did you see them arguing?" Honey asked. "Corcoran and Park?"

"I didn't see them arguing, no."

"You got any proof he was cheating?"

"Well, not proof exactly, but—"

"Do you know who he was cheating with?"

"Well, no, but he—"

"Are you sure Corcoran and Park were romantically involved to begin with?" Honey asked.

"They came to the dinner together," I said, a little defensively. "Bee actually told me she and Stephen weren't an item, but that was after he was already dead. Maybe she was lying to me to throw me off the scent."

Honey nodded.

"Okay. Well, I'll look into it," she reached into her briefcase to pull out a business card. "Listen, I gotta go, but please call me if you remember anything else."

"Honey, wait."

She turned around.

"You said the prosecutor would go after a case if it was an easy win, or something else. What is the something else?"

"The usual. Reward his friends, punish his enemies, or get a big donation for his re-election campaign."

Emma and I remained standing on the spot after Honey had left.

"Molly," Emma asked, "what is wrong with you?"

"What do you mean? You were on board with the Bee theory."

"Yeah, when we're talking about it between ourselves. But you say it out loud in front of a real lawyer and it sounds totally meshuggeneh."

"If there's nothing to it then there's nothing to it. But I don't think there's any harm in sharing our thoughts with her. Dang it. She probably does think I'm nuts now, doesn't she?"

"You still wanna go see your office or what?" Emma asked.

"Dan said we have the top floor," I said as we started down the hill.

CHAPTER TWENTY-SEVEN

"I HOPE MY NEW OFFICE doesn't look out this way," I said as we made our way along the narrow walkway through the trees. "I don't want to have to see where Stephen died."

"Molly. Don't you live next to a graveyard?"

"Another reason why I don't want to stare death in the face all day."

"You know this place was a *hospital*. Literally tons of people died here. And don't call me out for saying 'literally'. I do mean literally, cause all you need is ten or twenty people to make a ton. Even less if it's a bunch of fat guys."

"I know Stephen wasn't the first person to die here, Emma, I'm not an idiot. But he's the first person I know personally who died here. It's different."

The building entrance was a soap-green wooden door. Unlike the double doors at the entrance to the main hospital, this was not at all grand. Emma pushed the door open, and I followed her. Inside it was surprisingly bright. I looked up to see that the center of the building was an atrium, open all the way up to an expansive skylight.

"This is like that hotel I just stayed in for my conference in Phoenix," Emma said. "You step out of your room and there's like this low wall about waist high, and like fifty feet below is the lobby."

"It sounds dangerous," I said. "Wouldn't it be easy to fall right over?"

"No one died when I was there."

"Well, here's my new daily workout," I said as we started up the steps.

"Ho, this is pretty nice. *Helloooo*!"

"Emma, don't shout."

"What? You afraid I'm gonna wake up the ghosts?"

"No, I'm afraid your voice is going to destabilize the building like the Tacoma Narrows bridge and it's going to tumble down and crush us to death."

"Hello!" Came a man's voice. From the top of the stairwell, I could see the top of a shaved head.

"Pat!" Emma picked up speed and bounded up the steps. I did my best to keep up, but I quickly lost sight of her. Emma's canoe paddling keeps her extremely fit. By the time I had reached the top floor I felt like I was breathing sandpaper.

Pat was attired after his usual fashion, in black boots, grubby jeans, and a battered flannel shirt over a Joy Division T-shirt. He's pale, wiry, and tall. Emma is short, brown, and built for power. Standing side by side they look like an illustration of Diversity of the Human Species.

"This is it?" I exclaimed, after I'd exchanged a quick hug with Pat. "Just a landing and a couple doors?"

I backed away from the railing.

"You should stay away from the railing," Emma advised helpfully. "You're scared of heights."

"Yes, thank you for reminding me. Except there's not a lot of space up here."

"Hey Molly, sorry to hear about Donnie," Pat said.

"Thanks. It's been pretty stressful. Have you heard anything down at Mahina PD?"

Pat shrugged. "If it makes you feel any better, it doesn't seem like anyone there really thinks Donnie killed anyone."

"Eh, Pat, you know anything about this building?" Emma asked.

"I didn't even know it was here until today," I added. "Emma, you're making me nervous leaning over the railing."

"I'm not gonna fall over," she said.

Pat was snapping photos with his cell phone. "I'm gonna come out and say it's definitely haunted. At least for the purpose of my next installment of Mysterious Mahina."

"I thought your thing was called Haunted Hawaii," Emma said.

"It was, until the Mahina Chamber of Commerce started advertising in *Island Confidential*. They wanted something more distinctive and Mahina-centric. So now my column is called Mysterious Mahina."

"Is this the famous firewall between editorial and advertising that we're always hearing about?" I asked.

"Give me a break. I'm just trying to make up the difference between teaching intro comp and making a living wage." Pat tried the handle to Room 310; it was locked. He turned back from the door and looked around. "Hey. Where's Emma?"

I had a flash of panic, imagining Emma tipping quietly over the railing and plummeting to her death. Fortunately, Emma strolled out of the bathroom at that moment as the sound of gurgling water reverberated in the walls.

"Here she is," I said. "How's the bathroom?"

She shrugged. "Clean. Unisex bathroom though. So it's probably not going to stay clean with you an' three guys in your department. Hey Pat, guess what—"

"I'm going to go look at the bathroom." I jerked my head toward the bathroom. "Emma, you want to show me around?"

"Yeah, let me show you around," she said and followed me in.

Unlike the landing outside, the bathroom was humid and poorly-lit. A small globe fixture and a dusty breadbox-sized window were the only sources of light. A cloudy mirror was mounted over a cantilevered celadon-green sink. You'd think the combination of the dim light and the aged mirror would be flattering, but a quick glimpse of my reflection showed the opposite. Not only did I look waxy and undead, but my hair was going wild in the humidity. It was like every strand had decided it hated every other strand and they were bristling as far from one another as they could.

"Do you think these are the original floor tiles?" I asked.

The floor was covered in 2-inch hexagonal tiles in the same celadon green as the sink, the walls, and the rust-speckled metal stalls. The tiles were cracked and chipped, but clean.

"Molly, why are you acting so weird? I know you didn't bring me in here to talk about floor tiles."

"I thought you were going to tell Pat what Betty's daughter overheard. About your dean trying to talk the prosecutor into framing Donnie for Stephen's death."

"Yeah, I was, so?"

"Anything you tell him will end up in *Island Confidential.*"

"And then?"

"And then it could mess up whatever Honey might be planning. Maybe she doesn't want to tip them off that she knows what they're up to."

Emma sighed.

"Yeah, okay. Eh, check out this magic mirror, all blurry. Makes me look like a frickin' movie star."

Emma flicked her hair over her shoulder and sauntered out. I followed her out to the sunny landing.

"So, let's have a look at my choices," I said. "Which office will I least regret choosing?"

"Pat, tell her which office has the least ghosts living in it," Emma said.

"The *fewest* ghosts," I wanted to say, but didn't. You'd think people would appreciate helpful corrections like this, but I've found they don't.

Room 310 was on the wall to the left. On the right was the door to the restroom. In front of me were three doors in the same hospital green as the front door and the bathroom. They were labeled 311, 312, and 314.

"So what have you found out about this place?" I tried the door handles. But the offices were all locked.

"I have some good stuff on the main building." Pat had his hand braced on the railing.

"Pat, don't lean on that," I said. "You don't know how much termite damage there is."

He picked his hand up and folded his arms but didn't move away from the railing.

"They put in a lot of effort and expense considering it was a TB hospital in a territorial backwater," he said. "They got Carrara marble for the floors. Think about shipping marble from Italy to Hawaii. The family that financed this wanted the hospital to be a showplace. To put Mahina on the map. I found this quote. Hang on."

Pat brought something up on his phone.

"Here it is. 'Fair Mahina will outshine not only Honolulu, but will grow to rival the great capitals of the world.'"

"Great capitals of the world?" Emma snorted. "Mahina? Pat, you should do a series called Delusional Rich Idiots of History."

"So what was this building used for then?" I looked up at the skylight, which from the top floor looked enormous. It was rectangular, around eight by ten feet, of plain frosted glass. Four muntins formed a large rectangle in the middle and little squares in each corner. "Dan thought it might be nurses' quarters."

"Was it the nuthouse?" Emma walked over and punched my shoulder playfully. "Cause that'd be appropriate."

"This building was actually the Inebriate Asylum," Pat said. "Old-timey rehab."

"Eh, no look at me li'dat," Emma protested.

"What? I didn't say anything about you reeking of beer in the middle of the day," Pat said.

"I took the breathalyzer before we drove here, ah, Molly?"

"You have a breathalyzer?" Pat asked.

"In my glove box," Emma declared proudly. "Don't leave home without it."

Pat shook his head and recommenced taking pictures. Pat never drinks alcohol, and he never talks about it. And I've never asked him.

"It's true," I said. "She was below the limit. Emma won't tell me where she got that after-market liver installed, but I want one. Do you hear sirens?"

The sirens got louder, and then seemed to stop somewhere below us.

"Sounds like it's on that side," Emma said. "Behind those doors."

"Only one thing to do," Pat reached into his back pocket and hunched over the handle of the door marked 312. "Molly, you might want to turn away."

"From what? I see nothing."

It took Pat less than a minute to do whatever he was doing to the door. He stood up and pushed it open. The room was around ten by twelve feet. Two large crank-out windows admitted the hot afternoon sun. The walls were the familiar hospital green, and the linoleum square flooring was a checkerboard of green and beige. A putty-colored file cabinet, frosted with rust, was the only piece of furniture.

At first I thought the windows didn't have any kind of covering, but on closer inspection I could see yellowed Venetian blinds that had been pulled all the way up. The view was of the back of the main hospital building. From this angle I saw the hospital walls were streaked with black mold and the windows were black and dusty. If I pressed my face to the glass and looked down, I could see the terrace where Stephen spent his last living moments. Further to the left, nearly out of my line of vision, was the rickety wooden staircase leading from the emergency exit down to the ground.

"You get to look at that all day?" Pat asked me. "Depressing."

"I'll get used to it," I said, stepping back from the window. "Besides, if you look off to the right you can see trees."

"Over there!" Emma's face was pressed to the window. We rushed over to see an ambulance pulling away from the side of the building and out onto the main road. It gave a single whoop of its siren as it slowly moved out of our sight.

"I hope whoever it is, is okay," I said. "It's always kind of disturbing to hear an ambulance and imagine—"

"Hello," a voice echoed from somewhere in the building. "Anyone inside?"

CHAPTER TWENTY-EIGHT

"SECURITY," THE VOICE yelled as we scrambled to leave the office. "Anyone here? Gotta clear the building."

Pat quickly locked the door behind us and the three of us went thundering down the stairs. Pat's long legs could take the steps three or four at a time, but Emma still got to the ground floor first. I, of course, brought up the rear. The ground floor was abandoned when I got there. I eventually found Pat, Emma, and a security guard outside, next to Emma's car.

"Was someone hurt or what?" Emma was asking him.

The young man frowned.

"I not supposed to say nothing, Auntie."

"We should probably go," I said. "We can come back later—"

"Cannot," the young man said evenly. "Gotta wait for the police."

"I really have to get home," I objected. I was starting to feel pressure in my chest, and mentally kicked myself for not having brought my breast pump. Unfortunately, I didn't have my car with me. And Emma and Pat didn't seem like they were going anywhere.

Just as I had made up my mind to walk home, a familiar silhouette came lumbering around the corner.

Detective Ka`imi Medeiros.

He nodded to the three of us by way of greeting, and again to the young guard to dismiss him.

"Mister Flanagan," he said. "Professor Barda. Professor Nakamura. What brings you here today?"

"My dean told me to come here. So I did." I knew Medeiros thought I was a loose cannon, so maybe he'd be impressed by my compliance with authority.

"Your dean. Is that Geoffrey Gunderson?" Medeiros asked.

"No, Dean Gunderson is Arts and Sciences. My dean is Dan Watanabe in the College of Commerce. Our new offices are in that building over there. Dan asked me to go in and pick the office I wanted, so that's what I'm doing."

"How about you, Professor Nakamura?" He asked Emma. "What are you doing here?"

"I'm helping Molly make good choices," Emma replied.

"I'm doing research for my Mysterious Mahina series," Pat said before Medeiros had a chance to address him. "For Island Confidential."

"Did any of you see anything?" Medeiros asked. No one answered him. If we told Medeiros we had seen an ambulance pulling away, we might have to tell him that we saw it from the window of room 312, which would then bring up the awkward question of how we got into room 312.

"We heard a siren," Emma said. "Then da kine came in the building and yelled at us to get out."

"Detective, what is this about?" I asked. "Was someone hurt?"

"That's what we're trying..."

His eyes flicked to my shirt for a microsecond. He blinked.

"Okay. If you remember anything, any of you, please get in touch."

Detective Medeiros turned abruptly and walked off.

"What just happened?" I asked. "What did I say?"

"Probably time for you to get home," Emma said. "Look at your shirt."

Pat had his back turned to us and appeared to be examining his phone with great interest.

I looked down to see two dark-blue milk stains spreading on the front of my shirt.

CHAPTER TWENTY-NINE

THE THREE OF US WATCHED Detective Medeiros disappear around the corner of the old hospital building.

"What's the matter with him?" I asked. "Doesn't he see hacked-up bodies every day? I can't believe I scared him off with a little breast—"

"Aah!" Pat interrupted, clamping his hands over his ears.

"You're not a hacked-up body to Medeiros," Emma said. "You're Donnie's wife. I think it's different. Eh, you need a ride home?"

I looked down at my stained blouse.

"Do you mind if we kill fifteen or twenty minutes before we go? I'd like to get home after Margaret leaves. I'd rather Donnie saw me like this than Margaret."

"What, you think Margaret cares about your milk stains?" Emma asked. "Isn't she there exactly to do baby stuff?"

"Yeah, but she used to be my student. That makes it more embarrassing for some reason. Hey, where did Pat go?"

"I dunno. Oh, here he comes. Eh, babooze, couldn't handle a little grownup conversation about breast milk?"

Pat was sprinting up from the direction opposite to where Medeiros had gone.

"I'm going inside before they lock up the building," he panted.

"I like come," Emma said eagerly. "Molly, you can wait down here if you don't feel like keeping up."

"What? I can keep up. I'll just follow you guys. I don't want to just stand here oozing for twenty minutes. Where are we going?"

Pat led us around the other side of the hospital building, across an overgrown courtyard, through a splintery door, into a dark stairwell. Pat and Emma then bounded up what seemed like 17,000 flights of creaky stairs while I huffed and puffed behind them. Finally, Pat pushed open a door and we emerged into the end of a hallway.

"Sorry, Molly," he said. "I didn't want us to risk getting stuck in the elevator."

"No, it's fine," I wheezed, bracing my hands on my knees. "It's good. I can use the exercise."

"So how come we're here?" Emma asked.

"Molly, are you okay?" Pat bent down and tried to look at my face. I nodded, not wanting to waste valuable oxygen by speaking.

"I managed to talk to the security guard before he left," Pat said. "He was in pretty bad shape."

"Why?" I heard Emma ask. With my hands clutching my knees, I studied the floor and tried to control my breath so I wouldn't hyperventilate. The flooring here on the upper level was linoleum, just like in the Inebriates' Asylum out back. The fancy marble was reserved for the lower floors that the public would see. Or maybe marble was too heavy for anything but the ground floor.

"He told me he was walking around the building, and thought he saw something shining in the bushes," Pat said. "He went to check it out and saw it was a woman's blonde hair. That's when he called the police."

"Was it a wig?" Emma asked.

"Emma," I wheezed, "why would he call the police on a wig?"

"Cause maybe it was a *stolen* wig," she countered.

"Who would steal a wig and then hide it in the bushes? That doesn't make any sense."

"Sorry to have to tell you this," Pat said, "but the blonde hair was actually attached to a person. Sad to say."

I finally caught my breath and stood up.

"Do they know who it was?" I asked.

"He said she was a haole lady, and she was wearing what he called one of those white doctor coats."

Emma and I looked at each other.

"Bee!" we exclaimed.

"Yeah, that's what I thought too," Pat said.

"How do you know who Bee Corcoran is?" I asked him.

"Emma's been keeping me up to date," Pat said. "Good thing you have an alibi, Molly. In case it really was Bee down there."

"Me? Why would I want to hurt Bee?"

"Molly, you can't stand Bee," Emma said.

"Emma, Shh!"

"What? All the doors on this hallway are closed. No can hear me."

"You have no idea how loud your voice is," I whispered. "Anyway, it's not true. I don't hate Bee. Not at all. I *like* Bee."

"Even when she gives you unsolicited weight-loss advice?" Pat asked.

"She's only trying to be helpful," I said. "However misguided her efforts may be."

"The directory says her lab's on this floor," Pat said. "Should be about halfway down on the left."

"Emma, what did you tell him?" I asked.

Emma shrugged.

We followed Pat to Bee's lab. No need to do any lock-picking here; the door was unlocked. Pat walked right in, and we followed him.

The lab smelled like cedar shavings and mothballs, with a hint of stinky mammal. Mounted on the wall to our left was a grid of cages, each of which contained a single rat. On the far side of the lab, floor-to-ceiling horizontal blinds clattered softly, stirred by a breeze. Hazy sunlight filtered through the slats.

"Hello?" A slender young man with wide-spaced blue eyes emerged from behind something that looked like a refrigerator. He was wearing a blue t-shirt and jeans, and carrying a large cardboard Amazon box. Draped over the top of the box was a white lab coat. I quickly folded my arms over my milk-stained T-shirt and ducked behind Pat.

"Oh, hey," the young man said. "Did you guys move my stuff?"

"We just got here," Pat said. "What stuff?"

"Someone moved this," the young man nodded at the box in his arms. "Looks like everything's in there, though. No big."

"We're looking for Dr. Corcoran," Emma said. "Is she around?"

"I haven't seen her today," the boy replied.

"You work here?" Pat asked.

"Not anymore." He rested the box on the edge of a nearby counter. "I just came to get my things and say goodbye to my little buddies here. Refill their water, which *someone* forgot to do today." He nodded toward the white rats in their cages. Most of the animals were sleeping, but here and there a pink nose twitched through the metal mesh of the cage. Each rat had a water bottle mounted on the cage, and each bottle was filled to the top with clear water.

Maybe that's what I needed. A water bottle as tall as I was, mounted next to the glider chair in the master bedroom. Then I wouldn't have to beg people to bring me water when I nursed Francesca. I could just lick the ball bearing at the end of the metal tube.

"We'll just leave Dr. Corcoran a note, then," Emma said. We all stepped aside to let the boy pick up his box and leave.

As soon as he was gone, we separated and began poking around. I went over to open the blinds.

"I'll help," Pat said as he came over. "This window is way too big for this heavy of blinds. They should've used vertical ones."

"I never liked vertical blinds," I remarked, watching Pat manipulate the strings carefully to avoid the blinds going crooked. "They remind me of depressing grad-school apartments. But I guess I see the point of them."

"A balcony?" Emma exclaimed behind us.

"Pretty deluxe," I said.

"Yeah, not in a Biosafety Level 2 lab," Emma said. "There's not supposed to be a window that opens to the outside like—whoa!"

Emma and I stepped back as Pat finished lifting the blinds. A pair of tall French doors opened onto a narrow balcony surrounded by rusty metalwork railing. The center part of the railing had been broken through. An unobstructed breeze blew in, which would have been pleasant if we weren't standing on the fourth floor next to a busted railing where someone had probably just fallen to her death.

"What's down there?" I asked Pat. He'd placed one foot on the balcony and was holding on to the door frame with one hand and was leaning out. I could barely stand to look at him.

"Down there is where they found her," Pat said. "There's the road that goes around the hospital, and I can see a piece of yellow tape from here. Too bad my ghost cam wasn't positioned to catch what happened."

"Ghost cam?" I asked.

Pat came back inside and lowered the blinds carefully.

"I put a camera out to catch supernatural activity," he said. "But I set it up directly in the front. That's where the building looks the best."

"Do you really think that was Bee down there?" I asked. "The person that they found? Bee Corcoran is dead?"

Pat perched on a countertop and folded his arms.

"Yeah, I think so."

"That boy who was just in here," Emma said. "Think he did it? He said it was his last day here."

"You mean she fired him," I asked. "And for revenge, he pushed her out the window?"

"Yeah, I don't know," Pat said. "If he killed her, would he come back later to get his things?"

"Maybe to throw us off," Emma said. "Pun intended."

"That's a terrible pun, Emma," I said. "You're right, Pat. He was pretty calm for someone who had just murdered someone earlier in the day."

"Probably a psychopath," Emma said. "There's a lot of 'em out there, you know."

"Hey, I teach creative writing," Pat said. "You don't have to tell me about psychopaths. I don't know what's worse, the number of guys who write stories about murdering some girl who rejected them, or the fact that they all think they're being original and edgy. Okay, as long as we're here, I'm going to get some pictures."

"Here?" I asked. "Why?"

But Pat already had his phone out.

"You never know what's going to come in handy later," he said.

"Shouldn't we go?" I asked. "I don't want to be here when Detective Medeiros figures out their body is Bee and comes back here."

"Hey, look" Emma called out from a corner of the room. "The phone."

A black push-button landline phone sat on the countertop, the receiver lying off the hook. A crumpled paper towel lay next to it.

"There's nothing connecting it to the wall," I said.

"That's right," Emma said. "No wire. How does that fit in? Hmm. Murderer comes in, steals the phone wire so no one can call for help, pushes Bee out the window, closes the blinds, and runs away."

"Speaking of running away," I said, "can we go? And how does it help to steal a telephone cord? I'm sure Bee has a cell phone. Had."

"Eh Molly," Emma said, "I guess our theory doesn't work so good anymore, ah?"

"Yeah, whatever. No one left any fingerprints, right?" I asked as the door closed behind us.

"We have an eyewitness who can place all three of us here," Pat said. "I'm not sure fingerprints will make a difference."

"Oh. Right," I said.

"So, still think Bee killed Stephen?" Emma asked me as we followed Pat out.

"Molly," Pat asked, "you thought Bee killed Stephen Park?"

"No. Maybe." We followed Pat to the end of the hallway and into the emergency exit stairwell.

"Are Stephen's parents still on island?" Emma asked. "What did they think of Bee?"

"I don't know," I said. "I don't think *they* killed her though, if that's what you're asking. It doesn't seem like the kind of thing they'd do."

"A lot of murderers don't seem like murderers," Pat said. "You'd be surprised."

The stairs seemed a lot shorter on the way down than they had on the way up. But that might have been because we were all running.

It didn't really hit me until we were downstairs, standing around Emma's car.

"Oh my gosh," I said. "Bee Corcoran is dead."

"If it is Bee," Pat said. "But yeah, who else would it be? Blonde hair, wearing a lab coat?"

"I wonder if it was suicide," I said. "How sad."

"Why would Bee commit suicide?" Emma demanded. "She just got the life sciences research award."

"It doesn't work like that, Emma," Pat said. "You never know what kind of things people are struggling with in secret."

"I know one thing," I said.

Pat and Emma looked at me.

"Bee is transgender. Was."

"Nah!" Emma exclaimed.

"How did you know?" Pat asked.

"Stephen told me."

"How come you never told me?" Emma demanded. "I can't believe you kept it a secret. You're usually such a blabbermouth."

"It wasn't my place to say anything. If she wanted people to know, she would have told them. And you have no evidence for your claim that I'm a blabbermouth."

"Why did Stephen tell you about it?" Pat asked.

"Oh, probably to make sure I knew how interesting and awesome Bee was. I'm sure in his mind being trans gives you extra 'cool' points or something."

"Like how he went around fooling people into thinking he was half-Korean cause his last name was Park?" Emma asked.

"Yeah, that sounds about right," Pat said. "Anything to strike the right pose."

"I wonder who's gonna get her lab space," Emma said. "Her lab's got at least twenty percent more square footage than mines."

"I know you two think Bee led a charmed life," Pat said, "But Molly, if what you just told us is true...seriously, what would you do if you woke up tomorrow in a man's body?"

"Go to HR and demand my thirty percent raise," I said.

"Helicopter!" Emma raised her arms and rotated her hips.

"How about both at once?" I said. "That'd make an impression."

Pat sighed.

"Okay. I gotta go. Enjoy your straight cis privilege, ladies."

We watched Pat disappear into the hospital building's late-afternoon shadows.

"Wow. Tough crowd," I said.

"He should know I was just kidding about the helicopter thing," Emma said. "I can't even hula-hoop."

CHAPTER THIRTY

MARGARET'S CAR WAS still in front of my house when Emma dropped me off. Donnie wasn't home yet. I tried sneaking around the back. My plan was to get to the laundry room and grab a fresh shirt before Margaret saw me. But as soon as I stepped onto the back deck, there she was. She was sitting in one of the uncomfortable teak folding chairs, holding Francesca on her lap. I quickly crossed my arms to cover my chest, but as soon as I got closer I forgot about my stained shirt. Margaret's eyes were red and shining. She'd been crying.

I quickly took Francesca from her and held the baby close to me. Our hedge had grown high enough to block the view of the graveyard, so I couldn't see it. It was a small favor. This day was already weird enough.

"Margaret? Are you okay?

I sat next to her and popped the baby under my shirt. Francesca latched on with gusto, quickly relieving the painful pressure in my chest. Exactly the kind of thing we in the College of Commerce like to call a "win-win."

Margaret shook her head.

"I'm so sorry, Professor," she sniffled.

"About what? The baby's okay. The house seems fine. What's going on?"

She looked at me with her red-rimmed eyes.

"I'm leaving."

"You what? Why? Did you want to talk about the pay? Maybe we could—"

"I'm moving back to the mainland," she said.

"What? Where on the mainland?"

"Oregon."

"But what about the CPA exam?"

"I can take the CPA exam and practice there."

"Oh. You're sure about this?"

She nodded.

"Okay. Well, if that's what you want to do, then I'm happy for you. We'll just have to adjust and plan for a smooth transition. When are you planning to leave?"

"Tonight."

"Tonight?"

Margaret flinched.

"Sorry, Margaret, I didn't mean to raise my voice. I was surprised, that's all. I honestly don't know what we'll do without you."

"I'm so sorry," Margaret repeated.

"No, no, I'm not saying it to make you feel guilty. You've been wonderful with Francesca, and we're going to miss you. That's what I wanted to say. And this is all so sudden."

"I'll miss Francesca," Margaret sniffled. She was staring out at the hedge, in the direction of the graveyard. "I'll miss Hawaii. I'm so sorry, I know this puts you in a bad spot."

"Well, is there anyone you know who might be able to take the job?" I asked. ""Do you remember the young man you told me about, who was looking for a job? You said he loved animals?"

"Keola?" She turned to look at me. "We're moving to Oregon together."

"Ah. Okay. So that won't work."

"He said if he couldn't find another job by the last day of work, he was going to leave the islands. His last day of work was today."

A little advance warning would have been nice, I thought.

"Is the job situation any better on the mainland?" I asked.

"Oh, the job market's much better there. He's already got something lined up. With a food safety testing lab. And Hawaii's the worst state for CPAs when you count housing costs and available jobs. We're number 51."

"How do we rank fifty-one when there are only fifty states?" I asked.

"Washington, DC."

Margaret burst into tears. I hesitated, debating whether to give her a hug. Neither of us really wanted that, I decided. I went inside and got her a box of tissues.

CHAPTER THIRTY-ONE

DONNIE, BABY FRANCESCA, and I arrived at Honey Akiona's office exactly at two o'clock the next day. Honey had called Donnie to request a meeting and had asked him to bring me along.

Honey had moved her practice to a new office, on the bottom floor of an early 20th-century frontier-style building downtown. It was close to the Pair-O-Dice, but one street nearer to the bayfront.

Her assistant let us in to her office and we waited for a few moments. Honey finally came in, holding a manila folder.

"Aw, *cute*, the baby." Honey gave Francesca a smile and rubbed the top of her fuzzy head.

"Bah!" Francesca replied with a gummy grin.

"We didn't have anyone to watch her," I said as I pulled the baby to my chest and draped my shirt over her. "Excuse us. The baby's hungry."

"No worries. This won't take long. We got a situation." She dropped the folder on her desk and sat down. "Bee Corcoran is dead."

I nudged Donnie's foot, a nonverbal "I told you so." When I told Donnie what had happened, he had been infuriatingly skeptical. The body was probably a homeless person; there were any number of reasons Bee might not have been in her lab when we visited; the balcony railing had probably rusted out long ago.

I wasn't happy Bee was dead, of course, but maybe next time Donnie wouldn't be so quick to dismiss my conclusions.

"This could be a problem," Honey continued. "Bee Corcoran could confirm when you left the table, so you could say it's to your advantage to have her out of the way."

"Is someone saying I killed Bee Corcoran?" Donnie asked.

"Pang might try to go in that direction," Honey said. "Donnie Gonsalves murders his wife's ex-boyfriend out of jealousy, then kills a key witness. Pang solves two murders for the price of one and banks a big favor for the university."

"What do you mean, a favor for the university?" he asked Honey.

"Stephen Park's parents are suing the university for Stephen's death. The university would prefer to shift the blame somewhere else. Like to you, for example. Where were you yesterday morning?"

"I was at the Drive-Inn," Donnie said. "From seven in the morning until about three."

"How did Bee die?" I asked.

Honey opened the folder and traced her finger down the top piece of paper.

"No official cause of death yet, but probably head trauma."

"From the fall?"

Honey stared at me.

"Do you know anything about this, Professor?"

I had no reason to keep anything from Honey. I told her everything I could remember from the previous day. She seemed to be more open-minded than Donnie had been.

"We didn't do anything wrong, did we? I didn't think we were trespassing or anything." I stole a sidelong glance at Donnie.

"You say the door was unlocked?"

"To Bee's lab? Yes."

"You heard that someone had died, and her description sounded like your colleague. You went to her office—"

"Her lab," I corrected Honey. "Just to check on her."

"You went to your colleague's workspace, to check on her. The door was unlocked. Your actions were reasonable. What about the boy who was there? Any idea who he is?"

"I'm not sure. But I think he's Margaret Adams's friend Keola. Margaret said he had just left his job, and the boy in the lab told us it was his last day of work."

"Margaret Adams?" Honey raised her eyebrows.

"That's right, I forgot. She's your classmate. She's been watching our daughter in the mornings."

"She never went for her CPA? I thought she'd be working for one of the Big Four by now."

"She's studying for the CPA exam. In fact, she reads her study flashcards to Francesca. Puts her right to sleep. Well, she did, anyway. She—"

"Professor. Does the boy in the lab have a last name?"

"Oh. Sorry. If it's the same person, I think his name is Keola Shiner."

"You didn't tell me all this last night," Donnie said.

"I didn't think of it. I just remembered that Margaret had told me that Bee fired him from her lab."

"Fired?" Honey asked. "Interesting."

"He must be on the mainland by now," I said. "Margaret said they were going to fly out last night. That's why we have the baby today. We don't have anyone to watch her anymore. I guess you don't have Margaret's forwarding address."

"No," Honey said. "I'd appreciate it if you have it."

I pulled out my phone to search for Margaret's contact information.

"I can email it to you."

"Just write it down." Honey pushed a legal pad across the desk to me. Then, in response to my questioning look, "I like to be on the safe side. You know what they say. Email like the whole world's watching. And Mr. Gonsalves, we're going to need to contact some other witnesses to your whereabouts yesterday, besides your employees. Customers, anyone else who might've seen you. You understand."

As I was driving back home with Donnie, Francesca in her car seat in the back, my phone rang. It was Serena, the dean's secretary.

"Molly," she said, "You never got back to Dan about what office you want. I gotta get the assignments to Facilities by the end of the week. They just called to remind me cause they're gonna put up the signs outside your door that's why."

"Right. I did go over there yesterday, but—"

"Yesterday?"

"Yes."

"I heard someone found a dead body in the main building yesterday. You see anything?"

"I didn't see a dead body," I said, "but a security guard came into the building and chased us, me, out."

"Nah! Really?"

"I'll go back today and choose my office. Oh, what should I do if the doors are locked?"

"Call security and get 'em to let you in," Serena replied. "And call me or email me as soon as you decide. So I can cross it off my list. Don't try to tell Dan. He's about a thousand emails behind."

When Serena had hung up, Donnie said,

"It's okay. I'll take the baby."

"That's nice of you to offer, but I don't really feel good about having her at the Drive-Inn with all of the open flames and knives and things."

"Well, in our defense, no one's died at the Drive-Inn in the past week."

"Yeah, good point. Okay, you and Francesca go into the Drive-Inn and try to figure out who came in to buy breakfast yesterday. Make sure you have a rock-solid alibi."

"Do you want us to go with you?" Donnie asked. "I don't like the idea of you going to the old hospital alone. You don't know who's hanging around there."

"My office isn't in the actual hospital."

"It's not?"

"Nope. We're out back. In the Inebriate Asylum."

"Really?"

"Yes. Really."

"So are you going to tell your students to come to your office hours in the Inebriate Asylum?"

"That's exactly what I'll tell them. In fact, thank you for reminding me. I need to put it on my syllabus.

"Molly?" Donnie watched the road as he talked, so I knew he was serious now.

"Yes?"

"Please don't go investigating anything."

"I won't."

"Molly, I'm serious. Two people have already died up there. We don't know who might be hanging around."

"I'll get Emma to come with me."

Donnie gave me a sideways glance.

"Good. I think."

CHAPTER THIRTY-TWO

DONNIE DROPPED ME OFF at home. I called Emma, but her phone went straight to voice mail. My friend-finder app showed Emma in the middle of Mahina Bay. Darn it. She was out paddling and might not be back for hours.

I dialed Pat Flanagan's number. He, it turned out, was in town, and available. I hopped into my Thunderbird and drove over to the old hospital building. It was closer to my house than the main campus, I realized. One of these days, when we got our childcare situation squared away, I might even be able to walk to work.

I parked in front of the main hospital building, in the shade of a strip of jungle on the mauka (uphill) side. It would have been closer to park in the back, but I didn't want to spend any more time back there than I had to. It was bad enough that whichever office I chose would overlook that exact area, where Stephen had died. I turned on the local NPR station and listened to the Community Calendar. It was ninety percent events happening in Honolulu, and hardly anything in Mahina.

A few minutes later, Pat's vegetable-oil-fueled Mercedes diesel pulled up next to me, wafting a delicious french-fry scent. We exited our respective cars, locked up, and started walking.

"You okay, Molly?" Pat asked.

I nodded.

"Right before I came here, Donnie was telling me, don't stay any longer than you have to, be careful, don't go snooping, and I thought, oh, he's being overprotective as usual."

"No, in this case I can kind of see his point," Pat said. "Come on, I want to show you something."

We walked around the hospital to the old Inebriate Asylum. Surrounding it was untamed jungle. I could hear the roar of a river running through an unseen gorge.

"Look at the top floor," Pat said. "The windows."

"That's where we were yesterday." I shaded my eyes with my hand and tipped my head back to see.

"How many windows do you see on the top floor?" Pat asked.

"Can I count that one that's half hidden behind the tree?" I asked.

"Yeah."

"Four. Why?"

"There are only three rooms on this side on the top floor," Pat said. "311, 312, and 314."

"So one of the offices just has two windows. Hey, thank you for pointing that out. That's the one I want. Let's go have a look. Oh, Serena told me to call security to let us in."

I pulled out my phone.

"I can let us—" Pat began, but I shushed him.

"No B&E today, Pat. I have to do this by the book."

"You're just like Darren on Bewitched," Pat grumbled. "Not letting me use my powers for good."

"Pat, I'm a department chair now. I have to set a good example."

We trudged up the steps and waited. After around ten minutes, a security guard showed up. He was someone I hadn't seen before, and none of his keys worked in any of the locks.

"That's okay," I assured him. "Our department is moving into this floor. I just wanted to have a look around."

Once the guard had left us, Pat asked,

"Do you want me to—"

"Yes, please."

Pat picked the locks and opened the doors to each room in turn: room 310 on our left, and 311, 312, and 314, all of which faced the back of the hospital building.

I thought room 310 might be a good choice, as it was the only one that didn't look out at the back of the hospital. I was hoping it would have a view of the bay, because of its location. But I ruled it out as soon as I opened the door. In size and shape it was the mirror image of the bathroom, with the same narrow footprint, small window, and tiled green floor with a drain in the center. In the center of the room stood a rust-speckled stainless-steel contraption that looked like the offspring of an iron lung and a breadbox.

"No way!" Pat rushed to the device, grasped a handle, and lifted what I suppose you would call the lid. The device opened like an iron maiden. It seemed to be designed for an average-sized human to fit inside.

"What is that?" I hung back in the doorway, half-afraid that Pat was going to try to put me into the thing.

"It's a fever cabinet." Pat had his phone out and was taking pictures of the contraption from every possible angle. "This would have been considered the state-of-the-art medical care before World War 2. I wonder when they got this. Molly, have you heard of Julius Wagner-Jauregg?"

"No. Why? Did someone put him in that gizmo?"

"He won the Nobel Prize in 1927."

"Yay?"

"For his work in pyrotherapy. The use of fever to treat disease. He used malaria to treat late-stage syphilis, which up until then had been a death sentence. He had a soldier with malaria admitted into his ward, and he decided to draw the guy's blood and use it to infect his syphilitic patients."

"How...innovative. Did it work?"

"Yeah. Well. Except for the fifteen percent of patients it killed."

"Ah."

"Oh, and don't be tempted to celebrate him like he was some kind of hero."

"I wasn't going to, but okay."

"He was a member of the Nazi party, he sterilized patients who he thought masturbated too much, and he said working women were degenerate and unable to bear children or breast feed."

"Ha, joke's on him. I'm a working woman and I'm like a walking dairy over here. So what does all this have to do with that human toaster oven or whatever it is?"

"Yeah, sorry for getting off topic. I've been doing a lot of research on early twentieth century medical treatments for this series. It kind of is a human toaster oven. The idea is to give patients the benefit of fever therapy without infecting them with malaria. They'd shut patients into this thing and raise their internal body temperature to up to 107 degrees."

"That can't have been pleasant," I said. "How long did the patients have to stay in there?"

"Four to six hours at a time, for up to twenty sessions."

I shook my head and pushed back from the doorway.

"I don't think I want office number 310," I said. "Let's look at the other ones."

Rooms 311 and 312 each had a square footprint and a large window with a view of the back of the hospital. Room 314 was similar to the other two, but had koa paneling on the wall instead of green paint.

"I think you should take 314," Pat said. He had been quietly following me as I'd made my inspections.

"I like the wood paneling. But it seems like it's a little narrower than the others. Unless the paneling just makes it look smaller."

Pat took out his phone and pointed it at the far wall. Then he turned 90 degrees and did the same thing.

"You're right, it is narrower," Pat said. "Not from the window to the door, but about six inches wall-to-wall."

"I don't know if the fancy paneling is worth the smaller space." I went over to the window and looked out. It was overcast and raining. The back of the hospital building looked bleaker than ever.

"Good thing I didn't take my top down," I said.

"What?"

"My car."

I rapped on the wood paneling. "Pat, there must be something on the other side of this. There were four windows. But each office only has one, and there are only three offices."

I knocked on the paneling again.

"What does that sound like?" I asked.

"A paneled wall," Pat said.

A rap on the door interrupted us. It was a security guard, a different one from the last one. I hadn't seen him before either. Unlike the previous guard, this one was young, skinny, and officious. Maybe the other one had reported us snooping around.

"Excuse me, Miss," he said. "May I see your identification?"

I did not appreciate this pimply whippersnapper calling me "Miss" as if I were thirteen years old. At my age, the only people who answer to "Miss" are either drag queens or tragic figures in Southern Gothic novels.

"Of course." I pulled my school ID from my wallet. "I'm Molly Barda. Chair of the management department. College of Commerce. My dean, Dan Watanabe, asked me to come here and—"

"How did you get into this office?" he demanded.

"The door was open," Pat said. It was true—the door *was* open, after Pat picked the lock.

"And who are you, sir?" the guard asked Pat.

"Professor Barda's Feng Shui consultant," Pat said.

"Just a minute," the guard said, and left. A moment later, he was back.

"OK, you check out." He handed my ID back. He seemed to have thawed a bit now that he knew I was legit.

"I was wondering what's on the other side of this wall," I said. "Do you know?"

He shook his head.

"You gotta call Facilities for that, Professor Barda. But in the meantime, we got you down for Room 314. You should be getting a key within a few weeks. Okay, you two have a good day."

"Guess you just picked your office," Pat said.

"Yeah. I'll let Serena know. So she can cross it off her list."

CHAPTER THIRTY-THREE

EMMA CALLED ME THE next morning, just after Donnie had left for work.

"Emma, I had to pick my office without you." I pressed the phone to activate the speaker and hoisted the baby up to rest her head on my shoulder. I had abandoned the idea of spit up rags, opting instead to throw my shirt in the wash and get a new one when necessary.

"Molly," Emma's voice squawked from the phone on the table, "The paper just published Bee's obituary. And guess what they led with. That Bee Corcoran got the system research grant."

"Emma, you can't still be mad about Bee getting the award—"

"I was looking at the rules for the grant," Emma said. "And guess what. In the event the original awardee leaves the campus, turns down the award, or dies, the winning campus may select an alternate project."

"And?"

"And I'm thinking I should get to Gunderson and tell him to switch the award to my project," Emma declared. "Before the money goes somewhere else."

"Emma, no!"

"What do you mean, no?"

"How is that going to look?"

"Who cares how it looks?"

"Emma, if you try to get Bee's grant money, people will think you're the one who pushed Bee out the window. And your motive will be that you wanted her grant."

Emma was quiet for a moment.

"Emma?"

"Yeah, what? I'm still here."

"If they have to award the money to another project at Mahina State, there's a good chance they'll pick yours anyway."

"How do you know?"

"Fine, I don't know, okay? But I do know it's not a good idea to go steaming up to your dean before Bee's murder is even solved and asking him for Bee's grant money. You can see how that wouldn't look good, can't you? Besides, I don't trust your dean. If Betty's daughter was telling the truth, he's conspiring with the prosecutor to frame my husband for murder."

"Molly, I know what I'm doing. You don't have to be so maternalistic."

"Is that a word?"

"Yeah. It's like paternalistic except for ladies. Look, you should be worried about Margaret Adams. That boy she went to Oregon with is probably the one who killed Bee. Bee fired him, ah? How much you wanna bet he got mad an' pushed her out the window? Go worry about Margaret."

"I am worried about Margaret," I said, "I just don't know what I can do about it from here without risking making things worse. Emma, maybe you don't even want that award. Who knows what kind of strings Gunderson attached to it?"

"Ew, like sexual favors?"

"What? I was thinking more along the lines of kickbacks. Maybe Gunderson used Bee's research to get the system's grant money, and then he got her out of the way, so he could get his hands on the money himself?"

"I dunno," Emma said. "Gunderson wouldn't get the funds free and clear. You know grants don't work like that, ah? It's not like Gunderson can just take the money and go spend it all at Ye Olde Elbow Patch Shoppe or wherever he buys his clothes. He's still gotta spend it on legit stuff. Which, depending on how the grant's set up, could be pretty restrictive."

"Yeah, I remember you telling me—"

"Like the grant I have now, ah? Can't spend on meals, lei, manuscript preparation, stipends, books, dues, journal subscriptions, regular lab supplies, computers, printers, printer supplies, nothing. Okay, so back to my idea about sexual favors. What if Gunderson found out Bee's 'secret' and freaked out?"

"Emma, that's horrible. You think Gunderson killed her just because of who she was?"

"It happens."

"I know it happens. That's why it's horrible."

Francesca squirmed in my arms. I commenced my "baby march" around the living room, a bouncing gait that usually calmed her down.

"Emma, look, let's get your mind off this. Can you come over?"

"You sure? It's a little early for happy hour, but you could talk me into it."

"I wasn't suggesting happy hour. It's nine in the morning. I meant, we haven't had a rating party in a while."

"Oh yeah. Okay, I'll be there in a few. Don't go anywhere."

I rubbed Francesca's fuzzy little head.

"Don't worry. We'll be right here."

CHAPTER THIRTY-FOUR

A FEW YEARS AGO, SOME genius in our administration got rid of in-class teaching evaluations in favor of using a certain well-known online professor ratings site. Because anyone can go on the site and leave feedback, Emma, Pat, and I have made sure to curate our online ratings carefully.

Every so often we have what we call a ratings party, where we leave one another reviews on the site. We draw the line at writing our own reviews. For some reason, that feels wrong.

I brewed coffee and opened a bag of stone cookies. They're like biscotti, too hard to eat by themselves, but great dunked in coffee. I called Pat, but his phone went to voice mail. I texted him to tell him what we were doing.

The baby was fed and napping by the time Emma came by, so we were able to start right in.

First, we each logged in and left effusive, five-star ratings for Pat Flanagan's composition class. Pat is a part-time lecturer, who is hired semester by semester to teach one or two or five sections of composition. He can be let go at any time for any reason –or no reason at all. High online ratings give Pat a bit of an edge relative to the rest of the lecturer pool.

After we had finished heaping praise on Pat, Emma and I went on to write reviews for each other. You would think that Emma and I would give each other—that is, ourselves—positive reviews. But that's not what we do. Unlike Pat, both of us have tenure, which means we can only be fired if the administration actually makes an effort to come up with a reason and then do the paperwork.

Because our continued employment doesn't depend on our constantly convincing the administration of our worth, our main audience is potential students. So we give each other negative reviews to scare the slackers away from our classes.

Im a 3.5+ gpa student going to med school but could barley pass her class

Imposible 2 cheat cos she changes her tests every year. Unfair!

Her coffee mug is filled with the tears of her students.

I was in the middle of typing out a description of Emma's system for crushing the dreams of future doctors, when my phone beeped with a message from Pat.

Sorry can't join you. Filming lava flow. Check out Park's ratings.

"What's that?" Emma asked.

"Pat texted that he can't come because he's down filming the lava, but we should look at Stephen Park's reviews."

Across the table from me, Emma was already tapping on her phone.

"Gross," Emma said. "It's all reviews from Stephen's fan club. All positive. Everyone loved Stephen Park."

I pulled up Stephen's ratings page on my laptop and scrolled down.

"Not a single disappointed customer," I said. "Emma, how much do you want to bet he wrote these himself?"

"Look at the dates, Molly. The most recent ones were posted after he died. Oh, here's a bad one. 'Loves the ladies, the younger the better.'"

"Okay, maybe he didn't write all of them. Oh, come *on*. Someone posted a link to their blog? Someone went to the trouble of blogging about Stephen Park. Have you ever had a student blog about you?"

"Ew, no, and if I caught someone doing that, I'd call the FBI."

"I'm going to see what she wrote," I said.

"Whoa, before you click the link. It might be a phish whatever da kine."

"Oh yeah. Which one is spear phishing and which one is regular phishing?"

"I forget. Just don't click any links is all you gotta remember."

I stared at the review.

Stephen Park's class was one of my most unique experiences in Hawaii. Read more on my blog.

I picked out key words from the review and searched. Emma came over to sit next to me.

It didn't take long to find the blog. The author was an exchange student. She had been keeping a record of her Hawaii experiences for the benefit of her friends back home. Her latest entry was dated finals week.

The page featured a photo of the lava flow as a header.

"To Stephen, Who Taught Me About Theater And Life," Emma read.

"The word 'and' shouldn't be capitalized," I said.

"He let his students call him by his first name?" Emma asked.

"He insisted on it," I said. "Because he was a bold, unique iconoclast, exactly like all those other edgy cool profs who swear in class and sleep with their favorite students."

I felt Emma turn to look at me.

"Molly, let it go. He's dead. Weren't you saying you're not supposed to talk stink about the dead?"

"I was not talking stink. To describe is neither to endorse nor to condemn."

Emma leaned into the screen, blocking my view.

"Whoa. Look at this, Molly. 'One of the guys asked him how he got so jacked in such a short time. He said, I'm a guinea pig for a top-secret project. If I tell you about it, I'll have to kill you.'"

"What an original joke." I pulled the laptop toward me so I could see what she was talking about.

"Maybe it really was a secret, though, Molly. Maybe your idea about Bee killing Stephen wasn't so dumb after all."

"Thank you?"

"Think about it. He's hanging around Bee Corcoran, she's doing this muscle research, suddenly he starts growing muscles too? Just like the animals in her lab?"

I lowered the top of my laptop.

"So now you believe me? That Stephen was taking Bee's magic mouse juice?"

"She was working with rats, Molly, not mice. And it's not 'juice', she was using gene—"

"I know, but 'magic mouse juice' is catchy. Don't you think?"

"I don't care if it's catchy. It's wrong."

"So do you think maybe he found some bad side effects, and Bee was afraid he'd tell someone? She killed him before he could kill her career?"

"Hm." Emma rested her chin in her hand and stared at the table. "So who killed Bee then? Or you think with everything else going on in her life it was like the last straw, she regretted what she did and jumped out the window?"

"Or when she got the award, which remember she hadn't asked for, she realized people would be taking a closer look at her work and would find out what she'd been up to. Emma, I just remembered something. Margaret said that her friend told her that Bee's rats would end up in the wrong cages."

"What?"

"That's a problem, right? I mean, that's not normal, is it, that lab animals would get mixed up?"

"Uh, yeah, it's a problem. I don't do animal research myself, but I know there's all kinds of controls on it. You can't just go switching your animals around. I knew it, Molly. No one could get results like that unless they were faking."

"Well, wait though. She got results with Stephen, didn't she?"

"Maybe, if he really was taking the treatment himself. But what if he wasn't? What if he was just working out to impress Bee? Yeah, I dunno. It seems like too much of a coincidence, doesn't it?"

"Emma, I know it happens, but I don't understand how someone would fake their research results and think they could get away with it. I mean, wouldn't people find out eventually? Personally, I could never pull it off. I send my datasets to anyone who asks, and they can run their own analysis."

"Yeah, but that's assuming your data's good in the first place. If you wanted to, you could invent survey responses, and then enter 'em, yeah?"

"Oh. I guess so. But why would I do that? Even if I didn't care about ethics or integrity or anything like that, it doesn't seem worth the risk."

"Not to us, cause we already got tenure. We can get away with publishing in mediocre journals for the rest of our careers. Oh, and if Bee had investors interested in commercializing her research? More motivation for her to keep it going at all costs. Still too early for booze?" Emma got up and brought our coffee mugs into the kitchen.

"It's only ten in the morning, so yes, still too early," I called into the kitchen. "But I'll take another coffee as long as you're there."

"If Bee was faking her results somehow," Emma said as she returned with two steaming mugs of coffee, "and Stephen knew about it, that's a motive for Stephen's murder that points away from your husband. You should call Honey and tell her."

"I already told her, remember? You were there. Both of you were unimpressed by my theory."

"But you get more evidence now. You found a student's blog about Stephen Park, where he admits to being a guinea pig. Maybe Honey guys can find something else in there that could help Donnie's case."

"You're right," I said. "Worst case, Honey says she's not interested and doesn't want to know about it."

CHAPTER THIRTY-FIVE

I WAVED TO EMMA AS she drove off, then strapped Francesca into the baby seat in the back of my T-bird. I drove the few blocks down toward the ocean and pulled up to the curb right outside the Drive-Inn. I knew from hard experience that the lane between the Drive-Inn and the recycling center was too narrow for my car.

"Honey wants to talk to you again?" Donnie asked as he lifted Francesca out of her car seat.

"That's what she said."

"Well, if you can remember anything that'll help my case, that would be great. Tell me all about it when you get back." Donnie inserted Francesca into the baby carrier on his chest and grabbed the diaper bag out of the back seat.

"There are two bottles of milk in there," I said. "It shouldn't take long. I should be back in forty-five minutes at most."

"Take as much time as you need." Donnie patted the T-bird's top and turned to go.

I drove down to Honey's office feeling optimistic. But after her first few questions, I wondered why I had even bothered.

No, I didn't have any evidence that Bee had faked her results.

No, I didn't have any witnesses to Bee going out onto the terrace that night, much less pushing Stephen off it.

No, I didn't have any idea who Bee's investor might be, nor any evidence that she even had an investor.

Yes, I could see how Stephen's "but then I'd have to kill you" comment could have been simply a joke.

No, I had no evidence that Stephen Park had been taking any kind of experimental drug or treatment.

Honey had even more bad news for me. Betty Jackson's daughter was on the mainland visiting relatives and was unavailable for questioning. I didn't blame Betty for sending Verna away. Of course she would protect her daughter. I'd do the same thing in her place. Unfortunately for Donnie (and me), there was no one else who could corroborate Verna's account of the conversation between the dean and the prosecutor.

"Well, Professor," Honey said, standing up and offering a handshake. "I appreciate your keeping me informed. I'll talk it over with my investigator, and it'll be interesting to see what happens when the autopsy comes back."

I went back outside, started the engine, and let it warm up.

Honey's lack of interest was disappointing. Maybe she thought Stephen had been joking, but making something up about being a "guinea pig" wasn't the kind of thing Stephen would do. I considered telling Stephen's parents but decided against it. I didn't have anything solid for them, and I didn't want to be the one to tell them that their son was using an unproven experimental treatment. It would seem like I was calling Stephen vain and reckless. He *was* vain and reckless, but there was no point in rubbing their noses in it. Maybe I'd get some grocery shopping done and then go back and get the baby from Donnie. Then at least he wouldn't know how humiliatingly short my meeting with Honey had been.

As I shifted into Drive, my phone hummed. I engaged the parking brake again and picked it up.

Emma had sent me a text, so I called her back.

"Molly, you done already?"

"Yes. Unfortunately, I don't think Honey Akiona was very impressed by anything I told her."

"Did you tell her what Stephen said about being a guinea pig?"

"Yes, I did. As I said, she was unimpressed."

"What are you doing right now?"

"Sitting in my car in downtown Mahina with the engine running. Why? What are you doing?"

"I'm at the old hospital. Meet me on the fourth floor."

"Emma, isn't that where Bee's lab—"

But she had already hung up. Now I was decidedly curious. I shifted into drive and pulled out onto the road.

CHAPTER THIRTY-SIX

THE DOOR TO BEE CORCORAN'S lab was ajar, propped open with one of those contentious plastic door stops you can buy in packs of two at the hardware store.

I say "contentious" because those little wedges are at the heart of a conflict between two powerful factions at Mahina State. The Student Retention Office has decreed that we should keep our office doors open at all times in order to be welcoming to students. But Facilities has ordered us to keep our office doors shut to comply with fire regulations. To show they mean business, Facilities conducts random sweeps, confiscating door wedges and locking office doors behind them. Pity the unsuspecting professor who comes back from the bathroom to find herself locked out of her office right before class. Let's just say I've learned the hard way to take my key with me everywhere.

I pushed the door open. Inside Bee's lab, the lights were off. Sunlight filtered through the tall window, which was now crisscrossed with yellow police tape. The rat cages were empty, and the water bottles were gone.

"Emma?" I called softly.

"In here, Molly."

Emma had a cardboard box open. She was pulling out beakers and pipettes and other science-y-looking objects and setting them down on the counter.

"What are you doing?" I asked. "You're going to get your fingerprints on everything."

Emma gave me an exasperated look and held up her gloved hands for me to see.

"Grab a pair from that box next to the sink," she said.

I went over, pulled out two purple gloves, and tugged them on.

"What are we looking for?" I asked.

"Notebooks."

"What?"

"Come on, help me out. Where would you hide lab notebooks you needed to get to but didn't want anyone else to find?"

"Are you talking about actual paper notebooks?"

Emma sighed heavily.

"No, plasma notebooks. Yes, paper notebooks, Molly."

"It's the twenty-first century. Who uses paper notebooks anymore?"

"Anyone who works in the field. Or in a wet lab."

"Well, that's charmingly retro," I said.

"Yep, that's why we do it."

"Emma, are you sure this is a good idea? What if someone comes in and sees us rummaging around wearing gloves?"

"Molly, you can stay and help me, or if you're too chicken then you can leave. Just don't stand there kibitzing."

I considered pulling the gloves off and walking out, but I couldn't do it. My curiosity wouldn't allow me to leave. I went over to the far wall and started opening drawers.

"If she did keep notebooks, how do you know they're even here?" I asked. "What if they're at her house? Or in her car?"

"I keep mine in my lab," Emma said. "So do most people I know. Eh, what happened with the lawyer? How come she didn't care about our new evidence?"

"She said she'd mention it to her investigator." I slid open a drawer. It was empty, except for a sandwich bag full of plastic forks. "The thing is, we don't have any evidence for any of our brilliant theories. A second-hand report of a remark Stephen made to his theater class last semester doesn't count, apparently."

"Did you tell her we were thinking that there must've been an investor who had a stake in her research, then it turned out it didn't work, or it had some serious side effects?"

"If there was a secret formula, I'm pretty sure it worked. You haven't seen Stephen this summer, have you?"

"Nope."

"When I saw him he was a total 'after' picture. And it was different from all the other times his weight has yo-yoed."

"What about when he went through his exercise addiction phase and was at the gym all the time?" Emma asked.

"That's what I'm talking about. All he did was walk on the treadmill for hours, and he was emaciated then. I've only ever seen him scrawny or fat. The night he died was the only time I've ever seen him look muscular. Do you hear something?"

We both fell silent as footsteps echoed down the hallway outside. Emma ran to the door and peered out. Then she waved at me frantically.

"Act natural," she ordered, shoving me out into the hallway. She followed me out and pulled the door shut behind her.

"Hands in your pockets," she whispered. "Walk with me toward the exit sign."

"What? I don't have pockets."

I saw Geoffrey Gunderson walking toward us and quickly clasped my purple-gloved hands behind my back.

"Oh, hi Geoffrey," Emma said casually as we passed him in the hallway. "Hey, how's your summer going?"

Geoffrey Gunderson stopped walking, which meant we had to stop too.

"I've certainly had better, I must say. My goodness, just when you think one crisis has passed...and what brings you ladies in on this fine day?"

"Fine day?" I wondered whether Gunderson had been outside at all. It was overcast, drizzly, and steaming hot.

"Uh, Molly was just showing me the new College of Commerce offices," Emma said.

Geoffrey Gunderson gave me an odd look.

"Here in this building? Did Dan tell you he had space in the old hospital? I was given to understand that the College of Commerce offices were in the next building over."

"No, you're right," I said. "Dan did tell me that the College of Commerce has the building out back. We're here to look around. I was just reading about this building. How it was constructed in in the style of an Italian Renaissance palace."

I'd started reading *Island Confidential* again. Pat's latest installment of Mysterious Mahina had a history of the old Mahina Memorial building.

"Ahem. Well," Gunderson started over. "We're certainly fortunate to have such beautiful surroundings. And to rescue this wonderful historic building from the elements and the termites. Such a lovely opportunity. Although the termites can be so destructive, so, so destructive..."

The dean's gaze flicked briefly to a point behind us, roughly where Bee's lab was.

"Well, it was nice to see you, Geoffrey," Emma said. "Okay, Molly, back to your office, ah?"

As soon as we were in the stairwell I rolled the gloves off my hands. I was about to put them in my purse when I realized something.

"My purse is in Bee's lab," I said.

"You need it right now?" Emma asked. "This minute? While Gunderson's prowling around?"

"Well..."

"We can come back and get it later when we're sure he's gone."

"Okay. My phone's in there too. Can I borrow yours? I need to text Donnie and tell him I might be a little bit later than I planned."

CHAPTER THIRTY-SEVEN

"I FINALLY GET TO SEE your new office," Emma said, as I struggled to the top floor of the Inebriates Asylum building. "Molly, you okay?"

I held up my finger and she waited for me to catch my breath.

"That was unfortunate timing," I panted. "Your dean showing up. Geez, I hope I get used to these stairs soon. I feel like my heart's going to explode."

It had started to rain. The frosted skylight glowed silver, casting a sickly glow over the landing.

"Taking this many stairs is tough if you're not used to it." Emma went over to the railing and looked down. "You could take the elevator if you weren't so scared of it."

"I don't know. It's the old cage kind, and you know how things are maintained here—"

"Eh, Molly, how many ghosts you think are hanging around here? I bet there's a bunch of 'em watching us right now, ah?"

I stood with my back pressed against the door of office 311, watching Emma lean over the railing.

"If the dead really are watching us, Emma, they're probably asking themselves why you seem so eager to join them."

"What are you talking about?"

"Considering two people have just fallen to their deaths, why are you leaning on the railing like that?"

"That was the next building over," Emma retorted.

"Did you hear what Gunderson said about termites? You should get away from there."

"Fine. We can kill some time in your office, then go back and get your purse when we know Gunderson's gone. Does that work?" Emma finally turned away from the terrifying railing.

"Sure. Dang it. I should've pumped before I came here. Or brought my breast pump." I crossed my arms over my chest, feeling the familiar heaviness.

"Aw, why I gotta hear about that?" Emma complained. "Come on, show me your new office."

I tried the handle of 314, but it was locked.

"They never gave you the key?" Emma asked.

"Serena says it's going to take a while. They're going to wait until everyone's picked their office, and issue all of the new faculty keys at once."

"You gotta wait until Hanson Harrison gets back from Martha's Vineyard or wherever he goes all summer?" Emma asked. "Doesn't he always get back after class starts, with some story about how he missed his connection in Boston?"

"Yup. So I expect to get my key sometime around the middle of fall semester. I guess I'll have to call security to let us in. Can I use your phone again?"

"Nah, that'll take forever. Come on, move over."

Emma pulled something out of her jeans pocket and hunched over the door handle.

"You know how to pick locks?" I exclaimed as the door swung open.

"Pat showed me. You should learn."

"Ow," I crossed my arms tightly as I followed her in. "I really should've brought my pump with me. What was I thinking, leaving it in the diaper bag? It's not like Donnie can use it."

"I'm not listening," Emma declared. "Eh, this is nice. It's like the other one except you got koa on the wall. Bet you this office belonged to an administrator, ah? All deluxe."

She rapped on the paneling.

"Aren't you a biology professor?" I asked. "How are you squeamish about breastfeeding?"

"There's a reason I study plants, Molly. Eh, speaking of termites. I think you got 'em in the wall here."

"What? Where? How can you tell?"

"See how this gives, right here?" Emma pressed on the paneling.

As she spoke, an entire section of the wall gave way and swung open like a door.

CHAPTER THIRTY-EIGHT

BEFORE US LAY A SQUARE room, a mirror image of the one we were standing in. The only light source was the dusty window, shaded by the branches of a mango tree outside.

"The fourth window," I exclaimed.

"What fourth window?" Emma asked.

"From the outside you see four windows, but from the inside there are only three doors on this wall. Pat showed me. I forgot about it until now."

"Aw, that's cool." Emma strode into the little room, and I cautiously followed her.

The room smelled close and mildewed. I went over to the casement window and tried to open it.

"Having trouble?" Emma asked.

"It's stuck," I said.

Emma came over and muscled it open, releasing a cascade of paint flakes.

"How do you do that?" I asked.

"Canoe paddling, Molly. You could still join us for practice. It's not too late."

"Thanks again, and again, no thank you."

"Look at this, though, you got a secret room. How cool is this?"

The room was furnished with a simple bookshelf, a faded horsehair chair that used to have a floral pattern, and a small side table. Behind the table was a ghostly gray smudge on the wall.

"There's no lamp here. Or outlets." I looked up at the ceiling; there was no light fixture.

"And there's no exit door," I said. "Let's make sure this thing doesn't slam shut."

I pushed the door all the way open and then pulled the side table over to brace it.

"Molly," Emma said from the window, "you got a good view here. It's the end window so you see part of the hospital, but a lot of your view is trees. What do you think this room was for?"

"I don't know. There's not a lot here to go on, is there?"

I opened the drawer of the table in hopes of discovering some ancient hidden treasure, but it looked empty. Unthinkingly, I slid my hand to the back of the drawer. My fingers landed on something cold and metallic.

"Emma, look. What is this thing?"

Emma turned away from the window to squint at the object I was holding up. It looked like a fancy little trowel. It was adorned with scrolls and curlicues and coated in black tarnish.

"I dunno. Probably some torture device for the mentally ill. You should leave it here, Molly."

Out of some kind of rebellious impulse, I slipped the item into my bra.

"You're probably right," I said. "Okay, I think I need to get home. Are you ready to go?"

"Sure." Emma pushed the window shut as the rain started to pour down in earnest. We went back out the way we came in, closed everything behind us, and finally made sure the door to Room 314 was locked.

"Well, that was exciting," I said.

"Yeah, you got a double-wide office."

"Sounds extra classy when you put it that way."

"Let's try stop by Bee's lab," Emma said. "Gunderson's gotta be gone by now."

"I hope so. I'm swelling up like a prizewinning pumpkin. *Two* prizewinning pumpkins, if you want to be precise about it."

"Maybe we can find that notebook—" Emma caught a glimpse of my anguished expression and changed course. "Tell you what. You get your purse and go. I'll stick around and keep looking."

"I don't think that's a good idea," I said. "You shouldn't be there alone. Even if there's no murderer hanging around, what if a shelf falls on you or the floor gives way or something? The railing already gave way. If you're here by yourself, you won't be able to call for help."

Going downstairs took much less effort than going up. Going down I was able to listen to what Emma was saying when I wasn't gasping for breath.

"I don't wanna wait too long," Emma said. "I'm worried Facilities is gonna get their orders to clean out the lab, and they'll sweep everything out and dump it in the landfill. I wanna see if I can find Bee's notebooks before that happens. Tell you what, I'll take a super quick look around one last time, and then we can leave together. It'll only take a second."

"Fine," I said, hugging myself tightly. "But we really do have to be quick."

CHAPTER THIRTY-NINE

EMMA AND I TOOK THE side stairwell back up to Bee's lab. Emma had to keep stopping to wait for me because, frankly, I was a wreck. My legs were jelly, my chest felt like two bursting water balloons, and I was so hungry I felt like I was going to black out.

"I should buy a pedometer," I gasped, as we reached the fourth floor for the second time that afternoon.

"They don't make you any faster," Emma said, breezing ahead of me.

"I know that," I wheezed as I struggled to keep up with her. "I just want a quantitative measurement of my suffering."

Bee's lab looked the same as we'd left it earlier, filled with appliances that looked like bizarro versions of things you'd find in your kitchen. The autoclave was basically a desktop dishwasher. The incubator looked like a refrigerator, but when you opened it, it was warm inside, not cold. A fume hood served the same purpose as the hood over your stove, but it was huge, with a sealed-off workspace underneath.

The lab was close and stuffy, and I felt myself start to sweat. I spotted my purse sitting next to the sink and slung it onto my shoulder before I had the chance to forget it again. The box of gloves was right there, so I pulled on another pair.

"Okay, real quick," Emma said. "We're looking for anything that looks like a notebook. Open every drawer and cabinet. Think about where you'd put a notebook."

"I keep everything backed up online," I said.

"Just look, Molly. The sooner you find something, the sooner we can go."

"We have to find something?" I objected. "I thought you said it would just be a second."

"Molly, weren't you just on my case for standing too close to the railing? Get away from there and help me look, ah? Oh, I gotta take a bio break. Don't go anywhere. I'll be right back."

I realized I was standing next to the window. Two strips of yellow tape printed with the word CAUTION formed an X over the closed blinds.

I shuddered, backed away slowly, and banged my lower back on something. It was the corner of a long narrow counter that bisected the room.

The counter had a single shallow drawer at its end. You wouldn't see it unless you were standing by the window. I pulled it open. The drawer contained three boxes of purple nitrile gloves: Small, medium, and large. Something made me pick up the small box.

Underneath was a black-and-white composition notebook.

I picked the notebook up. National brand. *That's a strangely generic name*, I thought.

"Emma?" I called out, but remembered she'd gone to the bathroom.

"I'll take that," said a man's voice from the doorway.

Dean Geoffrey Gunderson strode in, holding out his hand.

He was coming right at me. From Gunderson to me to the open window was almost a straight line. All he needed to do was pick up a little speed. The blinds were closed, but they weren't much of a barrier.

This is what happened to Bee, I thought.

"Emma!" I yelled, as the weedy medievalist picked up speed.

Force equals mass times acceleration.

Why was my brain feeding me formulas from freshman physics, of all things? Gunderson didn't have a lot of mass, but he did seem to be coming at me pretty fast.

Momentum equals mass times velocity.

"She was keeping two sets of books," I blurted out.

"That is not your property, Professor Barda. Please give it to me."

Gunderson kept coming closer.

"If this comes out..." I started, then trailed off. What would be the point of running my mouth? It would just make him want to kill me even more.

Geoffrey Gunderson closed the distance between us and reached his arm toward me. I considered darting around him, but I was blocked by a wall and a file cabinet.

"Emma. *Emma!*"

My chest ached. All I wanted was to be home with Donnie and baby Francesca. Curiosity killed the professor. Why had I agreed to look for the notebook? Where was Emma? I had to think fast.

And then it came to me.

I dropped the notebook at my feet. With my right hand, I pulled my shirt and bra up with a single, well-practiced gesture. With my left hand I pressed my engorged breast.

A needle-thin jet of milk drummed against Gunderson's glasses, temporarily blinding him. As he clawed at his eyes, I saw Emma climbing up on the counter behind him. She looked around, picked up a large glass flask, raised it up, and brought it down hard.

"Ouch!" he cried, and rubbed his head. Which was not what we were expecting.

But Emma was not out of ideas. She snatched Gunderson's milk-splashed glasses.

"I'm calling the police," she declared, holding the glasses over her head.

"Yes, please do." Gunderson pulled a handkerchief from the inside of his suit jacket and dabbed his eyes.

"And don't you go anywhere," she warned.

"I don't suppose I can," he said in her general direction, "until such time as my spectacles are returned to me."

Emma stood on the counter and made the call while I put myself back together. We waited in uncomfortable silence until Detective Medeiros showed up.

CHAPTER FORTY

IF MY FAIRY GODMOTHER came to me and granted me the power to erase only one memory, I would probably pick that afternoon's interview at Mahina Police Department Headquarters.

Detective Medeiros herded us all into a single room with a small table at its center. I had always thought that witnesses were questioned one by one, but maybe Medeiros thought he could save some time with the focus group approach. He sat me, Emma, and Geoffrey Gunderson on one side of a scarred wooden table, and himself on the other.

"I'd like someone to tell me what's going on," Medeiros said. "Two people have died in that building, and now three Mahina State University professors are getting into a brawl and calling the police on each other."

"It was self-defense," Emma said. I nodded.

"These women were stealing university property," Gunderson countered.

"He's just saying that cause he killed Bee Corcoran," Emma retorted.

Gunderson turned to stare at Emma. If he had been wearing a monocle, it would have dropped into his lap.

"Emma!" he gasped. "Are you saying I killed Bee? How can you even think such a thing?"

"Why would he do that?" Medeiros asked patiently.

"Maybe he killed her because he found out her research results were fake," Emma said, "and he was afraid when it got out it would ruin his reputation. Cause he's the one who got her the system life sciences award."

"You say her results were fake?" Medeiros wrote on his tiny notebook and looked up at Emma. "Do you have evidence of this?"

"Detective," Gunderson pleaded, "From what I know of these two ladies, they are good, kind people at heart. But they appear to be in the grip of a *folie a deux*. I can think of no other explanation for this fanciful slander, to say nothing of the..."

Gunderson turned to stare at me.

"... assault upon my person!"

"Assault, ah?" Medeiros wrote in his notebook. "And how, precisely, did Dr. Nakamura assault you, Dr. Gunderson?"

"Me!" Emma exclaimed.

"Oh, no, it wasn't Emma. It was Molly here. I caught her taking property from the lab and asked her to hand it to me. And she...ahem."

Medeiros looked at me in a sort of appraising way, and then at Gunderson, and then back at me. As if he were struggling to reconcile the accusation of physical assault with the pencil-necked weaklings sitting in front of him.

"Well. You know she's from the *business* school," Gunderson added gratuitously, as if that were sufficient to explain my antisocial behavior.

"I was acting in self-defense," I said. "I thought he was going to push me through the window. He was coming straight at me. And I thought when it was happening that that's what probably happened to Bee Corcoran."

"And what did Professor Barda do to you, Dr. Gunderson, that you would characterize as assault?"

"Well, she... she ...er...the truth is, I didn't quite see everything that happened. *She* knows what she did."

All eyes turned to me.

"Would you like to explain, Professor Barda?" Detective Medeiros asked.

I flashed back to the sight of Gunderson's eyes widening with astonishment, just before the jet of milk blasted his bifocals like a hose turned on a window...

"No, Detective, I would prefer not to explain, if it's all the same to you."

Then I realized I had a way to change the subject.

"I know about the conversation at the Maritime Club," I blurted out. "About pinning the blame for Stephen's murder on my husband. Geoffrey Gunderson was there."

"With all due respect," Gunderson said, "you have no idea what you're talking about."

Gunderson's words were confident, but I could sense a rise in his anxiety level. I might have been picking up a subtle odor of flop sweat.

"Professor Barda?" Medeiros prompted. "Let's stick to the subject. Why does Professor Gunderson say you assaulted him?"

"I didn't touch him," I said.

"Well if you won't tell 'em, I will." Emma then provided an unnecessarily-detailed account of the incident, which I see no need to reproduce here. As she elaborated on her story, piling on the prurient details, Medeiros put the heels of his hands over his eyes. Just the way I do when I get those stabbing pains on the side of my head.

"Okay, now we got that out of the way," Emma declared, with the brisk air of someone dusting off her hands. "Molly, tell 'em about the conversation at the Maritime Club."

"Yes, why don't you do that?" Medeiros set his pad down and leaned back in his chair.

I had to proceed carefully. I knew prosecutors worked closely with the police. Accusing Pang outright might be risky. I would tell the story but leave the prosecutor's name out.

"Stephen Park died after a fall at the donor dinner," I said.

Medeiros nodded.

"He went out onto a lanai area adjacent to the dining room. There were no barricades or signs saying to keep off."

"It was a donor dinner," Gunderson interrupted. "We couldn't exactly put out orange traffic cones and flashing warning signs."

"Not even if it could have saved someone's life?" I said self-righteously.

Gunderson gave an indignant little sniff.

"The area was poorly lit, and the railing was too low to be safe," I continued, as Medeiros scribbled in his tiny notebook. "Stephen's parents are suing the university because they believe those unsafe conditions led to their son's death. But Dr. Gunderson tried to steer the investigation so that Stephen's death would be blamed on something or someone besides the university. My husband, Donnie Gonsalves, made a convenient scapegoat because years ago I was romantically involved with Stephen Park. Accusing my husband seemed like the path of least resistance. If Stephen was killed by a jealous husband, that would reduce the university's exposure."

"Why that's —" Gunderson sputtered.

"Professor Barda," Medeiros cut him off. "Do you have any evidence of this conspiracy to obstruct justice? Because that's what it sounds like."

"Yes. At a recent event at the Maritime Club, Dr. Gunderson was overheard in conversation with...another party, discussing pinning the blame on Donnie. My husband."

"Who was the other party?'" Medeiros asked, going directly to the question that I was hoping not to have to answer.

"I believe it was someone from the prosecutor's office," I said.

"Is it true, Dr. Gunderson?" Medeiros asked.

"Er," he said. He looked pale, and his fingers twitched. "Detective, might we continue our discussion in private?"

Medeiros looked at each one of us in turn.

"This is simply an informal interview," he said, finally. "You're free to go at any time."

Emma and I got up so fast we practically knocked our chairs over.

"You know the way out," Medeiros added.

"Molly will forward you the recording," Emma called back to Medeiros as we exited into the fluorescent-lit hallway.

"Recording? Of wha...yes, the recording," I repeated.

"Why did you tell him there was a recording?" I whispered as we hurried down the hallway toward the exit sign.

"Nah, it was good. It's gonna keep Gunderson honest if he thinks there's a recording."

We emerged from the police station into the hazy afternoon. Steam curled up from the puddles in the parking lot. I felt my bag vibrate and pulled out my phone.

"Ooh," I said. "I have a few messages from Honey Akiona. She wants me to come to her office right away. Darn it, I was hoping to go home finally."

We approached our cars. Emma's unlocked with a chirp when she rested her hand on the door handle.

"At least you figured out a way to get rid of your milk," she said as she climbed into the driver's seat.

"Emma," I said. "We will never speak of this again."

"Maybe *you* won't." She pulled the door shut, backed out of her space, and zoomed off.

I drove back to Honey Akiona's office, wondering what she wanted. She couldn't possibly know what had just happened.

Except that she did know. She had a police scanner, and friends in Mahina PD. She debriefed me, followed up with some pointed questions, and explained (at length) the importance of leaving crime investigations to the professionals.

After I swore to her never, ever, to interfere with any investigation ever again, Honey rewarded me with a morsel of good news about Donnie's case.

I drove home feeling chastened but encouraged. Despite everything that had gone wrong that day, at least one thing had gone right. Bee Corcoran's lab notebook was tucked under the floormat of my Thunderbird.

CHAPTER FORTY-ONE

"HOW DID IT GO WITH Honey?" Donnie asked, when we'd gotten seated at the kitchen counter. I knew it wasn't right to keep secrets from my husband (to say nothing of the general futility of trying to keep anything secret in Mahina). I tried to think of the best way to present the day's news. Positive first, I decided. Then I could hit him with the visit to Bee's lab and the subsequent trip to the police station. There wasn't going to be a better time. The baby was fed, and we were about to dig into plates of tasty Drive-Inn leftovers. Tonight it was Spam fried rice, chicken katsu, and potato mac salad.

"The good news is, Honey says they're having trouble building a case against you," I said. "She thinks Pang might give up soon if they can't get anything solid. Yes, he wants to bank a favor with the university, but he doesn't want it so badly that he's willing to do something risky like plant evidence or bribe witnesses. Also, you contributed to his campaign, so Honey thinks that helps a little."

"Maybe not," Donnie said grimly. "If he wants to make a show of being tough and principled, what better way than to bite the hand of one of your donors?"

"Well. That's my good news, anyway."

Donnie dug into his potato mac salad. "Hm. A little heavy on the mustard. What do you think?"

"Do you want to hear the rest of my news, or not?"

"I don't know. Is it good?"

I wrinkled my nose and shrugged. I was proud that I'd managed to secure Bee Corcoran's notebook, even if I couldn't decipher anything inside it except her initials. And I was looking forward to going over it with Emma tomorrow. But I doubted Donnie would feel as positive about it as I did. He'd probably just focus on the fact that I'd stolen something that belonged to a possible murder victim.

"So...how bad is it?" Donnie asked carefully.

"I wouldn't say bad exactly. Emma and I had kind of a little adventure today, that's all.

Everyone's okay, and no harm done. Know what?" I stood up. "Before we get into all that, why don't I get us some wine?"

CHAPTER FORTY-TWO

DONNIE DIDN'T SCOLD me, or yell at me, or even scowl at me. Instead, as I told him about the events of that afternoon, he sat very still. By the time I got to the part where I was being interviewed by Detective Medeiros, I realized I'd been doing all the talking. But I could tell Donnie had heard me, if only because of his white knuckles and thousand-yard stare.

When I finished he nodded, stood up, and without looking at me or saying a word, walked down the hallway and went to bed.

Things were almost back to normal the next morning. Before he left for work, Donnie hugged me extra-hard, begged me to stay safe, and hugged me again. Then he offered to take the baby to work with him, so that I could get some rest. I assured him that the baby would be safe with me. He seemed skeptical. When he left, he promised to check in on us as soon as he could.

I didn't tell Donnie this, but I was practically dancing with anticipation. Emma was going to come over and decipher the contents of Bee's mysterious lab notebook.

Unfortunately, it wasn't a matter of Emma walking in, cracking the book open, and instantly solving the mystery. The book was about three-quarters filled with handwriting that looked more like an inky scribble than like actual words. Emma sat at the dining table near the window to get the best natural light. She went over each page slowly, often flipping back a few pages. (This was very frustrating to me.) Frequently she would go to her phone to look something up.

Meanwhile, I walked the baby, brought Emma coffee, nursed the baby, drank about a gallon of water, refilled Emma's coffee, set out crackers, cheese, and chocolates, ate most of it, changed the baby, emptied the diaper holder, refilled Emma's coffee again, got the baby to sleep, and brewed more coffee.

"Anything?" I would ask Emma every so often.

She would shake her head as if shaking off an annoying bug.

Then, after an entire morning of this, Emma cried, "Oh!"

I came running over to the kitchen counter, holding Francesca. Francesca was wide awake at this point and in the mood to grab things. She reached for Emma's hair, and I pulled her out of range just in time.

"Hang on," Emma stalled me again, "Let me just make sure."

She continued to turn pages, muttering phrases like "milligrams per kilogram" and "tissue fibrosis" and something that sounded like "Sea Terminus."

Finally, she snapped the notebook shut.

"Okay," she said. "I figured it out."

"The murders?" I asked excitedly.

"How she got her *results*," Emma retorted, as if I should know that that was far more important. "I knew she was cooking the books. But now I know how she was doing it."

"Okay," I said, doing my best to hide my disappointment. "What does this have to do with her murder?"

"Molly. You wanna know what I found, or no?"

"Sure." I put Francesca into her playpen, sat down next to Emma, and feigned interest. "How was Bee cooking the books?"

"Okay, let's review. There's a thing our body makes that keeps our muscles from growing too big or too fast. Bee was trying to figure out a way to counteract it. And so are a bunch of other researchers around the world."

"I remember. Yeah, I probably have a double dose of it, whatever it is," I said. "I can't build muscle no matter what I do."

"You never know until you try, Molly."

"What do you mean? I have tried. Don't you remember, you talked me into signing up for that—"

"You wanna hear what I found or not?" Emma demanded.

"Sure."

"Okay. I'll make it real simple for you. She set up three groups of rats. One group, she just let them live their rat lives. She didn't give 'em drugs or nothing. That's what we call the control group."

"Thank you, Emma, I know what a control group is."

"The second group of rats got steroids, you know about those, yeah?"

"Yes."

"And the third group got the treatment that's supposed to suppress this muscle-limiting thing."

"I'm with you. Three groups of rats. Control group, standard no-big-deal treatment, fancy new Bee Corcoran treatment. So what happened?"

"They inflicted an injury and then saw how fast the muscle recovered."

"Oh no, poor rats."

"Yeah, like I said, I'm glad I work with plants. Anyway, the experimental group, the one with Bee's treatment? Had worse muscle recovery. And some of them died."

"Did more die in Bee's treatment group than in the other groups?" I asked.

"Yeah."

"Wow. That's bad. So the obvious question is, how did she end up winning the system research grant?"

Emma started to open the notebook and then shut it again.

"It's kinda complicated. I'll give you the English major version."

"Fine. Give me the English-major version."

"Okay. When a rat from her treatment group started dragging, she'd switch it with a rat from one of the other two groups. Then when it died, the death would be counted as one of the control group or the steroid group. Do that with enough rats and it looks like the treatment is just as safe as the other two conditions."

"She was switching the rats," I exclaimed. "Margaret's friend was right. Except Bee wasn't careless, she was doing it on purpose."

"Heck yeah, she was doing it on purpose. What about Margaret's friend?"

"The young man we saw in Bee's lab, who told us it was his last day on the job. That's why she fired him. Because he figured out that she was switching the rats around. Except he just thought she was being careless. Remember, I asked you whether you wanted to hire him, and you said no?"

"I did?"

"Yes. You said you didn't want some kid coming in and telling you how to run your lab."

"I don't remember that at all. Molly, your memory must be going."

"So when Stephen Park talked about being someone's guinea pig?" I asked. "Do you think he was developing some kind of side effect of the treatment?"

"Maybe."

"Like what?"

Emma leafed through the notebook.

"A lot of the rats died from fibrosis."

"What's fibrosis?"

"Like out-of-control scar tissue. But here's the thing, humans aren't rats."

"Yeah, *some* humans."

"You know what I mean."

"I'm calling Detective Medeiros," I scooted my chair back and stood up. "If Stephen knew about the treatment's failure, and was ready to blow the whistle, then Dean Gunderson would have a reason to kill them both to cover it up."

"And how you gonna explain to Medeiros how you got the notebook?"

I sat back down.

"Good point. Oh, how about if we send it to Honey Akiona? Anonymously, of course—"

A wet blast noise from the direction of the playpen interrupted me. I retrieved Francesca.

"I'll call her after I change the baby." I rushed down the hallway, holding the baby at arm's length.

"I'll call Honey," Emma shouted after me. "You go do your hazmat cleanup."

"Thank you," I called back. "You can explain it better than I can anyway."

I came back into the living room with the cleaned-up baby, to find Emma pouring herself a glass of vodka. Her phone was lying on the counter next to her glass.

"I told Honey about the rats," Emma said. "She wants to talk to you."

She handed me the phone and took the baby. With her free hand she picked up her glass and started drinking.

"Good news," Honey said. "Donnie's alibi for the time of Bee Corcoran's death holds up. Several regular customers and employees say he was there at Donnie's Drive-Inn."

"That is good news," I said. "Thank you."

Emma set her glass down and gave me a thumbs-up.

"The other thing you should know is that Geoffrey Gunderson also has an alibi for that time. He was in a meeting in Honolulu."

"So Gunderson couldn't have killed Bee," I said.

"That's correct."

"Well then what was he doing snooping around her lab?"

"He says he was in Dr. Corcoran's lab to look it over before Facilities came in. They're going to have to fix that busted railing before anyone else can occupy the space."

"So we're no further along than where we were before," I said.

"Well, I was just talking to Professor Nakamura. And I'll tell you what I said to her. I'll take a look at any information that comes my way. Regardless of where it comes from."

"Thank you," I exclaimed.

"No guarantees, though."

Emma handed me the baby as soon as I disconnected the call.

"I'll run the notebook down to her," she said. "Don't go anywhere."

CHAPTER FORTY-THREE

EMMA WAS BACK WITHIN half an hour, and Honey called soon after that.

"Medeiros guys have the notebook now," Honey said.

"Fantastic," I said. "That was fast. How did you...never mind. Hang on, Emma's here, so I'm going to put you on speaker. So what happens now?"

"They're gonna get an expert to look at it."

"They should hire me to do it," Emma called from the kitchen.

"Nah, all due respect, tell Professor Nakamura they got their own people."

"It was worth a try," Emma said.

The microwave beeped, and Emma came back into the dining room holding a plate of Drive-Inn leftovers.

"So with Donnie and Dean Gunderson both having alibis," I asked, "who do they think killed Bee?"

"They're probably gonna put it down as suicide," Honey said.

"Oh yeah," Emma cried through a mouthful of Korean chicken. "Cause da kine, ah?"

"Because that's their go-to when they don't have a suspect," Honey said. "What's da kine?"

"Oh, right," I said. "You know, being in the closet?"

"In the closet about what?" Honey asked.

Emma and I looked at each other.

"About being trans," I said.

"Sorry Professor Barda, about what?"

"You know, transgender?" I said. "Identifies as female but was assigned male at birth?"

I thought the phone had gone dead. But then Honey said,

"You're talking about Bee Corcoran?"

"Yes," I said. "She wasn't out about it. And she could pass pretty well. I only know for sure because Stephen told me."

"Stephen Park told you this?"

"I know he shouldn't have. It wasn't his story to tell. But I never told anyone else. Well, not while she was alive. Except Donnie, but that doesn't really count because—"

"Let's go back for a minute," Honey interrupted me. "What exactly did Stephen Park tell you about Bee Corcoran?"

"Well, let's see. He talked about how brave she was to live her truth, how her family wasn't speaking to her, how despite everything she was the most feminine woman he'd ever met, I don't know, I can't remember everything. Basically how awesome and courageous she was. In contrast to me, of course, because according to him I abandoned my true calling and sold out to the business school. That was a favorite theme of his, in fact—"

"Did he ever tell you straight up that Bee Corcoran was transgender?"

"Well, he—"

"Or that she was assigned male at birth?"

"I mean, I don't think he ever phrased it as clinically as that, but he got the message across. That's why her family cut off contact with her. Isn't it?"

"Bee Corcoran was an only child," Honey said. "Her parents passed away years ago. That's why she's not in touch with her family."

"Are you sure about that? Because Stephen—"

"Professor Barda, Bee Corcoran was, how do I put it? She was on her time of month when she died."

"Wow," I said. "They can do that now?"

"No. They can't."

"What do you mean?"

"Stephen Park misled you, Professor. Bee Corcoran was not transgender."

"What? But then why would Stephen...ugh, never mind, I think I just answered my own question."

When I hung up, I noticed that Emma was trying not to laugh.

"I'm glad you think it's funny," I fumed. "I feel like an idiot."

"Sorry, I'm not laughing at you." Emma got up and went into the kitchen. "Well, I kind of am. But it's just such classic Stephen Park. He lets everyone assume he's half-Korean cause his last name is Park, he lets you assume Bee's transgender, cause she's ripped. Eh, at least you never told Stephen's parents, right?"

"I guess. But of all the lies he could have told, why would he choose that one? Why would he try to make me think Bee was trans? It was like he wanted to convince me she had something I didn't. I mean, not like *that*, but it was like he was trying to tell me Bee's backstory was more interesting than mine. Why? What was the point?"

Emma came back out with a bottle of wine and two clean coffee mugs.

"Once again, you just answered your own question. Too early for wine?"

"Nope. Pour away. I can't believe it. What a jerk—"

"Whoa, what about speaking ill of the dead?" Emma slid one arm of the corkscrew under the foil and popped it off in one piece.

"I'm not speaking ill, I'm telling the truth. He's a jerk. It's an objective fact. You know, you're right. I shouldn't be surprised. Stephen is just a big phony. It's not any more complicated than that."

"*Was* a big phony."

"Do you know when he met me, he was going through a Bernardo Bertolucci phase? I'm starting to think that's the only reason we even got together."

"Sorry, I don't know who that is. Bernardo who?"

"A famous Italian director. Well, famous with people who care about that kind of thing, anyway. You know, now that I look back on it, I think the only reason he pursued me is because one, he thought I was Italian and two, I supposedly looked like that actress whose name I keep forgetting. Bee was just another prop for him. To show everyone how adventurous or progressive he was or whatever point he was trying to make. And he tricked me into being *nice* to her."

Emma rocked the cork out of the bottle.

"Tricked you? How'd he do that?"

"I thought she was marginalized because of her gender identity and you're not supposed to be a jerk to marginalized people. If I'd known she was just some fit blonde cis woman I'd have told her to eff right off with her stupid fitness advice. Come on, I'm letting my two-month-old get lazy by carrying her?"

"Molly," Emma whispered. "Let it go. They're both dead."

"*Good!*"

I immediately clapped my hand over my mouth.

"I didn't mean it," I whimpered.

"It's okay, bubbeleh." Emma filled a mug with wine and handed it to me. "We all grieve in our own way."

CHAPTER FORTY-FOUR

I CAME HOME FROM A well-baby checkup the following afternoon, to what I thought was an empty house. I put the sleeping baby down in her crib and started to undress for a shower. The sound of voices outside stopped me. I got dressed again, grabbed the baby monitor, and tiptoed down the hallway. The voices were coming from the back lanai.

I recognized one of the voices as Donnie's. Relieved, I went out to the back to see who he was talking to.

The other man was Detective Medeiros.

Both men stood when I came out back. Because there were only two chairs and three people, no one made the first move to sit back down.

"Professor," Medeiros greeted me.

"Where's Francesca?" Donnie asked.

"Sleeping." I held up the baby monitor to show him. "So what's going on?"

"Good news," Donnie said.

"Autopsy results came back," Medeiros said. "Stephen Park died of natural causes."

"Fibrosis?" I guessed, remembering what Emma had told me about the rat research.

"What?" Donnie asked.

"It's an overgrowth of scar tissue, and apparently it can be fatal...sorry. What were the natural causes?"

"The cause of death was abdominal aortic rupture," Medeiros said.

"Oh. What?"

"Since you seem to be interested in the details, the aorta is the main artery of the body, going from the heart down into the abdomen. It can spontaneously rupture, or break—"

"No, no," I interrupted him. "That's okay. Don't describe it. Stephen Park died of a medical condition, though, is what you're saying. Right?"

"Yes."

"He wasn't murdered?"

"No."

"Wow. Okay, so I was wondering, Sorry Donnie, but I have to ask. Detective, Stephen called my name that night as I was walking past. I ignored him. And I kind of assumed he tried again and leaned over too far and fell. I was wondering whether it was my fault he died."

"You were?" Donnie asked.

"Yeah. I was. I've kind of been obsessing about it, to be honest. Thinking, if I'd just stopped and acknowledged him, maybe he'd still be alive, and you wouldn't have had to go through this whole trumped-up...this whole ordeal. But it had nothing to do with me. Is that what you're saying, Detective?"

"Correct. Park's death wasn't caused by anything you did." Medeiros was staring out over the back hedge. Unlike me, he was tall enough to see the graveyard beyond it. "There's nothing you could have done besides call for help, which you did. He was gone before he hit the ground."

"So why do you think he called out to me?" I asked.

"My opinion? He probably realized he was having a medical emergency. It would explain why he left the dining room in the first place. He probably started to feel some discomfort at that time. But like I said, it happened quick. There's nothing you could have done."

"You're sure about that?"

"Yes."

I wanted to hug Detective Medeiros. But of course I restrained myself.

"Thank you," I said.

"Okay." Medeiros said.

Medeiros and Donnie did that handshake-backslap-hug thing that guys do, and then Medeiros gave *me* a hug.

"I gotta get going," he said. "You have a nice evening. Nah, nah, I'll see myself out."

"So how'd our baby do at the doctor's?" Donnie asked when Medeiros had gone.

"She had a tough afternoon," I pulled up the chair that Medeiros had just been sitting in. It was still warm. "Francesca likes getting shots about as much as I do. It was kind of heart-breaking to watch her, actually."

"What are you doing?" Donnie asked. "Is something wrong?"

"Sorry, I'm still feeling a little queasy after what Detective Medeiros told us. I'm going to keep my head between my knees and try not to think about exploding blood vessels."

The baby squawked over the monitor.

"It's okay," Donnie said. "You stay there. I'll go get Francesca."

After a few minutes I was able to sit up like a normal person.

"So, this is great news, right?" I said. "I mean, not great that Stephen died, of course that's tragic, but at least you're not a murder suspect now. Right?"

"That's right."

"And we can get the bail money back now?"

"M-hm. It'll take a few weeks but yes."

"Did Medeiros say anything about how something like that can happen to someone so young?" I asked.

"He said there are factors that can increase your risk. Smoking. Certain recreational drugs. Steroids."

"Well, I guess that's... steroids? Really?"

"M hm. He said a lot of the high school boys are doing it now."

"And they can tell?"

"Ka`imi said the toxicology report's going to take a little longer. They'll know more when it's done."

Francesca was dozing in Donnie's lap, her fat cheek resting on his forearm. I reached over and stroked her fuzzy head.

"This is such a relief," I said. "I'm so glad—"

"Your name was the last word Stephen Park ever spoke," Donnie said. "I didn't think about it until today."

"It was the last thing *I* heard. But maybe he said other stuff afterwards. Like when he fell over the railing he said some swear words or something. Would that make you feel better?"

Donnie frowned.

"No, of course not."

"I feel bad for his parents."

Donnie touched Francesca's cheek. "Yeah. I do too."

"I wonder what they're going to do now."

"Probably just go back home," Donnie said. "What else is there?"

CHAPTER FORTY-FIVE

THE NEXT MORNING, I was in the middle of filling out Student Retention Office forms when my phone rang. I saved my work and went to answer it. The caller ID was flashing Tiffany Schwartz's number.

I wasn't thrilled about having to talk to Stephen's mother, but at least it was a break from filling out Rodge Cowper's overdue paperwork.

Rodge hadn't filled out a single form all year, which meant I had to go back and do every single one for him in order to keep the department in compliance.

I reminded myself not to take it personally. This was the same Rodge who missed most of our department meetings and always turned in his grades late. Which mystified me, as he never gave out anything lower than an A, so what was the holdup? Rodge assigned no homework, he used class time to show videos or have "chat sessions," and his final exam was a beer party at his house. The only thing Rodge put any effort into was writing his own online reviews.

Because of his "student success" rates and stellar student evaluations, the Student Retention Office—the same Student Retention Office whose paperwork Rodge neglected—had once again anointed him Teacher of the Year. An honor that I had never once received.

But I wasn't bitter about it. Really.

"Molly, did you hear the news about Stephen? This is Tiffany by the way."

I brought the phone into the kitchen and poured myself a cup of coffee.

"I did hear about it. Detective Medeiros came to see us yesterday. Tiffany, I'm so sorry. If there's anything I can—"

"I just want to know who gave my Stephen steroids," she interrupted. "Was it that P.E. teacher friend of his?"

"You mean Bee Corcoran? Gosh, I don't know. I mean, poor Bee is gone too now, of course. And as far as I know, the toxicology report hasn't come back yet. I guess we'll know more when it does."

I was pretty sure Bee Corcoran had been Stephen's source. She'd been using steroids in her rat studies, so she knew where to get them and how to use them. But I didn't want to fan the flames by saying any of this to Stephen's mother. And I could always be wrong.

"Well we're not just going to go away quietly," Stephen's mother insisted. "We need to find out what happened to our son. Everyone seems to be stonewalling us."

"Maybe Honey Akiona can help," I said.

"Who?"

"She was Donnie's lawyer—"

"We already have a lawyer."

"But Honey is tied into the community. She went to school here and she has some good contacts. If you want to get to the bottom of this, I really think she's the one you want to talk to."

Stephen's parents got in touch with Honey Akiona. It turned out to be a good suggestion on my part, if I do say so myself. Honey contacted her old classmate Margaret Adams, who had recently relocated to Oregon. At Honey's request, Margaret persuaded Keola Shiner, who up until recently had worked for Bee Corcoran, to sit for an interview.

Keola didn't want to do the interview at first. But Margaret persisted, and finally, Keola agreed. He confirmed that he had worked in Bee's lab, and that he and Bee Corcoran had clashed because Bee kept "losing track" of the rats. She thought no one could tell the rats apart, he said, but he could. He'd had pet rats since he was a boy.

In the meantime, the toxicology reports came back on both Bee and Stephen. Both had traces of the identical combination of synthetic anabolic androgenic steroids. Which meant the whole time Bee had been preaching to me about the wonders of green tea and steamed broccoli and long walks, she'd been perfecting her own physique with illegal drugs. So Bee had been a bit of a phony too. Maybe she and Stephen deserved each other.

And then, as Honey Akiona was investigating for Stephen's parents, she dug up something else: Bee had been supplying Mahina State's football team with performance-enhancing drugs. (This was the biggest surprise so far. Our football team had an unbroken losing streak this season. How much worse would they have been without performance-enhancing drugs?)

Armed with this information, Stephen's parents made another run at the university. And this time, they were successful.

To make Stephen's parents go away (and quash any bad publicity about the football program), the university offered Stephen's parents a settlement. To Stephen's parents, it was insultingly small. When I heard the amount, though, I knew it was big enough to hurt Mahina State.

If we really had to fork over that much money to Stephen's parents, I knew we'd be buying our own toner and copy paper for the foreseeable future. Not that Stephen's parents didn't deserve some recompense, but still.

Stephen's parents decided they'd gotten the best deal they could, and prepared to return to California. Before they left, though, they wanted to say goodbye. Which is how Donnie and I ended up having lunch with them at the Lehua Inn Coffee Shop. (Their lawyer had already gone back to Los Angeles.)

We could hardly refuse their invitation, but I wasn't looking forward to it. Our good news, that Stephen had died of natural causes, was their bad news. While Donnie and I would be able to move on with our lives, Stephen's parents would be leaving Mahina bereaved and, in their view at least, practically empty-handed.

One thing I've always appreciated about Stephen's parents is that I never had to worry about awkward silences. As we waited for someone to come by and take our order, Stephen's mother went on (and on) about what a great influence I had been on Stephen. She told Donnie what a lifesaver I had been that time I bought Stephen a ticket and loaded him onto a plane, so his sister could meet him at LAX and take him straight to rehab.

"Did ye ken any o' this, Donnie?" Stephen's father asked.

"No," Donnie said truthfully. It had all happened before Donnie and I were dating, so I'd never seen any reason to tell him about it.

"What I don't understand is the steroid thing," Tiffany turned to me. "Are they sure about that?"

"I think so?" I stammered. Why was she asking me? I didn't do the autopsy. "I mean, that's what the medical examiner found."

"But what do you think?"

I shook my head. "I'm not a real doctor. As my mother often reminds me. But I do trust Honey Akiona. I know, it's hard to believe our football team has any kind of unfair advantage. I can't remember the last time they won a game."

"If you had stayed with Stephen this wouldn't have happened, Molly."

Poor Donnie. I reached under the table, found Donnie's hand, and squeezed it. He squeezed back.

"So many young men are using performance-enhancing drugs these days," I said. "Even in our high schools." That added nothing to the conversation, but I felt like I had to say some words.

"We'll be leaving wi' nothing," Stephen's father muttered.

"Less than nothing," Stephen's mother corrected him, "when you count what we paid for the lawyer. It's not like we need the money, Molly, but after how careless they were, your university should pay *something*. I mean, more than the pittance they're giving us. Don't you think? Angus, what about all of those safety things we have to do just to stay in business? Why should Mahina State get off without any penalty?"

"Our lawyer says if we tried to take it to court they'd drag it on for years." Stephen's father shook his head. "Like Tiff says, they're getting away wi' murder. It's no' right."

"Molly," Tiffany implored, "Tell me something. First your university tried to convince us our son had been murdered, just to get themselves off the hook. Now they've talked our lawyer into settling for crumbs. Do they not have a conscience?"

"Well, since you asked," I said. "The problem is we can't afford to have a conscience. We genuinely don't have enough money to fix up our university and make it comply with all the laws we have to comply with. I used to hear people talk about it, but I never really believed it until I became department chair and saw the budget for myself."

"Well I know lawyers cost money," Tiffany countered. "Mahina State sure seems to have lawyers out the ying-yang."

"They're the university system lawyers. They're already paid for. The reason our university drags things out like this is number one, as I said, we don't have money, and number two, any bad publicity is going to scare off donors and students and give the legislators a chance to flex their muscles on behalf of angry taxpayers by cutting our budgets even more."

"They shouldn't be able to get away with it, Molly." Tiffany's eyes were shining and rimmed with red now, although the rest of her face remained smooth and expressionless.

"Aye, they all expect us tae forget about our dead son and walk away," Angus agreed.

"Can't you think of something, Molly? You always were so clever."

Then, to my astonishment, Donnie said,

"I have an idea."

CHAPTER FORTY-SIX

"THINGS SHOULD BE FEELING normal again," I complained to Emma. "Stephen's death wasn't the university's fault, so the administration doesn't have to frame my husband for murder after all. We're going to get our bail money back soon, and life will go on. Why don't I feel relieved?"

"Because now you know our administration's so crooked they'd ruin your life to save themselves some money? And you know the prosecutor's in their pocket?"

"Yeah, those things are pretty disturbing. The other thing is that there were times when I thought Donnie really might have done it. I wish I didn't know that about myself. That I was capable of suspecting my own husband."

Through the window of my new office, I could see the old hospital building. I made a mental note to look for semi-sheer curtains. Something that would let the light in but obscure the view of the building where Bee and Stephen had both lost their lives.

"Funny that both of 'em died the same way, yeah? In the same building," Emma grunted as she ripped the packing tape from a box. She seemed to intuit what I was thinking. "Almost like they both—"

"No, no, no, no."

"No what?"

I pulled out a disinfectant wipe and squatted to wipe down the dusty baseboards.

"Emma, I'm relying on you to reassure me. With your no-nonsense, science-based, anti-superstition point of view. Your job is to convince me that it's mere coincidence that two people died in a way that looks like the last thing they saw..."

"Was a ghost?"

I sighed.

"Yes."

"Yeah, I was kinda thinking the same thing, actually," Emma mused as she shelved my books in random order.

"What? Emma, you don't believe in ghosts. Besides, Stephen died of an aneurysm."

Emma wiped her hands on the back of her jeans and then ripped open another box.

"I don't believe in ghosts. But just cause I don't believe in 'em doesn't mean they don't exist."

"How is that helpful, Emma? Hint: it's not. Not when I'm moving into this creepy old office."

"What's your problem, Molly? Scared of being in here by yourself?"

"No. Maybe."

"I can buy Park dying of natural causes," Emma went on. "He's been abusing his body for years, ah? With the smoking an' everything. But what made Bee bust through a fourth-floor railing? It's like she was running from something, scared for her life. An' they never figured out why, yeah?"

"Let's talk about something else," I said.

"Okay. Hey Molly, you wanna put anything in your secret room?"

"I don't know. I should at least air it out first. It's pretty musty in there." I felt the paneling for the soft spot, found it, and pushed. Nothing happened. Emma came up and gave it a shove, which did the trick. The door swung open.

The little room looked smaller than last time, probably because it had grown in my imagination.

"You gonna ask Facilities to put in a light?" Emma asked.

"No. I'm not going to tell Facilities about this space. They'll just take it away from me."

"Yeah, you're probably right. And they'll confiscate your door wedge while they're at it."

I went over to the window—which had much the same view as the other one—and unlatched it. I was able to muscle it open this time, although my efforts were rewarded with a shower of paint flakes.

"Eh, don't breathe that in, Molly," Emma warned. "It's probably full of lead."

"Shoot. Now I have to sweep it up."

"Ready to take a break?" Emma asked. "Let's fire up your coffee maker."

"Good idea. Remember how we used to sit around in my office with Pat and drink endless cups of coffee?

"Yeah. That was the good old days. Before you turned into a dorky suburban mom. Wanna call him?"

"Yeah, why not? All he can say is no."

It turned out Pat was at the downtown library doing research, and ready to take a break himself. He was at my office within five minutes. The coffee machine worked just fine and hadn't caused any fuses to blow or anything. The office smelled warm and homey.

"Whoa, did they finally buy you new chairs?" Pat exclaimed. Emma was already seated in one of my two matching mesh chairs, drinking her coffee.

"No, there's still no budget for office furniture. I had to pay out of pocket. My way of celebrating my new office. You want a coffee?"

"Sure. Wow, I get an actual chair!" He made a show of sitting down carefully, as if he had never seen an office chair before and wasn't sure what it was going to do.

"Molly's still sitting on her yoga ball, though," Emma said.

"I'm used to the yoga ball. A real office chair would feel weird now." I sat down on it with a bounce and brewed Pat a coffee. "These mugs are clean, by the way. Emma ran them through her autoclave. She says it's better than a dishwasher."

"You're welcome," Emma said.

Pat snorted as he took his cup. "What, like I care about germs? Coffee smells great, though. Thanks. Where's the baby?"

"Donnie has her."

"He brought her to the Drive-Inn?" Pat asked.

"Yeah, he wears the baby in that carrier thing," Emma said. "The girls think it's totally hot."

"They do?" I asked. "Which girls?"

"The girls that work there."

"What?"

"The customers, too. Come on, Molly, haven't you noticed? I mean, Donnie's already good looking. Strap a baby on him, and you can hear all the ladies ovulating when he walks by. Sounds like pennies dropping on a cookie sheet."

Pat shook his head and took a sip of coffee.

"Don't look at me. I'm not in this conversation."

"Let's talk about something else," I said. "Pat, are you still friends with that antique dealer? The one with the store down on the Bayfront?"

"He moved back to the mainland. Why?"

"Why is everyone moving back to the mainland? So inconsiderate of them. I wanted to see whether he could tell me what this thing was for. I found it here."

I dug the little engraved trowel out of my bag and handed it to Pat. He held it up to the window, looked at it from several angles, and set it on my desk.

"I'm stumped," he said. "Why don't you go online and do an image search?"

"We already did," Emma said. "The internet thinks it's a ski."

Pat set his coffee down on my desk and took out his phone.

"I still have his number. I'll text him a picture."

"Pat, you should take some more pictures while you're here," Emma said. "For your haunted Mahina articles."

"*Mysterious* Mahina," Pat corrected her.

"Whatever. It just stopped raining so the light's really good."

"I have more than enough pictures of this place," Pat said. "I just need to finish the installment I'm working on right now. That's what I was doing in the library."

"Didn't you say something about planting a camera somewhere?" I asked.

"Yeah, the ghost cam. It was a bust."

"Can't you just add some mysterious glowing lights or something to your video?" Emma asked. "What do the movie people say? Fix it in post."

"I'm not gonna add special effects. Give me some credit, Emma. I do have a few shreds of integrity left."

"Where were you filming?" I asked.

"The front entrance of the hospital building," Pat said. "I picked what I thought was the best angle. And before you ask, yes, I gave the police a copy of the video. Unfortunately, it wasn't any help. It didn't capture the place where Bee Corcoran died."

"But if you got the front of the building, they'd be able to see who went in and out," I said.

"The problem is a lot of people went in and out," Pat said. "And as you well know, Molly, the front door isn't the only entrance."

After a little prodding from Emma and me, Pat agreed to show us the video on his phone. I put on my reading glasses and watched as the building lit up with the sunrise. Over the next minute the light on the downhill side of the building grew brighter. First a trickle and then a flood of people flowed up the stairs, with only one or two going back down. Because the action was speeded up, the tree branches twitched comically, and the people swarmed like cockroaches.

"Wait a minute," I said. "Can you slow this down?"

Pat took the phone back.

"See something the police missed, did you?"

"Maybe I did, Mr. Know-it-all."

I watched the video again, finger hovering over the pause symbol. When I saw what I was looking for I paused the playback.

"Here," I held the phone so Emma could see it. "Do you recognize her?"

"The smudge with the black hair?" Emma asked.

I took the phone back and zoomed in.

"No. Her."

"Oh. The smudge with the light brown hair," Pat said.

"And the blue shirt," I added. "Don't either of you see what I'm seeing?"

"How can you tell who it is?" Emma asked. "I can't even tell if it's a boy or a girl. Most of their face is behind that other lady with the long hair."

"Okay, but now. Look."

I took the phone back, started the video up, and paused it again.

"There. That's her leaving."

"Who?" Pat asked.

"Pat, it's Margaret!"

"Oh, Margaret." Emma leaned in for a closer look. "Yeah, it looks like her."

"Who's Margaret?" Pat asked.

"Margaret Adams. She took Intro to Business Management from me years ago. She was in the same class as Honey Akiona. She was working down at the bed and breakfast back then. That's not important. But she's been coming to my house every day and watching the baby."

"Oh yeah. That Margaret. The accounting majors?"

"Really?" I said. "Accounting major is the one thing you remember about her?"

He squinted at the screen.

"Can you think of a better way to describe her in two words? Yeah, I guess it could be her."

"It is her," I said. "I remember she was wearing a light blue shirt, because that's the same color I was wearing that day."

"I remember the blue shirt," Emma said. "Yours, Molly, not hers. Cause the milk stains, ah?"

"Pat," I asked. "What was the time of death? Bee's death?"

"How would I know?" Pat protested. "They haven't released any official—"

"We know you know," Emma interrupted him. "Just tell us."

Pat sighed.

"Fine. But don't tell anyone I told you."

"Yeah, yeah, Ida B. Wells," Emma said. "We know. You gotta protect your sources."

"Time of death was estimated between 6:30 and 10:30am," Pat said.

"So it could have been Margaret," I said. "If this really is her in the video. She could have killed Bee and then come over..."

"To watch your baby," Pat finished the thought for me.

"I don't like the way you put that," I said.

"So are you gonna tell Detective Medeiros about this?" Emma asked me.

"I don't know," I said. "I feel like I should ask Margaret about it first."

"Seriously?" Emma demanded. "Tell the murderer you figured out she's a murderer and then ask her if she thinks you should tell anyone else?"

"But Emma, it's Margaret Adams. She's not a murderer. She's an *accounting* major for crying out loud."

Pat's phone made a "plink" noise, and he swiped to see the message.

"Got it," he said. "Mystery solved."

"The murder?" Emma asked.

"No. Not the murder. The mystery of what your little ski is for. It's an absinthe spoon."

"Oh!" I picked it up and took another look.

"A what spoon?" Emma asked.

"Absinthe is a liqueur distilled from wormwood and flavored with herbs," I said. "You put a lump of sugar on the spoon and pour the liquid through."

"Why not just mix in the sugar the regular way?" Emma asked.

"I don't know. Tradition."

"Oh, Molly, I almost forgot," Pat said. "I found something out about your office. I think you'll be interested."

"Haunted?" Emma asked eagerly.

"Kind of. I was looking through some of the old local papers, and there's a pretty good chance that this was Constance Brigham's office."

"Constance Brigham. *The* Brighams? Son of a missionary marries the daughter of a chief, family amasses incredible wealth and influence? The ones with the house on Russian Road?"

"Yup, that's the family," Pat said.

"And whose office did you say this was?"

"Constance Brigham. She was the supervisor of the Inebriates Asylum. The whole thing was her project."

"Really? I got the boss's office?"

"Yeah, she was pretty unconventional," Pat said. "She didn't have to work at all, much less devote herself to running a rehab facility. She was supposed to get married off and become a society lady. But she drove off all her suitors and dedicated her life to this."

"Why have I never heard of her?" I asked.

"Because no one's written her biography," Pat said.

"Maybe you should do it," Emma suggested.

"I was actually thinking of doing a series on her," Pat said. "For *Island Confidential*. There's a pretty credible story about her early career, where she caught one of the doctors, old married guy, being inappropriate with a young patient. She confronted him about it, and the next day he was found dead on the hospital grounds. He'd thrown himself from the top floor. Or *someone* threw him."

"Wow." I said. "I can't say I feel too sorry for the guy, though. Is that callous of me, do you think?"

"Wait. Constance?" Emma asked. "Like Miss Constance? The avenging Miss Constance?"

"Maybe Constance was a common name back then," I said.

"Oh yeah, that's kind of a funny story," Pat said. "The legend of Miss Constance. I looked into it."

"And?" Emma and I asked in unison.

"It's from a book of Hawaiian ghost stories that was published in the early seventies. There's no written record of the legend before then that I can find. It seems like the author took the one incident from Constance Brigham's life and ran with it."

"Nah!" Emma objected. "Cannot be. The nineteen seventies?"

"That's right," Pat said.

"But me and all my friends—"

"Did you ever hear your parents ever talk about Miss Constance?" I asked.

"No, but...aw, man."

"There was a real Constance," Pat said. "But she wasn't a patient here, she ran the place. And she never had a husband."

"If Constance Brigham devoted her life to running the Inebriates Asylum," I said, "I'd have to assume she was a temperance advocate, right? How do you explain the absinthe paraphernalia?"

Pat picked up the spoon and examined it.

"Maybe she confiscated it from a patient," he said.

"Nah. I bet she was drinking it in her secret office," Emma said. "And now you can continue the noble tradition, Molly. Don't worry, I'll help you. So you don't have to drink alone. It'll help you get your mind off thinking about Bee Corcoran anyway. I don't have to remind you how dangerous it is to go poking around unsolved murders."

"Please don't bring up the lava tube episode," I said. "But you're right, I should stop obsessing about it. Bee's death was ruled a suicide, Margaret is on the mainland, and most importantly, Donnie's off the hook. I'm through with murder investigations."

"That's more like it," Emma said.

CHAPTER FORTY-SEVEN

AS SOON AS PAT LEFT, Emma asked,

"You think Constance Brigham and Miss Constance are the same person? Like Pat said?"

"Probably," I said. "Pat's good at researching that stuff. I hope he does write up something about her life. I'd read it."

"I like the avenging ghost version better."

"Well, someone already wrote *that* book. In the seventies."

"So speaking of innocent-seeming young women who go around slaughtering people," Emma said, "you gonna call Margaret or what?"

"Call Margaret? Weren't you just telling me how dangerous it would be—"

"Aw, come on, Molly. I was just saying that cause Pat was here and he's such a worry wart. Besides, I know you want to call her and ask her how come she's on Pat's surveillance tape."

"What makes you so sure about that?"

"Am I wrong?"

"I just can't reconcile it in my mind. Margaret was so conscientious. That's why we were comfortable having her watch the baby."

"And now you're dying to talk to her because you have to reassure yourself that you didn't leave your baby with a crazy murderer. Plus she's thousands of miles away so she can't hurt you."

Rather than continue to argue with Emma, I called Margaret's cell number. I had no clear plan of what I would say to her.

She sounded glad to hear from me.

"How's Francesca?" she asked. "Oh, I miss her so much! How's that little bottom tooth?"

"Extremely sharp, thanks for asking. Margaret, listen. I'm really sorry to bother you with this. But your boyfriend, Keola—"

"Husband," she said.

"Whoa, what? You got married?"

I felt a little stung that I hadn't been invited to the wedding, forgetting for a moment that I suspected Margaret of murder.

"We kind of eloped," she said.

"Did Honey Akiona know that? She called you, right, and talked to Keola about Bee's rat experiment and why he left her lab?"

"Oh yes, Honey knows."

"Wow. Congratulations. I guess everyone knows but me. Anyway, here's why I called. Did you know about Bee Corcoran passing away? She was found dead the day you left the island."

"I...yes."

I looked at Emma for some kind of nonverbal moral support, but she was playing a game on her phone.

"Margaret, the police have video of you going into the hospital building the morning of Bee Corcoran's death."

It was true. The police did have the tape, even if they didn't know who was on it.

Margaret made a little squeak.

"And you're on the video leaving a few minutes later. You're wearing the same corn-flower blue top you were wearing when you showed up to my house to watch Francesca that day."

Margaret was quiet.

"Margaret, is someone there with you?"

"No. No, he's at work."

"Margaret," I persisted, "Did you kill Bee Corcoran, and then come over to my house and spend the day with my daughter? I'm not taping this conversation or anything, I just have to know."

"No, Professor, it wasn't like that. I would never hurt Dr. Corcoran. Or Francesca, if that's what you're thinking. I would never hurt anyone!"

But she wasn't denying having been at the hospital building when Bee died.

I remembered a phrase that I'd heard from an executive coach. When you want to grab someone by the shoulders and shake them, say this instead: *Help me understand.*

"Margaret, help me understand. What happened?"

"Professor, I don't know what happened. I mean, I do know, but I don't..."

"Can you tell me what you remember? Please?"

Emma looked up from her phone, interested.

"Did you go to Bee's lab?" I asked. "Dr. Corcoran's lab?"

"Yes. Professor, we only left Mahina because Keola couldn't find another job that paid as well as being Dr. Corcoran's lab assistant. If she'd hired him back, we could have stayed. So it was our last day, and I just wanted to talk to her myself. That's all. I just went to talk to her."

"So what happened?" I asked.

"The door was open, so I let myself in. Dr. Corcoran was standing over by the window, you know, at the end of that long counter? She looked like she was writing something in a book. I guess I was pretty quiet, so she didn't notice me come in."

Emma was now leaning into my phone and listening, wide-eyed.

"I walked over to her, but she didn't look up, and I didn't want to interrupt her. So I waited until she was finished writing and she closed the notebook and put it away, and then she looked up and saw me, and before I could even say anything..."

Margaret took some time to compose herself before she continued. "I guess I startled her. It was like, she kind of screamed a little bit when she saw me? And then she stumbled and went backwards out the window. It was open, I think to let some air in, because it was kind of hot and stuffy. Anyway, it was so fast. One minute she was there, and then next thing I knew she was gone...I started to go out after her, but I saw the railing was broken and I knew it wasn't safe to go out on the balcony. I'd left my phone in the car because I'd been charging it. I tried to call for help from the landline but it didn't work."

"You *tried* to call for help? *Did* you call for help?"

"The phone was dead. There was no dial tone. Then I saw a cardboard box sitting in front of the window, which I think was what she'd tripped over. I hope this wasn't wrong of me, Professor, but I saw Keola's lab coat sitting on top of it. I realized it was Keola's box. He'd been packing his things to leave, and he'd left his stuff there where he thought it would be out of the way, but it wasn't really, he'd left it in the worst possible place, because Dr. Corcoran...I moved the box away from the window. I hope Keola's not in trouble because of me."

"Does Keola know any of this?" I asked.

"No," she sniffled. "He doesn't know I went in that morning. I don't think he even knows about Dr. Corcoran being dead. We've both been so busy, you know I haven't told anyone about—"

"What did you do then?" I asked. "After you realized the lab phone wasn't hooked up?"

"I ran to the one open door on the hallway. It was the department office. The only person in there was a student worker. I told her to call nine one one, that Dr. Corcoran was hurt."

"Did she?"

"She looked around kind of confused, like someone had to give her permission, so I told her, hurry, and she said okay, and started looking around the desk for the phone. I left but I assumed she made the call."

"Why didn't you stay and wait for someone to show up, so you could explain what happened?" I asked. "It would have saved a lot of people a lot of grief."

"I'm so sorry," she said quietly. "If I could go back and do it over...I guess I wasn't thinking. All I was thinking was I couldn't be late."

"Late for what?"

"To watch Francesca."

"You'd just watched someone fall out a fourth-floor window and you were worried about being *late*? Margaret, I would have understood. Really."

"What's that sound?"

"Coffee machine." I glared at Emma, who was noisily brewing herself another cup.

She gave me a "what am I supposed to do?" shrug.

"Professor, what's going to happen now? I understand if you have to report us."

Margaret's story added up (if you will). I had found a notebook in the drawer at the end of that long counter. Now that I knew its contents, I understood why Bee wanted to keep it hidden. We had found the lab phone off the hook, which was consistent with Margaret having tried to make a call. It hadn't been hooked up, so she didn't get a dial tone. Margaret said she'd moved Keola's box away from the window, which was why the young man had asked us whether we'd moved his stuff.

It seemed clear to me that Bee's death had been an accident. Margaret couldn't have staged it if she'd tried. No one knew how fragile the railing was. Neither Margaret nor Keola (and probably not even both of them together) seemed capable of overpowering the athletic Bee and pushing her to her death.

And thanks to my own experience with student workers, I knew it was entirely plausible that the ball had been dropped on the 9-1-1 call, leaving the security guard to discover Bee's body.

"I don't think it's my place to report anything," I said. "If you want to pursue it, I think you should get legal advice. I recommend Honey Akiona. But they've already put it down to suicide. So maybe it's best to just let things be."

"Oh, thank you so much, professor."

"Okay, well, thank you for letting me know what happened. It's—"

"Professor? Wait, don't hang up. There was something I wanted to talk to you about. I was thinking about calling you, in fact. And now that you called me, I think it's kind of like a sign."

"Really? Okay. What is it?"

"It's about the Arts and Sciences dean. Geoffrey Gunderson."

CHAPTER FORTY-EIGHT

IT TURNED OUT MARGARET'S new husband Keola had been sitting on a lot more information than we knew.

Bee Corcoran's lab was supposed to have been upgraded to Biosafety Level 2, but the money for the improvements hadn't come through. Geoffrey Gunderson, it turns out, had been skimming money from the NIH grant that had been funding Bee Corcoran's lab.

Most of the funds had been diverted to Ray Pang's re-election fund. So Pang, in misdirecting Stephen's parents' lawsuit, wasn't just trying to bank a future favor with the university. He had been doing the bidding of a major campaign donor.

Gunderson wasn't the hapless messenger boy of some higher up; the plan, it seemed, was entirely his. The lawsuit from Stephen's parents, focusing on code violations in the old hospital building, would have brought unwelcome scrutiny, and risked exposing Gunderson's illegal activities.

Gunderson was not in cahoots with Bee Corcoran. She didn't know he'd been diverting money from her existing NIH grant, nor that he was planning to do the same with her system research award. Dean Gunderson, in turn, had no idea Dr. Corcoran was fudging her research results. He'd picked her research for the system life sciences award simply because he thought it had a good chance of winning. And he was right.

An investigation confirmed Keola's claims. Mahina State University had to pay back Bee's grant. Keola and Margaret got a whistleblower payout of thirty percent of the total, which was a big help to the young couple. As for Geoffrey Gunderson, he incurred the usual penalty meted out to administrators in such situations: A large severance payout and a quiet move to a higher-paying job at another institution.

I'm not sorry I squirted him with breast milk.

CHAPTER FORTY-NINE

I'D HAD ENOUGH OF UNIVERSITY events, but we couldn't really get out of attending the blessing ceremony for the official opening of the old Mahina Memorial Hospital building. Donnie, Francesca, and I found an empty table near the back of the dining hall. The place looked less glamorous in the daytime than it had at the donor dinner. The sun shone through the tall windows, highlighting every mismatched paint patch and missing ceiling tile. I texted Pat and Emma to let them know where we were, then took the seat closest to the wall and popped the baby under my top. Donnie went to get me a glass of water.

"Molly!" I heard a familiar voice behind me. It took me a moment to place it. I turned around to see Stephen Park's mother, Tiffany Schwartz. She wore a floor-length gown encrusted in flashing red sequins. It was a little dressy for Mahina, especially for an afternoon event.

"Tiffany! Hi! Sorry, I can't get up right now."

Francesca was vacuuming milk out of me with a vengeance. And I was so thirsty it was painful. Where was Donnie with that water?

"Oh, did you hurt yourself?" Tiffany asked.

"No, I just..." I glanced down at Francesca's little pink toes, curling and uncurling.

"Never mind," she said, "there's Angus. Angus! Over here, sweetheart!"

Stephen's father strode over, looking both stylish and sweaty. A blazer over a turtleneck was not what I would have picked for an un-air-conditioned building on a summer afternoon in Mahina. Most of the men in the room were wearing cotton aloha shirts.

"Oh, you're both here," I said. "How wonderful. Would you like to join us?"

"No, we're sitting up at the front table," Tiffany said. "We'd better get up there. Where's Donnie?"

"Right here." Donnie set two glasses of water in front of me. I picked up one and downed it gratefully, then started on the other one. Donnie hugged Tiffany and shook Angus's hand. Then Tiffany said,

"Did you tell her?"

"No," Donnie said. "I thought she'd get a kick out of being surprised."

When Stephen's parents had left, I said,

"Where did you get the idea I like surprises?"

"I didn't say you'd *like* it," he said, picking up the two empty cups. "I said you'd get a *kick* out of it. I'll be back with more water."

Pat and Emma showed up and took their seats at our table. Donnie came back just as Victor Santiago, Mahina State University's Vice-President for Student Outreach and Community Relations, stepped up to the microphone.

We sat through Santiago's brief history of the building. He talked up the architectural features and left out the part about it having been a tuberculosis hospital. Then came a series of speeches from various administrators I knew only by sight. Finally, the chancellor stepped up and said a few appreciative words about our donors.

Emma leaned over and whispered,

"What are they gonna name the building? I missed it."

"They haven't said," I told her.

Donnie smiled but didn't say anything.

An eruption of applause yanked my attention back up to the front. Victor Santiago was at the mic again, and Angus Park and Tiffany Schwartz were walking up to where he was standing.

"Why are Stephen's parents up there?" I whispered to Donnie. "They didn't donate money, did they? Weren't they just suing us?"

"The university agreed to give them naming rights to the building," Donnie said.

"What? Instead of money?"

"Exactly."

I stared at him.

"That's what you were suggesting at lunch that day?"

Donnie nodded.

"Donnie, you're amazing."

He settled his arm around my shoulders, and we watched our Vice-President for Student Outreach and Community Relations present Stephen's parents with a scale model of the building, complete with its new sign.

So Stephen's parents had gotten some compensation from the university after all, and I wouldn't have to pay out of pocket for my department's printer paper.

When the presentation was over, we all walked to the next building over to show Donnie my new office. He was mildly impressed by the extra room, but more interested in the secret doorway.

"This is solid." He ran his fingers down the door jamb and examined the recessed latch. "You don't find work like this anymore."

Emma and Pat were sitting in my visitor chairs. Emma was trying to goad Pat into a game of bumper cars by scooting her chair into him repeatedly.

"This is why we can't have children in the office," I said.

Donnie stood up, his hand still on the door jamb.

"Is Francesca okay?"

Pat placed one big boot on the base of Emma's chair, rolled her away from him, and held her at leg's length.

"I'm not talking about Francesca," I said.

"I was kinda surprised by the name they picked." Bored with bumper-chairs, Emma stood and went through the doorway into the secret room. "I thought they'd want to call it the Stephen Park Building or something."

Donnie frowned.

"I thought so too. But I suppose Park Beverly Hills Cosmetic Center Building was what they wanted. What are you going to use the extra room for, Molly?"

"I'm going to use it as a private place to pump milk," I said.

"It's a bar," Emma called out.

Donnie looked at me.

"I wouldn't call it a *bar*," I said. "I mean, it's not just a bar. I ran an extension cord in, so I have a coffee machine and a mini fridge. But yes, people can come here after hours to relax if they like. Including and especially my hardworking husband."

"Get some A/C in here and you got yourself a deal," Donnie said.

"Really?"

"Donnie," Emma called out, "you want some absinthe?"

"The liqueur?" Donnie asked.

"Yeah. You want to try it?"

"Uh, no thank you. It's a little early. In fact, I should probably head back to work."

"Aw, brah, you leaving already?" Emma came out holding a silver tray. On it were three plain glasses that used to be furikake jars, a green Pernod bottle, a bowl of ice, a smaller bowl of sugar cubes, and the fancy spoon I'd found in the back of the drawer.

Donnie checked his watch. "Maybe some other time, Emma. The dinner crowd's going to be coming in pretty soon."

"Papa's gotta work to build up that college fund," I nuzzled the top of the baby's fuzzy head. "Right, Francesca?"

"College fund?" Donnie put on an innocent look. "Oh, I have bigger plans than that. I was thinking if I keep at it and play my cards right, maybe one day this will be the Donnie's Drive-Inn Building."

The Fever Cabinet

DEDICATION

T

    o the unsung heroes
    in Facilities. May the events described herein never happen to you.

FIONA: NOT EXACTLY WHAT IT SAYS ON THE TIN

FIONA SPENCER WAS CLOSE to finishing her first term as Assistant Professor of Business Ethics at Mahina State University in Hawaii. Both the tenure line and the tropical location had provoked a satisfying level of envy among her graduate-school cohort. Best of all—or so she'd thought at the time she accepted the offer—the position would allow her to live with Emmett, a luxury academics did not take for granted. They would spend their first Christmas together as a married couple.

All tickety-boo. Until she set down in Mahina.

The "historic" new College of Commerce building turned out to be a disused sanatorium, across town from the main campus and currently under repair. Thanks to some bureaucratic cock-up, her office was officially listed as vacant, so the builders used it as a tip (or a "dump," as the Americans called it). Each morning she came in to find a new layer of plasterboard scraps and scaly old pipes added to the rubbish heap along the back wall of her office.

The two senior members of the management department, Hanson Harrison and Larry Schneider, did worthwhile scholarship. She would have gladly collaborated with either of them, but they were never there. Rodge Cowper, who hadn't published a thing since he got tenure, was forever stopping into her office, preening and trying to chat her up.

Home, unfortunately, was no refuge. The house Emmett had rented was ugly and cheap, surrounded by overgrown trees and vines that blocked out the sun. Emmett himself made her feel like an unwelcome guest; he only grew more distant after he was blamed for the boy's suicide. Last night they'd had a row, Emmett had stormed out, and she hadn't seen him since.

Fiona had shut her office door, despite the air con being out of order. She didn't want to talk to anyone today. Not Rodge, not her whingeing students, and especially not her nosy department head, Molly Barda. Not a day went by, it seemed, without the woman popping in and checking up on her. Fiona suspected Molly was watching for an excuse to sack her.

There are only two tragedies in life: one is not getting what one wants, and the other is getting it.

My life is a bloody Oscar Wilde quip, Fiona thought.

A sudden pounding on her door nearly made Fiona jump out of her seat.

"Fiona?" called a voice from the other side of the door.

Fiona's heart dropped. It wasn't Rodge. Or Molly. This was far worse.

"Fiona! I know you're in there. Do open the door, darling."

MOLLY: REFUSING A PERFECTLY UNREASONABLE REQUEST

"IT WOULDN'T BE AN ETHICS violation, Molly," Emma insisted. "You're exaggerating."

"Not unethical?" I was floored by Emma's nerve and scowled disapprovingly at my phone. This of course had no effect, as Emma couldn't see me.

"It's not an ethics violation to take university property and give it to my friends? Hey, how about I go over and ask Fiona about it? She's an actual business ethics professor. And before you make the business ethics is an oxymoron joke, I've already heard it, so don't bother."

Emma Nakamura is my best friend at Mahina State, and I would do anything for her—anything that's legal and won't get me fired. Unfortunately, she had called me to lobby for the fever cabinet, an antique medical device we'd found when the College of Commerce was moved into the old Inebriates Asylum.

"Don't bother her majesty," Emma said. "I know it would be wrong to give department property to me personally. That's not what I'm asking for. I'm saying the College of Commerce should do an interdepartmental loan to the biology department."

"So you, personally, can take it home and use it as a giant Crock-Pot for your luau."

"Not a Crock-Pot, Molly. An imu, for make kalua pig. And it's not my luau, it's Yoshi's."

"Oh, not for you, for your husband. Even better. It's a medical device, Emma. It's had sick people inside it. How can you even consider eating out of it?"

"I'm not gonna eat out of it. I just don't want those furshluginer dummkopf friends of Yoshi's digging a big hole in my backyard."

Emma grew up in Hawaii, right on this island in fact, just a few miles down the road from Mahina State University. But she went to graduate school in upstate New York, at Cornell. This, in her mind, entitles her to throw in Yiddish now and again as she pleases.

"Even if I said yes," I said, "how would you bring it home? The thing's enormous. It's like an iron lung. I don't know how they got it up here in the first place."

"We can take it apart. I'll bring a screwdriver."

"Oh, we can take it apart with a screwdriver? Yeah, sounds like a well-thought-out plan. Anyway, with all the construction going on in our building, they've been moving stuff around. I don't even know where the thing is now."

"You lost it?"

"Emma, I personally did not lose—ooh, speaking of construction, I better go. It sounds like the landing's caving in out there and I think I smell something burning."

This wasn't a ruse to put Emma off. The banging noise out on the landing was insistent enough to rise above the ordinary construction din in our building. And I really did smell something burning.

I hung up the phone, cutting Emma off mid-argument, and peeked out of my office. Across the landing I saw a disheveled figure hammering on Fiona Spencer's door. He held a smoldering pipe with his free hand. Which explained both the noise and the smell. What I didn't know was who this person was, and why he was bothering Fiona.

This was not good. My prime directive right now (according to Dan Watanabe, my dean) was to keep our new hire happy. And whatever was going on, it didn't look happy.

"Fiona?" The hobo had an English accent and pronounced it like "Fion-er." "Fiona! I know you're in there. Do open the door, darling."

Now what do I do?

Go back to my office, call security, and wait for someone to drive across town from the main campus? Or intervene, and risk getting myself tossed over the railing? Our building has an open atrium-style design. From the top-floor landing it's a straight forty-foot drop to the ground floor. And it's a hard floor.

"Fiona, darling, do let me in," the visitor persisted. This couldn't be Fiona's husband. From what I'd heard, Emmett Spencer was tall, good-looking, and American. This character had a fireplug build and wore a flat cap, a rumpled, oversized jacket, and wool trousers stuffed into knee-high rubber boots.

"Excuse me sir," I started to say, when Fiona Spencer yanked her door open.

"Oh, do try not to make a scene," Fiona snapped as her visitor entered her office. She glared at me and slammed her door shut.

I went back to my desk, looked up Fiona Spencer's phone number in the online campus directory, picked up the phone, and dialed. I could hear the phone ringing across the landing.

"Spencer," she answered.

"Fiona, this is Molly," I said. "I'm just calling to remind you about the budget meeting this afternoon."

"Yes, of course."

"I saw what just happened. Do you want me to call security?" I asked.

"No," she said emphatically. "Please don't. Thanks ever so much for your concern."

And she hung up.

Okay, fine. I mentally checked off my mandatory daily chat with Fiona Spencer. I pulled out the stack of reflection papers from my Intro to Business Management class and resumed grading. (Intro to Business Management—IBM—get it? It's business-y! The course titles and descriptions were already set before I was hired on. Changing them now would only confuse the students. But I want to make sure no one thinks these names were my idea.)

I finished grading the papers, stood up, and looked out onto the landing. Rodge's door was propped open. Larry's, Hansen's, and Fiona's were shut. Larry and Hansen weren't here, of course, but how Fiona could bear having her door closed was a mystery to me. The building's air conditioning was out of service because of something the construction workers were doing, so I had my window and door open as far as they would go. The banging of pneumatic tools, the traffic out on the main road, and even conversations on lower floors reverberated up the center of the building and directly into my office. But at least I had a breeze.

The sputter of an engine starting up outside cut through the other noise. I ran back into my office and looked out of my window, just in time to see a motorcycle disappear around the corner of the main hospital building.

Fiona was on the back of the motorcycle. Or at least, someone who sure looked like Fiona. Her thin, strawberry-blond hair peeked out from under a helmet, and her floral-print dress fluttered in the wind as the bike sped off.

MOLLY: A MEDIOCRE MENTOR

I DON'T USUALLY LOOK forward to budget meetings, but today I welcomed the break. I was drenched in sweat after spending most of the day in my un-air-conditioned top-floor office, and hours of grading freshman writing had made me cross-eyed. At a quarter till, I locked up my office and went down the four flights of stairs and across the utility road to the main hospital building.

I passed a man in a bright-pink Konishi shirt and a hard hat. He was standing in the shade of the cantilevered terrace, talking on his phone.

As unpleasant as it was for me to sit in my office and swelter, I realized I had nothing to complain about compared to the Konishi Construction crew. They had to do physical work in the soggy heat, wearing hard hats, long sleeves, jeans, and heavy work boots.

"Nah, no good," the man was saying. "Lava rock too hard. Cannot dig a hole big enough. Listen. I get one place. I get you the key. Top floor but we get the elevator working now. Eh, no leave one mess, ah?"

It was only later I realized the man was probably arranging for even more junk to get dumped into Fiona's office.

Our meeting was scheduled in the dining room on the ground floor. of the main hospital building. It's a gorgeous space, the same room where they held the donor banquet when the university first took over the old hospital complex. You'd think it was originally a grand ballroom, with its lofty stamped-tin ceilings and its tall French doors leading out to the terrace. In fact it had been a tuberculosis ward, before the discovery of antibiotics, when the state-of-the-art treatment was healthful quantities of sunlight and fresh air. With the French doors propped open to let in the trade winds, the temperature was actually tolerable.

Serena, the dean's secretary, was the only other person there. She was setting up the room, so I jumped in to help, shoving tables out of the way and unfolding metal chairs.

"This is so much nicer than our old building," I said.

"Hm," Serena said. "If you ask me, the university should've asked a few more questions before they moved us in here. Sorry, that's just my opinion."

"Why?" I asked. "Is there something wrong with the new space?"

"No," she said offhandedly. "Unless you mind your workplace being haunted."

"You mean the ghost of Constance Brigham?" The Brigham family heiress was rumored to roam the old hospital complex, occasionally tossing people out of windows or off balconies.

"Nah, not that," Serena said. "The thing about Constance Brigham was made up in the seventies to scare tourists. I'm talking about the baby's cry."

"The what?" I asked.

"If you're close to the hospital and you hear the baby's cry, it means you're gonna die. You only hear it if you did something bad, though. You should look it up."

Two of the marketing professors came in, and Serena put them to work unfolding metal chairs.

By the time the meeting started, everyone in the management department was present— except Fiona Spencer. It's not like she'd get lost in the crowd. We only had a couple dozen faculty in the College of Commerce, and only a few of those were women. I started to get concerned.

Worried for Fiona, of course; while she seemed to have gone off on the motorcycle willingly, it was no guarantee she was safe. But I was also concerned for myself, which I realize sounds a little selfish. I was afraid Dan Watanabe, my dean, would blame me for Fiona's absence. Not only was I Fiona's department chair, I was her assigned mentor, and the first in my college to participate in the new campus wide Encompassing Mentoring Initiative. Which meant I was singlehandedly responsible for cultivating Fiona's Sense of Community and Belonging at Mahina State University. And also in a position to embarrass the whole College of Commerce if I failed.

It's not false humility to say when Dan chose me as Fiona's mentor, he couldn't have picked a worse candidate. I have such a low tolerance for unstructured social interaction, on Sundays I time my arrival at Mass to avoid the Passing of the Peace.

But Dan didn't have many alternatives. I'm the only woman in the management department, and I'm also apparently the only one Dan can trust to take on extra work and do it properly. So I'm the one who gets to check in daily with Fiona to make sure she is feeling Fully Integrated into the Life of the College.

Fortunately for me, Dan Watanabe seemed to have more important things to do today than hassle me about the Encompassing Mentoring Initiative. Dan always looked kind of gray, with his graying hair, silver-framed glasses, and gray-and-beige reverse-print aloha shirts. But today he looked like his own ghost.

"Thank you for coming, everyone." Dan's weary voice rang and echoed in the great room. "You may have heard the rumors about an unexpectedly large budget cut coming down. Well, the rumors are true."

He looked around to make sure he had everyone's attention. He did.

"It seems," he went on, "the construction on this building has cost more than anticipated."

Outraged grumbling arose from the assembled faculty.

"This was entirely predictable, Dan." Hanson Harrison stood to speak. Hanson, one of the management department's senior members, was from old New England money. He looked the part: patrician posture, silver hair, tall. "You may recall before the county 'gifted' the old Mahina Memorial Hospital site to the university, the Mahina State faculty senate budget committee passed a resolution asking for a detailed estimate of the costs required to bring the buildings up to code. It was sent up to the chancellor's office, where, like all resolutions from the Faculty Senate, it sank without a trace."

"This is exactly why the county dumped it on us," Larry Schneider added. Larry was the other senior member of the management department. Unlike Hanson, he was slight and tenacious, and hailed from an unfashionable borough. If someone ever decided to make a movie about the College of Commerce with an all-dog cast, Hanson Harrison would be a Weimaraner, and Larry Schneider would be a terrier mix. (Rodge would be something shaggy that shed everywhere and humped your leg.) "They didn't want to pay for the remodeling. This place is still unfit for use, and all we're doing is lining the pockets of Konishi Construction, not to mention—"

"Thank you for your comments, Larry," Dan interrupted. "And Hanson. I understand the procurement process isn't always as transparent as we'd like. That's exactly what I'm here to talk about."

I sensed my colleagues settling down a bit. Despite being a dean, Dan Watanabe had for the most part managed to retain his integrity. We didn't always like his decisions, but we could count on him to be honest with us.

"Now, I'm going off the record here. It seems parts of these old buildings are valuable to collectors and restorers. Doorknobs, pieces of molding, even some of the old medical equipment. Konishi Construction's just throwing it out as they go, and...nobody write this down, please."

Serena, Dan's secretary, set down her pen. As did Iker Legazpi, from the accounting department, who always diligently took notes for his own edification.

"I'm not saying I officially approve of this," Dan continued, "in fact, I don't. But if we all work together, we can figure out a way to at least buy enough copy paper and toner cartridges to get us through the end of the fiscal year. Not through the university budget system, of course. But the Finance Club has agreed to help us out, in exchange for a small percentage."

"Are you saying we have to sell off pieces of our building simply in order to do our jobs?" Hanson demanded.

"Meanwhile our crappy football team spends two million dollars a year traveling to the mainland to get their butts kicked," Larry grumbled.

"What's the alternative?" Dan asked them. "Just keep an eye out for anything that looks unusual or collectible and bring it in to the dean's office. If it's too big to move, let Serena know."

I guiltily recalled the silver absinthe spoon I'd found in the unmarked space adjoining my office. The hidden room wasn't on any of our building plans. Neither Facilities nor Konishi Construction seemed to know about it.

I might turn in the spoon. But I wasn't going to breathe a word to anyone about my secret room. The extra space would only be confiscated and used for storage or given to some favored administrator. They certainly wouldn't allow me to stay there.

"We need to get the word out to all our faculty and staff," Dan went on. "Is anyone missing?"

Serena, Dan's secretary, said,

"Fiona Spencer. Management department."

Fiona was the only one who didn't show up? Even Rodge Cowper was here? Yes, there he was, by the window. Playing some game on his phone by the looks of it, but physically present.

"Molly?" Dan asked me. "Where is Fiona? Did you tell her about the meeting?"

"Yes, I did." I tried my best not to sound defensive. "I emailed the department, of course, and I phoned Fiona earlier today to remind her. She said she'd be here, but it seems something came up. I can let her know what we discussed."

I felt the resentful stares of my colleagues. Thanks to the latest round of budget cuts, the College of Commerce only got one new hire this year. The management department—my department—had landed the coveted faculty line.

And now, almost as soon as we hired Fiona Spencer, we'd gone and misplaced her.

"This is why we can't have nice things," one of the marketing professors quipped.

"That's not necessary," Dan admonished him. "Molly, I understand. You can't force Fiona to attend. Just make sure she comes to the next meeting."

"I'll do my best."

I braced for what was coming next:

"Remember," Dan said, "it's our responsibility to ensure our junior faculty are fully integrated into the life of the college."

By this time I could say it along with him, although I didn't, of course.

Dan went on to cover a few more topics of interest: an update on the air conditioning (currently scheduled to be working by late January), the revised Student Retention Office reporting forms, and the schedule for winter commencement. The agenda item that sparked the liveliest discussion was a curiously Schrödingerian statement on class attendance from the university system. It both supported taking attendance (because financial aid rules and our new automated Student Success System required the data) and argued against it (because who were we to sit in judgment of our students' complicated lives?). The upshot was it didn't matter what we decided to do about taking attendance. The instant a student complained, the administration would reprimand us for doing it wrong.

After the meeting, I found myself walking back to the College of Commerce building with Iker Legazpi. Iker's side-parted brown hair was perfectly in place as always, and his plump, ageless face radiated serenity. Talking to Iker is always a comfort for me, despite his sunny attitude. He usually has a kind word for everyone, and treats his students—even the underachievers, the plagiarists, and the grade-grubbers—with far more compassion than I am able to muster. I have a theory that Iker may be an angel in human form, except I can't work out why an angel would have been sent to earth to teach accounting.

Iker held the door for me as we entered the College of Commerce building.

"I'm worried about Fiona Spencer," I told him as we started up the steps. There's an elevator, but most of us don't trust it. "Iker, have you met Fiona's husband? What does he look like?"

"Emmett Spencer?" Iker frowned. "Yes, of course. I serve on the board of the St. Aelred School for Boys. Mr. Spencer is the new headmaster. Pardon me, perhaps I should not say he is new. He was appointed nearly a year ago."

"I thought you had to be a priest or something to work there, no?"

"Not any longer. It is a complicated history, that of the St. Aelred School for Boys."

"What does Emmett Spencer look like?" I asked.

We reached the landing where Iker's office was and stepped aside to let the people behind us pass.

"Emmett Spencer is one hundred and ninety centimeters in height, and of a slender build. He has brown hair and blue eyes, and he is thirty-six years old."

"A hundred and ninety centimeters is...?"

"Six feet, two point eight inches."

"So he's tall. Iker, how do you know his exact height?"

"As board treasurer, it is among my responsibilities to review the insurance policies. The details I share with you are not confidential. Why do you ask about the appearance of Dr. Spencer's husband?"

"Because Fiona...some guy came to meet her, and she left with him. It looked like she went willingly. But she hasn't come back. I was wondering whether the guy was her husband, but from your description, it doesn't sound like it's the same person."

"This thing happened today?" Iker asked.

I recapped the morning's events for Iker, ending with my seeing someone who looked like Fiona being spirited away on a motorcycle. I was already in trouble with Dan, so I didn't see any harm in telling Iker everything.

Iker shook his head.

"I do not know this figure with the odorous pipe and the rubber boots," he said. "But you say Dr. Spencer went willingly."

"Looked like it," I said.

"Perhaps she believes a drive in the fresh air on a motorcycle would be a cheering thing for her."

"Cheering? Why does she need cheering? Iker, she just got a tenure-track job in the same town as her husband. I know a lot of academic couples who would kill to trade places with her. Her students love her, even though she's mean to them. I mean, okay, this place isn't perfect, but can't she just once say thank you, or smile, or show even a glimmer of positive emotion at all? Why does she have to be such a dry stick? I'm sorry, Iker, I know I'm supposed to be her mentor, but I'll be honest. Fiona's a little hard to warm up to."

Iker retrieved his key and opened the door to his office. "Molly, we are not...do you wish to come in and talk more?"

"No, I don't want to keep you. And I need to get back. What were you going to say, though? We are not...?"

"Ah yes. We are not to show kindness only to the people who we find friendly and amusing. Kindness is not a purse from which we dispense little gold coins only to the deserving."

"I guess. So you're saying I should be charitable to Fiona regardless of her obvious contempt and ingratitude."

"To take a more worldly view," Iker added, "to lose Fiona Spencer would be a catastrophe for the College of Commerce. The Administration will say, we have given you a professor, and now you have lost her. We will not give you another."

"Oh, you're right about that. Dan reminds me every day. And you heard what happened in the meeting."

"It may be, Molly, that Fiona Spencer has a private sadness which you cannot see."

"I know, I know. I should give Fiona a break. She's in a brand-new job, she doesn't really know anyone, we still haven't gotten the situation with her office straightened out...I should try to be a little more understanding."

Iker was right. We were lucky we'd been able to hire anyone at all, let alone someone of Fiona Spencer's caliber. Dan had worked hard to convince the trustees to fill the business ethics position. (The previous Business Ethicist had departed years ago, under circumstances so tragically on-the-nose you'd think I was making the whole thing up.)

As Mahina State's enrollment flattened over the past few years, our approach to student retention grew increasingly desperate. The Student Retention Office's philosophy morphed from "every student should have the opportunity to reach their potential" to "every student can succeed" to "students don't fail; teachers do." "Failing" faculty are subject to mandatory "enrichment opportunities" where they are exhorted to better engage our "customers." My friend Emma Nakamura (a repeat offender) refers to these sessions as "de-education camp." ("Cause you come out dumber than when you went in," she says.)

Despite (or perhaps because of) this approach, enrollment and tuition revenue are down, and faculty haven't gotten a cost-of-living adjustment in years.

Now that faculty are quitting at an unprecedented rate, the administration is trying the same kinds of retention tactics on us.

What would I want if I were in Fiona's place? A workspace with functioning climate control. An office within walking distance of the classroom, not across town from it. A respite from the construction din reverberating through our building from 7:45 in the morning until exactly 4:30 in the afternoon.

The College of Commerce could offer Fiona none of these things. Instead, she got me as a mentor.

No wonder she was grumpy.

FIONA: AN UNEXPECTED VISITOR

FIONA HUNG ON TIGHT as the motorcycle sped along a one-lane road through a tunnel of green jungle, turned sharply up an even narrower road, and pulled off at a small clearing next to a waterfall.

Harriet Holmes pushed down the kickstand, removed her helmet, drew her flat cap from her pocket, and pulled it back onto her head.

"Brilliant, isn't it?" Harriet produced a pipe and tobacco pouch from the inside breast pocket of her field jacket and a small spray bottle from a different pocket. "It's almost too scenic. Oh, squirt some of this on yourself, darling. You know how the mosquitos will gobble you up given half a chance. You never did do well in the tropics."

Fiona took the proffered bottle and sprayed the mosquito repellent around her head and arms.

"I did not choose to have a reaction to the malaria pills. My deepest apologies for the inconvenience, however."

"Don't forget the ankles," Harriet reminded her through a cloud of pipe smoke. "Those little buggers love the ankles. Blood's close to the surface, you see. Come, sit."

Harriet led Fiona over to a recycled-plastic bench overlooking the waterfall. Beyond the treetops, the Pacific Ocean glittered in the distance.

"Now then, isn't this lovely." Harriet took an appreciative pull and blew an imperfect smoke ring. She tried again, this time with better results.

"There, you see?" Harriet waved her pipe at the perfect wreath of smoke floating over their heads. "Persistence pays."

"I'm supposed to be at a budget meeting."

"A budget meeting? You already know what it's about then," Harriet said. "It's only going to be gloom and doom. No bursar since the dawn of time has ever called a budget meeting to say, ripping news, everyone, we're rolling in dosh."

"Yes, I know all that," Fiona replied.

But bad news about our finances won't be all of it, she thought. The worst bit will be afterwards, when that Barda woman comes oiling up and tries to jolly me along and asks whether there's anything at all she can do for me, only there's no money to fix anything. And I'll have to say everything's going swimmingly, thanks, when what I really want to tell her is if you can't get the bloody air con fixed or keep the builders from piling up their rubbish in my office then leave me alone, you nosy cow.

"Something on your mind, darling?" Harriet asked.

Fiona smoothed her print dress over her slender thighs and watched the water tumble down the black lava rocks, a silvery column shattering into spray. She conceded the place was beautiful but could not bring herself to feel joy or appreciation.

"What was so very important that you had to bring me all the way out here to talk about it?" Fiona finally asked.

"Well, this is much more pleasant than that old workhouse or wherever they have you, isn't it?" Harriet waved her pipe at the waterfall. "The mosquito repellent's working, I hope, darling? Don't look at me like that. I took you away from your work because I didn't want you to make a scene."

Fiona's mouth set in a thin line. "You don't think you already made a scene hammering on my door?"

"I saw Emmett. I thought you might like to know."

This surprised Fiona, although she didn't want to give Harriet the satisfaction of letting on.

"I see him every day," Fiona shot back. "How long have you been in Mahina?"

"I only arrived Monday. Such a quaint little airport, reminds me a bit of Bathpalathang."

"You might've told me you were coming," Fiona said.

"Whatever for? I've got a place to stay. Wouldn't dream of imposing on the newlyweds. Anyway, here's what I wanted to tell you. I was planning to send off some note cards to let people know I was here. It seems there's only one proper stationer in Mahina. Mahina Printing and Stationers Incorporated. Such an old-fashioned little hamlet, this Mahina of yours. Not the sort of place I'd picture you, if I'm honest."

Fiona crossed her arms. "What's all this got to do with Emmett?"

"Well, I was having a look around the shop, I turned the corner, and there they were. You know how one's brain can be slow to process things. My first impression was of Emmett Spencer, respectable headmaster and devoted husband, squeezing someone's bum. My next thought was no, it's entirely impossible, because that's certainly not Fiona's bum he's squeezing."

Fiona glared at Harriet.

"Stop it. I've had quite enough of these filthy rumours. I'd think you, of all people, would be smart enough not to fall for it."

The pipe paused halfway to Harriet's mouth.

"It's nothing to do with rumours," Harriet said. "I saw them with my own eyes. I thought you'd want to know—"

"I don't believe it," Fiona declared.

Harriet took a pull on her pipe.

"Quite understandable. You threw in your lot with Emmett Spencer, you uprooted your entire life to be with him. You've invested quite a bit in this marriage, despite the warning signs, and I suppose you'd sooner die than admit—"

"Stop it." Fiona stood up. "Take me back. I'd rather sit through a bloody budget meeting than listen to this."

Harriet quietly put out her pipe, folded her cap, and tucked it into her pocket.

"Very well. I'll drop you back at the lunatic asylum, if you like."

"I'm sorry, Mum," Fiona said. "I know you're only trying to help. I've been a bit cross at Emmett myself lately, if I'm honest. And it's a former inebriates' asylum if you must know, not a lunatic asylum. For all the difference it makes."

MOLLY: LOST AND FOUND

EMMA NAKAMURA CAME over from the main campus the next day to join me for lunch in the cafeteria of the old hospital building. Our satellite dining center had the exact same yogurt cups, packaged sandwiches, and hard bananas available on the main campus. But the soaring ceilings and relative quiet of the old tuberculosis ward made lunch more pleasant.

I found Emma already seated at one of the round tables, munching a musubi and watching a video on her phone. Emma is short, freckled, and suntanned. Despite the silver threads in her wavy hair she's often mistaken for a student. But anyone who talks down to her is unlikely to try it a second time.

"What're you watching?" I sat next to her and pulled the foil top off my yogurt.

"This is me with the paddlers. Right after we finished the Molokai to Oahu race. We finally got the video posted."

I picked up Emma's phone to see a rowdy group of women on a small karaoke stage, clearly in a celebratory mood.

"Look how sunburned you all are. What are you doing?"

"We're doing a victory haka."

"You're what?"

"The haka is an ancient Māori tradition we use in the islands to display our strength and unity."

"I know what a haka is. That's not a haka."

"Oh yeah? What do you know about it?"

"Emma, you're playing air guitar."

"Colonizer." Emma snatched the phone back. "So what's new up here at the haunted hospital?"

I told Emma about Fiona Spencer's disappearance. She finished her musubi and licked the stray rice grains from her fingers.

"Did you get a picture of the guy who grabbed her?" she asked.

"No. Everything happened so fast. And he didn't grab her, that's the thing. She invited him into her office, and next thing you know she was riding off on his motorcycle. That's why I'm not sure whether this is something I need to report."

"You could describe the guy, though, yeah?"

"Sure. He kind of looked like a gardener. Or a hobbit? I don't know. He was wearing a lot of layers."

"What's Fiona look like?" Emma pulled the plastic wrap off her second Spam musubi and took a big bite.

"You've never met her?"

"Nope."

"Early thirties, fair hair, judgmental expression that says, 'I'm from Oxford and I disapprove of everything,' thin build, average height."

"Sounds like your new hire's working out great."

"Why does Fiona Spencer have to be my problem, Emma?"

"Cause you're department chair? Wild guess."

"I blame Dan Watanabe for appointing me." I gestured with my spoon for emphasis. "Anyone can see I'm not cut out for this."

Emma picked up a napkin and dabbed her eye.

"Easy there, Spatter McGee."

"Sorry about that." I set my spoon down. "I'm supposed to be keeping my faculty happy and productive and instead I go and lose one of them."

"Does she look like that?" Emma jutted her chin at a point behind me.

"Like what?" I twisted around to see Fiona Spencer sitting on the far side of the dining room, silhouetted against the tall window. She was eating alone.

"Emma, that's her! It's Fiona!"

Emma started to unwrap her third musubi.

"Glad I could help. You're welcome."

"What a relief. Let's go sit with her." I stood up.

Emma stayed put and scowled at me.

"Kinda looks like she wants to be by herself, Molly."

"I'm already behind on my Encompassing Mentoring check-ins. And also I'm supposed to encourage her not to miss any more meetings."

Emma made a face.

"Gotta make sure she's 'fully integrated into the life of the college' so she won't quit on you?"

"Exactly. Come on."

Emma didn't budge.

"Molly, in what alternate universe do people want their boss butting in on their peaceful lunch?"

"What are you talking about? I've had lunch with Dan Watanabe lots of times," I said.

"Yeah, but that's different," Emma shot back. "Your boss is Dan. Her boss is you."

Emma and I glared at each other for a minute, me balancing my half-eaten yogurt on my tray, her sitting there stubbornly.

"Your reasoning is unsound, and your conclusion is invalid," I said finally.

"Yeah, but I'm right," Emma retorted.

"I have to go talk to her, Emma. What if Dan comes in and sees her eating by herself and I'm over here with you enjoying my lunch?"

Emma sighed heavily, but she got up and came with me.

The deer-in-the-headlights expression on Fiona's face as we approached her table confirmed Emma was right. She wanted to be left in peace. But it was too late to back out now.

"Oh. Molly. I apologize for missing the budget meeting yesterday," Fiona said to me.

"Don't worry about it." I said.

"Well, ehm."

"Mind if we join you?"

We seated ourselves across from her, which probably made Fiona feel like she was facing a tribunal. But it seemed like a better choice than plunking down on either side of her. Fiona put aside the journal she'd been reading. Emma introduced herself, and Fiona introduced herself back.

"I put in another request to Konishi Construction," I said. "To have them get the junk out of your office."

I wanted to find out what had happened to her the previous day and who her visitor was, but it was a topic I'd have to ease into, and I couldn't really bring it up in front of Emma anyway.

"I'd be perfectly happy if they simply stopped bringing in more rubbish," Fiona replied. "Having the existing rubbish removed would be more than I could hope for."

"Whoa, three pretty ladies at one table."

We all looked up to see Rodge Cowper holding his lunch tray. The buttons of his rumpled aloha shirt strained across his belly. His thick, graying hair was cut short in the front and longer in the back. It occurred to me his hairstyle was probably older than Fiona.

Rodge placed his tray on the table, pulled out a chair, and sat down.

"Looks like today's my lucky day."

"Hey, Rodge, why don't you join us?" Emma said, once he was seated and had started in on his sandwich.

"She's a little firecracker, isn't she?" Rodge mumbled to Fiona, through a mouthful of egg salad and white bread. Rodge Cowper has an enduring crush on Emma despite (or possibly inflamed by) Emma's obvious contempt for him.

"You wouldn't know from her last name, Nakamura, but Emma's half-Hawaiian. That's why she's got that wild streak—"

"Rodge?" I said. "Do you remember our discussion with Maisie from HR?"

Rodge's face fell.

"I thought that was just for job interviews."

"No, it's for not getting written up by HR again."

"Eh, Fiona," Emma said, as if Rodge weren't there, "you going to the in-service tomorrow?"

"The Professional Development thing," I said, in response to Fiona's questioning look.

"That's tomorrow already?" Rodge asked Emma. "Are you going, Emma?"

"I forgot it was so soon," I pulled out my phone and scrolled through the Student Retention Office announcements. "Oh. Here it is. It's about how to understand text-speak so you can communicate better with your students."

"Surely we're not expected to share our private telephone numbers with our students?" Fiona asked.

"Oh yeah, you're new here," Emma said. "The Student Retention Office thinks professors should be on the clock providing outstanding customer service 24/7."

"Aw, give the SRO a break," Rodge said. "They're good people."

"Yeah, you're just saying that cause they keep nominating you for the stupid teaching award," Emma shot back.

"Our legal department says we don't have to share our personal contact information with students," I told Fiona. "I don't."

"Me neither." Emma narrowed her eyes at Rodge. "I believe in maintaining appropriate boundaries with students."

"Are the Student Retention Office and the university lawyers at odds then?" Fiona asked.

"Yes," I said.

"It's like the rule about our office doors," Rodge said. "We have to keep 'em closed for fire safety, but open so we look welcoming to students."

"Actually the thing about keeping the doors open is called the Rodge Cowper rule," Emma put in maliciously. "When a student's in your office you gotta keep your door open at least 45 degrees."

"There's a Rodge Cowper Rule?" Fiona asked suspiciously.

Rodge, his mouth once again stuffed with egg salad sandwich, gave Fiona a thumbs-up.

"Wait'll you hear about our new attendance policy," I said. "It's in the meeting minutes Serena sent out this morning."

"Hey, Fiona," Rodge swallowed his mouthful of sandwich. "You got any plans for Christmas?"

"That's right, we're almost to the end of the semester. Do you and Emmett have any plans?" I was proud of myself for remembering the name of Fiona's husband. Normally this is the kind of information that deserts me just when I need it.

"If you're going off island, you should know they jack up the prices exactly when school's out," Emma advised. "It's better if you guys can take off as soon as finals week's over."

"I suppose I'll travel back to England." Fiona rested her hand on her issue of Philosophy & Public Affairs. "Emmet won't be joining me."

"Whoa, pretty lady like you traveling that whole way all by yourself?" Rodge said.

"He can't get away from work, I'm afraid." Fiona's tone was flat.

"Isn't your husband the headmaster at St. Aelred?" Emma asked. "He can't take Christmas off to be with his wife?"

Fiona obviously didn't want to discuss this. I nudged Emma's foot under the table. She ignored me.

"Speaking of Christmas," I said, "Did you know in Japan, the traditional Christmas dinner is Kentucky Fried Chicken?"

I'll admit, I'm terrible at this.

"Are you freakin' kidding me?" Emma persisted.

"It's true," I said. "You have to place your order months in adva—"

"Didn't you move to the butt end of creation to be with him?"

"Emma!" I exclaimed.

"That's exactly what your dissertation advisor said about Mahina," Emma retorted.

"He was a little disappointed I didn't end up somewhere more high-profile, but Emma, you love living here. And so do I. Mahina is a wonderful place to live."

"Yeah, there's no place like it," Rodge agreed. "It's got everything you need. Did you know just about forty minutes south of here they got a clothing-optional—" I cleared my throat. Rodge shot me a guilty look and quietly started on the second half of his sandwich.

"It's rather silly and sentimental for a married couple to expect to spend all our free time together," Fiona said quietly.

"Nah, that's your husband talking," Emma declared. "You don't believe it for a second. You moved halfway around the world to be with him, and now he won't even spend Christmas with you? Come on, you don't have to put up with that."

"Emma! Fiona, I am so sorry. Emma, I think we should go. Rodge, maybe we should all let Fiona get back to her—"

Fiona burst into tears, stood up, and fled.

Rodge, Emma, and I sat and watched her leave.

"Whoa, catfight!" Rodge said.

Emma and I glared at him until he picked up his energy drink, mumbled something about getting back to the salt mines, and left.

"Nice going Emma," I said, when Rodge had left the cafeteria. "Why did you say those things to her?"

Emma reached across the table and grabbed Fiona's untouched tuna sandwich.

"I hate it when women put up with that crap. He makes her move all the way out here just to be with him, then he ditches her at Christmas. She's gotta dump him."

"Technically you're not wrong," I said. "But now I have to go do damage control. So thanks for that."

"Eh, I told you it was a bad idea to come sit with her. Next time listen to me."

I left Emma to dispatch the remains of Fiona's abandoned sandwich.

FIONA: FOUND AND LOST

FIONA MARCHED BACK up to her office, fuming. How dare that Emma creature say those things about Emmett? Why did Molly simply sit there, gawping, while Emma harassed her? And to top things off, there was that tiresome old fossil Rodge Cowper waggling his eyebrows at her.

Fiona was angry at herself as well. She shouldn't have let on about spending the Christmas holidays apart from Emmett. That titbit would be catnip for Mahina's nosy parkers.

Fiona hadn't tried to start a row. She'd only asked Emmett how long they were expected to live in the rented kit house while the St. Aelred's parsonage was being refurbished. She hoped the builders would be finished before the new year. Somehow it came up that Emmett already had plans for the Christmas holiday. Plans that didn't include her.

This was an obvious sign of trouble in their marriage. But it wasn't the first.

There was the time Fiona had popped into St. Aelred hoping to surprise Emmett for lunch, only to be told he was unavailable. On her way back out to the car park, she stopped in the ladies' privy (the one for female staff and teachers). She was in the far stall when two women walked in, chatting.

"I thought after Emmett's wife got here, he'd be more careful," said one.

The sound of running water drowned out the other woman's response.

"You really think the wife doesn't know?" The first woman laughed. "Eh, love is blind, but in this case it's gotta be deaf and dumb too, ah?"

"Yeah, dumb is right," the other woman had replied. They walked out cackling.

Fiona realized she was standing in front of her office door. She couldn't remember walking across the dirt path from the main building, nor mounting the stairs. She was that flustered.

Fiona unlocked her door and shoved it open. The Post-It Note with her name written on it fluttered to the ground. Her fury at Emmett gave way to feeling depressed about her working conditions.

She had no complaint about the size of her office. It was at least twice as big as any of the others on the floor. But whatever the room had been originally designed for, it certainly wasn't marking papers or meeting students. The tiled floor sloped gently toward a drain in the centre of the room. There was a single small window, up near the ceiling. Its size and position made it look like it was designed to prevent a person escaping. It certainly didn't admit much fresh air.

She sat down, set the stack of student papers in front of her, uncapped her red pen, and started to read:

The dictionary defines ethics as "moral principles that govern a person's behavior or the conducting of an activity."

She moved the paper to the bottom of the stack and started on the next:

Since the dawn of time, ethics has been a big problem in society.

She capped the pen and set it down. Despite the portable air conditioner wheezing away at her elbow, it was too hot for her to concentrate. She wondered whether she could steal away home for a quick shower and change but remembered once again that Emmett had taken the car.

When Fiona had suggested buying a second car, Emmett immediately dismissed the idea as wasteful. He'd been so confident in making his argument Fiona thought it useless to contradict him. Now she was angry at herself for not having put up a fight.

Someone knocked on the door and opened it. It was Molly.

"Fiona," Molly said, "I, uh—"

"Yes?"

Fiona had no interest in putting Molly at ease. Molly could have stopped what happened downstairs. Instead she did nothing. She could bloody well stand there in her uncomfortable-looking shoes.

"Fiona, I apologize for what happened just now. If I'd known how you—how those comments would land, I would have stopped it. Here's the thing, in Mahina? People here are really interested in other people's business. It took me a while to get used to it. When I was pregnant with Francesca, one of my students randomly congratulated me on having a girl, and I still don't know how she knew, because we didn't tell anyone the baby's sex."

Fiona said nothing.

"Emma means well," Molly went on. "Her comments came from a good place, even if it doesn't sound like it sometimes. Not sure I can say the same about Rodge. Sorry. Listen, is there anything I can do?"

"No," Fiona said. "I mean, yes, there is."

"There is?"

"If you wouldn't mind dropping me at St. Aelred?"

"The school?"

"Emmett's office has air con, and it's quiet. I'd rather work there. And I don't have the car just now."

Fiona hadn't had a car since Emmett had walked out. She'd been taking the sampan (Mahina's open-air taxi), going on foot, and now and again cadging a lift from a friendly neighbour. Fortunately, the shuttle between the College of Commerce and the main campus ran at regular intervals, which enabled Fiona to get to and from her classes.

"Oh. Sure." Molly glanced at her wristwatch. "Yeah, it's hard to get anything done here with all the noise. You want to go right now?"

Fiona did.

As they walked side-by-side down the stairs, Molly filled Fiona in on the mundane details of the budget meeting she'd missed. Fiona assumed Molly was simply making conversation, so she barely paid attention as Molly nattered on about the dean's scheme to scour the building for bits and bobs that could be sold off to supplement the budget.

The worst part of all of this was admitting her mother had been right about Emmett all along. That, more than anything else, was what Fiona found truly unbearable.

MOLLY: A DRIVE TO ST. AELRED SCHOOL

THE DRIVE OUT TO THE boys' school took longer than I thought. Or maybe it just seemed long because I was trying so hard not to offend the prickly Fiona Spencer.

Fiona might not be the most personable colleague I'd ever had, I reminded myself, but it could have been worse. We'd had so much trouble agreeing on a candidate, we could have ended up with a failed search.

Hanson Harrison's pick was a self-styled iconoclast who refused on principle (he claimed) to publish in peer-reviewed journals. Instead, his intellectual output was entirely confined to social media, where he proclaimed, "attendance policies are educational malpractice," and advised his followers "if you hate grading, stop doing it." Hidebound reactionaries who insisted on "standards" and "rigor" were destined for the ash heap of history (or the glue factory). Best of all, this young rebel's advisor happened to be one of Harrison's pals at Yale.

Unfortunately for Harrison, his pet candidate posted what he thought was a private message wherein he bemoaned the oppressiveness and injustice of the academic job market. As evidence he offered his own predicament, which he described as "stuck at a crappy little teaching college in Hawaii." He was promptly dropped from further consideration.

Hanson's nemesis, Larry Schneider, backed a young man whose research focused on debunking higher-ed myths. In addition to his publications, Larry's candidate maintained a lively blog, whose purpose was to mock fads like those espoused by Harrison's pick. Larry's candidate got as far as a phone interview with the Student Retention Office, after which he immediately withdrew from the search.

Rodge Cowper and I both supported Fiona Spencer; this was one of the few things Rodge and I had agreed on, ever. I liked her prestigious degree, which would go a long way toward reassuring local parents our quality was every bit as good as a mainland school. Her already-impressive research would ensure smooth(er) sailing for contract renewal and tenure. She seemed to connect well with the students during her teaching demonstration (mostly because they loved her accent).

Rodge favored Fiona Spencer because, as he put it, "No offense, Molly, but we could use some eye candy around here."

I made sure to put the top up on the Thunderbird before we started driving. After living in Mahina as long as I have, I don't mind a little rain now and then, but I couldn't expect Fiona to feel the same way.

We headed out of Mahina, down the two-lane highway toward the St. Aelred School for Boys. On both sides of the road was dense forest and bushy strawberry guava and staghorn fern, punctuated by the occasional corrugated metal roof.

"People complain about the rain here," I said, "but it doesn't bother me. I like how it keeps everything green. Honestly, I like living on the windward side. I think the other side of the island's too hot."

Fiona was silent.

"The thing is, it's warm rain, so even if you're caught without an umbrella, it's not the worst thing in the world."

No comment from Fiona.

What was her problem? She'd asked me for a ride, I agreed, and she was still grumpy. Maybe her mood didn't have anything to do with me, but when someone is sitting in the passenger seat, silent and fuming, it's hard not to take it a little personally.

As we picked up speed, the convertible roof started to squeak rhythmically.

"Your car is squealing," Fiona pointed out.

This probably annoyed her on top of everything else, but at least she was talking.

"I know," I said. "Sorry about that. I need to bring it in to Miyashiro Motors. I've been putting it off."

"Car servicing's expensive here." This could be interpreted as either commiseration or accusation.

"True," I agreed. "Plus every time I take my car in, I have to listen to Earl Miyashiro lecture me about how there are fewer and fewer places to buy parts and I should be driving something more practical, like a two-year-old Toyota. He has no aesthetic imagination. No concept of awe or beauty."

"Why don't you go somewhere else?" Fiona asked.

"He's a competent mechanic. Plus no one else on the island will even look at my car."

Fiona seemed to lose interest in the conversation and stared out the window.

I still wondered who Fiona's recent visitor was, the one who'd spirited her away and made her miss the budget meeting. But I'd seen how sensitive Fiona could be, so I kept my questions to myself. In any case, she'd willingly accompanied the person and had returned in one piece.

I shouldn't let Fiona's lack of friendliness bother me, I told myself. Of course like most people, I'd rather be liked than disliked. But as department chair, a certain amount of hostility came with the territory. It was my unhappy duty to represent the faculty's interests to the administration, and then to turn around and implement the administration's diktats over the objections of the faculty.

As Dan Watanabe, my dean, likes to put it, "it's lonely in the middle."

Almost too late, I saw the carved koa St. Aelred sign signaling the drive to the school.

"Turn in here?" I asked.

"What? Oh, yes, sorry. Right up here."

St. Aelred's private road was smoother and newer than the highway we'd just turned off. The glossy black asphalt drive cut through acres of velvety, perfectly-trimmed grass. We slowed at the guardhouse. The guard recognized Fiona and waved us through with a smile.

We drove on past a few single-story bungalows and classroom buildings, all decades old but perfectly maintained. I pulled up next to the administration complex, which housed the headmaster's office. As I shut off the engine, I spotted a stout, rumpled figure carefully stepping up the side of a grassy hill.

"Who is that?" I wondered whether this was the person I'd seen hammering on Fiona's office door.

"It's Mr. Ferman, The science teacher," Fiona said, just as I realized the man was someone I'd never seen before. He wore a tweed jacket with a woolen muffler, but his shock of white hair indicated he was considerably older than Fiona's visitor.

"He looks a little unsteady," I said. "Is he okay?"

Fiona gave a dismissive shake of her head.

"He's potty," she said.

"What about a potty?"

"Addlebrained. Emmett says he has a drinking problem." Fiona tried pulling the Thunderbird's door handle toward her to release the latch.

"Up and down, not toward you," I said. "Hang on, I'll get it."

I jogged around to the passenger side and saw Mr. Ferman stumble. With effort, he got back up, looked around, and rubbed his eyes.

I pulled open the heavy door and let Fiona out.

"Are you sure he's okay?" I asked. "Is there a nurse's office on campus?"

We watched Mr. Ferman steady himself and make his way toward the main highway, where we'd just come from.

"I'm certain he's fine," Fiona said as she started across the parking lot. "But I'll be sure to tell Emmett."

"Do you mind if I tag along?" I said. "We're going to be doing a recruiting push at St. Aelred's and I've never been. It'd be good to see the campus."

"If you like." Fiona walked ahead without waiting for me. "I imagine the families who send their sons here are setting their sights a bit higher than Mahina State University."

Charming, I thought. I followed her into the administration office, a one-story building with dark wood siding and frosted-glass jalousie windows.

The young man behind the koa counter wore a forest-green St. Aelred School polo shirt. When he turned to greet us, I realized I knew him.

Bryce Kahului was a first-year student in my Intro to Business Management class. He was a sweet kid, with an easy smile.

"Is Emmett Spencer in?" Fiona asked, without bothering to address him by name.

"Oh, hello, Dr. Spencer. No, he's not in at the moment. Oh, hey, Professor Barda."

He grinned, dimpling his cheek.

"Hi Bryce, nice to see—"

"Do you know where I might find him now?" Fiona interrupted.

Bryce's smile faded.

"I don't know. Sorry, Dr. Spencer."

"When did you last see him?" she demanded.

"Yesterday morning, I think—"

"Is Maureen here?" Fiona interrupted.

"Sorry, Dr. Spencer. She's in a meeting."

Fiona Spencer's mouth tightened.

"I see. Do you know when she'll be back?"

Bryce shook his head.

"Sorry. Would you like to leave a note?"

"No. Thank you."

Fiona pulled out her phone and stepped outside, leaving me standing there with Bryce. I was no longer surprised to run into current and former students all over town. At my credit union, where they could see my expenditures and balance; at the pharmacy, where they know my medical history; at the Galimba's Bargain Boyz cash register, where they offer unsolicited advice on my bra purchases.

"Bryce, I didn't know you worked at St. Aelred," I said.

"Yeah, I started when I was a student here." He brightened. "It's perfect for me. Part time, and lots of downtime so I can study."

"So you're an alumnus. Perfect. You know, the College of Commerce is going to be stepping up its recruiting here. Just out of curiosity, how did you happen to choose Mahina State?"

"Cheap, that's why," he said happily. "I wanna save up for grad school."

"Good plan," I said.

"Yeah, I told Mr. Spencer with in-state tuition, I could get through without taking out loans. He told me, Bryce, you're smart enough to go to a real university."

"He said what?"

"But I went Mahina State anyway."

You're smart enough to go to a "real" university? Nice way to talk about your wife's workplace, you undermine-y jerk.

I forced a smile.

"I'm glad you didn't listen to him, Bryce."

Fiona came back inside. Emmett wasn't answering his phone.

"I've no idea where he is." Fiona sounded flustered. "I hope he's not hurt."

Oh, do you? Because I hope he fell down a lava tube.

"Why don't I just drive you home?" I offered. "It's really no trouble."

She opened her mouth to say something, appeared to change her mind, and nodded.

"I'd appreciate it. Thank you."

FIONA: THE ONLY THING WORSE THAN BEING WRONG IS ONE'S MOTHER BEING RIGHT

AS MOLLY AND FIONA made their way back to the parking lot, Fiona stewed. She was furious with Emmett for putting her in this position. Why had she let him decide she didn't need a car of her own? She was angry at both Molly and Bryce, for having witnessed her humiliation. But the main target of her rage was the woman who had been right all along about Emmett Spencer. Her mother.

Harriet had seen it before they'd even married. Emmett had refused to buy Fiona an engagement ring. Harriet saw it as a red flag. Fiona had insisted Emmett was simply being sensible. The thin gold wedding band was all she required.

"You're quite mistaken about that, darling," her mother had countered. "Just wait until he has the chance to splash out on something he wants. See how sensible he is then."

It was true; Emmett economised ruthlessly when it came to furniture (which he didn't care about) and tea (which he didn't drink). But Emmett had arranged travel for the Christmas holiday, which must cost something. He wouldn't tell her where he was going, how much it would cost, or who else would be there. It was as if he wanted to be with her as little as possible.

The only time Emmett showed any affection for Fiona was when they were out and about.

"This is my wife, Fiona," he'd declare proudly as he introduced her to an acquaintance.

"Your wife?" the other person would reply, looking surprised. Or relieved.

Fiona was so wrapped up in her thoughts as she made her way down the walkway, she didn't realize Molly was no longer beside her. She stopped and backtracked, only to find her department head rummaging through a black plastic rubbish bin.

"e-waste. Hold for pickup," a handwritten sign was taped to the stuccoed wall. Molly's upper half had disappeared into the bin. She stood tippy toed on her pointy little shoes, her skirted backside sticking up into the air.

"Er, Molly?" Fiona approached her. "What are you doing?"

"They're throwing away these keyboards and they're brand new," replied a muffled voice from inside the bin. Molly stood up, clutching an armload of black computer keyboards, which she deposited on the ground. She pushed up her sleeves and dove back in.

Fiona hesitated; she thought she should help Molly instead of simply standing there, but there didn't seem to be room for two in there. Additionally, she had no desire to dig through rubbish.

"Got it!" Molly's muffled voice came from inside the bin. In the next moment, Molly held aloft a small cubic appliance.

"Look at this microwave," Molly said. "It's practically new. It'll be perfect for our little break table. You know, out on the landing, next to the ladies' room? Where we have the teakettle now? Okay, I think I'm ready to go."

"Do...you need any help?" Fiona asked.

"If you don't mind, could you grab the keyboards?"

Fiona scooped up the keyboards and followed Molly back to the car.

"Surely we can order these things," Fiona said as she tried to keep the keyboards from sliding out of their stack and dropping onto the ground. "Mahina State don't expect us to pick through other people's rubbish, do they?"

Molly turned and raised her eyebrows at Fiona.

"We cannot just order these things, believe it or not. Central admin's only released ten percent of our projected budget. There's zero money for office supplies. We have like twenty cents in our B budget right now."

As they approached the car, Molly shifted the microwave to balance it on her hip and fished her keys out of her purse.

"I probably shouldn't tell you this, but Dan Watanabe had to write a personal check to cover your last paycheck." Molly unlatched the boot and watched the massive blue lid swing up to reveal a cavernous storage area. It held a collapsible pram, a child's booster seat, a knapsack, and a pile of carrier bags. And it was mostly empty.

"Are you saying we're on our uppers?" Fiona asked.

"I don't know," Molly said. "What does that mean?"

"Insolvent? Broke?"

"Not any more than usual," Molly said. "I think it has more to do with your not having been added to the system yet. That's why they keep dumping construction junk in your office. Officially, your office is still unoccupied."

"But I've a key," Fiona objected. "Someone must realize I'm in there, surely."

"I know. I'm trying to get it straightened out, but Konishi Construction says it's a Facilities issue, and Facilities keeps telling me to talk to Konishi. Okay, here we are. Everything can go in the trunk. That's the wonderful thing about these old cars. Not great on gas mileage, but you could stash two or three bodies back here. Hey, speaking of construction junk, here's something to keep in mind. Some of the old fixtures in the building could be worth some money, and the Finance Club is going to help us out by selling them and taking a cut. When you have some free time, I can help you sort through the pile. Who knows, we might scrape enough together to actually send you to a conference or something. Yeah, now I'm saying it out loud, it kind of does sound like we're broke, doesn't it?"

"A bit."

Fiona could have refused the position at Mahina State. Emmett hadn't forced her to move out here. In fact, he'd warned her not to be too eager to accept the offer, to wait and think about it, to see what other opportunities presented themselves. Now she thought of it, he hadn't been very encouraging at all.

"Do you have children?" Fiona stacked the scavenged keyboards onto the pile of bags next to the collapsible pram. Molly gave the impression of being too scattered to be a mother. One imagined her dressing a baby in mismatched socks or misplacing it altogether.

"Just one child." Molly reached up with both hands and pushed the lid down until it locked into place with a thunk. "Francesca. She's seven months old. Although somehow with one kid and two adults, Donnie and I still feel outnumbered. Ready to go?"

Fiona looked around once more, as if Emmett might come bounding out to the car park to stop her leaving. Emmett, however, was nowhere in sight, so she reluctantly climbed into the passenger seat.

FIONA: NOT SNOOPING

FIONA HAD HOPED TO find Emmett at home when Molly dropped her off.

But the carport was empty. And as soon as Fiona stepped through the front door, she knew Emmett wasn't there. The interior of the house was gloomy. This was partly because of the overgrown foliage in the disused lot next door, and partly due to the low ceilings and stingy windows of the late-1980s kit home design.

Fiona realized with some annoyance that chasing after her errant husband had put her behind on marking papers. She sat down at her computer and logged into the plagiarism-checking program. She noticed two of the papers in the batch had been flagged as identical, which only worsened her mood. She assigned zeroes to the two plagiarists, hoping it wouldn't put her in the Student Retention Office's bad books.

The SRO had sent a broadcast email directing professors not to assign D or F marks as doing so "discouraged" students. Within minutes Dan Watanabe, the college's dean, had sent an email instructing the College of Commerce faculty to ignore the Student Retention Office and assign students the marks they'd earned. If anything, Dan wrote, the faculty should show a bit more "tough love" as the college's Friends in the Business Community had become concerned about grade inflation.

By the time she had finished marking, it was already dark outside. She wasn't accustomed to how quickly the sun set this close to the equator. She found she had no appetite, which was just as well, as she was stuck without a car and there wasn't much to eat in the house. Emmett never bothered to cook anything, and the few times Fiona had tried, he'd criticized her efforts. They'd defaulted to ordering out from Chang's Pizza Pagoda.

Fiona decided to order a pizza, just to give herself something to do. Perhaps by the time it arrived, she'd be hungry enough to eat it. If Emmett came home in the next hour or two, he would appreciate having something for dinner.

The login and credit card information for Chang's Pizza Pagoda was on Emmett's computer. He kept his computer locked, but she'd seen him type the password in, so it was a moment's work to get past the lock screen.

As soon as she entered the password, Emmett's email inbox filled the screen. Fiona clicked to open a new browser window, brought up the Chang's Pizza Pagoda website, and paused.

She wrestled with the urge to go back and check Emmett's inbox. She hated the idea of turning into the kind of wife who rummaged through her husband's emails.

But what if he was in some kind of trouble? He'd never been away from home this long without contacting her.

She decided finally she wouldn't rummage. Instead, she'd simply go back to Emmett's inbox and make a quick visual scan. If there was anything out of the ordinary, it should be obvious. She certainly wouldn't poke about in his private communications. That would be beyond the pale.

Thus justified, she selected vegetarian pizza and switched back to the in-box window.

At first, she saw nothing unusual. Most of the items appeared to be from the school secretary and were about things like parent visits and grade deadlines. There was one concerning Mr. Ferman. She already knew about poor old Mr. Ferman and his penchant for helping himself to the solvents from the chemistry classroom supply cabinet.

Fiona was about to close the window when an item at the bottom of the page caught her eye: RESERVATION CONFIRMATION.

She hesitated briefly and clicked. What would Emmett have a reservation for?

The email was a room confirmation for a Las Vegas hotel.

The dates spanned the St. Aelred School Christmas holiday.

And the reservation was for one adult: Mr. Emmett Spencer.

She leaned over and yanked the cord from the wall, counted to thirty, and plugged the computer back in again. That way, if Emmett thought anything was odd with his computer, he'd put it down to a power outage.

Fiona had forgotten to finish placing the order for the pizza. But it didn't matter. She wasn't hungry.

It was barely eight o'clock, but her papers were all marked, and she hadn't the mental energy to work on her research. It seemed pathetic to stay up to wait for Emmett.

She fell asleep quickly and slept heavily. Until the mobile phone on her nightstand rang.

FIONA: A MINOR MISDIRECTION

FIONA SNATCHED UP THE mobile eagerly. But it wasn't Emmett calling.

"Fiona," the caller said, "it's Maureen. Sorry to bother you. I hope you weren't asleep."

"No, of course not," Fiona lied, out of reflexive politeness. Why on earth was Emmett's secretary calling in the middle of the night? No, not the middle of the night. The time readout on Fiona's phone indicated it was only nine-twenty.

"Is Mr. Spencer there?" Maureen asked.

Fiona reached over to the other side of the bed. The covers were undisturbed.

"I'm afraid right now is not a good time, Maureen." Not an outright lie, but enough of a misdirection to throw Maureen off the scent.

"Aw, why you wen' answer the phone then?" Maureen chided, laughing. "Eh, sorry, ah? He missed a parent conference this afternoon, that's why, and they've been emailing to see when they can reschedule. I was hoping to get it straightened out tonight. No worries, I'll talk to Mr. Spencer tomorrow. We can get everything fixed up then."

Fiona disconnected the call, lay back, and stared up at the whirling blades of the ceiling fan.

It wasn't at all like Emmett to skip a work meeting without a good reason. Then again, Fiona wouldn't have thought it was like him to book a bachelor holiday in Las Vegas.

Fiona imagined Emmett's Las Vegas-bound plane plummeting into the Pacific Ocean in flames and billows of black smoke. The thought comforted her as she drifted back to sleep.

MOLLY: A VISIT FROM YOUNG BRYCE

AFTER I DROPPED FIONA off at her house, I drove back to the College of Commerce and lugged the microwave up the steps to the top floor. We already had a little break table set up on our landing, against the wall where the electrical outlet was. I plugged the microwave in, set the clock, and let myself into my office to recover. Emma is always on my case about not getting enough physical activity. I'd make sure to tell her I climbed four flights of stairs carrying a twenty-pound microwave, which should count as my weight-bearing exercise for the month.

I'd just started up my computer when I heard a knock on my office door.

It was Bryce Kahului, the student we'd just seen over at the St. Aelred School for Boys.

"Bryce. You got over here fast." I propped the door open (per the Rodge Cowper Rule). "Unless you have an identical twin. Would you like to come in?"

"Sorry Professor, I know it's not your office hours. An' you're probably ready to go home to your family." He took a seat in one of my visitor chairs. So he obviously wasn't that sorry.

"I'm not even close to going home," I said, which was true, now Bryce had parked himself in my office.

"Did you have another question about tomorrow's assignment?" I asked him.

"Oh, no, I already turned that one in. I stopped by because I wanted to say sorry for what I said about Mahina State. I could tell you were upset about it."

"Did you come all the way over here just to apologize?"

"It's okay, Professor. It's not that long of a drive. Honestly, it's a lot easier to find parking here than on the main campus."

"Well, I appreciate it. It was sweet of you to stop by, Bryce. Thank you."

"I think people stay away from here because of the baby's cry, too," he said.

"What baby's cry? We're not allowed to bring babies into the building."

"You never heard of the baby's cry?"

"No," I said. "I've heard of Constance Brigham's ghost throwing people off balconies. Wait, no, yes, I have heard of it. I think Serena said something about it. What's the story?"

"Back when this was a hospital, I don't know, in the nineteen twenties, I think? There was a man who worked on the plantation. He was married, but he got a girlfriend too. When his wife came hapai, he decided he didn't want to support her and their new baby. So when the wife had the baby, he set the nursery on fire."

"How horrible," I said. "I'm not sure I wanted to know that."

"The building was all wood, yeah? So it burned down real fast. But the nurses got all the babies out just in time."

"Oh, I'm glad," I said. "What about the man who set the fire?"

Bryce leaned his elbows on my desk and folded his hands.

"They say he was standing too close to the building and got killed when the roof collapsed. He was the only fatality."

"Ooh, karma," I said.

"Exactly." Bryce flashed his dimple-cheeked grin. "When you get bachi, you know, you did something bad? And you come close to where the old nursery was? If you hear the baby's cry you know something bad's gonna happen to you."

"Something bad? Like what?" Despite the heat, I realized I was rubbing my arms to smooth the goose bumps (or chicken skin, if you prefer the local expression).

"My mom's friend was driving up past the hospital one night with her aunty, and the aunty said, do you hear a baby crying? My mom's friend didn't hear anything. So the next day the aunty was on the roof fixing her gutter and she fell off and died."

"Oh no. Poor lady. Bryce, have you ever heard the baby's cry?"

Bryce shook his head.

"No, thank heavens. I know, chicken skin, yeah?"

"I was exactly thinking that, yes," I said. "Now I have something to think about when I'm here working late."

"You don't have to worry if you didn't do anything bad," Bryce said.

"Did your mom's friend's aunty do something bad?" I asked.

"Yeah, she was a good aunty, but she used to sell her pills. Anyway what were we talking about again? Me coming to Mahina State. You know what, whatever Mr. Spencer said about it, now I'm going here, it's actually not that terrible."

I was happy to be off the subject of the baby's cry. I'm not superstitious or anything, but you don't have to believe in something to be scared by it. After Emma convinced me to watch The Sixth Sense with her, I had to sleep with the lights on for a month.

"Now there's a slogan we can use for our ads," I said. "Mahina State. Actually not that terrible."

"I thought our slogan was 'Where Your Future Begins Tomorrow,'" he said.

"Yes. It is. Listen, for what it's worth, it was kind of a gut punch for me to hear what Mr. Spencer said about us, but no one's blaming you, Bryce. It's just Mahina State University does a lot for St. Aelred's. We serve on their board, we mentor their students in the science fair, we set up career days on their campus. I'm sure there's other stuff I'm not even thinking of. After all that, for him to turn around and badmouth us. Bryce, you know Mr. Spencer's wife, she teaches business ethics for us, did you know she earned her doctorate at Oxford?"

"For real?" Bryce's eyes widened. "Mr. Spencer never said anything about it."

"Doesn't surprise me. I understand he mastered out of his program, which is why he's Mr. Spencer and she's Dr. Spencer. Okay, well it is getting a little late, did you have any other..."

Bryce looked down at his folded hands.

"My boyfriend was supposed to come here with me, you know," he said. "To Mahina State."

"Oh." I had started to stand up, but I sat back down. "Where did he end up going?"

"He died."

I slid my tissue box over to his side of the desk. Maybe I should do something more than offer him a tissue. Should I whip out the Counseling Center's laminated information sheet and tell Bryce to scan the code with his phone? I think that's what they told us in our last training session. But it didn't seem appropriate right now.

"Do you think you might like to talk to someone?" I asked.

"I am," he said earnestly. "I'm talking to you right now."

"True. But I meant someone like a professional counselor. Our counseling center..." I remembered that our counseling center closed at noon now. It used to be open during regular business hours, but that was several rounds of budget cuts ago.

"Trevor was fearless," Bryce said. "He didn't care what anyone thought. One time he bought a new case for his phone. It was purple, all covered with glitter, and it said 'Princess' in silver writing. His dad was so mad when he saw it, he cut off Trevor's allowance."

"Over a phone case?" I said.

"Well, probably his grades had something to do with it too. Sorry, Professor." Bryce pulled out a tissue, looked up at the ceiling, and dabbed underneath his eyes. "I guess I'm not over it. Anyway, just wanted to come by to apologize for what I said about Mahina State. That's all. Sorry to take up your time."

"No, Bryce, it's no imposition at all, really..."

Bryce stood, grabbed a few more tissues, and walked out blowing his nose.

I locked up and started downstairs. Bryce was a likeable kid, but I wondered how credible he was with the story about the dead boyfriend. It all seemed like a little too much drama.

But I had my own drama to worry about. I had to pick up Francesca and I now had four minutes to get to daycare.

FIONA: STILL WAITING

ON FRIDAY MORNING, Fiona woke up to find the pillow next to her smooth and undented. Again. She went out to the kitchen, hoping she'd find Emmett sipping one of his twee little espresso drinks. But there was no sign of him there either, and the Nespresso machine was cold.

She opened the door to the carport. Emmett's Mini Cooper was still missing. There was only the congealed petrol splotch on the pavement.

Fiona didn't have time to wait for the sampan, and she didn't want to bother her neighbour again. Walking to campus (an hour, in the rain) would be impractical.

Molly Barda would have given her a lift, but Fiona was not inclined to call her and ask. It was bad enough her department head had seen the way Emmett had left her stranded the day before. If she called to ask for a ride now, it would be obvious Emmett was still missing, and worse, had stayed out all night without bothering to think of how his wife would get to work the next day. It would be too mortifying.

Besides, Molly had invited her to come along to some wretched garden club meeting tomorrow, and Fiona had agreed. All the more reason not to cadge a ride from her today. Fiona and Molly would be seeing quite enough of each other as it was.

Having no other options, Fiona made the call. Ten minutes later, Harriet Holmes' Triumph Bonneville roared up to her door.

Harriet was straddling the bike and puffing on her pipe when Fiona came outside.

"So he really has scarpered, has he?" Harriet asked as she handed Fiona a helmet. Harriet herself was bareheaded.

"I don't know." Fiona fastened on the helmet and climbed onto the back. Harriet held the motorbike steady with one hand and smoked her pipe with the other.

"Or only worked late and slept in his office again?"

Fiona bristled at the way Harriet emphasized the word "slept" as if it were a euphemism for something indecent. Fiona herself had noticed how spacious and private Emmett's office was. She wondered why he needed that new leather sofa, which was far nicer than any piece of furniture in their house.

"Maureen told me Emmett wasn't there at all yesterday afternoon," Fiona said. "He even missed a parent meeting."

Harriet took a long pull on her pipe and blew a perfectly formed smoke ring toward the grey sky.

"Missed a parent's meeting? My goodness. Even in Hawaii, I imagine one's still expected to show up to work occasionally."

"I wonder, what if something's happened to him?"

"Always looking for the silver lining, aren't you, darling?"

"That's a beastly thing to say, even for you. If anything happens to Emmett, I'll be stuck. Alone in the middle of the Pacific Ocean."

"Alone? Nonsense. I'm here."

"But it's only a visit, yes?" Fiona pleaded. "You're not here forever. Don't you have to be back before the start of Michaelmas term?"

"Unless I decide to take my retirement."

"Oh, it'll be ages before you retire, Mum," Fiona said hopefully.

"No, it won't. Oxford used to be like the Mafia. One only left feet-first. But they've just put in the Employer-Justified Whatsit Thingy now. Mandatory retirement at sixty."

"Surely not!"

"Sixty-something, I don't recall exactly. They'll be bunging me out soon enough, I can tell you that. It's legalized age discrimination, Fiona. They don't stand for it here, judging by some of the old fossils I see tottering around Mahina College."

"It's Mahina State University."

"I could retire, you know. Your father will be a free man within the year. Think how jolly it would be to have all three of us in Hawaii."

Fiona tried to rub her forehead, but her hand bumped against her helmet.

"I can't talk about this anymore. Please take me to my office."

Harriet paused and looked over her shoulder, her boot hovering above the kick starter.

"I'm awfully sorry, darling," Harriet said.

"Thank you, but there's no need for you, or anyone, to feel sorry for me. I should have known what I was in for when I married him. You tried to warn me, and I didn't listen. There. I said it. Ready to go?" Fiona pulled the visor of her helmet down.

"No, what I'm sorry about is it seems we can't leave just yet." Harriet stomped the kickstand into place, stuffed the smouldering pipe into a pocket, and climbed off the motorbike. Fiona lifted off her helmet and turned to see what Harriet was looking at.

Two policemen were walking up the drive.

FIONA: A VISIT WITH MAHINA'S FINEST

FIONA HOPED THEY HAD news about Emmett. Knowing where he was would be better than not knowing. Besides, she didn't wish Emmett ill, exactly, but his being incapacitated (or worse) would at least provide an excuse for his absence.

But the police hadn't come about Emmett, which was both a relief and a disappointment. Instead, they had questions about a Mr. Anatole Ferman, who taught science at the St. Aelred School for Boys.

"Why, what's he done?" Fiona asked.

"Ended up in the hospital is what," the younger policemen replied. "He's hurt pretty bad."

"The poor man," Harriet said pointedly. "What happened?"

"Hit by one bus yesterday," the older policeman said. "Driver said he stepped in front of it."

"Whatever for?" Harriet demanded.

"What in heaven's name is going on at that school?" Fiona added.

Fiona had expected to hear Mr. Ferman had suffered liver failure or alcohol poisoning. But not this.

"At this time, we don't know," the older policeman said. "We're looking into it. Is Emmett Spencer at home?"

Fiona and Harriet exchanged a glance.

"What does this have to do with Emmett?" Fiona asked.

"He's Mr. Ferman's employer, yeah?" the younger officer said.

"Ah yes, Emmett's the headmaster, isn't he?" Fiona felt like an idiot. "Yes, of course. I suppose he is Mr. Ferman's employer."

She wondered whether she should say anything about visiting the school and seeing Mr. Ferman stumbling and disoriented. She decided to keep mum. She didn't want to explain why she was at the school to begin with, searching for her missing husband.

"We haven't had any luck finding Mr. Ferman's family," the younger officer said.

"Did you call the secretary?" Fiona asked. "Maureen Dos Santos. She'd have the information."

"Already did," the older officer said. "She said Mr. Ferman's emergency contact is his ex-wife. He never updated it and the number's disconnected. She thought Mr. Spencer might have more information. She told us when she called here last night, your husband was at home. Can we talk to him?"

Fiona felt Harriet giving her a sharp look.

"Yes, of course," Fiona said quickly. "But he isn't here now. I'd expect he'd be at the school by this time."

Fiona knew better than to lie to the police. However, she had only said she expected her husband to be at work. She added, "I'll tell him to call you as soon as I talk to him."

"Car's gone," the older policeman said. The younger one nodded. Indeed, the carport was empty. This seemed to confirm for the police that Emmett wasn't hiding inside the house, at least.

The older officer handed Harriet his card.

"Officer De Silva," Harriet read. "We'll be in touch if we hear anything. Ta!"

Harriet and Fiona watched the officers head back down the drive.

"Was Emmett here last night?" Harriet asked as the police cruiser pulled away from the kerb and drove off. "I thought you said he hadn't come home."

Fiona shook her head.

"Maureen called and asked where he was. I couldn't very well tell her the truth, could I?"

"Why ever not?" Harriet asked.

"Maureen means well, but she's a frightful gossip. She'd be broadcasting it to everyone on the bloody island, wouldn't she? Don't look at me like that, Mother. It was only a little misdirection to save myself being humiliated."

"Fiona darling." Harriet fished the smouldering pipe from her pocket and puffed it back to life. "What if your husband truly has come to harm?"

"Don't be daft. I know it's easy to let one's imagination run wild, but nothing bad ever happens to Emmett."

"I hope you're right. Because if he has, your expedient little lie—excuse me, misdirection—is going to be a bit tricky to explain."

"Oh, I nearly forgot. I'll need to leave a note for Emmett to let him know I'm at campus."

"I see," Harriet said. "He'll show up when he pleases, and no questions asked."

Fiona went back into the house, leaving Harriet standing outside next to her motorbike, puffing thoughtfully on her pipe.

FIONA: BY THE RIVER'S EDGE

SATURDAY'S MEETING of the Pua Kala Garden Society, in the historic Brewster House on Russian Road, was exactly the kind of thing Fiona might have enjoyed under different circumstances. If she weren't preoccupied with the fact that her husband was still missing. For now, she'd have to keep her chin up and hope no one asked after Emmett.

Molly parked in front of a white house set back on a velvety lawn. Near the entrance was a lovely assortment of rosebushes blooming in shades ranging from pink to crimson. Sugar-pink roses dotted the trellis framing the front door.

As Fiona followed Molly down the back staircase, she heard bits of conversation floating up:

"She moved all the way out here for him, and it didn't stop him."

"If anything, he became more flagrant."

Fiona's stomach clenched.

"Well, she's better off without him."

Better off without him?

At the bottom of the staircase was the sheltered area underneath the house where the Pua Kala Garden Society met. Outside the shaded area, the sun blazed down on a garden of wild ginger, ti plants, and ferns that extended to the edge of the embankment. The roaring of the Hanakoa River below was louder here than it had been from the road.

The Pua Kala Garden Society members were seated in rattan chairs around a low coffee table. They stopped chatting and looked up when Fiona and Molly walked in.

Fiona recognized the impertinent Emma Nakamura, the agreeable Iker Legazpi, and Emmett's secretary Maureen Dos Santos.

"Fiona, come sit." Maureen waved and pulled out the chair next to her.

Fiona got on well with Maureen, although they had little in common. Maureen was a bit older and hadn't travelled much except to "go Vegas" each year. But Maureen had an easy laugh, and a way of making Fiona feel like an old friend, not like the boss's wife.

Ordinarily, Fiona would have been glad to see Maureen. But not today. She worried Maureen might ask after Emmett and wasn't sure what to say if she did.

The only person at the meeting Fiona didn't recognize was an elegant woman with upswept white hair and a floor-length caftan. This turned out to be Mrs. Masterman, their hostess.

I suppose I should do my best to be agreeable, Fiona thought as she took her seat next to Maureen. If Emmett's really done a runner, I may need to make some new friends.

MOLLY: BACK TO THE PUA KALA GARDEN SOCIETY

I PARKED OUTSIDE THE Brewster House and let the Thunderbird idle. I knew I had to get out of the car and go inside. Only I didn't want to.

Just push through it, I told myself. It'll be over in an hour.

I hadn't come to the Pua Kala Garden Society meeting to have fun or learn about flowers. I was doing my job. Specifically, I was here for the benefit of Fiona Spencer, who was currently sulking in the passenger seat.

Dan had reminded me once again that if we lost Fiona Spencer, the College of Commerce wouldn't be authorized for another full-time hire until sometime after the sun cooled. And it would be my fault.

"Just make her happy," Dan had urged me. "Maybe you can take her to that gardening club you and Iker belong to. English people like gardening, don't they?"

"Just" make Fiona Spencer happy? Good one, Dan.

If King Eurystheus had truly wanted to stump Hercules, he wouldn't have bothered with trifling tasks like slaying hydras and cleaning stables. No, he would have challenged Hercules to coax Fiona Spencer out of her perpetual snit. I doubted it was something even a demigod could pull off, let alone a socially inept department chair.

You might assume, because I'm friends with Emma Nakamura, that I can get along with anyone. But truly, Emma's not so bad. I mean, sure, we get on each other's nerves sometimes, but at least you know where you stand with Emma. If you invite her somewhere and she doesn't want to go, she'll tell you straight out, with some swear words added in to make sure there's no misunderstanding. She won't give you a hunted look and an affectless "yes, of course" as if she were being ushered up the steps of the guillotine.

I realized Fiona was already halfway up the walkway to the Brewster House, so I quickly locked up and followed her. The front door was unlocked. I slipped my shoes off and went in first. Fiona left hers on, which I didn't realize until I heard her behind me, clacking across Mrs. Masterman's polished eucalyptus floor in her hard leather-soled flats. I didn't say anything to her about the shoes. Mrs. Masterman could scold her about it if she wanted.

As we stepped into the shaded area under the house, the conversation stopped. I wondered at first whether they were talking about me. It was my first time attending a Garden Society meeting in a while. But to my relief I wasn't the topic of conversation at all; it turned out they were only gossiping about Nicole Nixon from the English department, or rather, her faithless ex-husband. Nicole wouldn't have minded at all. His caddish antics had inspired her recently-published memoir, which was enjoying some success in the literary world.

Iker Legazpi, the only man in our group, stood and greeted us with a neat bow. Emma was there, along with Mrs. Masterman and a dark-haired woman I didn't recognize. She wore a muddy-colored muumuu that flattered neither her complexion nor her figure, but she had a friendly smile. She and Fiona seemed to know each other, which I was relieved to see.

Mrs. Masterman made everyone introduce themselves, and I learned the woman's name was Maureen.

"Mrs. Masterman," Iker said, "I must say how fortunate we are that you have returned to Mahina."

"Yeah, what happened with that?" Emma asked. "We thought you was gonna stay in Honolulu, ah?"

Mrs. Masterman smiled and settled into her chair.

"The Brewster House has such a unique location. It has the great good fortune of being in both a high-risk lava zone and a tsunami zone. Well, no self-respecting mortgage lender would touch it. I had to finance the sale myself." She paused and gave us a Mona Lisa smile. "It seems the buyers had gambled their fortune on some kind of currency scheme—call me old-fashioned but I must admit, I never did quite understand it—and unfortunately, they missed a few payments. So as the mortgage-holder, I took possession of the property. I really had no choice."

"So you got your house back," Emma said, "plus you got the down payment an' whatever they paid before their investment thing wen' all kapakahi. Smart, you."

"I was simply lucky." Mrs. Masterman moved the cookie plate aside and lifted a blighted-looking orchid onto the glass-topped coffee table. "And fortunately the couple were not condemned to penury. They simply had to move to one of their other properties, I believe on Kauai. Well. I'm delighted to be back in Mahina, with my beloved garden and all of you wonderful Garden Society members. Oh, before we get started. This was found in the guest bathroom a few meetings ago and I keep forgetting to ask."

Mrs. Masterman put on her reading glasses, pulled out a crumpled piece of paper and smoothed it out on the coffee table. It was a regular letter-sized sheet, with a few typed words on it.

"Three thousand by Thursday or I tell," she read.

"It seems to be an extortion," Iker said.

"Quite so," Mrs. Masterman agreed. "If this was directed at anyone in this room, I am willing to do whatever I can to help you."

She lowered her reading glasses and looked around the room, but no one appeared to recognize the note.

"You may contact me privately if you wish." Mrs. Masterman put her glasses back on. "I have no patience whatsoever with blackmailers. If a deed truly needs to be exposed, why, do the right thing and expose it! Otherwise mind your own business. Now, who can tell me what's wrong with this poor little girl?"

Mrs. Masterman stroked a leaf of the plant.

"Cymbidium Mosaic Virus," Fiona said.

"Why, you're exactly right," Mrs. Masterman exclaimed, delighted.

For a while, it seemed things were going well. Fiona joined in the ensuing discussion of necrotic lesions and chlorotic rings. Now and then it almost seemed she was enjoying herself.

As we were wrapping up the meeting and getting ready to go, Mrs. Masterman invited Fiona to join her for dinner the following weekend, and to bring her husband.

I was a little envious; Mrs. Masterman had never invited Donnie and me to dine with her. But I was happy to see how quickly Fiona Spencer was getting herself "integrated into the community." I would have to tell Dan the good news.

"You're ever so kind to ask," Fiona replied, "but Emmett's still out of town. I'll be sure to ask him about it when he gets back."

Maureen, the woman who knew Fiona, said,

"But he was at home last night when I called, yeah?"

"Well, I thought I'd heard him come in," Fiona stammered, "but it seems I was mistaken. He called this morning and said he was delayed."

Maureen looked like she was about to say something but changed her mind and started gathering her things.

"Tell him to let me know as soon as he's back, yeah?" Maureen said, "so I can reschedule the parents' meeting. They're asking about him, you know."

"Yes, of course." Fiona stood up and slung her purse over her shoulder, avoiding eye contact.

Fiona's obvious discomfort made me feel uneasy. I wandered over to the side table, where Iker Legazpi was refilling his tea. It was warm for November, but Iker Legazpi was wearing his usual long-sleeved shirt and tie.

"How are things at St. Aelred School?" I asked him.

"Very well, thank you," Iker said.

"One of my students stopped by the other day and told me something about St. Aelred's. Bryce Kahului."

"He is an alumnus of St. Aelred," Iker said. "Mr. Kahului is perhaps not a top scholar, but he is kind and has a good character."

"He said he had a close friend at the school who was also going to come to Mahina State with him, but he passed away? The friend did, I mean. Do you know anything about it?"

"It was a very sorrowful thing," Iker said. "A student died by his own hand."

"Oh no. I'm so sorry to hear it."

"A boy of eighteen," Iker said. "It would be a tragedy in any event, of course, but in this case, there is the added complication. He is the son of Maureen and Apostol dos Santos."

Iker nodded in the direction of the newest club member, who was disappearing up the stairs.

"That Maureen?" I whispered. "She's married to Apostol Dos Santos? The Apostol Dos Santos?"

"Yes. You have heard of her husband, of course."

"Sure. He's on our Board of Trustees."

"Yes. He also serves on the Police Commission, the St. Aelred School Board, the Chambers of Commerce, and the Mayor's Advisory Board. He is a civic-minded and influential man."

"You know, I don't think I would recognize him.

"It is unsurprising. Despite his elevated profile, or perhaps because of it, he does not like to have his photograph taken."

"I hear dos Santos is someone you don't want as an enemy," I said.

"That is also my understanding," Iker sipped his iced tea. "It is said, you do not want to cross The Rancher."

"Why do they call him The Rancher?" I picked up a marble-sized tea cake from the cookie platter and popped it into my mouth. Delicious. I took another one.

"Perhaps he owns a ranch," Iker said. "But I am only speculating."

"The Rancher? What a missed opportunity. His name is Apostol Dos Santos. An apostle and two saints. He should definitely be called The Saint."

Iker looked at me quizzically.

"No?"

"But he is called The Rancher," Iker said.

I picked up a little square cocktail napkin and dabbed the powdered sugar from the corners of my mouth.

"Okay, fine. If you don't mind my asking, what happened, exactly? With the son?"

"It is said Trevor Dos Santos was a volatile and troubled young man."

"And?" I prodded.

"It seems the younger Mr. Dos Santos found a loaded firearm in the headmaster's desk and fatally shot himself."

"The headmaster meaning Fiona's husband?" I whispered.

Iker nodded.

"Fiona's husband left a loaded gun lying around in an unlocked desk?" I looked around but no one was close enough to listen. Mrs. Masterman was clearing away the tea things, and Fiona was on her phone. "Are you saying a student—Dos Santos's son, no less—got into the office and found a loaded gun? That's... I mean, I'm not a lawyer, but that sounds like criminal negligence or something, doesn't it? How does he still have a job there?"

"The weapon was purchased as a defense against what we call our helicopter parents," Iker said. "It is something of a paradox. The duller and more indolent the son, the more zealous and aggressive are the boy's mother and father. They cajole; they bribe; when those things do not work, they resort to threats. Mr. Spencer feared them."

"He should have bought a Taser or something," I said. "At least that's not designed to kill people."

"It was a tragic error in judgement, yes. One he very much regrets now, of course. There was talk of lawsuits and firing. Mr. Spencer is fortunate to have kept his employment."

"Wow. Poor Maureen. At least she doesn't seem to be holding it against Fiona."

"Indeed," Iker said. "It was Maureen Dos Santos who found the boy."

"No! Where?"

"In Emmett Spencer's private office. He took his last breath in front of the headmaster's desk. The very desk that held the loaded weapon."

I glanced over at Fiona, who was standing just outside with her back to us. She wasn't taking in the view of the Hanakoa River gorge. She was hunched over and looked like she was typing something on her phone.

"Why was Maureen in the headmaster's office?"

"It is her place of work. She is the secretary to the headmaster."

"Ohhh. Right. I see. That's how she knows Fiona. How horrible for her."

"So you see, Molly, it is incumbent upon us to show kindness to our colleague."

"You're talking about Fiona? I am kind to her. I'm super kind. I brought her to the meeting today. I've been driving her everywhere."

"These events, I am certain, have caused her much unhappiness and uncertainty."

"If anything, I think people should try to be nice to Maureen," I said. "She's the one who lost her son to suicide."

"Of course. We must take every opportunity to show kindness."

"I guess," I said, "Well, thank you for filling me in on the background, Iker. It explains a lot. You're right. I really should try to be nicer to Fiona Spencer. I mean, I'm already as nice as I can be in my actions, but in my mind, I've been maybe not so charitable."

Iker gave me a solemn nod.

"You will never regret showing kindness," he said.

Demonstrably untrue, I thought. But I guess it sounds nice.

FIONA: A GOOD DEED

IT WAS A PLEASANT SURPRISE to see Maureen at the garden society meeting, Fiona mused as she followed Molly back out to the car. Bit of a shock to see that Emma woman again.

Although things turned out alright in the end. Emma didn't harass anyone, Iker from accounting was lovely, and Mrs. Masterman gave her a little potted orchid as a welcome gift.

In fact, the meeting had gone rather well overall, certainly better than Fiona had expected. The blackmail note business was entertaining, reminiscent of one of those murder mystery parties. Mrs. Masterman had obviously concocted it for the amusement of her guests, but she was quite an actress and Fiona found herself nearly believing the note was real.

Things did go a bit pear-shaped when Mrs. Masterman invited Fiona and her husband to dinner. But it wasn't unusual for one's husband to be traveling, was it? Surely Mrs. Masterman didn't suspect anything was amiss.

Molly stopped at the front door to put her shoes back on.

"Sorry," Molly said when she straightened back up, "were you going to say something?"

"Ah. I suppose I was wondering, were we expected to remove our shoes?" Fiona asked.

"A lot of people do here. I've just gotten into the habit. Okay, ready to run?"

It was starting to rain. Molly sprinted back out to the car and held open the passenger door for Fiona. Fiona hurried into the car as quickly as she could manage.

"So, what did you think?" Molly asked as she climbed into the driver's seat.

"It was lovely, thanks." Fiona buckled the seatbelt.

"Was Maureen the same person you were asking about at the school? St. Aelred?" Molly asked.

"Yes. She's the headmaster's secretary."

"Ah. I figured a parent's meeting had something to do with school business, and how many Maureens could they have working there? Well, that works out then. I hope you were able to talk to her about whatever it was. Unless you managed to get a hold of her in the meantime...I mean, I'm not trying to pry or anything..."

Molly trailed off and concentrated on starting the car. It was an elaborate dance of ignition key and accelerator that seemed to require all her attention.

Fiona thought of a way to steer the conversation away from Emmett.

"Poor Maureen," Fiona said. "She's been marvellous, really. Considering all she's been through."

"I heard her son committed suicide?" Molly said as she twisted the key and tapped the pedal.

"Yes. You heard?"

"Hard to keep a secret in Mahina," Molly said. "I can't even imagine. Poor woman."

The engine finally engaged, and Molly pulled away from the kerb. They drove in silence down Russian Road, past expansive lawns and well-preserved houses.

"I think you really impressed Mrs. Masterman," Molly said, finally. "How do you know so much about orchid viruses?"

"A magician doesn't give away her secrets. That's the saying, isn't it?"

"I mean, not to imply that somehow you shouldn't know about orchid viruses," Molly said, "but I would've bet money Emma was the only person in the room besides Mrs. Masterman who could diagnose a sick plant on sight. What was the name of the virus again? Something like ceramic?"

Fiona let out a little snort of laughter. Molly glanced over, startled.

"I don't remember the name of it at all," she said.

"Really? So how did you come up with it then?"

"Emma Nakamura brought it up on her phone. She held it under the glass table for me to read. I should probably tell Mrs. Masterman. I do hope she won't be cross."

"Mrs. Masterman? No, I think she'd appreciate the effort."

Molly braked, causing the car's front end to plunge dangerously. She hand-over-handed the steering wheel to the right, making a wide arc uphill, onto the narrow road that led to the hospital. "Sorry, I just remembered something. Do you mind if we stop at Broadmoor? It'll just take a minute."

"I'm sorry, Broadmoor?" Fiona asked.

"That's what we've been calling our new building."

"Have we?"

"Well, not officially," Molly explained, "I think it was Pat Flanagan who started it, before he left, and it's kind of caught on. Pat taught English here at Mahina State, but he got a better offer in Honolulu, so he's there now."

"Broadmoor's a psychiatric hospital in Berkshire," Fiona said.

"Exactly," Molly said. "That's why we...you know, because our building used to be an inebriates' asylum. I mean of course you'd get the reference, you're from there. Not Broadmoor, I mean, you're from England. But you already know that."

Molly cleared her throat and focused on the road.

"I guess it's not really that funny," she said.

Fiona did not, in fact, find it funny. It was the sort of joke her mother might make.

"We're stopping by the office, then," Fiona said.

"Just for a second. You can wait in the car if you want, I'll just run up and I'll take you home right afterwards."

"I'll come with you," Fiona said, "I have loads of papers to mark and I've just remembered I left a stack of them in my office."

"Oh, that works out," Molly said. "Speaking of your office, any progress on getting the construction junk moved out?"

"No."

"What? Dang it."

"It might be my imagination, but it looks to me like the pile's getting bigger."

Molly sighed.

"I'm so sorry about that. Okay. When we go to campus I'll log in and submit another work order. They're not going to see it until Monday, but at least you'll be first in line." Molly slowed and guided the car around a narrow turn. "Boy, every time I drive up here, I'm amazed this is our one road to the hospital. Can you imagine trying to get an ambulance up here? If we ever have any kind of mass emergency we're done for."

"Do you mean the new hospital's up this road?" Fiona asked. "I assumed the signs were for the old hospital. Where our offices are."

Fiona remembered Mr. Ferman, the science teacher, was in hospital.

"Yup, the Mahina Medical Center's just about half a mile up the road," Molly said. "You've never been? Ever since we had the baby it seems like we're there every week. Tell you what, I can drive by so you can see where it is. I've just been through all the prenatal tests and birthing classes and everything, so go ahead and ask me anything you want to know."

Did Molly think Fiona had a baby on the way? No chance of that, she thought bitterly.

"It's nothing to do with babies," Fiona said. "Do you remember Mr. Ferman, the science teacher at the St. Aelred School?"

"The older gentleman? He seemed not to be feeling well? Yes, I do. Is he okay?"

"Ah. Well, he's in hospital, actually, and he doesn't have family. I thought I might look in on him."

"We can go now," Molly said. "And stop in the office on the way back down. Then we don't have to leave our stuff in the car."

A moment later, Molly turned into the hospital car park.

"Here we are," Molly said. "Totally normal hospital. Not haunted at all, unlike where our offices are."

Molly was right. The Mahina Medical Centre was modern and perfectly unmemorable.

"I suppose I should have brought a card," Fiona said to Molly as they headed to the main entrance. She realized she was holding the orchid Mrs. Masterman had given her. Perhaps Mr. Ferman needed it more than she did.

"I'm sure you can find a nice card in the gift shop," Molly said. "Would you like me to come in with you to see him? Do you think he'd appreciate an extra visitor? If not, I can wait in the lobby."

"It's best you come with me," Fiona said, "otherwise I may never find my way back. My sense of direction is pants, as my husband never fails to remind me."

Fiona was glad Molly was offering to join her in her visit to Mr. Ferman. She had no idea what she would say to him. She barely knew his Christian name. Was it Anthony? Anton? Anatole, that was it. She only ever called him Mr. Ferman.

But as she followed Molly into the tiny gift shop, Fiona wondered whether this visit was as pure an act of charity as she had originally thought. She had to admit to herself that her motives might not be entirely selfless. Mr. Ferman, after all, might know where Emmett was.

MOLLY: NOT EAVESDROPPING

FIONA SPENCER AND I ended up making an unplanned detour to the Mahina Medical Center, locally known as the "new" hospital. It was just up the road from the "old" hospital where our offices were. It seems Mr. Ferman, the elderly science teacher at St. Aelred's, was there and she wanted to visit him. I don't know where this sudden compassion of hers came from. The last time the topic of Mr. Ferman came up, Fiona had sniffily dismissed him as an old alcoholic who raided the supply cabinet for solvents to drink.

I wondered how well she even knew him. She didn't seem to know his first name. In the gift shop, she bought the first get-well card she grabbed off the rack, something with a cartoon dog with an ice bag on his head and a plaid blanket across his lap.

Maybe the fact he was in the hospital had made her realize he wasn't going to be around forever. Who knows? I was probably better off not trying to explain or predict Fiona's moods.

At least I was helping to brighten Mr. Ferman's day. Or so I hoped.

We hadn't planned our appointment ahead of time, so we were outside of regular visiting hours, but a sympathetic nurse led us to Mr. Ferman's room anyway. She told us we were the first visitors he'd had, aside from the police.

"If he's resting, let him be," the nurse advised as we stopped outside his door. "But if he's awake I think he'll be happy to see you. And he'll appreciate the flowers. So pretty, the color."

I realized Fiona was holding the potted plant Mrs. Masterman had given her. It was a pale-pink orchid, with three perfect blooms. Pink foil covered the small pot.

"Mrs. Masterman told me to keep it or give it so someone who needed it more than I did," she said, a little defensively. The nurse looked at me as if my opinion were somehow important.

"That's very kind," I said. "I think Mrs. Masterman would approve. In fact, I know she would."

"You don't think the flowers are a bit garish?" Fiona asked us.

"I think Nature is allowed to be garish," I said. "Things like orchids and sunsets should be colorful. I mean, who wants a tasteful rainbow, right? What would that even look like?"

"I agree," the nurse said. "If it was me in the hospital, I'd appreciate someone bringing me flowers. No one else got him anything, you know."

She turned and left us to cheer up Mr. Ferman.

Mr. Ferman had one arm in a sling resting atop the brown hospital blanket. A number of tubes and wires connected him to beeping machines. A crumpled IV bag hung on a pole. His thick white hair was pressed crooked by the pillow.

His eyelids fluttered, and he turned his head toward us.

"Ah, Mrs. Spencer," he rasped. "Do my eyes deceive me, or did you bring me flowers?"

"Hullo, Mr. Ferman." Fiona set the pot down on the small rolling table next to the headboard. "Yes, this is for you. Isn't it lovely? It's an orchid. I've no idea what kind."

"It's a moth orchid," I added. I'm no flower expert, but I have picked up a few scraps of information from the Pua Kala Flower Society meetings.

"And who's this delightful young lady?" Mr. Ferman tried to raise his head from the pillow. The effort was unsuccessful, and he sank back.

I introduced myself. He grasped my hand with his free hand. His skin felt dry and papery.

"How did you know I was here, Mrs. Spencer? I haven't told anyone."

"The police came round to my house to tell me about your accident." Fiona's tone was mostly stern but had a touch of compassion. "My goodness, you have been in the wars, haven't you? What on earth happened?"

"It seems I made a miscalculation," he said matter-of-factly. "Not a wise thing to do, where moving buses are concerned. It seems I'm lucky to be here and not downstairs in the morgue. That's what they tell me. Might've been better that way, come to think of it."

"I'll wait outside," I said. It sounded like the conversation was about to get personal and having a nosy stranger (me) lurking around wouldn't be comfortable for anyone. "It's very nice to meet you, Mr. Ferman. I hope you feel better soon."

I suppose I should have kept going down the hallway to give them some privacy. But I paused when I heard Fiona exclaim,

"Mr. Ferman, what in heaven's name is going on at the school?"

"My dear, as much as I'd like to lay the blame on anyone but myself—"

"First the boy Trevor, now you?" She retorted. "Who's next?"

I folded my arms and leaned against the wall, trying my best to look like I was relaxing and not eavesdropping.

"Oh, my dear. You are asking me for a rational explanation of things. I'm afraid I have no answers. Only many questions of my own. I can't remember a thing, you see. No, that's not quite right. I should say what I can remember makes no sense at all."

"It seems bad things are happening to people at St. Aelred's, Mr. Ferman. And now Emmett's gone."

Gone! That explained the odd exchange between Fiona and Maureen. Maureen had said the headmaster had missed an important parents' meeting, but Fiona had brushed it off as if it were normal for her husband to disappear without warning.

"Gone. Yes, he is, isn't he," Mr. Ferman wheezed. "Emmett Spencer, as you say, is gone. I remember now. Mrs. Spencer, you're making me nervous standing there like that."

The voices lowered, and I strained to hear what was going on.

"It's only that I'm worried about him," Fiona said, at a perfectly audible volume.

"Oh no, worry doesn't help, Mrs. Spencer. It won't change a thing."

"How can I not worry? A student kills himself, my husband's missing, now you've gone and stepped in front of a motor coach."

"I assure you, it wasn't on purpose. All I can recall is...no, not even that."

"It's quite a coincidence, though, you must agree," Fiona said.

"The boy's suicide isn't exactly a mystery," Mr. Ferman said. "It's the same old newsreel. I've seen it play through many times. A fellow's worried his son's not manly enough, not interested in girls, that kind of thing. But for some reason dear old dad thinks the answer is to stick the boy into an all-male boarding school. Don't know what the thinking is exactly. It'd be like me trying to get sober by moving into Hagiwara's Specialty Liquors. I mean, I'd enjoy myself, don't get me wrong, but it wouldn't change—"

"Yes, I get your point, Mr. Ferman," Fiona interrupted. "You're saying there is no connection among the events at St. Aelred. The circumstances of the boy's suicide had nothing to do with your accident, and neither has anything to do with my husband's disappearance. Have you any idea at all where he is?"

I strained to hear Mr. Ferman's answer. Just to be on the safe side, I had my e-reader out. If anyone asked, I wasn't listening in on a patient's private conversation. I was just hanging out in a hospital hallway catching up on my favorite mystery series.

"I am terribly sorry for any unpleasantness between you and Emmett, Mr. Ferman," Fiona said. "He's only done what he feels is best for the school. But that's all in the past, and everyone's moved on, and we..." and again, Fiona's voice became too quiet for me to hear what she was saying.

They kept talking, but at such a low volume that for all I knew they could have been muttering nonsense syllables at each other.

The conversation stopped and I heard a chair scraping on the floor. Fiona was getting up. I jumped away from the wall, sped down the hallway to a bench underneath a window, and feigned great interest in whatever was on the page of my e-reader. That's where Fiona Spencer found me waiting.

"Ready to go?" I dropped my e-reader into my purse and stood up, my face a mask of innocence. Or so I hoped. I also hoped Fiona hadn't noticed I'd been holding the device upside-down.

"Yes. All done." Fiona seemed impatient and unhappy. In other words, things were back to normal.

"That was nice of you to pay Mr. Ferman a visit," I said as we started down the hallway. "I'm sure he appreciated it."

We walked in silence back out to the parking lot. Fiona seemed like she wanted to say something. Finally, when we were getting into the car, Fiona said,

"Molly, would you mind terribly if we went back to St. Aelred?"

"Right now?" I asked. "Didn't you want to stop by the office—"

"Yes. But I do want to go round to the school first. I'm sorry. I'll pay for petrol. And I understand if it's all too inconvenient."

"It's no problem at all," I pulled out of the hospital lot and onto the road. I wondered what Fiona was trying to find out. "The main office?"

"The parsonage, actually," Fiona said.

"There's a parsonage?"

"Originally they had a minister serve as the school's headmaster. The headmaster's quarters are still referred to as the parsonage."

"Oh. But you're not living there? Even though your husband is the headmaster?"

"There was severe termite damage so it's under repair. I do hope I'm not putting you out."

"No, not at all. It's not far."

It actually was kind of far, but I felt bad for Fiona. If my husband and car were missing (I assumed the car had disappeared along with the husband, which was why she was having me drive her around), I'd want someone to help me out. Also, I was curious. What had Mr. Ferman said to make Fiona decide to rush back to St. Aelred's? What did she think she'd find there?

FIONA: THE LAST PLACE YOU LOOK

THE VISIT TO THE PARSONAGE site turned out to be an utter waste of time.

There had been no sign of Emmett at the site. Fiona and Molly had found only a wooden work bench, a pile of lumber with a wet tarp draped over it, and a few nails scattered on the concrete pad.

Mr. Ferman had told Fiona he had seen Emmett at the parsonage when he was out walking. But he didn't remember what day of the week it had been. Even at his best, Mr. Ferman tended to ramble. A fellow teacher had quipped that Mr. Ferman's brain had been "programmed with too many go-tos," which Fiona thought was a spot-on way to describe the man's meandering conversational style. Emmett (who, unlike Fiona, had never taken a course in History of Computing) didn't understand the reference and had refused to find it amusing.

The drive back up to the College of Commerce building was quiet. Fiona was too embarrassed to make conversation. She had just made her department head drive her all over Christendom. Molly probably thought Fiona was off her trolley.

And for all that, Emmett was still missing.

"Here we are," Molly said, pulling Fiona out of her thoughts. "I'm going to park next to the building. No one's around to hand out parking tickets on Saturday."

Molly followed the unpaved drive that wound around the back of the hospital building and pulled up underneath the terrace, alongside the old delivery bay. It was boarded over with mildew-speckled plywood. Molly locked up the car and the women followed a short footpath through the jungle down to the former Inebriates' Asylum.

The interior of the building was even warmer than outdoors.

"Can't wait till they get the A/C working," Molly said, bounding up the steps ahead of Fiona. "I don't know how people could stand working here before they had air conditioning. I guess they used to be able to open up that big skylight. Somewhere along the line they nailed it shut, I'm not sure why."

Fiona trudged behind, feeling utterly drained. How did the woman have so much energy? *How*, she thought resentfully, *did the woman have so much energy? Weren't new mums supposed to be exhausted?*

Or maybe it was Fiona who was unusually tired. Fiona had barely slept since Emmett walked out.

As they reached the top floor, Fiona caught a whiff of something savoury. She realized she was not only knackered; she was famished.

I should have eaten Mrs. Masterman's biscuits when I had a chance, she realized. I can't remember the last time I ate, come to think of it.

"Is someone cooking?" Fiona asked.

Molly's nose twitched.

"I don't smell anything unusual. But I might be coming down with a cold, so don't go by me."

The women went to unlock their respective offices. As the door of Room 310 swung open, the meaty odour intensified. Fiona felt her stomach rumble.

"The savoury smell's coming from my office," Fiona called out, and Molly hurried over.

"Your 'rubbish heap' looks like it's gotten bigger," Molly said as she came through the door. "Is that a toilet?"

"It seems to be," Fiona said. A chipped, soap-green toilet teetered atop the scraps of blackened lumber and mildew-speckled plasterboard.

"Fiona, I'm so sorry." Molly sounded sincere. "I keep sending in work orders to Facilities telling them Room 310 has an occupant, and they tell me I need to talk to Konishi Construction. But every time I try to talk to Konishi, they tell me they can't do anything because they only take their orders from Facilities. All I can do is keep sending in work orders."

Molly stuck her nose into the air and sniffed.

"Oh, I do smell it now. It smells good, kind of like bacon. Did you leave food in your trash can?"

Fiona didn't think so, but she went over to check the bin to make sure.

"It's empty," she said. "There's no food in there."

Molly tilted her head. "Do you hear a buzzing noise?"

The sound was coming from somewhere within the pile of construction debris. Molly and Fiona worked together to lift the toilet onto the ground (it was surprisingly heavy). They moved aside the rubbish until they made a small clearing. There they found the source of the sizzling sound: an electrical outlet with an old cord plugged into it. The wire to the plug was covered with woven fabric, black with white dots. It snaked back into the rubbish heap.

Molly yanked the plug out of the wall, yelped, shook her hand, and blew on it.

"Ow. What do you have plugged in back here?" she asked Fiona.

"Nothing."

They looked at each other.

"I've never gone back here," Fiona insisted. "I only use the front of the office, where the desk is."

"Okay, let's find out what's on the other end." Molly followed the cord, hand over hand, while Fiona moved things out of the way. They finally slid a ragged slab of fibreboard aside to reveal a great rust-speckled metal box balanced on a metal-and-wooden frame. It looked a bit like a breadbox, but it was much bigger, longer than Fiona was tall. It was radiating heat.

"The fever cabinet!" Molly exclaimed.

"The what?" Fiona asked.

"It was here all along. It's hot. Who plugged it in?"

"I'm sorry?" Fiona frowned at the contraption. "You know what this is then?"

"It's kind of a mechanical antibiotic, before they had actual antibiotics. On that end? If we cleared away the rest of that junk, you'd be able to see that there's a hole where the patient's head would stick out. They'd use a fan to blow air on their face to keep them comfortable."

"Fascinating," Fiona said. "So, it's not just rubbish cluttering up my office, it's historically significant rubbish. How do you know so much about it?"

"My friend Pat Flanagan, who I guess I mentioned, did a story about the old hospital for his news blog before he moved to Honolulu," Molly said. "I should send you a link to the article. Anyway, this is exactly the kind of thing our dean wanted us to keep an eye out for. Selling it off could keep us in whiteboard markers and toner cartridges for a year. Fiona, did you lend anyone your office key?"

"No," Fiona said.

"Okay. I'm going to have to call security, then. Someone's been in here plugging things in without your permission."

"Do you think it might've been the builders?" Fiona asked. "They've got keys."

"I did overhear one of the construction guys on the phone talking to someone about lending them a key. It might have been to this office. All the more reason to get security involved. They shouldn't be using your office as a dump, and they definitely shouldn't be going around creating fire hazards. What if we hadn't happened to come in today? This whole building could've burned down."

Molly punched in a number on her mobile and walked out to the landing, where the signal was stronger.

Later, Fiona couldn't remember whether she had been driven by hunger, curiosity, or a combination of the two. But the bacon smell continued to tantalize her, and it was coming from the metal box. Fiona guessed it was one of the builders heating up his dinner, in which case it would serve him out if Fiona found his meal and ate it first.

Fiona pushed aside a cobwebby slab of ragged plasterboard to reveal a black lever on the side of the contraption. She touched it. It was warm but insulated, so not intolerably hot. She pushed more decisively. When nothing budged, she rocked the lever back and forth. She finally moved it enough to crack the massive lid open about an inch.

Molly was still outside the door, with her back turned. Fiona pushed the lid up all the way.

And saw the source of the bacon odour.

She shoved the lid back down with both hands, barely noticing how the hot metal seared her palms.

Molly appeared out of nowhere and pulled Fiona upright. She led Fiona over to her desk and eased her into her office chair.

"Security's on their way," Molly's voice said, from somewhere in space. Fiona rested her head on her arms, like a child taking a nap at her desk. She wanted to stay as she was, eyes closed, while the room spun around her.

"Here," Molly said. "Drink some water."

Fiona lifted her head, took the mug Molly was offering her, and drank.

"Chicken Boy?" Fiona asked feebly, reading from the mug.

"You mean my coffee cup. It's a store in L.A. There's a giant chicken statue...I'll tell you about it some other time. Fiona, what happened? You were completely out. You know, you're right. It really does smell like someone was cooking in here."

MOLLY: THINK OF A HEDGEHOG. WITH A BONNET.

THE SECURITY GUARD was a round young man with an easygoing demeanor. It took me a couple of seconds to recognize him, out of context as he was.

"Micah?" I exclaimed. "I didn't know you worked here. Well, it's nice to see a familiar face."

Micah had been my student years earlier. He hadn't been particularly studious, but he was always cheerful and eager to help out.

"You okay, Professor?"

"Me, or her?" I asked. Fiona was at her desk, her head resting on her arms. I had pulled up a chair next to her, close enough to catch her in case she keeled over again. "Actually, neither of us is having a terrific day."

"Either of you hurt?" He picked up my wrist and felt for a pulse.

"Not physically, no."

I had made the mistake of looking inside the fever cabinet. Now I was trying to fill my mind with cute, pleasant things. Hedgehogs. Capybaras. Alice Mongoose and Alistair Rat having tea, with a capybara and a hedgehog as guests. I imagined the capybara with a Panama hat and the hedgehog wearing a bonnet.

Micah released my wrist and sniffed the air.

"Someone cooking in here? Smells ono."

Fiona raised her head from her folded arms to look at Micah. She had gone so green she practically matched the floor tiles.

"I'm fine, thanks," she replied robotically, and set her head back down. "Never been better."

"She's not fine," I countered. "She fainted."

"I got a report of unauthorized entry in three-ten." Micah stepped out of the office, checked the number to verify he was in the right room, and came back in. "Whose office is this?"

"This is Fiona Spencer's office," I said. "We haven't gotten her a permanent name plate yet. Micah, I'm the one who called you. Someone came in here, plugged in the fever cabinet, and left it on. It's a fire hazard."

"Mind if I take a look around? Can't find any obvious sign of forced entry." Micah ran his hand up and down the door frame, presumably checking for splintered wood. "Kalua pig, that's what I'm smelling. Smells good, you know. Not too much liquid smoke. That's a rookie mistake, ah? Too much smoke flavor. Pig's not supposed to taste like it died in a fire."

Fiona whimpered softly.

"Micah," I said, "please go look over there in the fever cabinet."

Having thus reminded myself of what I'd seen there, I was overcome by a wave of nausea. I bent over and let my head hang between my knees. I still felt queasy, only with more pressure behind my eyeballs.

"The what? Professor? You okay?"

"Big metal box," I said. "Hot. Be careful."

I heard Micah forging into the rubble to investigate. I heard the lid of the fever cabinet creak open. Something clattered onto the tile floor.

"Okay. I gotta call this in." Micah's voice was shaking. I took three slow, deep breaths and sat back up. Fiona was still slumped over her desk, and Micah was gone.

I heard his voice coming from out on the landing.

"Ambulance? Nah, no need," he said. "Six foot, six foot one maybe, brown hair. White boxer shorts. No jewelry or nothing. Kinda hard to tell. Haole, I think. Yeah, yeah. Nah. Yeah, fo'real. Like one huli huli chicken. Okay, hang on, ah?"

I was getting better at understanding Pidgin. I knew huli huli chicken was chicken cooked on a grill.

Micah came back into Fiona's office. She must have heard him, because she managed to push herself up to a sitting position.

"Anyone know who he is?" Micah asked.

"No idea," I said.

"I know who he is," Fiona said.

"What?" I said. "You do?"

"His name is Emmett Spencer," Fiona leaned her forehead on her hands. "He's my husband."

FIONA: WHOSE ASSISTANT (PROFESSOR) ARE YOU?

FIONA WAS FEELING A little better by the time the police showed up. Fiona, Molly, and the security guard had moved over to Molly's office. The security guard explained that Fiona's office was now a crime scene, and she might not be allowed back inside for a bit.

Fiona wasn't feeling well enough to move again and it wouldn't do to kick Molly out of her own office, so when the policemen came to interview Fiona, they dragged in extra chairs for themselves. Micah stayed as well, which made five people crowded into Molly's little office. At least Molly had a big window that opened to let in fresh air.

At first, Fiona thought all the policemen in Mahina must look alike. But she realized she had seen them before when they came round to her house to ask about Mr. Ferman.

"Just to confirm, you are Fiona Spencer?" Officer De Silva (the older one) asked Fiona. She nodded and he wrote something in a little notebook.

"The deceased was your husband, correct?"

"Yes."

"His occupation?"

"He was headmaster at St. Aelred School for boys."

The younger officer automatically crossed himself. He must have been a student there, Fiona thought.

"Your occupation?"

"Assistant professor of Business Ethics," Fiona said.

"And who do you assist?"

"It's just a job title," Molly cut in. "An assistant professor's not actually someone's assistant."

De Silva grunted and wrote.

"And what were you doing in room three ten?" he asked.

"It's my office, isn't it?" Fiona said.

De Silva's pencil paused in mid-scribble.

"That's your office?"

"It is," Molly said. "We don't have the name plate yet. But it is definitely Dr. Spencer's office."

"You're a doctor?" the younger policeman asked Fiona, wide-eyed.

"Okay, sorry I gotta ask this," De Silva said, "but do you know anyone who might have wanted to harm your husband?"

Mr. Ferman, whom Emmett had disciplined for stealing the ethanol from the supply cabinet in the chemistry classroom. The friends and loved ones of the departed Trevor Dos Santos (except perhaps for his mother Maureen, who seemed incapable of holding a grudge). To say nothing of that faction of St. Aelred trustees who had tried, unsuccessfully, to sack Emmett and replace him with their own candidate.

"Mrs. Spencer, I know this is difficult," De Silva persisted. "Can you think of anyone at all?"

And me, of course, Fiona thought. I wanted him dead.

"Mrs. Spencer?"

"Absolutely not," Fiona declared. "Everybody loved Emmett."

"Was he having problems with anyone at work?" De Silva asked.

"Remember Trevor Dos Santos?" the younger policeman said. "Killed himself in the headmaster's office. Wit' the headmaster's gun he left loaded. We could start looking there."

"Can I get anyone something to drink?" Molly asked. "Tea? Coffee?"

"No thanks," the policemen replied automatically.

"I like coffee," the security guard said.

"You know," Molly said. "I'd like some coffee too." She bounced up from the yoga ball she used as an office chair. The ball reminded Fiona of Rover from *The Prisoner*, the cult television series from the sixties. Emmett had seen every episode of *The Prisoner* several times and had made Fiona watch it with him. Fiona wondered whether Emmett really enjoyed the programme, or whether it only ticked a box on his Anglophile checklist.

Molly popped back into the office.

"Fiona, can I get you a cup of coffee?"

Fiona hesitated. She would have preferred tea. A cuppa would be lovely right now. But she didn't want to ask, and in any case, she didn't trust Molly to make it properly.

"I'll just fix you a cup," Molly said. "You don't have to drink it."

When Molly had gone, Officer De Silva said,

"You're familiar with the circumstances of Trevor Dos Santos's death." A statement, not a question.

"Yes," Fiona said. "He was a student at the St. Aelred School for Boys. He took his own life. It was tragic. We felt for his family, Emmett and I."

"People thought your husband was responsible." Another statement.

"Not the people who knew him well," Fiona said. "Maureen, for example. The boy's mother. She's Emmett's secretary. She's been quite supportive."

De Silva wrote in his notebook for what seemed like a long time.

"Anyone else you'd say knows your husband well?" De Silva asked.

"I suppose there's Bryce, the boy who works in the headmaster's office," Fiona said. "I expect it will be easy to find his last name. I don't happen to know it. Mostly he assists Maureen, I think. I don't believe he works directly with Emmett. Worked, I should say."

Fiona's sensitive nose twitched. But no one else seemed to notice the acrid odour.

"Anyone else you can think of who was a friend or acquaintance of your husband?" Officer De Silva asked. "Besides the secretary and the secretary's assistant?"

"There's Mr. Ferman," Fiona said. "The chemistry teacher."

"Can you tell me how to spell his name?"

Fiona stared at De Silva.

"You lot came round to my house to ask me about him. Don't you remember?"

De Silva frowned.

"Remember?" said the younger policeman. "She was at the house with Harriet Holmes. When we went to ask about Anatole Ferman after he wen' walk in front of a bus."

"Oh yeah," De Silva said. "Sorry, Mrs. Spencer, I didn't remember you at first. How was Mr. Ferman's relationship with your husband?"

"Our relationship with Mr. Ferman was perfectly cordial," Fiona said. "Dr. Barda and I went to visit him in hospital."

Molly came back into the office and set three steaming mugs on her desk.

"Who, Mr. Ferman?" Molly asked. "Yes, that's right. There's no coffee, sorry. I made tea. I tried heating up some cold brew in the microwave, but as soon as I turned it on there was a weird smell. At least the kettle works. Oh, you'll have to drink your tea plain. There's no sugar or milk unfortunately."

Fiona picked up a mug and sipped the unsweetened tea. It was bitter and made her teeth feel gritty, but it was hot, and certainly better than nothing. She was just starting to feel a bit better when Officer De Silva asked,

"Not counting today, when's the last time you saw your husband?"

MOLLY: THERE'S THE PRICE, AND THERE'S THE COST.

I OFFERED TO MAKE COFFEE while the police were questioning Fiona. I'd like to say it was because I'm generous and nurturing. In fact I was desperate to get out of my office and walk off some nervous energy. Why did I have to go and look inside the fever cabinet? What was wrong with me? It was as if I'd learned nothing from my high school Driver's Ed class, which I almost failed because I always passed out during those car accident movies.

I popped three mugs of cold brew coffee into the microwave. But after a few seconds, the whole landing started to smell like overheated brake pads. I stopped the microwave, took the coffee cups out, and sniffed around for the source of the stench. At first, I couldn't figure out what was wrong, because the microwave oven's interior looked clean and new. But when I lifted out the glass platform, I found a tiny, stinky lump of plastic.

This must be why the microwave had been in the e-waste pile at the St. Aelred School. Someone must have put a non-microwave-safe dish in there and melted it. How nice for St. Aelred's that they could afford to throw away practically-new appliances. I've been sitting on a fifteen-dollar yoga ball for years because we don't have a budget for faculty office furniture, and it was all I could afford out of pocket.

But I had a more pressing problem right now. I'd just ruined the last of the organic cold-brew coffee I had on hand. There were a few tea bags on the break table. The electric kettle wasn't where it was supposed to be, but I found it in the men's room. (Hanson Harrison brings it in there to fill it with water. Enter Larry Schneider, they get into a heated discussion about something or other, and Hanson forgets about his tea.)

When I came back into my office, Fiona was still answering questions. She seemed to be holding up pretty well.

Until Officer De Silva asked her,

"When's the last time you saw your husband?"

Fiona stared at De Silva as if he'd just accused her of committing the murder herself.

I considered leaving my office again to give her some privacy, but I would have had to get up and walk around everyone to get to the door, which would have been even more awkward.

"Did you and your husband have an argument?" De Silva persisted.

Fiona began to cry.

"Can she do this later, Officer?" I heard myself ask De Silva. I felt like a bit of a buttinsky, but what was I supposed to do? Fiona was bawling now, her thin shoulders heaving under her print floral dress. I couldn't let her get grilled like this, not after what she'd just gone through.

Fortunately, De Silva relented. I expected he might. Andy De Silva has carried a torch for Donnie's sister since they were all in high school. Even though she's married and living in California, and Donnie barely ever speaks to her, Andy De Silva seems to think of me as a connection to his crush.

De Silva said he wanted to talk to Micah anyway. This made Micah immensely happy, as he'd been waiting this whole time for his turn.

The younger policeman (I never did get his name) went into Fiona's office to get her purse, so she wouldn't have to go back in herself. I texted Donnie I was going to give Fiona a ride back to her house, and I'd be home soon.

Everything okay? Donnie texted back.

Not really, I replied.

Should I get Francesca?

Thank you. Yes. Will explain when home.

I carried Fiona's purse and my own as we walked down the stairs. I was glad she didn't suggest taking the elevator. I like to tell people I take the stairs to stay fit. In fact, the old elevator terrifies me, and I always imagine myself getting stuck in it and dying of thirst and heat stroke before anyone finds me.

"Fiona," I said, "I'm so sorry, I can't even imagine. If you need to take some time, we can arrange to cover your classes. We have bereavement—"

"No," she cut me off. "I'll teach my classes as usual. It's the best thing, really. I don't want to sit at home thinking about it."

"I understand," I said.

As we were about to get into the car, I realized I was still holding the plastic glob I'd pried out of the microwave. I dropped it into my bag. It could be like a lucky charm, except in this case it would serve as a reminder not to be such a cheapskate next time.

We were on the road, driving, before Fiona spoke again.

"I suppose I should have told him about the row Emmett and I had," she said. "About his holiday plans."

"I think you handled it well," I said. "You're not supposed to volunteer extra information, from what I understand."

"I suppose I'm free to make my own holiday plans now," she said.

I can't invite her to spend Christmas with me, I thought, panicked. My parents will be here.

My mother—was it something about being an Ob-Gyn, where once you bring a few lives into the world, you start to think you're omnipotent and everyone needs to hear your advice about everything? Or was it just her? And then there was my father, who despite having the best intentions, managed to be even more mortifying, if that were possible. I was still trying to live down the memory of my mother treating Donnie to an unsolicited lecture about sperm count. She'd then interrogated him about his choice of underwear.

"If you want to conceive, you gotta let your boys breathe," my father had chimed in helpfully.

I would have squeezed my eyes shut to banish the memory, if I hadn't been driving.

"I thought Emmett would be pleasantly surprised when I arrived early to Mahina," Fiona was saying.

Fiona's position had an official January start date, but somehow Dan worked a deal where we were able to get her here and start paying her a semester early. Some details—like her office —still hadn't been worked out. But Dan was afraid if we didn't give her the start date she requested, she might not come at all.

"He wasn't happy to see you?" I asked.

"No. It seemed my presence here was an intrusion."

"I'm sorry," I said, because what else can you say?

A swarm of bikers passed us, roaring into the oncoming lane just as the road took a turn and narrowed. I eased up on the gas pedal. We were driving through an older residential subdivision that had no sidewalks or bike lanes, only deep, narrow drainage channels between the asphalt and the front lawns. One moment of inattention and we'd be sideways with two wheels spinning in the air. The road was wet, and I hoped that neither we nor the bikers would run into a ditch.

"Fiona, I am so sorry," I said again. I had to steer the car and the conversation at the same time, and I wasn't doing a very good job at either one. It didn't help that my hands were still shaking. I slowed down even more to scale the first of a series of ridiculously tall speed bumps. The residents of this neighborhood had some pull with county services, apparently.

"Emmett had made me believe he was looking forward to my moving out here," Fiona said. "But when I showed up, he seemed cross. He doesn't like surprises, Emmett doesn't. I thought he'd come around. But he never did."

This was more personal revelation in thirty seconds than she'd done since the start of the semester. I wondered whether her sudden chattiness was a symptom of shock.

"He'd already planned his Christmas holiday without me," she went on. "He made it quite clear I wasn't welcome to join him, and that my arrival in Mahina had been a massive inconvenience for him. He told me I was being irrational for wanting to spend Christmas with him. It seems his definition of 'rational' means catering to his feelings and ignoring one's own."

I pulled up to the curb outside of Fiona's house to see the scruffy bikers that had passed us earlier, blocking her driveway. Most of them were grizzled, bearded men in leather vests. The one non-bearded biker, shorter and paler than the rest, but no less imposing for all that, strode toward Fiona's side of the car.

The woman gave the impression of being sturdy, although her shapeless jacket revealed little about her figure. I didn't realize where I had seen her before until she lifted a pipe to her mouth and took a puff.

I kept the engine idling and gripped the wheel tighter.

"Fiona," I said, trying my best to sound calm. "Would you like to go back to campus?"

The Thunderbird didn't have great acceleration, and I was pointed uphill. We wouldn't be able to outrun a pack of Harleys. On the other hand, the car was sturdy enough that with the doors locked and the windows up we would be safe inside, unless they started shooting at us.

"No, I'll be fine." Fiona opened the door. "My mum's here."

"Your mum?"

"You'll forgive me for skipping introductions. She'll talk your ear off if she has the chance."

"Are you sure? Because I can..."

But Fiona was already out of the car.

MOLLY: BRIGHAM & BREWSTER

ON THE WAY HOME I HAD a sudden impulse to stop at the Mahina Mall. There wasn't anything I needed to buy, but it had been an eventful day, to put it mildly. Our uncrowded little shopping center seemed like an ideal decompression chamber.

I pulled in and parked in the lot right outside the one-story Brigham & Brewster store that anchors the mall. Brigham & Brewster started as a dry-goods store in the mid-nineteenth century and is now a Mahina institution. It's where Mahina's merchant class buys their upscale aloha shirts, their sake sets, and their teenagers' prom outfits. Online stores haven't made a dent in Brigham's business. (People usually call it "Brigham's" for short. Calling it "B&B" is an outsider's faux pas, like referring to San Francisco as "Frisco" instead of "The City".)

As soon as I pushed open the glass door and stepped inside, I felt my blood pressure drop.

Brigham's silky pomander scent and perfectly tuned climate control were balm to my panicky, hyperventilating soul. I ambled over to the Shiseido counter and perused the selection of lipsticks. I strolled through the housewares department, admiring the stainless-steel cookware and the hand-painted Japanese bowls. It was pleasant to see what was on offer, even though between us, Donnie and I had more than twice the kitchen things we needed.

I was passing the lingerie counter (another look-don't-buy mission, as I still had a lifetime supply of bras I'd bought on sale at Galimba's Bargain Boyz) when I spotted Maureen Dos Santos. I was going to scurry past without saying anything, but she saw me and said hello.

So I had to stop and chat.

I'd only seen her that morning at the Pua Kala Garden Society meeting. But a lot had happened since then. Most notably, her boss turning up dead in Fiona Spencer's office. I assumed it wasn't yet common knowledge, and I certainly wasn't going to be the one to tell her about it.

"Maureen, hi," I said. "Wow, that's lovely. Is it silk?"

"Yeah, I'm returning it," Maureen said as the salesgirl scanned the price tag. "Wasn't really right for me."

The garment in question was a slip of heavy ivory-colored silk, with a wide lace border at the hem.

"I'm glad you brought Fiona to the Flower Society meeting today," Maureen said. "She needs to get more involved in the community, you know. Emmett's got so many other obligations as headmaster, she can't depend on him for her social life."

"No, she can't," I said. "You're absolutely right about that."

"I'm in the same boat. Apostol's so busy all the time. At least I get a nice allowance, I can go shopping whenever I'm in the mood."

The idea of getting an allowance from one's husband seemed horrifyingly retrograde to me. But I smiled and said, "have you started your Christmas shopping?"

Hawaii is ethnically and religiously diverse, but locals aren't offended when you assume they celebrate Christmas. Christian or not, everyone pretty much does.

"Not even Thanksgiving yet," Maureen laughed.

"Not too soon to think about it," the salesgirl said. "We get the decorations up already."

She was right. In the center of the lingerie department loomed a white flocked Christmas tree festooned with white ornaments and twinkling lights.

"I probably should be starting my Christmas shopping," I said. "But I had kind of a stressful day at work today, so I'm just here for some quick retail therapy."

The salesgirl hung Maureen's return up on a rack behind the counter. The slip was impractical but pretty, and it crossed my mind that I might like to buy myself something like it.

Then she opened the cash register drawer.

"Here's your refund, Mrs. Dos Santos," she said, and counted out three hundred and twenty-nine dollars and change, which Maureen quickly tucked into her purse.

I didn't need to buy a slip. When would I ever wear a slip?

"Aw, you had to work on Saturday?" Maureen clucked. "What, after the Flower Society

meeting? Poor thing. Know what, you ever try Brigham's chocolates? Over in the gift department, by housewares. Get the big box."

"I think I will," I said. "That's a great—"

The chorus of "Another One Bites the Dust" blasted from Maureen's purse. She pulled out
her phone and frowned at the screen.

"Mahina police department?" she said. "Funny. Why would the police be calling me?"

"No idea," I said. "I sure don't know. Why would I know? Probably a wrong number.
Anyway, thanks for the recommendation about the chocolate. I'll go check it out."

I speed-walked to the nearest exit and sprinted to my car.

That was enough relaxing at the mall, I thought as I peeled out of the parking lot. It was time to
go home and have a nice, normal evening with my family. I'd cuddle the baby on my lap and
give her a bottle. Donnie and I would have a glass of Sangiovese, or maybe a cool Pinot Grigio.
Donnie would tell me about his day at the Drive-Inn, and I would tell him about attending the
Pua Kala Flower Society meeting, visiting nice old Mr. Ferman in the hospital, and finding
Emmett Spencer's body in Fiona's office.

I did not expect to find Emma Nakamura at my house.

"She's here, Donnie!" I heard her yell as soon as I came in from the garage. From the back of
the house I heard the wail of a newly-wakened baby. I unslung my bag and hung it on its hook.
When I turned back around Emma was standing in front of me.

"Geez Emma, give me some warning!" I clutched my chest.

"Too stressed-out, you." Emma followed me out to the living room, where I plunked down
on the sofa. "You should be more like your husband. Home early from work to spend time with
the baby. It's called work-life balance. It's getting dark already. Where you been this whole
time?"

"Shopping," I whispered. "It's kind of a long story actually."

"No need whisper," Emma said breezily. "Baby's awake."

Donnie emerged from the hallway, carrying Francesca over his shoulder and marching with
the bouncy gait he used to calm her down. Her head was drooping, her chubby cheek squashed
on his shoulder.

"So? How's everyone?" I asked. "Emma, are you drinking already?"

Emma looked at the wine glass in her hand.

"Guess so."

"We're glad you're safe." Donnie came over, kissed the top of my head, and settled down
with the baby in one of the armchairs. "What happened?"

"How did you hear about it?" I asked.

"From me," Emma said. "I was driving up the old hospital road and I saw your car in the
parking lot and a bunch of fire and ambulance and stuff too. I tried to drive in but there was a
cop car blocking the way. So I came over to your house to find out what was going on. Donnie
was here so I decided to wait."

"There hasn't been anything on the news," Donnie said.

"So what happened?" Emma asked.

"Where to begin? How about I start with the good news? Emma, I found the fever cabinet."

FIONA: EMMETT'S GOOD WHISKEY

"DOES FATHER KNOW YOU'RE hanging about with the Hell's Angels?" Fiona whispered to her mother as the men shuffled into her house.

"They're not Hell's Angels, and yes, of course he knows," Harriet retorted.

"How does he know, Mum? Did you tell him?"

"Well, he shouldn't be surprised in any case."

"Why are they all taking their boots off?"

"Everyone takes off their shoes indoors," Harriet replied. "It's the Oriental influence. Loads of Japanese about, hadn't you noticed?"

"You're the expert now, are you?" Fiona grumbled, annoyed because her mother was right. Fiona had dropped a right clanger at the Garden Society leaving her shoes on.

The men were crowded into the available seats in the living room, so Fiona dragged in two of the white stacking chairs from the carport. She disliked the stacking chairs—one could never get them completely clean, for starters—but they were coming in handy just now. Besides, they weren't much worse than the orange-yellow living room suite Emmett had picked up at the liquidation sale of the Hanohano Hotel.

"Well, then." Fiona scanned the room and noted, to her dismay, that her mother was squeezed in between the arm of the couch and a man who looked like Genghis Khan. "Ehm. Anyone for tea?"

"Don't worry, darling, you don't have to be mother," Harriet said. "We've only dropped by to express our condolences. Then we'll be on our way."

The first man stood, approached Fiona, and clasped her in a bear hug so tight she noticed his beard smelt of coconut oil. He released her and stepped aside. The next man stepped up and gripped her hand briefly.

"Sorry, ah?" he said.

One by one, each man expressed sympathy in his own way. Finally, Harriet herself approached and placed her hands on her daughter's shoulders.

"Hard luck, darling," she said. She turned and herded the men out the front door.

A roar of un-muffled engines crescendoed, then faded as the bikers drove off.

Fiona walked into the kitchen, pulled out a teacup, and poured herself a generous portion of Emmett's good whiskey, something she had never done while Emmett was alive. Not that he forbade her outright. But he made her feel she lacked the expertise to truly appreciate it. That it was wasted on her, and she may as well drink something cheaper.

Fiona took her brimming teacup back into the living room to find her mother there, in the act of lighting her pipe.

"Mother!"

Harriet jumped.

"Ah, there you are, darling. Wasn't it lovely of the fellows to stop in and wish you well?"

Fiona clutched her teacup of whiskey and sank into the closest chair.

"Mum, you can't smoke in here."

Harriet pocketed the pipe and headed to the kitchen.

"Mind if I help myself to whatever you're having? 'Tea,' is it?"

"Bottom shelf, next to the fridge." Fiona called after her. "Have as much as you like."

Harriet came back out with a glass in her hand and got comfortable on the couch.

"You'll have to forgive me for asking," Harriet said as she took a sip, "but you're quite sure it was Emmett you found?"

Fiona nodded miserably and stared into the amber depths of her teacup.

"I can't imagine who could have done this to him," she said.

"Well, I can," Harriet countered. "He'd made a lot of enemies, hadn't he?"

"Not every passing thought needs to be spoken aloud. How did you know about it? It hasn't been in the news yet, has it?"

Harriet set down her glass.

"Not that I know of. It's a bit tricky to explain how I came to find out."

"I'm sure it is," Fiona replied. "And while I don't wish to appear ungrateful for the outpouring of sympathy from the horde of men you invited into my house and who now know where I live, what on earth possessed you to tell them about Emmett's death in the first place? They certainly were no friends of his."

Although, as she said it, Fiona realized she didn't know who Emmett's friends had been. She certainly had no idea whom he had intended to meet in Las Vegas.

"You've got it backwards, darling," Harriet countered. "I didn't tell anyone. It was Clyde who heard about it first from the police. He told me. Marvellous coincidence, don't you think?"

"Clyde? Who on earth is Clyde?"

"He was sitting next to me. He reminds me a bit of your father, in a way."

Fiona stared at her mother.

"Reminds you of Father? You don't mean the man with the plaited beard and the leather waistcoat?"

"Handsome man, don't you think?" Harriet replied.

"And how did he happen to know about Emmett?"

"It's rather a long story." Harriet took a sip and set her glass down on the side table. "Perhaps I'd better start from the beginning. Now, let me think."

"Take your time." Fiona gulped her whiskey and started to cough.

"You okay?" Harriet asked.

"Never better," Fiona gasped. Fiona was not much of a drinker and didn't see the appeal now. Her throat was burning, and she felt lightheaded. But she wanted to prove Emmett wrong about her not appreciating whiskey. "Now tell me, how did you find out about Emmett's death?"

"It seems one of the policemen who came to the scene had attended St. Aelred School. When he realized the body belonged to the headmaster at his alma mater, he rang up his wife to tell her."

"I wouldn't think they'd be allowed to do that if there's been a murder," Fiona said. "Seems a bit sloppy."

Fiona considered mentioning that the policemen who showed up at the murder scene were the same ones who had come round asking after Mr. Ferman but decided against it. She didn't want to derail the conversation.

"He told her the room smelt of kalua pig," Harriet continued. "That's the one they cook underground. Have you tried kalua pig? It's lovely, rather like a smoked gammon."

"You do realize the 'smoked gammon' was my husband," Fiona said.

"Yes, they found him in a sort of great roasting pan thingy, didn't they?"

"Yes." Fiona swirled her teacup and took another gulp of whiskey. "It was the first thing I noticed. A meaty sort of odour in my office."

"Your office?" Harriet exclaimed. "That's where he was?"

Fiona nodded.

"What on earth was he thinking getting murdered in your office? How horrid of him. Now you're getting me all distracted, darling. Let me think. What happened then?"

"The policeman's wife," Fiona said.

"Ah yes. The policeman's wife told her mother, who manages Mahina Printing and Stationers."

"Mahina Printing and Stationers? Why does that sound familiar? Is it where you told me you'd seen Emmett?"

"Quite. Lovely little shop. You didn't seem at all interested when I tried to tell you about it before."

Fiona slumped in her chair and took another slug of whiskey.

"I don't want to hear what happened in the shop. I want to know why everyone in Mahina seems to know Emmett was murdered."

FIONA: WORD GETS AROUND

HARRIET RETRIEVED THE bottle of Macallan from the kitchen, refilled Fiona's teacup, and topped off her own glass.

"Let me start again, darling, shall I? The policeman told his wife about finding the headmaster of the boys' school dead. Yeah? Then the wife told her mother, who manages the stationer's. The mother remembered seeing Emmett in the shop. And me as well. Then the mother told the daughter about our little contretemps—"

"Ah," Fiona said. "You're already infamous in Mahina, are you?"

"Do let me finish, darling. The mother told the daughter she'd seen Emmett in the shop, and the daughter told her husband, the policeman. The police went round to the stationer's, and that's how they found me."

"You were at the stationer's again?" Talking with her mother often made Fiona feel like she was trying to read a book that had random pages torn out.

"Not today. No, I haven't been back."

"How did they find you then?" Fiona asked. "You really must be infamous, mustn't you?"

"Oh, no one knows me. But I was with Clyde, you see, and it seems Clyde knows everyone in Mahina."

"You were with Clyde? Plaited-beard Clyde? You never said you were with Clyde."

"How am I supposed to remember every little detail if you keep interrupting me, darling? It seems the policeman's mother-in-law recalled the woman who was with Clyde Hamamoto—that's me, you see—had had words with the headmaster, so—"

"I'm almost afraid to ask, what sort of words exactly?"

"I gave Emmett a right bollocking, of course. Would you expect anything less?"

"Did you threaten him? Please tell me you didn't threaten him."

"Not a bit of it. All I did was tell him I had divorce papers all drawn up and ready, and there was a handsome incentive for him if he'd sign. I was improvising, of course, but he had no idea—"

"Mother!"

"Now don't 'Mother' me, darling, I was only trying to help. Anyone could see he was making you miserable. And I do see how it's all gotten a bit messy now, but how was I to know he was going to go and get himself murdered?"

Fiona closed her eyes.

"And did he accept your offer?" she asked quietly. "No, don't tell me. I don't want to know. Please allow me to cling to the conviction that my dead husband loved me."

"I haven't the faintest idea what he thought of my offer," Harriet said. "I was escorted from the premises before I could get an answer. They have some sort of plainclothes house detective there, did you know? I suppose to stop people nicking pens. Poor Clyde, I certainly didn't want to drag him into it."

"You shouldn't have brought him along, then."

"I don't suppose it would have made any difference. Clyde is my landlord."

"You're living with him?"

"Now don't look at me like that, it's not what you're thinking. He owns the Hanakoa Falls Bed and Breakfast. That's where the police found me."

Fiona shook her head and poured herself more whiskey.

"I don't believe there's any such place. I think you're making it up."

"Look it up if you like. Four and a half to five stars on all the travel sites. I've got a room with a private bath, balcony that looks out over the river, the view's brilliant. The police asked a few questions and told us what happened. Clyde already knew Emmett was my daughter's husband, because I'd had to explain to him what happened at the stationer's, you see. He insisted on getting the fellows together to come round and pay their respects. So here we are."

"I should like to ask something," Fiona said.

"Anything, darling."

"What if Emmett had come to see you? To accept your hastily improvised and poorly-thought-through offer of payment in exchange for divorcing me? Would you have gone through with it? Paid him, I mean?"

Harriet thought for a moment and shook her head.

"No. If he had come to see me? Much simpler to bung him over the balcony. The Hanakoa River's deadly. It would've swallowed him up without a trace. Not that I couldn't afford to pay him off, but why should he be rewarded for...you look a bit peaky, darling. Stay right here. I'll get you a paracetamol and a glass of water."

"It's in the medicine cabinet," Fiona called after her mother. "It's called acetaminophen here. No one in America's heard of paracetamol."

MOLLY: THE BABY'S CRY

BY SUNDAY MORNING, Saturday's gruesome discovery seemed very far away. My queasiness had faded, as had my determination to be a vegetarian for the rest of my life. I took Francesca to Mass and stopped by Donnie's Drive-Inn to pick up some lunch and see Donnie. (Sunday is the Drive-Inn's busiest day.) I had just gotten home and unloaded Francesca and all the baby paraphernalia when I remembered I had Student Retention Office paperwork due Monday. And I'd left the forms in my office.

So I buckled Francesca back into the car seat and headed to the College of Commerce. I felt a little strange going back into the building after what had happened yesterday. But Campus Security had sent out an announcement this morning, assuring us there was no danger to the Mahina State University community, but to be on the safe side, they were stepping up security at the old hospital complex.

My only problem was going to be keeping Francesca out of sight.

Right after we moved to the new building, one of the marketing professors brought his non-housebroken twins into work and let them run loose while he met with his students. The adorable tots managed to steal their father's cigarette lighter and set the hallway bulletin board ablaze. Fortunately, Serena, the dean's secretary, got there quickly with the fire extinguisher. But from then on, children were banned from the College of Commerce building.

Once inside my office I locked the door behind us. Then, balancing the baby on one hip, I pressed a slightly-worn spot on the koa-paneled wall and entered my secret room. It smelled like old leather with a whiff of mildew. I plunked Francesca into the portable playpen I'd set up and switched on my battery-powered desk lamp to supplement the natural light.

When Pat Flanagan, my reporter friend in Honolulu, was researching the old hospital, I asked him to find out what the hidden room was for. He thinks my office, together with the adjoining room, was the personal workspace of Constance Brigham, heiress to the Brigham fortune. Miss Brigham was from one of those old Hawaiian dynasties that sprang from the son of a missionary marrying the daughter of a chief. Constance herself devoted her life to temperance and charity, and the Inebriates' Asylum had been her life's work.

Whether Miss Brigham used the secret room to court donors, rendezvous with lovers, or simply relax with a glass of something otherwise not permitted on the premises, was unknown. For me, the room had been perfect as a private space to pump breast milk. Now Francesca was mostly weaned, I'd found it was a good place to do paperwork. My computer wasn't there to distract me, and with the panel closed, no one could barge in and interrupt me.

A breeze ruffled the stack of forms under the Alice Mongoose teapot I used as a paperweight. Francesca babbled happily as she played with her squeaky, jingly toys.

Filling out the Student Retention Office forms by hand was frustratingly inefficient, especially compared to the all-online system the Student Retention Office had until recently. But for now, there wasn't any alternative. Our procurement officer had discovered serious security issues with the Student Information Management System (that is to say, she caught her husband fooling around with the company's chief operating officer) so the contract was cancelled. The bidding process had to be started over. Until it ran its course, we were stuck with paper forms.

I heard a clicking sound outside on the landing. Who in the management department (besides me) would come in to work on a Sunday? I pressed the koa panel closed behind me, careful not to wake Francesca. The idea of leaving her unattended, even for a few seconds, spiked my anxiety, but I couldn't let it be known that I'd brought a baby into the building. In any case, the panel wasn't soundproof. So if she woke up, I'd hear her.

I went out to the landing to see Fiona's door was ajar. There was no police tape or anything to indicate her office had been a crime scene. They must have collected everything they needed already. I didn't feel like talking to Fiona, or anyone for that matter, but I realized I should probably pop in and see how she was doing. It was only yesterday she'd found her dead husband, after all.

"Fiona?" I knocked on the door frame and peeked in.

No one answered, and I didn't see anyone inside.

"Fiona?" What if she had passed out again and was on the floor somewhere? I walked into the office, knelt down and checked under her desk, stood up—and found myself face-to-chest with a large man in a hot-pink Konishi Construction shirt. He was wearing dark sunglasses, which seemed odd.

I yelped and stepped sideways, toward the door.

He stepped too, blocking my exit.

"Who are you?" he demanded.

"I'm Molly Barda." My voice sounded thin and tentative. "I'm the department chair."

He stared at me (or at least he aimed the sunglasses in my direction) as if considering whether to let me out. Who was this guy? My mind immediately went to the worst possible scenario. He was Emmett Spencer's murderer, he'd somehow gotten his hands on a Konishi Construction t-shirt and a key to Fiona's office, and he was back to make sure he hadn't left any incriminating evidence.

But why would a Konishi Construction guy want to kill Emmett Spencer? And if he wasn't a real Konishi employee, how would a random murderer get a key?

"I thought I heard Dr. Spencer come in," I said to the man, "so I came over to see her."

"You thought you was gonna find her on the floor?"

It was true, I had been looking under her desk.

"She fainted yesterday," I said. "I thought she, um..."

Nice work, Molly, you pretty much just told this guy you were here when Emmett Spencer's body was discovered. Smart move. The evidence he's looking to get rid of now includes you.

The man didn't move. He stood and stared. I couldn't think of anything to do but stare back. I hadn't even brought my phone with me, like an idiot.

And then I heard Francesca. Just one syllable: "Ba."

Francesca, hang on, I thought. We don't want the bad man to find you.

"Waaaaa!" Francesca cried.

"What was that?" the man turned his head a little, but he didn't move out of the doorway.

I was terrified, and angry. Poor Francesca, all alone in the musty little room.

But then I remembered what my student Bryce had told me. That if you were near the old hospital, you'd hear a baby's cry before something bad happened to you.

"What was what?" I said. "I didn't hear anything. Why, did you hear something?"

The man paled beneath his tan.

"You never heard that?" he demanded. "You deaf or what?"

I shrugged and tried not to flinch when I heard Francesca raise her voice again.

"Waa, waa, waaaaaaaaaaaaaaaaaaa!" Even more upset now because where was Mom? I ached to rush back to my office and hold her, but even if I could push past the man (I couldn't), I didn't want to lead him to her.

"WAAAAAAAAA!"

"Someone get a baby in here?" he demanded.

"Did you say a baby?" I put on a concerned expression. "Are you telling me you hear a baby's cry?"

He glowered at me for a few seconds, and I was afraid he was going to punch me. He swore, turned on his heel, and thundered down the stairs.

As soon as he was out of sight I rushed back to my office, pushed through the panel door, and snatched Francesca out of the playpen. After finishing up the diaper change (the baby's, in case you're wondering), I took out my cell phone and called Security.

At first there was no answer. I hung up again and this time someone picked up after the second ring. I babbled out my version of what had just happened, but the woman interrupted me to tell me they would be sending someone up to my office.

MOLLY: GOOD NEWS

"MICAH," I SAID. "WE are really glad to see you. Thank you for coming up."

"Oh, hey, little girl," Micah cooed, as Francesca stretched her chubby arms toward him. "Can I hold her? Francesca, yeah?"

How could I say no? Francesca was leaning away from me so hard I had to struggle to keep her from tipping out of my arms. Micah took her and held her. He must have been closing in on thirty, but he still had his chubby baby cheeks, which made him and Francesca look adorably alike. I'm not saying he looked like he could be the father of the baby; he looked like the actual baby. I would never share this observation with him, of course.

Francesca beamed at him, pushed away from his chest, and reached out to me again.

"I'm kinda surprised to see you back here, Professor," Micah said as Francesca twisted around in my arms and leaned back toward him. "After everything that happened yesterday. I thought you'd wanna take some kinda leave or something."

"Well I had paperwork to do," I said, "and I thought it would be good to get back up on the horse, so to speak. I thought it would be safe because, apparently, I'm an idiot. Micah, why don't you come in and sit down?"

He sat in my visitor chair with Francesca on his lap while I told him what had just happened over in Fiona's office.

"Sounds like it was just one of the Konishi Construction guys," Micah said. "They're allowed to be in here, you know. Construction is behind schedule that's why. They're working overtime and weekends."

"He was wearing one of those bright pink Konishi shirts," I said, "but that doesn't necessarily mean he was a real employee. Maybe he stole the shirt. Or counterfeited it. Or even found it at a thrift store. And who wears sunglasses indoors?"

"He must've had a key," Micah countered. "Cause you said he was already in Professor Spencer's office. We keep a log of everyone who has keys and you're not supposed to copy 'em. All the Konishi guys get 'em, but."

"If he was here for some innocent reason, why was he acting like that?" I asked. "Why prevent me from leaving the room? I think if Francesca's crying hadn't scared him off, he would've...I don't know what he would've done, but it would've been bad."

"Maybe he thought you were a suspicious intruder," Micah pointed out. "He doesn't know who you are, either, you know."

"Me? I'm the least threatening person imaginable."

Micah laughed. Francesca, still sitting on his lap, laughed too.

"If you could tell who was a criminal just by looking at 'em, law enforcement would be a lot easier," he said. "You can file a report if you want, Professor. Can't promise it'll go anywhere. It's up to you."

Francesca started to make discontented noises and act like she wanted to get down on the ground. I pulled a jingly butterfly toy out of my desk drawer and handed it over to her. She beamed and happily bashed the toy on my desk.

"Yes, I would like to file a report," I said.

"It's online," Micah said, so I fired up my desktop computer, and Micah talked me through filling out the form. As I typed out my recollection of the incident, I realized how weak my story sounded. I had gone into Fiona Spencer's office and found one of the Konishi Construction workers inside. He asked me what I was doing there—understandable. He eventually left. (I omitted the part about Francesca crying, of course, because I wasn't supposed to bring her to work in the first place.)

"I think this thing is affecting me more than I realized at first," I said when I had pressed the "submit" button. "I didn't sleep at all last night. I've never met Fiona's husband. Never even talked to him on the phone. I can't imagine how much worse this must be for Fiona. Even for me, the thought of him cooking to death inside the fever cabinet, it's so horrible. I can't get it out of my mind."

"They took the thing away you know," Micah said. "It's evidence, that's why."

"Come to think of it, that's right. I didn't see the fever cabinet in Fiona's office. Good. I'm glad they took it. I'd hate for Fiona to have to look at it after yesterday."

"I got some other good news too, you know," Micah said. Francesca stuck one of the butterfly's wings in her mouth and started to chew it.

"I'm here for good news," I said. "What is it?"

"It's not official yet, Professor, so don't tell nobody, but the cause of death wasn't the victim cooking to death like it looked like."

Francesca dropped the butterfly toy on the floor. After Micah retrieved it and handed it back to her, I asked,

"How did he die? Here I'll take her. And how did you hear about it?"

Micah handed Francesca across the desk to me.

"My cousin works at Mahina PD," he said. "Remember you didn't hear it from me. Don't want to get nobody in trouble."

"No, I understand. Of course."

"I know what you mean, Professor, about not sleeping. It was making me sick to think about the poor bugga getting cooked alive, you know."

"But you just said that's not what happened," I said. "Right?"

Francesca lobbed the butterfly toy straight at Micah. He caught it and handed it to her, which caused her to squeal delightedly.

"Yeah. So the good news is, he was already dead when they wen' put 'im in. Someone wen' shot 'im first." Micah rubbed the back of his shaved head for emphasis. "That's what my cousin said. Couldn't tell me nothing besides that, but he heard someone else talking about it."

"Well that's a small mercy," I said. "Listen, I know I'm probably worried about nothing, but do you mind walking us down to my car? I had a bunch of paperwork I was hoping to finish up, but I'll just come in early tomorrow morning.

MOLLY: A GREAT START

I MANAGED TO COMPLETE the Student Retention Office paperwork first thing Monday morning, thanks to a shortcut I cooked up for the dreaded Student Engagement Journal Entries. It involved a handwriting font, a random word generator, and some adjustments to my printer settings. No one in my department actually filled out the Journal Entries every week like they were supposed to, and I was fairly sure no one in the Student Retention Office actually read them, so I decided my solution should make everyone happy.

I even had some time to answer Pat Flanagan's email. Pat and I hadn't communicated much since he'd moved to Honolulu and taken a job at the weekly paper. I could tell he no longer found Mahina State University gossip particularly fascinating. And Pat's new beat (Honolulu city politics) is so complex that trying to keep up gives me vertigo. But he was just assigned a feature on the history of the big Labor Day canoe race / biker convention that takes place on this island, so once again we had something to talk about. I'd actually been to the event, and he hadn't, so I was able to give him a sense of the festive atmosphere. In his latest email Pat told me more about Mahina's oldest biker club, which apparently is more like a civic association than anything else. The former wife of one of our trustees was one of the first women to ride with them, he informed me, and a current member of the club even owns a popular upscale bed-and-breakfast.

In my reply I told him about dropping Fiona off at her house with all the bikers hanging around her driveway. I was sure he'd enjoy meeting Fiona and her mother, I wrote, and I encouraged him to fly back and visit any time he liked.

So I started the day with a pleasant feeling of having pulled ahead of my to-do list. I'd just bundled up the Student Retention Office paperwork for intra-campus mail, when Fiona marched into my office and dropped her frail backside into one of my visitor chairs. No knock on the door, no may I come in, nothing.

I set the stack of papers down and gave her my full attention. I hadn't seen her since we'd discovered her dead husband in her office the other day, so I assumed she was probably still feeling a little jangled. I wondered whether I should tell her about the guy poking around her office yesterday. Maybe eventually, but certainly not this minute when she seemed all stressed out.

"Molly, I'd like a word. In private. Do you have time right now?"

"Sure," I said. "Do you want to close the door?"

"In a moment."

Fiona pushed the chair back and went to the doorway.

"Mum?" she called out to the landing.

I'd seen Fiona's mother twice before, but this was the first time I'd gotten a good look at her. To me she looked exactly like a character from a BBC mystery series set in the English countryside. Sensible, practical, and horsey (in both senses of the word). You were always surprised when she turned out to be the murderer. In my archetypal TV show, I mean.

"Hullo. I'm Harriet." The woman reached across my desk and administered exactly the no-nonsense handshake I expected.

"It's a pleasure to meet you," I said, and we all got seated. My first impression of Harriet had been completely off. Harriet was bare faced, and she wore her hair in a no-maintenance crop. But she was hardly a hobo. Her clothing was tailored to outlast fickle fashion. Her field coat was rumpled and had some burn marks around the pockets, but a new one like it would set you back a month's rent.

"So..." I looked from Fiona to her mother and back to Fiona.

"She knows," Fiona said.

"I do," Harriet confirmed.

"About...Saturday?" I asked.

"Yes," Fiona said with some asperity. "Mum knew Emmett was dead nearly as soon as I did."

"Fiona's office still smells of ham," Harriet said cheerfully. "Quite upsetting, when you think about it. Fiona couldn't remember, what was that whatsit called you found him in?"

"It's called a fever cabinet," I said. "This building used to be a medical facility and there's still some old equipment lying around. They used it for pyrotherapy, which was basically raising the patient's body temperature and burning out infections. I think it was invented by a doctor who noticed some of his patients who got malaria were cured of their syphilis. Sorry, that's probably a lot more than you wanted to know."

"Not a bit of it. It's fascinating!" Harriet exclaimed. "How hot does it get?"

"A hundred and five degrees."

"Fahrenheit or Celsius?"

I glanced at Fiona. She was staring at her lap, her mouth a tight line. She didn't seem interested in hearing about the gripping history of this medical device.

"Fahrenheit," I said.

"Is that all?" Harriet snorted. "Barely hotter than bathwater. You can hardly cook a person like a Christmas gammon at that temperature."

"It was hotter than that," Fiona said flatly. "I nearly burned my hand on it."

I briefly considered sharing what Micah had told me—Emmett was dead when he was put into the device and hadn't been killed by the heat. But I wasn't sure Micah's information was correct and, even if it was, Fiona might get upset I knew something about the case that she didn't."

"Why ever did you have the thing in your office to begin with?" Harriet asked Fiona.

"It's not Fiona's fault," I said. "We completed her hire after the semester deadline so according to Facilities the office is still unoccupied and can be used as storage."

"It looks a right tip," Harriet said. "You should ask them to send someone in to tidy up."

"I've been sending in requests for exactly that," I said. "And actually, there was a guy in there yesterday. I don't know what he was doing, but he was wearing a Konishi Construction shirt."

"Finally," Fiona said.

I decided Fiona didn't need to know I'd reported the man to Security.

"So Fiona," I said, "did you want to initiate your bereavement leave?"

She shook her head.

"Hardly worth it for the three days they give you. I'd rather keep myself occupied. In any event, I'm not here about the leave."

"We need to find a lawyer," Harriet said, "and we're hoping you might recommend someone. I was going to take Clyde's recommendation, but my daughter forbade me."

"Clyde?" I asked.

"Not important," Fiona said.

I looked from Fiona to her mother and back.

"Of course it's your right to sue the university," I said. "But it would be hard to find a lawyer who's willing to take on something like that. Our legal department is really good at dragging things out—"

"Sue?" Harriet snorted. Fiona shifted uncomfortably next to her. "I'm not suing anyone. I'm about to be arrested for murder!"

MOLLY: ONLY TRYING TO HELP

"I CAN RECOMMEND A LAWYER." I pulled out a pad and started to write. "She happens to be a former student of mine, and she's helped me out a lot in the past."

"Helped you?" Fiona sounded incredulous.

"Yep. Despite my wholesome and inoffensive appearance, I actually have required the services of a criminal lawyer in the past. My grad school roommate came to visit, and I took her to a Garden Society meeting. She, I guess there's no polite way to say this, she died right there in front of everyone, and I was accused of her murder. Everything worked out in the end, I mean, here I am, not in prison, but yeah, it was a pretty stressful episode."

"Never," Fiona exclaimed.

"Well she's Italian, isn't she?" Harriet said to Fiona. "Bang tidy, the Italians, but a bit dangerous. If I were you, Fiona, I'd try a little harder not to get on her bad side, eh?"

"Molly, I do apologize for my mother," Fiona said.

"No, it's fine. My ancestry is Albanian, actually. Barda is an Albanian name. It's more commonly spelled with an 'h' but my...never mind, it's not important."

I happened to know "bang tidy" means "attractive," so Fiona's mother had basically just deemed me sexy and dangerous. It was a welcome compliment in my book. Especially since just the other day, Emma had pointed out that because I lived in the suburbs and had a daughter, I was technically a suburban mom. That, for some reason, was far more upsetting.

"Is she expensive, this lawyer?" Fiona asked.

"She's not cheap."

"Money won't be a problem," Harriet said. "As long as this person can ensure I'm not sent up to death row, I'll consider it money well spent. Not that I'm worried for myself, mind, but I imagine it would be terribly embarrassing for Fiona."

"Ship has sailed, Mum," Fiona muttered. "And Hawaii doesn't have a death penalty in any event."

"That's a relief, then," Harriet replied. "Well, I won't pretend I liked Emmett, and I can't say I wouldn't have topped him given the right circumstances. I daresay, I'm parched. I suppose tea's out of the question."

"Honestly, Mum, this is hardly the—"

"It's okay," I said. "I can make tea. We have a kettle."

"I'll make it," Fiona said. I guess she wasn't impressed with my tea-making skills.

"The kettle might be in the men's room by now," I said. "Make sure to knock first."

Fiona stood up.

"Yes, I know."

FIONA: NOT AN ABATTOIR

FIONA RETURNED WITH three brewed mugs of tea, to find Molly away from her desk, and Harriet about to light her pipe.

"Mum, put that beastly thing away. This is a no-smoking building."

Harriet's pipe paused in mid-air. She did some quick disassembly and tucked the components back into her coat. Another scorch mark, which Harriet seemed not to notice.

"Your department head seems a decent sort," Harriet said as Fiona took her seat.

"Where is she?" Fiona asked.

"She went to get us some milk for the tea," Harriet said. "This is rather a nice little office, isn't it? Why does yours look like an abattoir?"

"Don't be morbid. It looks like no such thing," Fiona protested, but in fact it wasn't hard to imagine blood being hosed off the green tiles, swirling down the drain at the centre of the floor. "I imagine it was an operating theatre at one time."

"Operating theatre, abattoir, tomato, tomahto. A hundred years ago it was more or less the same thing, wasn't it?" Harriet said.

"Got us some milk." Molly entered, holding a little red-and-white milk container. She opened the spout and set it down on the desk between Fiona and Harriet. "Oh, Fiona, thank you for the tea. I just realized when I was walking back up here, I never had a chance to say to both of you, I'm so sorry for your loss."

"Not much of a loss, let's be honest," Harriet said.

"Mother!" Fiona admonished.

"One of the schoolboys found Emmett's gun and topped himself," Harriet said to me. "Emmett nearly got sacked but managed to worm his way out of it. Can't imagine how the boy's family feels."

"That's not fair," Fiona retorted. "Naturally when there's a tragedy, people want to find someone to blame. But it wasn't Emmett's fault."

Harriet started to reach for her pipe pocket but stopped and poured a splash of milk into her tea instead.

"I supposed it depends on one's definition of fault, darling. If Emmett hadn't come to St. Aelred, the boy might still be alive."

Molly cleared her throat.

"So anything I can help with besides the contact information for the lawyer?" she asked.

"You can tell my mother not to go round incriminating herself," Fiona said.

"I'm doing nothing of the sort," Harriet retorted. "It's only because I caught him out with his bit-on-the-side and went spare."

"My mother confronted Emmett in a public place," Fiona explained, because Molly looked confused. "She yelled at him—"

"Never yelled," Harriet interrupted.

"I understand," Molly said. "You had an argument with Fiona's husband, and then he turned up dead. I can see how it looks bad. But I'm not a lawyer. Speaking of which, did you want her contact information—"

"I don't see how it counts against me," Harriet went on. "It should be the opposite, really. If I'd known he'd be getting murdered shortly, I would have pretended to be on the best of terms with him. I'll tell you what looks suspicious, Fiona. You lying about your husband's whereabouts."

"Mother! I did not lie!"

"But you did, darling. You claimed your husband was at home in bed when he was almost certainly already dead. I believe it's what the Yanks call a whopper."

MOLLY: THREAT ASSESSMENT

"YOU LIED TO THE POLICE?" I blurted out.

"Never to the police," Fiona said. "Only to Maureen."

"Why? Sorry, never mind, that's something to discuss with a lawyer. Speaking of which—"

"Yes, that's why we're here, isn't it?" Harriet said. "A recommendation would be much appreciated."

"Her name is Honey Akiona," I said.

Mother and daughter exchanged a glance.

"Very well. I suppose we should give her a ring." Fiona stood and her mother followed suit.

"Ta for the tea," Harriet said.

"Here's Honey's contact information." I wrote it down on a legal pad, folded the yellow lined paper in half, and handed it to Fiona.

"Thanks." Fiona sounded the opposite of grateful. "I believe we already have it."

"She's the one Clyde recommended," Harriet said, "but my daughter doesn't trust Clyde or some such nonsense, so she insisted we come here and waste your time getting the same information."

"Harriet, just out of curiosity?" I wouldn't have pried if it were just Fiona there, but I sensed Harriet wouldn't be offended by a nosy question. "The...discovery of the murder was day before yesterday, and you've already been arrested? Are you out on bail now, or how did things move so fast?"

"No, I haven't been arrested," Harriet said. I thought I heard Fiona mutter "worse luck" under her breath, but I could be wrong. "Clyde's been brilliant, he's been keeping me apprised. He's heard through the jungle telegraph I'm the prime suspect."

"Don't say jungle telegraph, Mum," Fiona said. "It's offensive."

"You can say coconut wireless," I suggested.

"I certainly hope this Honey person is good with difficult clients." Fiona yanked open my office door, and nearly ran into Micah, the security guard.

"Everything okay here?" Micah asked.

"We're fine, thanks," Fiona said. "My mother and I were just leaving."

"Oh, you're the mother?" Micah shook Harriet's hand. "So sorry what happened to your son in law."

"I think we need to let Molly get on with her work." Fiona sidled around Micah and out to the landing. "I suppose the next thing to do is call this Honey person."

Micah watched the women leave, pulled my office door shut, and sat down.

"You doing okay, Professor?"

"Yes, thank you for asking."

"Supposed to keep an eye on you and Dr. Spencer, that's why."

"Really? Why?"

"Cause you was both at the scene. Threat Assessment told us make sure you no hurt yourself or nothing." He took out a sheet of paper, unfolded it, and read. "Professor, you having thoughts of self-harm?"

"Self-harm? Hmm. I did briefly consider volunteering for the General Education committee, but I think I'm over it now."

"Mahina State University offers counselling resources for employees," he went on. "Refer your colleague or student to...just a minute professor."

He bent down and resurfaced holding a copy of the Counselling Centre's laminated information sheet.

"The Counselling Center's open till lunchtime usually," he said. "But it's good to call ahead."

"Thank you," I said. I didn't tell him I had my own copy of the Counseling Center's laminated information sheet with the outdated opening times printed on it. "It's nice to have someone looking after my well-being. But do you know what really does help? Just keeping me informed. The way you've been doing. Passing along whatever information you've heard."

"For real?" Micah looked skeptical.

"Yes. Listen, if someone dumped a body in your workplace and you had no idea who did it or why? How would you feel?"

Micah cleared his throat.

"Always on edge," he said. "Little bit paranoid kine. Wondering who's next."

"I'm sorry, Micah. I didn't even stop to consider you're dealing with this, too. How are you holding up?"

"I seen dead bodies lots of times at funerals," he said. "But this is the first time..."

I had never seen Micah in any mood but cheerful. Until now. He was looking in my direction, but not at me. I wondered whether this was what people called the thousand-yard stare.

"Eh, you know Professor Spencer's mother. Who was just here?"

"Yes," I said.

"She's a suspect, you know. Don't tell nobody, but. Eh, is that tea?"

Micah looked pale and tired, and very much like he could use a "cuppa," as Fiona might say. I wouldn't mind another cup myself. I collected the three mugs and stood up.

"Stay right there," I said. "I'll go make some more."

MOLLY: OVERKILL

SO HARRIET'S INFORMATION, wherever she'd obtained it, was correct. Or at least it was consistent with Micah's. Fiona's mother was a suspect in the murder of Fiona's husband.

"Why would they think Harriet did it?" I asked.

"Cause she got in one beef wit' the husband down at Mahina Stationers."

"What was it about? Do you know?"

"I heard it was cause he was cheating on the daughter."

"That's the least surprising revelation ever." I sipped my tea and set it back down. Fiona really was better at tea than I was. "Micah, do you really think Harriet could have done it? I don't know. It's hard for me to imagine."

"Domestic situations can get kinda out of hand, you know," Micah said.

"Yes, but like this? Why not do something simple like, I don't know, poison him? I mean, if I wanted to kill someone, I'd probably just dump some antifreeze into their margarita or something."

Micah set his tea down slowly.

"Not that I would ever actually poison anyone," I added quickly. "I would not. It's just, this is such an over the top, attention-seeking way to kill someone. Whoever did this would somehow have to get Emmett Spencer up to the top floor of the College of Commerce building and into the fever cabinet. I don't think he'd be that easy for an average-sized woman to move."

"She coulda marched him up at gunpoint, made him climb into da kine, then shot 'im."

"Oh, good thinking," I said. "I guess that would be pretty straightforward. But how would she get into Fiona's office then?"

"Maybe she had one accomplice," Micah said. "A partner in crime, know what I mean? She's like da kine, can get men to do da kine for her, you know?"

"What?"

"A femme fatale, that's what I was trying to think of."

"You're talking about Fiona's mother?"

Micah nodded shyly.

Harriet didn't square with my idea of a dangerous dame, but what did I know? My stereotype of a femme fatale came from Hollywood.

"Okay, let's play it out. Harriet says to some guy—let's say it's this Clyde person, whoever he is—help me kill my annoying son-in-law. They force him to accompany them to Fiona's office—would the husband have a key?"

Micah shrugged. "Not supposed to, but the wife coulda made an illegal copy."

"They make him open the office, make him climb into the fever cabinet, shoot him in the head except no one hears a gunshot, turn the fever cabinet on, and leave. Actually, Harriet might not need an accomplice if she did it that way."

"Agree," Micah said.

"Except. It's Fiona's office. Can you imagine Harriet saying, hey, here's an idea, let's kill my son-in-law and dump the body in my daughter's office in a way that causes her maximum trauma? See what I mean?"

Micah rubbed his chin.

"Yeah, good point. Maybe she didn't know which one was the daughter's office."

"Harriet knows where Fiona's office is," I said. "She's come to visit Fiona before. And it's the only one Emmett would have a key to. See, you and I sitting here can work out it couldn't have been Fiona's mother. I hope Mahina's justice system can figure it out as quickly as we did."

"How well do you know Fiona and Harriet?" Micah asked.

"Fiona started here this semester, and I met Harriet today. I guess I don't know them that well. I don't want Fiona's mother to be guilty. I want the police to find the real culprit. Then peace will descend on the Management Department, Fiona won't quit, and I'll be able to make the spring schedule without having to find an emergency substitute Business Ethics professor."

Micah sipped his tea and frowned.

"Professor, I was wondering, yeah? How hot is it supposed to get, da kine?"

"The fever cabinet? A hundred and five degrees Fahrenheit. It's supposed to simulate a malarial fever."

"Could it get up to a hundred fifteen?" Micah asked.

"I don't know. I mean, it must've been built in the thirties or even before, so I can't imagine the temperature control was that great. Especially if it was left on longer than it was designed to be. Why?"

"Cause that's hot enough to cook meat."

"What? I've never heard of that. So you could leave a roast outside in Palm Springs and it would cook?"

"Only reason people don't do is cause it's not hot enough to kill the bacteria," Micah said. "But you can get the meat falling off the bone at a hundred fifteen if you leave it in long enough."

"Ew, that's horrible!"

"Yeah, good thing you wasn't there to see it when they was trying to move the body. You know my auntie, when she makes kalua in the oven, she puts it on 225 for five hours. She says internal temp gotta be at least 140 to be safe."

"Micah, you said the heat's not what killed him, right? He was shot."

"Yeah."

"Do you know whether there's any progress on tracing the bullet? Was there a bullet?"

Micah shook his head.

"Nuh-uh. Victim was shot with a nail gun."

"A nail gun?"

Micah nodded.

"Like I could go down and buy from the hardware store?"

"Yeah."

"Okay, that's weird. A nail gun. Wow. So that's good, right? Narrows it down? Or something?"

Micah shook his head.

"Doesn't help the investigation, Professor. Cause it's not bullets, just standard framing nails. So there's no way to trace 'em."

MOLLY: A BANANA BAFFLEMENT

AFTER MICAH LEFT, I found it impossible to sit still and focus on my work. I emailed a reminder to my students about next week's midterm and decided to walk over to the main hospital building and get something from the cafeteria. Sitting in the high-ceilinged, sunny space always lifted my mood and cleared my head, and the short walk across the utility road was just enough exercise.

I took out my phone and texted Pat Flanagan:

Have some INTERESTING news from Mahina. How is your story going?

I realized I was feeling excited about being involved in another murder case. Which worried me.

So when I entered the dining hall and saw Iker Legazpi sitting by himself, I thought it might be A Sign. Virtuous people make me feel defensive and inadequate, so I generally avoid them. Iker Legazpi is an exception.

In fact, Iker is one of the three people in my life I turn to for advice. The other two are my husband Donnie, who always has the safe and politically-savvy answer for me; and my best friend Emma, who exhorts me to stand for my principles and battle the forces of evil regardless of the personal cost. (The forces of evil in Emma's mind include the Student Retention Office, the IRB, Athletics, the IT department, and for some reason the Humanities dean.)

Only a few other people were scattered around the room; it was well after the lunchtime rush and I had gotten in just before the cash registers closed. I bought the last strawberry yogurt and a rock-hard banana and headed over to where Iker was sitting.

Iker put aside what he was reading—an old paperback book in a language I didn't recognize—and listened patiently while I related the whole story, including the unusual murder method and the fact that Fiona's mother was now implicated.

"It is a terrible predicament for Fiona Spencer and her mother," Iker said. "And you are right to wish them well. Why does this trouble you?"

"Because to really help her I have to find out who the murderer is. I mean someone has to find out. That's what I meant. And I know it's what the police are supposed to be doing, but they're just going to pin it on Fiona's mother because it's the easy way out. She didn't get along with the son-in-law, case closed."

I tried to snap the nub off the end of my banana to peel it. The skin was too tough, and I could barely bend it.

"You are saying you hope for justice to be done," Iker said.

I gave up on the banana and started trying to pick the edge of the foil off the yogurt.

"Here's the problem, Iker. I'm not satisfied with hoping for justice. I referred them to the best lawyer in Mahina—not sure they're going to follow up, but I feel like there's more I can do.

Then again, am I just trying to inject some excitement into my quotidian suburban-mom existence? I know this sounds like a ridiculous amount of existential angst, but I have Francesca now. I feel like I should be a good example for her."

Iker picked up my banana, easily peeled it from the wrong end, and handed it back to me.

"Oh. Thank you. How did you do that?"

"You are concerned with what is in your heart," he said. "Whether your motives are pure. As Paul wrote to the Corinthian Church: *If I am without love, my great accomplishments will do me no good whatsoever.*"

"Exactly! Am I just being a thrill seeker? I mean, you know I've been involved in murder cases in the past, and I don't know, maybe I'm trying to recapture the excitement or something. Do you think it's possible?"

"Such misgivings are an encouraging thing, Molly. They are the sign of an active conscience. As we have cited the Apostle Paul, perhaps we invite James into the conversation as well. James 4:17 says: *to the one who knows to do good and does not do it, that is sin.*"

"Great. So I can do the right thing for the wrong reason, which ends up not being the right thing, or I can do nothing, which is also wrong."

"Molly," Iker said, "I have no doubt your intentions are good. However, I would offer a more practical caution. We do not yet know who did this thing to Fiona Spencer's husband. Nor do we know whether the grudge is against Emmett Spencer, Fiona Spencer, or even the College of Commerce. You should first of all ensure your own safety and stay out of danger. Now if you will excuse me, I must meet my afternoon class and I have missed the shuttle. I thank you for a pleasant and stimulating conversation."

Iker rose, gave me a little bow, and headed out to the parking lot. I felt a flush of guilt. He hadn't even finished half his sandwich, and he now had ten minutes to make the drive across town to the main campus, find a parking place, and get to his classroom. I watched him leave and took a bite of the remaining half of his tuna salad sandwich. Or maybe it was chicken salad, hard to tell.

But our conversation had reassured me. Wanting to help Fiona didn't mean I was a bad person, according to Iker. I didn't have time to dwell on the part about staying out of danger, because my phone started ringing.

"Molly, you done eating?" Emma's voice demanded from my phone.

"How did you know I was...oh."

I looked up to see Emma striding toward me, still on her phone. We both hung up.

"You want the rest of that?" Emma sat down in the chair Iker had recently occupied, picked up the sandwich half with the bite out of it and stuffed it into her mouth.

"Help yourself."

"Junk, this sandwich," Emma said through a mouthful of it. "What's it supposed to be?"

"I don't know," I said. "I didn't buy it. It was Iker's. He just left."

Emma took my napkin and wiped her mouth and fingers.

"Oh yeah, that's how come the chair's warm. Eh, maybe I just consumed some of his good karma. You got anything you gotta do right now?"

I looked at my watch.

"Not really. And I have some time before I have to get the baby. I don't feel like going back to my office yet. What's up?"

"Come help me pick out a Christmas present for Yoshi."

"Today? Christmas is more than a month away. I thought you liked the thrill of waiting until the last minute."

"They're having a sale on phones, and I might wanna get a new one for myself too. You're good at finding bargains, Molly. Plus we hardly get to hang out anymore."

MOLLY: CHRISTMAS SHOPPING

"WHY ARE YOU WALKING like that?" Emma demanded. "You trying to make me feel short?"

"No, I'm walking like this because the gravel wrecks the heels of my shoes if I walk normally."

"You tiptoeing across the parking lot looks way more ridiculous than scratched-up heels no one looks at anyway, just so you know. Where are you going?"

I stopped and carefully let my heels down to give my aching calves a break.

"Aren't we taking your car? The Thunderbird's kind of a gas hog. Yours is better for the environment."

"Uh-huh. You mean you want to leave your very recognizable car in the parking lot, so it looks like you're still here and not ducking out of work to go shopping?"

"Emma, your cynicism shocks me."

We got into Emma's car and buckled in. Emma pressed the ignition button, or whatever it's called on an electric car. It felt more like booting up a computer than starting an engine.

"Ready to sniff out some good deals?" Emma asked as we careened down the narrow road.

"Ha, speaking of 'sniffing' out good deals," I said. "I picked up a practically-new microwave from the e-waste pile down at St. Aelred's, and the first time I used it I found out why they tossed it. It smells like a toxic waste dump. I pulled out a little plastic glob from under the rotating plate, but it didn't seem to help."

"You didn't throw it away yet, did you?" Emma asked. "I need a microwave for my lab. I'll get one of my grad students to take it home and clean it out."

"Take it, please. Rodge Cowper used it to heat up his coffee this morning and it stank up the whole floor."

Emma wrinkled her nose.

"Ew, never mind."

"You mean the chemical fumes don't bother you, but the fact that Rodge used it once is a bridge too far?"

Emma parked in front of the hardware shop so she could plug her car into the free charger. From there it was a ten-minute walk through Mahina's intermittent rain to reach our destination. Emma declared the inconvenience completely worth it for what she called "free gas."

We arrived at the phone store to find it surprisingly empty. The mystery was cleared up by a sign in the window announcing the sale started next week. Emma acted like she had planned it this way all along. Her strategy, she claimed, was to stake out her purchase now and pick it up later at a reduced price.

I trailed after Emma as she walked the perimeter of the store, examining one rectangular black phone after another.

"I'm going to go look at the accessories," I said after about five fascinating minutes of comparing front-camera resolution.

"Don't buy phone cases here," Emma said, as she followed me over to the accessories rack. "They're a rip-off at the store, cause they gotta cover all the rent an' salaries. It's way cheaper to buy 'em online."

"Emma, shh," I whispered. "Your so-called wasteful overhead is that poor kid's livelihood."

The boy behind the counter looked like he was busy with something at the register, although Emma and I were the only customers in the store.

"That's how come we need universal income, Molly. The boy shouldn't be chained to his minimum wage job." Emma was generally apolitical, but when her husband Yoshi abandoned the MBA rat race to become a freelance artist, Emma became suddenly sympathetic to redistributive social welfare programs.

"You're right." I examined the price tags posted above the pegboard hooks. "These are kind of overpriced."

"Eh, Molly, you should get this one. The silverbacks in your department would plotz." She held up a glittery pink phone case with "Diva" written across it in gold script. "Could you imagine Hanson Harrison huffing and puffing about the Dignity of the Academy?"

"Not worth it," I said. "I can listen to Hanson huffing and puffing without buying an ugly phone case. Wait, this reminds me of something."

"We have more colors in the back," said a voice at my elbow. The young man from behind the cash register stood beside us with an expectant expression. I dearly hoped he hadn't heard my comment about the ugly phone case. "We got a big shipment in for the sale next week."

"Nah, we're just looking." Emma slid the package back onto the hook.

"Wait a minute," I said. "Do you have this in purple?"

"I'll go check."

"Molly, you serious?" Emma said as soon as the young man had disappeared into the back.

"Emma, look at this." I pulled the glob of purple plastic out of my purse and showed it to her. She took it from me and examined it.

"You starting a collection or what?" she asked.

"It's from the microwave. The one I scavenged from St. Aelred's. This is the stinky plastic glob I was telling you about."

"Oh yeah." Emma leaned in to examine the glob more closely but didn't touch it. "Did you take this out before or after Rodge used the microwave?"

"What? I don't know. Before. That's the thing. I took it out, but the microwave still smells terrible."

"So what does this have to do with you asking about whether they have the phone case in purple?"

"Okay, I'll stipulate from the outset, this is really none of my business, but—"

"Ha, when's that ever stopped you?"

"Fine, I won't tell you."

"Nah, come on," Emma pleaded. "I'm nosy too."

I peeked over the rack of phone accessories to make sure no one was listening.

"Okay. The St. Aelred's student who committed suicide. Maureen's son."

"Yeah, Trevor Dos Santos. What, he had a phone case like this?"

"Well, I was going for the build-up, but yeah. Maybe. I don't know. My student told me Trevor was his boyfriend."

"Wow, your students tell you some personal stuff, ah?"

"Sometimes, yeah. Anyway, according to him, Trevor bought himself a sparkly purple phone case, which his macho father did not appreciate. Dad cut off the kid's allowance. I wonder whether it all spiraled down from there. Bryce didn't come out and say it, but it seems possible Trevor's suicide could be related to what the father did."

"Aw, that's sad. So how does the microwave fit in? What, you think the boy Trevor burned his phone case in the microwave at the school cause he felt bad about his dad disowning him or whatever?"

"I don't know. Maybe?"

"So what are you gonna do with this thing?"

"I was thinking if this is really from Trevor's phone maybe Bryce would want it. I mean, I know it's not appropriate to insert myself into a student's personal life like that. On the other hand, if I were in Bryce's place, if someone had a memento from someone I'd lost, even if it was a little burned glob of plastic, I'd want it. What do you think?"

"Shh, Molly, the boy's coming back with your phone cases."

The young man was holding a set of three cardboard-backed packages fanned out as if they were oversized playing cards. The phone cases were glittery and purple, and all of them had *Princess* emblazoned across them in curly silver script.

"What model phone do you have?" he asked.

"This one." I plucked the biggest case out of his hand and held my plastic glob up next to it. The glob was burned black along the edge, but otherwise it was a match.

"I can keep that for you at the counter if you want to continue shopping," the young man offered. If he thought my comparing the phone case with a plastic blob was weird, he didn't show it. "You can take your time and come up when you're ready."

"I think I'm not going to make a decision on a case just yet," I said. "Thank you for bringing those out for me to look at, though. Oh, I will take this charger kit."

As Emma and I were headed back to her car, she said,

"I can't believe you just spent fifty dollars on a charger kit, Molly. You could get it online for less than half that price."

"He was very helpful," I said, "and I wanted him to get credit for making a sale. We might have been his only customers today."

"You're just getting ripped off and propping up an exploitative system."

"Well, until the Glorious Revolution occurs, this is the system we have. I can't tip him, that would have been weird. What would you have done, Comrade?"

"I dunno. Buy an overpriced charger kit, I guess."

MOLLY: GAY CASANOVA

EMMA HAD DODGED MY question about giving Bryce the plastic piece from (what I assumed had been) Trevor's phone. As she drove us back to my building, I brought it up again. Emma wasn't always tactful in giving advice (in fact I can't recall a single instance of Emma being tactful) but she usually had something useful to say.

"I dunno," Emma said. "How come you think Bryce and da kine, Trevor, had a relationship? Just from what Bryce says?"

"Well, yes, because not to be ghoulish or anything, but I can't exactly ask Trevor, can I? You sound like you don't believe it."

"From what Maureen was saying, it doesn't sound like Trevor had a boyfriend."

"She's probably in denial, Emma. They're at this conservative private school, the dad is this macho big-shot businessman, of course Maureen's going to edit the reputation of her late son." I was surprised Emma was being so naive.

"You're wrong, Molly."

Emma gunned the car into the left turn, barely missing a lifted truck speeding through the intersection from the other direction. Emma leaned on her horn for a good five seconds as we barrelled up the hospital road.

"Maybe we can discuss this when you're not driving," I said as the prickle of panic faded from my fingers and toes.

"Idiot. Not you. He shoulda slowed down."

"Great. After they scrape me out of your passenger seat, they can put that on my tombstone. So Maureen denies her son was gay. But—"

"I didn't say she denies it, Molly. It's the opposite. From what she says, the boy was like gay Casanova. He didn't have one boyfriend, he had plenty boyfriends."

"Emma, are you saying Maureen the school secretary at St. Aelred's called her own son gay Casanova?"

"I'm paraphrasing. But yeah, pretty much."

"In what context would that be an appropriate thing to say?" I asked.

"She said she wished she'd pushed the boy harder to get counseling. She thought he was looking for male affection cause he didn't get along with the father."

"How sad. So maybe Bryce thought they had something special, but Trevor not so much. Even so, do you think Bryce would still want something to remember Trevor?"

"A burned piece of plastic? Molly, that might not go over so good. And what if Trevor melted the phone case cause he wanted to get rid of it? Then you'd be going against a dead person's wishes."

Emma turned into the lot of the old hospital complex. My turquoise-and-white Thunderbird was one of only a few cars remaining.

"Yeah, you're right," I said. "I should probably stay out of it."

"*That's* what should go on your headstone," Emma said as she pulled up next to the Thunderbird. "Emma was right. I should've stayed out of it."

MOLLY: THE RODGE COWPER RULE

I THOUGHT I COULD SLIP back into my office unnoticed. I should have known better. I'd just emailed out a reminder about the midterm coming up in Intro to Business Management next week, so I came back to find a cluster of students waiting outside my office.

I had them come in one at a time, for the sake of privacy. I also kept my office door propped open to comply with the Rodge Cowper rule. Anyone waiting outside could hear every word spoken inside my office.

I hate being the excuse police, so I use a policy I borrowed from Emma: I don't let students postpone or make up exams. Instead, they can drop their lowest midterm grade, no questions asked. It's on the syllabus, but students read the syllabus about as carefully as I read the terms and conditions when I'm updating my operating system.

You have to miss the midterm because you're turning twenty-one and your family's taking you to Vegas to celebrate? I'll drop the zero and take the average of your remaining scores. It's your girlfriend's due date? Congratulations, that midterm won't count toward your final grade. You can't take the midterm that day because your pastor told you it's the date of the Rapture? Assuming I'm left behind to turn in final grades as the Apocalypse rages outside my office window, that'll be the midterm you drop. (And no, I don't understand that one either.)

When the last student had left, I went downstairs to find Dan Watanabe, my dean. Ever since we'd hired Fiona, Dan had been on my case to do whatever I could to help Fiona out. Finally, I had thought of something that would actually be helpful—get her some emergency aid for her legal fees. Honey Akiona was probably the best criminal lawyer on this side of the island, but she was also expensive.

Serena, Dan's secretary, produced the paperwork for me to fill out on Fiona's behalf. I'd have to get Dan to sign the form personally; it wasn't something Serena could use his signature stamp for. Dan had been in back-to-back meetings all day, but Serena assured me he'd be back at some point, because he'd left his car keys in his office.

First, Dan had met with our media team to put together messaging that placed Emmett Spencer's murder "in context" and didn't reflect poorly on the university's decision to move faculty offices into the abandoned hospital complex. Next Dan had strategized with Campus Security to figure out how to deal with snooping reporters and curious tourists. At the moment, she told me, he was in an emergency meeting with our Board of Trustees.

The trustee meeting was going to be "even worse than usual" for Dan, Serena told me. At best, the Board of Trustees showed all the nuanced understanding of the complex ecosystem of higher education you'd expect from, well, a Board of Trustees. Throw in a potential PR disaster involving a murdered headmaster turning up on campus, and things could get unpleasant.

"Serena," I asked, "if you had to guess, who do you think killed Fiona's husband?"

Serena was taking our incoming mail from a big plastic bin on a cart and sorting the envelopes into piles.

"Someone who hated him, probably," she said without looking up from her sorting. I noticed she tossed the mass-mail pieces directly into the recycle bin, having apparently decided on the faculty's behalf that we didn't need our junk mail.

"Do you think people blamed him for that student's suicide?" I asked.

"I blame him." she paused and looked at me. "Sorry, but who leaves a loaded gun lying around in his desk like that? At a school? Stupid."

"I can't imagine how the boy's parents feel," I said. "If I were in their place, I could see wanting revenge. Although I can't picture Maureen Dos Santos murdering anyone. What about the father, though? Do you think he'd kill someone who he thought enabled his son's suicide?"

Serena snorted.

"Nah. Apostol never like the boy, you know. Shame, having one mahu son."

"Really? Wow. How sad. Poor kid."

"Bad luck, the family. His first wife died in an accident, you know."

"Car accident?" I asked.

"Tanning bed. He got remarried and had a kid quick though. Didn't want to grow old alone, I guess." Serena reached for the ringing phone, signaling the end of our chat.

I wanted to ask more: Was Apostol Dos Santos so disappointed in his son that the boy's suicide didn't bother him? And how does someone die in a tanning bed accident?

But Serena's attention was on the caller, who was apparently leaving a message for Dan Watanabe.

I heard a noise behind me and turned to see Dan Watanabe rushing in. His hair was spiky with sweat, and he looked harassed.

"I only have a minute," he said to me as I followed him back to his office.

He plunked into his chair and stuck his hand into the giant jar of peach-colored antacid tablets on his desk. I averted my eyes when he crammed a handful of them into his mouth. I think they're supposed to taste like orange Creamsicles, but I tried one once and it tasted like a urinal cake. (Or at least the way I imagine a urinal cake tastes, never actually having eaten one.)

"It's for Fiona," I said. "She's going to have legal expenses. I filled out the paperwork for emergency assistance, and I was hoping you could—"

"Save yourself the trouble." Dan removed his glasses and rubbed his eyes. "Fiona Spencer is leaving."

MOLLY: IT'S THE OPTICS

"FIONA IS LEAVING?" I stared at Dan across his desk as he swallowed the remains of his antacid tablets. "How can she be leaving? Dan, she and her mother were just in my office this morning, asking about getting a lawyer."

Dan pretended to look through his desk drawers for something.

"Maybe she didn't feel engaged with the department," he said.

I threw my hands up and let them fall into my lap.

"Dan, I'm not the one who barbecued Fiona's husband and left him in her office. This is not my fault. How 'engaged with the department' would you feel if it happened to you?"

"Molly, no one's blaming you."

"Really? Because it kind of sounds like...sorry, I don't mean to be contentious."

Dan shut the desk drawer and looked at me.

"Fiona Spencer leaving by mutual agreement is probably the best solution overall."

"Except we lose a faculty line we never get back."

"It's not great, I agree. But the optics." Dan cleared his throat. "Apostol Dos Santos is on our Board of Trustees. His son Trevor took his own life in Emmett Spencer's office. It's just bad all around. None of it is Fiona's fault but, like it or not, she's caught up in it. Better for everyone, especially for her, if she finds a job somewhere else."

"Fiona's definitely caught up in it. I can't argue with you there. Okay, so if Fiona is leaving at the end of the semester, we have to figure out—"

"Maybe sooner than the end of the semester," Dan said.

"What?"

Dan averted his gaze again.

"Great," I said. "So how do we cover her classes?"

"I'm afraid that'll be your responsibility."

"Wait, me? Dan, you can't make me teach Fiona's classes and mine too."

"Technically I can. You're the department chair. You're responsible for ensuring coverage." He picked up a file folder from his desk and fanned himself with it. "Molly, I know you care about our students, and you'll do what it takes to make them successful."

"Couldn't we hire a lecturer just for the last few weeks?"

"Sure. If you can find someone who's qualified this late in the semester."

"Hang on. I'm not the only person in the management department. Maybe Larry, Hanson, and Rodge can each pick up one of Fiona's classes. We can offer them a prorated overload—"

"Molly, Larry Schneider and Hanson Harrison are both past retirement age, and they're holding it over me. The minute I dare to ask either of them to take on an overload, I'll get their notices of intent to retire the same day, and there's two faculty members gone I won't be able to replace."

"What about Rodge Cowper?" I asked. "He's not eligible for retirement yet, is he?"

"Rodge would agree to it just to get me out of his office and then he wouldn't show up to any of the classes."

"Is he allowed to do that? Just not show up?"

"I could fire him for insubordination. But it's the same thing. I'm down another faculty member I can't replace within my lifetime."

"Why is it such a fight for us to keep our positions?" I asked. "Emma's department doesn't seem to have any problem hiring new people."

"Funny you mention biology. Last time I brought up our situation with Marshall Dixon, she told me for the price of one College of Commerce professor she can get two biologists who will teach a three-three load, bring in a quarter million a year in grants, and are happy to have the job. Hard to argue with that."

"Dan, I'm not a business ethics expert. I teach resume writing. My degree's in literature. I had to do a ton of prep just to be able to teach Intro to Business Management. Sticking me into Fiona's classes would not be doing the students a favor."

"Well, maybe you'll do a better job than I could at convincing Fiona Spencer to stay. Good luck."

MOLLY: THE TANNING BED ACCIDENT

DONNIE WAS SITTING at the kitchen counter with Francesca hoisted over his shoulder. With his free hand he was sorting through the day's receipts. The baby was drooling happily down the back of his red Donnie's Drive-Inn shirt. I grabbed a prefilled formula bottle from the pantry, lifted the baby from Donnie's shoulder, and sat down to feed her.

I checked my phone with my free hand. Nothing interesting in my email, and Pat's reply to my text had been profoundly disappointing. He'd already heard about Emmett Spencer's murder, so I hadn't told him anything he didn't already know.

I single-thumb-typed another text to Pat:

Apostol Dos Santos first wife died in tanning bed "accident"?? Biker connection?

Pat had told me the wife of a trustee rode with the local biker club. I hoped he'd find my idea interesting.

"Donnie, did you feed the baby today?" I asked. Francesca was frantically gulping down the formula.

"I gave her a bottle about twenty minutes ago." He got up from the counter, ran a glass of water, set it in front of me, and sat down next to us on the sofa. "Tough day?"

"Yes, now that you mention it. Sorry, I didn't mean to imply you had starved her. She still seems hungry, that's all. Maybe she's going through a growth spurt. And thank you for the water." I took a sip to show his effort wasn't wasted. "It's not quite as important now that I'm not breastfeeding, though."

"You're right," Donnie said. "She does seem hungry."

We watched Francesca's cheeks pulsing as the fluid level in the bottle sank. The baby's eyebrows drew together, giving her a determined expression.

"Her whole world is focused on getting that formula out of the bottle," I said. "Only a baby could make complete self-centeredness look so adorable."

"So how was your day?" Donnie asked. "Want to talk about it?"

"I learned a new way to peel a banana."

"From the non-stem end?"

"You knew about that? I hate feeling like everyone knows things except me."

Donnie put his arm around me and gave me a gentle hug.

"Fiona's mother is a suspect in Emmett Spencer's death," I said. "Unless you already knew that too?"

"She was arrested?"

"Not yet. Fiona and her mother came in to see me about it this morning. I told them to call Honey Akiona."

"Good recommendation." Donnie took the empty bottle from Francesca, got up, and returned with a full one. Francesca grabbed the bottle and attacked it as if she hadn't eaten for a week.

"Yeah, turns out someone had already given them her name. Oh, one more thing." I stroked the baby's fuzzy black hair. "This afternoon, I found out Fiona told Dan she's leaving."

"I know you fought really hard to fill that position. Will you be able to replace her?"

"Probably not. But wait, there's more. Dan thinks she's going to leave before the end of the semester, so I'll have to teach all her classes."

"Why you? Can't any of the other professors help out?"

"Ugh, I don't want to talk about it. Is it okay if we invite Fiona over for dinner?"

Francesca was struggling to stay awake now. Donnie caught her half-empty bottle before it toppled onto the floor and took it over to the sink.

"Are you going to try to convince her to stay?" Donnie called over the sound of running water.

"Why, you think it's a bad idea?"

"No, not at all. But I can understand her wanting to leave."

"But to walk away from a tenure-track job?" I said.

"She just found her husband's dead body in her office."

"Good point. He's the main reason she came to Mahina in the first place. Now he's gone, we have to give her another reason to stay. Make her feel like part of the College of Commerce family."

"Didn't you say her mother's here?" Donnie shut off the water and came back out to the living room. "Sounds like she already has family."

"True, but I'm not sure it really helps. Imagine me and my mother, only times a thousand."

"Hmm."

"Fiona doesn't realize she has people here in Mahina who need her," I said. "Her students. Her colleagues."

"Her department chair who doesn't want to take over her classes," Donnie said.

"Exactly. So is it okay if I invite her over?"

"Sure." Donnie said. "When?"

"How about tonight?"

"Tonight?"

"I know it's last-minute."

"What are you thinking, an hour from now? If you're okay with leftovers. Here, I'll take the baby. Take a look. See what you think."

Donnie went to deposit Francesca into her crib. Inside the fridge I found stacks of large foil pans, neatly labeled with masking tape.

"It looks like we have chow fun, chicken katsu, teriyaki beef, and fried rice," I said to Donnie when he came back out. "I think that'll be fine. You're amazing. Thank you."

"Thank all the customers who didn't order chow fun, chicken katsu, teriyaki beef, and fried rice today," he said.

I gave him a big hug, and he planted a kiss on top of my head.

"Okay, I'm going to make the call now," I said. "Boy, I hope this isn't awkward."

FIONA: SURELY IT'S NOT THAT SIMPLE

FIONA SAT ON THE UGLY maize-coloured couch in the darkening living room, too dispirited to make the effort to switch on the light.

Fiona was no Pollyanna when it came to the American legal system. Her views had been shaped by studying its outstanding ethical failures: the Korematsu decision; the mortgage securities meltdown; the industry-fuelled opioid epidemic. Even so, she had been shocked by her conversation with Honey Akiona, reputedly the best lawyer in Mahina.

Honey had advised Fiona and Harriet to leave Hawaii before they could be arrested.

She hadn't come right out and phrased it that way, of course. She had prefaced her advice with, "Now I'm not saying you should do this..." and gone on to talk (hypothetically, of course) about what would happen if they were to leave before any formal charges were filed. The lawyer's best guess, based on her own experience, was that with the evidence they had, Mahina PD wouldn't bother to follow through. Especially if it was going to involve extradition from another country.

"Surely it's not that simple," Fiona had objected. "We're to just pick up and leave?"

"Sorry to be blunt," Honey explained, "but a lot of people think your husband got what was coming to him. Karma. Bachi. There's not a lot of sympathy for the victim here."

Fiona bristled. Certainly, Emmett had his faults. But for the entire town to dislike him as much as she did felt like an insult to her good judgement.

"There's something else you should consider, Dr. Spencer," the lawyer continued. "Your mother had a confrontation with the victim, which looks bad. But you lied to your husband's secretary and told her your husband was with you after he was already dead. That's even worse. Makes you look like you got something to hide."

Fiona hadn't tried to explain. She couldn't bring herself to admit she had lied to protect Emmett's reputation (and her own) and it had backfired horribly. It would make an interesting case study for her class, if it weren't all so mortifying.

Fiona didn't even have her mum about to commiserate with. Harriet had seemed more exhilarated than alarmed by the prospect of becoming a fugitive from justice and had gone out for a celebratory dinner with Clyde.

Fiona considered writing to her father to tell him about Harriet's friendship with Clyde. Unfortunately, it wouldn't make a bit of difference.

"Let her have her bit of fun," the perpetually unbothered Nigel Holmes would reply. Or worse, "That's my Harriet, absolute force of nature, don't you know. Always been a man magnet."

Fiona had never wanted a marriage like her parents'. She wanted a husband who stood up for himself, who cared for her enough to be just a little jealous. It hadn't quite worked out as planned, to say the least.

Meanwhile, against all reason, her parents' peculiar union had endured. It was all rather infuriating.

Fiona got up to fix herself a pot of tea, never mind it was already after five. She filled the electric kettle, the one that didn't whistle. Fiona had wanted one that whistled so she'd know when the water had boiled, but Emmett had insisted on a quiet one because he didn't like the noise. (Emmett himself drank coffee.)

Fiona realized she had few fond memories of her husband. It made the loss more painful. Because Emmett had left her with nothing.

Fiona abandoned the idea of tea. She switched off the kettle and helped herself to Emmett's good whiskey instead. She was on her second glass when her phone rang.

It was Molly Barda, her department head. With apologies for the late invitation, was she free for dinner? It looked like she bloody well was. No husband to worry about, and no mother either. Anything was better than hanging about, festering. Transportation was no longer a problem, as Maureen had managed to track down Emmett's car (it had been parked on the St. Aelred property the whole time) and rescue it from police impound.

Fiona punched Molly's home address into the map program on her phone and started down the hill.

FIONA: A NEW PERSPECTIVE

FIONA SPENCER WAS NOT an experienced drinker, so she was unacquainted with the effects of whiskey on an empty stomach. When she arrived at Molly's house, she felt tipsier than when she had left. She probably shouldn't have driven herself down, but she was here now. There was nothing for it but to carry on until her head cleared.

Fiona had prepared herself for an awkward evening. But from the moment Molly answered the door and invited her in, Fiona found to her surprise that the time passed quickly. She had never been impressed by her department head's social skills. But tonight, she realized Molly was a fantastic listener. So much so that she seemed fascinated by Fiona's every utterance. Molly's husband was dead charming too, although not at all the pale and slender type Fiona usually fancied.

Dinner was plain comfort food, served "family style" on platters and accompanied with wine, which Fiona did not refuse, lest she seem standoffish. The conversation flowed so easily, and the company was so agreeable, Fiona wondered whether Mahina might not be such a bad place to live after all. She might even miss it after she left.

"I've always distrusted passion, you see." Fiona was sitting at the kitchen counter, refilling her glass at regular intervals while Molly loaded up the dishwasher. "I suppose it's why I married Emmett in the first place. Well I liked his looks, too, didn't I? Can't ignore that side of things. Tall and ethereal, like some sort of angel. It was a challenge, at first, to try to make him happy. I even bought him a ten-thousand-pound watch as a wedding present."

Molly turned and gave Fiona a quizzical look.

"Did you say a thousand-pound watch? How does a watch—oh, you mean it cost a thousand pounds."

"Ten thousand."

"Whoa."

"Mum says buying a man an expensive gift makes a woman look desperate. Do you think it's true?"

"How does a watch cost ten thousand pounds? Can it fly or something?"

"It's a Vacheron Constantin. Platinum. Gorgeous blue-black alligator band."

Molly slotted the dirty plates into the dishwasher racks in neat rows. Fiona would have volunteered to help tidy up, but Molly seemed to have things under control.

"Do you have the watch now?" Molly asked. "I'd love to see it."

"No idea where it is. Funny, I haven't thought about the bloody thing in yonks. Looked lovely on Emmett's wrist. I can't even remember whether he was wearing it the last time I spoke to him. We had quite a row, you know."

"I think you mentioned it," Molly said.

"I was thinking he might've lost the watch. Or perhaps given it to someone."

"Things must have been good between the two of you at first, though, right?" Molly asked.

Fiona gave the question some thought as Molly rinsed and loaded dishes. Had they ever had what people called a "honeymoon" period? Finally, she said,

"When Emmett first asked me to marry him, he said he thought I'd be a 'suitable' wife. So no, I don't suppose there was ever a time when we were giddy in love or anything like that."

"You were okay with that?" Molly asked.

"Oh, yes. It sounded so rational. So different to my parents. They like to think they're all about passion, living their truth, and all that tosh."

"Following your passion and living your truth doesn't sound so bad if you can afford it," Molly said.

"It is when it lands you in prison."

"Prison? Who's in prison?"

"My father, for one."

Fiona wouldn't have opened up so readily if Molly's husband had been there, but he'd long since gone to put the baby to bed and hadn't returned. For some reason it was easy to confide in Molly.

Molly finished up at the dishwasher, pulled up a barstool next to Fiona, and poured herself some wine.

"I'm sorry to hear about your father," she said. "If you'd like to talk about it? I don't want to pry."

"Oh, no need for sympathy. He's quite proud of himself if you must know. He was sentenced to twelve months for protesting a tree-felling scheme in his neighbourhood."

"A whole year for participating in a protest? Sounds kind of harsh."

"Oh, he fancies himself quite the martyr. He's only got a few months left on his sentence so he's in a bit of a rush to finish writing his prison memoir."

"Okay," Molly said.

Fiona stared into her glass.

"Molly, all I wanted was routine. Consistency. To live an unexceptional, predictable little life. Like yours."

"Um, thanks?"

"Life with Emmett in Mahina seemed to suit. Married to a headmaster in a little village thousands of miles away from anything. Teaching at an obscure college no one's ever heard of. It seemed like a lovely plan."

"You sound exactly like my dissertation advisor." Molly put her glass down. "Except he didn't think it was at all lovely. It was bad enough for me to end up at a university he'd never heard of, but teaching in the business school? That was a mortal sin as far as he was concerned. He said I was wasting my 'fine critical mind' teaching 'a bunch of slack-jawed baseball caps how to pad their resumes.' But you know what? I could've done a lot worse. Mahina is a great place to live, Fiona. We don't have a symphony orchestra, or a ballet company, or five-star restaurants, but we do have the County Band and world-class hula. Not to mention the Maritime Club and the Pair-O-Dice Bar and Grille. I like it here. I do. It probably sounds like I'm trying to sell you on Mahina."

"A bit, yes," Fiona replied.

"Maybe I am. Dan told me you were thinking of leaving."

Fiona felt her face grow hot.

"I didn't think he'd go and tell everyone," she said.

"He didn't tell everyone. He told me, because he thinks it's my job to talk you out of it."

Molly drained and refilled her wine glass.

"He says it's my fault you're leaving," Molly went on. "I'm the one who's supposed to be engaging you. Making you feel like you belong here. Ensuring you're fully integrated into the life of the college."

"What a bloody load of rubbish." Fiona was unsure whether to feel flattered or manipulated.

"Exactly!" Molly tried to point at Fiona, but her aim was slightly off, and she had to grab the countertop to keep from toppling off the stool. "That's what I've tried to tell Dan. Depending on me to charm people into making good life choices is a ridiculous load of...what you said. But. Here's the thing, Fiona. Losing you would be a disaster for the management department. You're the best teacher we have. By far."

Better than the two quarrelling silverbacks and Rodge the superannuated sex pest? Fiona wondered. Faint praise indeed. Unless Molly was including herself in the comparison.

"And I count myself, by the way," Molly added. "Fiona, the students really like you. They'd be heartbroken if you left."

"Never."

"It's true," Molly insisted. "They love your lectures, your syllabus, everything. They're always telling me how much they enjoy taking a class from Mary Popp—pop, popular, you're very popular, is what I'm trying to say. You're doing such a great job, Fiona. We're lucky to have you. I'm sorry if I haven't made it clear."

Fiona was astonished to find herself blinking back tears. Yes, she knew Americans exaggerated horribly, and she was certain no one truly loved her lectures. Still, it was the first time anyone had paid her a compliment in donkey's years. Apart from Rodge.

"I know this whole situation has been horrible for you," Molly went on, "and you need to take care of yourself first. But if there's anything I can do? To, you know, make you feel supported, at least so you don't feel like you have to drop everything and leave before the end of the semester? There's an emergency employee loan we can get you to help with your legal fees. I've already filled out the form. We should have had you over for dinner earlier. It's just that with the baby—"

Fiona burst out laughing.

"What's so funny?" Molly's confused expression made Fiona laugh even harder.

"I'm not leaving because the department's not friendly enough," Fiona sputtered. "I'm leaving to avoid a murder charge."

MOLLY: SEVERAL BOTTLES WERE HARMED IN THE MAKING OF THIS CHAPTER

DINNER WITH FIONA SPENCER didn't go at all the way I'd expected. First of all, she was half in the bag when she showed up. I confiscated her purse as graciously as I could ("here, let me take that") and hid it in the kitchen. She wasn't going to get her car keys back until I was sure she'd sobered up.

Drunk Fiona was a lot chattier than the version I was used to. She complimented our remodeled plantation house, which was nice of her, at first. But this soon turned to her complaining about her own domicile, which segued quickly into a disquisition on the relative merits of our respective husbands. She made unsettling comments about Donnie's "vigor" and "stamina" and managed to come up with various reasons to touch him and squeeze his biceps. Eventually he made an excuse about putting the baby to bed, left the living room, and never came back.

It was close to midnight before I was able to steer the conversation to where I could ask Fiona the big question. We were sitting at the kitchen counter, killing a bottle of Sangiovese.

I told Fiona what Dan had said to me and asked her whether it was true. Was she really planning to leave Mahina?

I was prepared for her to be offended, or at least evasive. I did not expect her to burst out laughing.

"I'm not planning to leave because the department's not friendly enough," she snorted. "I'm leaving to avoid a murder charge."

I was confused, to say the least. Just this morning it was her mother who was under suspicion. Had I misunderstood? Was Fiona a suspect too?

"Shouldn't you talk to Honey Akiona before you just take off?" I asked. "Or if you're not comfortable with Honey, you should get some kind of legal advice from someone. Don't you think?"

"Mum and I saw Honey Akiona today," Fiona said. "Right after we came to see you."

"Oh. So what did she tell you?"

"Our leaving the States was her idea."

"Are you serious?" I realized I was talking a little too loudly. Donnie and the baby were probably both asleep by now.

"Are you serious?" I asked again, more quietly. "Honey Akiona told you to leave town while the police were investigating the murder of your husband? Isn't there some rule about not leaving town or something?

"She said now's the best time," Fiona said. "No one's been charged yet."

"Doesn't running away make you look guilty?"

Fiona refilled her wine glass.

"Mum asked her the very same thing. Honey Akiona told us if we go back to England, your police won't bother to extradite us. Too much trouble and paperwork. Humbug, I believe she called it."

"Really? Could I kill someone and move to England, and get away with it because it's too much trouble to chase me down?"

Fiona shrugged.

"So long as you choose an unsympathetic victim. Like my husband. It seems most of Mahina thinks he got what he deserved."

"Got what he deserved for what?"

"Leaving a loaded gun lying about so Maureen's son could kill himself."

"Oh, right. That."

I wondered what Trevor Dos Santos was doing in the headmaster's private office to begin with, and why he chose to end his life there. But it didn't seem tactful to ask about it and, besides, Fiona probably didn't know anyway. We'd emptied our bottle of wine, so I opened another one. Fiona and I sat side-by-side at the counter and drank quietly for a few moments.

Finally, I asked,

"Fiona, do you have any idea who killed your husband?"

Fiona shook her head.

"No. But there were times I wished him dead."

"You had some anger and frustration, which you did not intend to act on, and now that he's really gone you feel irrationally at fault," I said. "I've been there, believe it or not."

"Really?" Fiona whispered. "You wished your husband would die?"

"No, no, not Donnie. Someone from the Student Retention Office."

"Ah. I've heard you don't get on with them."

"You have? Wait, what have you heard exactly?"

"Was it Linda you wanted dead?" Fiona asked.

"What did you hear about me and the Student Retention Office?"

"I wouldn't blame you for wanting to murder Linda," Fiona said.

"Which Linda are you talking about? They have more than one."

"Do you remember when she tried to make me give passing marks to that student? I don't remember his name now. Even if I had tried to go along with it, I couldn't have done because he wasn't even registered in my class. But I do appreciate your coming to my defense."

"Oh, that Linda. Yeah, I remember. No, it wasn't one of the Lindas. Her name was Kathy. She was canoe paddling with Emma. I saw her out there on the water and I imagined lightning striking...it's a long story."

Fiona tossed back another glass of wine.

"I don't know who would do something like this to Emmett," she said. "Although...I wish I could be certain of my mother's innocence."

"You think your mother did this?" I asked.

"We don't always get on, Mum and I," Fiona said. "But she cares for me, in her own way. She thought Emmett was making me unhappy. She was right, of course."

"For what it's worth," I said, "If I were going to murder my daughter's rotten husband, I wouldn't leave his body in her office for her to find. I'm sure your mother wants to protect you, not traumatize you."

"She had a row with him in public," Fiona said. "Loads of witnesses. I'm not saying she murdered Emmett with her bare hands, but she's quite good at enlisting people in her schemes. She may have an accomplice. A Thomas Becket sort of thing."

"Will no one rid me of this turbulent son-in-law?"

"Quite. She's got a friend here named Clyde. He's devoted to her. I think he might've done it."

"So it sounds like your mother might have to leave town," I said, "which is a shame, of course, but Fiona, you don't need to leave, and walk away from a tenure-track job."

"I lied about Emmett's whereabouts," Fiona stared into her wine glass.

"Yeah, why did you do that? Did you actually lie to the police?"

"No. To Maureen. I told her he was beside me in bed. He wasn't. He hadn't come home. I was making excuses for him."

"I see."

I did see. When the wife runs around on her husband, everyone says it's the wife's fault. When the husband runs around on the wife, everyone says it's the wife's fault. I couldn't blame Fiona for trying to save face.

"In hindsight I can see it was a stupid thing to do. I only wanted to avoid being gossiped about. Bloody Maureen, she of all people should understand."

"Why Maureen of all people?" I asked.

"Maureen had her son four months after her wedding. Mahina knows how to do simple maths. Quite a scandal at the time, I understand, with him recently widowed."

"Ah," I said.

"It's a shame, really." Fiona poured herself yet another glass of wine, stopping only when the meniscus threatened to overtop the rim. "Husband's turned out to be a bit of a brute. Keeps a tight hold on the purse strings. Maureen has to buy things on her credit cards and return them for cash just to get a bit of spending money. When the husband cut off Trevor's allowance, Maureen did everything she could to make it up to the boy. Even sold her jewelry."

That explained Maureen returning the three-hundred-dollar slip with the price tag still attached. She probably never intended to wear it. I didn't tell Fiona I'd seen Maureen in Brigham's. I already felt squeamish about poking into the poor woman's unhappy domestic life.

"Wow," I said. "I feel bad for Maureen."

"And after all she did for him, he went and topped himself." Fiona sipped from her brimming glass. "Not to speak ill of the dead, but Trevor was a spoilt child. Oh dear, I've gone and finished the bottle."

I took the hint and opened yet another bottle. I couldn't let Fiona drive home. After I refilled our glasses, I went to make sure the guest room bed was made up. By the time I came back to the kitchen, Fiona had fallen asleep with her head on the kitchen counter, and she was snoring softly.

MOLLY: BFFS

I WOKE UP THE NEXT morning to discover Fiona had gone. She'd managed to find her purse and car keys, which I had cleverly hidden on the kitchen counter the night before. Her absence was a relief, to be honest. Dealing with Drunk Fiona had been quite an experience; I was in no rush to meet Hungover Fiona. Donnie had left already with the baby, so I had the house to myself.

I called Honey Akiona's office and switched on the speakerphone so I could talk while I got dressed. Honey was the one who had talked Fiona into leaving. Maybe she could talk her out of it.

Honey told me she couldn't discuss the specifics of Fiona's case, of course. But she did permit herself to opine in a general sense about events in the news. The wheels of justice turn slowly in Mahina, Honey assured me, and for the time being it seemed the police didn't have enough evidence to make an arrest in the case of Emmett Spencer's murder.

"Honey," I asked (back when she'd been my student, I had a hard time calling her "Honey," but I was used to it by now), "Can you recommend a good private investigator? Say, I wanted to find out who really killed Emmett Spencer?"

"I can't think of anyone," she said.

I finished applying my smudge-proof lipstick and waved my hand in front of my face to dry it.

"What about your investigators? Do they freelance?" I asked.

"No," Honey replied.

"Getting this resolved would make my life a lot easier." I closed one eyelid and painted on eyeliner. Just a thin line, no fancy wings. I didn't have time to mess with wings today. "If Fiona Spencer leaves the country, well, she can't, that's all. We can't afford to lose her."

I closed the other eyelid and painted a matching line.

"You're not paying for my advice," Honey said, "but I'll give it to you anyway. You really wanna make your life easier, let the police do their job and stay out of it. Listen, I gotta go. Nice to talk to you again, Professor. Stay in touch."

And that was the end of our conversation.

I opened my eye and frowned at myself in the mirror. What just happened? It was pretty clear Honey wanted nothing to do with this case. If I wanted to figure out what happened, I'd have to find some other way to do it. I finished getting dressed and drove to work.

If you assumed our wine-fueled heart-to-heart had turned Fiona and me into BFFs, you'd be wrong. I saw little of Fiona that day, despite the fact that her office was across the landing from mine. She was there for her required office hours, but she kept her door shut. (Of course she was probably massively hung over, so I couldn't really blame her.) Instead of knocking, her students would hover in front of Fiona's office door as if it might sense their presence and swing open on its own. When it didn't, they gave up on Fiona and came to my office.

Why me? Larry Schneider and Hanson Harrison weren't there. (It was no use trying to force them to keep their scheduled office hours; they'd only threaten to retire.) Rodge Cowper was in his office, and it was well known he welcomed students, particularly the pretty, young, female ones. But students—particularly the pretty, young, female ones—seemed disinclined to visit him.

So I met with Fiona's students, and the conversations went something like this:

1) Student wants to know when an assignment is due, doesn't know what percentage of the grade the final exam is, or wants to know what grade they're getting in the class.

2) I pull up Fiona Spencer's syllabus online and point out where their question is answered. Occasionally I remind them how to calculate a weighted average.

If you are wondering why students would rather make a special trip across town from the main campus to the College of Commerce building to obtain this easily-accessible information rather than taking five minutes to find it themselves, I would direct you to my colleague Betty Jackson's excellent annotated bibliography on learned helplessness. (Just ask for it in the library, they get requests for it all the time.)

I was so busy advising students and shuttling to and from the main campus to teach my classes, I barely thought about Emmett Spencer's murder. But that afternoon a chance comment from a student brought it back up. He had come to see me because he was on academic warning. He didn't like school, he told me, and wondered aloud why he was bothering with the effort and expense of college at all.

I pulled up his online transcript and tried not to grimace.

"What originally inspired you to come here?" I asked carefully. We were under strict orders from the Student Retention Office not to say anything that might encourage a student to leave.

It was all very well for faculty to provide guidance, as long as we didn't suggest taking a gap year or transferring somewhere else. Our prime directive was to keep our students enrolled and paying tuition.

"I came here to get a decent job," he said.

"Well, there you go."

"Yeah, but my friend who graduated last year? He's still working the cash register at Galimba's Bargain Boyz except now he's got a bunch of loans to pay off."

"Well, the job market in Mahina is limited," I said.

"But the Konishi Construction guys get good jobs. They all got nice trucks and cool watches and stuff. I was thinking, I should quit school, go work construction."

"Okay, but you have to remember, construction is a cyclical...did you say watches? What kind of watches?"

"I saw one guy the other day, he had on this cool blue watch. I never saw anything like it."

"Dark blue or light blue watchband?" I asked.

"Dark blue. Almost black, but not black, know what I mean? White face, real clean looking. You could tell it was expensive."

It might not have been the watch Fiona had bought for her husband. Maybe there was a blue-watchband craze sweeping Mahina I hadn't noticed. But it seemed worth looking into.

"Where did you see this person again?" I asked.

The young man shrugged. "I dunno. Somewhere on campus."

"Here in the hospital complex, or on the main campus?" I asked.

"Here, I think."

"Would you excuse me please? I just remembered, I have a meeting."

I hustled the bewildered student out of my office, called Mahina PD, and asked to speak to Detective Medeiros. I had no idea whether Medeiros had been assigned to this particular case, but I trusted him. He and I go way back. Also, he and Donnie have known each other since high school at least. He would pass the information along to whoever needed to know it.

Detective Ka`imi Medeiros listened to what I had to say and expressed his gratitude by encouraging me to mind my own business.

It's almost as if they don't want to solve this case, I thought grumpily as I hung up the phone.

MOLLY: WHO WATCHES THE WATCHES

I CAME TO WORK THE next morning on high wristwatch alert. The first thing I noticed was hardly anyone wore a "real" watch anymore, only fitness monitors and smart watches.

I was wearing a smart watch these days too; Donnie and I both bought them after we had Francesca, so we wouldn't miss each other's texts. Having my watch buzz in the middle of a meeting and light up with the message "baby has runny poop" was a small price to pay for the peace of mind.

I strolled all four floors of my building, checking out the wrists of every Konishi Construction worker I came across. I saw one blue watchband, but it was rubber and the watch had a black oblong face.

Pat texted me back to tell me it was the wife of another Mahina State trustee who was the biker. Also, Dos Santos's first wife hadn't exactly died in a tanning bed accident. She had over-dosed on barbiturates and alcohol, and then passed out in her tanning bed. She was burned so badly the medical examiner claimed he had a tough time identifying the body.

The watch thing seemed like a dead end. Until later that afternoon. I stood up from my desk to get the blood moving in my legs and saw Konishi Construction had started work on the rail-ing. In front of the work area stretched a garland of yellow safety tape. A worker was lying on his back, with the soles of his boots facing me and his head resting at the edge of the four-story drop to the first floor.

He was using a power screwdriver to loosen the fasteners holding the railing together. The railing leaned out over the abyss. When he reached up to catch it, his cuff pulled back to expose a dark-blue watchband.

I could see why the student had noticed the man's watch. The midnight-blue leather glowed richly, and the crisp platinum-and-white face was minimalist elegance itself.

I downed my lukewarm coffee (for courage? I don't know why) and crossed the landing to Fiona's office. Her door was ajar, so I rapped on it and pushed it open without waiting for an invitation.

Fiona was sitting with a student, going over a marked-up paper. Apparently Fiona had chosen to ignore the Student Retention Office's ban on using red ink on student work, because the paper looked like a crime scene. (The Student Retention Office had at one point tried to block the department secretaries from ordering red pens. It didn't go well. As powerful as the Student Retention Office may be, no one pushes the secretaries around.)

"Oh hey, Professor Barda," the student said.

"Hi," I replied cheerily, completely unable to remember her name. She'd been in my Intro to Business Management class last year. "I'm so sorry to interrupt. I need to have a quick word with Dr. Spencer."

Fiona followed me over to her doorway.

"The worker over there, lying on his back," I whispered to her.

"He's awfully close to the edge." Fiona's voice sounded hoarse. "Is he dismantling the balustrade?"

"I'm sure he'll put it back together when he's done. My question is, do you recognize his watch?"

We watched him work for a moment, which was very stressful for me. I kept imagining him sliding head-first off the balcony and plunging to a bloody death forty feet below. Fortunately that didn't happen.

The man raised his hand, and I heard a little gasp from Fiona.

"Is it the watch you gave Emmett?" I asked.

"Yes," she said quietly. "Or very like. What should I do?"

"If it is his, I assume you want it back?" I asked. She nodded. "Is it engraved or anything? So you can identify it as your husband's?"

Her face fell.

"No. We were—I was going to have it engraved. But Emmett said it was perfect as is and he didn't want to ruin it."

"Okay. I'll see what I can find out."

She nodded again and slipped back into her office. Finally, I could do something useful for Fiona.

I didn't want to bother the man again while he was working on the ledge, so I waited inside my office with the door propped open. I kept an eye on him until he had finished up and was brushing the dust off his jeans.

The student who had been in Fiona's office wandered in and sat down in my visitor chair.

"Oh hi, Ashley." I stood up to signal that I had to leave. At least I had remembered her name, finally. The man with the watch was already starting down the steps, toolbox in hand.

"Sorry to bother you," she said earnestly, "but I was hoping you could help me check my graduation progress. Dr. Spencer says trying to figure out our Gen Ed requirements was making her woozy."

"Sure thing," I said. "I just need to talk to that man for a second. Wait right here."

I tucked a clipboard under my arm and started down the steps. The man was gone, probably disappeared into the elevator on the third floor. I raced down to the bottom of the steps and to the back of the ground floor lobby and waited in front of the elevator.

Eventually the bronze doors creaked open, and the man walked out past me.

The watchband looked black now in the dim lighting of the ground floor.

"Excuse me," I called after him, and he slowed down to let me catch up. "I couldn't help noticing your watch. I was wondering where you got it."

He looked at his wrist.

"Yeah, nice, ah?"

"Very. I was thinking, my husband might like one like it."

I had to walk quickly to keep pace with him, so I couldn't tiptoe on the muddy utility road. I'd have to worry about my shoes later.

"Mr. F gave it to me." The man was able to talk and carry a heavy toolbox without slowing down at all. "I don't know where he got it from, but."

"Mr. F?"

"Teaches science down at St. Aelred."

"You mean Mr. Ferman? The one who was in an accident and ended up in the hospital?"

"Shame, ah? Good man, Mr. F."

"May I see the watch again?"

The man stopped walking and held his wrist out for me to admire. Out in the sunlight the band looked dark blue again.

"If you know Mr. F, you could ask him where he got it," he said. "Anyway, I gotta go, ah? You have a good evening, Mrs. Gonsalves."

The man hurried off. I shouldn't have been surprised he knew who I was. Or, rather, who my husband was. Everyone in Mahina knows Donnie Gonsalves, founder and owner of Donnie's Drive-Inn. So much for me being a clever spy.

I tiptoed back to our building, cleaned the mud off my shoes in the first-floor ladies' room, then went upstairs to tell Fiona what had just happened.

She agreed that this must be her husband's watch. The Mr. Ferman connection couldn't possibly be a coincidence. She dialed Mahina PD and asked for Officer De Silva. He wasn't there so she left a message. She described the watch in impressive detail, although all she seemed to recall of the man was that he was "dressed like a builder."

After she hung up, I asked,

"Why didn't you say anything about Mr. Ferman?"

"I don't believe Mr. Ferman killed my husband," she said. "I'd only be giving the police an excuse to harass the poor man. The builder's probably lying about where he got it in any case."

"Oh. I didn't even think of that."

A quiet knock made us both look up.

"Ashley! I'm so sorry." I had completely forgotten about the student waiting in my office. "Okay, let's go have a look at your transcript...hang on, what just happened? Where did they all come from?"

A line of students had formed in front of my door and stretched down the stairs.

"They just sent out a text alert about early spring registration opening," Ashley said as we walked back over to my office. "So you can help me plan my spring semester schedule too."

MOLLY: A PURPLE GLOB

I HAD TO PUT THE QUESTION of Emmett Spencer's watch out of my mind temporarily. You don't want to hear the details of navigating our Byzantine course registration system—really, you don't. Just trust me when I tell you that trying to help students work out their class schedules is as challenging as solving a murder mystery, and much less fun.

The last student in line was Bryce Kahului. By the time he was up, my brain was so wrung-out I was happy I even remembered his name. He set up his laptop on my desk, and I asked him how he was doing.

"Kinda hectic at St. Aelred," he said. "They're hiring a search firm to look for a new headmaster. I think Maureen's got it under control though."

Must be nice to work at a private school where you can replace people when you lose them, I thought.

I was tempted to tell him about my conversation with the Konishi Construction employee and ask him whether he knew anything about Emmett Spencer's watch. Specifically, how it might have ended up in Mr. Ferman's possession. But as curious as I was, it didn't seem right to drag a student into this.

"You call your boss Maureen?" I asked. "Not Mrs. Dos Santos?"

"Nah, she never like being called Mrs. Dos Santos. She says, Mrs. Dos Santos is my mother-in-law, call me Maureen."

A twinkly noise filled my office. Bryce pulled his phone out of his messenger bag and shut off the sound. I wondered whether his hot pink phone case had caused him any grief with his relatives.

"Sorry about that," he said. "It's my sister calling again. I don't have the money to fly home for Thanksgiving and she's giving me a hard time about it."

Should I invite Bryce to our Thanksgiving potluck? Donnie would be okay with it. But to avoid the appearance of favoritism, I might then have to invite every student in the College of Commerce, something I definitely wasn't prepared to do.

I took Bryce through an audit of his past classes and current requirements, switching windows among the table of historic course number changes, the schedule of currently available courses, and the maps of which courses (which may or may not be offered in the current semester) fulfilled which Gen Ed requirements. The faculty have repeatedly asked for all this information to be consolidated on one site, so we wouldn't have to open several different browser windows and PDF documents each time we wanted to advise a student. But migrating data takes resources, and faculty labor is apparently unlimited and free, so the answer is always no.

Fiona Spencer's spring classes were filling fast, I noticed. There were a lot of students who wanted to experience a class with "Mary Poppins," a nickname I didn't think Fiona would appreciate.

"Do you have someplace to spend Thanksgiving?" I asked Bryce when we were finished with his course scheduling.

"Oh yeah. St. Aelred's. The dining hall does a nice meal for the boarders and staff. I'll be having Thanksgiving dinner there."

"That's wonderful," I said. "Oh. One more thing."

I pulled the purple plastic glob out of my bag. Poor kid, if he couldn't spend Thanksgiving with his family at least he could have this little memento.

"Bryce, I think this might be from Trevor's phone. Do you want it?"

Bryce frowned at the charred glob on my desk.

"Why do you think this is from Trevor's phone?" he asked.

"Because, remember you told me about Trevor's sparkly purple phone case, and how it caused so much trouble between him and his father? When I saw this, I remembered what you told me. Sparkly, purple, that's how I made the connection."

I didn't tell him the part about matching the piece to the cases at the store. It would have seemed weird.

"Where'd you find it?" Bryce asked.

"There was a new-looking microwave in the pile of e-waste on the St. Aelred School campus," I said. "So I picked it up for the department. This piece of plastic was stuck inside, under the rotating glass plate."

"Can I see it?" Bryce picked up the glob and shook his head. "Doesn't match. Trevor's one was a different color. Where's the microwave you're talking about?"

"It's the one right out there on our break table. We're not really using it, because every time someone turns it on our whole floor smells like toxic waste. If you know anyone who needs a stinky microwave, it's there for the taking."

"I could use it," Bryce said.

"Really? Well, okay. Sure. Help yourself."

Bryce slung his messenger bag onto his shoulder, went over and unplugged the microwave, and carried it down the stairs.

FIONA: THANKSGIVING

AS SHE WAS GETTING ready for bed that evening, Fiona's phone rang. It was the lawyer, Honey Akiona.

"Dr. Spencer."

Fiona thought Honey Akiona's tone sounded grim. She sat down on the bed.

"Yes?"

"Looks like someone's kicked a hornet's nest. Things have started to move pretty fast."

"Oh?" Fiona felt queasy.

"Do you remember our conversation?"

"Yes. Are you saying my mother and I—"

"I think your mother's okay for now, actually," Honey said. "But you somehow got on the wrong side of someone important."

"I did? How ever did I manage that?"

All Fiona had done was leave a message for Officer De Silva about the builder who was wearing what looked like Emmett's watch. De Silva hadn't returned her call and upon further reflection, she realized it wasn't much to go on. She didn't have a good description of the man wearing the watch, and perhaps it hadn't really been Emmett's watch after all. The man could have invented the story about Mr. Ferman, who after all, was famously eccentric.

"I'm not sure what you did," Honey said. "But someone's putting pressure on Mahina PD. It's not a healthy climate for you right now."

"How much time do I have?" Fiona asked. "Do I have the weekend at least?"

"Oh yeah," Honey said. "As long as you're out of here by Christmas you'll be okay."

So Fiona quietly arranged her departure and, in the meantime, did her best to keep up appearances. She taught, and graded, and kept office hours, although with the door shut so very few students dared bother her.

Wary of letting the mask slip, she avoided any unnecessary contact with people. She especially evaded her mother. Harriet was both perceptive and indiscreet; no secret was safe around her.

But on a rainy, lonesome Thursday, when Americans were celebrating their Thanksgiving holiday, Harriet roared up to Fiona's house on her motorcycle. Harriet shanghaied (her phrase) her daughter for what she called "a jolly Thanksgiving do by the seaside."

Fiona's escape plan was well enough along by now that even if Harriet found out about it, she couldn't cock it up. Emmett's Mini Cooper Convertible would already be down at the harbour and would ship out today or tomorrow. The only thing left for Fiona to do was to notify her department head she wasn't coming back on Monday. She would do that later today.

Fiona accepted her mother's invitation, even though it meant riding on the back of Harriet's 1966 Triumph Bonneville in the rain. Getting rained on in Mahina wasn't so bad, really. It was like stepping into a warm shower.

"The Maritime Club is the social centre of Mahina," Harriet shouted to her daughter as they pulled into the nearly-full car park. "And they have a gorgeous spread today."

"Don't you have to be a member to eat here?" Fiona asked.

"I joined, didn't I tell you?" Harriet took Fiona's helmet and her own and locked them up. "Clyde put me up for membership. He's quite well-known around Mahina."

Harriet secured the bike and they hurried into the weather-beaten little clubhouse. At first Fiona didn't recognize any of the diners. But as she took in the room, she saw a man she thought looked awfully like Mahina's state senator, and over there by the window was the mayor with his wife. The walls were chock-a-block with black and white photographs of the Maritime club and its members throughout the years. The maître-d greeted Harriet by name, wished her a Happy Thanksgiving, and led Fiona and Harriet to a small table next to a window overlooking the ocean.

Hanging above their table, directly next to the window, was a black-and-white photo taken at a Maritime Club Christmas party. (Many of the people in the photo were wearing Father Christmas hats.)

"Well, isn't this interesting," Harriet exclaimed.

"Do you see someone you know?" Fiona asked.

"Just a who's who of Mahina. Including the little tart from the stationers who was snogging your husband."

"Oh yes, I remember. When you publicly incriminated yourself and me as well." Fiona deliberately did not look at the photo. Little tart? This was new information. Who was the little tart, Fiona was dying to know? "Happy Thanksgiving to you too, Mother."

"I shouldn't have mentioned it," Harriet said. "I am sorry."

"Well you did mention it, didn't you?" Fiona retorted. "It's a bit late to take it back."

A waiter came by and placed a basket of miniature baguettes and a tub of butter on the table.

"Get you ladies something to drink?" he asked. "In addition to coffee, tea, juice, and soft drinks, we offer prosecco, which is a sparkling wine."

"No need to introduce us," Harriet said. "Prosecco and I are old friends. Two, please."

"Just coffee for me," Fiona said quietly. She was annoyed that Emmett's infidelity had intruded on what should have been a tolerable meal.

But she was also curious.

When the waiter left, Fiona forced herself to look at the photo. A quick scan didn't reveal any faces young or attractive enough to raise suspicion.

"You may as well tell me who it was," Fiona said, adding pointedly, "I'm sure I have the self-control to refrain from creating a public disturbance."

"Right there, in the leopard print." Harriet finished buttering a bit of baguette and pointed with her knife. "I don't understand the attraction, but there's no explaining that sort of thing, is there?"

Fiona looked to where Harriet was pointing. Then she stared.

"Let's not dwell on it, darling," Harriet said. "No point in being cross about it now, is there? Look, is that a chocolate fountain? I'm ravenous. Come on, let's get something to eat."

"You go first." Fiona pressed her hands to her temples to keep her skull in one piece. She barely noticed when the waiter set the coffee down in front of her.

Fiona needed fresh air more than she needed caffeine. She went out the side exit door and found herself standing on a bit of lawn just a few feet above the crashing surf. She took out her phone and scrolled through her emails. There was the Thanksgiving invitation from Molly, complete with street address and phone number.

She dialled Molly's number. Might as well get this bit over with, at least.

MOLLY: THE S-WORD

WHEN DAN WATANABE MOVED up from department chair to College of Commerce dean, I became department chair. I also inherited the department tradition of hosting Thanksgiving potluck. Today Rodge was the only one from the management department who showed up, his contribution to the Thanksgiving banquet a bag of tortilla chips from Galimba's Bargain Boyz. Emma and Yoshi brought a pot of kim chee chili. (It sounds like it would taste weird, but it's really good. The kim chee adds crunch and heat, like onions but less onion-y.) Iker Legazpi from the accounting department had come with a savory homemade chicken and vegetable stew. Some of the kids that worked at Donnie's Drive-Inn were there too. One of them happened to be a student in one of my classes.

Emma was on her best behavior, doing her utmost to hide her loathing for Rodge. Rodge, fortunately, had the decency to refrain from trying to flirt with Emma while her husband was sitting right there. I called my student "Riley" and afterward remembered his name was "Ryler," and "Riley" was someone else. I hoped no one noticed.

So things were going pretty smoothly until my phone rang. I took it into my office and was surprised to hear Fiona on the line.

When the call was over, I wandered back into the dining room, feeling a little dazed.

"Iker and Emma," I said, "could you help me bring in more drinks from outside?"

Donnie stood up to help.

"It's okay," I said. "We got it. Thank you."

"Let me know if you need me." He gave me an inquiring look and sat back down.

I led Iker and Emma out the side door and onto the back lanai.

"Where are the drinks we are to carry in?" Iker asked.

Emma didn't waste time looking for the nonexistent bottles. She made herself comfortable on one of the wicker chairs, gazed out at the graveyard beyond the back hedge and took a sip of wine.

"What?" she said, when she saw me looking at her glass. "I knew it was a ruse. If there was really something heavy to carry, you'd have sent Donnie out."

"It's true," I said to Iker. "I brought both of you out here under false pretenses because I need your advice. Please sit down. We have a situation."

"Uh oh," Emma said eagerly.

"That was Fiona calling," I said.

"Will Dr. Spencer be joining us today?" Iker asked as he took the chair next to Emma.

"No. And she told me something I found kind of hard to believe, so Iker, I wanted to check with you. Are you still on the board of St. Aelred's?"

"Yes, I am," he said carefully.

"Whoa, Iker," Emma exclaimed. "High maka maka you, hanging out with the tech billionaires and the heiresses. How'd you score that gig?"

"When one is trained in accounting and willing to serve as treasurer, it is a simple thing to gain entry to the board of a nonprofit," Iker said. "I find I am turning down many such invitations."

"Did the board ever discuss the headmaster's personal conduct?" I asked Iker. "Specifically, did Emmett, to your knowledge, um, break his marriage vows?"

Iker's cheeks flamed pink.

"These proceedings of the personnel subcommittee of the board are confidential," he said stiffly.

"In other words, yes," Emma volunteered.

"Was the other party Maureen Dos Santos, his secretary?" I asked.

Iker blushed even brighter.

"Maureen? Whoa, almost spilled my wine." Emma drained her glass and set it down on the side table. "Our Maureen? From the Flower Society?"

"Yes," I said. "I don't know any other Maureens who are the headmaster's secretary."

"No way. Fiona told you Emmett was, wait, how's the British way to say it, getting a leg up on Maureen? Bubbling her squeak? Iker, you learned British English. What's the right phrase?"

"Fiona said 'shagging'," I said.

"Fiona said that?" Emma exclaimed. "Wow, I'm surprised. I think shagging's considered a rude word in England, isn't it?"

"Yeah, well. Fiona's pretty mad," I replied.

"So what else did she tell you?" Emma asked.

"It wasn't a long conversation. She won't be coming back after the weekend, good luck finding a replacement, sorry for the short notice, and oh by the way that b-word Maureen was s-wording her husband the whole time."

"You don't have to say 's-word'," Emma said. "You already said shagging. She's leaving cause of that?"

"I don't know."

I told Emma and Iker about Honey Akiona advising Fiona and her mother to leave the country before charges were filed.

"So maybe Fiona really did kill her husband," Emma said, "and now Mahina PD's closing in."

"So you're saying you think Fiona knew about Emmett and Maureen all along?" I asked. "She's a pretty convincing actor, then. It sounded to me like she just found out."

"Didn't you say she was all fainting and staggering around when she found Emmett's body?" Emma asked. "Maybe that was acting too."

"Why was one of the Konishi Construction workmen wearing Emmett's watch then, claiming Mr. Ferman at St. Aelred's gave it to him?" I asked. "How does that fit in?"

"The simplest explanation is the man found the watch on Mr. Spencer's remains," Iker said. He seemed to have recovered from the recent trauma of discussing Emmett Spencer's affair. "Konishi Construction is performing work on the College of Commerce and also at the parsonage at St. Aelred, therefore it is possible the same workman has spent time at both sites and knows of our Anatole Ferman. He invents the story as a way to explain his possession of the costly watch. And Mr. Ferman, he is one who rambles in his words. It is difficult to get what is called a straight story from him."

"Ew," Emma cried. "You think one of the construction workers stole a watch right off Emmett Spencer's dead body?"

"It is not difficult to imagine," Iker replied. "One can reason as so: The dead man can no longer enjoy the watch. If I take the watch, I can exchange it for food or medicine. If I do not take the watch, someone else will find it. And so it is justified for me to remove the dead man's watch."

Emma and I both stared at Iker for a moment. It occurred to me Iker never talked about his childhood. It was just as well, probably.

"How do you think Fiona killed him then?" Emma asked. "He was shot, right? Did they ever find the gun?"

"I heard it wasn't a gun gun," I said. "Micah, my former student who's one of our security guards now?"

"Yeah, we know Micah," Emma said.

"Okay, well Micah told me he'd heard it was a nail gun. Easily accessible, totally untraceable. Listen, the reason I called you out here is I think Fiona is going to go after Maureen. And then she's going to leave the country. Shouldn't we try to stop her?"

Donnie stuck his head around the corner.

"Everything okay out here?"

"Donnie, I'm so sorry," I said. "Thank you for entertaining the guests."

"Molly thinks Fiona killed Emmett Spencer," Emma announced, "and now she's going to murder Maureen Dos Santos and leave the country."

Donnie came out and took the last unoccupied chair.

"Was that Fiona on the phone?" Donnie asked.

"Yep," I said. "She told me she won't be back after the Thanksgiving weekend. And she thinks her husband was having an affair with Maureen. Which she was not happy about. Once you murder someone, isn't it easier to kill again?"

"Yes," Iker said sadly. "The first time one takes a life one must also kill one's own conscience. With the conscience gone, the next killings are easier."

"Do you think we should call the police?" I asked. "Where's my phone? Oh, I'm holding it."

"Did Fiona tell you when or where she's going to commit the murder?" Donnie asked me.

"Oh." My finger hovered over the phone's number pad. "I guess that would be helpful to know. No, she didn't even say she was going to kill anyone. She just seemed really angry. I know, you think I'm being ridiculous."

Donnie stood up.

"Not at all. I'm surprised it hasn't already happened."

"You already knew about Maureen and Emmett?" Emma exclaimed.

"Why didn't you tell me?" I asked. "And how did you know?"

"I didn't know," Donnie said. "But now you tell me, I can see it. There are small things that add up."

"Oh, like when Maureen defended Emmett after her son's suicide," Emma said. "Even though the boy used Emmett's gun he stupidly left loaded and sitting in his desk."

"Things like that," Donnie agreed. "Okay, I'm going back in. Rodge seems like he's getting ready to leave, by the way."

"Oh no, Rodge," I said. "We're the only people here he really knows."

"Don't apologize to Rodge," Emma said. "He brought a bag of tortilla chips to your potluck."

"I will go," Iker stood up. "Although I have many disagreements with Rodge Cowper, and I do not think he is a good teacher, I would not like for Rodge to feel he is without a friend on this day of Thanksgiving."

When Donnie and Iker had gone back inside, Emma said,

"So you think Fiona's gonna go after Maureen?"

"I don't know. Fiona doesn't strike me as someone who has a good handle on her emotions."

I hadn't told anyone about Fiona's uninhibited behavior at dinner. It would only embarrass everyone involved. But I'd been relieved when she hadn't accepted the invitation to our Thanksgiving potluck.

"No kidding," Emma said. "I could totally see her whacking someone. Eh, call her back and ask her what she's gonna do."

"I did call back. Twice. The call went straight to voice mail." I slapped a mosquito on my forearm.

Emma leaned forward with her elbows on her knees and stared into my face.

"Molly, you're the one who talked to her. If your first impression was, she's gonna go hunt down Maureen, there's probably something to it."

"Well, what am I supposed to do, drive all over Mahina looking for her only to find her at home having a quiet tea with 'Mum'? And in the meantime, I've left poor Donnie here to deal with all the guests by himself?"

"Look at it the other way," Emma said. "What if you had the chance to prevent a murder, and you decided not to? And you had to live with it for the rest of your life?"

"Dang it, Emma."

"We gotta take the T-bird, though. Otherwise Yoshi's got no way to get home."

FIONA: CLOSURE

FIONA PUT HER MOBILE away and took a moment to gaze at the Pacific Ocean. It was grey and choppy. A disturbance in the water might have been a whale—November, she'd been told, was when one started seeing them—or it might have been simply the wind whipping up the waves. She had rung off rather abruptly and now she wondered whether she had dealt with things properly. She considered calling Molly back. But the mobile signal had dropped to zero bars.

Fiona went back inside to find her mother digging into a chocolate-syrup-drenched stack of pancakes.

"Lovely out there, isn't it?" Harriet asked. "One doesn't even mind the rain. Did you see the whales breaching?"

"I need to talk to Maureen," Fiona said.

"Not right this minute, I hope," Harriet replied. "I was going to get some salmon next."

"You're having salmon after chocolate pancakes?"

"Why ever not? That's what the prosecco's for, to cleanse the palate."

"I'll wait." Fiona folded her hands in front of her and stared at Harriet.

"Is that her name? Maureen? You know who she is, then."

"She's Emmett's secretary," Fiona said.

Harriet briefly choked on her pancake and washed it down with prosecco. She signalled the waiter for a refill.

"Never," Harriet exclaimed, when she'd recovered. "Emmett was getting his leg over with the secretary? Fiona, the man's a walking cliché."

"Still waiting for you to finish eating," Fiona said, knowing she was being annoying.

"What's the rush? I'm sure you can get into a hair-pulling fight with your husband's secretary any time you like. Why don't you wind your neck in and try to enjoy your supper?"

"I only want to wish her happy Thanksgiving and no hard feelings," Fiona said. "Closure, I believe it's called."

"Nonsense."

Fiona glowered at her mother.

"Do you know what I think, darling?" Harriet said through a mouthful of pancake. "I think you're feeling angry and betrayed. You may say you want reconciliation and all the rest of it, but you're not being honest with yourself, are you? I think you should enjoy your weekend and see how you feel about it Monday."

By Monday, of course, Fiona would be on her way back to England.

"Just this one favour, Mum. I'll be quick about it and then I won't mention it again."

Fiona wheedled and pestered until Harriet finally relented. They finished up their meal and rode the Triumph through the drizzle down to the St. Aelred School for Boys. The dining hall seemed to be busy, so they went there first. It was full of chattering boys eating turkey, pumpkin pie, and mounds of rice from rectangular paper trays. But Maureen was not in evidence.

"Well that's that. Shall we?" Harriet turned to leave.

"She might be in the office," Fiona said."

"I do hope you don't make a scene darling," Harriet said.

"No, we would never want to do that, would we?"

Bryce Kahului was behind the counter.

"Hullo Bryce," Fiona said. "Working on your holiday, I see."

"Oh, happy Thanksgiving Dr. Spencer. How can I help you today?"

"Is Maureen here?"

"Here?" He seemed surprised. "I thought she was with you."

"Why on earth would Maureen be with us?" Harriet asked.

"Bryce, this is my mother, Harriet Holmes," Fiona said. Harriet and the boy shook hands.

"She said she had to..." Bryce's forehead creased. "She's running an errand."

"Where did she go?" Fiona asked.

Bryce ran his finger around the collar of his St. Aelred polo shirt.

"Sorry. I'm supposed to tell you Maureen's in a meeting. She says it's unprofessional if people think the secretary's not on site."

"I understand. Thank you, Bryce."

As Fiona turned to leave, the office phone rang.

"Excuse me," Bryce said, and went to answer it.

"St. Aelred School." Bryce said cheerily into the phone. "How may I help—oh, hello, Mr. Dos Santos, happy Thanksgiv— no, you just missed her."

Fiona stopped, and Harriet bumped into her.

"What are you doing?" Harriet whispered.

"Listening in," Fiona whispered back.

Bryce's back was turned, so he didn't see Fiona and her mother still standing there.

"Oh, pretty soon, I think," Bryce said. "She went to take the headmaster's car down to the ship. Yeah. Oh yeah, I didn't think about that. I don't know how she was gonna get back, maybe call a taxi? Yeah, yeah, good idea. Okay, good. Aloha."

Fiona pulled her mother out of the office before Bryce could hang up and see them standing there.

"Why is this Maureen taking Emmett's car to a ship?" Harriet asked as they hurried back out to the car park.

"Mum, do you know the way to the port?"

"The port? Fiona, honestly—"

"Please, Mum."

MOLLY: A TRUE FEMME FATALE

I KNOCKED ON FIONA'S door and rang the doorbell. No one answered, and the carport was empty.

"What now?" Emma asked as we got back into the car.

"I don't know. Where else would Fiona Spencer hang out? Maybe with her mother, but I have no idea how to find her."

I twisted the key in the ignition and delicately toed the gas pedal.

"Actually," Emma poked my shoulder and said something I didn't catch.

"What?" I was concentrating on my pedaling technique. Just enough gas to give the thirsty V-8 what it needed, but not enough to flood it.

"I said it doesn't matter where Fiona hangs out," Emma shouted at me.

The engine caught and roared to life. I lifted my foot off and let it idle.

"I can hear you," I said in a normal voice.

"What I was saying is, the real question is where does Fiona think Maureen is? I dunno where Maureen lives though. Do you?"

"Me? No. Oh, do you know who we could ask? Bryce Kahului. My student."

"You got his number? Can you call him?"

"I can do better than that. I think I know where he is right now." I shifted into gear and started down the hill. "He said he was having Thanksgiving at the school."

"Doesn't he have a family?"

"I think they're on another island. Okay, here's the intersection. What do you think? Do we go left or right?"

"Go right," Emma urged me.

"Right it is." I eased onto the highway, toward the St. Aelred School for Boys. "So you don't think I'm worried about nothing? I can't decide whether we're saving the day or whether we just left our husbands alone on Thanksgiving for no good reason."

"Molly. Remember that time in the cafeteria when you introduced me and Fiona, all I did was say hello and she busts out crying?"

"Not exactly the way I remember it, but yes."

"And what about when she came over to your house and was groping Donnie? That's not someone with good impulse control."

"Emma, how did you know about that second thing? I didn't tell anyone about it."

"Donnie just told me today."

"He did? Donnie told you? When?"

"He said if Fiona came over today, he'd have to make sure there was always a piece of furniture between them. He said not to tell you what he said, cause he didn't want you to feel bad about it."

"Poor Donnie. I hope he's okay handling the guests by himself."

"Fiona's not there to harass him, so I think he's fine," Emma said.

"Okay, here we are."

I parked the Thunderbird as close to the main office as I could. We sprinted in and found Bryce Kahului behind the counter. I wished him a happy Thanksgiving, introduced Emma (unnecessarily, it turned out, as he had taken her biology class), and asked him whether he happened to know where Maureen Dos Santos might be at the moment.

"That's funny," he said. "Someone else was just here looking for her. Maureen should be back soon."

"It was Fiona Spencer," said a raspy voice behind me. "Can you blame her?"

I turned around to see Mr. Ferman. He was thin, leaning on a cane, and his tweed jacket hung loosely. But his white hair was combed neatly into place, and his red bow tie looked festive. He certainly looked better than when I'd seen him in the hospital.

"Mr. Ferman?" I tentatively extended my hand. He balanced his left hand on his cane and returned my handshake. His grip was warm and papery. "I'm Molly Barda. I don't know whether you remember me. I came to see you a few days ago. This is my colleague, Dr. Emma Nakamura."

"You're Fiona's friend," he said. "So you must have known. Everybody knew. Except the respective spouses, of course."

"Knew what?" Emma asked innocently.

"Apostol thought Maureen could do no wrong," Mr. Ferman said. "But that girl, she was never a one-man woman. Even I could see it. She was trouble. A true femme fatale."

Bryce came out from behind the counter.

"Mr. Ferman, are you ready? The next seating's in five minutes. We don't want to miss the *pule*."

"I don't want to keep you from your Thanksgiving dinner," I said, "but we would like to find Maureen."

"They were in a hurry, I can tell you that," Mr. Ferman said.

"They?" Emma asked.

"Fiona Spencer was riding with some fellow on a motorcycle, and they were going like a bat out of Hades."

"Where were 'they' headed?" I asked.

Bryce frowned. "Mr. Ferman, do you mind going ahead? I'll catch up."

Mr. Ferman gave a salute and shuffled out of the office in the direction of the dining hall. I wanted to ask him about the elegant watch with the dark blue band, but that would have to wait.

"Fiona Spencer and her mother came here a few minutes ago looking for Maureen," Bryce said. "What's going on?"

"Fiona just found out about her husband hooking up with Maureen," Emma said. "She's pretty mad about it and we're afraid she's gonna do something dumb. Bryce, is it true?"

"Awkward," Bryce said. "Maureen should be back soon if you wanna talk to her."

"When do you expect her back?" I asked.

"Mr. Dos Santos just has to drive her back up from the port, so it should be—"

"So she's at the port?" Emma interrupted.

"What? Nah, I never said—"

"Thank you, Bryce," I said. Emma and I sprinted back out toward the car.

Bryce ran after us.

"Professor Barda, Professor Nakamura, I know you want to help. But you really don't want to get involved with this."

"No?" I asked. "Should we just call the police?"

"No. No, that wouldn't be a good idea. Listen, I have to catch up to Mr. Ferman. Eh, you want to join us for Thanksgiving dinner? It's okay, plenty food, you know. And it's pretty good."

"Thank you for the invitation," I said, "but we actually have our own Thanksgiving dinner to get back to. You're right, Bryce, it's probably best we stay out of it. Have a wonderful Thanksgiving and tell Mr. Ferman Happy Thanksgiving too."

MOLLY: A PRETTY GOOD LIAR

"WHOA, MOLLY," EMMA cried, "I'd rather get there alive, ah?"

"Sorry about that." I'd peeled out onto the highway a little too fast, and the back end of the car had swung wide. "The road's wet, though. It's not my fault."

"The road's always wet." Emma snapped her seatbelt shut. "You live in Mahina, remember?"

"We're not going back to the house," I said.

"Yeah, I figured. You know, you're getting to be a pretty good liar."

"It's sweet Bryce feels protective of us, but it sounds like he knows something bad's going to happen. In fact, I think this might be a good time to call the police."

"Okay," Emma said. "I'm gonna use your phone though, cause 911 get caller ID."

"Why does that matter?" I asked.

"I don't want everyone to think I'm a snitch."

We got to the highway's end and made the right turn to the potholed road that goes down to the Port of Mahina. The weather was usually sunnier in this part of Mahina, and today was no exception. The clouds thinned out as we drove, and before long the sky was shiny and blue.

The Port of Mahina sign was half-hidden behind overgrown monstera, but I spotted it in time to make the turn. The chain-link gate was open, although there was no guard posted. I pulled into the lot and parked in the shade of a lifted Tacoma. On both sides of the lot were corrugated-metal buildings surrounded by trees and vines. A cargo ship loomed on the water side of the lot.

"That must be the ship that's taking the car," I switched off the ignition. "But where's Maureen?"

"I see her! She...uh-oh."

We exited the car as quietly as possible, slowly pressing the heavy doors shut with a "thunk." I stood on tiptoe and peeked over the bed of the lifted truck. Emma was too short to see over the truck bed, so she stood to my right and peered around the back.

By the edge of the water, next to a guardhouse, I saw Maureen Dos Santos and a tall, heavy-set man. He was dressed like an average Mahina businessman, in a designer aloha shirt and black slacks.

"Is that her husband?" I whispered. "Apostol Dos Santos?"

"I think so," Emma said.

I had seen him before, I realized. In Fiona's Spencer's office, wearing a hot-pink Konishi Construction shirt and dark sunglasses.

We couldn't hear what they were saying. Maureen stood with her arms folded. Apostol seemed to be pleading with her. The cargo ship's multicolored containers made a colorful backdrop, stacked like Lego bricks.

Maureen was not wearing the baggy muumuu I'd seen her wearing at the Garden Society meeting. She sported an off-the-shoulder gold lame top, snug black leggings, and spiky heels. She clutched the handle of a leopard-print rollaboard suitcase.

"Because I love you, Maureen," we heard the man cry out. "I'll die without you."

Maureen shook her head and stepped back. Emma leaned out a little too far to get a better look, and almost toppled over sideways.

"Steady on." The sound of the strange voice practically made me jump out of my shoes. Emma and I looked around wildly to see where the voice was coming from.

"Down here."

We crouched down to see Harriet and Fiona, seated comfortably underneath the lifted truck. Harriet's field coat was spread over the asphalt like a picnic blanket. A car parked on the far side of the truck shielded the women from being seen.

"What are you two doing here?" Fiona whispered as Emma and I scooted under the truck to join them. She sounded more mystified than angry.

"Looking for you," Emma said.

"Why are we all sitting under a truck?" I asked.

It wasn't a bad place to wait things out. Harriet's coat was well-padded, and the truck was lifted high enough that we didn't have to worry about bumping our heads.

"Fiona was planning to have a word with Maureen," Harriet said, "but Maureen's husband turned up. One doesn't like to interfere in a family discussion."

"He ran after her shouting her name," Fiona said. "It got dramatic rather quickly, so we thought it would be best to stay out of sight."

"And now we're stuck here, watching the drama unfold," Harriet said, "We've learnt ever so much, haven't we darling? For example, we know what happened to Emmett, don't we?"

"What?" Emma and I asked in unison.

"Maureen's husband killed him," Fiona whispered.

"With a nail gun?" I asked.

"You knew about the nail gun?" Harriet exclaimed.

"Mum, shh."

"You got any more detail?" Emma asked eagerly.

"Maureen's husband got Emmett to come round to the parsonage," Fiona said. "Under the pretense of asking him about window casings or some such thing. They're rebuilding it for us, you know. Were rebuilding it for us, I should say."

"Of course it was all a ruse," Harriet said. "He had brought Emmett there to confront him about Maureen. Fiona, darling, do they know about Maureen and Emmett?"

"Yes," I said.

"It's kinda why we're here," Emma added.

"He seems to have quite a grudge against Emmett," Fiona said. "He accuses Emmett of taking his family from him."

"Quite," Harriet said. "He blamed Emmett for his son's suicide, and of course he wasn't terribly happy about Emmett getting his end away with his wife. So he confronted Emmett at the parsonage, Emmett turned his back, and he picked up the nail gun."

"Which was conveniently loaded up and lying about on the site," Fiona said.

"Yes, for a crime of passion it does seem rather well-planned," Harriet said. "Mr. Dos Santos emptied the nail gun into the back of Emmett's skull. All out of affection for Maureen and their late son, of course."

"So how did Emmett's body end up in your office?" I asked.

Fiona and Harriet looked at each other.

"He didn't say," Fiona replied.

"No idea," Harriet added.

"So Fiona, you gonna kill both of 'em then?" Emma asked.

"I'm sorry? Me?"

"Yeah, you. We came down here cause Molly thought you were gonna kill Maureen cause of the affair. Now you gotta kill 'em both, sounds like, cause Dos Santos killed your husband."

Fiona turned to me.

"Molly. You thought I was planning to murder Maureen?"

"Emma did too," I said. "Maybe not outright murder her, but the whole reason we came here is because you were understandably upset about the affair, and we wanted to stop you from doing something you might regret."

Fiona looked hurt.

"I only wanted to talk to her," she whispered.

"About what?" Emma asked.

Fiona shook her head. "I can't remember."

"It seemed ever so bloody important at the time, though, didn't it?" Harriet said. "Oh, I say, has either of you brought your mobile?"

"Both of ours are still packed away in her saddle bag," Fiona said glumly. "We had to move quickly to hide ourselves."

"I already called the police," Emma said. "When we were driving down."

"I'll say this for Emmett," Harriet said. "He's got to have been the stupidest man alive, to be having it off with that man's wife. Whatever could he have been thinking?"

"Maureen!" Dos Santos roared. We all looked at each other.

"I'm just going to take a quick look," I said.

"Don't let 'em see you," Emma warned.

I scooted back out from under the truck and peeped over the truck bed.

Apostol was pleading, arms outstretched. Maureen did not seem impressed by his show of devotion. She was backing away, wobbling on her high heels.

I ducked back down and told Harriet, Fiona, and Emma what I'd seen.

"I hope the police get here before it's too late," Fiona said.

"The police station's only a couple miles away," Emma said. "They should be here by now."

"I'm going to call Bryce again," I said.

"Who?" Harriet asked.

"He works for Maureen at St. Aelred's," Emma said. "Plus he's our student, that's how come Molly knows him."

"Oh, him," Harriet said. "We just saw him, didn't we, Fiona? Cute as a button, and nearly as bright. Not terribly useful, though."

"Do you think he can help us?" Fiona asked.

"I don't know," I said. "I hope so. Couldn't hurt, might help. And I don't have any better ideas."

MOLLY: BIG SCRAP

MAYBE I SHOULD HAVE called Donnie, but I already felt bad about leaving him to entertain our guests by himself. And I held on to the hope he'd never have to know about this.

I called the St. Aelred main number, and let it ring until it went to voice mail. I tried again, and this time Bryce picked up. I heard festive cafeteria noise in the background.

"Bryce, it's Molly Barda," I said. "Is there a party going on in your office?"

"I forwarded the office phone to my cell in case anyone called," he said. "I'm still in the dining hall. What's going on?"

I quickly brought him up to date on the situation.

"Are you saying Maureen's husband killed Mr. Spencer?" he asked after a long pause.

"Yes. And they're both here."

"Maybe you shouldn't be there, Professor."

"We would all like very much not to be here but, at the moment, we're hiding under a truck because we don't want him to see us. Wait, is it his truck?" Fiona and Harriet nodded. "Great. We're cowering under Apostol Dos Santos's truck. Bryce, is there anything you can tell me that might help us here?"

"Why do you think I know anything?" Bryce sounded wary. "You should call the police. Don't tell them it's about Maureen or Apostol though."

"What do you mean? Why not?"

"Apostol Dos Santos pretty much owns the police."

"Are you kidding me? So the police won't show up if they know Dos Santos is involved?"

"Good to know," Emma muttered, and punched 9-1-1 into her phone. Apparently, everyone could hear both sides of my conversation with Bryce.

"Don't leave, Maureen," we heard Apostol Dos Santos sob in the distance. "I'll die without you. I mean it."

"Who was that?" Bryce asked. "Is it Mr. Dos Santos?"

All four of us turned toward the sound, even though we couldn't see anything but the car next to us.

"Yes, that's Mr. Dos Santos," I said. "He and Maureen are arguing, nothing physical so far. Is there anything else you can tell me that might help us?"

"I wish I could help, Professor. Sorry."

"Wait. Dang it. Bryce, are you there?"

"Hello, Emergency?" Emma spoke into her phone. "You gotta send someone down to the port right now. There's a, um, a fight going on."

"I'm still here," Bryce's voice was scratchy. "Bad connection, ah?"

"Please, Bryce," I said. "This is important. What are you not telling me?"

"What makes you think I'm not telling you something?"

What did make me think that? His walking off with the microwave? Although I had offered it to him. The fact he'd tried to discourage us from following Maureen? Although it probably would have been smart to heed his advice. The way he claimed the piece of plastic wasn't from Trevor's phone? Maybe he was right. But I was still convinced he was hiding something from me.

"You asking me who's the individuals involved?" Emma said to the dispatcher. "It's Maureen—"

I shoved her shoulder and shook my head at her.

"What? Oh yeah, right. It's, um...no one you know. Just some homeless guys. No, wait, tourists. Yeah, that's what I said. Homeless guys versus tourists, big scrap."

"Whoa," Bryce said. "Sounds like you got a lot going on down there. Okay, hope everything works out—"

"Bryce, listen. We don't know what's going to come out when this situation is over. If I do make it out alive, I promise I will do my best to protect you from any consequences arising from anything you tell me right now. Is there anything else you know about this situation that could help us?"

"You mean it about protecting me?"

"Of course," I said.

I heard him take a deep breath.

"You promised, yeah?"

MOLLY: HIS POOR GRIEVING MOTHER

BRYCE KAHULUI WAS A scholarship kid at the St. Aelred School for Boys. Working as assistant to the headmaster's secretary was part of his aid package. And it was how he met his first real boyfriend, Trevor Dos Santos, the secretary's son. Unlike Bryce, Trevor never had to worry about money. He bought sneakers, video games, candy, and whatever else took his fancy, whenever he liked.

Until his father cut off his allowance.

Trevor set about finding a new income stream. At first, he stole ethanol from the chemistry supply cabinet, watered it down, and sold it to the other boys. Bryce found out and convinced him to stop. Unfortunately, when inventory was done, it was Mr. Ferman, the chemistry teacher, who got the blame.

Trevor was running low on funds again when he had a stroke of luck: he discovered his mother was having an affair with the new headmaster.

He decided to blackmail her.

One afternoon at work, Bryce noticed Maureen seemed agitated. She told Bryce to come in an hour later than his scheduled time the next morning. Bryce became suspicious, so he came in early instead. He found the office locked but let himself in with his key.

He heard a conversation coming from the headmaster's private office. He recognized the voices of Maureen and Trevor, and crept close to listen.

"Let me see the pictures," Maureen said. Bryce couldn't hear Trevor's reply.

"I have the whole amount right here," Maureen said. "We can keep each other's secrets, yeah?"

Bryce heard a drawer slide open, some rummaging and scraping. A pop, like a firecracker.

Bryce ran out the back door. He circled around the building and walked casually back in through the front. He found a crowd had already gathered around a sobbing Maureen.

When Maureen spotted Bryce, she dried her eyes and came over to give him a hug.

She whispered in his ear,

"We can keep each other's secrets, yeah?"

"What do you mean?" Bryce tried to play dumb. It didn't work.

"Who they gonna believe, honey?" she murmured. "Trevor's poor grieving mother? Or his gold-digging boy toy?"

The police found Trevor dead on the floor with a single gunshot wound to the head. Emmett Spencer's gun was lying near the boy's left hand. It was ruled a suicide. Only Bryce and Maureen knew any different.

MOLLY: I CAN'T BEAR TO SEE A MAN GROVEL

I THANKED BRYCE, HUNG up, and gave Emma, Harriet, and Fiona, a summary of what Bryce had told me.

All four of us crept out from underneath the truck and peered over the top of the small car next to it. We saw Apostol Dos Santos on his knees. Maureen was backing up the gangplank of the cargo ship.

Harriet straightened up and strode out from between the two cars.

"Mum!" Fiona stage-whispered. Harriet ignored her.

"Dos Santos!" Harriet bellowed.

Apostol Dos Santos turned toward the sound of Harriet's voice.

"Don't be a bloody fool, Dos Santos. Your son didn't kill himself. Maureen shot him."

"Mum," Fiona squeaked. "What are you doing?"

"I can't bear to see a man grovel," Harriet declared.

Dos Santos wasn't groveling now. He picked himself up slowly. Maureen was too far away for me to see her facial expression, but I could read her body language. She had been defiant and dismissive. Now she was scared.

"She's lying!" Maureen shrieked. "It's not true!"

Apostol Dos Santos roared and charged up the gangplank. His bulk obscured Maureen for a moment.

Three loud pops sounded, like firecrackers.

Apostol Dos Santos flailed his arms, toppled sideways over the skinny railing, and fell into the water with a "sploosh."

Maureen stood on the gangplank, staring into the water, still grasping the gun with both hands.

Then she looked up. Sirens wailed in the distance, steadily growing louder.

Maureen tossed the gun into the water, in the general direction of her late husband. Ignoring Harriet, she turned and sauntered up the gangplank, pulling the leopard-print rollaboard behind her.

MOLLY: YOU SHOULD TALK TO SOMEONE

EMMA, DONNIE, AND I were at an outdoor table at the Maritime Club, enjoying the cool breeze and the view of the waves crashing and foaming on the black lava rocks. Emma has the Maritime Club membership, but her husband Yoshi didn't want to come ("all those pretentious, dressed-up people," he'd said, which if you knew Yoshi when he first moved here, you'd find hilarious) so she'd invited Donnie and me along.

We were discussing the case of Maureen Dos Santos, who had been apprehended trying to flee the island on a container ship. She was currently awaiting trial for the murders of her son and her husband. It was reported that Mrs. Dos Santos would have escaped had it not been for a group of unnamed witnesses who were either homeless people, or tourists, or both.

"I thought Mahina was too gossipy for anyone to keep secrets," I said. "But I guess I was wrong. Fiona had no idea her husband was cheating on her."

"It's always the one who's getting cheated on who's the last to know," Emma remarked as she stuffed shrimp into her mouth.

I turned to Donnie.

"Don't look at me like that," he said. "You and the baby keep me busy as it is. I don't have time for a whole other woman in my schedule."

"Good," I said.

"Eh, service is slow tonight," Emma said. "I'm gonna go to the bar. Don't give away my seat."

Donnie found my hand under the table and squeezed it.

"I'm glad you're safe," he said.

"Me too. Believe me, if we'd known Maureen was going to start shooting, we wouldn't have gone down there. I wouldn't have gone down there, anyway. Emma might've."

"Molly, I know you wanted to do the right thing, and it's great that you helped out, but I have to admit, I'm selfish. Your safety is more important to me than anything. So please, next time—"

"I was never in any actual danger," I said.

"Really?" Donnie looked skeptical.

"I should've called you, though. Next time I feel like I'm in trouble at all, I will call you."

Donnie seemed like he was about to say something but changed his mind.

"You okay?" I asked.

"It's hard to believe The Rancher is dead." Donnie squeezed my hand again. "It's the end of an era. Apostol had a lot of influence in Mahina."

"Hey, a power vacuum," I said. "Here's your chance. To be King of Mahina or whatever Dos Santos was."

Donnie laughed.

"No thanks. I'd have to fight Konishi for it."

"Al Konishi?" I asked. "Konishi Construction?"

Donnie nodded.

"He's Dos Santos's cousin."

"Hey, Professor Barda, Mister Gonsalves."

We looked up to see Micah, my former student and erstwhile security guard. He wore a white shirt and black trousers, and was holding an order pad.

"Micah? You work here?" I asked, unnecessarily. "At the Maritime Club?"

He nodded enthusiastically.

"Yeah, I quit the security job. Couldn't handle, after da kine, in Dr. Spencer's office. I kept seeing it in my head when I was trying fo' go sleep, you know? Mr. Gonsalves, the guy was all cooked like one huli huli chicken. You know when they moved the body he just fell apart—"

"Sounds like you made a good decision," Donnie said.

"That's a traumatic thing to live through, Micah," I said. "I know exactly what you mean. Maybe you should talk to someone about it."

"Oh yeah, good idea." Micah pulled out the fourth chair and sat down at our table.

"Micah, I didn't mean—"

"Professor Barda, glad you never get hurt. Mr. Gonsalves, bet you was worried, ah?"

"Yes," Donnie said.

"Micah," I said, "we don't want to take you away from your work."

"It's okay. It's a little slow right now. Eh, so my cousin at Mahina PD told me—oh hey, Professor Nakamura."

Emma had a glass of beer in each hand.

"That was nice of you to bring extra," I said, "but Donnie and I are drinking wine."

"Huh? These aren't for you. This is so I don't have to get up again. Eh, Micah, looking sharp, you."

"I dressed for work, that's why."

"Listen, if you want anything to drink, you gotta get it yourself," she said. "Service is junk today."

"Micah was going to tell us what he heard from his cousin who works with Mahina PD," I said.

"Oh yeah?" Emma got seated and started on her first glass of beer. "So is it really true? Maureen killed her son in the headmaster's office and made it look like suicide?"

"It's true," Micah said. "The boy was gonna tell the father about the mother's affair."

"What a little snitch," Emma said. "Not that I'm excusing Maureen for killing him. But still."

A bearded man in an aloha shirt materialized next to our table.

"Is everything okay here?" he asked. "Micah?"

Micah scooted the chair back and jumped to his feet.

"Oh, hey, Mr. K. Sorry, I was just—"

"It's my fault," I said. "Micah was sharing some history with us. At my request. I understand if you can't spare him."

The manager glanced at his watch.

"We do want our staff to engage our members," he said. "And we're proud to share our club's history. But Micah, we're a little busy right now, and we have customers waiting."

MOLLY: WE ABSOLUTELY DISAPPROVE OF MURDER

MICAH CAME BACK TO our table to chat after the rush was over. According to his cousin at Mahina PD, the purple glob in the microwave really was from Trevor Dos Santos's phone. After Maureen shot her son, she cooked his phone in the microwave to get rid of the photos he'd taken. She managed to ruin the microwave. But she didn't destroy the incriminating images, which the police were able to retrieve from a remote server.

I picked up a little more gossip from Bryce Kahului, my student, when he stopped by my office during Christmas break. Bryce has lunch regularly with Mr. Ferman, who has been sharing his recollections as they surface.

The workman who had been wearing Emmett Spencer's watch was telling the truth about where he got it. Apostol Dos Santos had just killed Emmett Spencer and was about to walk away from the body when Mr. Ferman happened by on his morning stroll.

To distract Mr. Ferman from the nail-studded corpse lying prone on the workbench, Dos Santos removed the headmaster's distinctive watch and handed it to Mr. Ferman. Disoriented by what he had just witnessed, Mr. Ferman regifted the watch to the first person he saw—the Konishi employee I'd seen at our building. He then wandered out onto the highway and into the path of a tour bus.

Fortunately, Mr. Ferman's body and his memory are steadily recovering.

Pat Flanagan was finishing up his feature on the Labor Day Race and preparing to pitch a story on The Dos Santos murders to his editor. I gave Pat my eyewitness account of Dos Santos's death and Maureen's attempted escape. Pat reciprocated with the solution to the Mystery of Emmett Spencer's Christmas Plans: Fiona's husband had reserved a single-occupancy room in a Las Vegas resort. The same resort where Maureen and Apostol Dos Santos spent the holidays. The apparent plan was for Maureen and Emmett to sneak off while Apostol gambled.

No wonder Emmett didn't want Fiona to accompany him.

The Dos Santos case was, unsurprisingly, the main topic of discussion at the December meeting of the Pua Kala Garden society. We deduced that the extortion note Mrs. Masterman's housekeeper found in the bathroom had probably been discarded there by Maureen. When Mrs. Masterman asked the group about it, Maureen pretended she had no idea what it was.

There was a general feeling among the Pua Kala Garden Society members of having been hoodwinked; we'd all thought of Trevor Dos Santos as a tragic victim of suicide, not a ruthless blackmailer. We agreed that while we absolutely disapproved of murder, it wasn't easy to eke out much sympathy for the young racketeer.

Serena, the dean's secretary, told me it was Fiona's mother who had kicked off the entire chain of events. Harriet's chewing-out of Fiona's husband in the middle of Mahina Stationers was immediately the talk of Mahina, Serena told me. The gossip got back to Maureen's husband, who could no longer remain in denial. He took advantage of his position on the board of the St. Aelred School for Boys to lure his wife's lover to the isolated parsonage site behind the school.

The physical evidence indicates that Emmett Spencer's last act was turning his back on the older man—an unforgivable gesture of disrespect.

Dos Santos arranged with his cousin's company, Konishi Construction, to dispose of Emmett Spencer's body. The conversation I'd overheard on my way to our budget meeting was probably part of the plan. Konishi Construction was using Fiona Spencer's presumably-unoccupied office as a temporary storage site. According to Micah's cousin at Mahina PD, a Konishi employee admitted to assisting Dos Santos in the "storage" of unspecified "rubbish." Dos Santos had originally asked them to dig a hole, but it would have taken too long to dig through the lava rock. Instead, Dos Santos was given a key, a Konishi Construction t-shirt, a 55-gallon drum, a dolly, and directions to the "vacant" office. The Konishi employee insisted that no one at Konishi knew a dead body was involved. Of course no one at Konishi Construction asked too many questions. No one questioned Apostol Dos Santos.

Konishi knew the fever cabinet was in Fiona's office, so Dos Santos likely knew about it as well. Dos Santos might have remembered the difficulty of identifying his first wife's body after the tanning bed incident, and assumed Emmett Spencer's identity could be similarly obscured.

This is Mahina PD's working explanation for Emmett Spencer's placement in the fever cabinet. Dos Santos, of course, isn't talking, so we'll never know for sure.

After our college got the fever cabinet back from the police (who were happy to return it as it took up most of the free space in the evidence room), the Finance Club auctioned it off online. With the proceeds, the College of Commerce was able to buy a teakettle, coffee maker, and microwave for each floor of our building. And we had enough left over for two years' worth of copy paper, toner, and whiteboard markers.

Without a murder conviction hanging over her head, Fiona Spencer decided to cancel her trip back to England and finish out fall semester. She left after commencement for a position in New Zealand. Her students threw her a little party and gave her a fancy umbrella as a going-away present, which I hope she assumed was a reference to rainy Mahina.

I had been dreading trying to find a replacement for Fiona, but fortunately there was a candidate available. A recently-retired Tutor in Law at Balliol College, Oxford University. Miraculously, she's perfectly content with our paltry lecturer wages, and with her office assignment. It's Fiona's old office, Room 310, which she cheerfully refers to as "the abattoir."

Her name? Harriet Holmes.

FIONA: DEAR OLD OSCAR

FIONA STEPPED OUT OF the motor coach in front of the extended-stay hotel, and took a deep draught of cool, foggy air. She'd feared New Zealand's upside-down seasons would mean a warm December, but here at the southern tip of South Island at least, it was cooler than she'd expected.

It would feel like a proper Christmas after all. This cheered her. Driving on the left-hand side of the road had lifted her spirits as well. Fiona had the oddly pleasant sensation of coming home to someplace she had never been.

She extended the handle of her rolling bag and hooked her new umbrella onto it. As a moving away gift her students had given her a British-made umbrella, black, with a malacca crook handle. It was meant as a sort of joke; the students called her "Mary Poppins" on the sly. Fiona thought this rather sweet, and far preferable to some other nicknames she'd heard of.

She checked her watch: a men's Vacheron Constantin with a dark-blue alligator band. It looked huge on her slender wrist, but Fiona liked the boldness of it. The Mahina police had been lovely about getting it back for her. She'd heard the builder who had been wearing it was only too happy to return it when he found out where it had come from.

Another entry on the plus side of the ledger: Harriet had stayed behind in Mahina.

Fiona's mother had negotiated a semi-retirement with the Bursar in order to teach at Mahina State. Because she had been a Tutor in Law at Oxford, she was deemed qualified to teach the College of Commerce Business Ethics classes. Harriet was happy to make do on a lecturer's salary. She was minted and didn't need the money, and she thought the whole thing a jolly wheeze.

As much as Fiona didn't want to admit it to herself, she was relieved to find it wasn't too much trouble to travel between Hawaii and New Zealand. When she was ready, she could pop over and visit Harriet. And with only a few more months before Fiona's father was out of prison, there was a fair chance all three would be able to meet soon, perhaps somewhere on the upcoming book tour for his prison memoir.

Children begin by loving their parents; as they grow older they judge them; sometimes they forgive them.

Dear old Oscar. There was no avoiding him, it seemed. Fiona smiled and pulled her rolling bag up to the hotel's check-in counter.

THE INFLUENCER

THE INFLUENCER

TO THOSE WHO have never tasted fame: May you always appreciate your good fortune.

CHAPTER 1

DR. EMMA NAKAMURA IS my best friend. We both teach at Mahina State University in Mahina, Hawaii, where, according to our TV ads, "Your Future Begins Tomorrow." Over the years, we've come to know each other well. So I can tell right away when Emma is up to something.

Emma was trying to convince me she had dropped by my house for a cup of coffee because she "happened to be in the neighborhood." I knew better. In fact, she was angling to meet social media sensation Jandie Brand, who had recently moved into our new rental unit, separated from our main house by a mere quarter-acre of lawn. I'd tried explaining to Emma that Jandie and her husband had chosen our quiet street for the express purpose of avoiding pestering fans. Somehow Emma didn't think any of it applied to her.

Steadfastly ignoring Emma's increasingly-obvious hints, I opened the pantry to an eye-level stack of toilet paper and paper towels and a brickwork wall of blue Spam cans. A tropical storm was headed our way, so before Donnie left for the mainland, he had stocked us up on the essentials. I managed to dig out the coffee without knocking anything over.

"I knew I had a new box of coffee in here somewhere," I said. "Here we go. Mizuno Mart house brand."

"Maybe your tenants get some better coffee we could borrow," Emma said. "Let's go ask 'em."

"Seriously Emma?"

"What?"

Emma sat at my kitchen counter with an innocent look on her face. Looking innocent is easy for Emma. She's five foot nothing, with round, sun-freckled cheeks and wavy black hair pulled back in a casual ponytail. Thanks to all the canoe paddling she does, Emma is built like a very fit teddy bear. She also has tiny, childlike hands, something she hates having pointed out (I've had to learn this the hard way).

"Emma, you just told me you stopped by for a cup of coffee. Which is great, because I always like seeing you. This is the coffee I have. You want the coffee or not?"

"Yeah, Mizuno Mart coffee is fine. You're right, I didn't just come over to see you."

"A-ha! I knew it."

"My *schmendrick* brother is staying at my house. I needed a break."

Emma grew up just a few miles outside of Mahina, speaking Pidgin like everyone else around here. Then she went back east for grad school and picked up some Yiddish, which she uses frequently, mostly to enrich her insult repertoire.

"Jonah's at your house? Last I heard, he was living in Washington."

"He is. Guess it was too complicated for him to actually let me know in advance he was visiting. The first I heard of it was when he called me from the airport. I had to move out of the guest room so he could stay there."

"The guest room? Emma, why are you sleeping in the—know what, never mind, it's none of my business."

"No big deal, just Yoshi snores. It's like sleeping next to a running chainsaw. Or like when there's a hurricane and the rain's coming down real hard on the metal roof. Oh, speaking of hurricanes, Molly I bet your tenants aren't prepared for the hurricane like you are. Maybe we should—"

"So we've made our way back around to my tenants now, have we? The hurricane is going to be down to a tropical storm by the time it hits us."

"Yeah, but do they know they're supposed to go out and buy extra toilet paper and Spam? I bet they don't. They're gonna starve to death, Molly, and it's gonna be our fault. Cause we didn't reach out an' help when we had a chance."

I finished brewing our two coffees and brought them over.

"Remarkable. Emma, I don't think I've ever seen you so starstruck before."

Emma snatched her coffee mug from me.

"I'm not starstruck. I just like following Jandie's feed and I think it's cool she moved to Mahina. To my best friend's house, even. What are the chances?"

"And you know why she came to Mahina, right? So she can take a break from her adoring public for six months."

"Molly, she doesn't need to be protected from me. I'm not one of her crazy fans. Know what I think? I think you just wanna keep her all to yourself."

Emma didn't actually say "so there!" but the way she drank her coffee implied it.

"Emma, I—"

"We should print out the hurricane checklist and bring it over. You don't want them getting swept away in a flood, do you?"

"We had the builders install steel foundation piers. No one's getting swept away."

"Molly, what is your problem, come on!"

"Look. Suppose we do walk over there. I'll say hey, you heard about the storm coming, here's the hurricane prep checklist, by the way, this is my friend Emma Nakamura, everyone says oh nice to meet you, and then do we walk away like normal people?"

"That's right," Emma said.

"No, because then you'll just *happen* to mention how people are always telling you how much you look like Jandie, and you'll make her stand there while you try to get a selfie with her—"

"Not." Emma crossed her arms and we glared at each other for a few seconds.

Finally, I said,

"Okay fine. But you have to give me your phone."

"Aw Molly, come on."

She handed me her phone in the end, because otherwise I would have refused to go at all. I printed out the Emergency Preparedness checklist from the County Civil Defense website, and Emma and I crossed the soggy lawn to the house next door.

I raised my hand to knock, but Emma stayed my hand.

Someone inside was talking. Not Jandie. A man's voice.

"I think it's time to pull the trigger."

"How long?" said another man.

The voices lowered to a murmur.

"But that's what I'm trying to *saaaay*!"

Emma nudged me. We both recognized Jandie Brand's childlike voice.

"I'm not gonna bite the hand of the gift horse that feeds me."

"That's Jandie," Emma whispered.

"I know," I whispered back. "This is getting interesting."

"Okay, you two brain geniuses, riddle me this." This was Jandie again. "What about the landlady? She has a problem minding her own business. And she's kind of a crackpot, if you ask me."

"Hey," I mouthed. "*I'm* the landlady."

"Shh!" Emma shoved me.

"Now Jandie," said one of the male voices, "Ed's right. Know what they say, get it done now, you can always cry later."

I stood up straight and rapped the door. The conversation inside stopped dead.

"Someone's at the door," said the other man.

"Sorry, we're busy," Jandie shouted. "Can you come back later?"

"This is Molly from next door," I shouted back. "I brought over the hurricane checklist."

The door opened, and Edward Ladd stood there. I was struck by how far he was from his wife on the conventional-attractiveness scale. He was bald, beak-nosed, and older than Jandie by a generation or two.

I inwardly scolded myself for being superficial. Ladd must have a delightful personality. No, that, too, was a mean thought. *Try not to be so shallow, Molly.*

I cleared my throat and handed him the checklist.

"Hi. Hope you guys are doing okay. You've probably heard the weather reports. This is from the County Office of Civil Defense. In case you don't already have a copy."

"I'm Emma," said Emma.

"I can't have the power go out," he said as he looked it over. "Are you telling me I'm supposed to buy a generator now?"

"We've provided you with a portable generator," I said. "It's in the carport. You can run your refrigerator, whatever else you need. Just don't try to use a microwave and a blow dryer at the same time."

"Where are we supposed to get two gallons of water per day?"

"The bottled water's going to be all sold out by now. Wipe out your bathtub with bleach, fill it up with water, and add another capful of bleach. It'll be safe to drink."

"Do you want us to show you guys how to use the generator?" Emma asked.

"No. We'll figure it out."

He closed the door without further niceties.

"What a *putz*," Emma remarked as we walked back up the grassy hill toward the road. "Totally blocked us. Not even a little peek."

"Maybe she asked him to keep people away. I told you they wanted privacy. Hey Emma, did you hear what Jandie said about me?"

"No one was talking about you."

"She called me a crackpot. Why would anyone say I'm a crackpot?"

"Molly, no one thinks you're a crackpot. Guarantee. I mean, you can be inflexible, obsessive, neurotic—"

"Thank you, Emma, I get it."

"Self-centered, kind of un-self-aware—"

"Yes, thank you, Emma. What are you OW!"

Emma was clutching my arm. It was pretty painful, to be honest. Emma has an alarmingly strong grip, especially considering how tiny her hands are.

And then I saw the cause of Emma's alarm.

"It's her," I stammered. "What's she doing here?"

CHAPTER 2

STROLLING DOWN OUR side of Uakoko street was a blonde woman in a long-sleeved muumuu. The two Yorkshire terriers she was walking had been groomed to look like silky mops. All three of them, the woman and the two Yorkies, wore matching yellow hibiscus flowers tucked behind their ears.

"I can't believe it," Emma said. "I thought Linda retired."

"She did," I replied. "Being retired just means you don't have to go to work, though. It doesn't turn you invisible."

Linda Wilson had been a higher-up in the Student Retention Office at Mahina State. Emma teaches introductory biology, which makes her the designated dream-crusher for aspiring health professionals. There was no way those two were ever going to see eye-to-eye. Because I was Emma's friend, Linda had always had it in for me too.

"Linda," I squeaked. "What a pleasant surprise!"

"What are you doing here?" Emma demanded.

"Molly, Emma, it's so nice to see you. Pele, Hiiaka, and I are just going for our daily walk."

The two leashes went taut as the Yorkies sprang at us with their teeth bared.

"How nice. That's exactly what we're doing too. Walking." My reflex, even now, was to appease Linda by agreeing with whatever she said. "Gotta get those steps in, right? Look at us. What are the chances? All of us here, walking on Uakoko Street?"

Linda motioned us closer and I caught a whiff of cigarette smoke.

"Do you know who lives in that new ohana building?" Linda whispered to Emma. She was pointing to my rental unit. "Social media influencer Jandie Brand."

"Who?" I asked innocently.

"Oh, Molly." Linda shook a playful finger at me, rattling her gold bangles. "You think we're just little country bumpkins out here in Mahina. 'Who' indeed."

"No, I didn't mean—"

"Jandie Brand is actually very famous on the internet," Linda explained to Emma.

"That's great, Linda," Emma replied flatly.

"And Molly knows her better than any of us, don't you, Molly?"

"I don't interact with her much," I said. "I try to give them their privacy."

"Well, the next time you see Jandie, you can tell her I have a message for her."

"A message? Okay, no problem." I had zero intention of passing on any message from Linda Wilson. But Linda didn't need to know that.

"Tell her it's fine to post all the food and flowers and waterfalls, just like every other visitor to Mahina, but do you know what would really improve her feed? Some cuddly fur babies."

"Cuddly fur babies. Sure." I stepped back as the Yorkies lunged and snapped at my ankles.

"I know she would enjoy meeting Pele and Hiiaka. Everyone does. Molly, you *will* introduce us, won't you?"

"Umm..." I glanced at the sky, which had taken on an ominous greenish cast. "Now isn't a good time with the storm coming. We're all battening down the hatches. In fact, we probably shouldn't even be out walking."

"Of course. Perhaps in a day or two, after the rains have passed," Linda said sweetly.

"Linda," I said, "please don't tell anyone Jandie's here. She and her husband value their privacy and the last thing she needs is to get swarmed by fans."

Linda said nothing, a stiff smile frozen on her face.

"I mean, I'm sure she would love to meet *you*, and your adorable...fur babies, of course. But please don't tell anyone *else*."

Linda unfroze.

"Yes, of course. I'll be in touch."

Linda continued to glide up the street in her long muumuu, her two little mop-dogs scampering angrily around her feet.

Emma and I rushed into the house. I shut the door behind us and locked it firmly.

"How did Linda find me?" I gasped. "And how on earth did she know about Jandie Brand?"

"Yeah, that was a bad surprise. I need a drink."

"Emma, it's ten in the morning."

"Bloody Mary it is. Where's your vodka?"

I sank onto my couch.

"On the counter next to the toaster. The bloody Mary mix is in the door of the fridge. Emma, Linda's going to blab to everyone about my having a celebrity tenant. People are going to come swarming around to harass them. This is exactly what I promised wouldn't happen."

"Unless you arrange an introduction for Linda and her little hellhounds." Emma plunked down next to me with a glass in each hand and handed me one. I took a cautious sip and quickly set the glass down.

"What is this, half vodka?"

"I would've put in more, but that's all there was in the bottle."

"What was Linda doing on my street? How did she know my personal business?"

"Are you seriously asking, Molly?"

"I know. It's Mahina. Everybody knows everyone's business. Of course Linda knew, somehow. Dangit."

"You should be used to it by now," Emma said. "Remember that time you was buying a whole bunch of booze and underwear at Galimba's Bargain Boyz an' it turned out the boy at the cash register was one of your students?"

"I had no reason to be embarrassed," I said. "Those were all perfectly legitimate purchases."

"Exactly! Who cares if everyone at Mahina State knows your exact bra size? Same thing when you was going to see the shrink—"

"I'm not sure this is helpful—"

"Oh yeah," Emma said, "and remember that thing with Stephen Park? Your students knew he was cheating on you before you did."

"Emma, what is your point?"

"I'm just giving you examples of how you can't expect to have any privacy in Mahina. So don't stress yourself out about it."

I chugged the remaining contents of my glass.

"There's seriously no more vodka?" I asked.

"Nope. We drank the last of it."

"It's not the privacy issue, Emma, it's the Linda Wilson issue. I thought when she retired that was it. I'd never have to deal with her again. And today she pops up right in front of my house with her snarling little 'fur babies'. Not what I needed right after overhearing my tenant complain about her nosy landlady."

"To be fair, Molly, you wouldn't have heard it in the first place if you hadn't been—"

"Oh, and I didn't even tell you, here's another layer on my spring break stress cake. Victor

Santiago, the donor relations guy, wants my students' business plans featured at this year's Senior Showcase."

"Isn't that good?" Emma asked. "Senior Showcase is a big deal."

"No, not good. Because if my students' presentations are anything other than perfect and one hundred percent inoffensive, I'll be vilified for alienating our donors. And if everything is flawless and anodyne, I'll get in trouble for boring them. And if I refuse to participate, I'm not a team player. Emma, after the latest budget cuts, external donations are our lifeblood. I'm afraid I'm going to mess things up for everyone."

"You'll be fine, Molly. You got this. Didn't you just go to some donor dinner thing last year?"

"You mean the one where Donnie and I were forced to sit at the same table as my ex, I sprang a breast milk leak that ruined my favorite blouse, and oh yeah, *someone died*, and I got blamed for it? *That* donor dinner?"

Emma cleared her throat.

"Uh, no, I meant a different one. Eh, someone's at the door. I'll go see who it is. If it's Linda I'll tell her you left."

Emma ran over to the front door and pressed her eye to the peephole. The relief in her body language signaled it wasn't Linda.

My visitor was Mr. Henriques, my retired next-door neighbor. At least I assumed he was retired, based on the fact that he seemed to spend his days at home, observing the comings and goings of Uakoko Street.

"Eh Mr. Henriques," Emma said. "Nice to see you. Come in. You like some coffee?"

CHAPTER 3

MR. HENRIQUES WAS ABOUT my height, with a moon face and a few strands of black hair spread thinly over a large head. I couldn't help it: I found Mr. Henriques thoroughly annoying. I also felt guilty about this because I could tell he was lonely.

"Oh, hello Mrs. Nakamura. Mrs. Gonsalves. Just a glass of orange juice, please." He came in and sat on the couch cushion next to Emma. "What's the matter with the Ladds? They're making so much noise I cannot hear my shows."

"I don't have any orange juice," I said. "Did you say something is going on next door?"

He braced his hands on his knees and stood up.

"I like show you."

Emma and I followed Mr. Henriques out the front door and onto the wraparound lanai. He led us around to the back. From the corner of the lanai, we could see the rental unit through the leggy papala and bushy strawberry guava that I kept at roof-height for privacy's sake. On the far side of the rental unit was Mr. Henriques's house. It was a little shabby, and the metal roof needed repainting. But he kept his lawn neatly-trimmed and his carport well-organized, and he never let mail or newspapers stack up.

"I don't hear anything," I said. "Really, they were making enough noise to disturb you inside your house?"

"Well it's quiet now," he admitted.

"What did you hear before?" Emma asked.

"They was arguing," he said. "Like, real loud kine."

"Mr. Henriques, if you think there's an actual emergency—"

"I know. Call 9-1-1 right away," he said sheepishly. "Otherwise give 'em their privacy."

"It's wonderful to hear your concern for your neighbors' well-being, truly," I said.

"Well, I got no one else to look after these days. Might as well make myself useful, ah?"

Instead of using the conversational pause to take his leave, Henriques leaned on the railing of the lanai as if he were settling in for a long chat.

"Eh, Mrs. Gonsalves, your husband here?"

Emma started to answer but I cut her off.

"Donnie's out at the moment." If Mr. Henriques knew that Donnie and baby Francesca were traveling on the mainland and that I was here alone, he would only ramp up his helpful visits.

"I was wondering how come Donnie's Drive-Inn was all closed up," he said. "You're not closing for good, ah?"

"No, not at all. It's just for a couple of weeks."

"You and Mr. Gonsalves getting divorced? That's gonna be hard for you, single working mom with a new baby."

"No! Of course not. We're just doing some renovations. We thought this would be a perfect time. The college and high school spring break both happened to fall on the same dates this year, so half of Mahina's vacationing in Vegas right now."

Including my husband and daughter. Donnie thought it was important for Francesca to meet his family members. His uncle in Las Vegas, for one, wasn't getting any younger. My appalling stepson Davison lived there too, and had a kid of his own, about Francesca's age.

Mr. Henriques frowned.

"You think I should talk to Mr. Ladd? You know, give him some hints about how to treat the wife? It's not right for them to be shouting at each other like that."

"I don't think Molly's gonna let you," Emma said.

"Look," I said, "It's true, I am being protective of Jandie and her husband. When they signed their lease, they specifically said they wanted to live somewhere quiet, where fans wouldn't bother them. At first I thought they were being a little extreme, but now? I'm starting to understand. I mean, just today I had someone I thought was my best friend, pretend to come by to visit me, but all along it was a ruse to wangle a face-to-face with Jandie."

"Hey!" Emma objected.

"And then a former coworker who I haven't seen in years pops up and demands I arm-twist Jandie into featuring this woman's horrible little dogs on her social media. The whole reason Jandie and her husband are in Mahina in the first place is because they want a break from the spotlight."

"Oh yeah, Jandie, maybe," Mr. Henriques said. "But I think Mr. Ladd would like to have a little bit of that spotlight shining on him again."

CHAPTER 4

BY THE TIME MR. HENRIQUES finally left, it was close to lunchtime. Emma wandered into the kitchen and opened the freezer side of the refrigerator.

"Wow, Donnie set you up good. There's like a year's worth of food in here. What a *mensch*."

"I know. It was thoughtful of him. It's strange not having Donnie and the baby here. The house seems so empty. I think I'm starting to miss them."

I heard the microwave run. Emma wandered back out to the living room holding a bowl piled high with steaming chow fun and pulled a chair up next to where I was working.

"What are you doing, Molly?"

I lifted my hands from the keyboard.

"What do you mean, what am I doing? I do all kinds of stuff on the computer."

"Yeah, but you're doing it secretively. I can tell cause the sneaky way you're typing."

Emma stared at me accusingly as she chewed her chow fun.

"Fine. I was searching for Edward Ladd. My tenant. It's a common name, unfortunately."

Emma pointed at me dramatically.

"Aha! Stalking your tenants. After you told everyone else to leave 'em alone."

"Yeah, well, the difference is, what I'm doing doesn't bother them because they don't know I'm doing it."

Emma scooted her chair closer and peered at my computer screen.

"What are you looking for? You find anything good?"

"Not yet. I was wondering what Mr. Henriques meant about Ladd missing the spotlight. Should I know who he is? Is he some infamous serial killer or something?"

"Why don't you just ask him?"

"What, ask my tenant if he's a serial killer?"

"No, ask Mr. Henriques what he meant. He's lonely, Molly, can't you tell? He'd love for someone to listen to all his conspiracy theories an' stuff."

"I'd really rather not."

Emma shoved my shoulder.

"Eh, Molly. Try Ed Ladd. Instead of Edward."

"I already did."

"How about Teddy or Ted?"

"Oh, good idea. Hm. No, nope, no. Oh my goodness, that is *definitely* not him."

"Put safe search on," Emma suggested.

"Oh yeah, good idea. Okay, let's try again. I'm still not...wait a second. What? No way. Seriously?"

Emma bounced impatiently in her chair.

"What is it, Molly?"

"Hang on, let me show you something."

I went to my bookshelf and pulled down a book. I was unpleasantly surprised to see it was speckled with brownish-orange mold. The pages looked chewed around the edges.

"What's that?" Emma asked.

"I guess I haven't read this in a while. Mahina weather isn't great for books, is it?"

Emma took the book from me.

"Ew. You should buy a dehumidifier. Where'd you get this?"

"I bought it for myself as a treat after I left my corporate job."

"Seriously, Molly? You used to have a real job? How come I never knew this?"

"It didn't last long. It's not something I care to discuss."

"Huh." Emma leafed through the pages. "I thought about going into industry, you know. Lotta my old classmates ended up there. Working at seed companies, or chemical companies. It's good money. How'd you like it?"

"I didn't," I said. "Everything was about bringing in money and tying yourself in knots catering to entitled, unreasonable clients."

"Oh yes, so very different from teaching at Mahina State."

"I am aware of the irony."

"You should toss this and get a new copy." Emma handed the book back to me. "It's falling apart."

"No, I'm keeping it," I said. "It's out of print. And it's signed by the author. Maybe it'll be worth something someday."

"The author? Who you think is living in your rental unit right now?"

"It could be him. What do you think?"

Emma turned the book over and scowled at the author photo on the back cover.

"This guy has hair."

"Well, it's been a couple of decades."

"Eh Molly, you know who would be interested in this? Pat."

"Emma, that's a great idea! Pat can get to the bottom of this."

Pat Flanagan used to work the crime beat for our local paper, the *County Courier*, before they laid off most of their staff. He started his own newsblog, *Island Confidential*, and took a job teaching composition at Mahina State, which is how Emma and I met him. The three of us were inseparable, until he moved to Honolulu to take a job at an acclaimed alternative weekly. The move was great for Pat's career, a completely rational decision on his part. But I still missed him. I'm pretty sure Emma did too.

"Should I call him right now?" I asked.

"Good idea. I'll get us some wine."

"I guess it is after noon. But not Donnie's good wine, Emma. It costs a fortune, and I would never say it to him, but I honestly can't tell the difference. Can you go into the pantry and grab a box? Try not to knock over the wall of Spam."

CHAPTER 5

BY THAT EVENING IT was raining so hard it would have been dangerous for Emma to drive home, even if she had been sober. I set her up on the living room couch with a blanket and pillow. She was out by nine. It took me a little longer to get to sleep. People describe the sound of rain falling on a metal roof as "restful." Which, sure, if you like the sound of someone pouring buckshot into a metal garbage can right over your head.

The next morning I thought at first I had gotten up early. But I hadn't. It just seemed dark because of the dense cloud cover.

I walked out to the kitchen and brewed myself a cup of coffee. Emma was fast asleep on the couch, unbothered by the rumbling of the coffee maker. I took my cup out to the lanai and watched sheets of rain sweep across the cemetery behind my house.

I saw something move out on the lawn. A big red-and-white golf umbrella propelled by a scurrying little pair of legs. My neighbor Mr. Henriques was heading my way.

I ran around to the front door and headed him off before he could knock and wake up everyone in the house. But then I remembered Donnie and the baby were on the mainland and the only person inside was Emma.

Mr. Henriques shook out his umbrella, spattering both of us. He apologized and set it down on the porch. I invited him inside and tried to jostle Emma awake, but she muttered something and pulled a pillow over her head.

"Would you like a cup of coffee, Mr. Henriques?" I asked.

"Do you have orange juice?"

"No, I'm afraid I still don't."

"Coffee's okay then."

I brewed him a cup, and a second cup for me, and set out the cream and sugar on the dining table.

"Sorry to bother you again," he said as he got seated. "Thanks for the coffee, ah? I thought I should tell you right away."

Mr. Henriques dumped the entire contents of the cream carton into his coffee cup, leaving me to drink mine black.

"So, Mr. Henriques, what is it you have to tell me? It must be important to come out in this weather." I sipped and tried not to wrinkle my nose. Mizuno Mart house brand coffee without any cream in it tastes like paving tar.

"There's no one in the house," said Mr. Henriques.

"I don't understand. You and I are sitting right here, and Emma is over there on the couch. Wait. You don't mean..."

"Mr. Henriques looked embarrassed.

"My *renters'* house? Were you spying on Jandie and her husband?"

"Nah, nah, not spying. I saw the jalousies was open. The rainwater was going to get in an' cause damage."

"Oh. Well that seems reasonable, I guess."

"I went over an' knocked and no one answered. I wanted to make sure everything was ok. I know you said stay away from 'em, only I suspected something was wrong. I was worried about their safety."

"Do I smell coffee?" I heard Emma ask from the couch. "Eh, howzit, Mr. Henriques."

"Mr. Henriques was just telling me he saw the windows open on the rental unit," I said. "And when he knocked, no one answered."

"I'm listening. I'm gonna make myself some coffee." Emma ambled into the kitchen.

"So what happened then?" I asked.

"Well I went inside to see what was going on."

"Okay. I think that's technically breaking and entering. So what did you find? A dead body or something?"

"No." He fidgeted. "Nobody there, the house was empty. They was gone."

"Gone like empty? Like they'd packed up and left?"

"No, the furniture and everything was there."

"So you broke into the rental unit when the occupants were away."

Mr. Henriques concentrated very hard on sipping his creamy coffee.

"I'm glad you're being honest with me, Mr. Henriques, but do you understand why it was a bad idea to go inside? What if someone had been inside and thought you were a burglar? You could've gotten shot."

Emma brought her coffee over and sat down at the table with us. She picked up the cream carton, shook it, and put it back down. She sighed and spooned four heaping spoonsful of sugar into her cup.

"You see any broken windows?" Emma asked. "Blood spatters anywhere?"

"No," I said before he could answer. "They just happened to be out. Let's hope they don't notice and please, Mr. Henriques, never go into their house unless they specifically invite you."

"But where'd they go? They shouldn't be out in this weather," he objected.

"*You* were out in this weather," I said testily. "You walked over here."

"But they left the windows open," he said.

"Good for you, Mr. Henriques," Emma said. "You stopped the rain from coming in and now Molly and Donnie don't have to pay to fix water damage."

"I appreciate your good intentions," I said. "Next time you see something amiss, please just knock. If they don't answer, come here and let Donnie or me know. We'll figure out what to do."

"A lot of people have guns, you know," Emma said. "You coulda been shot."

"I already told him that, Emma."

His eyes widened.

"Do you think Jandie would shoot me?"

"Nah, I can't see Jandie shooting anyone," Emma said. "But the husband might, you know."

"Eh, when I was inside, I saw they got da kine, a big saltwater aquarium."

"They what?" I said.

"I got one aquarium too, you know," Mr. Henriques said. "Small kine. Eh, I just caught a couple snowflake eel down at the tidepools. Maybe I could give 'em one."

"Did you see any water damage?" I asked.

Emma reached over and shoved my shoulder. "Who cares about water damage, Molly? You get *Jandie Brand* staying at your house."

"Yes I do. Jandie Brand and her saltwater aquarium."

I watched Mr. Henriques tip his cup back to finish the last drop of his cream-with-coffee.

"Thank you so much for this, Mrs. Gonsalves." He wiped his mouth with the back of his hand.

"No problem," I said. "Always a pleasure."

"Cream in my coffee is a real treat for me."

"I know. I like it too."

"I don't get to enjoy it much. I'm on a fixed income, you know."

"Oh." Well, *that* made me feel bad. "Um, look, Mr. Henriques, when we closed down the Drive-Inn to do the renovations? We had to bring home a lot of food. More than we could possibly eat. Could I get you to take home a tray or two? It's frozen, so it'll last."

"Oh, I don't know, Mrs. Gonsalves..."

"Please. It's just taking up room in the freezer. You'd be doing me a favor."

Emma and I stood on the porch and watched Mr. Henriques make his way back to his house. In one hand he held his giant golf umbrella. In the other he clutched a Mizuno Mart shopping tote containing foil trays of chow mein and chicken katsu. One protein and one vegetable.

"It *is* kind of weird for Jandie and her husband to be out when the weather's like this," Emma said.

"Maybe they were spending time with friends, and they got stuck and had to stay overnight. Just like you did," I said.

"Sure," Emma said. "Maybe."

CHAPTER 6

BY THE TIME EMMA AND I had gotten the dishes washed up, the rain had diminished from "deluge" to "normal for Mahina." I did my express-dress (quick shower, minimal makeup, glop on some hair product and hope for the best) and made the short drive to morning Mass at St. Damien's. My showing up baby-less did not go unnoticed. A pack of aunties intercepted me on the way back to my car and would not let me leave until I had assured them that Francesca was fine, Donnie was perfectly capable of providing her safe passage to the mainland and back, and the closure of Donnie's Drive-Inn was only temporary. We'd soon be back in business better than ever, I insisted. It was more social interaction than I'd bargained for, and I sped home with the sole objective of collapsing into bed.

By the time I pulled up to my house, the rain had ceased, leaving the street steaming in the sun. Mr. Ladd—Tedd Ladd, as I now knew him to be—was in his carport, hosing off the tires of his truck.

I parked in the garage and walked down to the rental unit to say hello. He'd seen me pull in, so it would seem antisocial if I just ignored him and went inside. I was also curious about two things: Was he in fact the formerly-famous cartoonist who had signed my book decades earlier? And did he have any idea Mr. Henriques had been snooping around inside their house?

"Looks like we have a new water feature," he remarked. I followed his gaze to the graveyard that backed up to the edge of our properties. A vast, shimmering lake (or so it seemed) was studded with the tops of gravestones.

"I happened to notice your car wasn't in the carport earlier today," I said. "I was a little worried. Because of the flash flood warning. They say to avoid driving long distances. You know, turn around, don't drown."

"*You* just drove somewhere," he retorted.

"Yes. I went to Mass this morning. St. Damien's is less than half a mile away. I actually could've walked."

"Mass, huh? Whatever gets you through, I guess. Anyway, looks like we're all safe and sound. So nothing to worry about."

"OK, great. Well, have a nice Sunday." I turned to go back to my house.

"Jandie wasn't feeling well," he said.

I turned back around.

"We went to look for a drugstore. You know. Female stuff." Ladd gestured vaguely at the front of his cargo shorts.

"Well, next time, if she needs some ibuprofen or a heating pad or something, she can come over and borrow it," I said.

"It's no big deal," Ladd started winding up the hose. "She'll be fine."

"Good. I'm glad. Okay, you both have a great day."

"How'd it go?" Emma said when I walked in. "I saw you talking to the husband. Does he know Mr. Henriques went into his house?"

"I wish he really had stolen his stupid fish," I said.

"Who stole whose fish, what?"

"Nothing."

"Eh, your hedge in the back is looking kinda raggedy, yeah?" Emma said. "Is Kaycee still doing your yardwork?"

I went over to the window and saw that the back hedge could in fact be described as raggedy.

"She's supposed to come by today," I said. "In fact she's supposed to be here now. I don't know what's going on. She normally does good work."

Kaycee Kabua was a Mahina State agriculture graduate who had started her own landscaping business. She had been doing Emma and Yoshi's yard and Emma had recommended her to me. It seemed to me Kaycee's work had been slipping lately, but I didn't want to say anything that would make Emma think I didn't appreciate the referral. Besides, if Kaycee was having any personal issues, I didn't want to make things worse for her by talking her down to Emma.

CHAPTER 7

WHEN KAYCEE STILL HADN'T made an appearance in my backyard an hour later, I moved from annoyance to worry and decided to call her. But when I went out to the back lanai where the reception is better, I spotted her on the other end of the yard, behind the rental unit. Fair enough, she was supposed to be looking after both properties. Although it struck me that since the new tenants had moved in, she seemed to spend a lot more time on their side of the lot.

When she saw me walking toward her, she put down the long-handled implement she had been poking into the trees.

"Eh professor," she said.

"Aren't you hot?" I asked. She was wearing a hoodie, with the hood fastened so tightly that only her eyes and nose were visible. Kaycee was in her twenties but still cute in the way that babies are cute, with plump cheeks and round, dark eyes.

Kaycee shrugged.

"The little fire ants like drop down the back of your neck, that's why."

"Oh. Is it better to come by when it's cooler?"

"Nah, I'm fine."

"Okay. Well. Do you think you'll be able to get to the other part of the hedge today?"

A single hedge ran along the back of the property, separating the backyards of 25 Uakoko Street (where Donnie and I lived) and 25b (the rental unit) from the cemetery beyond. The hedge behind the rental unit was neatly-trimmed and free of weeds. Our side, by contrast, looked like it had gone on a three-day bender.

I shouldn't have been surprised. Kaycee was a Jandista (a fan of Jandie Brand) so I could understand why she'd linger close to Jandie's house, trimming leaves while hoping to catch a glimpse of her idol.

"Sure, I'll get to it today. Eh," She cleared her throat and looked around. "The wife went missing or what?"

"Not that I know of. But if you see anything out of place, please let me know."

"Okay Professor, will do. Eh, no worries, I'm gonna get to the other side today, even 'em up, make 'em look nice, yeah?"

When I got inside, Emma was sitting at the dining table with her laptop open, drinking wine out of a mug and reading the news.

"More rain coming," she said. "That's not gonna be good. Not gonna be able to paddle for a while."

"Why not?"

"A bunch of cesspools are gonna overflow and it's all gonna run into the ocean. All the farm runoff too."

"Thank you for reminding me why I never go into the ocean."

"We'll get you out there one of these days."

"Nope."

"Oh, I emailed Pat about da kine. Cartoon guy."

"Heard back?" I asked.

"Not yet. I gotta finish up this report, and get some grading done, and then I'm done for the day. I know, I'm a heathen for working on Sunday."

I tidied up the kitchen and then folded laundry until Emma was done. Laundry doesn't count as work in my mind, because I don't get paid to do it.

"Finally." Emma closed her laptop and pushed up from the couch. "Time for happy hour."

"What was taking so long?" I opened a new bottle of wine (my cheap and cheerful red blend, not Donnie's fancy Sangiovese) and filled two repurposed furikake jars.

"Stupid online class. Right on," Emma said as she took a small jar. "You got the Mahina stemware."

"Yeah, I don't see the point of an actual stem on your glass," I said. "It just makes it more prone to tip over."

"Want to go outside?" Emma said. "I've been indoors all day."

"Okay. Let me check and make sure Kaycee's finished up."

"Why?"

"I told her to work on the whole hedge and not just the part near the rental unit. I don't want her to think I'm checking up on her or don't trust her to do her job properly."

"You don't trust anyone to do their job properly," Emma said.

The hedge was evenly trimmed, giving Emma and me a clear view into the cemetery from the back lanai. The twilight had an unusual reddish tinge to it. The air hung close and heavy. I felt mosquitos lurking nearby, sniffing for a gap in the repellent I'd doused myself in.

"Your hedge looks good," Emma said. "Kaycee does good work, yeah?"

"Once you can get her to stop lingering around hoping to catch a glimpse of her idol."

"Give her a break, Molly. It's not like we get a lot of celebrities in Mahina."

"Conform in Speech, and Dress and Thought," I said, "And you'll Be Promoted When You Ought."

"What is that from?" Emma asked.

"Safety Worm. Tedd Ladd's cartoon character," I said. "Safety Worm is like an amoral Jiminy Cricket for careerist office workers. There's a second line. Speak the Truth and Have Your Say, and You'll Get Two Weeks' Severance Pay. Wow, I hadn't thought of that in years. But it came right back. It's been lurking in my subconscious this whole time."

"Catchy," Emma said. "You should put that in your email signature. It would be perfect for you College of Commerce guys."

"Do people even get severance pay anymore?"

"You okay?" Emma asked.

"Mr. Henriques and Kaycee have both noticed Jandie's gone," I said. "It's not just me."

"How did the husband seem when you talked to him?" Emma asked. "Did he seem nervous or like he had a guilty conscience?"

"Not at all. He seemed smug and dismissive."

"He goes out in the middle of a storm, comes home by himself, hoses off the car, no trace of the wife," Emma said.

"He claimed she was inside," I said. "Or implied it, anyway."

"Uh huh. Do you believe him?" Emma asked.

"Emma, I don't want to get sucked into some *Rear Window*-type voyeuristic obsession with my renters."

"In *Rear Window*, there was an actual murder," Emma reminded me.

"He said she wasn't feeling well. She has 'female trouble' apparently."

"Couldn't ask for a better opening," Emma said. "We're female."

"It's already dark. I don't want to do anything dumb after dark."

"Tomorrow then," Emma said.

"Fine."

CHAPTER 8

THE NEXT MORNING, EMMA and I were in the kitchen, packing up a "Feel better" package for Jandie Brand. Or rather, I packed while Emma noodged me. She would say "supervised."

"Okay, we've got ibuprofen, caffeine pills, eyeshades, and a bottle of wine" I said. "I don't know about the heating pad, though."

"What's wrong with the heating pad?"

"Something chewed through the cord. Ew, what's living in my closet and chewing through things?"

"Look, there's mold on it," Emma added.

I dropped the heating pad into the garbage can.

"Lemme call the house." Emma dialed the phone.

"If we're just doing all this to call Ladd's bluff, Emma, I don't know that we need—"

Emma waved her arm to shush me.

"No, I wanna go home, and make sure my doofus husband and my idiot brother haven't burned the house down. Oh, hey, Jonah. Howzit. Yeah, good. Good. She's fine. Listen, I'm gonna come by real quick an' grab the heating pad. It's...you did what?"

Emma leaned her elbows on the kitchen counter and planted her free hand on her face.

"No, Jonah, it's not. It's a *terrible* idea. Lucky you never get electrocuted...oh yeah? Well you deserved it. I'll just use the hot water bottle. Yeah, the red one...what do you mean it doesn't work? Never mind, I'll be right over. Don't go anywhere. In fact, don't do anything. That's right, I do mean stand still and hold your breath till I get there."

I barely had time to finish a cup of coffee before Emma was back.

"You must've been lucky with traffic." I took the hot water bottle from her and placed it into the gift bag "This looks fine. What's wrong with it?"

"Nothing's wrong with it. My idiot brother didn't realize that even though it's called a hot water bottle, you still gotta heat the water up yourself before you put it in. Ready to go?"

"Ready as I'll ever be."

Emma and I squelched across the wet lawn to the rental unit. The rain had cleared but the ground was saturated and soggy.

"Emma, do you think Jandie's really sick?"

"You think her husband's lying."

"No. Yes. Maybe. Fifty-fifty. I don't know. OK, look. If he's telling the truth, then we're being good neighbors."

"And if he's not, we're on our way to visit a murderous psychopath who just killed his wife."

I stopped.

"Should we go back?"

"Nah. He probably already saw us out the window anyway. Come on."

"There are so many places to hide a body around here," I said. "Lava tubes, rivers, a whole ocean—"

"There's a whole freakin' cemetery right next door, don't forget," Emma said.

The door of the rental unit opened as we approached it. Tedd Ladd was unshaven and looked gaunt.

"Eh, good morning," Emma said. "We brought over some things for your wife."

"For Jandie? Why?"

"You mentioned she wasn't feeling well," I said.

"Lady troubles." Emma elbowed me, which reminded me I was holding the gift bag.

Ladd held the door open just wide enough to reach out through the crack.

"I'll make sure she gets it."

"Maybe we can come in and help her set up the hot water bottle," Emma said. "They're tricky for some people."

"No thanks. We're fine." Ladd tried to push the door shut but couldn't. Emma had placed her foot over the door stop, and she was wearing hiking boots. She'd planned ahead for this, apparently.

"Why don't you want us to come in?" Emma challenged him.

"Emma," I said, "we can just go..."

Ladd stepped back and Emma and I fairly tumbled into the living room.

"She's not here." Ladd crossed his arms and looked at the floor. "I didn't want to tell you. The truth is, I don't know where she is. You might as well come in."

We stepped inside and he closed the door behind us, which made me a little nervous. Right away I saw the aquarium Mr. Henriques had been talking about. It was huge, occupying the entire length of the counter that separated the living-dining area from the kitchen. The emergency generator had been moved inside from the carport and sat underneath the counter, apparently ready to rescue the aquarium if the power went out.

I walked over for a closer look.

"Lovely aquarium." I know little to nothing about aquariums. I wanted to check for water damage on the countertop without being obvious about it. The aquarium *was* lovely, in the usual way aquariums are. It contained waving greenery, a swarm of tiny electric-blue fish, a clump of fleshy anemones, and a couple of those things that look like flat lemons swimming around. Sitting on the bottom was a brown lump with a ridge of lacy spines and a grouchy expression. The countertop seemed free of water damage. So far.

"I can watch it for hours," Ladd said. "I think my next addition will be a snowflake eel. My sources tell me you can find them in the tidepools in Pohaku."

I knew which tidepools he was talking about. They were right outside the Maritime Club. Emma was a club member. I don't know whether Ladd knew this, or whether he was angling (ha!) for an invitation from her, but Emma didn't say anything.

"So what's going on with Jandie?" I asked. I thought that would be his cue to invite us to sit down, but he didn't. Instead the three of us stood and stared at the aquarium. It looked like something that belonged in a hotel lobby, I thought. It was completely out of place in a little rental house. Still, I found myself staring at it.

"She went out, and she hasn't come back," Ladd said. "I don't know anyone here, so I didn't...Jandie's a free spirit, and I don't want to seem overbearing. She would hate it if I called the police just because she happened to be out of cell phone range."

"There's a lot of places on the island that are out of range," Emma took out her phone. "You been checking her posts?"

Ladd rubbed the back of his neck.

"Of course I have. I mean, not in the last five minutes."

"This one's timestamped this morning. Mahina rainbow." Emma held out her phone for Ladd to see.

Ladd took the phone from her, shook his head, and handed it back.

"That's a pre-scheduled post. She took it a while ago."

"Is it usual for her to go out on a photoshoot overnight?" I asked.

He shrugged.

"She's never done it before without letting me know first. Is there anything dangerous she might not know about?"

Emma strolled over to the living room couch and plunked down on the couch. I followed her over, and Ed Ladd followed me.

"Mr. Ladd. Edward. May I call you Edward?" Emma said.

"Ed's fine."

"Ed, this is a beautiful island, which is probably why you came in the first place. But what a lotta newcomers don't realize is there's a million ways to die here."

"Emma," I said, "I don't know whether—"

"Molly," Emma interrupted me, "he asked if there's anything dangerous here. An' it's good he asked, cause lots of tourists don't ask the right questions."

"I wouldn't call us *tourists* necessarily—" Ladd said.

"They assume the whole island chain was designed by Disneyland safety engineers or something," Emma went on. "Until someone gets swept out to the ocean, or drops into a lava tube, or falls off a cliff while they're hiking—"

"Emma!" I shook my head.

Ladd held up his hand.

"No, I asked. I need to know."

"Hey, at least no get poisonous snakes," Emma reassured him.

"I believe you mean venomous, not poisonous," Ladd said. "A poisonous snake can only hurt you if you try to eat it. But I take your point."

Emma's lip twitched dangerously. She does not like being corrected.

"Well we should go." I went over to Emma and pulled her up from the couch by the elbow. "So try the fire department first, they're good with rescuing hikers. Or just call 9-1-1 and let the dispatcher decide. Better Jandie gets mad at you for being concerned than have her stuck at the bottom of a ravine with a broken leg and no one to help her. Okay, bye, let me know if you need anything."

"What's the rush?" Emma shook me off and straightened out her T-shirt as we walked back toward the house.

"You were going to do something bad to him."

"Molly, *I* know the difference between poisonous and venomous. I said poisonous for *his* benefit."

"I know."

"It's like if I knock on your door, and you say who is it, I don't say it is I. I say it's me. It's casual conversation, I'm not in front of a classroom. It's da kine, what's that thing you English majors call it?"

"Maybe he was trying to be helpful. He doesn't know you're a biology professor."

"*Putz.* Him, not you. Know what? I think he killed Jandie."

"You think he murdered his wife? Because he corrected you?"

"Because he's a freakin' psychopath. And I know that's not a real thing and it's actually called antisocial personality disorder so don't correct me."

"I wouldn't dream of it. Emma, you go on inside. I'm going to pick up the mail. I know I shouldn't say this, because they prepaid a six-month lease. But I don't really like him either."

CHAPTER 9

ON THE WAY TO THE MAILBOX I noticed a folded piece of lime-green paper tucked under one of the windshield wipers on Emma's car. I plucked it out and brought it inside.

Emma was already set up at the kitchen counter with a box of wine and two full glasses.

"Eh, no look at me all judgmental li'dat Molly. It's...hang on a second."

She pulled out her phone and frowned at the screen.

"Fifty-seven, fifty-eight, fifty-nine, okay, *now* it's after noon."

"You got mail." I handed her the folded flyer. It turned out to be a "friendly" warning from the Uakoko Street Homeowner's Association. Emma gulped her wine and plunked the glass down aggressively on the paper, right over the clip art of the smiling sun.

"Since when am I not allowed to park on the grass?" she demanded. "What, I'm supposed to park on your narrow little street and block traffic?"

"I guess so, because apparently if you don't, I have to pay a fine. Dangit. When did they become so zealous? Honestly, I didn't even know we had a homeowner's association. I mean, not an active one. This is the first time I've ever seen anything from them besides the postcard in the mail reminding me to pay the annual fee."

"Maybe it's cause you get Jandie living here."

"Well joke's on them, because Jandie's missing. Seriously, you think they've gone all activist about keeping cars off the lawns just because we have a minor celebrity living here?"

"Not just a celebrity, Molly. An influencer. Her whole *shtick* is taking pictures and sharing them with the entire world. Maybe your association thinks a car on your lawn's bad for the neighborhood image."

"Image? Uakoko Street? I mean, I like living here, but I think I'd describe it as 'unpretentious' at best."

"You got a better explanation?"

"I guess not. Hey, since it is actually lunchtime, you want something to eat?"

"Are you cooking?" Emma asked suspiciously.

"No. Donnie left us a bunch of frozen food from the Drive-Inn."

"Oh, yeah that sounds perfect. Eh, I forget to tell you Pat's on his way over."

"Pat Flanagan? Is on his way here?"

"Yeah. I texted him about da kine, Ladd. Turns out his editor thinks an article about a washed-up cartoonist living in the backwoods of Mahina sounds interesting. Go figure."

I checked the oven to make sure it was empty (an old habit from before I was married, when I used the oven as shoe storage overflow). I set it to heat and selected a tinfoil pan from the freezer. Chicken katsu and teriyaki beef, according to the masking-tape label.

"Do you want to invite Yoshi and Jonah to join us?" I asked Emma.

"Nah. Yoshi's got a thing with his paddling club and Jonah's going with him. I can set the table."

Emma got up and started clearing away the glasses and the empty bottle.

"Oh, thanks for clearing that off."

"Yeah, I don't need Pat getting all judgey about us day drinking."

"Yoshi and your brother aren't going paddling in this weather, are they?"

"Nah, they're going down there to move the canoes away from the bayfront. In case there's a storm surge. Afterwards they're all gonna go back to the house and party."

"Sounds festive."

"Yeah, after a couple drinks the ukuleles come out and then the singing starts."

"It sounds nice," I said.

"Sure, it is. For the first seven or eight hours."

"Do you want to stay here tonight?" I asked.

"Oh yeah, that's a good idea. We can catch up with Pat and not worry about driving home in the bad weather."

"I'd offer you a spare toothbrush but I'm guessing when you went home this morning you brought back a packed overnight bag."

"You know me so well. Seriously, though, I owe you. If there's one sound that's worse than Yoshi snoring, it's him trying to sing 'Hawaiian Superman' after a few beers."

Pat showed up at my door about half an hour later. His head was still shaved but he'd grown a goatee, which I was surprised to see was graying. I'd always thought of Pat as young.

"I forgot how much I hate riding in the Sampan," was the first thing he said as he walked in. I watched the open-air wagon waddle back down the street.

"I like the Sampan," I said as I closed the door. "It's old-timey, and it's very Mahina."

"Pat hates it 'cause his legs are too long." Emma came out of the kitchen. "Eh, Pat, good to see you."

Pat hugged Emma, then me. His leather jacket smelled wet and cold.

"Sure it's okay if I stay over?" he asked. "Donnie doesn't mind?"

"I'm sure he wouldn't. Go put your stuff in the guest room, come back and we'll have lunch. I hope you're hungry."

When he'd gone into the guest room I remembered Emma was spending the night too.

"Sorry, Emma, you can have the nursery. I'll bring an air mattress in."

"No worries. I like the couch. Eh, Pat looks good, yeah, with the beard?"

"He looks distinguished," I said. "Unsettlingly so. Huh. I wonder whether he's seeing someone."

"I'm right here," Pat said as he seated himself at the table.

"That was fast," I said. "So are you seeing someone?"

"A gentleman doesn't kiss and tell. Hey, they did a good job, whoever built your rental unit. The style matches your house."

"Konishi Construction," I said. "They're the only game in town, so good thing they know what they're doing."

I pulled the pan out of the oven and carefully positioned it on the three potholders Emma had placed on the table. I'd asked her to set out four, one for each corner of the pan, but she'd insisted three was more stable, like a camera tripod.

"Oh, the food looks great," Pat said. "All I've had to eat today is an overpriced airport muffin."

"Thanks," I said. "Reheated katsu and teriyaki beef served in its original foil pan, just as nature intended. Nothing but the best for my guests."

"It's from Donnie's Drive-Inn," Emma assured him.

"Oh right, in case you were afraid it was something I'd made."

"So how's it going with your celebrity tenants?" Pat asked.

"The wife's missing," I said.

"Jandie Brand," Emma added.

Pat set the serving tongs down and straightened up from his customary slouch.

"Missing? Officially?"

"They went out for a drive, and only the husband came back," Emma said. "And then we went over this morning and he admitted she was missing."

"In the middle of a hurricane and a flash flood warning," I added.

"Is anyone gonna look for her?" Pat asked.

"The husband said he was gonna get help," Emma said. "I'm not sure I believe him."

"So you think he's *the* Tedd Ladd, huh?" Pat downed his coffee went to the kitchen to brew himself another.

"Maybe?" I said. "It's hard to tell. Edward Ladd is a common name. And it has to be ten years since he was actually famous. Pat, how can you drink coffee all day? Doesn't it keep you up?"

Pat came back and set down his coffee.

"Come on, doesn't that smell great? *Ten* years ago? Try twenty. That's when Tedd Ladd was in his heyday."

"Twenty years? Are you sure? Wow, we're old."

"Yeah, I can't see it being the same guy," Emma said. "Jandie's husband just seems like some middle-aged loser who likes to stare at his fish tank."

"It's a pretty spectacular fish tank," I said. "It takes up the entire kitchen counter."

"Worried about water damage in your new rental unit?" Pat asked.

"Why would you assume that would be my main concern?"

"It tracks though," Pat said. "Ever notice how many celebrities get sick of dealing with people and decide they'd rather be around animals instead?"

"I don't think I ever heard of this guy Ladd before," Emma said.

"He might not have been that popular in Hawaii," Pat said. "You think he's involved in his wife's disappearance? It's usually the spouse."

"Yes," Emma said.

"No," I said.

"He's a has-been and can't stand his wife's success," Emma said.

"Emma doesn't like him. Emma, I thought you just said you didn't think he was the famous Tedd Ladd. How can he be a has-been?"

"Who cares?" Emma retorted. "He's old enough to be her dad. And he looks like a jerky stick with glasses."

The roar of a motorcycle stopped abruptly outside my front door.

"Now, old boy!" somebody was saying in a plummy voice. "Steady, old chap! I've got something for you."

CHAPTER 10

I LOOKED OUT THE FRONT window and saw our business law instructor, Harriet Holmes, dismounting her 1966 Triumph Bonneville. She bent down to reach something on the ground. I realized she was feeding something to one of the neighborhood's feral cats.

"Why is Harriet here?" I said. "And how does she know where I live?"

"Harriet Holmes?" Pat asked. "Wow, I showed up at the right time."

Pat Flanagan had never met Harriet Holmes, but he knew very well who she was.

Harriet Holmes's arrival in Mahina had coincided with certain events newsworthy enough to make the national media outlets. Harriet currently taught law and ethics in the College of Commerce. Recently retired from Oxford, she thought teaching in "the tropics" (Mahina) would be a "jolly wheeze." As chair of the management department, I was technically her supervisor, to the extent anyone could "supervise" Harriet Holmes.

She bounded up the steps and hammered on the door. As I opened up she barged inside.

On first impression, Harriet Holmes is not glamorous. She is in late middle age and squarely built, with chopped mouse-gray hair that perpetually looks like it's been squashed under a hat. (Because it has.) Harriet eschews cosmetics, reeks of pipe tobacco, and dresses like she's on her way to muck out the stables. Men find Harriet irresistible.

"Ah, what ho, Barda, Nakamura." Harriet removed her flat cap and stuffed it in one of the pockets of her field coat. "Hullo, who's this fair Fenian?"

Pat sprang up from the dining table so fast he practically knocked his chair over.

"I'm Pat Flanagan. It's great to meet you."

"Tea?" I offered. Harriet cheerfully (if unflatteringly) replied, "I'll make it."

I helped Harriet locate the kettle and our rarely-used supply of loose tea. Having exhausted my usefulness in the matter, I left her to it. Pat, Emma, and I seated ourselves at the counter so we could converse while Harriet worked her tea magic in my kitchen.

"Harriet, this is such a nice surprise," I said. "What brings you by?"

"Nigel and I are looking to let a cottage," she said, "We've found something just up the street. Would be jolly fun to be neighbors, eh, Barda? We can ride to work together. Save you a bit on petrol."

"Now *there's* an idea." That I planned never to follow up on. I imagined myself riding on the back of Harriet's skinny-wheeled Triumph, splashing through muddy potholes while hanging on for dear life.

"What's wrong with the place you got now?" Emma asked. "You're right on the Hanakoa River. How come you wanna move?"

"The river's beastly at the moment. It's all muddy water and debris churning past, not pleasant to look at in the least. Nigel says he feels he's about to tip straight into it every time he steps out onto the lanai. Oh, and he doesn't get on with Clyde."

Emma reached under the counter and nudged Pat's knee.

"Clyde Hamamoto." Emma whispered. "Harriet's good friend from the motorcycle club. He's their *landlord*."

Pat nodded knowingly.

"Uakoko Street suits us both down to the ground," Harriet was saying. "Nigel's taking ages to finish his manuscript. He needs to be somewhere quiet where he can write without the rushing water breaking his concentration."

"What's Nigel writing?" Pat asked.

"His prison memoir," Harriet replied proudly. "The location's perfect. One couldn't hope for quieter neighbors than yours."

I was confused for a minute, as I didn't think the residents of Uakoko Street were particularly noiseless.

"She means the cemetery, Molly," Emma said.

"Right. I knew that."

"Nigel rather fancies living next to a graveyard." Harriet poured the boiling water into the teapot, refilled the kettle, and switched it on again. "He plans to have it as the background of his author photo. On the book jacket."

"You'd also be living near a celebrity influencer," Emma said. "Jandie Brand and her husband are renting the house next door."

"Oh ah, now that you mention it, it's possible I've heard of her," Harriet said a little too casually. "It might be handy, mightn't it, to know an influencer when it comes time to publicize Nigel's book."

The electric kettle clicked off and Harriet filled the teapot for a second time, this time with the tea leaves in it. "He'll have to do it all himself, you know. Publishers don't lift a finger these days for their authors. Shocking, really."

"Jandie's missing, you know," Emma said.

"Missing?" Harriet brightened. "How exciting. Perhaps we should organize a search party."

"Listen, everyone," I said, "let's not go barging into their business. Maybe she doesn't want to be found."

"Maybe the husband's topped her," Harriet countered.

"That's what I think," Emma said.

"It's usually the husband," Pat agreed.

"She could be moldering under the floorboards right now," Harriet added cheerily as she came over and poured tea.

"Or he cut her into pieces and fed her to his fancy fish," Emma said.

"That's an angle," Pat said. "Ha! So to speak."

Emma socked him in the shoulder.

"Good one, Pat."

"Everyone, *please* do not harass the tenants," I pleaded. "The only reason they're here is because they wanted to live in a quiet neighborhood."

"Not much of a quiet neighborhood, is it?" Harriet handed me a brimming teacup. "What with everyone going round murdering each other."

CHAPTER 11

HARRIET PERSUADED US to walk up the street and give her our opinions on the house she was considering. The rain had started up again, so I handed out umbrellas from the spare-umbrella basket we keep by the front door. Emma and Pat each took one, but Harriet chose to walk under Pat's instead of taking one for herself.

The house Harriet was interested in looked very much like the other early twentieth-century plantation houses on the street. It had dark green vertical plank siding, white trim, and a corrugated red metal roof. It was on the same side of the street as my house, and like mine, it overlooked the cemetery. The drop-off from the backyard was a steep fifteen or twenty feet. We walked to the low retaining wall and looked out over the rolling lawn. It was vibrant green—no sprinklers required in Mahina—and dotted with glistening gravestones.

I caught a whiff of smoke. Harriet was puffing away on her pipe. I moved away to avoid breathing too much of it in. The smoke didn't seem to bother Pat, who was still sharing an umbrella with her. They were talking about something, but I couldn't hear over the sound of the rain pattering on my own umbrella.

I sidled back in close enough to hear the conversation.

"Easier to plant a hedge or something," Emma said. "You could do it yourself."

"Yeah, a landlord springing for an actual safety improvement?" Pat said. "What was I thinking?"

"Hey now," I said. "We're not all evil exploiters. Some of us try to take good care of our renters. Are you guys talking about the retaining wall?"

"Nigel and I won't be out here dancing on the precipice," Harriet assured us. "We've loads of space in the screened-in lanai."

"Ooh, screened-in lanai sounds nice," I said. "Imagine sitting outside without having to douse yourself in bug spray first."

"I never get bitten when I'm at your house," Emma said.

"Yeah, me neither," Pat added.

"That's because I'm there," I said, "and they're biting me and not you. Next time you guys can try sitting out there by yourselves."

"You must be giving off loads of carbon dioxide, Barda," Harriet said. "Best we keep moving then."

We followed Harriet and her trail of pipe smoke around the side of the house. Pat, who was by far the tallest member of our little party, tried to use his phone flashlight to peer into the windows, but the glass jalousies had a pebbled texture that made it impossible to see inside.

"So what do you think?" I asked Harriet as we headed back down the street. "It looks nice enough from the outside. I mean, if you want to live next to a cemetery, I know it's not for everyone. Moving is a big decision. Moving all your stuff and everything."

"Bit spendy, but worth it, I think. It's an investment in Nigel's career, after all. Someplace quiet to get his writing done. We do so want his book to be a success."

We were approaching my house when Harriet said this, and I thought I saw her glance in the direction of my rental unit. Great. Add Harriet Holmes and her husband Nigel to the list of people who are going to be pestering me for an introduction to Jandie Brand.

"Well, it would certainly be delightful to have you as neighbors," I said. "Although I have to be honest. If you'd asked me last week, I would have said the neighborhood was safe. But now, with Jandie Brand disappeared? I don't know what to say."

"Oh, I expect it's not as bad as all that," Harriet said. "Nigel abducted by rabid fans? We should be so lucky, as the song says. Ah, here we are."

Harriet climbed onto her Triumph and roared off, calling back, "Cheerio!"

Pat, Emma, and I hosed off our muddy feet and left our footwear to dry on the front porch. Thanks to days of incessant rain, the atmosphere inside was close and damp. I cranked the ceiling fans up to top speed in an attempt to dry things out.

"An investment in Nigel's career. Did you hear her? This is about me getting them an audience with Jandie Brand." I headed into the kitchen to get two wine glasses. "Pat, help yourself to coffee or whatever you want to drink at this hour. Emma and I are having wine."

Emma hitched herself up to sit at the kitchen counter, and Pat took my invitation to make himself a cup of coffee."

"Wow, Harriet's a lot," Emma said. "I mean, I like her, but. Eh, you really think she's moving in to be close to Jandie?"

"I'm sure of it," I said. "Everyone seems to want to get close to Jandie. Even my friends, who I thought liked me for myself and enjoyed my company. Emma."

"Maybe this wasn't the right time for me to come visit." Pat finished fixing his coffee and took a seat next to Emma. "I mean for the sake of getting a story about her husband. Of course, it's always worth it to visit you guys. *I* enjoy your company, Molly."

Emma socked Pat in the shoulder. He laughed.

"Pat, I don't think Jandie's husband would mind talking to a reporter," Emma said. "I think he'd enjoy it. As long as the conversation is all about him and how smart he is. Eh, Pat, your mother never told you not to put your elbows on the table?"

Pat straightened up. "This is a counter, not a table. But whatever. I was surprised how much my editor loved the idea. Believe me, she doesn't love anything. Washed-up mainland celeb discovers the 'real' Hawaii and tries to reinvent himself, even as his young wife eclipses him and he realizes he'll never recapture even a fraction of his former fame and acclaim."

"Ouch." I handed over two furikake glasses to Emma, followed by the wine box. "It does sound like the kinds of depressing stories your paper likes to run, though."

"Yeah, it's right on brand for The Bleakly." Pat finished his coffee in one gulp. "Hey, you got any more of that tea? It was good."

"Sure, but I'm not sure I can replicate what Harriet did. You're welcome to try."

I traded places with Pat. He went into the kitchen to fill the electric kettle with tap water, and I sat down at the counter to fill myself with grocery-store cabernet.

"Is Mahina water still as good as it used to be?" Pat asked.

"Of course it is," Emma said. "Not like your nasty Honolulu water,"

"I liked meeting Harriet," Pat said. "I think she'd be fun to have as a neighbor."

"It might be," I said. "If I weren't her department chair. Wait a minute. Pat, you have a crush on Harriet?"

"Maybe a little one."

"You know she's married, right?" I said.

"Obviously, to someone named Nigel." Pat checked the oven clock and poured boiling water into his cup. "Don't worry, it's completely chaste and above board. You have to admit, there's something about her."

"Maybe it's the 'posh' accent," I said. "The students seem to be bewitched by it. Even when she says things that would normally be super-offensive, I only get one or two complaints at most."

"Could be the pipe," Emma said. "How many women do you know who smoke a pipe?"

"I don't know anyone who smokes a pipe besides her," I said. "And for the record I do not find it charming. It's a constant battle trying to get her to comply with the on-campus smoking ban. Enforcement of which is my thankless responsibility, by the way. Somehow it always slips her mind that she's not allowed to smoke in the building. 'Oh dreadfully sorry Barda, made a bollocks out of it again haven't I,' and then I can't even be mad at her because she seems genuinely contrite even though I know she's not."

"So you're having fun being department chair?" Pat brought his tea over and joined us at the counter. "Hey, by the way. I invited someone to come by. I hope that's okay."

"Come by where?" I said. "Here? To my house?"

"The places downtown we'd normally meet are closed because of the flood warning. He's going to be here in..." Pat glanced at me and something in my expression must have motivated him to add, "Sorry, I can call and cancel."

"It depends," I said. "Who is it?"

"His name is Howell. He's a nice kid, writes for the *County Courier*."

CHAPTER 12

"PAT, YOU INVITED A stranger into my house?"

I sped into the kitchen and started flinging dirty dishes into the dishwasher.

"Don't worry, your house looks fine," Pat said.

"No it doesn't, you huge liar. But it will. Can you clear all the stuff off the coffee table? Just bring it in here. I'll figure out what to do with it later. Why on earth are you helping someone from the *County Courier* anyway?"

"Why shouldn't I?" Pat asked.

"Because the *County Courier* laid you off, along with all the other decent reporters, and now they're basically a collection of ads for car dealers and furniture stores? Where did Emma go?"

"I'm in the bathroom," came a disembodied voice. "Don't talk to me."

"He's trying to get a start on his career, and I want to help him out." Pat brought over an armload of coffee cups and junk mail and dumped everything on the counter next to the sink. "Good karma, pay it forward, and all that nonsense."

"It's very nice of you." I popped a detergent pod in the dishwasher, pushed the door shut, and got the cycle started. "I was thinking you were maybe cultivating him as an unwitting source or doing some Machiavellian 'keep your friends close but your rivals closer' kind of thing. Darn it, there are still all these dirty cups. I'll have to wash them by hand."

"Here, I'll do it." Pat got up, filled the sink with soapy water, and swept the dishes into the sink. "There. Now you can't see them under the bubbles. Molly, you don't seem thrilled about Howell coming over. I thought you'd be interested in meeting a reporter. You always like hearing the village gossip."

"I do. But not when I'm in the middle of it. Pat, you came over to do a piece on a formerly-famous cartoonist. Okay, fine. But now his celebrity wife has disappeared, and you just invited over a reporter from the local paper?"

"Sorry, Molly, like I said, I can call him and cancel."

"No, then he's going to ask you why and it's just going to seem like we're hiding something and it's going to turn into this big murder case. How am I going to explain this to Donnie? What if he sees it in the newspaper while he's over on the mainland? Things always sound worse when they make it onto the national news. Remember that story about the eruption, where they claimed the lava flowed all the way to Honolulu?"

"I wouldn't worry about getting your name dragged into this story, Molly. Look, I really appreciate you letting me do this. I didn't realize it was gonna cause so much stress."

Emma came out of the bathroom, wiping her hands on the back of her jeans.

"Eh, the place looks good," she said.

"I guess it does look okay. Thanks for helping me tidy up, Pat." I sat back down at the kitchen counter and refilled my wine glass. "I've been a little stressed out about this Senior Seminar thing."

"Oh, the business planning class?" Emma hitched herself up next to me and filled her own glass.

"Is that the class they called BP?" Pat asked.

"Yes. They still call it that. Anyway, you know Victor Santiago, the fundraising guy whose title I keep forgetting? Big Head Cheese of Money Raising or whatever he's called?"

"Vice-President for Student Outreach and Community Relations," Emma said.

"How on earth do you remember that Emma? Anyway, my business planning students have a command performance at the Senior Showcase. You know the end-of-the-year dog and pony show where they invite all our VIP donors and Friends in the Business Community? This year Jerry Mizuno is going to be there. They've been trying to cultivate the Mizuno family for years. Victor told me this is probably our most important Senior Showcase ever. With the latest budget cuts from the ledge, we're more dependent than ever on private donations. He made sure I knew that he will not tolerate a repeat of what happened last year with the theater majors."

"So what's the problem?" Emma asked. "I mean, I don't think your business students are gonna put on pig masks and critique capitalism through poetry and burlesque."

"No, thankfully. But Victor wants to project a proper, dignified image of our school. My students are just turning in their first drafts now, and, well, the best plan by far is for something called Party Pooper."

"What is it?" Pat asked.

"It's a handheld device meant to carry in your pocket or purse. It's a combination noise-maker and deodorizer dispenser, for when you're away from home and nature calls."

"Eh, sounds like a great idea," Emma said. "Tell me when they start selling it. I'll buy a bunch for the next time Yoshi has his paddler friends over to our house."

"This is Jerry Mizuno as in Mizuno Mart?" Pat asked. "I mean, Mizuno Mart sells toilet paper and stuff like that. I don't see how your Party Pooper product is gonna offend them."

"I don't know. I hope you're right."

"Molly, at least they're coming up with their own ideas," Emma said. "Count your blessings, ah? Remember last year when I found a bunch of my students buying their homework solutions online?"

"What did you end up doing about that?" Pat asked.

"No more research papers or homework. Nothing you could pay someone to do for you. I'm only assigning in-class exams and presentations now."

"How does that work in your online classes?" I asked.

"A hundred percent of the grade is oral exams. There's no hiding it if you don't know the material. Really separates the wheat from the chaff."

"Ouch," I said. "I can't imagine the Student Retention Office is happy about that. Their whole mission is No Chaff Left Behind."

"Yeah, well, no big loss there. I'm already on the Student Retention Office's 'Party Pooper' list. But the good part is, the students who make it through my class? They know their stuff now, when they go on to the higher-level classes. You know da kine, who teaches anatomy and physiology? She's ready to name her firstborn after me."

We were interrupted by a quick knock.

"That's him." Pat jumped up and bounded to the front door.

"What was his name?" I asked.

"Howell," Pat said. "Howard Howell."

Howell looked to be in his mid-twenties, with auburn hair and a friendly, freckled face. He wore typical Mahina business attire, an aloha shirt tucked into slacks, but he struck me as not being local.

Great, I thought. I've turned into one of those provincial small-towners who sizes people up and decides they're "not from around here."

"Call me Howdy." The young man reached out and grasped my hand. His flat Midwestern accent confirmed that he was not, in fact, "from around here." And his gap-toothed grin forever cemented in my mind his resemblance to Howdy Doody.

We were all standing around awkwardly now, so I invited everyone to sit in the living room.

"I'll make coffee." Pat headed into the kitchen.

"Decaf for me if you don't mind," Howdy called after him, "thank you Mr. Flanagan!"

"I'll do decaf for everyone. It's easier."

I wished Pat had let me make the coffee so I wouldn't have to make conversation with this complete stranger, but at least Emma was there with me.

"I'll go put together some snacks," Emma said, and got up and disappeared into the kitchen.

Fortunately Howdy Howell was good at keeping conversation afloat. When he found out I taught in the College of Commerce at Mahina State, he asked how I liked working in the repurposed Inebriates' Asylum, and did I think it was haunted? I replied that I liked the old building very much, and I half-hoped it was haunted as I would love to meet the ghost of the Inebriates' Asylum founder, Constance Brigham. The spirit of the eccentric heiress was rumored to roam the old hospital complex.

"I was surprised to find out Mahina had its own university," Howdy said. "I don't mean anything bad by it. Nothing at all wrong with small towns, I always say. I cover high school sports for the *County Courier*, and let me tell you, it's just like back home. People sure do love their high school football."

"Our university get football too." Emma came into the living room and set down a tray of goodies. "Go Fighting Moons."

I supposed I could forgive Emma for abandoning me. She had pulled together whatever snack-like items she could find in my kitchen, including nuts, tortilla chips, and some long-forgotten chocolate buttons that had developed a white bloom.

Pat came out holding four pre-poured cups of coffee and handed them around.

"You notice they're the *Fighting* Moons, not the *Winning* Moons," he said. "At least with the high school teams you got a chance. Hey Howdy, did you tell her about the story you're doing?"

"Story?" I looked from Pat to Howdy and back.

"He kind of beat me to the punch," Pat said. "He's doing a story on your tenants. The influencer and the has-been."

CHAPTER 13

"WHAT?" I NEARLY DROPPED my coffee cup. "Look, Pat, Howdy, I'm sorry, I can't be party to violating my tenants' privacy. When they signed their lease, they were very clear—"

Howdy blushed.

"Oh golly no, Professor Barda, it's not like that. I'm not invading anyone's privacy. In fact, Jandie reached out to me."

"It turns out they're fine with publicity," Pat said. "On their own terms, of course."

"Emma," I asked, "did you know about this?"

Emma shook her head.

"But if they wanna talk to someone, you can't stop 'em, right?"

"Anyone can talk to whomever they like," I said. "I just feel like an idiot standing up for their privacy this whole time."

"Nah, you're doing the right thing," Emma said. "Screen out the riff-raff. But maybe you don't have to be so *farbissen* with your friends."

"It's a great story," Howdy said. "Celebrity couple moves to the middle of nowhere, they find inner strength they didn't know they had. They rediscover themselves and their love for each other."

"The middle of *nowhere*?" Emma glared at Howdy. "The celebrity couple slumming it with us backwards country bumpkins? Is that what you're going with?"

"No, no, not at all, Professor Nakamura. It's only, that's how Mr. Ladd..." Howie ran his hand through his already-unruly ginger hair. "Mr. Ladd called it the middle of nowhere. But I'm sure he means it in a good way."

Emma pointed her stubby forefinger at Howdy.

"Well, you tell him he's wrong. Mahina's the biggest town on the island. We get paved roads, county water, and we're connected to the electrical grid. Some of us even get sewer hookup. It's not like we're down in Kuewa."

"Way to convince him we're not a backwater, Emma," I said.

"You're right, Professor Nakamura," Howdy said cheerfully. "I actually have been to Kuewa. I know exactly what you're talking about. Jandie took me down there, to show me where they were originally thinking of settling down. They liked how affordable it was. But she needs good internet so that was a dealbreaker for her. Professor Barda, what do you think about Jandie and Mr. Ladd? Are they as perfect a couple as they seem?"

"I try not to talk about people behind their backs," I said.

Pat snorted, which I thought was extremely uncalled-for.

"Sure, I understand. Say, I have another question, did any of you happen to see Jandie today?"

Emma and I exchanged a glance.

"No, not today, that I recall," I said cautiously. "Why?"

"I was supposed to have an interview with her this morning, but she wasn't at home."

"She didn't share her plans with me," I said. "Oh look, we're getting low on coffee. Emma, can you help me find the new coffee I just bought?"

Emma followed me into the kitchen. We ducked into the mud room, and out to the lanai. From there we had a view of the rental house and the cemetery, quiet under the green-gray sky.

"Jandie Brand missed an appointment with a reporter this morning," I said. "What social media personality does that? The husband's already told us he's worried about her. Something is weird here."

"The husband is what's weird. If anyone did something shady, it's him. Eh, I got another question. You think he calls himself Howdy to mess with people cause he knows he looks like Howdy Doody?"

"I was wondering the same thing! I didn't know you knew what Howdy Doody looked like."

"Only cause of that weird hipster t-shirt you have that says it's Howdy Doody time, whatever that means."

Emma hoisted herself up and perched on the railing.

"Don't worry," she said, "I'm not gonna fall down. I get excellent balance from paddling."

"I'm still not joining your paddling crew. Nice try though. Okay, about this situation. What should we do? Should we tell her husband about the missed appointment?"

"Not if he's the reason she's missing."

"You don't trust him."

"Molly, do you?"

"No, not really. You know this is the first time in his adult life that Donnie's taken a vacation. He trusted me to hold everything together while he was traveling. Won't he be surprised when he comes back to a house of chaos and murder."

"Jandie getting murdered by her husband isn't your fault, Molly."

"What if nothing's changed by the time Donnie and the baby get back, and now poor little Francesca's living next door to a murderer? Emma, what should I do?"

"What, you're gonna let him stay here after he murdered his wife?"

"No, of course not. But the only alternative is I'd have to evict a murderer. We're just going to have to move, that's all."

"You should go back inside," Emma said.

"Yeah, you're right. I'm being a bad hostess. Wait, what do you mean *I* should go back inside? Where are you going?"

"I gotta go pick up the mail and check on my idiot brother and my doofus husband."

"Okay. Well, send them my love. Sounds like they need it."

Pat and Howdy were still talking when I went back inside. I didn't have the energy to reinsert myself into the conversation, so I went into my bedroom to check my email. There was a new message from Donnie, with a photo. Donnie was holding Francesca in front of a scaled-down Eiffel Tower. They had made it to Vegas. Francesca was beaming. She looked bigger than when I'd seen her last—was that possible? Donnie was unshaven and looked exhausted.

I missed Donnie and Francesca. I wouldn't even have minded visiting Donnie's grandson, Davison Hiapo Keali'i Gonsalves Balusteros (aka Junior). Junior was a little older than Francesca and was technically her nephew. But I was happy to keep my distance from Junior's father (and my stepson), Davison Gonsalves. Davison had been my student once upon a time. In my years of teaching at Mahina State, I've had many wonderful students whom I remember with fondness. Davison is not one of them.

I wrote back telling Donnie I missed them and wished I could be there with them. Now, how much news to share? Donnie had enough to worry about, traveling with the baby. There was no point in telling him things that were just going to stress him out.

"Donnie, our renter disappeared, and we think her husband murdered her! Or maybe a deranged fan did her in. There's probably hundreds of those skulking around!" No, that wouldn't do.

CHAPTER 14

DONNIE WOULD WANT TO know whether there had been any hurricane damage. I wrote that the bottom of Uakoko Street had flooded temporarily, but our property was safely out of harm's way. I told him Pat and Emma had both come to visit, so he didn't have to worry about my being alone in the house. He would be amused to hear that Harriet Holmes' husband Nigel had apparently gotten a publisher interested in his memoir about the time he'd spent in prison for protesting a tree-felling scheme in his neighborhood. I sent my sincere love and best wishes to the Davisons, père et fils. I wasn't sure whether Junior's mom Tiffany was still in the picture so be on the safe side, I didn't mention her.

What else? Oh, of course, food. I told him how much I was enjoying all the food from the Drive-Inn that Donnie had left in the freezer. And that the aunties had mobbed me at St. Damien's yesterday, telling me they couldn't wait until Donnie's Drive-Inn reopened so that they could once again walk over and enjoy their after-Mass coffee.

I pressed "send" and was about to go back into the living room and pretend to be a good hostess, when I saw a notification pop up in my in-box.

A submission had been uploaded to the Business Planning class. I clicked over to see what else had been turned in. Something that would wow our potential donors and compel them to open their wallets, I hoped. Or at least something that would appease Victor Santiago, Lord High Inquisitor of Community Connections or whatever the heck his title was.

The proposed product was a deodorizing spray for pet accidents. Not particularly innovative, but overall a solid business idea.

I read through the outline of the plan. Other than the product name possibly causing Victor Santiago's monocle to drop into his teacup, it looked fine. In fact, it was quite good. A huge improvement on the student's previous work, almost as if it were written by a different...

Oh no.

I was already stressed out enough about the Senior Showcase. Now I had to deal with plagiarism on top of everything else.

I downloaded the paper to my computer and uploaded it into the plagiarism checking site. Nothing popped out. I wanted to believe this was the student's own work, and he had simply been inspired to his highest levels of performance by my exceptional teaching.

Yeah, right. I'm as prone to self-serving bias as the next person, but I'm not delusional.

I had done everything I was supposed to do to avoid plagiarism. Design unique assignments that can't be found online. Have students turn in consecutive drafts instead of having one big paper due at the end of the semester. But none of it helps if the student is paying someone else to do the assignments.

I called Emma. She didn't pick up, so I left a message and went through the rest of my email. I hoped by the time I emerged from my bedroom, Howdy would be gone.

Howdy stood up when I entered the living room.

"Thanks so much for your hospitality, Professor Barda," he said. "I'm going to get going now. Thanks for everything, Mr. Flanagan."

"I'm gonna call it a day," Pat said when Howdy was gone.

"Pat, was he waiting for me?"

"Yeah, he didn't want to be rude and leave without saying goodbye. Okay, good night. Hey, thanks for letting me stay over."

"I figured your independent weekly wasn't exactly going to put you up at the Hanohano Hotel," I said.

"You got that right. They didn't even cover my plane fare." Pat yawned and sauntered off to the guest room.

I was still clearing off the coffee table when I heard a sharp knock on the front door, followed by someone jiggling the knob.

"Hang on Emma, I'll be right there."

When I opened the door, Emma sped past me and made a beeline to the kitchen. She filled two furikake glasses with wine and plunked them down on the counter.

"I got your message. So you got an essay mill situation going in your class, ah?"

"Maybe. I was hoping you could help me figure it out, since you've dealt with this before. Hey, how's everything at home? Is your house still standing?"

"Barely. I don't wanna talk about it. Eh, you don't know how to repair drywall, do you?"

"Me? Of course not. Pat might, though. Ask him tomorrow, he's already out for the night."

"Pat went out? Where? What's open on Monday night besides the Pair-O-Dice? Oh no Molly, it's open mic improv night at the Pair-O-Dice. We gotta stop him."

"I meant he's 'out' as in out like a light. He's asleep."

"Oh. Yeah, that makes sense. So what's the assignment you think is plagiarized?"

I set my laptop on the counter in front of Emma. She squinted at the screen.

"Urine Luck?"

"That's the product name."

"Oh, I see. 'Looking for a solution to smelly household accidents? Urine luck.' That's kinda clever."

Emma sat up and turned to me.

"Almost *too* clever," she added.

"Exactly! See what I mean?"

"How's it compare to the student's other work?"

"Very different," I said. "It's like he vaulted ahead ten grade levels in half a semester. Plus the SWOT analysis is flawless."

"The what analysis?" Emma asked.

"Strengths, Weaknesses, Opportunities, Threats. SWOT."

Emma sat back and folded her arms.

"Hmm. Yeah, definitely suspicious. You should have 'em come into your office and explain it to you."

"What if it really is his own work, though? It'll look like I'm falsely accusing him."

"Eh, you're letting the Student Retention Office get inside your head now. Know what, I got some pre-meds in my class I can talk to. If there's anyone who knows more about cheating than your business majors do, it's the pre-meds. Lemme ask around. Eh, I got some news for you, Molly. Know how come I was able to get over here so fast after you called? I was checking out the house."

"Checking out what house?" I asked.

"I think you need more wine. I'm just gonna bring the box over."

"Emma, I'm not even done with the glass you just gave me. What house? What is going on?"

Emma plunked the wine box on the counter and hitched herself up onto the bar stool next to me.

"I got back here about an hour ago."

"You've been here the whole time?" I asked.

"Yeah. I noticed Edward Ladd's big stupid overcompensating truck wasn't there. So I figured I'd go inside and check it out."

"Inside the rental unit? That's breaking and entering!"

"No it's not," Emma retorted. "You're the owner, you have something in your contract that lets you go inside any time, right?"

"Well, yeah, I do. But you went in, not me."

"So you gave me permission."

"Emma, I did not—"

"I was acting on your behalf to check on the well-being of the occupants."

I should have been angry at Emma for going into the house without permission. But I was too curious to be mad.

"Whatever. Where did he go? Do you think he went out to look for Jandie?"

Emma shrugged.

"Maybe he went out to check where he hid the body."

"So what did you find?" I asked.

Emma took an infuriatingly long draught of wine.

"Her bed was messy."

"Is that unusual?" I asked.

"It is for Jandie. On camera it's always perfect."

Emma handed me her phone. The screen showed a photo from Jandie Brand's account. Pink-and-white ruffled throw pillows were perfectly placed on a smooth, sugar-pink bedspread. The window framed a sunny day outside, and the soft-focus background filter was cranked up so far that the graveyard in the background looked like a gauzy meadow.

"You know," I said, "it's possible that in real life her room doesn't always look as perfect as it does on camera. Emma, what would you have said if someone walked in and caught you snooping around Jandie's bedroom?"

"I woulda told 'em you authorized me to be there."

"Great. So aside from a messy bed, did you actually find anything?"

"Nah, but I wasn't in there that long. I was just seeing if there was something obvious, like a dead body in the freezer or something. Eh, thanks for not getting too mad about it."

I set down my empty wine glass.

"No, Emma, you bring up a good point. I am allowed to go in and inspect the unit. It's in the contract. Maybe I should go have a look."

"Whoa, wait, Molly, what?"

I slid off the chair and stood tall, quickly grabbing the edge of the counter for balance. I had skipped dinner, so two glasses of wine may have packed more of a punch than usual. I wasn't afraid at all. In fact I was brimming with courage and curiosity.

"I'm going, Emma. You can't stop me."

"Hey, don't go without me." Emma drained her glass and followed me out to the cold, dark yard.

CHAPTER 15

THE CHILLY NIGHT AIR had a sobering effect. By the time we were at the door of the rental unit I wanted to turn around and go back home. But I couldn't, not with Emma right there.

The floor plan of the rental unit was a scaled-down, mirror image of the main house. Which meant the carport was to my left...this was so confusing.

"Emma, you should take the lead," I said. "You already did the, you know. Recon-saponce...responkabonk...pre-looking."

"Reconnaissance?" Emma said.

"Yes! That's what I said."

Maybe the cold night air hadn't been that sobering after all.

I followed Emma as she moved seemingly at random from one spot to the next, opening drawers, sticking her arm down between the bed and the wall, and crawling along the baseboard.

"Emma," I said, "you're like a human Roomba. Just bouncing around."

"The Roomba algorithm works," Emma retorted, from underneath the bed. As she was backing out, she kicked over a wastebasket. I righted it, thankful that it was empty. Then I saw a hot pink sticky note stuck to the inside. I quickly plucked the piece of paper from the waste-basket and pocketed it. Realizing I had just touched a stranger's garbage, I ducked into the bathroom and washed my hands for a solid sixty seconds.

We covered the rest of the small dwelling quickly but didn't find anything out of place. Jandie had a reflector set up next to the window in the third bedroom, so she was probably using that as her photo studio.

"See?" I said to Emma. "She doesn't even sleep here. That bed is just a prop. This room is her photo studio."

"Maybe she does sleep here," Emma retorted. "You don't know where Jandie sleeps."

I went over to the bed and knocked on it. It was hard, and made a hollow sound. I lifted up the pink bedspread to expose plywood.

"So she sleeps on plywood," Emma retorted. "That's not a crime. What's your point?"

"I forget."

We looked through the rest of the house, paying particular attention to the freezer (which contained a half-empty carton of strawberry cheesecake ice cream and nothing else).

Finally we decided we had conducted as thorough a search as possible under the circum-stances and decided to head back to the main house.

"So what do you think?" I asked Emma as we squelched across the wet lawn. The rain was starting up again, so we walked faster.

"Nothing really looked out of place," Emma said. "Although we can't be sure that nothing's missing, cause we don't know what was there before."

"Well, there were no suspicious odors or loose floorboards," I said. "That's something."

"Eh Molly, what if the husband doesn't come back? What if they're both missing? What about your rent?"

"They paid the six-month lease in advance," I said.

"Aha! Now I'm thinking maybe *you* whacked 'em."

"Hilarious."

Did they have two cars or just one?" Emma asked.

"I've only ever seen the big black truck that the husband drives. I think Jandie takes the Sampan when she needs to go somewhere."

"Oh yeah, that's right. She get a lotta posts with her riding in the Sampan."

When we got back to my house Pat was awake, relaxing in the living room and drinking coffee.

"If you want to know anything about their private life, you could just ask Howdy," Pat said.

"What?" Emma said.

"Howdy Howell. The reporter. He's interviewed them a few times now. He'd be happy to talk to you."

"What are you talking about?" I asked innocently.

"I'm talking about your tenants, whose house you two were just snooping around in."

"Shame on you spying on us!" Emma said.

"I wasn't spying. I saw you through the window, coming out of their front door."

"I'm the landlady," I said. "I have the right to inspect the house. It's in the contract."

"What were you looking for anyway?"

"Jandie," Emma said.

"What, you mean you were looking for her dead body?"

"No," Emma said.

"Maybe," I said at the same time. "Oh! Pat. I just remembered something I was wondering about. Why did Tedd Ladd stop drawing? He was doing his cartoon, he was super popular, and then he just stopped. He never explained why."

"I asked Howdy the same thing," Pat said. Emma and I plunked down on either side of him on the couch.

"And then?" Emma prompted him.

"Probably just grief," Pat said. "It happened around when his first wife passed away."

"His first wife died, ah?" Emma stood and went to the front window. Outside, sheets of rain, illuminated by my porch light, glinted in the dark. "So was it really grief? Or guilt?"

CHAPTER 16

"LADD'S FIRST WIFE DIED of cancer." Pat got up from the couch and went into the kitchen to fix himself a cup of coffee. "But sure, Emma, accuse a grieving widower of murder."

"I hope they're not on the road right now," I said. "Pitch dark, hard rain. Not a good combination."

Our rural island had few streetlights, and the ones we did have were deliberately kept dim to minimize any light pollution that might interfere with the telescopes.

"I have Jandie's cell phone number," I said. "Should I call her?"

"You have her cell number?" Emma whirled around to glare at me. "How come you never called her when she went missing?"

"Sorry, I didn't think of it. Okay, I'm calling her now."

I dialed Jandie's number, but I got an "all circuits are busy" message. Same thing on the second try.

"I should have tried her phone before," I said. "I think I should call the police. Her husband said he was going to, but I don't trust him. If they yell at me for being a nuisance, fine. I'd rather that than know I could've done something and didn't."

"It's possible you're overreacting," Emma said. "But I wouldn't bet Jandie's life on it."

"I agree, you've already annoyed the police as much as anyone possibly could," Pat added helpfully.

"Oh yeah, remember that time they had to mobilize every emergency vehicle on the island to find her?" Emma said. "I thought Detective Da Kine was gonna blow a gasket."

"That unfortunate situation was not my fault, and you both know it." I called the non-emergency police line and left a message describing the situation. I honestly didn't expect to hear back. But to my amazement, not ten minutes later a police cruiser pulled up in front of my house.

I opened my door.

"...Detective Medeiros?"

The detective was broadly built, and tall enough to hit his head on my door frame if he didn't duck. His thick black hair was tied back in a ponytail, and he had a small goatee. He wore a colorful, presumably custom-tailored aloha shirt (I don't think they're available off-the-rack in his size).

But something was different about Detective Medeiros. Had he gotten new tattoos? A haircut?

"Aloha." He put out a beefy hand. I hesitated. The friendly gesture was way out of character for Detective Ka`imi Medeiros, whose attitude toward me ranged from annoyance to exasperation.

"Detective Brian Medeiros," the man said. "You called about your tenant, Jandie Brand?"

"Oh! *Brian* Medeiros. I thought you were—"

"Yeah, I get that a lot. Ka`imi is my cousin. He's the brains of the family. I'm the handsome one."

"Ah!"

"May I come in?"

"What? Oh. Yes. Yes, of course! Thank you for coming so quickly. Please."

I led him into the living room and introduced Pat and Emma, who gawked at him rather rudely, in my opinion. They hadn't heard our exchange and were clearly shocked to see Detective Medeiros being so cordial.

I, too, wondered what had earned me this VIP treatment, but I wasn't going to question it. No need to bite the hand of the gift horse that feeds me, as poor Jandie would say.

"I'm so glad you came," I said. "The thing is, I'm worried about my renters. They're kind of new here, and they went out just as the bad weather is coming in. I can't reach them by phone."

"Lucky for your tenants, the mayor has a personal interest in their well-being," Medeiros eased down onto the opposite end of the couch from me. I felt my side of the couch lift until my feet dangled above the floor.

"The *mayor*?" Pat, Emma, and I exclaimed at once.

"Does the mayor know them personally?" I asked.

"Not yet. I think he'd appreciate an introduction, but. The wahine, not the husband."

"Good choice," Emma said. "So our mayor's a Jandista?"

"What is that?" Medeiros asked.

"Someone who's a fan of Jandie Brand," Emma said.

Medeiros looked pained.

"In a way, I suppose you could say. But it's not about her music or whatever."

"There's no music involved," Pat said. "She's an influencer. Famous for being famous."

Medeiros heaved a sigh.

"Okay, the thing about it is, Jandie Brand is making Mahina look like a real appealing destination with all her photos and da kine that she puts up. She's been good for our economy."

"So it's about tourist dollars," Pat said. "Sorry, I mean *visitor* dollars."

"More importantly, yen, yuan, and euros," Medeiros said. "The international visitors spend more. If something happens to Jandie Brand, it's bad for our restaurants and hotels and da kine. Anyway, that's probably more than you needed to know."

"No, thank you for giving us that background," I said. "It's very helpful."

As a naturally inquisitive person, I appreciated the detective's openness. Detective Brian Medeiros's cousin, Detective Ka'imi Medeiros, always acted like he'd get his pay docked if he dared to give me any information.

Detective Medeiros went on to ask all of us the expected questions about the missing couple, and some unexpected ones as well. What was my relationship with the tenants, did I get along with them, were they having money problems, had I noticed unusual behavior from the neighbors?

My warm feelings toward the "good" Detective Medeiros (as I now thought of him) cooled a bit when I noticed his questions becoming unnecessarily repetitive, as if he were trying to catch one of us out in a lie. Or perhaps some sin of omission. Like omitting the fact that Emma and I had been snooping in the rental house.

Unfortunately, his method turned out to be effective.

"You entered their *house*?" Medeiros looked from me to Emma and back, not bothering to conceal his surprise. "Both of you? When they wasn't there?"

"She went first," I said.

"Yeah, well she came in afterwards an' helped."

"Blaming each other isn't gonna work," Pat said. "You're both getting kicked out of paradise."

"We didn't do anything wrong, Detective Medeiros. It's *my* house." Even to myself I sounded whiny and defensive. "According to the lease I can inspect it at any time."

"Do you go into your tenants' house regularly?" Medeiros asked.

"Well...no. This was the first time."

"Why today then?"

"The same reason we called you," I said. "Because they're missing, and we're worried about them. Oh, and they were supposed to meet someone and missed the appointment. Pat, your friend Howdy, I can't think of his real last name."

"Howdy Howell," Pat said. "Yeah, that's true."

"I'll need his contact information from you." Medeiros turned to Emma. "Did you remove anything from the house?"

She shook her head.

"You?" He turned to me.

"No, I didn't...oh, hang on."

I remembered the sticky note I'd found stuck to the inside of the trash can. I dug it out of my bag and held it out to Pat.

"Why are you giving this to me?" Pat asked.

"You have your phone out. Take a picture. Please."

Pat snapped the picture and handed the paper back to me. I leaned across the couch and handed it to Medeiros. He glanced at it, folded it in half, and stuck it in his shirt pocket.

"You shouldn't have removed anything from the house," he said.

"That note was in the trash."

"Is the house a crime scene?" Emma asked.

"Is it?" I asked.

Medeiros braced his hands on his knees and stood. My side of the couch thunked back down to earth.

"Not that we know of. I'm going to go check it out right now. Will you be here in case I have any more questions?"

We assured him we would.

As soon as he was gone, I heaved a sigh of relief.

"What a day." I went into the kitchen to check whether the rice in the rice cooker was still good. It was fine, maybe a little hard around the edges. "How many people did I have to interact with? Edward Ladd, Harriet Holmes, Howdy Doo—Howdy Howell, Detective Medeiros 2.0."

"What about me and Emma?" Pat asked.

"You guys don't count. It's strangers and acquaintances that wear me out. You're the kind of friends I can ask to set the table while I heat up dinner. Oh yeah, anyone else up for a late dinner? I'm famished."

CHAPTER 17

"I LIKE THIS DETECTIVE Medeiros better," Emma said through a mouthful of kim chee chili and rice. "The other one is so uptight."

"It's because Molly's a landlord now," Pat said. "Of course the police are gonna be nice to her. The agents of class control work for the oppressor class."

"Oh, *I'm* an oppressor now? Pat, you're the one who's always saying individual choices don't matter within the context of a capitalist system. Besides, I thought you said you liked the rental unit."

"I do like it," Pat said. "I'm not judging, I'm just observing."

"Speaking of people judging me," I said, "I still can't figure out why Jandie Brand called me a crackpot."

"She what?" Pat asked.

"We went over to their house to warn them about the hurricane," Emma said. "We overheard 'em talking, and Jandie was saying what about the landlady, she has trouble minding her own business and she's kind of a crackpot."

"You can't argue the point about minding your business," Pat said. "You only heard her say it because you were eavesdropping at the time."

A knock on the door interrupted the conversation.

"I'll get it." Emma hopped up and opened the door to Detective Medeiros.

"Eh, Detective, you like come in?"

"No, I just wanted to let you know I'm leaving now."

"You find anything suspicious?" Emma asked.

"If you see anything unusual, call and let me know. You can leave a message if there's no answer."

Medeiros handed his card to Emma and left.

We cleaned up and Pat disappeared into the guest room. Emma and I agreed that it wasn't a good idea for her to drive on such a dark and stormy night. Well, maybe not exactly stormy, but it was drizzling. And the cloud cover definitely made it dark.

Emma got comfortable on the living room couch and called Yoshi to tell him she was staying with me. She launched into a narrative of the day's events, starting with our visit to the rental unit and Edward Ladd's admission that his wife was missing. There didn't seem to be any harm in it. Medeiros hadn't sworn us to secrecy or anything, and I supposed Yoshi must be as eager for news as anyone. Even more so, in fact, because Yoshi loved being the expert and the first to know things. This quirk of his was amusing at a distance and really annoying otherwise. I flipped the porch light on and went to bed.

The rain was so loud on the metal roof I had trouble falling asleep. The instant I did, or so it seemed, I was awakened by a banging on the front door.

Now what? I walked by the couch and shook Emma awake, and then we both tiptoed to the front door. I put my eye to the peephole.

Harriet Holmes was standing on my front porch, calmly shaking the water off her umbrella. I opened the door and quickly hustled her inside, glancing around to see who might have been pursuing her.

No one was.

No, it just happened that in Harriet Holmes's mind, ten o'clock at night in the hammering rain seemed like a perfectly appropriate time for a neighborly visit.

Before I knew it she was in my kitchen. She pulled out three matching furikake glasses from the dishwasher.

"I wouldn't have popped round," Harriet said, "only I saw you had your light on. Cheers. Or should I say, *sláinte*. Speaking of which, where's young Flanagan?"

"Asleep in the guest room," I said. "He can sleep through anything. Evidently."

Harriet sat at the dining table and placed the glasses down. From somewhere within the various pockets and folds of her battered field coat, she produced a full-sized bottle of whiskey and set it on the table.

"Whoa, nice!" Emma hurried into the kitchen. "I'm gonna get the Chicken Boy mug. Molly, are the dishes clean?"

"In the dishwasher? Yes. I ran it this afternoon. Emma, what's wrong with the furikake glasses?"

"Nothing, I just like Chicken Boy."

The furikake glasses hold about six ounces. The Chicken Boy mug has about three times that capacity.

"Oh yeah, still warm," Emma said as she retrieved the mug. "Eh Harriet, you make a decision on the place up the street?"

"We did," Harriet said. "Nigel and I went round and signed the lease this afternoon. It's official. We're neighbors."

Emma and I joined Harriet at the table. She pulled off the top of the bottle and poured us each a generous amount.

"That's great news, Harriet, welcome to the neighborhood." I raised my glass halfway and set it down. I so dearly wanted to be back in bed at this point, I didn't even have the energy to drink.

"You decided you rather have a view of the cemetery?" Emma asked.

"Mm." Harriet sipped her whiskey. "Be a welcome change, to be honest. Clyde, he's my landlord you know, he's been rather a dry stick ever since Nigel's come to Mahina."

Harriet still pronounced it "Ma-HIGH-na." I'd tried correcting her a few times, but it never stuck. I eventually gave up.

"Oh yeah, I get it," Emma said.

"I expected Clyde and Nigel to get on," Harriet said, "They've so much in common. They both have a bit of the outlaw about them, haven't they?"

I didn't see the similarity myself. Nigel Holmes was a retired law professor, the kind of person who would wander around for an hour looking for his glasses only to realize they've been perched on his forehead the whole time. Clyde Hamamoto, on the other hand, had the insignia of his motorcycle club tattooed on his neck.

"But when it comes down to it," Harriet was saying, "Clyde can be appallingly conventional, never mind the plaited beard and the leather waistcoat and all the rest of it. Bit of a disappointment, really. I say, on the topic of rentals, Barda, there's been a bit of activity around yours, what?"

"Detective Medeiros come by today," Emma said. "Looks like the mayor's taking Jandie's disappearance seriously, so Mahina PD is too. Molly and me, we think the husband killed her."

"We do not necessarily think that, Emma" I countered. "Oh, sorry, Harriet, please no smoking inside."

Harriet reluctantly tucked her pipe back into the recesses of her field jacket.

"Both tenants seem to have disappeared, now, though," I said. "First her, then him."

"And they missed an appointment with a reporter," Emma added.

"Well, I can report that Ladd is alive in any event," Harriet said.

"He is?" I was suddenly wide-awake. "Where is he?"

"Guest of the state," Harriet said. "Safe and sound in the Mahina PD cell block."

"Jandie's husband was arrested?" Emma took the bottle and poured herself more whiskey. "Eh, Harriet, you kinda buried the lede there, ah?"

CHAPTER 18

"MOLLY, YOU WANT AN ice pack?" Emma asked. I realized I had my elbows on the table and was digging the heels of my hands into my eye sockets to push back against the throbbing.

"Yes please."

"She gets migraines when she's confused," I heard Emma explain to Harriet. "She gets 'em a lot lately."

"Stressed, not confused," I objected. "Okay, I'm also confused. Harriet, how do you know where Edward Ladd is, and why is he in jail? And most of all, why do I have no idea what's going on here?"

I felt like my eyeballs were about to pop out of my skull. Only the firm pressure I was applying with my hands was holding them in place, I was certain.

"I do a bit of pro bono work," Harriet said. "Wonderful way to get to know where the bodies are buried. Not merely a figure of speech, it seems."

I felt Emma nudge the ice pack into my hand. I took it from her and planted my face in it. The cold immediately dialed the headache down from agonizing to merely uncomfortable.

"What happened?" Emma asked. "How'd they catch him?"

"They nicked him at the airport," Harriet said. "He had a one-way ticket to Honolulu."

"That's insane," I said. "He thought he was just going to hop on an airplane and somehow no one would notice?"

"Probably not thinking straight," Emma said.

"Well even if he's not as smart as he thinks he is," I said, "he has to be smarter than *that*."

I pressed the cold pack tight against my head, and took slow, deep breaths. With each exhale I visualized the pain seeping out of my eye sockets like used motor oil. It sounds gruesome, but it actually works.

"Edward Ladd wouldn't leave his precious aquarium," I said.

"Molly, he's a sociopath," Emma said. "He murdered his wife. You think he cares about some fish?"

"Brilliant," Harriet exclaimed. "So we're investigating then."

"What? No!" I pressed the cold pack into my forehead as hard as I could. "No, we are not investigating anything. The Mahina Police Department is on it, they've already made an arrest, and I know from bitter experience that they do not welcome help from well-meaning citizens."

"Oh, pish-posh," Harriet declared. "Rumor has it both of you been involved in a case or two."

Harriet herself had recently been accused of murder. Emma and I had been unavoidably pulled into the situation, but things had turned out well in the end. More or less.

"It was certainly an experience," I said. "Not one I care to repeat."

"We could just look into it a little," Emma said. "Molly, come on, don't you care about a murder happening on your own property?"

"You want to stick your oar in, you go ahead. Both of you. Welcome to it. But I'm not inclined to sign up for anything like that again."

"I say, Barda," Harriet said, "do you know the story of the horse that wandered out of a village and could not be found?"

I set down the cold pack, which was no longer cold. Trying to understand where Harriet was going with this would just make my headache worse. I decided to nod along but be careful not to commit to anything.

"I don't believe I know the story, no."

"Well, the best minds of the village failed to locate the horse. But one day the village idiot walked into town, leading the missing animal by the bridle. When they asked him how he had done it, he said: 'Well, I just thought what I'd do if I was a horse, and then I went and did it.'"

"I see," I said, humoring her.

"I don't," Emma said.

"And neither do you, Barda. I'll give it another go. Now, what are we trying to do?"

"Prove Jandie Brand's husband killed her," Emma said.

"Let the police do their jobs," I said.

"You don't believe Jandie's husband killed her?" Emma shot back.

"It doesn't matter what I believe. The professionals, whose actual job this is, will figure it out."

"Barda, Nakamura," Harriet interrupted, "I'll thank you to call me Mr. Ladd for the next day or so."

"What?" Emma and I said at the same time.

"I will inhabit his mind. I will become him," Harriet said. "Rather Zen, don't you think so, Nakamura?"

"Ladd's mind is not someplace I'd want to inhabit," Emma said.

Harriet refilled her glass and drained it in two gulps.

"I am Edward Ladd. I am a formerly celebrated cartoonist fallen from fame, middle-aged and bald. My much-younger wife has surpassed me in every way. More famous, more beloved, and Heaven knows, far more attractive."

"If you wanna be realistic," Emma said, "no can talk all fancy li'dat. Ladd doesn't have an English accent. Oh yeah, and the real Edward Ladd tells everyone how smart he is every chance he gets."

"Well this is going to be interesting." I stood up. "Harriet, I mean 'Mr. Ladd', It's getting close to midnight, and I certainly don't want to keep you."

Harriet stood up too.

"Say, looks like it's time to blow this joint and get some shut-eye." Harriet's nasal tone was apparently intended to evoke an American accent. "I'm gonna take a powder. Adios, amigos."

"I'd like Ladd better if he actually talked like that," Emma said when Harriet had gone.

"At least we have the rest of the week for her to get it out of her system before classes start again," I said. "Emma, I am so tired, I'm probably going to sleep late tomorrow. If you get up before I do, you and Pat can help yourselves to whatever you want for breakfast."

"Oh yeah, I know," Emma said.

CHAPTER 19

THE NEXT MORNING I woke up at seven a.m., much to my annoyance. I hadn't slept well. The rain had been hammering on the roof all night, and the power had gone out sometime during the early morning. Pat and Emma were still asleep. I dragged the portable generator out of the garage and plugged the refrigerator in. I hoped I wouldn't have to throw any food out. I went back into the garage to look for our long extension cord, but just as I found it, the power came back on. When I came back into the kitchen, the digital clocks on the stove and the microwave were blinking and needed to be reset.

Emma popped her head up from the couch.

"Molly, you're up early. I slept good, you know." She stretched her short arms over her head.

"I wish I could say the same."

"Eh, I forgot to tell you. You know those papers you were worried your students were buying? I got a lead for you. Check out OutsourceMyHomework dot com. That's the one that everyone's...oh no, Molly."

Emma flung her blanket aside and hopped off the couch.

"Whoa, Molly, you look bad."

"Thank you?" I said.

"I know how it is. You get older, no can hold your liquor so good."

"It's not that, Emma, I just didn't get to sleep—"

"Eh, I got my sweatpants on already. I'll get us breakfast at 7-11. You like Spam musubi?"

"Yes please."

I wasn't on death's door; I was simply tired. Also, Emma had seen me before I had a chance to put on any makeup.

I wound up the power cord on the generator and dragged it back into the garage. By the time Emma got back I had made coffee for myself and was feeling better. Emma had a bag of Spam musubis, a 12-pack of Mehana Red Ale, and a copy of the *County Courier*.

"Check this out." Emma pushed the paper across the table to me. The headline above the fold read: *Social Media Star Disappears, Husband Detained.*

"Howdy Howell has the byline," I said. "I thought he was just doing upbeat human-interest stories."

"Things are a little different now with the husband in jail," Emma pointed out. "Eh, I know you got your problems with Harriet Holmes, but you gotta admit, she knows what she's talking about. She knew about Ladd going to jail before it was in the paper."

"Emma, I do not have a problem with Harriet. She's highly qualified and Mahina State is lucky to have someone of her caliber. Although I do have to ask, what kind of person gets sent to sexual harassment training and then makes improper advances toward one of the facilitators?"

"Maybe she took 'sexual harassment training' literally."

"Funny, Emma."

"It wasn't *unwelcome* improper advances, at least," Emma reminded me.

"Oh, I am aware. Now my headache's back. Ow."

"You stay right there, Molly. I'll get your ice pack."

Emma took the newspaper back and read to me while I pressed the cold pack against my eyeballs. No one had seen Jandie leaving Mahina, according to Howdy Howell's story, and she was well-known enough to be recognized. She would have had trouble leaving town without anyone noticing.

The one ray of hope was the fact that no body had been discovered. Ladd hadn't posted bail, and he wasn't talking.

"Maybe he figures he's safer in custody," I said.

"Oh yeah, he's right about that," Emma replied. "Jandie's fans wanna dismember him."

Pat came over to join us at the table.

"You're a fan, Emma. So does that mean you want to dismember him?"

"Not if it means I gotta touch him. Ew."

"Good morning Pat," I said.

"Oh, no, Molly. Headache again? You want some hydrocodone?" he asked.

"No thank you. Makes me queasy."

"Eh, check this out." Emma handed Pat the copy of the *County Courier*.

"Walking around the airport with a one-way ticket?" Pat said. "That's funny. Almost like he wanted to get caught. Who is he protecting?"

"That guy, protecting someone?" Emma countered, "I think he's just a moron. Criminals aren't always masterminds, you know."

"It's almost lunchtime," Pat said. "Don't you guys have to be at work or something?"

"It's spring break," I said through the ice pack I had pressed to my face.

"Pat, you got somewhere to be?" Emma asked.

"Kind of. I'm meeting Howdy Howell for lunch."

"Tell him we all liked his reporting this morning," I said.

"Where are you meeting?" Emma asked.

"Not sure. We were gonna meet at the Pair-O-Dice, but I just found out the whole street's still closed off because of the flooding. We were gonna compare notes on the Jandie Brand disappearance. Not sure we wanna call it a case yet."

"Have him come here," I said. "I have a big pan of char siu fried rice in the freezer so as long as everyone's okay with that."

"You're okay with him coming here again?" Pat asked. "Last time you hid in your bedroom."

"If it makes things easier, Pat, I am happy to have you invite your colleague here."

"In other words," Emma said, "Molly's anti-socialness is defeated only by her nosiness."

"Okay, first of all, thank you for putting the most negative possible spin on my gracious offer of hospitality. Second, it's not 'nosy' to want to find out how my own tenant disappeared."

CHAPTER 20

"GOSH, PROFESSOR BARDA, this is awful nice of you to invite me to lunch." Howdy unfolded his napkin and tucked one corner into the top of his aloha shirt. I set the pan of fried rice down on the table and spooned a generous portion onto his plate.

"Howdy, do you think Jandie's husband had something to do with her disappearance? I'm not being *nosy*, I'd just like to know whether there's a murderer living on my property. Surely you can understand."

"I honestly don't know, Professor Barda, this was all so sudden. I never expected it. Although now that I think back...no, I better not say anything. In this country you're innocent until proven guilty."

He tucked into his fried rice, and I sat down, a little disappointed.

"For a smart guy, that attempted getaway was a dumb stunt," Pat said. "Ladd must've known he couldn't just try to fly out without someone noticing. Why didn't he go hide out in Kuewa, or stow away on a cargo ship?"

"So you think there might be someone else that might be involved, Pat?" I asked. "And Ladd is taking the fall for some reason? If someone else is involved, that means that even while Ladd's in jail, I could be in danger. At least Donnie and the baby are off-island but when they come back...is someone knocking at the door?"

It was Kaycee Kabua, our landscaper.

"Eh Kaycee, howzit!" Emma came up behind me, leaned out, and gave her a fist bump.

"I just left my sprayer in your carport on Sunday, and I wanted to let you know I was getting it," she said.

"Hello there," said a voice behind me. "I'm Howdy."

Kaycee wasn't wearing her hoodie today. Her dark curls were loosely tied back, and her round face was prettily made-up. Howdy was so obviously impressed with her, he was practically wringing his hat (except he didn't have a hat) and tracing circles on the ground with his toe.

After I made introductions, Howdy offered to accompany Kaycee out to the carport to help her carry anything that needed carrying. Kaycee accepted his assistance, even though she didn't need it. She was easily capable of carrying the sprayer with one arm and Howdy with the other.

Howdy returned in an upbeat mood.

"Gee, what a terrific girl!" Howdy took his seat at the dining table and spooned a huge second helping of fried rice onto his plate.

"Right. Kaycee's great. So, where were we? Jandie Brand is in danger or possibly dead, her homicidal husband's in jail, we don't know who else is involved, our rental is a murder house, and I might be next."

Emma gave me a look.

"Am I wrong?"

"Aw don't be so pessimistic," Howdy said cheerfully "Know what they say, may as well look on the bright side. If things go bad, you can always cry later."

You can always cry later?

I turned to Howdy.

"You," I said. "Howdy, you were here with the Ladds. The day I dropped off the hurricane information sheet."

Howdy didn't deny it.

"Sure," he said. "It's possible. I've been over there a few times."

"What were you trying to talk Jandie into?" Emma asked.

"Talk her into? Why, nothing that I recall."

"Jandie said something about her landlady being a nosy crackpot," I said.

"Well I sure don't remember that particular conversation. But I can tell you where we had a little bit of, I don't want to call it a disagreement, let's say something that was under discussion. The *County Courier* expects its human-interest stories to have an uplifting tone. That's what I was shooting for. I hate to say it, but the way the couple was with each other wasn't at all what I was hoping for. I was ready to write about a wife whose husband supported her fame and success. And a husband whose life was entering a second act, with his wife's support and a new generation of fans."

"So how come it wasn't what you were hoping?" Emma asked. "She hated him, I bet."

"I'm not sure it's right for me to go into too much detail," Howdy said.

"You must have been there that day," I said. "I heard two male voices in the house. Why would Jandie call me a crackpot?"

Howdy looked genuinely confused.

"I can honestly say, Professor Barda, that your name never came up."

"See?" Emma said to me.

"So what do you talk to them about when you go over there?" I asked.

Pat stood up.

"Don't mind me. I'm getting a cramp in my leg."

"Gosh, now that I think about it, I realize we always end up talking about Mr. Ladd's new book."

"He did say something about working on his writing," Emma said. "I thought that big *trombenik* was just saying it to sound important."

"Is there going to be a new book of cartoons?" I asked. "I'd be interested in reading it."

"Maybe it's a murder mystery where a husband does away with his younger and more successful wife," Emma suggested.

"No, it's neither of those things." Howdy pulled his satchel out from underneath his chair and produced a black, one-inch binder and a red-and-white flash drive. "I have a pre-publication copy right here. I didn't find much in here that I could use, but Mr. Flanagan, I thought you might be interested."

"Does Ladd know you have these?" Pat took the flash drive and binder from Howdy, handling them as gently as if they were baby birds.

"Oh sure, Mr. Flanagan, he's the one who gave them to me. He wouldn't mind you having them. He told me his publisher was having trouble lining up reviewers and if I knew anyone who was interested, I should share it with them."

"Is it about his life with Jandie?" Emma asked eagerly.

"No, she barely makes an appearance," Howdy said. "Missed opportunity, if you ask me. There's a lot of people out there who would buy anything having to do with Jandie Brand."

Howdy ran his hand through his hair.

"I know I shouldn't say this, but here goes. I think if you're married to someone, you should want them to succeed, and you should be proud of them when they do succeed. I think Mr. Ladd resented his wife's success. He thought he was the one who deserved to be famous, not her. I think he even thought she was standing in his way, if you can believe it."

Emma turned to me.

"You're a fan of this *putz*?"

"I did like his cartoons," I said. "Boy. That saying about never meeting your heroes is true, isn't it? Everything is disappointing."

"Oh, except this fried rice, Professor Barda," Howdy said brightly. "You're a great cook."

"I'll take credit for heating it up," I said, "but it's from Donnie's Drive-Inn."

"Can I keep this?" Pat asked.

"Oh, sure, Mr. Flanagan," Howdy said. "Like I said, I already read it. I'm no literary critic, but I gotta tell you, it's not something I'd put myself through again."

As soon as Howdy left, Pat inserted the flash drive into Emma's laptop. The three of us crowded together and read from the screen.

It was obvious why Howdy didn't want the book back. Ladd's memoir was an aggrieved, rambling screed, the main point of which seemed to be that the world seemed to be set up in a way that Edward Ladd found personally inconvenient. Ladd particularly seemed to resent the social pressure to treat as equals those he thought of as his inferiors. Which was just about everybody.

Pat stood up and walked over to the window.

"Don't mind me, I just need a break."

"Me too," I said. "I'm going to get something to drink."

"Bring the box," Emma called after me.

"If you plan to keep reading, you two should get on the liver transplant list now," Pat said. "From what I know of the guy, I don't think it's gonna get any better. Did you know he calls himself a certified master of persuasion?"

"I believe it," Emma said. "He musta been pretty freakin' persuasive to get Jandie to marry him. I'm thinking telekinetic."

"Here we go." I sat back down and placed the wine box on the table. "Have all you want. We can always buy more."

"Someone's at the door," Pat said. "I'll go get it."

It was detective Brian Medeiros. Pat invited him in, and we all moved to the living room. Detective Medeiros wouldn't have fit at the dining table.

"Is it true Edward Ladd was arrested last night?" I asked.

"That's correct," Medeiros replied. "I came by as a courtesy, to let you know he made bail. So don't be alarmed when he comes around."

"Did he tell you where Jandie is?" Emma asked.

Medeiros sighed.

"No."

"Great," I said.

"Look," Medeiros said. "Don't go out of your way to contact him or anything like that, but if you see anything suspicious, you can call me. You have my card. Professor Barda, are your friends gonna stay with you?"

"Yes. You are, right?"

Pat and Emma nodded.

I nodded.

"Good," Medeiros said.

CHAPTER 21

THE NEXT MORNING, THE story of Jandie Brand going missing had made it to the *County Courier* website. The comments on the online article were as constructive and enlightening as comments on the websites of local newspapers usually are. I closed the browser window feeling dumber for having read them. Enough internet for today, as the kids say.

The rain was hammering the metal roof, so I knew taking a walk was out of the question. Pat was in the guest room and Emma had gone to check on her house. I had already taken care of all outstanding laundry, dishes, and bills. One of my papers-in-progress had been revised and resubmitted and I was waiting to hear back from the editor. My other paper was currently with one of my coauthors.

For the first time in recent memory, my to-do list was empty. I got up to fix myself a big pot of tea. I'd finally get back to that murder mystery I'd been reading...

And then my computer beeped a notification. Another draft business plan uploaded to the course website.

I sat back down at my computer. I'd realized long ago that it was better to get grading done as assignments came in, instead of letting them accumulate into a demoralizing pile.

The draft business plan was flawlessly formatted and clearly written. There was so little room for improvement, I couldn't even call it a draft. If this had been turned in as a final assignment, it would be an A paper.

The product described therein was a unisex undergarment equipped with a sort of replaceable filtration system. The executive summary led off with the product name and slogan:

Toot Sweet. Because your freedom ends where someone else's nose begins.

The company logo was an anthropomorphized can of baked beans, wearing a World War I-style gas mask.

It read exactly like the plans for "Party Pooper" and "Urine Luck." Structured as the assignment required, and free of spelling and grammar errors. There was no way these plans were written by three different people. And certainly not by the three different people whose names were on the assignments.

I noticed then that the rain had let up. I didn't have to deal with this right this minute, I thought. A walk would clear my head. I pulled on my shoes, grabbed an umbrella, and started walking uphill. The lush lawns and metal roofs gleamed from the recent downpour, and the air smelled electric. I went all the way to the cul-de-sac at the top of Uakoko Street, then turned around and went back down to the bottom. Feeling energized, I turned right and kept walking until I reached the lava rock marker at the entrance to the cemetery. The vast cemetery lawn was brightened with flower arrangements that families had left for their loved ones. I hadn't seen another person on the street, and I felt like I had Mahina all to myself. I inhaled deeply. The air was clean and fragrant. I wondered why I didn't go out walking more often.

And then the rain started to pelt down. I put up my umbrella, only to have a blast of wind immediately blow it inside-out, breaking two of the ribs.

I arrived home drenched and tossed the umbrella in the garbage. I couldn't put it off anymore. I was dealing with an obvious case of academic dishonesty, and I was going to have to confront it.

Emma came back that evening with a big bag of avocados from her tree. Pat emerged from the guest room, and I set up a quiet dinner for three at the table. Pat told us he'd spent the day researching Tedd Ladd, but didn't find much other than that his old books of cartoons were abundant and cheap at online second-hand bookstores. He also mentioned that he'd tried to finish reading the manuscript Howdy had handed him.

"Any good dirt?" Emma asked.

"No. It's a completely self-indulgent sludge of Ladd's musings on life and on how awesome he is. It manages to be both boring and embarrassing."

"Maybe if he's that un-self-aware he'll let something slip," I said.

"You know, you're welcome to read the whole thing for yourself," Pat said.

"Not tempted at all," I said. "Emma, where did you go today?"

"There's that paddler party still going on at my house," Emma said. "I had to go check on the damage."

"I didn't know Jonah was into canoe paddling," I said.

"He's not. But him and the guys are all there partying right now. A couple of the paddlers from Kauai got their flights cancelled so they're stuck here."

"Kauai's getting hit hard right now," Pat said.

"Poor Kauai. Every time. Eh, Molly, you find anything out about those plagiarized assignments?

"I think I got another one." I told Emma and Pat about Toot Sweet.

"These are actually good ideas," Emma said. "Toot Sweet, Party Pooper, what was the other one?"

"Urine Luck," I said. "I can't just ignore this."

"So then do the paperwork," Pat said. "Report them."

"Have you ever done the paperwork, Pat?" Emma asked.

"Not that I remember."

"Oh, you'd remember," I said. "The minute you upload a report, the Student Retention Office is all over your case. 'Can you prove the student knew he was supposed to turn in original work?' 'How can you be 100% sure that she didn't accidentally turn in the wrong document?' 'If you were a more caring teacher, your students wouldn't feel like they had to cheat.' They just keep making your life miserable hoping you'll give up."

"So don't do it," Pat said.

"Oh sure, sounds simple," Emma said. "Except if you let it go, you could get in trouble anyway. Remember that cheating scandal last year? Our administration was 'shocked, shocked' to find that plagiarism was going on. They blamed the faculty for not reporting when they should've. Eh, know what I realized? Our administration is exactly like army ants."

"They can skeletonize a cow in under two minutes?" Pat asked.

"They keep everyone walking around pointlessly in circles till they drop dead."

"Why do they do that?" I asked. "The ants, I mean."

"They're blind, so if they don't have any direction or leadership, they just follow the ant in front of them. Then more and more of 'em join in and pretty soon you got a big rotating disk of army ants walking themselves to death. It's kinda cool and disturbing at the same time. Look up ant mill if you wanna see it for yourself."

"That is interesting," I said. "Anyway, can we talk about my plagiarism issue now? I downloaded the three documents and checked the metadata. I didn't see anything suspicious. But then I noticed that one of the papers had the letters 'OMH LLC' in the footer. But only in the bibliography section."

"Did you look it up?" Pat asked.

"Yeah, I got almost a million results. An office cleaning company, financial services, grocery store, some little video game company. I don't know what it is."

"OMH is probably OutsourceMyHomework," Emma said.

"That's right," I said, "you did mention it before, didn't you?"

"That's the easy part," Emma said. "Now you gotta prove it."

"Speaking of proving things," Pat said, "what's Harriet up to? Is she still investigating your neighbors?"

"Oh yeah," Emma said, "she's getting inside Ladd's mind. Pretending to be him."

"Like method acting?" Pat asked.

"Yes," I said. "Including an American accent that seems to be payback for whatever Dick Van Dyke did in Mary Poppins."

"It sounds kinda nuts," Emma said, "but Harriet seems to know what's going on. Don't forget, she's the one who told us about Ladd getting arrested at the airport before the police did."

That night, despite the incessant drumming of rain on the metal roof, I managed to drop off to sleep. Only to wake up around midnight. Through the front window I saw the tawny glow of the sodium streetlight reflecting on the wet road. Everything seemed normal, and yet...I grabbed my phone, went out through the sliding doors onto the lanai and tiptoed around to the back of the house. From there I could see across the lawn to the rental unit. I watched it for a few minutes. At first it was dark and still, but then I saw light flickering inside, as if someone were creeping around with a flashlight.

I tapped on the window of the guest room to wake Pat, but he was sleeping soundly.

I remembered I had my phone with me and dialed the Mahina Police Department non-emergency number. It rang and rang without going to voice mail. Then I called 9-1-1. The dispatcher picked up, but unfortunately, I'd connected with someone who was very serious about her responsibility to be frugal in her allocation of the county's resources. I was unable to convince her that a light in my rental unit constituted an emergency. She advised me to call back after 7:45 the next morning, when the non-emergency receptionist was on duty.

I marched back inside and found Emma was dozing on the living room couch. I shook her awake.

"Someone's in the rental," I said. "I can't wake Pat up. The police don't think it's important. I know this is a bad idea, but I think we should go take a look."

CHAPTER 22

EMMA AND I TIPTOED across the wet lawn and quietly let ourselves into the rental unit. We followed the sound of snoring to the master bedroom.

It was too dark at first to recognize the intruders. But when one of them stirred and the moonlight hit her face, I'm afraid I shrieked in surprise. The man next to her sat bolt upright, clawing at his sleep mask.

"Nigel!" I exclaimed. At the same time, Emma cried, "Harriet!"

"What on earth is going on?" I asked.

Harriet cleared her throat. "Say toots—"

"You don't have to do the accent," I interrupted her. "It's just us. Please tell me what's going on here."

"Right." Harriet groped at the night table for her glasses and slipped them on. "Ah, here we are. Oh I say, Barda, Nakamura, rather an inconvenient hour for a visit, what?"

"Harriet," I persisted, "Nigel, why are you two sleeping in my tenants' bed?"

Harriet removed her glasses, examined them, and put them on again. "Nigel didn't want to be left out of the investigation, you see, and I've already taken the role of Edward Ladd. So Nigel's Jandie Brand, world-famous social media influencer and the center of our little drama."

"Hashtag-rather-a-cracking-good-adventure," Nigel said.

"Bit long for a hashtag, darling," Harriet said. "Did you sleep well?"

"Never better, my murderous little minx."

Nigel kissed Harriet's cheek, then jumped up and pulled on a flowered hapi coat that had been hanging on a bedpost.

"Fancy a cuppa, darling?" he asked Harriet.

"Is he wearing Jandie's robe?" I asked Harriet as Nigel sashayed out of the bedroom.

"He is," Harriet said. "Surely you don't want him running about in nothing but a pair of pink leggings."

"Listen, Harriet, I really do appreciate all the effort you and your husband put into this, and really, thank you for being concerned about my renters, but I wish you'd checked with me before you decided to stay the night here. What if Ladd had come back and found you two asleep here? I mean, we don't know what he's capable of."

"Fair point, Barda." Harriet threw aside the covers and started to pull on a pair of trousers over her long underwear. "I don't believe I'd have come to harm, not with Nigel here as protection. Still, I suppose one can't be too careful in lawless Mahina."

"Well, you've certainly committed to the Method, I'll give you that. Did you get any insights?"

"Oh yeah, you figure out what that psycho did with Jandie?" Emma asked.

Harriet frowned.

"The experiment was not a success, I'm afraid. Perhaps I'm too fond of Nigel. Committed as I was to the role of homicidal husband, I simply couldn't stomach the thought of doing away with him. Sounds a bit treacly when one says it out loud, but there it is. I say, is someone at the door?"

"I'll get it darling," we heard Nigel call.

Emma and I left Harriet to finish getting dressed and went out to the dining room. We found Nigel sitting at the Ladd's dining table having tea with Mr. Henriques, the next-door neighbor. The early morning sun slanted through the window, lighting up Nigel's colorful robe and snowy hair, and cruelly illuminating Mr. Henriques's bald head beneath his combed-over strands. I was so exhausted, it all felt like a dream. Although in retrospect the scene would have seemed surreal regardless of how well-rested I might have been. Unfortunately, this was my house, and it was up to me to take control of this mad tea party. I would have preferred to walk out and go straight back to bed.

"Mr. Henriques," I said, "what a surprise. What are you doing here?"

He jumped a little, sloshing his tea, then replaced his cup down carefully in the saucer.

"I was checking on Mr. Ladd's aquarium." Henriques said.

"How come?" Emma asked.

"I noticed activity inside the house, and I thought someone might be after the fish."

We all turned to look at the aquarium. The fish in question flicked back and forth serenely. "Who would be after the fish?"

"Oh, no one in particular," Mr. Henriques explained. "But I promised Mr. Ladd I'd take care of his fish for him."

"How would you have gotten in if Nigel hadn't been here to answer the door?" I asked.

"Mr. Ladd gave me the key." Mr. Henriques beamed proudly.

I tried to remember whether there was anything in the rental contract forbidding the renters from sharing the key with someone else. Even if there were, what would be the point in enforcing it? Everyone would be mad at me, and I'd probably get stuck taking care of the stupid fish myself.

"You did a good job, you, Mr. Henriques," Emma said. "The fish look happy."

"Yes, they're lovely," Nigel said. "Bit fiddly I understand, maintaining a saltwater aquarium."

"Oh yes," Mr. Henriques said eagerly. "It's a labor of love."

"Well I hate to be a buzzkill party pooper," I said, "but I'm going to ask everyone to clear out. Thank you for feeding the fish, Mr. Henriques."

"Want some coffee?" Emma asked as we re-entered my own house.

"No. Help yourself to whatever's there, though. Oh, I forgot you brought avocados. Hey, you can make avocado toast. Or guacamole."

"Nah, these are your avocados," Emma said. "Get plenty more at home."

"I'm too tired to eat right now. I'm going to try to get some sleep. Thanks for helping me clear everyone out and clean up."

"No worries. You're running low on cream though. I'll put a note on the refrigerator, so you don't forget."

CHAPTER 23

THE NEXT DAY I SNEAKED regular, nervous peeks at my rental unit. Detective Medeiros had told me to expect Edward Ladd to return after he'd paid his bail. Ladd finally did come back that evening. I knew right away. Not because of my unceasing surveillance, but because he actually came by and knocked on my door. When I opened it and saw him standing there, I practically had a heart attack.

I was alone. Emma and Pat had left to do some grocery shopping and get takeout at Chang's Pizza Pagoda.

"No offense to Donnie's cooking," Emma had said. "But Chang's Pizza Pagoda got a two for one special on their cheesy kung pao shrimp pizza."

"I'll be moving back in, just wanted to let you know," Ladd said. "So you wouldn't think there was an intruder and call the police."

"Heh, call the police...that's a good one." I tried to force myself to smile. At that moment I would have been happy to refund the entire amount they'd paid for the lease, just to have Edward Ladd out of my life entirely.

Ladd stood on my porch, waiting. For me to ask him about Jandie? For me to say I was glad to have him back? For me to invite him in?

"Can I...help with anything?" I asked.

"No, I just wondered what you thought of my manuscript."

Ladd knew we had his book? Were we supposed to have it, or was he trying to trick me into admitting I'd read it? What exactly had Howdy Howell told us? My brain helpfully reminded me that serial killers say the second murder is easier than the first, so I should be careful about what I say to Edward Ladd. *Thanks a lot, brain, now how about telling me exactly what I am supposed to say to this guy?*

"Your book?" I stalled cleverly, hoping the "master of persuasion" couldn't also read minds.

"I gave it to Howell," Ladd said. "He said he was going to give it to everyone he knows. That includes you."

"Oh, Howdy Howell. The reporter. I've only met him a couple of times, but I'll have to ask him about it next time I see him. A book, you say."

Misleading, but not an actual lie.

"If you want to assign it to your students, you don't need to ask permission," Ladd said. "Just make sure they're not buying bootleg copies."

"You have my word," I said. "I will never encourage my students to buy bootleg copies of your book. By the way, have you heard from Jandie? We're all really worried about her."

Ladd shook his head and without a word, turned and walked away.

Harriet came by that night about ten o'clock, with a big bottle of Irish whiskey. Before I could thank her, she told me it was a present for Pat.

"Why Pat?" I asked. "It's not his birthday or anything."

"It's Saint Patrick's Day," she said.

"Today's the eighteenth. St. Patrick's Day was yesterday."

"Was it? So easy to lose track during the spring holiday."

Harriet pulled out a chair and sat down at the dining room table. I joined her there.

"I know," I said. "I'm not really watching the calendar too closely either, but Pat and Emma went shopping today and came back from Mizuno Mart with a bunch of half-price marshmallow shamrocks and green candy corn."

"I see. I'm a day late. Can we call it Irish punctuality then? Where's yer man?"

"Pat's already asleep," I said. "It'd be like trying to wake the dead. Besides, he doesn't drink."

"Not really? Nakamura told me, but I thought she was taking the Mickey."

"No, it's true. Coffee's Pat's psychoactive of choice. But it would be a shame to let your generous gift go to waste."

"So it would." Harriet unboxed the whiskey. I went to the couch to shake Emma awake.

"So Ladd's back," Harriet said, once we were all at the table. "Any news about young Jandie?"

"So creepy, that guy," Emma said. "Doesn't even seem to bother him that his wife's missing. If I'd been here, I woulda said so to his face. I don't care, I'd take him on."

"It's probably better you were out then," I said. "I don't think you kicking him in the shins would advance the cause of justice. Also I appreciate all the food you guys brought home, so thanks."

"Eh, Harriet, this is how narcissistic he is. He asked Molly what she thought of his book."

"Ladd's got a book, has he?" Harriet raised her glass. "Any good?"

"No," Emma and I said at the same time.

"Any idea who the publisher is?"

"None," I said. "We just have the manuscript, not the final printed version."

"Hard to find a reliable publisher these days. Nigel's seems a bit dodgy. I'm not complaining, mind you, we're quids in, but their paperwork's a dog's breakfast. Filing our U.S. taxes is going to be an adventure."

"Speaking of money," Emma said, "it's weird that Ladd managed to make bail. Last I heard he was using the public defender and she was trying to argue the amount down cause he couldn't pay the original amount. I hope he hasn't gotten his murderer hands on Jandie's money."

"Ah, yes, funny that," Harriet said. "It seems a benevolent stranger paid his bail."

Emma and I turned to look at Harriet.

"Well he hadn't the money to pay it, had he? Here, go on." Harriet refilled our glasses.

"Seriously, Harriet?" Emma demanded. "*You* paid that psycho's bail?"

"Harriet," I said, "what are you going to do if he skips town this time? They already caught him trying to fly out of Mahina. If he leaves, you're going to be the one left holding the bag. I mean, you teach law, you obviously know this. I just...why?"

"He's not going to do anything useful while he's locked up," Harriet said cheerfully. "Far more instructive to observe the man in his natural habitat."

Emma opened her mouth to argue, but apparently changed her mind.

"Yeah, I see your point," she said.

"Emma, you what? This is insane. No. No one is observing anyone."

"Oh, and you say *I'm* bossy?" Emma retorted.

"I'm not bossing anyone. You two can do whatever you like. Just keep me out of it. I'm not involved in this at all."

"Plausible deniability, eh, Barda?" Harriet said.

"Yes," I said. "Sorry to be no fun, but I'm exhausted and I'm going to bed."

"Oh I say, you won't mind if I hang about tonight."

"What? Okay, why not. As long as no one does anything that could get me sued or arrested, both of you, stay as long as you like. Help yourselves to anything in the pantry or the fridge. There's plenty of green candy corn. Harriet, thank you for the whiskey. It was delightful."

I thought Emma and Harriet would stay up for a while, drink some more, go to bed, and forget about everything by the next morning. I was wrong.

CHAPTER 24

I WOKE UP THE NEXT morning to find Harriet Holmes still in my house. She was sitting upright in one of the armchairs in the living room wearing over-ear headphones and making notes in an old-fashioned notebook. Emma sat at the dining table sipping coffee and reading a paper copy of the *County Courier*. I started to say good morning, but Emma quickly put a finger to her lips. I made coffee as quietly as I could and brought my laptop over to the table.

"Man, make up your mind you baboozes," Emma muttered to her laptop.

"How long has Harriet been sitting there?" I whispered.

"She was there when I got up. Didn't want coffee or nothing. Eh Molly, can you help me with this?"

"Why are you filling that out now? We're not teaching this week."

"I know. It's from last week. I'm late. Again."

"Well. I should remind my faculty how lucky they are to have me fill those things out for them."

Emma lowered the laptop lid and stared at me.

"You're allowed to have your department chair fill them out?"

"Technically, no," I said. "But I fill these things out for my faculty anyway."

"How come?"

"Oh, let's see. Larry Schneider objects to everything the Student Retention Office does on principle and refuses to cooperate with them. Rodge Cowper has never met a deadline in his life. Hanson Harrison doesn't believe in email. And the first and last time Harriet Holmes uploaded her weekly classroom assessment, HR called me in and threatened to send my whole department to sensitivity training."

Emma lifted her eyebrows and turned to look at Harriet. Harriet was pressing her headphones to her ear with her left hand and scribbling furiously with her right.

"What'd she write?" Emma whispered.

"They wouldn't even tell me. So it's easier for me to just fill these things out myself. As long as I don't get caught. Please don't rat me out."

"Okay, what am I supposed to put on this line?" Emma turned her laptop around to show me the screen. "I never know what to write for this part."

"Ah. Here's what you do. Rephrase the question and then append the phrase, by encouraging a growth mindset and honoring the students' individual learning styles."

"Seriously?" Emma asked.

"It hasn't failed me yet. So for this item your answer would be, In BIO 101 I ensure understanding of the foundational course content by encouraging a growth mindset and honoring the students' individual learning styles. For the next one, I construct a safe and affirming learning environment in BIO 101 by encouraging a growth mindset and honoring the students' individual learning styles."

"No way. That's all I gotta do? I wish you'd told me sooner." Emma turned the computer back around and resumed typing.

"You're welcome."

"Oh yeah, thanks, ah?"

"Where's Pat?" I asked.

"He went for a walk."

I glanced out the front window. Sunlight glared off wet metal roofs across the street.

"I hope he took an umbrella," I said.

"Oh I say," Harriet blurted out, loudly enough to make Emma and me jump. "Ladd's got a visitor."

"Who is it?" Emma called back.

"Quiet," Harriet boomed. "I'm sussing it out now."

Emma stood up and pulled out her phone.

"I'll be right back."

Emma went into the kitchen, grabbed the bag of avocados, and walked past Harriet and out the front door. Harriet didn't seem to notice.

"It's a right knees-up now," Harriet said after about thirty seconds. "Someone else just arrived. A female. Don't think it's Jandie. Voice is pitched too low. She's saying something about avocados. Could be a secret code."

"Harriet, that's—"

Harriet held up a finger for silence and pressed it to her ear. Then she wrote something in her notebook.

The front door eased open, and Emma came in quietly. She was empty-handed. I motioned her over to the table.

"You gave them my avocados?" I whispered.

"It was worth it," Emma said.

"So what happened?"

"Howdy Doody's over there with Ladd. They didn't invite me in, obviously, but at least I got to see who it was. Don't look at me like that, Molly. You weren't gonna eat half a dozen avocados by yourself in the next twelve hours, were you?"

"Did you leave me one, at least?"

"Yes, I left you two. I'm not a monster."

Harriet continued to listen and write. Emma worked on her weekly report. I read Donnie's latest email. Francesca seemed to be sprouting a new tooth, and Donnie's Uncle Brian had taught her to say "Vegas," which she pronounced "Bay-gus." Donnie didn't mention our renters, so perhaps the news of Jandie's disappearance hadn't reached him yet. Perhaps the whole thing would get resolved before Donnie had a chance to find out about it.

Through the window, out of the corner of my eye, I saw a Sampan drive by, heading down the street. It didn't stay in my field of view long enough for me to see the passengers.

"Well, that's sorted for now." Harriet lifted the giant headphones off her head, leaving her cropped gray-brown hair sticking out in all directions. "The sound quality's a bit of a disappointment. I didn't catch the names of the visitors."

"The man was Howdy Howell, the reporter," Emma said. "The woman was me. I brought over avocados to make 'em open the door so I could see who was there."

"Ah. Brilliant." Harriet scribbled more notes.

"What did you hear?" I asked.

"I thought you didn't wanna be involved," Emma said.

"Ladd and Howell were discussing the possible whereabouts of Ladd's wife," Harriet said. "Ladd's still claiming he doesn't know where Jandie is. Wouldn't be the first time someone's lied to a reporter for self-serving reasons."

"Did you find out *any* new information?" I asked.

Harriet stood and ran a hand through her hair. It looked exactly the same.

"No, not really. Something about Kuewa. It's where all the hippies and flower children live, isn't it?"

"And drug dealers, and people in witness protection," Emma said.

"They thought she might turn up there for some reason. She hasn't, of course. Rather a jolly wheeze listening in, though, makes one feel a proper spy. Can't wait to tell Nigel all about it."

CHAPTER 25

HARRIET FINALLY WENT home Friday afternoon. The following morning, Pat went out to spend the day at the library, and Emma settled in to finish up her Student Retention Office paperwork.

"Emma," I asked, "what was the name of that essay mill website again?"

"OutsourceMyHomework," she said, without looking up from her computer. "Dot com. Molly, they do custom-written assignments. You're never gonna find the evidence you need. You gotta give your students individual oral exams. Otherwise you're just gonna be playing whack-a-mole."

"Well, oral exams aren't in the syllabus." I brought over my own laptop to the dining table and set it up. "If I try to introduce them now, I'm going to get pushback and I'll get overruled by our administration in the end anyway."

"Yeah, that's true," Emma said. "Just plan 'em for next semester."

I started up my browser. The OutsourceMyHomework site had a welcoming layout and a cheery color scheme.

Welcome to outsourcemyhomework.com. We match up your order details with the most qualified writer in your field. We guarantee that your order is completed on time and to the highest standard. Find out how much your paper will cost.

I used the pulldown menu to select Business Plan, Undergraduate.

"Emma," I asked, "how much does your biology textbook cost?"

"I dunno. Couple, three hundred, I think. It's got a lot of color pictures though, that's why."

"So a custom-written business plan costs less than a biology textbook," I said.

"Yeah, but is it a thousand pages with color pictures?"

"Do you want to hear the customer reviews?" I asked.

"No."

"What about the ones from Hawaii?"

Emma looked up.

"There's reviews from Hawaii?"

"Yes! Listen to this. OutsourceMyHomework dot come is my go-to service whenever I need my homework done fast and quality," I read aloud. "They also do all kinds of unpopular subjects like arts, entrepreneurship, and pre-med."

"Sad." Emma went back to working on her computer.

"Here's another one," I said. "The speed of your writer are good. Your team is quick in replying and very helpful."

"I feel sorry for whoever ends up hiring that kid," Emma said.

"Aha!"

Emma looked up.

"Absolutely magnificent," I read. "I was very impressed by the speed and the quality of the assignment delivered. I could not imagine that homework services like outsourcemy-homework.com even exist. Finding this company is one of the best things that happened to me. For a reasonable price I got a business plan about a product called...Oh, for crying out loud."

"What?" Emma asked.

"I think I found our mysterious business plan writer. Emma, this must be for my class."

"So you gonna wait for someone to turn it in?" Emma asked. "And then bust 'em?"

"No, I'm going to give the cheater a chance to turn back. I'll send out a message to the class warning them against using essay mills. And I'm going to tell them if anyone is thinking of turning in a business plan for a product called 'Wee the People,' they should seriously reconsider."

"You're too nice," Emma said.

"Wow, that's not something I hear very often."

CHAPTER 26

ON SUNDAY MORNING, at what I can only describe as an unholy hour, my phone jangled me awake.

"I say Barda, have you seen the *County Courier* this morning?"

"Harriet?" I said. "The *County Courier*? Um, no, I haven't. What time is it—"

"I think you ought to check up on Ladd."

"Me? Harriet, what are you—"

But she had already hung up.

I went out to the living room, where Emma was snoring on the couch. I shook her awake.

"Molly, go back to bed," she mumbled. "What time is it anyway?"

"Harriet Holmes just called. She said I should check on Ladd. She didn't say why. I don't want to go over by myself."

"Make Pat go with you." Emma turned over and pulled the pillow over her head.

Pat and I found Ladd in bad shape. He answered the door wearing nothing but striped pajama bottoms. He was drinking from a coffee mug, but he reeked of sour booze. He was clutching the Sunday issue of the *County Courier*.

"You okay, man?" Pat asked.

"Uh, good morning," I said. How would I explain why we'd come by? "We just thought we'd check in."

"I guess you saw this." Ladd handed me the newspaper. The *County Courier's* top of the fold headline was *Body Found at Base of Cliff*. Pat leaned in to read over my shoulder.

A woman's body had been found at the bottom of seaside cliffs in the Kuewa district. The area was so inaccessible, the body had to be lifted out by helicopter. Her name was being withheld pending notification of her family, and anyone with information about the incident was asked to contact the police non-emergency line or Crime Stoppers.

"No, I hadn't seen this," I said.

"You think it's her?" Pat asked.

Ladd ran the heel of his hand up the side of his face.

"I hope it's not Jandie. But I haven't been able to reach her. Still. She doesn't answer her phone. She hasn't posted anything since she...for days now."

Ladd seemed genuinely distressed. If it was an act, it was a convincing one.

Or maybe his agony was real, only it wasn't over the Jandie's death. It was because he thought he'd hidden the body and it was only his bad luck it had been discovered.

Ladd didn't seem inclined to invite us in, and I had no particular desire to go into his sour-smelling house. I asked him to let me know if he needed anything. He (probably equally glad to end our interaction) assured me he would.

"Someone should keep an eye on that guy," I said once we were back inside my house. Emma was toasting bagels. The scent of seared starch was irresistible.

"Isn't that what we were just doing?" Pat asked.

"What happened over there?" Emma asked.

We told her about the newspaper story and how Ladd thought the dead woman might be Jandie.

"I think I know where that place is. Where they found her." Emma came over to the counter and held out a plate with four buttered bagel halves. Pat and I each took one. "Paddlers stay away from there after a heavy rain, cause it's where all the *schmutz* comes pouring out into the ocean. Man, I hope the body they found isn't Jandie. How did Ladd seem? Suspicious?"

"He seemed pretty upset, actually," Pat said. Emma looked at me.

"He really did," I said.

"Oh, you don't believe me, but you believe Molly?" Pat objected.

"Maybe he was upset about the body being found," Emma said.

"That's what I thought too," I said.

"I'm gonna keep an eye on him." Emma grabbed a napkin, wiped her buttery fingers, and went to the front door.

"Where are you going?" Pat asked.

"To ask Harriet what she thinks. I bet she has some ideas."

"Oh, yes, let's get Harriet even more involved in this than she already is," I said to the closing front door.

"Jealous?" Pat got up and refilled his coffee cup.

"What? Jealous of Harriet Holmes?"

"You have to admit," he shouted over the noise of the coffee machine, "she's much better at this than we are."

I held off answering until Pat sat back down.

"Better at what, exactly?"

"She's creative. I hate the phrase, think outside the box, but that's what she does. She's not limited by—"

"Not limited by what? Tact? Manners? Decency? The rules everyone else has to abide by?"

"Whoa, Molly, did I hit a nerve?"

I sighed.

"Sorry, Pat. I didn't mean to snap at you. It's just that Harriet breezes around, doing whatever strikes her fancy at the moment, everybody loves her, and yet somehow she does things that always end up making more work for me."

"You're both independent adults, Molly. You're not responsible for her."

"Oh really? Tell that to HR. Did you know she told one of our marketing professors she'd been to his country and found it quite charming for a banana republic? Guess who got called into the principal's office? Not Harriet."

"I guess that's why they pay you the big bucks."

"What, to be a department chair? Ha, I wish. It's going to be interesting having Harriet living right up the street." I grabbed the last bagel half, which by now was room-temperature and a little leathery. "Okay, I still have time to get dressed and make it to Mass. By my calculations I'll get there just as they're finishing up the Passing of the Peace."

CHAPTER 27

WHEN I GOT BACK FROM Mass, Emma was lounging on the couch, playing a game on her phone.

"How was Mass?" she asked, without looking up. "You dodge the Passing of the Peace?"

"Mostly. What did you and Harriet get up to today?"

"I thought you didn't wanna know. Cause plausible deniability."

"I know, but I'm curious. Want a coffee?"

"Nah, I'm good."

I went to make a cup for myself and joined her in the living room.

"We tailed 'im," Emma said, almost causing me to spray my coffee.

"Ladd?"

"Uh-huh," she said.

"Emma, if he really is a murderer and he catches you following him, he's going to kill both of you, and I'll have to find someone to teach biz law in the middle of the semester. Unless he comes over and murders me afterwards, then it's not my problem anymore I guess."

"No worries. We kept outta sight."

"Is Pat here? He'd probably like to hear about this."

"I already told him the whole story. He's been holed up in his room. He says he has to file something before some deadline."

"He's not going to write about you spying on Edward Ladd, is he?"

Emma set down her phone on the floor and sat up.

"He better not, I said not to."

"So how are you so sure your target didn't see you?"

"Know what? That coffee smells good."

Emma came back with her own cup and sat on the couch.

"We used Harriet's da kine. The big headphones and that horn-looking thing you point in the direction you wanna listen. Works good, that thing."

"Is that legal?" I asked. "Never mind, she's a law professor. She would know. So what happened?"

"First, we hadda go into the cemetery right behind the rental unit to get a clear shot."

"So you and Harriet are standing in the cemetery, on a bright Sunday morning, wearing giant headphones and pointing the H.G. Wells ray gun at Ladd's house. Very low-key."

"You wanna hear about it or no?"

"Yes. Now I'm hungry though."

I opened the refrigerator and looked for the leftovers was sure I'd seen in there this morning.

"Hey, are you hungry?" I called from inside the fridge.

"Nah, I already ate your leftovers."

"Green candy corn it is." I poured some onto a paper towel and rejoined Emma in the living room.

"Anyway, we was taking turns, one of us with the headphones, the other one holding the umbrella. So when Harriet had the headphones on, she heard the front door opening and closing. So we decided to split up with me following him. I got in my car and caught up to him pretty quick cause he was walking."

"You followed a pedestrian in your car?"

"Yeah. I had to drive slow."

"He didn't notice a car driving next to him at three miles an hour?"

"Come on Molly, I know better than that. I drove behind him. An' the electric car's quiet. He didn't notice me. Anyway I followed him all the way down to Long's."

"Okay, and?"

"He bought some allergy medicine, a frozen burrito, and a bottle of Wild Turkey 101."

"Not exactly a smoking gun, Emma."

"Okay, get this. The cashier asked him for his birthday. So now I know his birthdate. It's cause of that law, yeah, they gotta card everyone who buys booze, even they're super old."

"Shoot, thanks for bursting my bubble. I always took it as a compliment when they carded me."

"Anyway Molly, I know what his birthday is now."

"Emma, I already know what his birthday is. It's on the rental application. Did he go anywhere else? Did he lead you to a body, or a cache of hidden murder weapons or something?"

"Honestly, I thought he was gonna. After he checked out, he took his paper bag an' walked all the way down to the hill to the ocean. He just stood there for a long time looking at the water."

"Oh. Then what happened?"

"After that he just walked back up the hill and went inside his house. So I came back here, and then you came in."

Pat came into the kitchen.

"Hey, ladies. Emma tell you about her gumshoe adventures?"

"Molly wasn't too impressed," Emma said.

"Hey, did you hear about my top-notch detecting?" I said. "Actually, our top-notch detecting. Emma was the one who told me about OutsourceMyHomework dot com. I think that's where some of my students have been buying their business plans."

"I don't know why you bother," Pat said. "Why do you care more about academic integrity than your administration does?"

"You cared about it when you were teaching here," I said.

"At first, maybe," he said. "But I caught on pretty fast. I just started giving everyone A's as long as they turned something in. It made life easier for everyone."

"You *what*?" Emma exclaimed.

Pat ambled to the refrigerator and opened it. "I wasn't getting paid nearly enough to deal with all that B.S. with the Student Retention Office. You want me to work miracles? You're gonna have to pay more than minimum wage. You ladies hungry?"

I stood up.

"I am. I can heat up a tray of chicken katsu and teriyaki beef if I know I'm not the only one eating. Shoot, now what?"

I went to answer the door. Howdy Howell stood in the doorway, looking glum. I invited him in.

Howell plumped down on one end the couch and stared at his knees.

"I can't believe it. Jandie's gone. She's really gone."

Pat joined him on the couch. Emma and I quietly sat down at the dining table to give Pat and Howdy some space.

"Why do you think it's Jandie?" Pat asked.

"Who else could it be?"

A hearty pounding on the door made Howdy jump.

"I'll get it." Pat made his way to the front door in two long strides. "Oh, hey, Harriet."

Harriet Holmes swept into the room.

"Flanagan, brilliant to see you up and about. I say Howell, you look absolutely shattered. Yoo hoo, Nakamura, Barda, no, don't get up." She plopped down on the couch where Pat had been sitting. "You've all seen the news, I expect."

Pat took his displacement in stride and sat in a nearby chair.

"I can't believe Jandie's gone," Howdy repeated.

"Buck up, the body's not been identified yet." Harriet said encouragingly.

Howdy wiped the corner of his eye with his wrist.

"I hope you're right, Professor Holmes. But it sure is a coincidence, isn't it?"

"It's a wonder the body turned up at all." Harriet said. "It's rough seas down there. If it weren't for a daring 'opihi-picker, they'd never have found her."

"'Opihi-pickers are hard core," Emma said. "We lose one or two of 'em a year, just on this island."

"Really?" I said. "That's surprising. They're pretty experienced with the ocean, aren't they?"

"Even so. They fall off cliffs, or get trapped in rough surf," Emma said. "Just going by the numbers, 'opihi kill more people than sharks do."

"All that for limpets? Hardly seems worth all the fuss," Harriet said, "Manky little buggers. Taste like fishy rubbers to me."

"She means erasers," Pat said to Howdy. "Probably."

"What do we think?" Harriet said. "Misadventure, or murder?"

"It could have been an accident," I said. "Isn't it possible Jandie, assuming it is Jandie, was trying to get a photo and got too close to the edge of the cliff?"

Emma snorted.

"What are you thinking, Professor Nakamura?" Howdy asked.

"I think the husband did it."

"Wow. I sure don't like to think Mr. Ladd could have done something like this," Howdy said.

"You gotta think about it, Howdy," Emma said. "Even if you don't wanna admit it's possible. Reporters are supposed to be objective."

"I know." Howell looked dejected. "It's really hard. When I was interviewing them, I got to know them both pretty well. Jandie was a great girl. Down to earth, kind."

"Yeah, and the husband?" Emma said. "Egotistical pompous *schmuck* who probably killed his wife."

Howie shook his head.

"I never had any trouble with him, Professor Nakamura. Mr. Ladd could be real charming when he wanted."

"Just out of curiosity, Howdy." I said, "why do you call the husband Mr. Ladd but the wife Jandie?"

"I was raised never to call older people by their first names, Professor Barda. It's disrespectful."

Emma elbowed me. "Glad you asked?"

CHAPTER 28

AND JUST LIKE THAT, it was Monday again. Spring break was supposed to have been a time to recharge, but now it was over, I felt more frazzled than ever.

Maybe walking to work would burn off some stress. I left my car in the garage and walked down Uakoko Street. It was a good decision, I thought. The storm had blown over, and the sky was shiny blue. I arrived at the old Territorial Inebriates' Asylum building (where the College of Commerce is now located) at seven-twenty and had the satisfaction of being the first member of my department to arrive.

Retrofitting the old Territorial Inebriates' Asylum had been no simple task. After several false starts, a black mold scare, and an excavator malfunction that somehow shut down the plumbing for several days, Konishi Construction had finally gotten the climate control working. The only problem now was that the air conditioning seemed to be permanently stuck in the open position. I stepped into my freezing office and opened the window a crack to let some warm air in. Wasteful, I know, but my only other option was to sit there getting blasted by frigid air until my sweat formed an ice shell over my entire body.

Still feeling in a sunny mood from my walk, I settled down to deal with my in-box. My cheeriness ebbed as I went through the messages, starting from the most recent: A past-deadline assignment from Intro to Business Management. Then a few more. The campus newsletter. An announcement for a destination conference associated with an academic society I'd never heard of. A letter from one of my students complaining how unfair it was that she had worked so hard to get her assignment in on time only to have me postpone the due date at the last minute.

I stared at the email, baffled. I'd been so consumed with the issues in my Business Planning class over the break, I hadn't given much thought to the intro class. But I was certain I hadn't changed any deadlines on them. I used to hate it when my professors would change the syllabus around on a whim, and I was careful never to do the same to my own students. What was going on?

I found the solution to the mystery in the very next email, in the form of a campuswide announcement from the Student Retention Office, sent late Sunday night. The Student Retention Office welcomed everyone back from spring break with the announcement that "teachers" (by which the Student Retention Office meant the faculty) would accept late work without penalty because of the storm. And in case the "teachers" were uncooperative, the SRO helpfully provided a hotline for students to call and report them.

My phone rang. Harriet had come in to work and was calling from her office across the landing. She told me she had just seen the announcement from the Student Retention Office. It was utter bollocks, she informed me, and she had no intention of accepting any late assignments. But that wasn't what she was calling about, and could I drop by as soon as I possibly could? I got up, crossed the landing, and knocked on Harriet's door frame.

"Ah, there you are. Brilliant." She stood up. "The SRO gets right on my wick. I've just changed my email settings. They're going straight into the spam folder from now on. Come along, we haven't much time. Nakamura's coming too."

"Coming where?"

"No time to waste, Barda. Off we go."

I locked up my office and followed Harriet down to the parking lot, where Emma was standing by her little electric car.

"Wanna drive, or walk up?" Emma asked us. "It's not that far."

"Not that far to where?" I asked.

"No time to walk." Harriet pulled open the passenger door and climbed into the back seat. I sat up front next to Emma. Emma drove uphill for two minutes and pulled into the parking lot of the Mahina Medical Center.

"There he is." Harriet pointed out Edward Ladd, who was walking into the side entrance. "Let's hang back a bit. We don't want to get too close."

"Why are we at the hospital?" I asked. No one answered me.

As soon as Ladd had gone inside, we got out of the car and went into the building through the same side entrance. Harriet pushed open an emergency exit door and led us down echo-y concrete fire escape stairs to the basement level. We emerged into a long, dimly-lit hallway, at the end of which was a grimy set of double doors. An ancient metal sign, black stamped lettering on pale yellow background, hung over the doors: MORGUE.

"Ladd's identifying his wife's body," Harriet whispered. She led us into a recessed doorway perpendicular to the morgue entrance and produced the listening gizmo from the folds of her field coat. "Can't be a fly on the wall, but this is the next best thing."

"Where were you hiding that?" I exclaimed. "And why am I here? I shouldn't be here. None of us should be he—"

"Shh!" Emma glared at me.

Harriet fiddled with some controls on the contraption and aimed it at the morgue doors. She produced a pair of headphones and set them on her head.

"Just the one pair, sorry," she said to us. "We can all listen after."

I could hear murmuring voices behind the doors, punctuated by the occasional scrape of metal. Judging by Harriet's shifting expressions, she was hearing a lot more than we were.

The doors swung open suddenly. The three of us backed up and ducked out of sight as Ladd walked out, with the much taller and wider Detective Medeiros right after him. We waited a few minutes to make sure the coast was clear, then retraced our steps back to the parking lot.

"Good to be back in the land of the living," Emma said when we stepped outside into the sunshine.

"I've never actually been down to the morgue," I said. "It is creepy. Even more than the College of Commerce building, and I'm pretty sure the College of Commerce building is actually haunted."

"Thought you'd like it," Harriet said.

We got back into Emma's car. Harriet took the front passenger seat this time, so I squeezed into the cramped back seat. As Emma started back down the road, Harriet took out her listening gizmo, twiddled some dials, flipped some switches, and plugged a cable into the dashboard of Emma's car.

"Showtime," Harriet said.

We heard a squeaking sound at first, like metal wheels. Then a quiet conversation. Men talking. At first it was hard to make out what they were saying. But I did recognize the voices of Edward Ladd and Detective Brian Medeiros.

Suddenly Ladd cried out. His voice was cut off, as if he'd clapped his hand over his mouth.

"Is this your wife?" Detective Medeiros asked gently.

"Yes, that's Jandie," Ladd said. "It's such a shame. She was so beautiful."

"Hard to look one's best in the circumstances," Harriet remarked.

"Weird," Emma said. "He doesn't sound too upset."

"Maybe it's closure," I said, "like it's better to know than to keep wondering what happened?"

"Ssh!" Emma waved her free hand at me.

"No water in the lungs," Medeiros was saying. "So she didn't drown. It's not official yet. Autopsy results haven't come in. But I thought you'd want to know."

"Oh dear," Harriet said cheerily. "She was found in the ocean, but she didn't drown. Murder with a body dump then."

CHAPTER 29

EMMA AND I WERE SITTING at the dining table having our morning coffee when we saw a police cruiser driving up the street.

We hopped up and ran through the kitchen, out to the lanai where we could get a good view of the rental unit. We watched two uniformed officers cross the lawn and approach the front door.

Ladd seemed to be expecting them. He followed the two officers right back out without any argument, carrying what looked like an overnight bag.

"Arrested, released, sees his dead wife at the morgue, arrested again," I said.

"Can they do that?" Emma asked. "Arrest him, let him go, arrest him again?"

"I guess they can," I said. "They just did."

Emma and I watched the police car make its way up the narrow street, do an 18-point turn at the dead end, and drive away.

"Wow, the guy can't catch a break," I said.

"He doesn't deserve a break, Molly."

"You're right, he doesn't. Come on, let's go back inside. I need another coffee. I bet you do, too."

"Eh Molly, you know what's weird?"

"He seemed completely unsurprised to be arrested again?"

"Exactly," Emma said. "I bet he doesn't mind getting arrested cause it's making him as famous as his wife."

When we got back inside, I headed to the kitchen to make coffee. Emma sat down at her laptop, which was already open on the dining table. She typed while I brewed.

"A-ha!" she cried.

"What is it?" I fixed up two coffees, brought them over, and sat in the chair next to her.

"Look at this," she turned the computer toward me. "Ladd's cartoon books are so old they're outta print. There's only secondhand copies available. Look what they're going for now."

"Wow, those are some premium prices. People are really paying that much? But Emma, these are all private sellers. Ladd doesn't get any of that money."

"It's not just the money, Molly. It's the fame. He killed her cause he wanted her fame for himself and now he's getting it."

"What, really? Okay, granted, he only cares about himself. Still, think about it. Would you kill your spouse to boost your used-book sales, if it meant there was a good chance you'd spend the rest of your life in prison? Come on, who would sign up for that deal?"

Emma snapped her laptop shut.

"Molly, you and me, we can't see into the soul of someone like that. Assuming he *has* a soul. Maybe it's worth it to him. You know what Pat always says, about pride and spite being the main things that motivate people?"

"That's such a bleak view of humanity. I would hate to think Pat's right about this."

"Yeah, that's your pride and spite talking. Eh, let's talk about this later. I gotta get to class."

That evening, Emma and I were having an early dinner and discussing the day's events when Howdy Howell stopped by.

"Say, Professor Barda," Howell said. "Is Mr. Flanagan here? We were supposed to meet up a little later, but I was in the neighborhood."

"He's taking a nap," I said. "Would you like to come in?"

"Eh Howdy," Emma called from the dining table, "we're having leftover green candy corn for dinner. Want some?"

"And wine," I said. "We were just talking about Edward Ladd getting arrested again. Did you know about it?"

Howdy hesitated, as if unsure how to answer.

"Come in, have a glass of wine," Emma said.

"Come on," I urged, "join us."

He hesitated and looked at his watch, and at me.

"Thanks, Professor Barda. I suppose I can throw a little fuel into the engine."

For appearance's sake I quickly assembled a plate of crackers and cheese and placed it in the center of the table. I got a glass and a small plate for Howdy.

"Oh, *now* you set out the good stuff," Emma said.

"Emma, if you wanted crackers and cheese, you could've said something. You can have whatever you want, you know that. So Howdy, how are you?"

Howdy paused and set down the cracker he was eating.

"I'm okay, Professor Barda. In fact, I'm better than okay. It looks like Jandie's finally going to get some justice."

"You wanted Ladd to get arrested?" Emma asked.

Howdy sighed.

"Not at first. It took me a while to come around to reality. But yeah, as disappointing as it is, you gotta face the truth. Kaycee thinks Ladd's guilty, too."

"Kaycee Kabua? Our landscaper?" I asked.

Howdy nodded.

"Sure, we're friends now. Good friends. Professor Barda, I can't thank you enough for introducing us—"

"You know what, you can just call me Molly," I said. "Only my students call me Professor Barda."

"Oh, I don't think so, Professor, thanks all the same. Pat told me I should call you Professor Barda and Professor Nakamura. Especially Professor Nakamura."

Emma narrowed her eyes. "*Especially* Professor Nakamura? How come?"

Howdy rubbed the back of his neck.

"Um, he just, I mean, he said it was what I should do."

"Pat gave you good advice, Howdy," I said. "It's always a good idea to use people's proper titles, but Emma's especially sensitive about being talked down to because of her h-e-i-g-h-t."

"You think I can't spell?" Emma pushed her chair back and stood up.

"What? Oh, shoot, sorry. I'm used to doing that around Francesca. Emma, I didn't—"

Emma made a rude hand gesture and stomped off toward the guest room.

"Pat!" she yelled. "What are you saying about me you bald-headed babooze?"

"I see what you mean," Howdy whispered to me. "She's kind of touchy, isn't she?"

"I heard that!" Emma bellowed from down the hallway. "I should come out there and knock that stupid straw hat right off your head."

"Emma, you're thinking of Mortimer Snerd," I called back.

"What?" Howdy said to me.

"What?" I said to Howdy. "I'm sorry, what were we talking about?"

Howdy brought a quaking glass up to his mouth, splashing wine all over his hand.

"I can't remember."

"Are you okay?"

"Yes ma'am, I mean, yes, Professor Barda. I'll just wait here for Mr. Flanagan. I expect his nap is pretty much over."

CHAPTER 30

THE NEXT DAY NEWS OF Edward Ladd's arrest was everywhere. Pat Flanagan and Howdy Howell had a double byline on the front page of the *County Courier*, but the story was big enough to go beyond Mahina. The Honolulu paper and the wire services had picked it up: Social media star missing, presumed dead. Husband arrested. Some of the longer stories would mention, a few paragraphs down, that Edward Ladd had at one time penned a popular cartoon under the pen name Tedd Ladd. But, the writer would add, Mr. Ladd had been out of the public eye for many years.

It was a struggle to keep class on track. My students already knew, of course, about my celebrity tenant. I was used to discouraging their efforts to pry.

"Jandie and her husband chose Mahina because we treat them like neighbors, not like novelties," I would explain. "Jandie already posts about where she goes on the island, what she buys, what she eats. We can always read her timeline if we want to know more about her. That should be enough to satisfy our curiosity. Otherwise, let's let them live their lives and be happy here."

But my usual deflections weren't enough to fend off the questions I was getting today. How did he kill her? (We don't know for a fact Jandie's husband killed her, I told them.) Were there any signs they weren't getting along? (Not that I saw, but I hardly ever saw them because I tried to mind my own business.) After my tenant was murdered, was I scared for myself? (No, I told my students. This was a lie.)

I came home that evening emotionally exhausted, to find a pile of what looked like bills and junk mail on the dining table. Emma must have brought the mail in.

I poured myself a glass of wine and sat down to deal with the mail. A happy surprise was a postcard from Donnie, which had been sent from the airport in Las Vegas the first day they landed. A not so happy surprise was a letter-sized lime-green flyer folded in thirds. The return address was the Uakoko Street Homeowner's Association. Underneath my name and address was stamped, Unauthorized Rental Violation: First Warning.

This I did not need. My homeowner's association was hassling me now, over my respectively murdered and incarcerated tenants? I hadn't even known it was against the rules to have renters. Who can remember all the different things you sign when you buy a house?

I started to unfold the paper and noticed there was no postage stamp. That meant it hadn't been properly mailed; someone had just stuck it in my mailbox. I had heard only the Post Office was allowed to stick things in people's mailboxes. Was that still true?

A quick online search confirmed my hunch. I may have committed an infraction against the Uakoko Street Homeowner's Association, but whoever stuck this piece of paper into my mailbox appeared to have violated Federal law.

Too bad I don't know any lawyers who would be interested in this, I thought. Then I realized I might know one after all.

Petty, I know. But in my defense, I'm not the one who started it.

I phoned Harriet Holmes. She picked up right away and urged me to come by in person. By the time I'd made the short walk up the street she was standing in her open doorway, waving me in. Even from the sidewalk, I could smell pipe smoke.

I followed Harriet inside. Because her hands were full (pipe in one hand, and a glass of what looked like whiskey in the other) I closed the front door behind us.

"Oh, ah, hello." Nigel, Harriet's husband, was ensconced in the telephone nook with a small laptop open in front of him. His bushy white eyebrows drew together, prominent on his purplish-red face.

"You remember my department head, darling," Harriet said. "Molly Barda."

"Molly. Quite." The eyebrows relaxed. He ran a hand through his already-tousled white hair. "Yes, of course. Delightful. Delightful."

The last time I'd seen Nigel Holmes, he had been wearing Jandie's flowered hapi coat and pink leggings. The occasion was obviously more memorable for me than it had been for him.

"This is the first time I've seen your place since you moved in," I said. "It looks nice."

But Nigel had already tuned me out. He was staring at his computer screen, typing away.

"Don't mind him, Barda, he's rushing to meet a deadline." Harriet led me over to a rather impressive bar, set her glass down, and with her pipe clenched in her teeth, poured me what looked like a double shot of excellent whiskey. It would have been rude to refuse, of course.

"Let's leave him to it," she said. "It's lovely out on the lanai right now. Don't worry about the mosquitos. We've got it screened in."

"He's working on his, uh, prison memoir?" I asked as I followed Harriet outside. We got seated at a stylish teakwood table with matching (and surprisingly uncomfortable) chairs. Harriet set the whiskey bottle on the table. Next to it she placed a small wooden stand that turned out to be a resting place for her pipe.

"Mm. The publisher's an absolute tyrant about deadlines from what Nige says. But he doesn't seem to mind. Keeps his mind engaged, he says."

The sun sinking behind the mountains rendered the vast cemetery two-dimensional in the shadowless twilight. I decided I preferred the view from my own backyard. If I didn't feel like staring at a graveyard every time I went outside, I could just tell Kaycee to let the foliage grow up a little higher. But Harriet's house was further up Uakoko Street and at a higher elevation than mine. There was only the low retaining wall separating the backyard from the graveyard below.

"Harriet, thank you for having me over on such short notice." I produced the plastic bag that held the green folded flyer. I'd already touched it, but I didn't want to contaminate it more than necessary. "This was left in my mailbox. It's not actual mail. It's a crime to tamper with the U.S. mail, isn't it?"

"Ah yes? May I?"

Harriet opened the bag and pulled out the paper.

"Oh, I was trying to avoid fingerprints—"

"This sort of paper doesn't hold fingerprints well," she unfolded the paper and smoothed it on the table. "And nobody's going to test for fingerprints in any event. It's a few hundred dollars' fine at most. No prison time, if that's what you're hoping for."

"Of course not." Prison for putting a flyer in someone's mailbox did sound a little excessive when she said it out loud.

"Ah yes, our ever-vigilant homeowner's association. Hmm, nuisance, vacate immediately, daily fine, oh, it's all here, isn't it? No, she can't do any of it."

Harriet folded the paper and handed it back to me.

"She?" I asked.

"Head of the homeowner's association. Asked me for legal argle-bargle she could use to sort out a resident who was running an illegal rental. Had no idea it was you she was after, Barda. Terribly sorry."

I gazed out at the dark cemetery and sighed.

"I did not realize renting was against the rules. I mean, I know we read through the CC&Rs when we bought the house, but I had about a thousand papers I had to sign and initial. I'm starting to wish we'd never build that rental in the first place. Harriet, what can I do?"

"Ignore it."

"Really? Sounds like kind of a daring legal strategy."

"Linda likes to make herself feel important," Harriet said, "but when it comes down to it, she can't do any real harm."

"Are you sure? Because...wait a minute. Did you say Linda? Likes to feel important? As in wielding what little actual authority she has in the most obstructive, bureaucratic, and misery-making way possible?"

Harriet took a deep pull on her pipe and blew a stream of smoke into the night air.

"Sounds like you know her."

"I think I may. Is her last name Wilson by any chance?"

"Indeed. Linda Wilson. Ah yes, of course. Recently retired from the Mahina State University Student Retention Office."

CHAPTER 31

HARRIET REFILLED MY glass up to the top. I did not object. Not only was the whiskey excellent, but the teak slats of Harriet's stylish outdoor chair were cutting into my backside. Harriet was wearing her heavy field coat. She probably had no idea how uncomfortable her furniture was.

But worse by far than my physical discomfort was the prospect of Linda Wilson, my nemesis from the Student Retention Office, in charge of my homeowners' association.

"Dangit. I had no idea she lived on my street, much less that she was the head of the homeowners' association. I even chipped in for her retirement gift. She's never going to stop persecuting me about this rental, is she?"

"I wouldn't worry. Know what I think? She's put out that she never was able to meet Jandie Brand. Feels snubbed. But she can't admit it to herself, so instead she bangs on about peace and quiet and the unique character of our beloved Uakoko Street. Once this murder business is over it won't be a problem."

"Why? What's to dissuade her from what is apparently her lifelong mission to make my life miserable? And now she's retired, she can spend all day harassing me, can't she?"

"Well, she's not exactly got the moral high ground here. She's renting to Nigel and me, after all."

"Linda Wilson is your landlady?"

Harriet nodded and released another plume of pipe smoke into the night air.

"Wow. A few weeks ago I didn't even know Linda Wilson even lived around here," I said. "I thought I'd never have to think about her again after she retired. Now I find out she's in charge of the whole place."

"She's harmless, really." Harriet set her pipe down and refilled our glasses with her excellent whiskey. "Now, I've got a question for you. Our missing girl, Jandie Brand. Always dressed to the nines, was my impression."

"Mine too. Whenever I saw her, she was always put together. Trendy clothes, fancy eyebrows, the whole thing. I think I remember her telling me designers sent her clothes and makeup for free. Hoping for the exposure. She never had to go clothes-shopping if she didn't want to."

"I thought as much. Barda, would it surprise you to learn that when she was found, she was dressed in drab and definitely unfashionable clothes? Like one would find at the Oxfam."

"The what? Oh, Oxfam. Second-hand clothes. Here it would be Goodwill or Salvation Army. Sorry, that's not really important. Yeah, it's not like Jandie to wear thrift store stuff, but if she wanted a disguise...wait a minute. Harriet, how do you know what Jandie was wearing when she died? We didn't see the body."

"Never mind about that. My point is, there's a theory the poor girl may not be Jandie Brand after all. If she isn't Jandie, two interesting questions arise. Who is she? And where is Jandie?"

"Well now, hang on. If I were Jandie, trying to escape from my abusive husband, I would do something out of character to throw him off."

"Fair point. Sad to think she went to all the effort for nothing. It's something to think on."

It had gotten completely dark while we were talking. The cemetery was now a sea of shadow, studded with moonlit gravestones. I took my leave and headed home. It was a good thing I had come on foot. Harriet was a generous hostess, and her whiskey was, as I may have already mentioned, excellent.

When I came back in, the house smelled comfortingly of pizza and coffee. Pat and Emma were at the dining table.

"Where've you been?" Emma demanded as I poured myself a glass of water and joined them. The Chang's Pizza Pagoda box lay open in the middle of the table, containing a few slices of veggie pizza. I told them about my conversation with Harriet.

"Linda Wilson lives right here on your street?" Emma exclaimed. "No way. And she's in charge of the homeowners' association?"

"I thought it was just bad luck we ran into her that one time," I said. "Nope. She was patrolling her territory."

"No way. Molly, you gotta move."

"Emma, I'm not going to let Linda Wilson chase Donnie and me out of our own home."

"How's Nigel's prison memoir going?" Pat asked.

"He was working on it when I went over there. According to Harriet, his publisher is keeping him to some strict deadlines."

"Maybe," Pat said.

"What do you mean maybe?" Emma reached for another slice of pizza.

"I don't know. Maybe Harriet is exaggerating to make Nigel's work seem more important and sought-after than it really is. This whole thing with Ladd got me thinking. People will pull some pretty outlandish stunts to promote their books. Remember when Emma started a riot at that speakers' event on campus?"

The accusation caught Emma mid-bite.

"Not," she protested through a mouthful of pizza.

"You kind of did, Emma," I said. "So Pat, you don't think Nigel Holmes' gritty tale of minimum-security prison is the blockbuster Harriet says it is?"

"Has she told you the dollar amount of the advance, or is it all just 'loads of dosh' or whatever?"

"It would be weird if she went around telling people the exact amount, Pat."

"He's been going over Ladd's manuscript, that's why," Emma said.

"Oh, brave man." I slid a slice of pizza onto my plate. Bamboo shoots and bean sprouts aren't my favorite pizza toppings, but I hadn't had anything solid for dinner. "I couldn't get past the first couple of pages. Are there any clues in it about Jandie's murder?"

"I thought you couldn't make money by writing a book about your crimes," Emma said.

"Son of Sam Laws," Pat added. "Although, those only say you can't profit from writing about the actual crime. And even with that narrow interpretation, they haven't always held up in court. That's not really relevant here anyway. There's practically nothing in there about Jandie. He says something once about how other guys are jealous of him cause his wife is young and hot."

"Here he is married to one of the biggest celebrities in the world," Emma said, "and somehow he thinks people would rather read about him."

"Do you think he was having an affair?" I asked.

"Only with himself, as far as I can tell," Pat said.

"Hey, that reminds me, Molly," Emma said. "Remember that Post-It you found in the house?"

"You know, I forgot about that." I pulled up the photo on my phone. "Here it is. It's hard to read the writing, and the picture quality's not great. Do you think it means anything? As far as this case?"

Emma leaned in to look.

"You shoulda focused better and held still. It's kinda blurry. I bet you moved, that's why."

"At least I remembered to take a picture of it. This looks like a number. Hornet? C-o-s-h. A cosh is something you hit someone with." I said.

"Yeah, that doesn't mean anything to me," Emma said.

We cleared off the pizza box and paper towels. Pat went to bed, Emma took her usual place on the couch, and I settled in to read Edward Ladd's manuscript on my computer. To the extent there was a plot, it was this: Edward Ladd was an "intimidatingly intelligent" and bookish child, who, we are told, bested bullies with his wit (although the specifics were absent). As a college student he chafed at "useless" breadth requirements and "stultifying" classes. He eventually dropped out of college, vowing never again to Let Schooling Interfere With his Education. Edward Ladd, in his telling, was the smartest guy in the room, the hero of every story.

"Find any clues yet?" Emma called over from the couch.

"Pat was right," I said. "No murder here. Unless you count him boring the reader to death. The only good thing about it is it's mercifully short. What are you doing?"

"Looking through Jandie's posts," Emma said.

"That sounds way more interesting. Find any clues? A sinister figure lurking in the background of one of her photos?"

"Nah. It's just her in different places around the island." Emma flipped through the posts. "There's a lot of cooking and recipes. Farmer's market. Hey, here she is at Donnie's Drive-Inn."

"I remember that. It was nice of Jandie to feature the Drive-Inn. Donnie told me we had a little bump in business after her posts."

"Here she is at the Bayfront. Hey, that's our canoe halau in the background. Ooh, sketchy boardwalk, must be Kuewa. She actually makes it look good in the picture though. Here's a plate with dragon fruit and a cut-open papaya. Jandie eating loco moco pizza rolls—"

"Chang's Pizza Pagoda?" I asked.

"Yup. Ooh, here's hot malasadas. Man, this is making me hungry."

I plunked down on the chair next to Emma's couch.

"I don't know why we're doing this," I said. "The police are on it. The mayor is even interested. What do we know that they don't?"

"We know Jandie personally, Molly."

"Did you ever actually meet her?"

"We can't just ignore her murder, pretend like nothing happened and everything's fine. Besides, the mayor doesn't care about Jandie. He just doesn't want any bad publicity getting out about Mahina."

"I guess so."

Emma sat up and gave me a friendly punch in the upper arm.

"That's the spirit, Molly!"

"Well, I've looked through Ladd's manuscript," I said, "and I haven't found anything resembling a clue."

"Yeah, I've gone through Jandie's timeline like ten times. Nothing out of place. She's posting like normal, then it just stops."

"So now what?" I asked.

We sat quietly for a moment. Emma brightened and shoved me excitedly.

"Molly! Call the number!"

"Great idea. What number would that be?" I rubbed my upper arm.

"The number on the Post-It we found. That you took a picture of."

I pulled my phone out and found the picture. I showed it to Emma.

"This one?"

"That picture's junk. I can't tell whether those are ones or sevens," Emma said.

"Me either. And that could be a 4 or a 9."

"We can read the rest, so that's three digits with two possibilities each," Emma said. "Two to the third is eight possibilities. So we only gotta try at most eight phone numbers."

"So on the seven-eighths chance it's not the right number, what do you say when someone picks up?"

"I get them to identify themselves then say sorry, wrong number."

"And on the one-eighth chance it's not a wrong number, you might be making contact with an actual murderer. Know what? If this were a movie, right now I'd be screaming 'just call the police, you ding-dongs' at the screen. So how about tomorrow I call Detective Medeiros and share your brilliant idea with him?"

CHAPTER 32

THE FIRST THING I DID the following morning was call the Mahina PD non-emergency line. Emma made us coffee while I spoke with Detective Medeiros.

To my surprise, Medeiros had actually followed up on the Post-It note I'd found.

"That phone number is Little Jack Horner's," Medeiros told me. "It's a bakery down in Kuewa."

"Oh yeah, I've heard of it. It's supposed to be good. That's why the note said *Horn*," I said.

"Yes. We already investigated the area. No sign of Jandie Brand."

"What about cosh? Why was that about?"

"Not sure."

I hung up. Emma was watching me.

"So?" She handed me a cup of coffee, already sweetened and doused with cream.

"The phone number is Little Jack Horner's," I said.

"Oh yeah, the café in Kuewa. Jandie did a photoshoot from there like a month ago."

"Makes sense. Darn it, what was I thinking, a murder clue on a sticky note would be right there in the house for me to find? And of course the police have already checked it out. It's their actual job."

"Let's go there anyway," Emma said.

"Why? Do you think there's something the police might have overlooked?"

Emma held up her phone, displaying a photo of a smiling Jandie Brand, sitting at an outdoor table, brandishing a pair of chopsticks at what looked like an entire cheesecake in front of her. The caption was stuffed with hashtags:

#lilikoi #pie #passionfruitpie #Hawaii #Hawaiilife #cakevspie #sweet #jungle #beautiful-hawaii #tropicaldreams #islandlife #Jandistas

"Jack Horner's got the famous lilikoi chiffon pie," Emma said. "I always wanted to try it. You no get class today, ah? We could go now."

"All the way down to Kuewa? It's a long way to drive for pie," I said. "But you're right, I'm not teaching today, and I don't have to be in until later. Are you sure?"

"I got a progress report due tomorrow and it's due noon East Coast time. Which means I really gotta submit it today. And I am teaching class this afternoon. But if we start now, we can get back in time."

I took our coffee cups to the sink.

"Just to be clear," I said, "we are not interfering in a police investigation. We're just going to Kuewa for pie."

"Oh yeah, hundred percent," Emma agreed.

Little Jack Horner's was about forty minutes out of Mahina. The narrow, intermittently-paved road was crowded on both sides by strawberry guava bushes and staghorn fern, and canopied with Albizia trees. Emma almost drove past the hand-painted sign marking the location of Little Jack Horner's. Tacked on to the main sign was a cardboard placard announcing "Fresh" Eggs Today!!

Emma slammed on the brakes, backed up, and steered into a gap in the foliage. I was thankful we hadn't taken my car. Having my 1959 Thunderbird scraped up by wayward strawberry guava branches would have broken my heart. At the end of a long gravel driveway was a dirt lot with around half a dozen parked cars. Two of them were late-model Mustang convertibles, obviously rentals. The bakery itself was a tin-roofed plantation-style house with a wrap-around lanai. A few patrons were eating and taking selfies at the outdoor tables.

Emma pulled over to the side of the gravel lot and parked. We stepped out into the hazy sunshine.

"I can smell the coffee from here," Emma said. "Man, I'm hungry."

"This place must be pretty good for people to come all the way out here on a weekday morning," I said. "Hey, thanks for driving."

"Yeah, good thing we didn't bring your car, Molly. I don't think it woulda fit up the driveway."

"I was thinking the same thing," I said.

Directly inside the bakery building was a counter where we were to place our orders. A woman in her forties seemed to be in charge. She was a certain Kuewa type: leathery tan, sun-bleached strawberry blond hair, wrist tattoo that had blurred over time. She wore a dark-green apron tied over a blue-and-green batik dress.

"You still get eggs for sale?" Emma asked when we had reached the front of the line.

"Sure do. How many dozen you want?"

"Just one dozen," Emma said.

"A dozen for me too," I added.

"Rainbow!" the woman barked. The woman called Rainbow appeared from somewhere in the back. She looked to be about the same age and general type as her boss, but the years had been harder on her. "Two dozen eggs for these ladies please."

"Two dozen eggs," Rainbow repeated to herself, and went back the way she'd come in.

"Do you have lilikoi pie?" I asked.

"Our lilikoi chiffon pie? Only one piece left."

Emma and I looked at each other.

"She can have it," we said at the same time.

"Eh, look at us," Emma said, "All like da kine, Solomon."

"We can split it," I said.

"She's paying," Emma added. "What? I drove."

"That's fair."

"We make our lilikoi chiffon pie fresh every day," the woman said. "You should check in next time you're in the neighborhood. Now, you can't make a breakfast out of half a piece of pie. How about our omelet aux fines herbes? It's our specialty. Eggs are from our own happy hens."

"I don't think I'm hungry enough for an omelet," I said. "Just pie and coffee for me, please."

"I like try one omelet," Emma said.

There were no other customers lined up behind us, so we got to chatting while our food was being prepared. Our chatelaine's name was Phoenix. This was not her birth name, obviously, and in fact she wasn't the first "Phoenix" I'd met here. Phoenix is a common name among people who have moved to the island to reinvent themselves. Sometimes after escaping a bad marriage or quitting a tedious job. Often after enrolling in witness protection.

"Were you here when Jandie Brand did her photoshoot?" Emma asked.

"Who?" Phoenix lifted the lone pie slice out of the display case.

"Little hapa girl, straight black hair, high voice?" Emma said. "She's a social media influencer."

"We get a few of those. They buy one or two things and take up a table for two hours while they take pictures of their food." Phoenix handed me a tray with two skinny slices of pie (she'd pre-split it for us) and two coffees. "Rainbow will bring out your omelet. Be patient. She's new."

"Oh. Is she from...next door?" Emma asked.

Phoenix turned to Emma.

"Be kind. That's all I'm gonna say. We can all use a little kindness."

Emma and I found a table out on the lanai. We were surrounded by jungle. It was warm but not too hot, and the coffee smelled delightful.

"What's 'next door'?" I asked as soon as we sat down.

"It's a rehab place for women. Not one of the fancy kind. More like a halfway house."

"How do you know so much about it?" I asked. "You've been here before?"

"Yeah. With the paddlers. We were checking out the sewage situation."

I paused mid-sip and slowly set my coffee cup down.

"No worries, Molly, their water supply's fine."

"Are you sure?"

"Yeah, it's just the wastewater. Their heart's in the right place, you know, trying to help these women out. But they get more people staying there than they're supposed to. So their cesspool's overloaded and the stuff leaks out and ends up in the ocean. All these rains we had haven't helped, you know. The paddlers were trying to raise money to help them close the cesspool and get a septic tank instead. Costs a lot more than you'd think, and there's the maintenance too."

"What's the difference between a cesspool and a septic tank?" I asked. "I thought they were the same thing."

"A septic tank is enclosed and has to be pumped out every so often," Emma said. "A cesspool is just a hole in the ground lined with rocks. Eventually the stuff leaks out. Yeah, you should wrinkle your nose Molly, it's gross."

"Just letting sewage ooze out into the groundwater? How is that allowed?"

"Lotta places down here in Kuewa are on cesspool. Somehow people trust it to act like some frickin' enchanted well that magically sanitizes everything. Newsflash, it doesn't work like that."

"Well. I just learned something. Now I'm going to try to stop thinking about cesspools and enjoy my tiny piece of pie. Mm, it is good. Emma, how many people do you think know there's a halfway house next door? If you hadn't said anything, I would never have suspected."

"They keep a low profile. No sign outside, and they let the trees grow up an' hide the building."

The woman called Rainbow brought out our eggs. She plunked the mismatched cartons on our table and left without saying a word. I opened the cartons to make sure the eggs weren't cracked. They were intact, and smaller than store-bought eggs and varied in color: white, brown, and blue-green. They also needed to be washed.

"Hey look," Emma showed me her phone. "Jack Horner's has vacation rentals."

I looked at the online listing.

"I bet they don't have a homeowner's association hassling *them*. Where do people stay though?"

"Probably over there." Emma pointed to a cluster of tiny houses on the far side of the property, just visible behind a screen of trees.

"Those look exactly like the emergency shelters from the last lava eruption," I said.

"Maybe they are," Emma said.

"I've always been curious about those little houses. What do you think they're like to stay in?"

"Why, you gonna set some up on your property? Like some kinda super slumlord?"

"No, I was thinking when Donnie comes back it might be fun to spend a night down here. Francesca would enjoy seeing the chickens too."

Emma and I stopped by the counter again on our way out to buy some creampuffs we'd seen in the display case.

As Emma started to back out of the parking spot, something occurred to me.

"Emma, that place next door. It's a women's shelter?"

"More like a halfway house, but yeah, pretty much."

"Is it possible Jandie's there? Hiding out from her husband? Maybe she planned her escape when she did the photoshoot."

"How do you explain the body they found then?" Emma countered. "Her husband said it was her."

"Maybe he's bluffing," I said. "Maybe he misidentified the body on purpose."

"What for?"

"So the police will stop looking for her and leave him free to track her down? I don't know."

"How's he gonna look for her if he's in jail? I know, Molly. It would be awesome if Jandie was still alive. But I don't think she is."

I couldn't argue with that. Emma guided her car back down the narrow driveway. The only sound was the scraping of branches against the car doors.

"You know the Cloudforest isn't far from here," I said. "Do you want to stop and say hi to Mercedes Yamashiro before we go back? I don't know, maybe we don't have time."

"I'm about to go on the highway. Right or left? Pick one. You gotta be more decisive, Molly."

"Right."

"I know I'm right."

"I mean turn right. I don't get down to the Cloudforest that often. Also, might as well check how things are going with our interns.

CHAPTER 33

I HAD STAYED AT THE Cloudforest Bed and Breakfast when I first arrived in Mahina. Mercedes Yamashiro, the proprietor, had taken me under her wing. She'd even tried to introduce me to Donnie.

I wasn't interested. At the time I was dating Stephen Park, the theater professor. Stephen had turned out to be faithless, self-absorbed, and a terrible human being all around. I should have listened to Mercedes and not dismissed Donnie the "plate lunch salesman" out of hand.

Emma drove hard over a pothole, which broke my chain of thought.

"So anyway," Emma was saying, "I told 'em, yeah, fine, it's supposably legal now, but it doesn't mean you can use my house as a...Molly, are you listening?"

"Of course. You're telling me a story about...your brother?"

Safe guess.

"Jonah can be such a pain in the *tochas*," Emma said. "How does a grown man end up being such a useless waste of carbon?"

"Didn't you try to fix me up with him?"

"I never," she said.

"You set up a meeting at Sprezzatura," I said. "You, me, and Jonah. At the fanciest restaurant in Mahina. And then you backed out at the last minute, hoping that with just your brother and me there, it would magically turn into a date."

"Yeah, so?" Emma demanded. "What's wrong with Jonah? I still think you two woulda made a good couple."

Emma's little brother Jonah is undeniably good-looking, but notoriously scatterbrained.

"Emma, *you're* the one who told me he's 'dumber than an empty box of stupid'."

"He is. And you're smart. So if you had kids, it'd balance out. Eh, you gotta admit, my brother's a better catch than Stephen Park. What a *putz* he was. Glad you dumped him."

"Can't disagree with you there."

"Shame, ah? Bad representation for Koreans."

"What are you talking about? Stephen wasn't Korean."

"Half Korean then."

"No. Emma, we talked about this. Park is a Scottish name. Stephen Park was zero percent Korean."

"But then how come—"

"Stephen let everyone think he was half-Korean because in his mind being hapa was cooler than being some plain old white guy whose wealthy parents subsidized his theater career with the profits from their Beverly Hills-Adjacent plastic surgery center."

"Oh wait," Emma said. "I think I remember something about that."

"Don't you remember how Stephen used to sneer at me for abandoning my literary education? How 'degrading' he thought it was for me to be working in the, gasp, horrors, *business school*? And here he was, a bigger phony than I could ever *dream* of being."

"Wow, Molly, sounds like you're still mad at him."

"What? Of course I'm not," I said. "That would be petty."

"You should be mad at him. Remember when he lost track of time and missed your birthday cause he was *schtupping* his theater student?"

"Oh, *that* part you remember. Hey, here we are. I didn't realize the Cloudforest was so close."

"Time flies when you're trashing your ex." Emma steered into a parking spot.

The young woman at the desk was one of the College of Commerce interns. I knew her from Intro to Business Management class the previous year, so we got to chatting about her internship. She told me she liked Mercedes and enjoyed most of the guests, and she was learning to deal with the occasional difficult customer. Mercedes wasn't there, so I left a message. Emma bought a jar of guava butter from the display behind the counter.

"Oh, tell Professor Harriet I hope her thumbs feel better soon," the young woman said as we turned to leave. I turned back.

"Professor Harriet Holmes?" I asked.

"Yeah, Professor Harriet is great. I'm taking her business law class this semester. I always heard b- law was boring but Professor Harriet makes it super interesting."

"I'm happy to hear it," I said.

"She get all these stories about high maka maka British guys she knows, like politicians and archbishops and stuff. Did you know what a 'rent boy' is?"

"What happened to Professor Harriett's thumbs?" I asked. "Why did you say you hope they feel better?"

"Oh our class did pretty bad on our last midterm. Someone asked her aren't you supposed to make sure we all pass? And she told us the grades would stand but she expected the Student Retention office would have her in thumbscrews for it."

"I think it was just a figure of speech," I said. "The Student Retention Office doesn't have actual thumbscrews."

"Really?" Relief washed over the young intern's face.

"It *is* the Student Retention Office though," Emma said. "You never really know what they're capable of."

CHAPTER 34

WE GOT BACK TO MY HOUSE around lunchtime and found Pat sitting at my dining table, working on his computer and drinking coffee. I set out the box of cream puffs and we sat down to catch him up.

"And look at these." I opened the carton of eggs to show him. "Authentically farm fresh, complete with dirt."

"So they don't need to go in the fridge," Emma said.

"Wait, really?" I said.

"Yeah, really. Don't look at me like that, Molly."

"Yeah, according to my mom they never refrigerated their eggs back in the old country," Pat said.

"Okay. I guess I won't put them in the fridge then. Pat, anything interesting happen while we were gone?"

"Someone named Kaycee called," Pat said. "Is she the one who does your yard?"

"There is a Kaycee who does our yard," I said. "Thanks, I'll call her back."

"She said don't call her. She wants you to call Howdy Howell."

"Why should we call Howdy?" Emma asked. "Isn't he your friend, Pat? You call him."

"No one asked *me* to call him." Pat went back to whatever he was doing on his computer.

"That doesn't sound right," I said.

"Here's Howdy's number if you want to call it." Pat held out a sticky note.

"Guess we're calling Howdy." Emma plucked the paper out of Pat's hand.

"Ow!" Pat shook his hand. "Paper cut!"

Emma dialed the number on her phone. I was happy to let her deal with it. I tidied up in the kitchen and tried to make as little noise as possible.

"Hey Howdy, it's Emma Nakamura. Kaycee called. Yeah. Uh huh. Eh, why don't you just come over here and help us figure out what's going on."

"What is going on?" I asked when Emma had disconnected the call.

"He didn't want to talk about it on the phone. Pat, do you know what's this about?"

Pat stopped typing and looked up from his computer. "No. I hope he's okay, though. I don't think he's ever done a real crime story before."

"What, you think it's gonna mess him up or something?" Emma asked.

Pat shrugged. "It can take a toll on you."

A few minutes later, Howdy Howell stood on my front porch, looking disoriented.

"I can't believe it." He wandered into my living room, looking around as if it were his first time there. "I just can't believe it."

"Come in," I said. "Sit down. We have coffee and cream puffs."

"Thanks so much, Professor Barda. Professor Nakamura."

Howdy sat at the dining table. Pat pushed the pink Jack Horner's pastry box over to him. Howdy flinched.

"Sorry, Mr. Flanagan," he said. "I can't think about eating right now."

"You gonna be okay?" Pat closed his computer and set it under his chair.

Howdy shook his head.

"I'm not worried about myself, Mr. Flanagan."

I set a fresh cup of coffee down in front of Howdy. He accepted it gratefully.

"What on earth is going on with Kaycee?" I took the last empty seat at the table. "Why did she tell us to call you?"

Howie sipped his coffee and set it down.

"Wow, thanks, Professor Barda. Kaycee's in jail."

"Kaycee?" I exclaimed.

"For what?" Emma asked.

"For murder," Howdy said.

"Nah, nah, nah. I can't believe Kaycee would murder someone," Emma said. "It's not like her at all. And believe me, I don't say that about all my students. Who did she murder, supposably?"

"Jandie Brand," Howdy said.

"Kaycee loved Jandie Brand," I said. "What possible reason would she have to hurt her?"

"Doesn't necessarily let her off the hook," Pat said. "Remember 'fan' is short for 'fanatic.'"

"So what's her bail?" Emma pulled out her phone, presumably to check her bank balance. "I can chip in. I know she won't skip town."

"They're holding her without bail," Howdy said. "Professor Barda, Kaycee said you could help because she works for you, and she was your student at Mahina State."

"She was Emma's student, not mine," I said. "But she does do yardwork for Donnie and me."

"She's hoping you can convince them she's not a flight risk," Howdy said.

"I mean I'll tell them she's a great landscaper and a reliable worker," I said. "I can't say I know her that well."

"I'll vouch for her," Emma said. "What is wrong with people?"

"What about Ladd?" Pat asked. "Is he off the hook?"

Howdy shook his head.

"I think the theory is they planned it together. Kayce Kabua and Edward Ladd. So they could be together, I guess."

"Wait," I said. "They think Kaycee was having an affair with *Ladd*? What on earth is her motivation?"

"Ladd's rich and famous," Pat said.

"He's not *that* famous," Emma said. "I mean, no one recognized him at Long's."

"And we ran their credit report before they moved in," I added. "They're comfortable, but I wouldn't call them rich. I mean, if they were rich, they'd be staying at one of the resorts, wouldn't they? Not renting a single-wall plantation house next to a cemetery in Mahina."

"People can surprise you," Pat said. "I mean, if I had a nickel for every time I've thought, ew, no way are *those* two having an affair, I'd have a disturbingly large amount of nickels."

"I really like Kaycee," Howdy said. "She's a great girl. And I came here because she asked me to ask you for help, and I said I would. But…I mean, I'm not an expert. Who am I to think I know better than a judge?"

"So you want us to try change the judge's mind or no?" Emma demanded.

Howdy shook his head. "I don't know, Professor Nakamura. Poor Kaycee. Maybe she's safer where she is? It's all so confusing."

"What evidence do they have against Kaycee?" I asked Howdy.

"I don't know, Professor Barda."

"Does she have a lawyer?" Emma asked. "Honey Akiona's the best, if you want my advice. Expensive, though."

"I don't have a lot of savings," Howdy said. "But I'll pitch in what I can."

"I wanna go talk to her," Emma said. "Molly, you come with me. Pat and Howdy, you go do your investigative reporting thing."

"But—" Pat started.

"What, you got something better to do?"

"Yeah, okay. Whadda you say, Howdy," Pat said. "Should we try to make ourselves useful?"

CHAPTER 35

IT WAS QUICKER TO GET a phone call with Kaycee at the Mahina police cellblock than to schedule an in-person visit, so Emma and I dialed in the next morning. Kaycee sounded surprisingly cheerful as she filled us in on her situation.

An anonymous tipster had directed police to Kaycee's carport, where they had retrieved a shovel with traces of blood on it.

Kaycee told us she had no idea who might have called in the tip, or how her shovel had gotten blood on it. She was always careful to clean up after a job, she said. She would never put away a bloody shovel with her other tools. When Emma told her about the theory that she'd been having an affair with Jandie's husband, Kaycee laughed out loud. Why would she want to get with some grumpy old fut like him? She liked Jandie Brand and would never want to harm her, who would be dumb enough to think she would? Kaycee told us jail wasn't so bad. One of the guards was a friend from high school. So were a couple of the inmates.

Kaycee didn't seem to grasp the fact she was in real trouble. She seemed to think it was all a big mistake that would get cleared up quickly.

"What do you think?" I asked Emma when we'd hung up. "Is Kaycee lying about not having an affair with Ladd and covering for him? He killed Jandie, and she's taking the blame?"

"Who was the snitch?" Emma asked. "That's what I'd like to know. Who called the police and told 'em about the shovel? Who would wanna pin this on her?"

"I don't know. Maybe she slighted someone and didn't realize it, and they're getting back at her?"

"That's a heck of a way to get back at someone," Emma said.

Pat came into the kitchen, rubbing his face, and set up a cup of coffee for himself.

"Morning, sleeping beauty," Emma called into the kitchen.

"Late night?" I asked.

"Yeah, but worth it." Pat brought his coffee out to the table and joined us.

"So we have a cause of death." Pat sipped his coffee. "For Jandie Brand."

"For the mystery corpse we *assume* is Jandie Brand," I said. "Although the only person casting doubt on her identity is Ladd, so it's probably her."

"Oh, I know," Emma said. "Beaten to death. With the bloody shovel they found in Kaycee's garage."

"Wrong," Pat said.

"Drowned?" I suggested. "Someone pushed over the cliff into the ocean?"

"Wrong again."

"I give up," I said.

"Not me," Emma said. "Wait. Okay, I give up too."

"Overdose," Pat said. "There are significant injuries, but they're postmortem."

"I would not have guessed an overdose," I said. "Is it wrong for me to be relieved to hear it? I mean, that she wasn't alive to suffer?"

"I kinda agree," Emma said.

"Did you get to talk to Kaycee yet?" Pat asked.

"We just finished," I said.

"Did Kaycee tell you why she had a bloody shovel in her garage?"

"She had no idea how it got there," Emma said.

"Carport, not garage," I said. "So someone could have planted a bloody shovel there. Or smeared blood on one she already owned. We were wondering who would've called in the tip."

"Ladd?" Emma suggested.

"But he's in jail too, isn't he?" I said. "Can you call in an anonymous tip from jail?"

"You can snitch in jail," Pat said. "It's kind of a tradition, in fact."

"Implicating Kaycee wouldn't clear Ladd anyway," I said. "It would just support the theory that the two of them were having an affair and conspired to get rid of his wife."

"Except Ladd could say Kaycee was obsessed with him and killed his wife so she could have him to herself and he's the real victim," Emma said.

I stood up and headed to the kitchen.

"Ugh. I need a drink, but it's only nine-thirty in the morning so that drink's going to have to be coffee. Also I'm hungry now, which is weird."

"Maybe someone really, really wanted Jandie dead," Pat was saying when I came back with my coffee and a plate of reheated wontons and chicken katsu. "Overdosed her, beat her with a shovel, then threw her into the ocean. Real belt-and-suspenders approach."

"How much of this is public?" I asked Pat.

"They're not releasing her cause of death," Pat said. "They want to keep the murderer in the dark. So don't you two say anything."

Howdy Howell stopped by the house later that afternoon. He thanked Emma and me for calling Kaycee and told us she really appreciated our reaching out to her. He and Pat went out to the lanai to talk privately. I didn't mean to eavesdrop, but the warm breeze carried the men's voices through the open window.

"Mr. Flanagan, I'm telling you this in strictest confidence," Howdy Howell said. I should have stopped listening then and there, but humans can't exactly seal off their ears, can they? "I liked the Ladds a lot, and I always thought Mr. Ladd was a decent man, but now...Kaycee is telling me the shovel they found isn't hers. She says someone planted it at her place. Does that make any sense to you, Mr. Flanagan?"

I glanced over at Emma. She was relaxing on the couch and reading one of her plant biology journals. Maybe she couldn't hear the conversation going on outside.

"So who are you thinking it was?" Pat asked.

"I hate to make an accusation," Howell said quietly. "He was always real decent to me."

"But?" Pat prompted him.

The wind must have changed direction. Either that, or Pat and Howdy started talking more quietly.

"Dang it." Emma sat up.

"Emma, were you eavesdropping?"

"Oh yeah, like you weren't." Emma came over and pulled a chair up next to my desk. "We gotta find out what Howdy told Pat. I bet he was talking about Ladd. How are we gonna get Pat to spill, that's the question."

"I wish I could stay and help," I said. "But I have a homeowners' association meeting in about an hour."

"Ugh, really? Since when is your stupid HOA more important than squeezing the truth out of Pat?"

"Since I learned our nemesis Linda Wilson was in charge of it," I said. "I need to be prepared for whatever knavery she's planning to inflict on me next."

"Yeah, okay. You get a pass."

"Want to come?" I asked Emma. "They're having it at Harriet and Nigel's place."

"No way. If I die without ever laying eyes on Linda Wilson again, I'll consider it a life well lived."

CHAPTER 36

THE FRONT DOOR OF THE new Holmes residence was ajar. I let myself in and placed the heated-up tinfoil tray of chicken katsu on their kitchen counter with the other potluck dishes. When Donnie had brought home the foil trays from the Drive-Inn and packed them into the freezer, I thought it was way too much food for the short time he'd be out of town. I was wrong. The frozen food stash was coming in handy.

I found the standing-room-only crowd out back, packed into the screened lanai overlooking the cemetery.

Presiding over the meeting was my erstwhile nemesis from the Student Retention Office, Linda Wilson. Even though it was a warm evening, Linda wore one of her signature long-sleeved muumuus. She passed out meeting agendas printed on lime-green paper. The meeting itself was routine—treasurer's report, modest increase in annual dues—until the last item.

Vacation rentals.

"We all moved here to Uakoko Street because it was such a *peaceful* neighborhood," Linda announced, making eye contact with me for the first time that evening. "Although I haven't been able to determine any specific rules or covenants which have been broken with regard to rentals..." (and how disappointing for *you*, I thought) "...I think recent events will serve as a warning to all of us to screen our tenants carefully. On that note, let us thank *my* tenants, Nigel and Harriet Holmes, for the use of their house this evening."

"Hullo," Harriet called from somewhere in the back.

"Delighted," her husband Nigel added.

When the meeting was over the crowd moved inside to enjoy the potluck offerings. Harriet came over and clapped her hand on my shoulder.

"I say Barda, things do seem a bit tense between you and old Linda."

"It's completely unfair," I said. "Harriet, you know me. I'm not brave enough to fight the Student Retention Office. I always cooperated with them. Emma was Linda's real nemesis. Linda's problem with me was just guilt by association." There was a little more to it than that, but Harriet didn't need to know everything.

"Our gentle little Emma Nakamura? Never. However did it all start?"

I glanced across the room. Linda was far enough away to be out of earshot. Still, to be safe, I motioned Harriet outside. We stood next to the retaining wall separating the Holmes's backyard from the cemetery below.

"It all began back when the Student Retention Office had a campaign to go after classes with high failure rates. BIO 101, Emma's class, popped up on their radar. Linda Wilson went after Emma, trying to arm-twist her into giving more generous grades. According to Linda, Emma was crushing the dreams of future doctors and nurses. When Emma wouldn't cave, Linda went straight to Emma's dean."

I looked around to make sure no one was eavesdropping. Most of the guests had gone inside, and a few lingered on the lanai, drinking and chatting.

"So now Emma's dean is all upset about getting in the crosshairs of the Student Retention Office. He goes to Emma and tells her she has to fix things with Linda, but of course without lowering standards in BIO 101. Now Emma was in an impossible position. So she wrote out the whole story and published it to the campuswide listserv. She wrapped up by saying she would quit before she took advice on teaching biology from someone who didn't know Gregor Mendel from Josef Mengele. I don't know whether Linda got the reference, but she knew she was being insulted. She retaliated by referring Emma to Faculty Development."

"Ah yes." Harriet lifted her whiskey glass. "The Student Retention Office struggle sessions."

"Emma calls it de-education camp, because you come out dumber than when you went in. Anyway, I'm sorry you've had to deal with that, Harriet. Not the friendliest welcome to Mahina State."

"De-education camp, that's brilliant. Actually, I don't mind it. Rather a jolly wheeze, if you must know. One spends the day in a palatial sort of conference room with working air con, loads of snacks, and shockingly decent coffee. And if we're lucky, we get a little speech from Victor Santiago from alumni and community whatsis."

"Yeah, Victor Santiago kind of scares me too. Have you noticed he never smiles?"

"Victor scares you? I think he's dead sexy. I mean to say, I'm a happily-married woman, but what's the word? *Caliente*."

"Okay. Listen, Harriet, it was really nice of you and Nigel to open up your house for this meeting. It made me feel a little less like I was entering enemy territory. Where is Nigel? I thought I heard him earlier."

"Back at his desk, I expect, working on his manuscript," Harriet said. "He's fallen a bit behind schedule, it seems."

I felt a cramp in the back of my leg and propped my foot up on the retaining wall. A stone dislodged and tumbled down to the cemetery below.

"Oh no, sorry about that." I took my foot back down. "Harriet, speaking of Linda, you might want to ask her to get this retaining wall looked at. I'm not a structural engineer or anything, but I don't think retaining walls are supposed to have pieces falling off them."

"I jolly well will ask her to fix it. I've become rather attached to this place and I'd rather it didn't slide into the graveyard. I say, speaking of Linda, I'd heard she was having it off with one of our lecturers, and you and Emma found them out. I'd assumed it was why she disliked you."

"Emma and I didn't set out to expose her," I said. "We had no idea. We were looking into something completely different. But once you start turning over rocks..."

"Ah yes. No telling what sort of slimy abominations will come wriggling out. Oh I say, Henriques, you're a quiet one. You gave me quite a start."

Mr. Henriques, my next-door neighbor, had materialized next to us. In the moonlight, his big round moon head looked more moon-like than ever. He reeked of sour booze.

"Good evening Professor Holmes. Professor Barda. How are you on this fine evening? Or *is* it a fine evening?" Mr. Henriques's voice cracked. "Poor Jandie. Poor, poor girl."

Out of one of the multitudinous pockets of her field coat, Harriet produced a crisply folded handkerchief and handed it to Mr. Henriques. He blew into it with a loud honk.

"He didn't deserve her," Henriques sniffled. "Shame we don't have the death penalty in Hawaii."

"You think the husband's guilty then," Harriet said.

"I'm not talking about the age difference." Henriques tucked Harriet's handkerchief into his back pocket. "Nothing wrong with a girl wanting to be with a mature man. When's the last time he brought her flowers, you think?"

"I expect you know the answer." Harriet seated herself on the crumbling retaining wall, dislodging another stone. Mr. Henriques and I sat on either side of her. The stone was cold and damp, but there was no other place to sit.

Henriques pulled out his phone and showed us one of Jandie's photo posts, from about a month earlier. It showed a pretty but inexpensive coffee-can flower arrangement of waxy red anthuriums, torch ginger, ferns, and ti leaf, the kind you might buy at the Farmers' Market for ten dollars.

"Nice composition," I said.

"I sent the flowers. Me." Henriques pocketed the phone. "Anonymously. I didn't want credit. I just wanted to make her happy. The husband, all he cares about is his aquarium. He deserves to get the needle, that's what I think."

Having made his point, Henriques stood and made his unsteady way inside, heading in the general direction of the potluck dishes.

"Well, that was unexpected," I said.

"Was it really?" Harriet countered.

"I guess not. He's always struck me as a little odd. Linda!"

Linda Wilson materialized in a cloud of gardenia perfume and stale cigarette smoke.

"Hello Harriet. Molly. How nice of you to show up to one of our little association gatherings. I hope you didn't find it too boring."

"Never boring, Wilson," Harriet said. "I say, where are little Whatsis and Thingummy?"

"Pele and Hiiaka get stressed around crowds," Linda said. "Bob's watching them at home."

"Is that what they're called?" Harriet exclaimed. "Wilson, you named your dogs after two revered Hawaiian goddesses? Careful, that's the sort of thing that'll get you packed off to sensitivity training."

"I love the potluck idea," I interrupted. "And I always enjoy seeing people's houses and getting decorating ideas. I'm really glad I came tonight."

"Well, I must see to the other guests." Harriet stood. "Snacks and bevvies inside, whenever you're ready."

I watched helplessly as Harriet disappeared into the house, leaving me alone with Linda Wilson.

"Such a shame about Jandie Brand," Linda said. "I hope this doesn't ruin the image of our neighborhood."

"It's terrible," I said. "Everything that's happened. Poor Jandie."

"Yes. We should all try to be careful about screening our renters. I know I am. Well, you're new at this. You'll learn, I hope."

"You're absolutely right, Linda. I am new at this." I tried to figure out what Linda's game was here. Linda would have jumped at the chance to have Jandie Brand as her own tenant. But now things had gone pear-shaped, as Harriet might say. I figured there were now two possibilities. Linda was either:

(a) gloating at my misfortune, cured of her celebrity fever, and relieved Jandie's murder hadn't happened on her watch, or

(b) gloating at my misfortune, and convinced things would have turned out differently if only *she* had been the one renting to Jandie Brand and Edward Ladd.

"How did you get Jandie interested in your place to begin with?" Linda asked.

Ah, so the answer was (b).

"I actually asked Kaycee to help us advertise the place, I said. "I'm not sure exactly which listing brought them in. She's good at social media. She uses it to publicize her landscaping business."

"But after they saw your house up close, they still agreed to rent it?"

"Yes, they did," I said. "It's brand-new, and we spent the money to make it nice. Oh, that reminds me, Linda, you might want to have someone come out and look at this retaining wall. It's a little...crumbly."

"You're always so full of interesting ideas, Molly," Linda said stiffly.

"I mean, I'm not a structural engineer or anything, I just...oh goodness, look at the time." I checked my wrist (a symbolic gesture, as I wasn't wearing a watch). "I have to get back home. Thank you so much for all your organizing and leadership, Linda. Okay, see you around."

I cut through the yard and speed walked straight home, without saying goodbye to Harriet or anyone else. Retired or not, I was still a little afraid of Linda Wilson from the Student Retention Office.

CHAPTER 37

I DON'T KNOW WHAT WOKE me up at two in the morning. Maybe it was the smoky smell. Or the glow outside my window, too early and too orange to be sunrise.

I grabbed my phone and ran out onto the lanai, around to the corner where I had a view of the rental house. Orange light flickered behind the pebbled glass jalousies. After what seemed like minutes of fumbling, I managed to dial 9-1-1.

While I was panic-shouting at the dispatcher I ran back through my bedroom and into the living room where Emma was sleeping. I shook her awake. We both went and pounded on the guest room door to wake Pat.

We had a fire extinguisher in the pantry. I finally found it on the floor, lying sideways behind a stack of toilet paper.

By the time the three of us got outside, the rental unit was engulfed in flames and the air smelled like a rained-on campfire. The little fire extinguisher wouldn't have helped, even if we could safely get close enough to use it. The blaze lit up the lawn and the cemetery. We could hear the sirens coming up the short drive from downtown.

The yellow fire truck pulled up and firefighters jumped out. I wanted to watch them but a tap on the shoulder distracted me. Detective Medeiros was standing behind me.

"Professor. You got a minute?"

I realized I was standing out on the street wearing nothing but my fleece bathrobe. The grass was wet and cold. I thought of squirmy creatures under my bare feet.

"Of course," I said. "Should we go inside?"

Medeiros shook his head.

"Your house might've been targeted as well. Safest not to go back in for now."

"Targeted?" I repeated. "Me?"

I'd like you to come down to the station to make a statement."

"Can I just grab some slippers from the front porch?" Medeiros glanced at my bare feet and nodded. I dashed up and grabbed a pair of Donnie's slippers, or flip-flops as they're called outside of Hawaii. They were ugly blue plastic and way too big for me. They made loud comical slapping noises when I walked. But at least I wasn't going to the police station in bare feet. My car was in the garage—also not safe, and possibly wired to blow up for all I knew—so I hopped into the back of Medeiros's big SUV for the short drive downtown.

"Where are Pat and Emma?" I asked.

"Who?"

"Pat Flanagan? Emma Nakamura?"

"Oh. Don't know," he said.

For a wonder, Medeiros didn't treat me like a suspect. Instead of the bare, uncomfortable interview room (which I was familiar with by now, unfortunately), he let me sit in a chair in his office like a regular visitor. Wearing a fuzzy bathrobe and my husband's giant slippers, but still.

"First thing, Professor, you got any idea who did this?"

"No. Believe me, this was a surprise. Although now I think of it, Linda Wilson, the head of my homeowners' association, had a grudge against me. I think *she* wanted the celebrity renters and resented our getting them first."

When I said it out loud, it sounded silly. Linda Wilson was spiteful and underhanded, but a literal arsonist? Well, maybe, but I couldn't prove it.

"You heard of Justice for Jandie?" Medeiros asked.

"No. You mean, justice for Jandie Brand?"

"Yeah. It's a trending hashtag. Might be her fans, might be someone who got a beef with the current prosecutor, might be people with too much time on their hands. Or could be something else. You never heard of it?"

"No. I try to avoid social media. For my own peace of mind." I pulled my robe tight around me. Why did they have to keep it so cold in the police station? "Why would these people burn our house down? What would it accomplish?"

"We think it may have to do with your tenant Edward Ladd."

"What about Kaycee Kabua? Has anyone targeted her? I heard a rumor about Kaycee and Tedd Ladd conspiring together. I hope she's not a target."

"I don't know, Professor. We're trying to gather up the facts."

"I sure wish I could be more helpful. Detective, I really appreciate your letting me know all this. My experience with Mahina PD...you guys haven't always been so forthcoming."

Medeiros picked up a pen and tapped it on the desk.

"I've found it's best to be open with people. You don't tell 'em stuff, they fill in the blanks themselves. So I'm gonna tell you something else now and I want you to tell me what you know about it."

"Okay."

"Ladd says his wife is still alive," Medeiros said.

"What? But he identified her in the morgue. He said it was Jandie. Remember? When he was talking about how it was a shame, she was so beautiful, which I thought was kind of creepy, honestly. Does he think unattractive people deserve to die?"

Medeiros lifted his eyebrows and leaned back in his chair.

"How do you know what Mr. Ladd said? I don't believe we released the transcript to the public."

Whoops.

"Mr. Ladd talked to me about it," I said, which was true.

"And at the time you discussed it with him, did he seem to believe the deceased woman was his wife?"

"I think so? It was an uncomfortable conversation. He and I are not particularly chummy."

Medeiros leaned forward and placed his elbows on his desk.

"Mr. Ladd is claiming he was mistaken. He says now the dead woman is not his wife. He says the whole thing was a publicity stunt that got out of hand."

"Can't you do DNA tests or something?"

"Sure. DNA can tell us a lot. But it's not like on TV, where you always get a clean sample and then the lab sends you results instantly. And even when you do have results, it's not always so clear what they're telling you."

A percussive noise behind me made me turn around. It was Emma, knocking on the door frame. She wore black leggings and a red Cornell sweatshirt. Like me, she was wearing what she'd been sleeping in. But her ensemble seemed more dignified than my fuzzy bathrobe and ill-fitting slippers.

"Thought I'd find you here," Emma said. "Eh, howzit Detective."

"Professor Nakamura." Medeiros pushed his chair back from his desk.

"You done with her?" Emma asked. "I'm gonna take her home now, if can."

Medeiros held up a finger and made a phone call. He listened and nodded.

"Yeah, they swept the house. It's okay to go back in. Please let me know if you see anything out of the ordinary."

I pulled my fuzzy robe tight around me and followed Emma out to the parking lot, keeping my eyes focused on her back. I tried to ignore the loud slapping sounds of my oversized slippers. I hoped none of the characters sitting around the Mahina police station at this hour were my current or former students.

"So?" Emma said as she drove me home.

"Have you ever heard of something called Justice for Jandie?" I asked.

"Oh yeah. It's a big movement online. They want whoever killed Jandie to face the consequences. I mean, I do too. Don't you?"

"Could wanting 'Justice for Jandie' be a motive for someone setting fire to the house? To get back at Jandie's husband? Some unhinged fan who took things a little too far?"

"Nah, no way they'd burn it down. Jandie lived there. That house would be a shrine to them."

"I guess that's reassuring. But also disturbing. A *shrine*?"

By the time we were back home the sun was coming up. I fell into bed and pulled the covers tight around me, feeling I had burned through every last drop of adrenaline my body could eke out.

CHAPTER 38

I WOKE UP WITH THE sun shining rudely into my eyes. I flung my arm over my face and groped at the night table with my free hand until I found my phone.

According to the clock on my lock screen, it was already Sunday afternoon.

I showered, got dressed, and did my makeup. It was something I could do to feel normal, even if I wasn't going to see anyone today. Except for Pat and Emma, who were pretty much members of my household by this point. Our insurance office wasn't going to be open until tomorrow. I'd call them and deal with the fire damage first thing tomorrow morning. What should I tell Donnie? I'd put off thinking about that until tomorrow too.

Pat and Emma were at the dining table. Pat was on his phone, and Emma was reading the *County Courier*.

"You okay Molly?" Emma set down her newspaper.

"I'm fine."

I fixed myself a cup of coffee and joined them at the dining table.

"You slept through Mass," Pat said. "For shame."

"Give her a break, Pat." Emma scowled at him. "Her new 'ohana just burned down, she had to spend half the night sitting in the police station in her bathrobe, and worst of all, she had to go to a homeowners' association meeting with Linda Wilson."

"Thank you, Emma. Oh, there's one bit of good news." I sipped my coffee. "I sent out a message to my class telling them certain assignments had been identified as having been purchased from OutsourceMyHomework.com, and academic dishonesty would result in a failing grade and expulsion from the school."

"Could someone really get expelled for plagiarizing?" Pat asked.

"Technically, yes," I said, "although in reality the Student Retention Office would never allow us to expel anyone. I just wanted to scare the students into doing the right thing. Give them a chance to turn back. So I told them if anyone wanted to change their business idea, they should delete their previous submission and they could submit a different idea for their next draft."

"What a softie," Emma groused. "You gave the cheaters a free do-over."

"What am I supposed to do, Emma? I can't prove anything."

"Did anyone remove their submissions?" Pat asked.

"Yes, they did," I said. "Specifically Urine Luck, Party Pooper, Toot Sweet, and yes, 'Wee the People.' They all got taken down."

"Someone actually turned in Wee the People?" Emma asked. "After they admitted online they bought the paper from OutsourceMyHomework? What a *dummkopf*. What was it, anyway?"

"It was a design for a unisex public bathroom," I said. "It's a shame. It was actually pretty well thought out. And there was one more plan I hadn't even gotten around to grading yet. It was called Bloody Marvelous."

"What kind of product was that?" Pat asked.

"You don't want to know. Well, all my class's best business ideas just disappeared, but at least I'm not going to have any plagiarized business plans in the Senior Showcase."

"That you know of," Emma said darkly.

"Molly," Pat said, "did you learn anything from Detective Medeiros yesterday? You were down there a long time."

"Oh, yeah. He told me Ladd is now claiming the dead woman isn't Jandie after all. That's a twist, huh?"

Emma snorted.

"Ladd's an idiot if he expects anyone to believe that. He's just saying it now cause he's in trouble."

"I dunno." Pat scratched his chin. "He might be telling the truth. Molly, your coffee smells good."

"Help yourself," I said, although Pat would have gone and made himself coffee regardless.

"What are you talking about, Pat, he might be telling the truth?" Emma demanded. "We heard him identify her in the morgue, you know."

"Yeah, it was really disturbing to listen in," I said. "You know what sticks with me? The squeaking metallic sound. I don't know whether it was wheels on a dissection table, or one of those long drawers, or what, but it's the soundtrack of my nightmares now."

"Let me show you something." Pat came back to the table and set down his fresh cup of coffee. He took out his phone, navigated to a popular bookstore website, and showed us the result.

"Is that the book Jandie's husband wrote?" Emma asked. "The one we saw?"

"Uh huh," Pat said. "His memoir. It's still on preorder, but based on the ranking, sales are gonna be through the roof as soon as it's released."

"That's a shame," Emma said. "Ugh, he really called it *Rhyme and Reason*?"

"And people are buying it anyway," Pat said. "There's something else. Jandie Brand's account. Even though there haven't been any new posts in a while, for obvious reasons, her followers have more than doubled since her disappearance."

"So people have morbid curiosity," Emma said. "What else is new?"

"That's exactly it," Pat said. "Scandal sells. If it bleeds, it leads. Is it so far-fetched for a publicity-minded couple to have planned something like this?"

"Jandie would never," Emma declared. "Besides, someone died for real. There's a dead woman in the morgue. *That's* not a stunt. So who is the dead woman, and where is Jandie, if she's not dead?"

"Yeah, I haven't figured that part out," Pat said. "What did you two find out at the egg farm place in Kuewa? What was it called, Peter Pumpkin Eater?"

"Little Jack Horner's," I said.

"Oh right," Pat said. "I think Peter Pumpkin Eater would've been better."

"Jandie was there," I said. "She took a picture of their lilikoi chiffon pie and everything."

"The woman who works there told us Jandie had come in a while ago but hadn't been there recently," Emma said.

"Has your friend Howdy Howell been looking into it?" I asked. "He's talked to Jandie and her husband more than any of us have. What does he think?"

"He's been busy trying to get Kaycee out of jail," Pat said. "He hasn't really been paying attention to much else."

"Are those two a thing now? Kaycee and Howdy?" Emma asked. Pat shrugged.

"Do you know who strikes me as someone the police might want to talk to?" I said. "Mr. Henriques from next door. He came up and talked to Harriet and me yesterday at the HOA meeting. He seems weirdly obsessed with Jandie."

"Just cause he can't read social cues doesn't make him a murderer," Pat said. "I think he's just lonely. I know how it can be."

"You are nothing like Mr. Henriques, Pat," I said. "Hey, here's a theory. Linda Wilson. She's obviously still jealous that Jandie rented from me and not from her. Maybe Linda killed my renter out of spite."

"Oh, and then she went and burned down your rental unit," Emma said. "Finish the job and get rid of any evidence. Makes sense to me."

"You two really don't like Linda, do you?" Pat said.

"It's not a matter of like or dislike," I said.

"We know what she's capable of," Emma added.

Pat sighed.

"Emma, she made you go to a half-day seminar. Let it go."

"Is anyone else hungry?" I asked. "I just realized I am."

"Little Jack Horner's is open Sundays," Pat said. "I didn't get to go with you last time."

CHAPTER 39

"PAT," EMMA ASKED, "YOU wanna drive all the way down to Kuewa for breakfast?"

"Emma, if you drive, I'll buy." I jumped up and took the coffee cups to the sink. "I feel like a big slug after sleeping in all morning. It'll be nice to get out of the house."

By the time we got down to Little Jack Horner's, the Sunday brunch crowd had already come and gone so we mostly had the place to ourselves. We chose a table on the shady side of the lanai. There was plenty of lilikoi chiffon pie this time, so we each got a full slice, and Emma ordered a whole frozen pie to take home.

Rainbow, the haggard dark-haired woman who had waited on us last time, remembered Emma and me. She gave us a shy hello when she brought out our pie and coffee. Pat introduced himself and began to chat easily with her. Pat claims he's an introvert, but after years of plying reluctant sources, he's learned how to get conversation flowing.

Rainbow told us she and the other waitstaff were residents of the facility next door. It was a second chance for women whose lives had gone off track, she said. They didn't allow any alcohol or drug use. Pain meds had to be over the counter only. Sometimes the women couldn't handle it and walked away. In fact, one of the other waitresses had stopped showing up to work. Fortunately, Rainbow and another girl could cover her shifts for now.

"Did Jandie Brand ever visit here?" Pat asked.

"Yeah, I heard about it. I don't really go on social media."

"I heard a rumor that Jandie's alive and well," Pat said. "Ow!"

Emma and I had both kicked him under the table.

"But they found her body," Rainbow said. "I read it in the paper."

"So many rumors get started when you have a high-profile case like this," Emma said. "I'm sure we all wish she was still alive."

Pat told Rainbow he was a reporter and gave her his card. She winked at him and tucked it into her apron pocket before going to attend to the other diners.

"Pat," I said when she'd gone, "Detective Medeiros trusted me! The theory that Jandie is still alive, that was confidential!"

"No it wasn't," Pat said. "Medeiros wouldn't have told you if he didn't want it broadcast all over Mahina."

"*I'm* not the one doing the broadcasting, *Pat.*"

"Nah, he's right," Emma said. "There's a reason Medeiros told you. I think he wants to give Ladd a false sense of security, so he slips up."

"Oh, so he only confided in me because I'm a reliable blabbermouth?" I objected.

"You say it like it's a bad thing," Emma said.

"I'm gonna stop in and drop off my card with the owner," Pat said as we were walking out. "What's her name again?"

"Phoenix," Emma and I said.

"Me and Molly are gonna be in the car," Emma told him. It was a good decision. We waited in air-conditioned comfort inside Emma's tiny electric vehicle while Pat took his time chatting up the proprietor.

"Hey, isn't the Cloudforest around here?" Pat asked as he climbed into the front seat. "Wanna stop by and say hi to Mercedes Yamashiro?"

"Last time we went she wasn't there," I said.

"Did you call first?" he asked.

"I was already driving," Emma said. "Molly sprung it on me at the last minute."

Pat dialed his phone and confirmed Mercedes was in.

"Yeah, tell her Molly, Emma, and Pat are coming by," he said. "Oh, do you have birria today? Right, yes, I know what it is. The goat stew. Yeah. Can I get a family size to go?"

Mercedes Yamashiro greeted us at the front desk of the Cloudforest Bed & Breakfast, and immediately shooed us into the dining room. As soon as we were seated, one of the interns (not the one I'd talked to during our earlier visit) brought out coffee, tea, and a tray of chocolate-dipped shortbread cookies.

After we'd settled in, Mercedes swept into the small dining room of the Cloudforest Bed and Breakfast. Her violet and yellow hibiscus muumuu set off the lavender streak in her bobbed hair. I have trouble remembering people at all if I haven't seen them for a few weeks, so I am always impressed by Mercedes' memory. She asked after Donnie and the baby and told me she hoped they were enjoying Vegas. She told Emma to bring her brother Jonah down to the Cloudforest for a visit while he was on island. She said to Pat, "I hear you have a special someone in Honolulu. Congratulations, Patrick."

"Pat?" I said. "The world's biggest misanthrope? You actually are seeing someone? You found someone you can stand?"

"Babooze, how come you never told us nothing!" Emma socked him.

Pat shrugged and rubbed his upper arm where Emma had punched him.

"Like I said. A gentleman doesn't kiss and tell."

"Molly," Mercedes asked, "what is happening with the poor girl that was renting out your `ohana? Such a shame, yeah?"

"You been keeping up with the Jandie Brand story?" Emma asked.

Mercedes tucked her hair behind her ear, revealing a dangling gold-and-lavender-jade earring.

"Well. I had never heard of her before, but after she moved to Mahina, I thought oh, good for her, you know? Shining a light on our little island. I became a fan. And then came this terrible news."

"Did you know she stopped at Little Jack Horner's a while ago?" Emma asked.

"I did," Mercedes said. "I was thinking of inviting her to visit the Cloudforest, but I decided against it. I'm sure she gets those kinds of requests from people all the time and I didn't want to be a bother."

"I think she would have liked the Cloudforest," I said.

"Mercedes," Pat asked, "what's your take on Little Jack Horner's? You must know them."

"Oh yes, of course I do. We all know each other down here. Phoenix Desertspring has turned out to be a real standup member of the community. Some of us had our doubts at first, but she's good for Kuewa."

"Phoenix Desertspring's not her real name, though," Emma said.

"Well it might not be the name she was born with," Mercedes said, "but it's the one she goes by now. So it's her real name as far as I'm concerned."

"She has some kind of arrangement with the halfway house next door," Pat said.

"I know what people are saying," Mercedes frowned at Pat. "But she's giving those ladies a second chance, maybe a third or fourth chance. As an employer, you're taking a risk. It's not realistic to expect people in that situation to get paid minimum wage."

"Wait a minute," I said, "Little Jack Horner's, arguably the trendiest and definitely one of the most expensive coffee shops on this side of the island, doesn't pay minimum wage?"

"Molly, those ladies get plenty problems. Who else is going to hire them? A lotta them lost their driver's license and if they work at Jack Horner's they can walk to their job next door. Anyway their expenses are subsidized with a county grant, so the residents don't have to pay much rent."

"They were supposed to install septic with all those people living there," Emma said. "All da kine goes straight into the ocean."

"Emma, I know the girls on your paddling crew are worried about the water quality. But the ocean is big, it can handle a little bit of kūkae. Where else are those poor women supposed to go? Oh Pat, I think your order's ready. I'm so glad you all stopped by."

When we got home, Emma put the lilikoi chiffon pie in the fridge, and Pat tucked his carton of goat stew into the back of the freezer. We were still full from our visit to Little Jack Horner's, plus the cookies and coffee we'd had at the Cloudforest Bed and Breakfast. It was too late for coffee and too early for wine. We sat down at the dining table anyway, out of habit.

"I like Mercedes," Pat said, "don't get me wrong. But business owners, they're a special kind of ruthless."

"Lotta my dad's friends are small-business tyrants," Emma said. "I think you can either go into business for yourself, or you can have empathy for other people, but both? No can."

"Hey, I think I want to go out and take a look at the rental unit," I said. "What's left of it. The insurance company is going to send someone by tomorrow and I feel like I should be prepared."

"Sure you want to do this?" Pat asked.

"Yeah, I'll be fine."

"We'll come with you," Emma said. She and Pat followed me outside. Even now, the campfire smell hung in the air.

"They taped off the front," Pat observed as we approached the burned-out front of the rental unit.

Mr. Henriques must have been watching for us. The moment we reached the front, he came trotting down to join us. He seemed more subdued than he had the previous evening, and his complexion was a little greenish. Which made his round head look more like a moon than ever.

"Howzit, Mr. Henriques," Emma said. "Eh, it's not as bad as I thought it was gonna be."

I had expected to find nothing but smoking rubble and was surprised to find the house mostly intact. The exterior was charred, and the front door was missing. Someone had stretched an "X" of yellow tape over the opening.

"How did this happen?" Mr. Henriques sounded indignant.

"That's what I'm hoping someone will figure out," I said. "Did you see anything, Mr. Henriques?"

"Are you going in to look at the damage?" he asked. "I'll come with you."

"I think the police tape over the door means we're not supposed to go inside," I said. "It's probably not—"

Before I could finish my sentence, Mr. Henriques ducked under the tape and was inside the house.

We found him in the dining area, staring into the fish tank that occupied the length of the kitchen counter. The fire hadn't reached this far inside. The aquarium was humming away happily. Colorful fish darted back and forth among the fronds of seaweed. Looking closer I could see tiny, pulsating jellyfish, as translucent as sandwich bags.

Emma peered into the tank.

"Looks pretty good, considering," she said.

"But it smells bad," I replied. The smoky stench was overwhelming. I wondered how long the smell would linger. Not forever, I hoped.

"Can I take them home?" Mr. Henriques was staring into the fish tank, his slender fingers pressed lightly against the glass.

"Those belong to Mr. Ladd," I said. "I can't just give his fish away."

"But won't the insurance cover them?" Mr. Henriques didn't take his eyes off the aquarium.

"Mr. Henriques," I said, "I appreciate your offer to help, but I am not going to commit insurance fraud. I will get in touch with Mr. Ladd and see what he wants to do—"

"That's not fair!" Henriques turned to me. "He said I could take care of them when he was gone. He gave me permission!"

"Edward Ladd? He called you from jail?" I asked.

"No. It was before all of this happened. He told me if he ever has to be away for any reason, I'd be the one he trusts to take care of his aquarium. I know how to manage an aquarium. I have one of my own, you know. Did you know, Jandie was going to post a picture of my aquarium. She was. She told me. Mr. Henriques, you should be proud, that's what she told me."

"You have a saltwater fish tank too?" Emma asked.

"You guys wanna come over and see it?" Mr. Henriques asked.

"Maybe later, Mr. Henriques.," Emma said. "But thanks, ah?"

"I have to take special care of the yellow tang," he said. "They're very sensitive to heat."

"Okay, look," I said. "Mr. Henriques, I'm going to talk to my insurance people tomorrow. Maybe they'll have some ideas about what to do with the fish. Who knows what they're going to say? But right now, let's get out of here before something caves in."

CHAPTER 40

AS SOON AS EMMA AND I got back to my house, I poured two glasses of wine, sat down at the dining table, and called Detective Medeiros. Emma sat across from me to listen in.

He picked up right away.

"Sorry to bother you on a Sunday, Detective," I said. "But you said to tell you if I saw or heard anything out of the ordinary."

"Sure. Shoot."

"I was just talking with our next-door neighbor, Mr. Henriques. He says Edward Ladd gave him permission to come in and take care of his fish."

"And then?"

"You said Ladd is now claiming his wife's disappearance was a stunt, and the body at the bottom of the cliffs wasn't really her. Well Mr. Henriques claims Mr. Ladd told him, Mr. Henriques, that he, Mr. Henriques, could take care of Ladd's fish in case Ladd has to be gone for any reason. So doesn't it sound like Mr. Ladd was planning for the possibility of going to jail?"

"I gotta be honest, Professor Barda, what you're telling me, it isn't exactly a smoking gun. Are you sure Henriques is telling you the truth? That's a nice aquarium, you know. Some real valuable aquatic life. Maybe Henriques is trying to get his hands on it."

"Yeah, I could see that."

Emma, who was listening to both sides of the conversation, shrugged. Then she got up to refill her glass.

"The thing about Jandie Brand being alive still, maybe it's true," Medeiros went on, "but if it is true, Mr. Ladd needs to tell me where his wife is. And convince me the dead woman isn't her. Eh, you're talking to your insurance tomorrow? About the fire?"

"Yes. Is there anything I should tell them?"

"Give them my contact info."

"Where's Pat?" I asked Emma when I'd hung up.

"He's in his room. I think he's taking a nap."

"We're calling it *his* room now? Well at least he's comfortable here."

An abrupt hammering on the door made us both jump.

Harriet Holmes stood on my front porch, bottle of excellent whiskey in hand.

"Our telly's out," she said. "Mind if I watch here?"

Harriet marched in without waiting for an invitation.

"Sure. Watch what?" I quietly closed the door behind her.

"Ladd's going to be on the evening news. Oh I say, Flanagan!"

Harriet's voice was so hearty, I could sense the walls vibrating. Pat stumbled into the living room, rubbing the sleep from his eyes.

"Ah, Flanagan. Always a pleasure. Ready to watch the Sunday evening news?"

Pat dropped his hand.

"The regular TV news? Why would we watch that?"

"Edward Ladd's gonna be on," Emma said.

"Apparently," I added.

"Really?" Pat was instantly alert.

"I was just talking to Detective Medeiros," I said. "I wonder why he didn't say anything about it."

"Detective Medeiros tells you what he wants you to know," Pat said. "Nothing more."

"So when's it supposed to start?" Emma asked.

"In about a minute," Harriet said. "I'll pour us drinks."

"What about Nigel?" I asked. "Did he want to join us?"

"He's working on his manuscript," she called from the kitchen above the rattle of glasses. "Been rather all he's thinking about lately. I say, Barda, you have any proper whiskey glasses?"

"I just have my Mahina stemware," I called back. "Recycled furikake glasses. I'll get some snacks. Pat or Emma, can you figure out how to get the TV working?"

"Do you not know how to turn on your own TV?" Pat asked.

"I used to, but it's been so long I don't remember now."

It took Pat and Emma a while to figure out how to tune in to the local news on our living room TV. Donnie and I hadn't watched regular television since Francesca was born. Our media consumption had been nothing but educational videos for the baby. These were regularly sent by my parents and generally geared towards children five to ten years older than Francesca. We had to watch them all from beginning to end, because my mother would call at random times (with my father hovering in the background) for a report on how Francesca liked the most recent one, what exactly she liked and didn't like about it, and what exactly she had learned.

Eventually, Pat and Emma got the regular TV working and found the right station.

Edward Ladd's interview was underway. We had missed the introduction. It looked like the interview was being filmed in a bland-looking office. But I recognized the setting as the library of our local jail. Ladd showed the wear and tear of his ordeal. The rims of his eyes were red, and he looked like he'd aged a few years.

"He's had a tough time," I said. "Look at him."

"He's just sorry he got caught," Emma retorted.

"Maybe not that sorry," Pat said. "Look at the stack of books next to his left elbow. Our right, his left."

We all leaned in to read the writing on the book spines.

"Rhyme and reason," Emma read. "Oh, his stupid book."

"There's a subtitle too," Harriet pointed out. "A semi-autobiographical meditation on rationality and art. Oh I say, there's a fellow with a lot of confidence."

"Is he seriously using his wife's murder to promote his book?" I said.

"It's a good job Nigel's not here to get any ideas," Harriet said.

The interviewer was a familiar-looking man wearing an aloha shirt. A local newscaster.

"So your theory is your wife is still alive," the man said, "and perhaps staying with friends. Do you have a particular group of people in mind, and if so, have you asked them about her whereabouts?"

"We haven't been on this island too long," Ladd said, "but in the time we have spent here, Mahina has welcomed us with a great deal of aloha."

"What about the fire at your house?" the man countered. "Would you consider that an expression of aloha? Most people wouldn't."

Ladd's expression glitched like a bad TV signal.

"Did you say fire?"

"He'd no idea." Harriet leaned forward, elbows braced on her knees. "Look at his expression. He's only now learnt of it."

"Last night there was a fire at the house you shared with your wife Jandie Brand," the newscaster said.

Ladd opened his mouth and closed it again. He'd clearly been knocked off balance by the news.

"I don't know anything about it," he said. "If the fire was deliberately set, it was the act of someone vicious and mean-spirited. Jandie would never want that. In fact, as I wrote in *Rhyme and Reason*, my semi-autobiographical—"

"Listen to him, taking every opportunity to go banging on about himself," Harriet exclaimed. "Right narcissist, he is."

"Exactly," Emma said.

Ladd set the book down and turned to look directly into camera.

"Jandie, if you're out there, please come home. Please. It's...it's time."

He appeared to blink away tears, shook his head as if he were embarrassed, and stood up. The camera followed him. It caught a few other people who didn't seem to have planned to be in the shot. A lighting guy, a sound guy, and a tall man with a shock of red hair.

"Isn't that Howdy Howell?" I asked.

"Yeah, it sure is," Pat said. "He did a good job, getting in there. I didn't even know this thing was happening tonight. I guess we'll see his byline again in tomorrow's *County Courier*."

The camera swiveled back to the anchor, who was arranging the pages of his script. He snapped to attention and improvised a wrap-up.

"Poor Howdy," Emma said.

"Poor Howdy?" Pat said. "He's getting a great scoop."

"Pat, his girlfriend's in jail," Emma said. "And those rumors about her and this guy? Ladd? if I was Howdy, I'd be sick to my stomach thinking about my girlfriend with that...soulless stick of beef jerky."

"Okay, but hear me out," Pat said. "Wouldn't a beef jerky stick *with* a soul be even worse?"

"Kaycee one hundred percent denies having any kind of affair with Ladd," I said.

"Where's the story coming from then?" Harriet asked.

"Someone in the DA's office had to figure out a motive for Kaycee Kabua killing a woman she barely knew," Pat said. "That's what they came up with."

"It was good enough to keep her in jail apparently," I said. "Boy. I'll feel better when I find out who set the fire."

"Or maybe you'll feel worse," Emma said. "Depending on what they find out. What if you're the target? Hey, what if Linda Wilson did it?"

"Linda Wilson is a bit cross with you," Harriet said.

"She's one to talk," I said. "Getting on my case for subletting and she's doing exactly the same thing. Anyway, Linda's been 'cross' with me ever since I came to Mahina State."

"It's a Student Retention Office thing," Emma said. "They all got a huge inferiority complex. You know how people are always talking about who's the smartest person in the room? Notice how they never ask, who's the dumbest person in the room? That's cause everyone knows it's always the person from the Student Retention Office."

"Do you ever think Linda felt you two were a little condescending to her?" Pat asked. "I mean, just a guess."

Pat's phone rang.

He got up quickly and left the room. When he returned, he said,

"Wrong number."

Harriet stayed for quite a while after the broadcast ended. The four of us spent a little more time speculating about Jandie Brand's disappearance. Then Harriet, Emma, and Pat moved on to dishing our colleagues and administrators. Mindful of the need to be a responsible department chair and role model, I didn't participate. It occurred to me that with Nigel preoccupied with his publishing deadlines, Harriet might be starved for grownup social interaction. As amusing as Harriet could be, I was technically her supervisor. I didn't feel like I could let my guard down around her, the way I could with Pat and Emma. Although I did enjoy sitting quietly and soaking up all the gossip.

When the whiskey bottle was empty, Harriet bid us good night and left.

As soon as she was out the door, Pat said,

"That was Rainbow who called me. From the bakery place in Kuewa."

"Little Jack Horner's," Emma said.

"Right. She called me about the interview."

"How come she called you?" Emma asked.

"I left my card."

"Not how come she called *you*, Pat," I said. "How come she _called_ you?"

"That's exactly what *I* said," Emma confirmed.

"She told me if Jandie is alive, she's not going to feel safe as long as 'that man' is running free."

"Interesting," I said. "Do you think Rainbow would've called you if she didn't think Jandie was still alive?"

"Yeah, what else does she know?" Emma said. "Did she say anything else?"

"Not really," Pat said. "She said she had to go, and she hung up."

"Maybe she's just trying to find an excuse to talk to Pat," Emma said. "I bet it gets lonely down there in Kuewa."

"Maybe she's afraid they'll just let Ladd go to avoid the bad publicity?" I said. "I mean, it wouldn't be the first time that happened around here."

"Oh yeah, I bet you're right, Molly," Emma said.

"Huh," Pat said. "Maybe I should look into this a little more."

"Be careful," I said.

"Why would I be careful?" Pat retorted. "You don't get good stories being careful."

CHAPTER 41

THE INSURANCE AGENT'S representative arrived promptly at 9 on Monday morning. I was waiting for him by the rental's burned-out front door. As he sauntered down the sloping lawn, clipboard in hand, I realized the round-faced young man looked familiar.

"Micah?" I exclaimed. It was nice to see a familiar face. I used to feel awkward running into my former students, but by now I was used to it. College of Commerce graduates (and dropouts) have popped up at my doctor's office, my credit union, and most of the places I shop. If you don't like the idea of your former students knowing your bank balance, your wine-buying habits, or your age, weight, and current prescriptions, all I can say is don't pursue a teaching career in Mahina.

Micah closed in quickly and gave me a big hug before I knew what was happening.

"Professor Molly, good to see you! Tough break, ah? No worries, we'll get everything straightened out for you."

"Well this is a surprise," I gasped as he released me. Micah always had a high level of energy and enthusiasm, and apparently upper-body strength to match. The local practice of greeting acquaintances with hugs instead of handshakes was something I was still trying to get used to. "You're with the insurance company? I thought you were working down at the Maritime Club."

"Yeah, I'm still there, nights an' weekends. It's good tips, an' nice people. But this has benefits, and I'm using my College of Commerce degree. You still teaching at the college?"

"They haven't fired me yet."

I had intended to be humorous, but Micah simply nodded and said,

"Lucky. Okay, let's see what we got here."

Instead of walking straight in through the front door opening, he went around the left side of the house, into the carport. I followed him up the steps to the side door. It was unlocked. Micah went ahead of me into the laundry room.

"How does it look?" I immediately realized what a dumb question it was. "I mean, you can't see any damage here. The smoky smell is everywhere though."

"I'm just here to do the preliminary. Depending on what I find, I might have to call in the arson people."

"I guess that makes sense," I said.

"Anyone been in here since the fire?" Micah poised his pen over his clipboard.

"Me," I said. "I know I shouldn't have come in, but I wanted to see for myself what kind of damage there was."

"Anything of value in here that you know of?"

"There's a saltwater aquarium," I said. "It didn't look like it was affected by the fire, but I don't really know. Does the aquarium count as valuable?"

"Oh yeah," Micah said. "Aquarium fish are big business. One of our commercial clients over on the west side, pet store owner, just got hit with a five thousand dollar fine for illegally collecting aquatic life. He thought we'd cover it as a business expense. I had to tell him his policy doesn't cover illegal acts. We do sell policies like that, you know. But the premiums are higher."

"Interesting," I said. "Should you be telling me this? About one of your clients?"

"We keep our client's details in strictest confidence," Micah said proudly. "You notice I never said the name, yeah?"

From what Micah had just told me, I could hop online and find the man's identity in five seconds. Which, I calculated, was about as long as it was going to take for the coconut wireless to be humming with the news of my own situation.

Micah and I emerged into the kitchen. I was glad to see it was tidy, with no dirty dishes or food sitting out. The aquarium was still bubbling away on the counter. Brightly-colored fish darted around the undulating green fronds. A few paces beyond the aquarium was the burned-out hole where the front door used to be. The yellow "X" of tape still held in place.

"I've never seen the tank from this side," I said. "I've only ever come in through the front door. I guess it's a creative way to separate the kitchen from the living and dining room, as long as you don't need the counter space."

"This is a nice one," Micah said. "It looks like the ones in those fancy kine Chinese restaurants in Honolulu." Micah walked around the counter to the dining room side and stopped short, his eyes fixed on the floor.

I came up behind him and saw what he was looking at: A man was sprawled face-down on the laminate floor. I recognized his palaka shirt and the combed-over black strands of hair clinging to his moon-like head.

Micah took a step back, right onto my foot, and nearly took us both down.

"Someone should check for a pulse," Micah said.

"Someone?"

We looked at each other.

I'm not particularly brave about this kind of thing, but I happened to know Micah was even worse in these kinds of situations than I was.

"Okay. I'll do it. Excuse me." I set down my bag on one of the barstools and took out my hand mirror. I knelt down next to Mr. Henriques. His face was turned away, toward the base of the counter. I placed the mirror in front of his mouth to see whether he'd fog it. My wrist touched the side of his face.

I dropped the mirror and scooted back, knocking Micah off-balance.

"Is he alive?" Micah asked as soon as we'd both righted ourselves.

"No. He didn't fog the mirror. And he's cold."

"How long has he been...da kine?"

"Well, he was here yesterday. Alive. He was here, and alive. We should leave. No, we should call for help. Then we should..."

I turned around to see Micah was already gone. I was alone with the late Mr. Henriques.

"Don't worry, Mr. Henriques." I could barely hear my own voice over the sound of the aquarium bubbling overhead. "I'm going to call Detective Medeiros. Whoever did this to you, they won't get away with it."

I dialed Medeiros's direct number and walked out the front of the house, ducking under the tape. I found Micah leaning against the side of my house, hands braced on his knees, still panting from his short sprint across the lawn.

"I'm calling the police right now," I said. "Micah. You look...why don't you come inside and sit down?"

Micah followed me into the living room and sank down onto the couch.

I left a message on Medeiros's voice mail, hung up, and called 9-1-1. I explained the situation to the dispatcher.

"Someone is on their way," she said. "Are you okay, ma'am?"

"Me? Okay? No, not really. I was just talking to a dead body inside my burned-out house."

"I see. And was the dead body talking back, ma'am?"

"No. It was just me talking. It was poor Mr. Henriques. He was my neighbor. He—"

"Ma'am, get yourself a glass of water and try to relax. Someone will be there very soon."

Micah and I were sitting side-by-side on the couch drinking from matching glasses of tap water when Pat came strolling in.

"Oh hey, Micah. You guys waiting for the insurance company people?"

"Howzit, Mr. Flanagan," Micah said weakly.

"Call me Pat."

"Micah *is* the insurance company people," I said. "You're a claims adjuster, right?"

"Administrative assistant to the claims adjuster."

"Isn't that great? Good for you, Micah. Anyway, Pat, come sit down."

"What?"

"Sit down," I insisted. "I need to tell you something."

Pat pulled over a chair and sat.

"Mr. Henriques is over there in the rental unit," I said. "I called the police and they're on their way."

"He won't leave? I can talk to him."

"No. No, Pat, he's dead. Mr. Henriques is dead."

"Does he have a pulse?" Pat asked.

"Does who have a pulse, the man who's dead?"

"I mean, did you check for a pulse? Maybe he's just unconscious."

"He didn't fog a mirror, Pat. He's cold."

"Oh. Man, that's terrible."

We sat uncomfortably for a few moments.

"Pat, you're fidgeting. Go ahead and get up. I just didn't want to throw the news at you out of the blue."

Pat sprang up and headed to the coffee machine.

"I wonder if it has something to do with Jandie Brand," he called from the kitchen.

"I heard she faked her death, you know," Micah said.

"Oh that's right," I said, "I forgot your cousin works at the police station. What have you heard?"

"The husband is saying it was a publicity stunt gone wrong. I don't know what she needed to do that for. She's already famous."

"I imagine he'd like some publicity for his book," I said.

"Jandie's husband wrote a book?" Micah's eyes widened. "Is it about Jandie?"

"No, it's about him. What was the title of it, Pat? *I Am Very Smart*, or something."

"*Rhyme and Reason*," Pat came back holding a coffee mug. "Sorry, did you guys want coffee?"

"No thank you," I said. "We were instructed to drink water. So that's what we're doing."

"So Micah, what do you think?" Pat eased back into the chair. "Do you think Ladd's telling the truth now?"

"I don't think so," Micah said. "Cause if Jandie's alive, how come no one's seen her? And if the dead girl isn't Jandie, how come there's no missing persons report matching the girl's description?"

"Good points," Pat said.

"There's something else too," Micah said. "I'm not supposed to say nothing about it, but the husband, yeah? He says there's a reporter who can back up his story. But the police went and talked to the guy—"

"A reporter?" Pat interrupted. "Is it Howdy Howell? Red-haired guy?"

Micah shrugged.

"I dunno the name."

"Sorry for interrupting," Pat said. "Go ahead, Micah."

Micah leaned forward, his elbows on his knees.

"Here's how come I'm not supposed to tell anyone. Cause the police went and talked to the reporter, and the reporter guy told 'em Ladd's lying, but he's not gonna say anything about it in public cause he's scared of Ladd."

Pat stood up.

"I should call Howdy."

"Don't tell him what I told you," Micah pleaded. "I wasn't supposed to say nothing."

"No, I know, Micah." Pat ambled into the kitchen for a second cup of coffee. "I'm just going to check in, see how he's doing."

CHAPTER 42

I HEARD A KNOCK AT my front door. When I opened it to invite Detective Medeiros in, I saw an ambulance pulling away slowly down the street. I was relieved Medeiros hadn't made us go look at the body.

"Just a few questions for you," Medeiros motioned us to sit back down, and I realized Pat and Micah were hovering behind me. "All of you, please. Okay."

He took a notebook and pencil out of the front pocket of his aloha shirt.

"We've confirmed that the deceased appears to be Reynolds Henriques, of 31 Uakoko St," Medeiros said.

"Reynolds?" I said. "Huh. I guess I never knew his first name."

"Did Mr. Henriques have any conflict with anyone you know of?" Medeiros asked.

"Molly thought he was a little creepy," Pat said.

"Pat! I never said that. Micah, it's not true, just so you know. I always tried to be nice to Mr. Henriques."

Pat shrugged. "I'm just saying. If he made that kind of impression on you, he might've rubbed someone else the wrong way too."

Medeiros wrote something in his tiny notebook and addressed the next question to me.

"Did you notice anything out of the ordinary, as far as Mr. Henriques's behavior, or the things he was talking about? Did he seem concerned for his own safety, or was there anyone he had a conflict with?"

"I spoke to him at our homeowners' association meeting," I said.

"When was this?" Medeiros asked.

"Friday," Pat said. "Remember, Molly? You and Emma were scheming about giving me the third degree about my conversation with Howdy, and then you remembered you had to go to your meeting."

I shot Pat the stinkiest stinkeye I could muster before answering Medeiros's question.

"It seems we have a fact-checker-in-residence," I said. "How fortunate. Yes, Pat is correct, it was Friday evening. I was talking with Harriet Holmes. Mr. Henriques joined our conversation and started going on about how it was too bad Ladd wasn't going to get the death penalty, how he wasn't good enough for Jandie, and so on. He had a crush on Jandie, from what I could see. He told me he sent her flowers."

"See?" Pat said. "Creepy."

"Hm." Medeiros wrote in his tiny notebook. "Anything else you can think of?"

I couldn't think of anything to add. We all sat quietly until Micah broke the silence.

"He was next to the aquarium," Micah said. "Maybe he was looking at it when he died. An' someone snuck in through the front door behind him."

"The aquarium!" I exclaimed. "Thank you, Micah. Remember, Pat? Mr. Henriques told us Ladd had told him to take care of the aquarium in his absence."

Medeiros set down the notebook.

"If Mr. Henriques was angry at Edward Ladd, why would he agree to take care of Mr. Ladd's aquarium?"

"Well he wasn't angry at the fish," I said. "I think he saw it as more of a privilege than a chore. But assuming Mr. Henriques is...was telling the truth, why did Ladd plan for someone to watch his fish in the first place?"

Medeiros wrote something in his notebook, tucked it back into his shirt pocket, and pulled out a folded piece of paper.

"Here, let me show you something." Medeiros unfolded the paper and handed it to me. It was a photocopy of the back of a postcard.

I'll be there tonight. Don't keep me waiting.

"This handwriting look familiar to anyone?" Medeiros asked.

We passed the paper around and examined it in turn, but none of us recognized the writing. The letters were printed, not cursive, and not particularly distinctive.

I went to my file cabinet and pulled out the rental contract. The only handwriting of Ladd's was his signature, which looked like a tangle of thread. I handed it to Medeiros so he could take a closer look.

"That's the only sample of his writing I have. Sorry."

"Don't you have an autographed book?" Pat said.

"Shoot, why didn't I think of that? I do. Good thinking, Pat."

I pulled the book down and opened the yellowed pages to the inscription on the front. I set the photocopied note next to it.

To Amelia, the inscription read. *Always Play it Safe.* Followed by "Tedd" Ladd's scribbly signature.

"He misspelled your name," Pat was peering over my shoulder. "Why is it so hard to write Amalia?"

"I was at the bookstore with a whole bunch of people waiting behind me in line. I didn't want to make a fuss."

"Why didn't you just tell him to write Molly?" Pat asked.

"Because people misspell Molly too. Doesn't matter. Do these two samples look like the same handwriting to anyone?"

"No," Pat said.

"Nuh-uh," Micah said.

"May I borrow this?" Medeiros asked.

"This book has sentimental value," I said. "And the pages have gotten kind of crumbly. If you don't mind, I'll take a picture of the inscription and email it to you."

Micah insisted on returning to work. He wouldn't hear of going home and resting. I was sure the insurance company would have given him the day off given the circumstances, but he seemed eager to get back (and, I assumed, tell everyone what he'd seen).

When Micah and Detective Medeiros had left, I stood up and stretched.

"So I'm already late to the Gen Ed committee meeting," I told Pat. "I need to get going. If you see Emma can you tell her what happened?"

Emma called me that afternoon when I was driving home.

"I'm coming over," she said. "You want me to bring a pizza?"

"If you want pizza. I do have food, though."

"Not in the mood for chicken katsu and chow mein again, no offense to Donnie's Drive-Inn. You like pepperoni and sausage?"

"Yes. Extra cheese too please if you don't mind."

CHAPTER 43

"WOW, POOR MR. HENRIQUES." Emma lifted a slice of pizza onto her plate. "So you think Ladd had him killed?"

"What's Ladd's motive?" Pat asked. "It'd be kinda stupid of him to arrange the hit for when he's in jail but get the guy killed right inside his own house where anyone could find it."

"Maybe he knows something about how Ladd killed Jandie," Emma said. "You know how nosy Mr. Henriques was. I bet he saw something he shouldn't have."

"That could've been one of us," I said. "We all went poking around in there. Harriet and Nigel too, come to think of it."

"Maybe it was one of Jandie's crazy fans," Pat said. "Could be they thought Henriques was Ladd. Although they don't look much alike."

"Pat," Emma said, "Jandie's husband is so nondescript, Molly didn't even recognize him even though he'd signed a book for her in person."

"It was twenty years ago," I said. "He still had some hair. But yeah, fair point."

"Now, let's talk about this call I got from our friend Rainbow," Pat said. "About how Jandie, if she were alive, wouldn't feel safe until Ladd was behind bars."

"Maybe Rainbow thinks Jandie's husband killed her, and she wants to make sure he's punished for it," Emma said. "It's a reasonable position to take."

"Except it's not a campaign," Pat said. "She only called me. I got ahold of Howdy and he said he hadn't heard from her."

"Well you went out of your way to go down to Kuewa and leave her your card," I said. "Did Howdy do that?"

"Do you remember the phone call?" Emma asked.

Pat leaned back, folded his arms, and closed his eyes.

"It was after Ladd came on the evening news," he said. "My phone rang. I left the room and answered it. It was Rainbow from Little Jack Horner's. I hope it's okay to call you, she said. You left me your card. Yeah, great to hear from you, I said. She sounded nervous and I wanted to make her feel comfortable. Then she said, I'm not saying Jandie's still alive or anything, but if she is, she's not gonna show her face until that man's behind bars for good."

Pat opened his eyes and helped himself to another slice of pizza.

"Call her back," Emma urged Pat.

"I don't know. I'm not sure I trust her story."

"Why not?" I asked.

"I'm not sure she's reliable. I mean, you know."

"Cause she's from the halfway house?" Emma said. "What, you think she's not trustworthy cause she made some bad decisions in life? It's only the right kind of people who have a monopoly on the truth? What kind of elitist are you anyway, Pat?"

Pat grumbled about Emma knowing how to push his buttons, but he pulled out his phone and dialed. He listened, introduced himself, and listened some more.

"We're at Molly's house," he said. "No, not her. The other one. The one who sent her water glass back because she thought it looked dirty. Yeah. Yeah, I know."

He looked at me.

"Molly, she wants to talk to you."

I took Pat's phone and put it to my ear.

"This is Molly," I said. "Look, sorry about the glass, I didn't realize it was part of the design—"

"You got a good internet connection where you are?" Rainbow asked.

"I think so."

"I'm gonna give you a link," she said. "You got something to write with?"

I frantically pantomimed writing. Pat handed me a pen and folded down the pizza box so I could write on it.

I was going to repeat the website address back to her to ensure I got it right, but she'd already hung up.

CHAPTER 44

THE NEXT MORNING, I made a personal trip to the Mahina police station to see Detective Medeiros. He was skeptical. At first, he didn't even want to watch the video I'd downloaded. But when I finished playing it for him, he demanded to see it again. He told me he'd handle it from there.

By that evening, Detective Medeiros had arranged a press conference. The local evening news was there, represented by a single cameraman. The print press was there as well, in the form of Pat Flanagan and Howdy Howell. The conference took place in the Mahina PD main meeting room. A few uniformed police officers hung out in the back, watching.

Detective Medeiros didn't want Emma and me in the room, but he couldn't stop us from lurking outside in the hallway. The wooden double doors had glass windows, crisscrossed with black wire in a diamond pattern. The wire may have reinforced the glass but didn't affect the visibility. The doors weren't soundproofed either, fortunately for us.

Medeiros loomed behind a tiny podium at the front of the room.

"I'm here tonight," he said, "to share with you a development in the disappearance of Jandie Brand, a new resident of our island. Ms. Brand went missing on March fifteenth. Tonight, we have new evidence that may shed light on the situation."

Pat and Howdy Howell stood side by side against the wall. Pat typed on his phone while Howdy scribbled in a steno pad.

Medeiros stepped away from the podium and a television monitor mounted on the wall behind him flickered to life.

The video showed a darkened bedroom, as cramped as a monk's cell. The image was tall and narrow, as if it were being filmed from inside a closet or through a partly-open door. Something that looked like a heap of blankets lay on the narrow bed. The camera zoomed in and out and focused near the top of the pile of blankets. The image snapped into focus, showing a tangle of dark hair protruding from the blankets.

We heard a hammering noise, and then a man's slurred voice.

"Jandie? Jandie, where's the light. Jandie. Talk to me."

Medeiros walked to the back of the room, toward us. He planted himself in front of the door, blocking our view. The pattern of his aloha shirt filled the window.

"Why doesn't he want us to see?" I whispered to Emma.

"Ssh, we can still hear," Emma said. "Besides, we already watched it."

"I know, but I want to see the reaction."

"Too good fer me?" the man on the video cried out. "Yrr too good fer me, 's that it?"

We heard a low-level commotion in the conference room. Voices murmuring, a chair scraping.

From memory, I knew the press conference attendees were now watching a man enter the darkened room, his back to the camera. The camera shook a little but kept its focus on him.

"Y' gonna say somethin' to me?" The man cried. "You gonna lie there an' ignore me?"

I hadn't recognized the voice right away the first time I'd seen the video. But now, hearing it a second time, it was unmistakable.

Inside the room, it grew quiet. I knew they were watching the man in the video raising something over his head, preparing to bring it down full force onto the bed.

"Still wish you were watching?" Emma whispered to me.

"No," I said.

"You shoulda gone with me," the man on the video cried. "You had your chance!"

The rest of the soundtrack was sickening thuds, slurred swearing, and panting as Howdy Howell brought down the shovel as hard as he could, over and over, until he was exhausted.

The video ended with Howell wiping the shovel on the bedspread and walking out of the shot.

Emma and I stepped aside as the doors swung open. We watched Howdy Howell being led out of the room in handcuffs by the uniformed police officers. Howdy was not taking advantage of his right to remain silent.

"Golly, I don't get it," Howdy was objecting. "You don't really think it was me doing those awful things, do you? Guys, this is an awful misunderstanding."

"Whoever was filming, how come they didn't they stop him?" Emma said.

"So there would be two murder victims instead of one?" I replied. "If I'd been the one hiding in the closet and filming, I'm not sure I would've been brave enough to jump out and intervene. Would you?"

"Yeah, I dunno."

We watched the cameraman and the other reporters follow Howdy Howell down the hallway. Finally Detective Medeiros came out. Instead of following the crowd, he came over to Emma and me.

"Professor Nakamura. Professor Barda. You did the right thing leaving the investigation to us."

It wasn't exactly the outpouring of gratitude I thought we deserved. I was the one who had given Medeiros the video, after all. But it was probably as much appreciation as I'd ever get from Mahina PD. At least when Detective *Brian* Medeiros told me to butt out, he was tactful about it.

"What about Mr. Henriques?" I asked Medeiros. "Did Howdy kill him too?"

"No," Medeiros said. "Mr. Henriques died of heart failure. We haven't said anything publicly because we haven't been able to find any surviving family members to notify. Would you happen to know his next of kin?"

Neither of us did.

CHAPTER 45

IT WAS A CLEAR, SUNNY morning. I was getting ready to walk up to my office when someone knocked on the front door. I peered through the peephole and yanked the door open.

Jandie Brand stood on my front porch. Her trademark baby face looked a little less chubby than I remembered, and her sparkling black eyes had hollows underneath them. Her skin was bare, and her hair was pulled back. She was still quite pretty, but not as dressed-up as I was used to seeing her.

"You're alive," I exclaimed observantly. "Come in. Let me call in to work. I'll tell them I'm working from home this morning. No, wait, let me call Emma first. Pat?"

"Yeah?" Pat called from the kitchen.

"Can you make an extra cup of coffee? Jandie Brand is here."

I heard a ceramic mug crash onto the tile floor.

"Sorry," Pat called out. "Be right there."

Pat brought out the coffee just as someone pounded on the door.

"That's probably Emma," I said. "I'll get it."

"What was so freakin' important that I had to come over here right now?" Emma stood defiant on my front porch, her tiny fists planted on her sturdy hips. "I gotta get this babooze to the airport."

Only then did I notice Emma's brother Jonah standing next to her.

"Hey," Jonah said to me.

"Jonah," I exclaimed. "Good to see you. Wow. You haven't changed. At all."

It was true. He even had on the same Mr. Zog's Sex Wax t-shirt I remembered him wearing into Sprezzatura.

"Postpone your flight," I said. "This is worth it. Come in."

"You're the one who was writing about my husband Eddie," Jandie was saying to Pat. She sipped her coffee. "Soon to be ex-husband, I'm happy to say. Oh, I'm gonna miss real Kona coffee."

Jandie was being polite about the coffee. She was drinking Mizuno Mart house brand, which was zero percent Kona coffee.

"Jandie," I said, "There's someone who wants to meet you."

Jandie turned around to face us. Emma opened her mouth as if to say something, and froze in place.

"This is Emma Nakamura and her brother Jonah," I said. "Emma and Jonah, Jandie Brand. Jandie, they're two of your biggest fans."

I had no idea whether Jonah had even heard of Jandie Brand, but I figured he'd go along with it.

"Hey," Jonah said to Jandie.

Emma remained as immobile as if I had just introduced her to Medusa.

Jandie jumped up and clasped Emma in a hug, which seemed to reanimate her. Jonah's hug was next, and it lasted longer.

"It's so great to meet you both," Jandie squealed. As Jandie, Jonah, and Emma took selfies together, I dragged over a chair from the living room so all five of us could all sit around the table.

"Jandie," I said, when the selfie session was done, "it's really good to see you. I'm thrilled you're alive. How are you alive? After...what we saw in the video?"

"I'll explain later," Emma whispered to her brother.

"That wasn't me on the bed. I was the one filming." Jandie held up her coffee as if to take another sip, and with the other hand held out her phone and snapped a picture of herself. "Hey, what do you think of my no-makeup look? I mean, I just escaped a deadly, life-threatening situation, I shouldn't seem too worried about filling in my eyebrows, right?"

"You look really good, Jandie," Emma said. "I like the natural aesthetic."

"Yeah," Jonah agreed.

"Oh Molly," Jandie said, "How did our house burn down?"

"I don't know," I said. "The insurance company is still investigating."

"Was it hashtag-Justice-for-Jandie?" she asked eagerly.

"The name did come up," I said.

"I bet it was Justice for Jandie. Cause they thought Eddie hurt me and they came back to punish him. Oh my fans are the best! Do you think they used those mazel tov cocktails?"

"Sure. It was probably Justice for Jandie." I didn't know, so I figured I may as well agree with her. Jandie clearly preferred that explanation and didn't seem bothered by the prospect of her adoring fans setting her house ablaze. "Do your fans know you're okay?"

"They will," she said. "But only after Howdy confesses. I'm not letting him off the hook."

"Good choice," I said. "What a horrible person he turned out to be. So Jandie, who was under the covers if it wasn't you? Was it a mannequin or something?"

"No. Where would I get a mannequin?"

"So the whole disappearing act," Emma interrupted. "Did you go along with it willingly? Or did someone make you do it?"

"It was my idea to begin with," Jandie said. "Do you know who Aimee Semple McPherson was?"

"Charismatic preacher from the 1920s," Pat said, "built the Angelus Temple in Los Angeles, founded the Foursquare Church."

"Talk about an *influencer*!" Jandie set her coffee cup down. "She had her own radio network, and millions of fans. One day, when she was at the peak of her fame, she went out swimming and didn't come back. It was a huge news story. Then one day she reappeared, and said she'd walked through the desert or something, and her shoes weren't even worn out. She made headlines all over the world. I thought, hey, I could learn something from her!"

"What could go wrong," I said.

"What *did* go wrong?" Pat asked.

"Howdy Howell, that's what. He got it into his head that the two of us were gonna run off together. As *if*."

"So where *were* you this whole time?" Emma asked. "Was it the halfway house next to Little Jack Horner's? You know we went down there a couple times. But only cause we thought you were in trouble."

"You were close," Jandie said. "I was staying in one of the tiny houses on the Little Jack Horner's property. Phoenix Desertspring set the whole thing up. At first, I didn't really trust her. She seemed like kind of a crackpot and I thought she was asking too many questions. But we were doing everything in cash, with no paper trail, so I guess she had to check us out and make sure we were gonna come through."

"Did you say *crackpot*?" I asked. "You were talking about Phoenix?"

"Yeah, I mean, what kind of person calls themselves Phoenix? Why would you name yourself after some boring city in Arizona?"

"You paid *cash*," Pat said. "Not 'cosh', cash."

"We found a note with Jack Horner's name and number and a word that looked like 'cosh'" I explained.

"Oh," Jandie said. "That was probably something Eddie wrote. His handwriting is terrible."

"Jandie," I said. "Who, or what, was Howdy Howell attacking in that video? What was under the blanket?"

"Can you believe Howdy?" Jandie said. "The Universe was really looking out for me that night. I think Nell saved my life."

"Who's Nell?" I asked.

"My friend," Jandie said. "She was the one under the blanket."

"You filmed someone beating your friend to death with a shovel?" Pat asked.

"No, of course not!" Jandie protested. "Nell was already dead. She was one of the rehab girls."

"From next door?" Emma asked.

"Yeah. Phoenix hires them to do cleaning and baking and stuff. It teaches them life skills. Nell and Rainbow brought my meals and did my housekeeping. I was stuck inside with my phone turned off. All I had was a phone to the front desk, but I couldn't call out or anything. I talked to Nell and Rainbow every day and we kind of became friends. Anyway, Nell. She'd been doing pretty good with her treatment, but one day, some of her old friends came to visit and they all snuck off and partied. Afterward she came over and said if she went back to the Center, they'd know she'd fallen off the wagon and they'd kick her out. So I told her she could sleep it off in my room. Anyway, she never woke up."

"I'm so sorry, Jandie," I said.

"I guess when you quit using, your tolerance goes down," she said. "You can't party like you used to."

"So your friend passed away in your room," Pat said. "What happened then?"

"I was about to call the front desk to ask Phoenix what I should do, and my room phone rang. It was Phoenix calling me! To tell me she saw Howdy on his way to my cabin. By that time he was being kind of a pest. I got the idea to leave Nell on the bed and cover her with a blanket. I thought Howdy was gonna come in and try to argue with me or something. I just wanted to scare him. I knew Nell wouldn't mind. She'd wanna help me out. I didn't expect Howdy to come in and...Ugh! That could've been me! Anyway after Howdy finished he started crying and ran away. I called Phoenix. She came right over. We wrapped Nell up and rolled her into the river. In a really respectful way, of course."

"Why didn't you call the police?" I asked.

Jandie looked at us blankly.

"I don't know. Phoenix said Nell would have wanted it that way. I'm sure she reported it to...whoever, I dunno. Rainbow didn't like it when she found out, but Phoenix is the boss. Actually, now that I think of it, Phoenix didn't want to tell anyone about the postcard either. Rainbow got it from the trash and snuck it to the police."

"What postcard?" Pat asked.

"It was from Howdy," Jandie said. "It said *I'll be there tonight. Don't keep me waiting.* It didn't get there till the day after anyway. Phoenix was real good at not telling anyone where I was, but I think she kinda got carried away with all the secrecy stuff."

"Phoenix is a financial partner with the rehab center next door," Pat said. "I'll bet that's why she didn't want to report the death right away. They get paid per client. The longer she can delay reporting Nell's death, the more money in their pockets."

"Well, thanks for everything," Jandie said. "Okay, I'm gonna get going before Mr. Henriques figures out I'm here."

"Jandie?" I said. "Mr. Henriques passed away."

"Oh no, that's so sad! Well, I guess he was pretty old. No offense. How did it happen?"

"They found him in your house," Pat said. "Under the fish tank."

Jandie's eyes grew wide.

"Oh, no. Did he die in the fire? Is Justice for Jandie gonna get in trouble?"

"No," I said. "No one was hurt in the fire, thank goodness. But before he passed away, Mr. Henriques said your husband asked him to watch the aquarium."

Jandie wrinkled her nose.

"I don't believe it. Eddie trusted *Mr. Henriques* with his precious fish?"

"He didn't trust you?" Pat asked.

"No! He was always telling me, don't stick your hands in there, don't touch the jellyfish, stay away from Mr. Grumpy's spines, blah blah blah."

"Mr. Grumpy's spines?" Pat said.

"Yeah, not like the spine in your back. He means like a stick that...sticks out of the fish. I call him Mr. Grumpy. He's kind of ugly, but also beautiful in his own way."

"You got a picture?" Emma asked.

Jandie scrolled through her phone and handed it to Emma.

"Here it is. Look at his expression, old Mr. Grumpy!"

Emma showed the photo around the table. A brown-and-white fish rested on the floor of the aquarium. The fish's body looked like a lump of mud. But the translucent white spines protruding from its back and fins were as delicate as lace.

"That's a stonefish," Jonah said. "They got 'em in Australia. If you step on one, it can kill you."

Jandie lit up.

"I've always wanted to go to Australia," she said.

"You surf?" Jonah asked.

Jandie dimpled at him.

"I'd love to learn."

"Should we tell someone?" I asked. "About the stonefish? Maybe Mr. Henriques reached into the tank and that's what caused his heart failure."

"He did have a habit of putting his hands where they didn't belong," Jandie said. "Anyway, I better get going. Thanks for an awesome adventure."

"Are you staying in Hawaii?" I asked Jandie.

"I don't know. I'll have to see what the future brings."

She cast a shy smile at Jonah.

"Jandie, one more thing," I said as she was hitching her purse onto her shoulder. "I used to be a big fan of your husband's, I mean soon to be ex-husband's cartoons. And then one day he just stopped drawing them and he never said why. Do you know what happened?"

"Oh, that one's easy," Jandie said with the casual air of someone tossing a lit match over her shoulder. "His wife, I mean the one before me? *She* drew the cartoons. *He* took the credit. When she got sick and died, no more cartoons. You won't find *that* in his stupid book."

CHAPTER 46

ONCE THEY HAD HOWDY Howell (not his real name, it turns out) in custody, Mahina PD quickly matched him to a man wanted in Michigan for the murder of his wife. Her body had been found in the woods, wrapped in a blanket. It was determined that she had died from blunt force trauma. As of this writing he is serving a 30-year sentence in his home state.

Edward Ladd moved out without saying goodbye. Driving home one day, I had to pull off to the side to let a moving truck make its way down Uakoko Street. I checked the burned-out rental unit when I got home and found it empty. No aquarium, no fake plywood bed, nothing. The rent was prepaid for a few more months, so there were no hard feelings on my part.

Phoenix Desertspring, proprietor of Little Jack Horner's and employer of first resort for the residents of the sober living facility next door, was called in to testify in front of the County Council. They concluded resident deaths and departures were not always reported promptly and the facility was exceeding its occupancy limits. No one could figure out what had happened to the money that was supposed to be used to convert the cesspool to septic. But people weren't exactly beating down the doors for the chance to manage a halfway house in Kuewa, and somebody had to do it. So it was soon back to business as usual for Phoenix Desertspring and her business partner, Mercedes Yamashiro, owner of the Cloudforest Bed and Breakfast.

Kaycee Kabua was none the worse for her stint in Mahina lockup. Jandie Brand, apparently feeling a little guilty that Kaycee had been dragged into her drama, gave Kaycee a free spot on her social media feed. Kaycee was a natural. She described how Howdy Howell had tried to frame her by planting the attempted-murder weapon in her carport. But Howdy's evil plan was doomed to failure, Kaycee explained, because she would never have a bloody shovel lying around. She always kept her tools clean, to prevent transmission of plant diseases such as Rapid ʻŌhiʻa Death. And that, she concluded, is why you can depend on K.C. Landscaping for your home and small business landscaping and maintenance needs.

Pat moved quickly to investigate Jandie's claim about the true authorship of Tedd Ladd's cartoons. The culmination of Pat's research was a feature in the *Weekly*. In Pat's telling, Edward Ladd was a self-promoting impostor who had taken credit for the work of his first wife and was now trying to revive his career on the coattails of his second. The story was picked up by other outlets and went nationwide just as Ladd's book was released. *Rhyme and Reason: A Semi-Autobiographical Meditation on Rationality and Art* garnered terrible reviews and was jeered into remainder bins all over the nation.

When a particularly scathing review of his book appeared in a major national newspaper, Ladd livestreamed a sweaty tirade (he had apparently spent the past few hours drinking) against book reviewers, ex-wives, and the female sex in general. He quickly gained a small but ardent online following of disaffected young misogynists who call themselves "Tedd's Ladds" and spend a lot of time agitating for the repeal of the 19th amendment. So Ladd managed to make his way back into the spotlight after all.

Jandie Brand continued to gain followers and fame, as well as a new fiancé. Emma is happy for her brother. She remains fond of her future sister-in-law, albeit increasingly unimpressed with her intellect.

"I love 'em both," Emma will confide, after a few glasses of wine. "But no way should those two be allowed to reproduce."

When Donnie and Francesca returned from their mainland trip, Donnie was surprised to see the rental unit under construction. I hadn't mentioned the fire to him. I'd wanted him to enjoy a worry-free trip with baby Francesca. So Donnie was a little unnerved when I told him everything that had happened in his absence. He blamed himself for leaving me alone in Mahina. I tried to assure him that none of it was his fault, and in fact it was a good thing baby Francesca was thousands of miles away when all of this unfolded.

One evening, when Donnie and I were relaxing at home (as much as one can relax with a toddler in the house), Micah from the insurance company called me. After weeks of investigating the origin of the fire, the investigators had secured video from a home surveillance camera across the street. It showed a prowler, lurking around the rental unit, peering in the windows, and smoking. Something alarmed the intruder, causing her to drop her lit cigarette by the front door and flee—almost tripping over the tangled leashes of her two little Yorkshire terriers.

Mrs. Aragaki, the owner of the surveillance system, had at first been reluctant to stir up trouble by coming forward with the evidence against Linda Wilson. But when she received a notice (printed on lime-green paper) ordering her to tear up her low-maintenance gravel yard and replace it with grass, Mrs. Aragaki decided it was time to strike a blow against tyranny.

The fire was deemed to be accidental, so no criminal charges would be pursued. Linda Wilson's insurance would simply have to reimburse my insurance. Since Linda had the same home insurance company Donnie and I did, the case would be wrapped up with minimum fuss.

I hung up and told Donnie what happened. He was playing peekaboo with Francesca.

"Don't ever start smoking, baby," Donnie said to Francesca. "Smoking is bad for you. Icky!"

"Smoking!" she exclaimed.

"I bet she's not even embarrassed about burning our house down." I picked up Francesca and held her to me. "No smoking, okay?" I murmured.

"Smoking!" she yelled, pushing back from my chest. "I smoking! I smoking!"

Donnie took the baby from me and handed me a brimming glass of wine.

"Molly, it's a good thing Linda's not embarrassed. We don't want her to be upset. No more feuds. Don't you think?"

"Yeah, you're right. Speaking of landlords. Now that the renovation's wrapping up we should think about finding renters again. I'm already getting inquiries from these morbid types who want to stay in a Death House. But I don't think those are the kinds of tenants we want."

"I found out Davison's having some relationship issues," Donnie said. "He talked to me about moving back to Mahina and renting the place from us. Francesca, go give mommy a big hug."

I sank down onto the couch, not believing what I was hearing. Francesca came toddling over and I absently snatched her into my arms. My awful stepson, living right next door? Having his sketchy friends over there partying noisily at all hours, letting his dogs tear up the lawn and poop everywhere, and no doubt conveniently forgetting to make his rent payments? I'd call Jandie and get the name of her divorce lawyer before I let that happen.

"Donnie, Davison cannot—"

"I told him no," Donnie said.

"You told him what? Donnie, you did? You told Davison no?"

The only thing Donnie and I had ever really fought about was his son Davison. And now Donnie was actually contemplating not giving Davison everything he wanted? This was a turning point.

"He's a grown man now, Molly. He and Tiffany have to be there for their son. I told Davison they need to work through whatever issues they're having. He can't keep running away from his problems, and I'm not always going to be there to bail him out. Do you think I was too harsh?"

"No! No, you're right, Donnie. Your advice sounds really sensible."

I felt a surge of affection and admiration for my wonderful husband. It had taken a few years, but he'd finally stood up to his spoiled son.

A pounding on my door interrupted us. Still holding Francesca, I ran to answer it.

Harriet and Nigel Holmes stood on the porch.

"Oh I say, Barda," Harriet exclaimed, "this is an uncharacteristically maternal look for you."

"Hullo, look at the little sprog." Nigel reached out and chucked Francesca under the chin.

"Spog!" Francesca announced. "I smoking!"

Donnie came up behind me.

"Harriet, Nigel. Would you like to come in? You have time for a glass of wine?"

"Why, Harriet," Nigel said, "Doesn't that sound absolutely—"

"Not now, pumpkin," Harriet interrupted. "Barda, there's something you need to see."

"Harriet darling, perhaps they're busy—"

"Nonsense. I think you need to see this."

CHAPTER 47

DONNIE, THE BABY, AND I followed Harriet and Nigel up the street to their house.

Or, to be precise, to where their house used to be.

"Well, Barda." Harriet sounded almost accusing. "Seems you were right all along."

"Me?" I stared at the sloping pile of rubble, dark and ominous in the twilight. "What do you mean? What happened to your house?"

"What house?" Donnie asked. "Where?"

"Dass not a house!" Francesca giggled. "Dass a rocks!"

"Rotten luck, what?" Nigel said.

"You were right about Linda Wilson, that self-important, bloviating cow," Harriet fumed. "She's a mean, cheeseparing skinflint who refuses to maintain her property to a decent standard and doesn't give a fig about people's houses sliding into graveyards when they least expect it."

"The retaining wall gave way?" I asked.

"Didn't even put up a fight. Just as you predicted, Barda."

"What did you predict, Molly?" Donnie asked.

"I'm not an expert or anything, Harriet. I was only asking about it because it looked a little unstable to me. I mean, rocks kept breaking loose and falling down into the cemetery."

"Are you saying there was a livable house here?" Donnie asked. "I'm sorry, I haven't spent a lot of time walking around the neighborhood."

"Until just a few minutes ago," Harriet said. "The only warning was a sort of vibrating sensation underfoot. Nigel and I got out just in time."

"Did you call Linda?" I asked.

"She's not picking up," Harriet said. "We went round to knock on her door and she's not answering that either."

"We've nowhere to go," Nigel added. "I suppose we're lucky to be alive."

Donnie and I looked at each other. He gave me a nod.

"Our rental unit's just been fixed up," I said. "They've repaired the fire damage. I mean, if you don't mind that Mr. Henriques...um..."

"Why don't you come spend the night?" Donnie interrupted.

"Ah, just like old times, eh darling?" Nigel said to Harriet.

"What?" Donnie said.

"Barda, you've got a vacancy then?" Harriet said to me. "This is opportune."

"A vacancy? Yes. Yes, I guess we do."

"Okay, great," Donnie said. "I'll go get my car. We can move a few of your things down before it starts raining again. Seems a lot has happened since I've been gone."

"I'll come with and fill you in." Harriet trotted downhill to join Donnie and Francesca. "Back in two shakes."

This was terrible luck for Harriet and Nigel, but all things considered, it was a stroke of good fortune for us. We weren't likely to get better tenants than Harriet and Nigel Holmes. They were eccentric, sure, and my being Harriet's department chair was a little awkward. But they weren't going to throw noisy parties or vandalize the property. And I knew I could count on them to pay the rent.

Linda Wilson wouldn't be happy about our poaching her tenants. Too bad. She didn't maintain her property. It was a wonder no one was hurt. Linda had no one to blame but herself. Not that it would make any difference to her. She would still think of some way to blame me.

Nigel was already poking through the remnants of the collapsed house.

I went over to join him and examined the rubble to see what I could safely salvage.

"Here, let me help," I said. "I don't know what's important, but—"

"No, no, please," he insisted. "We're already causing you enough trouble."

"No trouble at all." I saw the corner of a check stub poking out of the rubble and tugged it free. "We keep new toothbrushes and spare sweats just for guests. Tomorrow's a school day, and..."

Something on the check stub caught my attention.

"OMH dot com?" I read. "Why does that sound..."

I looked up to meet Nigel's gaze. Nigel's complexion normally tended toward the florid, but in the sodium light he looked practically purple. And despite the cool evening, he was sweating.

"Silly for us to be poking about in the dark like this," he stammered. "Not sure what I was thinking, really. We might as well head over to yours, take care of this tomorrow when it's daylight."

"Nigel," I said. "OMH dot com? Is this *OutsourceMyHomework dot com*? What is this?"

Nigel gulped.

"You mustn't tell Harriet," he pleaded.

"*You* wrote those business plans for my students. It was you, wasn't it?"

"Well, I..."

"Party Pooper?" I demanded. "Toot Sweet? *Urine Luck*?"

"Yes, that was rather good, if I do say so—"

"You taught at Balliol College! And here you are enabling academic dishonesty! What were you thinking?"

"You don't understand, Molly." Nigel looked down at the rubble beneath his feet. "Harriet thinks I've found a publisher for my memoir."

"There are other ways to make money besides writing for an essay mill," I said. "Legal, non-scummy ways."

"It's not to do with money," Nigel said quietly. "We've got loads. It's just that Harriet is so proud of me. She'd be crushed to know the truth."

I saw the headlights of Donnie's car coming up the street.

"I won't tell Harriet," I said. "Okay? But Nigel, you have to promise me two things. First, if you're going to be renting our place, no more of this essay mill business. I'm legally liable for any criminal acts you commit on my property and the last thing I need is to get caught up in something like this. Tell Harriet you've already gotten the full amount of your advance and have that be the end of it. Don't worry about royalties. Most books don't earn out anyway."

"Fair enough." Nigel dabbed his eye with the back of his wrist. "What's the second thing?"

CHAPTER 48

THE SENIOR SHOWCASE, the end-of-the year event where Mahina State's Friends in the Business Community came to admire our best student work, was as scandal-free as I (and Victor Santiago) could have hoped. The business plans on display were an uninspired assortment of sports bars, party planners, and online clothing stores. The miscreants who had purchased their assignments from OutsourceMyHomework were not represented at the Senior Showcase. I had already assigned them failing grades for the course and reported them to the Office of Student Conduct. There they suffered severe consequences for their intellectual larceny, if by "severe" you mean "gently guided into an independent-studies program and allowed to complete their degrees by sleight of paperwork."

Despite my class's unremarkable showing, Victor Santiago, Vice-President for Student Outreach and Community Relations, was in a cheerful mood. The reason? He had just received news of an anonymous and shockingly generous donation to the university. During the closing remarks of the Senior Showcase, Santiago called me up to stand next to him as he made the announcement.

Please accept this gift to the Mahina State University College of Commerce, given in appreciation for the Department of Management and its department head, Dr. Molly Barda. Her tireless devotion to academic integrity has inspired this donation. In short, she's bloody marvelous.

As I watched Victor Santiago read those words, I thought I saw him smile.

DEATH AT THE EFFIGY

DEATH AT THE EFFIGY

PAT FLANAGAN TOOK out his notebook and wrote:

Opening night at the Effigy. Exposed ducting, flat black paint, blacklight. Underneath he added, *DJ looks like Marilyn Monroe in mourning.*

Trusty was supposed to be taking pictures but (unsurprisingly) hadn't shown up yet. Betty Benitez, Trusty's girlfriend, hoisted herself onto the barstool next to Pat and signaled to the bartender.

"You're looking extra yuppie tonight," Pat shouted into her ear. "You're probably the only one in here with a day job."

She glanced down at her broad-shouldered taupe pant suit and leaned over to yell, "Working late. These guys can't get it through their shiny bald heads it's 1984, not 1954. You can't have official company functions at the strip club. You can't show topless training videos to the interns. You can't bring in birthday cakes shaped like...I mean you can, if you don't care about getting sued."

The bartender returned with two highball glasses filled with pale golden liquid on ice.

"Perfect timing." Betty clicked her glass against Pat's. "Congratulations on your first real reporting assignment."

Upon graduating from San Diego State with his engineering degree, Pat had interviewed at one of the local tech companies. He hadn't gotten the job, but he had hit it off with Betty Benitez from the legal department. Through Betty's connections, Pat had landed a position at *Voltaire's Quill*, a free weekly chronicling San Diego nightlife and culture.

Pat took a sip and raised his eyebrows. "Not bad. What is it?"

"Cinzano Bianco," Betty replied. "Speaking of idiot men, where's—oh hiya Babe!"

"Hey, Boops." Trusty's white-blond hair and puka shell necklace shone in the blacklight as he leaned forward to nuzzle Betty's neck.

"You know how to work that thing?" Pat asked.

"Eh brah, no worries." Trusty patted the expensive Leica hanging around his neck. "I'll start with the DJ. Star's looking sexy tonight. Looks like she lost some weight. Betty, how come you're dressed for work?

Betty stood abruptly.

"Need a break," she mouthed to Pat, and strode toward the back of the club. Trusty, unbothered, ambled over to the DJ booth.

Pat swiveled his barstool around to watch the dance floor and take notes: *Black walls, black clothes, white faces.* He immediately crossed it out. He meant to refer to the dancers' pale makeup, but Harriet, his editor, might think he was implying the club was racist.

Trendy new drink chintzano (chk spelling). "Normal Heights comes to Pacific Beach?" Music so loud I feel my organs vibrating. Hope nothing ruptures.

Pat was considering a line about lint glowing under blacklight when he noticed the dance floor energy ebbing. One by one, the dancers paused. Betty strolled out from the back, holding a half-smoked cigarette.

"Party over already?" Betty checked her watch. "It's only—" She stopped midsentence when she saw what everyone was staring at.

Trusty lay crumpled on the dance floor, flecks of light from the rotating disco ball playing over his still form.

HARRIET MONTGOMERY, whose living room doubled as the *Voltaire's Quill* newsroom, peered over Pat's shoulder. Her tar-black hair showed mousy roots. "Still wrestling with writer's block, Sullivan?"

"Flanagan," Pat Flanagan said. I took notes, but—"

The front door banged open, cutting Pat off midsentence. Betty Benitez stepped into the room. Star Billings, the blonde DJ, trailed after her.

"You two look like a dog's breakfast," Harriet observed.

"We haven't slept." Betty handed Harriet a small cardboard box. "We got your camera back though. What's left of it."

"Any usable photos?" Harriet put the box on Pat's desk without opening it.

"Might have been," Betty said. "If Trusty had remembered to load the film."

"Ah. And how is young Trusty this morning?"

Betty and Star exchanged a look.

"Dead," Star squeaked. "He hit his head and got a dramatic brain injury."

"Oh dear. How unpleasant," Harriet said. "Drinks?"

As the group followed Harriet into the kitchen, Pat caught up to Betty. "Sorry about Trusty," he said. Betty gave his hand a quick squeeze.

They sat around the kitchen table, a tumbler of Harriet's good whiskey in front of each of them. From somewhere within her layers of clothing, Harriet pulled out a pipe and a pouch of tobacco.

"Well?" Harriet asked Betty.

"Trusty fell off the catwalk," Betty said. "Technically it's a lighting truss. Injuries were consistent with the 35-foot drop."

Harriet pulled at her pipe and frowned.

"Why was he up there?"

"He wanted overhead photos of the dance floor." Star picked up a cocktail napkin and blew her nose. "I never thought—"

Betty threw her arm around Star's thin shoulders and gave her a squeeze. "Hey, it's not your fault. Trusty chose to take the risk."

When Betty and Star left, Harriet motioned to Pat to stay seated.

"Congratulations, Sullivan."

"Flanagan," he countered.

Harriet blew a wobbly ring of pipe smoke.

"I've assigned you to investigate Trusty's death."

"What about Effigy's—"

"We'll get the advertising contract in hand before we publish anything."

"What's there to investigate?" Pat objected. "Sounds like it was an accident."

Harriet contemplated the white-on-turquoise interlocking boomerang pattern on the kitchen table.

"There's loads to investigate. What was he looking for up there? A camera angle? Or something else? Second, surfers have superb balance. Unless someone drugged him? Write it down."

"Harriet, Trusty was perfectly capable of drugging hims—"

"Suicide? Unlikely. He'd just had a pay rise. He was chuffed about it."

"You gave Trusty Spivey a *raise*?"

"To keep him from defecting to that poseur rag *Revolt in Style.*"

"Why not let him go?"

"I couldn't let Trevor snatch him up. Not much of a worker, our Trusty, but lovely to look at, and eager to please. Who do you think might've wanted Trusty dead?"

Pat threw up his hands. "I dunno. Me? Harriet, Trusty was supposed to be taking pictures for our story. Instead, he forgot to load the film, and wrecked your camera. It's not the first time he's left other people to clean up his mess. Sorry, I didn't mean—"

"Who else was there?" Harriet pointed her pipe at Pat Flanagan. "Think, Flannery!"

"Star and Betty. The bartender. The usual night crawlers. Some guy on the dance floor doing this snake dance with a pair of silver fans."

"Brilliant. You interview him?"

"Nah. Those types are always more interesting to look at than to talk to. Anyway, Star didn't leave the DJ booth. Betty took a smoke break, but I don't think Betty—"

"Betty could've knocked him down with a blow gun. Blow gun! Write it down."

"Harriet, I—"

"No, you're right. Betty would be more subtle. Antifreeze in his Midori Sour, that sort of thing. I could almost believe it was an accident."

"Except?" Pat asked.

Harriet reached into a pocket, drew out a folded yellow Post-It, and handed it to Pat. "Found this in my desk yesterday."

Something fishy at VQ. Effigy next? Signed, anonimus.

Pat sighed. "Looks like Trusty's writing. And spelling. Any idea what he's talking about?"

"None whatsoever. Buck up, Finnegan. We've got work to do."

IT TOOK PAT AN HOUR to motor up Highway 101. His Honda Civic had one window that wouldn't shut, which made his car shudder at freeway speeds. By the time he arrived at Betty's condo in Encinitas, both he and the takeout dinner sitting on the passenger seat were cold.

Betty answered the door holding a tumbler full of pink liquid. She took the food container from him with her free hand. As she headed to the kitchen she called back affectionately, "Hey, you stringy old chicken hawk, what're you drinking?"

"No jacuzzi wine for me please. You got any beer?"

Pat shut the door and followed Betty inside. The monochrome decor coordinated with Betty's black stirrup leggings and gray sweatshirt. Indoors was warm and smelled like menthol Virginia Slims and vanilla. (Betty was convinced vanilla air freshener disguised the cigarette smell).

"Let's eat at the coffee table," Betty said. "The kitchen table's piled with work stuff. Our top salesman's been taking prospects south of the border for a boys' night out. Then threatening to show the Polaroids to the wives. Don't worry, I will quit. As soon as I pay back my law school loans. What's the occasion?" Hey, this looks great. Lemme zap it in the microwave."

"Italian Flag Special from Stefano's in Hillcrest." Pat tried to get comfortable on Betty's black leather sofa. "It has red marinara, white alfredo sauce, and that green poseur stuff you like."

"It's called pesto and I do like it." Betty set the two heated plates on the coffee table and sat next to Pat.

"Harriet wants me to investigate Trusty's death," Pat said.

"Trusty was an idiot." Betty twirled a forkful of pesto linguine and popped it into her mouth.

"Not the reaction I expected from the grieving girlfriend."

"His parents coddled him his whole life, and now they're mystified he can't take care of himself like a normal adult. They couldn't wait for me to marry him and take him off their hands. So, what's to investigate? Wasn't it an accident?"

While Betty sipped her white zinfandel, Pat told her about the note.

"How does Harriet know it was from Trusty?" she asked.

"He misspelled *Anonymous*. And she recognized his handwriting."

"Why didn't Trusty say something to Harriet in private? I'm pretty sure he had plenty of opportunities to do *that*."

"He wanted to remain—"

"Anonymous. I get it. So, Trusty sees something funny going on, he leaves Harriet a note, cause he doesn't completely trust her. Next thing you know, he's dead. Is that it?"

"You summed it up."

"Glad I could help. Hey, you tell your parents yet you're not an engineer?"

"Still putting it off."

"Know who else has an engineering degree? Star Billings."

"The airhead DJ?" Pat immediately regretted saying it.

"You are such a *pig*!" Betty socked Pat's shoulder. To change the subject, Pat picked up the *San Diego Reader* from the side table and read, "*The Incision Decision: Why people undergo cosmetic surgery.* This is why I hate San Diego. It's like a bunch of insecure people decided to construct an entire culture based on ads from airline magazines."

"You think that's bad? Dare you to check out the personals."

Pat turned to the back pages. "*ATTRACT GIRLS!*" he read. "*Attractant 10 Pheromone Spray.* Maybe that's what Trusty was using on you."

"As good an explanation as any."

"*Seeking a woman who can keep up with me. Own my own tux. People say I think too much.*"

"Imagine the poor guy with his tux, never knowing why everyone finds him so annoying."

"*SINGLES BIG DANCE PARTY Saturday at the Viscount Hotel (formerly the Travelodge) 1960 Harbor Island Drive. 21 and over. Open-minded nonsmokers only. Reading these makes me sad.*" Pat folded the Reader and set it aside.

"Before you start feeling too superior, remember those ads pay your salary. Not those ads specifically, but *VQ* has ones exactly like it. Mind if I smoke?"

"Go ahead. I'm heading out. Thanks for making me depressed."

PAT STAYED ON NORTH Torrey Pines Road instead of following Genesee. The ocean breeze blasting through the open window ensured he was wide awake by the time he parked and entered Effigy.

Effigy wasn't the kind of club where you asked someone to dance. You claimed a space on the floor amidst the Siouxsie Sioux and Robert Smith clones, and you performed solo. This suited Pat; being alone raised no suspicions. Pat strolled around looking for a way to climb up to the lighting truss. He found an access door, but it was locked.

Between the beer and the bladder-thumping music, Pat needed to make a pit stop. Exiting the bathroom, he passed a large man talking on the pay phone in the narrow hallway.

"And I'm saying the price went up," the man said. "No, but after last Saturday...yeah. I'll see you there."

Last Saturday was when Trusty had died.

Pat decided to follow the man. He managed to keep the Harley-Davidson in view, through a winding stretch on the 5 freeway and down Harbor Drive. They passed the naval base, turned left on 8th street, and entered a lonely stretch of industrial buildings. Pat pulled over when the biker stopped at a white building with a single light out front. Five minutes later the man came out, jumped onto his bike, and roared off in the direction they'd come from. Pat noted the building address and name: Harbor Chemical Supply.

Before Pat could shift back into drive, a white F-150 emerged from the back of the building, sending up a spray of gravel and momentarily blinding Pat with its headlights. Pat followed.

He spotted the truck ahead of him, approaching a red light. The truck didn't slow down. It accelerated straight into the intersection, backed up, pulled a U-turn, and sped off. A late-model Mercedes sat at an angle in the intersection, its front bumper dented. Beside it lay the crumpled Harley. A man stepped out of the car holding something to his ear. One of those cellular phones. It was a good thing too, as there didn't seem to be a pay phone nearby. Pat waited in his car until the SDPD black-and-white pulled up.

A young officer approached Pat's Honda and rapped on the window. His brass name bade read Kitagawa. Pat stepped out of the car and followed Kitagawa to where the driver of the Mercedes, a middle-aged man in a brown suit, was standing.

"Tell him I had the light," the driver implored Pat. "You saw it. Tell him!"

Officer Kitagawa took notes as Pat told what he'd witnessed.

"Where's the rider?" Kitagawa asked. Pat and the driver looked at each other. The intersection was poorly lit, surrounded by vacant lots overgrown with weeds.

"I can help you look for him." Pat didn't expect the police to let him poke around a murder scene, but it was worth a try.

"Fine," Kitagawa said. "Yell if you see something. And don't touch anything."

PAT GOT TO WORK AROUND noon the next day. He didn't see Harriet, but he found DJ Star at the kitchen table, drinking from a pilfered Perry's Café mug. Harriet was still asleep, Star told him, but Pat could go wake her up if he wanted.

Pat waited until Star left. He marched to the back of the house and pounded on Harriet's door.

"Is it noon already?" Harriet sounded hoarse.

"I think you'll want to hear this," Pat shouted through the door. "Kitchen. I'll make tea."

Harriet minced into the kitchen wearing a satin leopard-print dressing gown, a Rosie the Riveter head scarf, and blackout glasses. She patted the table as she sat down, as if she were blind. Pat set a mug of strong black tea in front of her and related the events of the previous night.

Harriet perked up a bit. "Did you find the body?"

"Not me personally. The cop found it."

"And there's a notebook?"

"Yeah. It was stuck under a chain link fence. It has all these bars and clubs listed, with dates. I'll turn it over to the police, but I wanted us to read it first."

Harriet waved away the notebook and stood up slowly. "Let's talk when you've done pasteup. Well done, Finnegan."

Pat tuned the radio to 91X. Pasteup had been the one job Trusty was good at, probably because it wasn't that difficult. Pat checked the Lectro-Stik's temperature and was arranging the three-inch-wide strips of text on the board when he read: *SINGLES BIG DANCE PARTY Saturday at Moose McGillycuddy's 1165 Garnet Ave 21 and over. Open-minded nonsmokers only.*

It was the ad he'd seen at Betty's house, in the *San Diego Reader*. Only with a different date and location. Pat checked the notebook he'd found at the accident scene. Good thing Harriet hadn't taken it after all.

Moose McGillycuddy's was listed in the notebook.

Pat went to the shelf and pulled down the most recent issues of *Voltaire's Quill*.

Each issue had a *SINGLES BIG DANCE PARTY* advertised in the back pages. The location changed each time. Confetti's in Mission Valley. The Zebra Club downtown. The Bacchanal on Clairemont Mesa Boulevard. The Belly-Up Tavern in Solana Beach. The same clubs appeared in the notebook, along with a date, a dollar amount, and another number Pat couldn't decipher.

Pat ran back to Harriet's bedroom and hammered on her door. Hangover or no, she'd want to hear about this.

PAT SHOWED UP AT THE *VQ* office early Sunday morning to get his disappointing report over with. Star Billings was at the kitchen table, drinking coffee. "Harriet told me you're working on something interesting," she said.

Pat sat down. "Probably a dead end. I went to Moose McGillycuddy's last night for the 'open minded singles' party. Nothing that I could see. Except a bunch of drunk idiots in stonewashed jeans and dumb bi-level haircuts."

"What made you think of going to Moose's? Stay there, I'll make a fresh pot." Star rose and rummaged in the cupboard behind Pat. He was about to respond to her question when his skull exploded with white fireworks.

PAT DIDN'T KNOW WHERE he was, but he smelled booze. And menthol Virginia Slims. Slowly he realized Betty and Harriet were helping him up off the kitchen floor and into a chair.

"Bloody cow was going to burn my house down," Harriet fumed.

"And murder Pat," Betty added pointedly.

"Is that what she was doing with my Wild Turkey 151?" Harriet was indignant. "She wouldn't tell me. Buggered right off when she saw me."

Pat closed his eyes and rubbed the rising lump on the back of his head.

"How well do you know her?" Betty asked Harriet. "I mean, I've hung out with her, but ...I don't even know her real name."

"Star's a bit mysterious," Harriet said, "Seems a right plank, but she's got an engineering degree."

"Those are overrated," Pat muttered.

THAT EVENING OFFICER Warren Kitagawa stopped by Harriet's. He sat at the kitchen table with a glass of water in front of him. Harriet and Betty had wine coolers. Pat, still feeling woozy, drank ginger ale.

Kitagawa was not surprised by the attack. He told them Star Billings, aka Stella Baker, was part of a crystal meth distribution network. The drug, manufactured at Harbor Chemical Supply, was sold at "singles parties" advertised in San Diego's free weeklies. Star gained access to the clubs as a DJ.

"Trusty Spivey pasted up the ads at VQ," Pat told Kitagawa. "He must've noticed the pattern."

"If he figured it out, 'Star' had a motive to kill him," Kitagawa said. "But witnesses have her in the DJ booth the whole time."

"She tried to kill Pat," Betty pointed out. "Can't you get her for attempted murder, at least?"

"If we find her. And Mr. Flanagan is brave enough to testify."

Why brave?" Betty asked.

"These people are ruthless," Kitagawa said. "Pat saw what they're capable of."

"Are we going into witness protection?" Harriet asked hopefully.

"We don't have the resources. But unofficially..."

PAT STEPPED OFF THE jetway and inhaled the thick, humid air. Mahina, on the lush windward side of a sparsely populated Hawaiian island, offered the ideal combination of opportunity and obscurity. Officer Warren Kitagawa had called in favors from relatives and gotten Pat the next best thing to official witness protection.

Pat was the new crime reporter at the *County Courier*, Mahina's premier (in fact only) newspaper.

Inside Mahina Airport Pat stopped to watch a performance of *kahiko* hula—the ancient style accompanied by percussion. He stood transfixed, feeling the vibrations as the women stomped, whirled, and chanted in perfect synchrony.

He knew how Star had killed Trusty.

Pat grabbed his duffel bag and sprinted to the airport's lone pay phone.

"Resonant frequency," he told Officer Kitagawa. "When soldiers march across a bridge they break stride, so the resonance of their steps doesn't destabilize it. Star studied engineering. She'd know that. The song she put on right before Trusty fell had a marching beat and the volume was turned way up. If Trusty was up on the catwalk taking pictures, it wouldn't take much to shake him loose."

PAT CLIMBED INTO THE taxi and directed the driver to the Hanohano Hotel. He would miss Betty, and *Voltaire's Quill,* and even Harriet. But his new life was in Mahina. He'd call his parents after he settled in. His engineering degree had come in handy after all.

ABOUT THE AUTHOR

Frankie Bow writes two mystery series: *The Professor Molly Mysteries*, and licensed works in the Miss Fortune World.

Like Professor Molly, Frankie works in higher education. Unlike her protagonist, she is blessed with delightful students, sane colleagues, and an adequate office chair.

Follow Frankie at frankiebow.com.

ABOUT THE PUBLISHER

Hawaiian Heritage Press publishes Hawaii's finest classic and modern literature.

www.ingramcontent.com/pod-product-compliance
Lightning Source LLC
Chambersburg PA
CBHW080721020726
47503CB00010B/2745